THE IDOL O⟨...⟩R

Cautiously, Joe and Marge crept up the stairs in the Dark Tower of Witchwood. Finally they emerged into a brightly lighted chamber. There were no furnishings, but at the far end of the room was a huge, hideous, multi-armed idol made of some dark stone.

Its face was a travesty of a human woman's face. It sat in the lotus position, and eight arms came from its distorted torso. Each of the hands held a different deadly weapon. Its eyes were blazing red rubies of nearly impossible size and perfection.

"Look at those stones!" Marge gasped.

Joe shook his head. "I wouldn't touch it. It's probably cursed a thousand ways from Sunday."

"Actually, I'm not," the idol said. "If you looked like this, would you need much in the way of curses?"

By Jack L. Chalker
Published by Ballantine Books:

THE WEB OF THE CHOZEN
AND THE DEVIL WILL DRAG YOU UNDER
A JUNGLE OF STARS
DANCE BAND ON THE *TITANIC*
DANCERS IN THE AFTERGLOW

THE SAGA OF THE WELL WORLD
Book One: *Midnight at the Well of Souls*
Book Two: *Exiles at the Well of Souls*
Book Three: *Quest for the Well of Souls*
Book Four: *The Return of Nathan Brazil*
Book Five: *Twilight at the Well of Souls: The Legacy of Nathan Brazil*

THE FOUR LORDS OF THE DIAMOND
Book One: *Lilith: A Snake in the Grass*
Book Two: *Cerberus: A Wolf in the Fold*
Book Three: *Charon: A Dragon at the Gate*
Book Four: *Medusa: A Tiger by the Tail*

THE DANCING GODS
Book One: *The River of the Dancing Gods*
Book Two: *Demons of the Dancing Gods*
Book Three: *Vengeance of the Dancing Gods*
Book Four: *Songs of the Dancing Gods*
Book Five: *Horrors of the Dancing Gods*

THE RINGS OF THE MASTER
Book One: *Lords of the Middle Dark*
Book Two: *Pirates of the Thunder*
Book Three: *Warriors of the Storm*
Book Four: *Masks of the Martyrs*

THE WATCHERS AT THE WELL
Book One: *Echoes of the Well of Souls*
Book Two: *Shadow of the Well of Souls*
Book Three: *Gods of Well of Souls*

THE DANCING GODS

GODS

PART ONE

THE RIVER OF DANCING GODS

DEMONS OF THE DANCING GODS

Jack L. Chalker

A Del Rey® Book
BALLANTINE BOOKS • NEW YORK

A Del Rey® Book
Published by Ballantine Books

ISBN 0-345-40246-4

Manufactured in the United States of America

First Edition: December 1995

10 9 8 7 6 5 4 3 2 1

CONTENTS

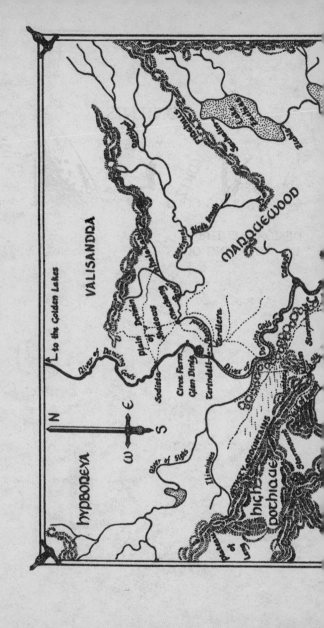

THE RIVER OF
DANCING GODS

TABLE OF CONTENTS

ENCOUNTER ON A LONELY ROAD

People taken from other universes should always be near death.
—The Books of Rules, XX, 109, 234(a)

JUST BECAUSE YOUR WHOLE LIFE IS GOING TO HELL DOESN'T mean you have to walk there.

She was walking down a lonely stretch of west Texas freeway in the still dark of the early morning, an area where nobody walked and where there was no place to walk to, anyway. She might have been hitching, or not, but a total lack of traffic gave her very little choice there. So she was just walking, clutching a small overnight bag and a purse that was almost the same size, holding on to them as if they were the only two real things in her life, they and the dark and that endless stretch of west Texas freeway.

Whatever traffic there was seemed to be heading the other way—an occasional car, or pickup, or eighteen-wheeler with someplace to go and some reason to go there, all heading in the direction she was walking from, and where, she knew too well, there was nothing much at all for anybody. But if their destinations were wrong, their sense of purpose separated the night travelers from the woman on the road; people who had someplace to go and something to do belonged to a different world than she did.

She had started out hitching, all right. She'd made it to the truck stop at Ozona, that huge, garish, ultramodern, and plastic heaven in the middle of nowhere that served up anything and everything twenty-four hours a day for those stuck out here, going between here and there. After a time, she'd gotten another ride, this one only twenty miles west and at a cost she was not willing to pay. And so here she was, stuck out in the middle of nowhere, going nowhere fast. Walk, walk, walk to nowhere, from nowhere in particular, because nowhere was all the where she had to go.

Headlights approached from far off; but even if they had

7

held any interest for her, they were still too far away to be more than abstract, jerky round dots in the distance, a distance that the west Texas desert made even more deceptive. How far off was the oncoming driver? Ten miles? More? Did it matter?

It was at least ten, maybe fifteen minutes before the vehicle grew close enough for the woman to hear the roar of the big diesel and realize that this was, in fact, one of those haunters of the desert dark, a monster tractor-trailer truck with a load of furniture for Houston or beef for New Orleans or, perhaps, California oranges for the Nashville markets. Although it had been approaching her from the west for some time, its sudden close-up reality was startling against the total stillness of the night, a looming monster that quickly illuminated the night and its empty, vacant walker, then was just as suddenly gone, a mass of diminishing red lights in the distance behind her. But in the few seconds that those gaping headlights had shone on the scene, they had illuminated her form against that desperate dark, illuminated her and, in the cab behind those lights, gave her notice and recognition.

She paid this truck no more attention than any of the others and just kept walking onward into the unseen distance.

The driver had been going much too fast for a practical stop, a pace that would have upset the highway patrol but was required to make his employer's deadline. Besides, he was on the wrong side of the median to be of any practical help himself—but there were other ways, ways that didn't even involve slowing down.

"Break one-nine, break, break. How 'bout a westbound? Anybody in this here Lone Star truckin' west on this one dark night?" His accent was Texarkana, but he could have been from Maine or Miami or San Francisco or Minneapolis just as well. Something in the CB radio seemed automatically to add the standard accent, even in Brooklyn.

"You got a westbound. Go," came a reply, only very slightly different in sound or tone from the caller's.

"What's your twenty?" Eastbound asked.

"Three-thirty was the last I saw," Westbound responded. "Clean and green back to the truck-'em-up. Even the bears go to sleep this time o' night in these parts."

Eastbound chuckled. "Yeah, you got that right. I got to keep pushin' it, though. They want me in Shreveport by tonight."

"Shreveport! You got some haul yet!"

"Yeah, but that's home sweet home, baby. Get in, get it off, stick this thing in the junkyard, and I'm in bed with the old lady. I'll make it."

"All I got is El Paso by ten."

"Aw, shit, you'll make that easy. Say—caught something your side in my lights about three-two-seven or so you might check out. Looked like a beaver just walkin' by the side of the road. Maybe a breakdown, though I ain't seen no cars on your side and I'm just on you now. Probably nothin', but you might want to check her out just in case. Ain't nobody lives within miles o' here, I don't think."

"I'll back off a little and see if I can eyeball her," Westbound assured him. "Won't hurt much. That your Kenworth just passed me?"

"Yeah. Who else? All best to ya, and check on that little gal. Don't wanna hear she got found dead by the side of the road or something. Spoil my whole day."

"That's a four," Westbound came back with a slight chuckle.

"Keep safe, keep well, that's the Red Rooster sayin' that, eastbound and down."

"Y'all have a safe one. This is the Nighthawk, westbound and backin' down."

Nighthawk put his mike into its little holder and backed down to fifty. He wasn't in any hurry, and he wouldn't lose much, even if this was nothing at all, not on this flat stretch.

The woman was beginning to falter, occasionally stumbling in the scrub brush by the side of the road. She was starting to think again, and that wasn't what she wanted at all. Finally she stopped, knowing it was beyond her to take too many more steps, and looked around. It was incredible how dark the desert could be at night, even with more stars than city folk had ever seen beaming down from overhead. No matter what, she knew she had to get some rest. Maybe just lie down over there in the scrub—get stung by a tarantula or a scorpion or whatever else lived around here. Snake, maybe. She considered the idea and was somewhat surprised that she cared about that. Nice and quick, maybe—but painfully bitten or poisoned to death by inches? That seemed particularly ugly. With everything else so messed up, at least her exit ought to be clean, neat, and as comfortable as these things could be. *One* thing in her life should go right, damn it. And for the first time since she'd jumped out of the car, she began to consider living again—at least a little bit longer, at least until the sunrise. She stopped and looked up and down the highway for any sign of lights, wondering what she'd do if she saw any. It would just as likely be another Cal Hurder as anybody useful, particularly at this ungodly hour in a place like this.

Lights approaching from the east told her a decision was near, and soon. But she made no decision until the lights were actually on her, and when she did, it was on impulse, without any thought applied to it. She turned, put down her bags, and stuck out her thumb.

Even with that and on the lookout for her, he almost missed her. Spotting her, he hit the brakes and started gearing to a stop by the side of the road, getting things stopped fully a hundred yards west of her. Knowing this, he put the truck in reverse and slowly backed up, eyeing the shoulder carefully with his right mirror. After all this, he didn't want to be the one to run her down.

Finally he saw her, or thought he did, just standing there, looking at the huge monster approaching, doing nothing else at all. For her part, she was unsure of just what to do next. That huge rig was really intimidating, and so she just stood there, trembling slightly.

Nighthawk frowned, realized she wasn't coming up to the door, and decided to put on his flashers and go to her. He was not without his own suspicions; hijackers would use such bait and such a setting—although he could hardly imagine somebody hijacking forty thousand pounds of soap flakes. Still, you never knew—and there was always his own money and cards and the truck itself to steal. He took out his small pistol and slipped it into his pocket, then slid over, opened the passenger door, and got out warily.

He was a big man, somewhat intimidating-looking himself, perhaps six-three, two hundred and twenty-five pounds of mostly muscle, wearing faded jeans, boots, and a checkered flannel shirt. His age was hard to measure, but he was at least in his forties with a face maybe ten years older and with very long, graying hair. He was dark, too—she took him at first for a black man—but there was something not quite of any race and yet of all of them in his face and features. He was used to the look she was giving him and past minding.

"M'am?" he called to her in a calm yet wary baritone. "Don't worry—I don't bite. A trucker going the other way spotted you and asked me to see if you was all right."

Oh, what the hell, she decided, resigning herself. *I can always jump out again.* "I need a ride," she said simply. "I'm kind of stuck here."

He walked over to her, seeing her tenseness and pretty much ignoring it. He picked up her bag, letting her get her purse, and went back to the truck. "Come on. I'll take you for a while if you're going west."

She hesitated a moment more, then followed him and permitted him to assist her up into the cab. He slammed her door, walked around the truck, got in on the driver's side, released the brakes, and put the truck in gear. "How far you going?" he asked her.

She sat almost pressed against the passenger door, trying to look as if she weren't doing it. For all he knew, she *didn't* realize she was doing it.

She sighed. "Any place, I guess. How far you going?"

"El Paso. But I can get you to a phone in Fort Stockton if that's what you need."

She shook her head slowly. "No, nobody to call. El Paso's fine, if it's okay with you. I don't have enough money for a motel or anything."

Up to speed and cruising now, he glanced sideways over at her. At one time she'd been a pretty attractive woman, he decided. It was all still there, but something had happened to it, put a dull, dirty coating over it. Medium height—five-four or -five, maybe—with short, greasy-looking brown hair with traces of gray. Thirties, probably. Thin and slightly built, she had that hollow, empty look, like somebody who'd been on the booze pretty long and pretty hard.

"None of my business, but how'd you get stuck out here in the middle of nowhere at three in the morning?" he asked casually.

She gave a little sigh and looked out the window for a moment at the black nothingness. Finally she said, "If you really want to know, I jumped out of a car."

"Huh?"

"I got a ride with a salesman—at least he said he was a salesman—back at Ozona. We got fifteen, twenty miles down the road and he pulled over. You can guess the rest."

He nodded.

"I grabbed the bags and ran. He turned out to be a little scared of the dark, I guess. Just stood there yelling for me, then threatened to drive off if I didn't come back. I didn't—and he did."

He lighted a cigarette, inhaled deeply, and expelled the smoke with an accompanying sigh. "Yeah, I guess I get the picture."

"You—you're an Indian, aren't you?"

He laughed. "Good change of subject. Well, sort of. My mom was a full-blooded Seminole, my dad was Puerto Rican, which is a little bit of everything."

"You're from Florida? You don't sound like a southerner."

Again he chuckled. "Oh, I'm from the south, all right. South of Philadelphia, anyway. Long story. Right now what home I have is in a trailer park in a little town south of Baltimore. No Indians or Puerto Ricans around, so they just think of me as something a little bit exotic, I guess."

"You're a long way from home," she noted.

He nodded. "More or less. Don't matter much, though. I'm on the road so much the only place I really feel at home is in this truck. I own it and I run it, and it's mine as long as I keep up the payments. They had to let me keep the truck, otherwise they couldn't get no alimony. What about you? That pretty voice sounds pure Texas to me."

She nodded idly, still staring distantly into the nothingness. "Yeah. San Antone, that's me."

"Air Force brat?" He was nervous at pushing her too much, maybe upsetting or alienating her—she was on a thin edge, that was for sure—but he just had the feeling she wanted to talk to somebody.

She did, a little surprised at that herself. "Sort of. Daddy was a flier. Jet pilot."

"What happened to him?" He guessed by her tone that something had happened.

"Killed in his plane, in the finest traditions of the Air Force. Sucked a bird into his jets while coming in for a landing and that was it, or so I'm told. I was much too young, really, to remember him any more than as a vague presence. And the pictures, of course. Momma kept all the pictures. The benefits, though, they weren't all that much. He was only a captain, after all, and a new one at that. So Momma worked like hell at all sorts of jobs to bring me up right. She was solid Oklahoma—high school, no marketable skills, that sort of thing. Supermarket checker was about the highest she got—pretty good, really, when you see the benefits they get at the union stores. She did really well, when you think about it—except it was all for me. She didn't have much else to live for. Wanted me to go to college—she'd wanted to go, but never did. Well, she and the VA and a bunch of college loans got me there, all right, and got me through, for all the good it did. Ten days after I graduated with a useless degree in English Lit, she dropped dead from a heart attack. I had to sell the trailer we lived in all those years just to make sure she was buried right. After paying out all the stuff she owed, I had eight hundred dollars, eight pairs of well-worn jeans, a massive collection of T-shirts, and little else."

He sighed. "Yeah, that's rough. I always wanted to go to college, you know, but I never had the money until I didn't have the time. I read a lot, though. It don't pay to get hooked on TV when you're on the road so much."

She chuckled dryly. "College is all well and good and some of it's interesting, but if your degree's not in business, law, medicine, or engineering, the paper's only good for about thirty-eight hundred—that's what I still owe on those loans, and it'll be a cold day in hell before they see a penny. They track you down all over, too—use collection agents. So you can't get credit, can't get a loan, none of that. I got one job teaching junior high English for a year—but they cut back and laid me off. Only time I ever really enjoyed life."

"So you been goin' around from job to job ever since?"

"For a while. But a couple of years of working hamburger joints and all those other minimum-wage, minimum-life jobs gets to you. I finally sat down one day and decided it was fate, or destiny, or something. I was getting older, and all I could see was myself years later, sitting in a rented slum shared with a couple of other folks just like me, getting quickies from the night manager. So I figured I would find a man, marry him, and let *him* pay my bills while I got into the cooking and baby business."

"Well, it's a job like any other and has a pretty long history," he noted. "Somebody's got to do it—otherwise the government will do *that*, too."

She managed a wan smile at the remark. "Yeah, well, that's what I told myself, but there are many ways to go about it. You can meet a guy, date, fall in love, really commit yourself—both of you. That might work. But just to go out in desperation and marry the first guy who comes along who'll have you—that's disaster."

"Works the other way, too, honey," he responded. "That's why I'm paying five hundred a month in rehabilitation money—that's what they call alimony these days in liberal states that abolished alimony—and child support. And she's living with another guy who owns an auto-repair shop and is doing pretty well; she has a kid by him, too. But so long as she don't marry him, I'm stuck."

"You have a kid?"

He nodded. "A son. Irving. Lousy name, but it was the one uncle he had on her side who had money. Not that it got us or him anything. I love him, but I almost never see him."

"Because you're on the road?"

"Naw. You'd be surprised what you can work. I'm supposed to have visitation rights, but somehow he's always away when I come visiting. She don't want him to see me, get to know me instead of her current as his daddy. Uh-uh."

"Couldn't you go to court on that?"

He laughed. "Honey, them courts will slap me in jail so fast if I miss a payment to her it isn't funny—but tell *her* to live up to *her* end of the bargain? Yeah, they'll tell her, and that's that. Tell her and tell her and tell her. Until, one day, you realize that the old joke's true—she got the gold mine in the settlement and I got the shaft. Oh, I suppose I could make an unholy mess trying to get custody, but I'd never win. I'd have to give up truckin', and truckin's all I know how to do. And I'd probably lose, anyway—nine out of ten men do. Even if I won—hell, it's been near five years." He sighed. "I guess at this stage he's better off. I hope so."

"I hope so, too," she responded, sounding genuinely

touched, with the oddly pleasing guilt felt when, sunk deep in self-pity, you find a fellow sufferer.

They rode in near silence for the next few minutes, a silence broken only by the occasional crackle from the CB and a report of this or that or two jerks talking away at each other when they could just as easily have used a telephone and kept the world out.

Finally he said, "I guess from what you say that your marriage didn't work out either."

"Yeah, you could say that. He was an Air Force sergeant at Lackland. A drill instructor in basic. We met in a bar and got drunk on the town. He was older and a very lonely man, and, well, you know what I was going through. We just kinda fell into it. He was a pretty rough character, and after all the early fun had worn off and we'd settled down, he'd come home at night and take all his frustrations out on me. It really got to him, after a while, that I was smarter and better educated than he was. He had some inferiority complex. He was hell on his recruits, too—but they got away from him after eight weeks or so. I had him for years. After a while he got transferred up to Reese in Lubbock, but he hated that job and he hated the cold weather and the dust and wind, and that just made it all the worse. Me, I had it really bad there, too, since what few friends I had were all in San Antonio."

"I'd have taken a hike long before," he commented. "Divorce ain't all that bad. Ask my ex."

"Well, it's easy to see that—now. But I had some money for the first time, and a house, and a real sense of something permanent, even if it was lousy. I know it's kind of hard to understand—it's hard to explain. I guess you just had to be me. I figured maybe kids would mellow him out and give me a new direction—but after two miscarriages, the second one damn near killing me, the doctors told me I should never have kids. Probably couldn't, but definitely shouldn't. That just made him meaner and sent me down the tubes. Booze, pot, pills—you name it, I swallowed it or smoked it or sniffed it. And one day—it was my thirtieth birthday—I looked at myself in the mirror, saw somebody a shot-to-hell forty-five looking back at me, picked up what I could use most and carry easy, cashed a check for half our joint account, and took a bus south to think things out. I've been walking ever since—and I still haven't been out of the goddamned state of Texas. I waited tables, swept floors, never stayed long in one spot. Hell, I've sold my body for a plate of eggs. Done everything possible to keep from thinking, looking ahead, worrying. I burned out. I've had it."

He thought about it for a moment, and then it came to him. "But you jumped out of that fella's car."

She nodded wearily. "Yeah, I did. I don't even know why, exactly. Or maybe, yes, I do, too. It was an all-of-a-sudden kind of thing, sort of like when I turned thirty and looked in the mirror. There wasn't any mirror, really, but back there in that car I still kind of looked at myself and was, well, scared, frightened, maybe even revolted at what I saw staring back. Something just sorta said to me, 'If this is the rest of your life, then why bother to be alive at all?' "

He thought, but could find little else to say right then. What *was* the right thing to say to somebody like this, anyway?

Flecks of rain struck his windshield, and he flipped on the wipers, the sound adding an eerie, hypnotic background to the sudden roar of a midsummer thunderstorm on a truck cab. Peering out, he thought for a moment he saw two Interstate 10 roadways—an impossible sort of fork he knew just couldn't be there. He kicked on the brights and the fog lights, and the image seemed to resolve itself a bit, the right-hand one looking more solid. He decided that keeping to the white stripe down the side of the road separating road and shoulder was the safest course.

At the illusory intersection, there seemed for a moment to be two trucks, one coming out of the other, going right, while the other, its ghostly twin, went left. The image of the second truck, apparently passing his and vanishing quickly in the distance to his left, startled him for a moment. He could have sworn there wasn't anything behind him for a couple of miles, and the CB was totally silent.

The rain stopped as suddenly as it had begun, and things took on a more normal appearance in minutes. He glanced over at the woman and saw that she was asleep—best thing for her, he decided. Ahead loomed a green exit sign, and, still a little unnerved, he badly wanted to get his bearings.

The sign said, "Ruddygore, 5 miles."

That didn't help him much. Ruddygore? Where in hell was

that? The next exit should be Sheffield. A mile marker approached, and he decided to check things out.

The little green number said, "4."

He frowned again, beginning to become a little unglued. Four? That couldn't be right. Not if he was still on I–10. Uneasily, he began to think of that split back there. Maybe it *was* a split—that other truck had seemed to curve off to the left when he went right. If so, he was on some cockeyed interstate spur to God knew where.

God knew, indeed. As far as *he* knew or could remember, there were no exits, let alone splits, between Ozona and Sheffield.

He flicked on his interior light and looked down at his road atlas, held open by clips to the west Texas map. According to it, he was right—and no sign of any Ruddygore. He sighed and snapped off the light. Well, the thing was wrong in a hundred places, anyway. Luckily he was still ahead of schedule, so a five-mile detour shouldn't be much of a problem. He glanced over to his left again for no particular reason. Funny. The landscaping made it look as if there weren't any lane going back.

A small interstate highway marker, the usual red, white, and blue was between mile markers 3 and 2, but it told him nothing. It didn't even make sense. He was probably just a little crazy tonight, or his eyes were going, but it looked for all the world as if it said:

∞ ? What the hell was *that*? Somebody in the highway department must have goofed good there, stenciling an 8 on its side.

At the 2, another green sign announced Ruddygore, and there was also a brown sign, like the kind used for parks and monuments. It said, "Ferry—Turn Left at Stop Sign."

Now he knew he had gone suddenly mad. Not just that he knew that I–8 went from Tucson to San Diego and nowhere near Texas, but—a ferry? In the middle of the west Texas desert?

He backed down to slow—very slow—and turned to his passenger. "Hey, little lady. Wake up!"

She didn't stir, and finally he reached over and shook her, repeating his words.

She moved and squirmed and managed to open her eyes. "Um. Sorry. So *tired* . . . What's the matter? We in El Paso?"

He shook his head. "No. I think I've gone absolutely nuts. Somehow in the storm we took an exit that wasn't supposed to be there and we're headed for a town called Ruddygore. Ever heard of it?"

She shook her head sleepily from side to side. "Nope. But that doesn't mean anything. Why? We lost?"

"Lost ain't the word," he mumbled. "Look, I don't want to scare you or anything, but I think I'm going nuts. You ever hear of a ferryboat around here?"

She looked at him as if he had suddenly sprouted feathers. "A what? Over *what*?"

He nodded nervously and gestured toward the windshield. "Well, then, you read me that big sign."

She rubbed the sleep from her eyes and looked. "Ruddygore—exit one mile," she mumbled.

"And the little brown sign?"

"Ferry," she read, suddenly awake and looking very confused. "And an arrow." She turned and faced him. "How long was I asleep?"

"Five, maybe ten minutes," he answered truthfully. "You can still see the rain on the windshield where the wipers don't reach."

She shook her head in wonder. "It must be across the Pecos. But the Pecos isn't much around here."

"Yeah," he replied and felt for his revolver.

The interstate road went right into the exit, allowing no choice. There was a slight downgrade to a standard stop sign and a set of small signs. To the left, they said, were Ruddygore and the impossible ferry. To the right was—Oblivion.

"I never heard of any town named Oblivion, either," he muttered, "but it sounds right for these parts. Still, all the signs said only Ruddygore, so that's got to be the bigger and closer place. Any place they build an interstate spur to at a few million bucks a mile *has* to have something open even this time of night. Besides," he added, "I'm damned curious to see that ferry in the middle of the desert."

He put on his signal, then made the turn onto a modest two-lane road. He passed under the highway and noted glumly that there wasn't any apparent way of getting back on. Well, he told himself, he'd find it later.

Up ahead in the distance he saw, not the town lights he'd expected, but an odd, circular, lighted area. It was particularly unusual in that it looked something like the kind of throw a huge spotlight, pointed straight down, might give—but there were no signs of lights anywhere. Fingering the pistol, he proceeded on, knowing that the road was leading him to that lighted area.

And it *was* bright when he reached it, although no source was apparent. The road, too, seemed to vanish into it, and the entire surface appeared as smooth as glass. Damnedest thing he'd ever seen, maybe a thousand yards across. He stopped at the edge of it, and both he and the woman strained to see where the light was coming from, but the sky remained black—blacker than usual, since the reflected glow blotted out all but the brightest stars.

"Now, what the hell . . . ?" he mused aloud.

"Hey! Look! Up ahead there, almost in the middle. Isn't that a man?" She pointed through the windshield.

He squinted and nodded. "Yeah. Sure looks like somebody. I don't like this, though. Not at all. There's some very funny game being played here." Again he reached in and felt the comfort of the .38 in his pocket. He put the truck back in gear and moved slowly forward, one eye on the strange figure ahead and the other warily on the woman, whom he no longer trusted. It was a great sob story, but this craziness had started only after she came aboard.

He drove straight for the lone figure standing there in the center of the lighted area at about five miles per hour, applying the hissing air brakes when he was almost on top of the stranger and could see him clearly.

The woman gasped. "He looks like a vampire Santa Claus!"

Her nervous surprise seemed genuine. Certainly her description of the man who stood looking back at them fitted him perfectly. Very tall—six-five or better, he guessed—and very large. "Portly" would be too kind a word. The man had a reddish face, twinkling eyes with laugh lines etched around them, and a huge, full white beard—the very image of Santa Claus on all those Christmas cards. But he was not dressed in any furry red suit, but rather in formal wear—striped pants, morning coat, red velvet vest and cummerbund, even a top hat, and he was also wearing a red-velvet-lined opera cape.

The strange man made no gestures or moves, and finally the driver said, "Look, you wait in the truck. I'm going to find out what the hell this is about."

"I'm coming with you."

"No!" He hesitated a moment, then nervously cleared his throat. "Look, first of all, if there's any danger I don't want you between me and who I might have to shoot—understand? And second, forgive me, but I can't one hundred percent trust that you're not in on whatever this is."

That last seemed to shock her, but she nodded and sighed and said no more.

He opened the door, got down, and put one hand in his pocket, right on the trigger. Only then did he walk forward toward the odd figure who stood there, to stop a few feet from the man. The stranger said nothing, but the driver could feel those eyes following his every move and gesture.

"Good morning," he opened. What else was there to say to start things off?

The man in the top hat didn't reply immediately, but seemed to examine him from head to toe as an appraiser might look at a diamond ring. "Oh, yes, you'll do nicely, I think," he said in a pleasant, mellow voice with a hint of a British accent. He looked up at the woman, still in the cab, seemingly oblivious to the glare of the truck lights. "She, too, I suspect, although I really wasn't expecting her. A pleasant bonus."

"Hey, look, you!" the driver called angrily, losing patience. "What the hell *is* all this?"

"Oh, dear me, forgive my manners!" the stranger responded. "But, you see, *you* came *here*, I didn't come to you. Where do you *think* you are—and where do you want to be?"

Because the man was right, it put the driver on the defensive. "Uh, um, well, I seem to have taken a bum turn back on Interstate 10. I'm just trying to get back to it."

The big man smiled gently. "But you never *left* that road.

You're still on it. You'll be on it for another nineteen minutes and eighteen seconds."

The driver just shook his head disgustedly. He must be as nutty as he looked, that was for sure. "Look, friend. I got stuck over here by accident in a thunderstorm and followed the road back there to—what was the town? Oh, yeah, Ruddygore. I figure I'll turn around there. Can you just tell me how far it is?"

"Oh, Ruddygore isn't an 'it,' sir," the strange man replied. "You see, *I'm* Ruddygore. Throckmorton P. Ruddygore, at your service." He doffed his top hat and made a small bow. "At least, that's who I am when I'm here."

The driver gave an exasperated sigh. "Okay, that's it. Forget it, buddy. I'll find my own way back."

"The way back is easy, Joe," Ruddygore said casually. "Just follow the road back. But you'll die, Joe—nineteen minutes eighteen seconds after you rejoin your highway. A second storm with hail and a small twister is up there, and it's going to cause you to skid, jackknife, then fall over into a gully. The overturning will break your neck."

He froze, an icy chill going through him. "How did you know my name was Joe?" His hand went back to the .38.

"Oh, it's my business to know these things," the strange man told him. "Recruiting is such a problem with many people, and I must be very limited and very selective for complicated reasons."

Suddenly all of his mother's old legends about conjure men and the demons of death came back from his childhood, where they'd been buried for perhaps forty years—and the childhood fears that went with them returned as well, although he hated himself for it. "Just who—or what—*are* you?"

"Ruddygore. Or a thousand other names, none of which you'd recognize, Joe. I'm no superstition and I'm no angel of death, any more than that truck radio of yours is a human mouth. I'm not causing your death. It is preordained. It can not be changed. I only know about it—found out about it, you might say—and am taking advantage of that knowledge. That's the hard part, Joe. Finding out. It costs me greatly every time I try and might just kill *me* someday. Compared with that, diverting you here to me was child's play." He looked up at the woman, who was still in the cab, straining to hear. "Shall we let the lady join us?"

"Even if I buy what you're saying—which I don't," Joe responded, "how does she fit in? Is she going to die, too?"

The big man shrugged. "I haven't the slightest idea. Certainly she'll be in the accident, unless you throw her out ahead of time. I expected you to be alone, frankly."

Joe pulled the pistol out and pointed it at Ruddygore. "All right. Enough of this. I think maybe you'll tell me what this all is, really, or I'll put a hole in you. You're pretty hard to miss, you know."

Ruddygore looked pained. "I'll thank you to keep my weight out of this. As for what's going on—I've just told you."

"You've told me nothing! Let's say what you say is for real, just for the sake of argument. You say I'm not dead yet, and you're no conjure spirit, so you pulled me off the main line of my death for something. What?"

"Oh, I didn't say I wasn't involved in magic. Sorcery, actually. That's what I do for a living. I'm a necromancer. A sorcerer." He shrugged. "It's a living—and it pays better than truck driving."

The pistol didn't waver. "All right. You say I'm gonna die in—I guess fifteen minutes or less now, huh?"

"No. Time has stopped for you. It did the moment you diverted to my road. It will not resume until you return to the Interstate, I think you called it."

"So we just stand here and I live forever, huh?"

"Oh, my, no! I have important things to do. I must be on the ferry when it comes. When I leave, you'll be back on that road instantly, deciding you just had a nutty dream—for nineteen minutes eighteen seconds, that is."

Joe thought about it. "And suppose I do a flip, don't keep going west? Or suppose I exit at Fort Stockton? Or pull over to the side for a half hour?"

Ruddygore shrugged. "What difference? You wouldn't know if that storm was going to hit you hard because you were sitting by the side of the road or because you turned back—you can never be sure. I am. You can't avoid it. Whatever you do will take you to your destiny."

Joe didn't like that. He also didn't like the fact that he was taking this all so seriously. It was just a funny man in a circle of—"Where does the light come from?"

"I create it. For stuff like this, I like to work in a spotlight. I'll turn it off if you like." He snapped his fingers, and suddenly the only lights were the truck headlights and running lights, which still illuminated Ruddygore pretty well.

Suddenly the vast sea of stars that was the west Texas sky on a clear night faded in, brilliant and impressive and, somehow, reassuring.

Joe heard the door open and close on the passenger side and knew that the woman was coming despite his cautions. He couldn't really blame her—hell, this was crazy.

"What's going on?" she wanted to know.

Ruddygore turned, bowed low, and said, "Madam, it is a pleasure to meet you, even if you are an unexpected complication. I am Throckmorton P. Ruddygore."

She stared at him, then over at Joe, half in shadow, and caught sight of the pistol in his hand. "Hey—what's this all about?" she called to him, disturbed.

"The man says I'm dead, honey," Joe told her. "He says I'm about to have a fatal accident. He says he's a conjure man. Other than that, he's said nothing at all."

Her mouth opened, then closed and she looked confusedly from one man to the other. She was not a small woman, but she felt dwarfed by the two giants. Finally she said to Ruddygore, "Is he right?"

Ruddygore nodded. "I'm afraid so. Unless, of course, he takes me up on my proposition."

"I figured we'd get to the point of all this sooner or later," Joe muttered.

"Exactly so," Ruddygore agreed. "I'm a recruiter, you see. I come from a place that's not all *that* unfamiliar to people of your world, but which is, in effect, a world of its own. It is a world of men—and others—both very much like and very different from what you know. It is a world both more peaceful and more violent than your Earth. That is, there are no guns, no nuclear missiles, no threats of world holocaust. The violence is more direct, more basic—say medieval. Right now that world is under attack and it needs help. After examining all the factors, I find that help from outside my world might— *might*—have a slight edge, for various reasons too long to go into here. And so I look for recruits, but not just *any* recruits. People with special qualities that will go well over there. People who fit special requirements to do the job. And, of course, people who are about to die and who meet those other requirements are the best recruits. You see?"

"Let me get this straight," the woman put in. "You're from another planet?" She looked up at the stars. "Out there? And you're whisking away people to help you fight a war? And we've got the chance to join up and go—or die?"

"That's about the size of it," Ruddygore admitted. "Although you are not quite right. First of all, I have no idea if *you* will die. I had no idea you would be in the truck. And, as an honorable man, I must admit that he might be able to save you if, after returning to the road, he lets you off. Might. He, however, *is* in the situation you describe. Secondly, I'm no little green man from Mars. The world I speak of is not up *there*, it's—well, somewhere else." He looked thoughtful for a moment.

"Think of it this way," he continued. "Think of opposites. Nature usually contains opposites. There is even, I hear, a different kind of matter, anti-matter, that's as real as we are yet works so opposite to us that, if it came into contact with us, it would cancel itself and us out. When the Earth was created, my world was also created—a by-product, you might say, of the creation. It's very much like Earth, but it is in many ways an opposite. It runs by different rules. But it's as real a place as any you've been to, and, I think, a better, nicer place than Earth in a number of ways."

Far off in the distance there seemed to come a deep sound, like a boat's whistle, or a steam train blowing off. Ruddygore heard it and turned back to Joe.

"You have to decide soon, you know," he told the driver. "The ferry's coming in, and it won't wait long. Although few ride it, because only a very few can find it or even know of it, it keeps a rigid schedule, for the path it travels is impossible unless you're greatly skilled *and* well timed. You can die and pass beyond my ken to the unknown beyond, or you can come with me. Face it, Joe. What have you got to lose? Even if you somehow could beat your destiny, you're only going through the motions, anyway. There's nothing for you in *this* world any more. I offer a whole new life."

"And maybe just as short," the driver replied. "I did my bit of soldiering."

"Oh, it's not like that. We have many for armies. I need you for special tasks, not military ones. Adventure, Joe. A new life. A new world. I will make you young again. Better than you ever were."

Something snapped inside the driver. "No! You're Satan come to steal me at the last minute! I know you now!" And, with that, he fired three shots point-blank at Ruddygore.

The huge man didn't even flinch, but simply smiled, pursed his lips, and spat out the three spent bullets. "Lousy aim," he commented. "I really didn't catch any of them. I had to use magic." He sighed sadly. The whistle sounded again, closer now. "But I'm not the devil, Joe. I'm flesh and blood and I live. I am not a man, but I was once a man, and still am more than not. There are far worse things than your silly, primitive devil, Joe—that's part of what I'm fighting. Come with me— now. Down to the dock."

Joe looked disgusted, both with Ruddygore and with the pistol. "All right, Ruddygore, or whoever or whatever you are. It don't make any difference, anyway. I can't go. Not if I can save her. You understand the duty."

Ruddygore nodded sadly. "I feared as much when I saw her in the cab. And for such a motive I can't stop you or blame you. Damn! You wouldn't believe how much trouble all this was, too. What a waste."

"Hey! Wait a minute!" the woman put in. "Don't *I* get to say anything about this?"

They both looked at her expectantly.

"Look, if I had a million bucks, I'd bet that I'm still sound asleep in that truck up there, speeding down a highway toward El Paso, and that this is all a crazy dream. But it's a great dream. The best I ever had. I'm on my way to kill myself. I've had it—up to here. I gave up on this stupid, crazy world. So I'm dreaming—or I'm psycho, in some funny world of my own. Okay. I'll take it. It's better than real life. There's no way I'm going back to that life. No way I'm getting back in that truck, period. I've finally done it! Gone completely off my rocker into a fantasy world that sounds pretty good to me."

Ruddygore's face broke into a broad, beaming smile. He looked over at the driver. "Joe? What do you say now?"

"Well, I heard her story and I can't say I blame her. But I'm the one who's gone bananas, not her."

"Dreams," Ruddygore mused. "No, this is no dream, but think of it that way if you like. For, in a sense, we're all just dreams. The Creator's dreams. And where we travel to is out there." He gestured with a cane, gold-tipped and with a dragon's head for a handle. "Out across the Sea of Dreams and beyond to the far shore. So take it as a dream, the both of you, if you wish. As a dream, you have even less to lose."

The pistol finally went down and was replaced in Joe's pocket. He looked back at the truck. "Maybe we should get our things."

"You won't need them," Ruddygore told him. "All will be provided to you as you need it. That's part of the bargain." The whistle sounded a third time, very close now, and Ruddygore turned to face the dark direction of its cry. "Come. Just follow me."

Joe looked back at his truck again. "I should at least kill the motor and the lights," he said wistfully. "That truck's the only thing I got, the only thing I ever had in my whole life that was real. This ferry—I don't suppose . . . ?"

Ruddygore shook his head sadly. "No, I'm afraid not. Your truck wouldn't work over there. The captain would never allow it, anyway, because we couldn't get it off the boat and it would take up too much room. But don't worry about it, Joe. It's not really here, you see. It's somewhere back there, on your Interstate 10."

With that the truck faded and was gone, lights, engine noise, and all, and they were in total darkness.

The whistle sounded once more, and it seemed almost on top of them.

CHAPTER 2

ACROSS THE SEA OF DREAMS

Travel between universes shall be difficult and highly restricted.
—XXI, 55, 44(b)

THE FERRY CAME OUT OF THE DARKNESS, FLOATING ON A SEA of black. It surprised them that it looked very much like the old ferryboats—an oval-shaped, double-ended affair with a lower platform for cars, and stairways up both sides to the upper deck, where the twin pilothouses, one at each end of the boat, flanked a passenger lounge of some sort with a large single stack rising right up the middle. The sides of the car deck weren't solid, but were punctuated by five large openings on each side, openings without windows or other obstructions, yet the car deck could not be seen through them.

Each one of the huge, round holes had a gigantic oar sticking out of it. The oars were in a raised position, seemingly locked in place. It was clear from the engine sounds and the wisps of white from the stack that the captain was using his engine.

"I never saw a ferry except in pictures," the woman remarked, "but I bet nobody ever saw one with oars before."

Ruddygore nodded. "The engine's in good shape for settling in on this side, but, once out on the sea and to the other shore, that kind of mechanical power just isn't possible to use." He paused a moment. "Ah! It's docked! Shall we go aboard?"

Joe stood there and stared for a minute. "Funny," he muttered, mostly to himself. "I swear I've seen this thing before someplace. Way, way back and long ago. When I was a kid." He scratched his head a moment, then snapped his fingers. "Yeah! Sure! The old Chester ferry. Long, long ago." He peered into the gloom, but the illumination from the passenger deck allowed him to see what he was looking for. "Yeah. There on the side. Kinda faded and peeling, but you can still make out the words 'Chester—Bridgeport.' I'll be damned!"

Ruddygore nodded. "It takes many shapes and many forms,

27

for it's shaped from history and from memories, the backwash of the world flowing backward into the sea whence it came. It is as it is because of your memories, Joe. But—come! I don't want to keep it waiting; as I said, it has a schedule to keep." He paused briefly. "You're not having second thoughts now, are you? Either of you?"

Joe looked at the woman, and she shrugged and gestured ahead with her hand. "Guess not," Joe replied dubiously. As Ruddygore led the way, first she and then the trucker followed, still more than a little uncertain of it all.

Even stepping onto the ribbed metal of the car deck, they both felt an air of dreamy unreality about the whole thing, as if they were in the midst of some wondrous dreaming drug or, perhaps, comatose and in some fantasy world of the mind. Still, both looked in at the cavernous car deck—and saw nothing. Nothing at all. It was totally and completely dark in there, with not even the other end of the boat showing.

Ruddygore led them to the right stairway and saw them peering into the dark. "I wouldn't be too anxious to see in there," he cautioned them. "The ones who row this ship are best not seen by mortal human beings, I assure you. Come. Climb up to the lounge with me and relax, and I will try to answer your questions as best I can."

Hesitantly, they both followed him, still glancing occasionally at the total dark that masked whoever or whatever could manage oars that had to weigh a ton or more each.

It was quickly obvious that they were the only passengers, and the lounge, as Ruddygore had called it, was deserted—but they had obviously been expected. A number of wooden chairs and benches were around, looking a bit shopworn but not too bad; in the rear, around the stack and its housing, was a large buffet table filled with cold platters and pitchers of something or other.

"Just take what you want whenever you feel hungry," the sorcerer told them. "The red jugs are a fair rosé, the yellow a decent if slightly warm ale. Use any of the flagons you see— they're public."

The engines suddenly speeded up, and there was the faint but definite sensation of moving, moving back out into the dark. But moving where? And on what sea?

"What are we floating on—desert?" the woman asked.

Ruddygore cut himself a hunk of cheese, poured some wine, tore off a large chunk of bread, then sat down in a chair that creaked under his great weight and settled back.

"We are heading across the Sea of Dreams," he told them between large bites and swallowed.

Joe decided he might as well eat, too, and followed Ruddygore's lead, except for taking some sliced meat as well and the ale rather than wine. "I never heard of a Sea of Dreams," he noted. "And it sure ain't in Texas."

Ruddygore chuckled, "No, Joe, it sure ain't. And yet, in a way, it is very close to Texas—and everyplace else, for that matter. It is the element that connects the universes. It isn't anywhere, really, except—well, *between*."

The woman wandered out onto the deck for a moment and stared down at the inky blackness. There was the strong feeling of movement; wind blew her hair, wind with an unaccustomed chill in it, but there was no sound of water, no smell of sea or brine.

She shivered in the cold and came back in to join the others. "That sea—is that water?"

Ruddygore reloaded with meat and half a loaf of bread and settled back. "Oh, no. But it has the consistency of water and the surface properties of water, so you treat it that way. In truth, I couldn't begin to explain to you what it actually is." He thought a moment. "The best way to give you at least a sense of it is to provide you with a little background."

Both passengers settled down. "Shoot," Joe invited him.

"Go back to the beginning. I mean the *real* beginning. The explosion that created your universe and mine. Where was the Creator before He created the universes?"

Joe shrugged. "Heaven?"

"But he created the heavens and the earth, also," Ruddygore reminded them. "Well, I'll tell you where He was. Here. And when He created your universe, He also created all the natural laws, the rules by which it all operates, and He generally has played by those rules, particularly in the past couple thousand years or so. But when He created your Earth, there was a backwash from all that released energy. As it surged from here toward your universe, an equal suction of sorts was created that resulted in the creation of another world—indeed, another whole universe on the other side of here. The force of it was such that it was totally complete—but it wasn't the universe *He* was interested in. Realizing, though, that it was there, He turned it over to associates who were around. Angels, you might call 'em, although that's far too simple a term."

Ruddygore paused to stuff his face with gobs of meat and cheese, washed everything down with most of a pitcher of wine, then continued.

"The other universe was, of course, a mess, since it was more or less a backwash of yours. Much natural law held, but not enough to make any real sense out of it. It was chaos. How it was in reality is totally beyond imagination, I assure you, but it was an environment more alien than any other planet in your universe. It was madness beyond imagining, and it was obvious to those—angels—in charge that it must be stabilized, must have *rules* like those in the universe you know. But these were, after all, angels, not the Creator, and they could only shape what the Creator had wrought, not really change it. The result was a set of Laws, absolute Laws, governing how my universe and my world would operate. These Laws incorporate the basic physical laws needed for such a place to exist at all, but only the Creator can think of *everything*. Thus, the Laws of my world are, shall we say, soft. The simple ones, particularly on the local level, are subject to change."

"Huh?" the woman responded. "You mean, nine out of ten times that you drop a rock it goes down the way it should—but one in ten times it might go up? Or just stay there, suspended in midair?"

"Ah, something like that," the sorcerer replied. "Basically, that rock will drop every single time—unless someone with the knowledge and the will applies them to that specific rock. It won't do otherwise on its own, I assure you."

"This—place we're goin'," Joe put in. "It's got people and stuff?"

Ruddygore chuckled. "Yes, Joe, it's got 'people and stuff.' It didn't at the start, but the angels implored the Creator, once they'd gotten it set up, and He shifted a small group from your world over to mine. From that first tribe come the populations of today. And in the millennia that have passed since then, they've developed into different races, different cultures, just as on your Earth. Not quite as diverse, but diverse enough, and this despite the fact that there are far fewer languages there than on your Earth. It's not as important as you might think, that different language business. In your world almost all those peoples to the south of your own country, and many in your country, speak Spanish, I believe—yet there are many cultural differences among those peoples, and many countries that are quite different from one another. Geography and isolation do as much to make people diverse as language."

"You know a lot about our world," the woman noted. "Do your people visit us?"

"Oh, my, no!" Ruddygore laughed. "If they did, they'd soon be corrupted beyond belief. In fact, very few can cross the Sea of Dreams, and none as of now can do it until and unless *I* will it. You see, this is *my* ferry, and it's the only one. Oh, others can see the Sea and others can try the crossing, but it is tricky and dangerous. Impossible to cross, in fact, unless you know *exactly* how to do it. Fail and you will merge with the Sea, returning to the mind of the Creator—and you, yourself, will cease to exist. This is more than death. Your very soul is swallowed and merged back into the primal energies below us. You are gone in true death."

"You're telling us that there is a soul—an afterlife?" the woman pressed eagerly. "That's what it sounds like."

"Well, there is a soul, yes, Miss—just what *is* your name, anyway? We can't keep calling you 'that woman' all the time."

"Marjorie's my real name," she told them, "but mostly I just go by the nickname of Marge."

"All right—Marge," the sorcerer said, nodding. "At any rate, yes, you have a soul. All the humans have souls, and a few of the others. But as to the fate of those souls—there are a lot of things that can happen. Evil can destroy a soul—outside as well as internal evil—and leave the body empty. The soul can wander, or it can be trapped, or a million other things can happen. Otherwise it definitely goes *somewhere*, a *somewhere* from which it occasionally, but very rarely, returns. And there are, it seems, a *lot* of somewheres for that soul to go. Let's not get into that now."

"Okay," Joe agreed. "But I noticed you said all the humans have souls, and a few of the others. What kind of others do you mean?"

Ruddygore sighed. "An infinite variety, really. Those without souls are, of course, the creations of the original angels. To compensate, most are immortal or nearly so, meaning they don't age. They can still, of course, be killed—although, even there, they have a lot of charms and protections. They are not killed in the same way people are, usually. To that original band have been added, over the millennia, ones from your own world who were involved in the original creation but who have, through the dominance of man, been displaced and, by luck, or charm, or the help of me and my predecessors, or the mercy of the Creator, have made their way to my side of the Sea. A one-way trip, though. Some of these have souls, as the Creator Himself willed."

"What sort of—others?" Joe pressed nervously.

"Elves, gnomes, leprechauns—those sorts. The stuff of your legends the world over. The other folk who once shared your world, but for whom man had less and less need and far less room and tolerance. The stuff of your fantasies and legends. Their ties to their native Earth, in fact, are bridges between the worlds across the Sea of Dreams, in a way, for even today those artists and writers of fantasy and the fantastic in your world see them, experience them, if only in dreams, and write of their exploits. The fantasies, the myths, the dreams of your world, are the reality of mine."

Ruddygore sighed. "Look. We cross the Sea of Dreams, and the Creator is even now all around us. He sleeps, and as He sleeps He dreams. Some of the dreams are pleasant ones. Some are nightmares. But *His* dreams take root and flow to one side of the Sea or the other, entering the dreams of one and the reality of the other. This war we now face may be but one of His nightmares. Even now, some dreamer on your world may perceive it in his own mind and write it as a fantasy. You ought to think about that, anyway. You might well be the stuff of an epic fantasy novel in your own world, the dreamer there unknowing that he writes of your reality."

"I'd rather not think about that one," Marge said sourly.

"At any rate," the sorcerer continued, "you're going to a world that will be at once totally different and very familiar to you both. Like this boat. It is a familiar thing to Joe, yet it has not existed since he was a child. It is familiar—yet it is something else. Listen! Have you sensed that the engines have shut down?"

They were all suddenly quiet, attentive to the noises—and

found that he was right. The thrumming of the engine had ceased, and along with it, the vibration against the glass windows of the lounge.

After a few moments of silence, they could hear the groanings of grommets larger than they as the massive oars were seized, freed, and dipped in unison down into the Sea of Dreams.

Below them, on that dark and mysterious car deck now began a deep, hollow sound, rhythmic and somewhat intrusive. It sounded like some giant drummer beating a slow tempo on some great kettledrum. It was all around them, yet not quite pervasive enough to drown out conversation.

"I know what that is," Joe said. "I saw *Ben Hur* nine times. They're rowing to the beat."

Ruddygore nodded. "That's exactly what they're doing. And they'll speed up when they can and maintain it for a long while."

"Just who are—they?" Marge asked apprehensively, thinking of the size of the boat and those oars.

"Monsters," Ruddygore replied casually, getting more cheese. "Real ones. Lost balls, you might say. One-of-a-kinds that didn't make it in either your universe or mine. Once evil and all defeated, they had no real choice. They row the boat, or they are cast adrift in the Sea of Dreams, unable to swim to any shore, even in dock. Oh, don't look so shocked. All of them deserve what they got, and all are volunteers, in a sense. I offered them a chance to row or sink, and they all chose to row. They are comfortable and reasonably kept and they are all now doing something constructive rather than the terrible things they did to destroy, way back in the past."

Marge shivered a little, suddenly even more aware of the beat of the great drum, and tried not to think of what might be beating it. She got up and went back over to the doorway, looking out at the darkness once more.

"Hey! There's something out there!" she called to them. Joe and Ruddygore walked over and joined her. The sorcerer slid back the door and walked out onto the deck. The other two followed.

The creak and groan of the great oars below was noticeable, but with their present better speed and rhythm, they and the drumming could be more or less tuned out. The breeze was still cool. Ruddygore stood at the rail a moment, staring off into the gloom and listening above the sound of the rowing and creak of the ship. "Just what did you see?" he asked her.

She shook her head in puzzlement. "I—I'm not really sure. Some large shapes and odd lights."

"You're liable to see just about anything out there if you stare long enough," the sorcerer told them. "All that was is drawn back to the Sea, and all that will be is formed and dispatched from it. Only what *is* is elsewhere."

In the night, after a while, they all could see what Marge had seen and more. Shapes, some familiar, some unfamiliar. Skylines and odd buildings, then at another time what looked like the fully deployed three masts of some great sailing ship, although the ship itself could not be seen. There were sounds, too—vague, low, yet omnipresent. The sounds of millions of voices talking together far off in some void; the sounds of great machines, of explosions, of building and destroying, all merged into a vague whole. For a while they were caught in its eerie spell, but finally Joe asked, "How long until we get to—wherever it is we're going?"

"A few hours," Ruddygore told him. "You might want to stretch out on one of the benches and catch some sleep—both of you. You've had quite a time so far this night."

"Maybe I will," Joe responded, scratching and yawning a bit.

Marge just shook her head. "No way for me. I'm afraid if I go to sleep I'm going to wake up on the outskirts of El Paso."

Ruddygore chuckled. "I understand your worry, but it won't happen, I assure you. Once we cast off from your world, you were committed irrevocably and forever. Only a few from my side may travel back and forth at will. For those like you, it is a one-way trip."

Joe did stretch out and after a while was snoring softly, but Marge was as good as her word, both anxious and too keyed up to sleep now. She sat down near Ruddygore, who was eating again, and tried to find out more.

"This place we're going to—does it have a name?" she asked him.

He nodded. "Oh, yes. It hasn't just one name, but many. Of

course, the planet itself is simply called the world, or earth, just as you call yours. Why not? It's logical. But the nations and principalities are quite differently named and very distinct. We are bound for Valisandra, my chosen land, to my castle there."

"You're the ruler of a country?"

"Oh, my, no!" He laughed. "Valisandra is a kingdom and quite well and fairly governed. The day-to-day administration of a nation is far too complex and boring for me, I'm afraid, and I'd probably do a very poor job if I ever got the chance. I'm more a—sorcerer in residence, you might say. Long ago I did a trifling service for the current king's grandfather and was given my castle and some land around it as a gift of thanks. With so much magic loose in the world, it gives comfort to the king and his people to have a powerful sorcerer living among them. I have great affection for the land and its people. I have been one among them for a very long time, and I have the same stake in its well-being and preservation as they do. They know this—and they also know that I have no political ambition whatsoever, and thus am no threat to them. There are few ranking sorcerers in the world today—thirteen, all told, including myself—although there are hundreds of slightly lesser lights that may one day replace us."

"This—Vali—"

"Valisandra."

"Valisandra, then. What's it like?"

He sat back, took another long swig of wine, and smiled. "It's a pretty country. The climate is mostly temperate, except in the far north, and the land is rich in good, black earth made for growing things. The people—about three million, all told— are pretty well divided between free farmers and townspeople and those on feudal holdings. The central government's fairly strong, with its own army, so the feudal hold is weak—more like sharecropping than the semi-slavery state some places have. There are still wild areas, too, where the unicorn and deer play free and the fairies come out to dance. Yes, it's a very pleasant place indeed."

She smiled. "It sounds nice. But you said something about a war. That doesn't sound so pleasant."

"It's a different world from yours," he reminded her. "In some ways more peaceful by far. There are no laser-guided battle stations in orbit, no ICBMs and strategic bombers ready to destroy the world at the slip of a politician's nerve. But there is war, and jealousy, and greed, and, yes, death there as well, as they are in every place that mankind exists. Think of a world where magic, not science, is supreme. There are no hospitals, no miracle cures or shock trauma units; and that means a higher mortality rate. There is, of course, medicine—folk and herbal, which can be surprisingly effective sometimes—and magical healers as well. No electricity or great engines for good *or* evil. Power is the wind and water and muscle, as it was in the old days on your world, although there is a cleverness in civil engineering that builds dikes and aqueducts and the like. On the surface, a more primitive, simpler world—but only on the surface. It would be a mistake to think of it as a medieval Earth, for the world is very complex and far more diverse than yours, and the magic is as complex in its own way as nuclear physics is in your world."

She nodded. "It sounds like a fairy story."

"It *is* a fairy story. It is the origin of all such tales. But it is very real—and right now, my part of it is in trouble."

"The war."

"Yes—the war," he responded. "The overall district is called Husaquahr. It's almost fifteen hundred miles from north to south, and more than half that from east to west. There are six countries, as well as five City-States around the mouth of the river which dominates the land. The River of Dancing Gods."

"The River of Dancing Gods," she repeated. "It's a charming name."

"It's more than charming. The river itself winds its way from the Golden Lakes in the north to the Kudra Delta far to the south. It is the blood of Husaquahr—its arteries are its many tributaries, and the system is life itself to the millions of humans and fairy folk who make up its population."

"Why is it named Dancing Gods?"

"There are all sorts of legends and stories about that, but I suspect its divinity derives from its importance to its people. The dancing part may have a thousand reasons in legend, but it is perhaps because it is a very old river that meanders greatly, so much so that to travel on the river the fifteen hundred straight-line miles to the delta from the lakes, you would actually travel over twenty-four hundred miles. It is a primary water source for irrigation, and it is navigable from the point where the Rossignol joins it to form the southwestern border of Valisandra. It is the Nile, the Mississippi, the Ganges, the Yellow, the Volga—and more, all rolled up into one. And, in a sense, it's what the war is about."

"Yes, we're back to the war."

He nodded. "The enemy force includes every destructive element in Husaquahr and from elsewhere besides. Evil, greedy, petty—you name it. It is a frightening force, commanded by a charismatic general known only as the Dark Baron. Who or what he actually is, is unknown, but he is, for certain, a great sorcerer who takes some pains to escape being identified. That makes me believe that he is the worst of all enemies, a fellow sorcerer on the Council that oversees the magic of the entire world. One of my brothers. Or, perhaps, sisters. The Dark Baron is so totally cloaked that it might be either."

"But if the sorcerer is one of your own—doesn't that narrow the field?" she asked. "I mean, it should be simple to discover which of only twelve others he or she might be."

"You'd think so," Ruddygore agreed, "but it's not that simple. Our skills may differ, but our powers are equal—and we are bound by our own rules and laws. No sorcerer may enter the lands or castle of another without the permission of the owner. Distances are great. Magical power being equal, there is no way to tell who is doing what. I assure you that it is quite possible to appear to be in two or even a dozen places at once. Spies within a fellow sorcerer's lairs are impossible—we smell each other too easily. And, of course, even if we knew, it would require incontrovertible proof before any action could be taken. Most of my brothers and sisters on the Council refuse to believe that one of their own could turn this way, and the Council would have to act in concert to defeat and destroy this enemy once and for all. So they sit idly by while the Dark Baron's armies march on Husaquahr, and unless those are defeated in battle, there's nothing that can be done. The Council will not stop something as petty as a war. They are almost traditional."

"But you're meddling," she pointed out.

He nodded. "Someone has to, I fear, and since I suspect that I am at least one primary object of the war, it is in my own self-interest to do so."

"You? They want to kill you?"

"No. I believe that the Dark Baron, with some of his great and powerful allies, could kill me if he wished. Kill me—but not capture me. You see, he has most certainly allied himself with the forces of Beyond—you might call it Hell itself—and that tips the scale in his favor. Oh, he's very clever about it—if I could prove that alliance, it would be the evidence needed to force the Council into action—but *I* know."

"This is starting to get complicated," she noted. "Who or what are these forces of Beyond?"

"Well, you know the story basically, I'm sure. Some of the angels of the Creator rebelled against Him and were cast out. Since that time those forces have been trying to get back, working through the actions of evil ones in your world and mine. Well, now they have their most powerful ally, and the assault's on my world, not yours, and thus more likely not to worry the Creator. They've been terribly frustrated that your own world hasn't yet blown itself into atoms despite their agents' best efforts. But now they have a chance—by getting back into Husaquahr and then, they hope, by forcing an accommodation with me—literally to invade your world, using my powers as a bridge."

She looked shocked. "You mean you'd *do* it?"

He shrugged. "They're not terribly interested in my world, because it's not a primary creation of the Creator. It's yours they want. But it's *my* world, after all. If they can seize and dominate it, they might force a swap, a trade. If they can gain control of the River of Dancing Gods, they will have Husaquahr by the throat, and that's exactly what they're trying to do. It's a slow, brutal conquest—but they are winning."

She sat back, a little dazed, and considered what he had said. The forces of Hell were after Earth—her native Earth—and were willing to conquer and destroy a whole different world to do this. She could appreciate Ruddygore's position, too. He alone knew the way across the Sea of Dreams. He alone could ferry them safely through the very mind of the Creator Himself. And since he controlled the pathway, he could be rid of them—by sending them one-way into Earth.

"Why don't you just send them all over and be done with it, then?" she asked him. "Wouldn't that solve your problem?"

He looked at her strangely and was silent a moment. Finally

he muttered, "Yes, your world *has* treated you most unkindly, I see." He cleared his throat, and his voice grew loud and firm once more. "You seem to forget that your world is the *primary* object of creation. What you suggest is that I precipitate Armageddon. Disregarding the billions of souls I would have on my conscience for a moment, let me remind you that Armageddon would engulf everything, involve the Creator directly. My world would no more survive it than yours, and with less promise of rebuilding thereafter. There will be no Armageddon laid against my soul's account! I do not intend that—even if it means the total destruction of Husaquahr. But they will never believe that. Or they may believe, but not believe that they can not somehow get the secret, anyway. But I have a different plot in mind.

"I intend to beat them at their own game. Send them back into the abyss from which they crawled, they and all their ilk."

CHAPTER 3

"A PROPER HERO AND HEROINE"

Barbarians must be tall, dark, and handsome, exotic in race but of no known nationality.

—XL, 227, 301(a)

SHE SLEPT THEN, THE DEEPEST, SOUNDEST, MOST PEACEFUL sleep she'd had in recent memory, and so hard was it that she barely stirred when shaken the first time. Finally she became aware that somebody was trying to wake her, but she resisted. It was so very peaceful and felt so very good, and it had been such a long time . . .

At last she muttered, "All right, all right," to the mysterious shaker and, in a moment more, managed to open her eyes. She gave a little gasp and rubbed her eyes, a slow smile creeping over her lips. What she saw was the impossibly named and improbably dressed Throckmorton P. Ruddygore. "So it *was* real," she breathed.

He grinned. "Oh, yes. Come. Time to get up, get something into you, and get ready to begin. We're almost there now."

She yawned, stretched, got up, and looked casually out the

windows of the lounge. It was still dark right around them, but off in the distance day seemed to be slowly breaking.

Joe was already up and he nodded to her as she went back to the food table. It had changed somehow during the night and was now filled with pastries, cheese, crackers, brown bread, and condiments that made up a solid European-style breakfast. The pitchers and flagons, she found, were filled with various kinds of fruit juices—and there was a large pot of coffee.

Suddenly conscious of her hunger, she started in.

"No eggs or sausage or nothin'," Joe grumped. "A man's got to have something solid in him to start a day."

Ruddygore laughed. "I'm afraid you'll have to get used to this sort of thing, both of you. Everything's a bit more primitive in Husaquahr, and without refrigeration your American-style breakfasts just aren't practical. I wouldn't complain too much, though. There are times when you'll wish you *had* a breakfast like this."

"I don't mind at all," Marge assured him. "I never was much for the breakfast stuff, anyway."

Ruddygore looked at her with a satisfied expression. "You seem a lot more chipper today," he noted.

She nodded and sipped at the coffee, which was strong and bitter, but still what she needed to complete the waking-up process. "I woke up and you're both still here. That's enough."

Joe wandered over to the windows and looked forward. "Funny, I can see the dawn over there, but it's still dark as pitch right overhead."

"That's because it's never dawn on the Sea," the sorcerer told him. "What you're seeing is not dawn but the edge of the Sea of Dreams. You'll know we're out of it when we come into full light, although I've arranged for a bit of a fog. It wouldn't do to be seen putting in, you know."

Marge went over and looked out at the approaching sky. "How long?"

"An hour, maybe less," the sorcerer replied. "It's actually quite close, but particularly in this area we're going against the current."

Joe scratched and stretched. "I could use a shower."

"Me, too," Marge seconded, feeling just how grubby she'd

let herself become. It was the first time in a long time that she cared about it one way or the other.

"Sorry. No facilities on the boat," Ruddygore told them. "You've seen the pitiful little johns—and they're more modern than you'll likely see again. There's little for showering at the castle, either, I fear, but I'm sure I could arrange for a bath. Just hold on until we get there."

Marge looked back out at the approaching division in the sky, then turned toward the sorcerer. "How long from when we land until we get to this castle of yours?" she asked him. "I seem to remember last night you said it was way up near the source of this big river."

"Indeed it is," Ruddygore told her, "but that won't bother us. The Sea of Dreams contacts all points in all universes. We will land within walking distance of the castle, I assure you. I could arrange even now for us to be met, but I think the walk will do us all good—and you'll get a look at the land." He turned and gestured toward the food table. "In the meantime, let us eat, drink, and be merry."

"Yeah, 'cause tomorrow we die," Joe responded grumpily. Clearly he was very much out of his element and most uncomfortable about it.

"We've broken through!" Marge called to them, and both men came to join her at the window. The darkness was gone—totally gone, with no sign fore or aft that it had ever been. They were now in a dense, white fog that obscured everything. Somewhere up there, though, was a bright point of light that had to be a sun, and that cheered both of the newcomers.

They heard the beat slow, heard oars being shipped, and realized now that they were drifting with a far different kind of current from that of the Sea of Dreams. There was no mistaking the feeling that the boat was coming in to dock.

They went outside on deck, and Marge in particular was cheered to find it comfortably warm, although the dense fog threatened to soak them through. She walked forward, around the pilothouse, and the two men followed. Neither Joe nor Marge could resist looking in the pilothouse, but there was nothing to be seen. Whoever or whatever the captain of this ghostly ferry was, he, she, or it was definitely not visible in the daylight, although the large wooden wheel moved with a deliberateness that said that something, someone, was there.

"The captain and deck crew are nice folks," Ruddygore told them, "but rather sensitive about being seen. Among other things, unlike the rowing crew, *they* can and occasionally do go ashore, and what the passengers don't know about them can't someday be betrayed to an enemy."

Marge took a last look back at the apparently empty wheelhouse and shivered slightly despite the damp warmth. She wondered idly if Ruddygore was being completely honest and straightforward with them. Not that it made any difference right now. They were totally in his hands and at his mercy.

Somewhere aft, a loud bell clanged four times, and again some of the oars came down as the boat performed a steering maneuver. There was a sudden lurch, then a great bump that went the length of the boat, and abruptly the oars shifted again and the boat came to a complete stop.

"Well, we're home!" Ruddygore announced cheerfully. "Follow me." With that he made his way down one of the side stairways.

Joe looked out at the all-encompassing fog and shook his head. "Some home," he muttered to himself, but followed the other two.

They walked across the ribbed metal car deck and saw that there was a smooth area beyond the boat. Ruddygore stepped off onto it unhesitatingly, and after a moment, Marge and Joe did likewise.

The fog began to fade only a few paces from the boat, and before they'd gone fifty yards it had completely vanished, revealing an unexpectedly beautiful scene.

They were in a small wooded area beside a large river, the woods following and hugging the river itself, which seemed to be a thousand yards or more wide and whose other shore was apparently dense forest.

But ahead was cleared land, gently rolling and lushly green with tall, unmowed grasses. Everywhere, too, were wildflowers by the thousands, of countless colors and shapes and varieties, sticking up through the deep green grass. Insects, many very familiar-looking, buzzed and twitted to and fro; here and there small birds circled, dipped, or landed and hopped around in the grass.

Beyond was a hill, not very high, really. Beyond it was a bluff dominating the scene, and on top of the bluff was a castle of the kind both newcomers had seen only in picture books.

"Just like Disneyland," Joe muttered.

"Colder, draftier, but a lot bigger and more useful," Ruddygore responded. "That is Terindell. My home."

"It's beautiful," Marge told him. "Even more beautiful than you described last night."

Ruddygore led the way along a path that seemed well-worn, leading through the lush fields to the castle in an indirect, meandering fashion. It was not paved, but was dry and solid black earth and rock and proved no problem.

"The path is circuitous mostly because of erosion," the sorcerer explained. "As you might guess from the richness of the vegetation, this region gets a lot of rain, and a straight path would have worn its way into a crevasse by now."

"I don't mind," Marge assured him. "It's so beautiful here, and I never felt better in my life."

Joe looked back dubiously. "Where's the boat?"

"Oh, it's not here," Ruddygore replied. "It never quite makes the whole trip either way. You might as well forget that boat, Joe. You'll never see it again."

The walk up to the castle took the better part of an hour, but it was time well spent in just enjoying life and feeling good. Marge was like a kid again, laughing and smelling flowers and chasing butterflies; even Joe seemed to be affected with a sense of well-being after a while. He didn't join in, but at least he laughed along with her.

Shortly before reaching the castle itself, the path intersected the main road leading up to it. It was a dirt and gravel road and not used very much, judging by the lack of real impressions in it, but it was well maintained.

As their elevation increased, they could look down and see the panorama that was Ruddygore's normal view.

"The river we just came from, back there, is the Rossignol," the sorcerer told them. "A gentle river that sings sweet, sad songs, but is a grand old lady in her own right. Over there, now, you can see her child, and the child of many other rivers great and small. The River of Dancing Gods."

Even this far north, there was no comparing the great river with its tributary. It flowed, shimmering golden in the sunlight, a broad, wide, powerful river. Although here it was not much wider than the Rossignol, they could see where the two rivers joined, and where they seemingly flowed along together in the same bed off into the distance, the dark of the Rossignol seemingly resisting the mix with its golden master. But when they joined, the River of Dancing Gods grew enormously, already a mile or more from bank to bank, a great river indeed, with more than a thousand miles left to grow in power and strength even more.

"The other side of the Dancing Gods is Hypboreya, a very different sort of country," Ruddygore told them. "Across the Rossignol is Marquewood, a republic that is even now threatened on its southern border by the forces of the Dark Baron. This little spot of Terindell is but a small finger of Valisandra pointing southwest."

After a last, long look at the stunningly beautiful scene, they regretfully continued around the castle and up to its great outer gate with its massive wooden doors.

Somewhere inside, a trumpet blared briefly, echoing through the inner courtyard, and a great gong sounded three times. At the third gong stroke, the huge doors opened inward, revealing, to the newcomers' surprise, a moat. The inner castle was still a good forty feet beyond. Now from the inner castle, the drawbridge lowered slowly on rusting hinges with a clatter of chains and a moaning of protesting timbers.

"Wow. Just like Robin Hood," Joe muttered, a bit awestruck in spite of himself.

The drawbridge hit with a clang, and, allowing Ruddygore to lead the way, they entered the inner castle.

The entire castle was more a complex than a single building—and complex was the word. The outer wall, including small guard towers and turrets, was thick enough to have almost an avenue along its protected top; inside, it presented a complex of ledges connected by elaborate stairways, all made out of granite. Beyond this was the moat—an ugly affair, oily on the surface and smelling as stagnant as it must be.

The inner castle was a second, thicker shell that definitely had rooms throughout. How many it was impossible to tell, but from the positioning of the windows they could see that there were at least four floors. It was perhaps a hundred feet thick.

Inside this structure was a broad, green courtyard, well kept and maintained, with decorative shrubbery and flower beds; it was broken by a series of blocky stone buildings of various sizes.

They stopped at the edge of the courtyard, and Ruddygore beamed with pride. "Terindell was built more than six centuries ago," he told them. "It has a grand and glorious history, since its position here commanded the heights overlooking the two great rivers and their junction—and, therefore, what commerce and use the rivers made possible. It is quite a fortress, and its location is still vital; but so long as it is mine and I am here, it is safe from the kind of violence it was built to withstand."

"They'd have a tough time getting anybody out of here who didn't want to go," Joe agreed. "They'd have to surround you and starve you out, most likely, and that would put *their* backs to the river in case you wanted out."

Ruddygore looked surprised at his new recruit. "You seem to understand the military factors of my world very well for someone from such a technological culture as your own. Do you have any experience in this sort of thing?"

"Naw. It just seemed logical, is all," the former trucker replied.

"Hmmm . . ." Ruddygore muttered to himself. "Remind me never to confuse ignorance and stupidity again." He cleared his throat and regained command of the conversation. "Staff quarters are in the inner ring, as we call it. I also do a bit of teaching here, and those students also stay there. Inside here we have the central kitchen, then the adjoining banquet hall. The two-storey, blocky L-shaped building over there contains my library, laboratories, and quarters. Come—we'll go there first."

He led the way across the courtyard. For the first time the two newcomers noticed others in the vast castle complex. Smoke was coming from the great chimney that abutted the kitchen, and from inside could be heard talking and the sounds of hard work. Around the courtyard, a few small boys were caring for flower groupings or trimming bushes. No, Marge saw, not small boys. About the size of nine- or ten-year-olds and dressed in green leotards and jerkins, but definitely not boys. One, at least, had a graying beard, and there was something odd, almost inhuman, about their wiry bowleggedness, oversized hands and feet, and disproportionately enormous and slightly pointed ears. Ruddygore caught her thoughts.

"Elves," he told her. "Nice, pleasant folk. Nobody better for landscaping and grounds maintenance work."

Even as they followed the sorcerer, both Joe and Marge could hardly keep from staring at the little men busily at work.

They reached Ruddygore's building and headquarters and were met at the door by a tall, exotic, and, again, not quite human creature. He was close to six feet and stood ramrod-straight, but he was oddly elongated. Joe thought of him as a four-foot-six man stretched somehow to that height. His face, too, was incredibly lean and thin, his ears large, thin, and sharply pointed. His skin was yellowish, and his eyes, black orbs set in deep red where white should be, darted this way and that like those of some beast of prey sizing up its victims. He was dressed in the same sort of jerkin and leotards as the elves, but his were a muddy brown. He wore no shoes; both hands and feet were long and had lengthy, eaglelike talons instead of nails. His jet-black hair was cropped very short, but a shock of it rose up and drooped slightly over his forehead. He was a formidable and fearsome sight, that was for sure.

"Welcome back, sir," the creature said in the stiff, emotionless tones of a butler or other professional servant. He neither looked nor sounded as if he were genuinely glad to see Ruddygore or anybody else. "Did you have a pleasant and successful trip?"

"Yes, yes, indeed," Ruddygore replied and started to go in. He was suddenly aware of his two guests' hesitancy, stopped, turned, and beckoned them in. "Please come in. Poquah— well, I won't say he doesn't bite, but he certainly doesn't bite friends."

Poquah gave what was probably meant as a disarming grin, but he showed an awful lot of sharp, pointy teeth and what looked like a black, forked tongue. The effect was more intimidating than it was hopefully meant to be.

Giving the creature something of a wide berth, they entered and found themselves in a large, two-storey open room completely lined by bookshelves going from floor to ceiling. The floor was covered with thick carpeting with elaborate designs in gold and silver against a burnt orange background. Around a central fireplace were four large, overstuffed chairs. The fireplace itself was reinforced with brick and stone and had a funnellike cap a few feet from the top that sucked up smoke and took it out the roof.

"My quick-reference library," the sorcerer told them with pride. "The bulk of the books are in storage rooms below the castle itself. The whole hill is really a man-made honeycomb of chambers."

They looked around the great library, and one thing immediately struck Marge, at least. "Very impressive," she told him. "I see all sorts of sizes and bindings on books on three of the walls—but all the books on that far wall look the same, with that red binding."

Ruddygore looked over at the wall and nodded. "Indeed, you're right in that they are related. You'll find a set of those in every town center, in every main city, and in the home of everyone wealthy enough to buy them or with any interest in the magical arts. Those, my dear, are the Books of Rules. Five hundred and thirty-seven leather-bound volumes with every little Rule that makes this place tick."

Poquah cleared his throat behind them. Marge jumped, not having heard him move at all. "Pardon, sir," the creature said, "but it is now five hundred and thirty-eight. A new one came in while you were away."

Ruddygore threw up his hands and looked to heaven. "By all the gods and demons and the Creator! This Council is the worst batch we *ever* had! No wonder the world is going to hell!" He let out a big sigh, then motioned to Joe and Marge. "Have a seat, you two, and I will try to explain this idiocy to you. Poquah, can you see about some cold ale for us and then rejoin us here? You're going to be involved in this, too, you know."

The creature bowed. "At once." He was gone so quickly they could hardly realize he had left.

Taking comfortable seats in the padded chairs, the two recruits waited for Ruddygore to begin.

"First of all," he said, "you have to remember what I told each of you in our different conversations last night. How this world was pure chaos, and how the angels in charge created order out of it."

They both nodded, each realizing now that the other had been given the same information.

"All right," the sorcerer went on, "What they did, they did just to stabilize the place. They delivered the Laws. Needless to say, those Laws are complex and involved, and you could no more make sense of them than you could make sense of esoteric particle physics. But they're operating Rules for the place. You follow me so far?"

They both nodded, and he continued.

"All right, then. Those Laws should be sufficient for everybody. They're very general and very universal, but they're all we really need. Unfortunately, several centuries ago, when this castle was an outpost in a major war, a new bunch of sorcerers came to the Council who were, let me say, rather pedestrian. All the really powerful magicians of the time had either perished in the wars or gone on to higher planes. This new Council was made up of pretty petty men—it was all male then, although that's changed—who decided that the Laws contained a large number of loopholes. They weren't specific enough. They didn't address modern problems. With that, the Council ceased being the guardian of the Laws and the integrity of magic and our way of life and became, alas, a bureaucracy. Oh, it was a creeping little thing—you never really noticed it, it was so agonizingly creeping—but, after a while, what we had were the Books of Rules to cover everybody's pet idea, theory, moral code—you name it. Anything they could get a majority of the Council to consider and pass on. Every generation of sorcerers brings some new stuff, and that's what you see behind me here. As long as none of the Rules break any of the Laws—nobody can do that—they are as binding and restrictive as any law of nature."

"Sounds like income tax," Joe commented sourly. "They started with a simple little tax, I'm told, on just the very rich, and got to the point where there were hundreds and hundreds of books of tax laws. I never could know 'em. Last year I had to pay over two hundred bucks to have my taxes done. And even the guys at the IRS admitted nobody really understood the whole thing. It was just too much of a big mess."

Ruddygore smiled. "Exactly! That is exactly it! I doubt if anybody anywhere understands all that's in those volumes. Fact is, you just live in the world and you aren't even aware that what you live with is one of the Rules. It's just the way things are. And they're constantly being revised and rewritten.

Biggest mistake we made was forming a subcommittee to look over the Rules and throw out the bad and resolve some of the basic contradictions that came up. Instead, the fatheads just increased the amount of Rules."

"It's the tax code, all right," Joe said agreeably.

"Only it's worse, since what's in there affects everything and everybody," Ruddygore pointed out. "You have no choice in the matter. And you have no idea—yet—just how petty it can get. And how silly. In fact, that's one thing we will have to attend to right away with the two of you. Right now you're aliens in this land and still pretty much outside the Rules. If we don't attune you to them before you leave Terindell, all those dumb things will fall on you at the same time, and the Creator alone knows what sort of terrible things might happen to you. Poquah, is the lab in good shape?"

"Excellent, sir," the creature replied, and both Joe and Marge almost jumped out of their chairs. Poquah was standing there with a service cart filled with pitchers and tankards—for how long he had been present, they couldn't say. There hadn't been a sound from either him or the service.

Ruddygore chuckled at the two. "I admit Poquah takes some getting used to. He is my closest aide and boss of this place, second only to myself in authority. However, he is an Imir—a race distantly related to those elves you saw, but *very* distantly. The Imir are large, as you can see, and a warrior race if there ever was one."

Poquah served the tankards to the three of them in a good, professional butler manner, but then poured a fourth for himself and took the last chair. He still looked something like a stickman, bending only at right angles.

The Imir took a swallow from the tankard and put it down on the carpet. "We deny relation to elves," he said proudly. "Except, perhaps, the other way around. We have little in common, elves and Imir."

"His people have a basic gift of faërie,* though," Ruddygore

---

* *Faërie* refers to the heritage, magic nature, power, and "realm" of fairies in general; it has a connotation of that which is withdrawn from human ken. *Fairy* refers in more specific manner to individuals, races, traits, and abilities of the fairy folk; its connotation is more that of a normal, day-to-day existence.

told them, "honed in the Imir's case to a fine edge. You simply will not see or notice them until and unless they want to be seen or noticed. It is a trait many of the magical folk have, but in their case it is a defensive one, triggered by startlement, apprehension, or fear. In the case of the Imir, they can turn it on and off at will—a very handy thing for warriors."

"I can see that," Marge agreed.

"Well, Poquah, what do you think of our two new recruits?" the sorcerer asked.

Poquah looked over at the two of them, those red eyes surveying first Joe, then Marge. "Interesting choices," he said at last. "But as a pilot project, they may do. I am surprised at the presence of the woman, but it adds symmetry to the entire affair."

Ruddygore smiled. "The Imir are not known for tact and diplomacy," he told them. "They tell you exactly what they think."

"Diplomacy and tact are basic dishonesties developed by races who cannot fight," the Imir responded casually. "They are unnecessary to the Imir."

Ruddygore sighed and got up. "Very well, then. Let me get a change of clothes, and we'll see to making a proper hero and heroine out of the two of you."

CHAPTER 4

HOW TO MAKE A GOOD APPEARANCE

All persons brought from other universes must be physically acclimated to this one and bound to the Laws and the Rules.
—XX, 210, 116(a)

WHAT RUDDYGORE CALLED HIS LABORATORY WAS A STRANGE cross between a real lab and something out of the Middle Ages. There were compartments, basins, beakers, and flasks very much like those in a school chemistry lab, and there was even a source of natural gas with small Bunsen burner-type nozzles on flexible hoses. There was drainage in the basins, too, although water was strictly a hand-pump affair from several locations. Other parts of the place, though, were what Joe called "strictly voodoo."

There were open areas with all sorts of mystic and cabalistic designs on the floors; long candelabras and incense burners in the shape of odd and demonic idols stood about. Here, too, were braziers and all the other paraphernalia one would expect of an ancient court magician or high priest. There was even an area with an unpleasant-looking altar set into one wall.

Even in the modern part, with its hundreds of little drawers and compartments, things were less than usual. Bat's blood, a jar of eyes of newts, and other things even less pleasant revealed themselves when Joe opened a few compartments out of curiosity. A drawer full of live spiders, quickly slammed shut again, ended his meddling in a hurry.

Ruddygore entered from the rear, near the altar, looking quite different from how he had looked earlier, resplendent now in flowing robes of sparkling gold and wearing a skullcap of the same material.

He smiled and nodded to them, then went over to one of the clear areas near the altar and glanced down in disgust. "Damn. Have to get a mop first and wait for the floor to dry. Damned adepts with their love spells . . ."

Still grumbling, he got a fairly ordinary-looking mop out of the base of an exotic offering stand, pumped out some water from one of the well basins, soaked the mop, and quickly erased the designs on the center of the floor. Replacing it all, he wiped his hands on a towel and came over to them.

"I'll have to wait for the whole thing to dry," he said. "I need to sketch out a few new designs down there." He sighed. "Well, we can use the time a bit to discuss your future."

"That interests me a lot," Joe told him, and Marge nodded.

"Well, let me start with you, Joe. Did you ever imagine yourself off in some other time and some other place as the hero of a big epic? You seem fond of show business, by your remarks. Ever imagine yourself as one of those big, strong heroes?"

Joe thought a moment. "Not really. Not from movies or TV anyway."

"Not even when you were a kid?"

He thought a moment more. "Yeah, I guess so. I'm more than half native American, you know, mixed with Seminole and whatever part of Puerto Rican is from the old days. I used to like to hear the old folks' stories about how it was before the white man. You know, the great civilizations of the past. A lot of times I saw myself as the great warrior chief, riding down with super power and wisdom, turning back the white man and saving the old ways. Kind of silly for a kid from South Philly, I guess, whose idea of wilderness was Fairmont Park, but it does something to a kid when all the other kids are playing cowboys and you know what you are."

Ruddygore nodded thoughtfully. "I can see that. Can you think back to it clearly? I mean, can you visualize that warrior chief? What he looked like?"

Joe considered. "Yeah. I think I can. Sort of."

"Okay, then. Just hold that vision and don't let go." The sorcerer turned to Marge. "And you? Any super cowgirls? Beautiful princesses? Amazonian warriors?"

She smiled wistfully. "Yeah."

"Which one?"

"All of 'em."

The sorcerer chuckled. "Well, if you had to pick one, some vision of yourself—perhaps as the warrior queen, gutsily defending her splendid golden castle . . ."

She thought it over and closed her eyes for a moment. "Yeah. I can think of a dozen novels I've practically lived again and again."

"All right. Just keep that vision in mind." He looked over at the floor. "I see it's dry now. Let me make my preparations."

He reached inside the mouth of a hideous bronze idol set in the wall and took out what proved to be a piece of thick, soft chalk. Working rapidly, he positioned first Joe, then Marge, about eight feet apart in the clear area, then started drawing around each of them on the smooth slate floor with the chalk.

The designs were identical. Pentagrams, clearly and solidly drawn, and outside each pentagram a six-pointed star. He got up from the floor and said, "Now, neither of you move. Not an inch outside those pentagrams—not until I tell you. Understand?"

Joe looked nervous and uncomfortable. "The real conjure stuff," he murmured uneasily.

The sorcerer nodded. "The real stuff, Joe. You in particular should understand that you stay where you are at all costs.

Marge, you take it seriously, too." He backed up a distance from both of them, then drew a new, larger pentagram around the two recruits, this time with Ruddygore inside. From a small valise also inside the outer design he removed candles and long candlesticks, which he proceeded to set at each of the five points of the outer pentagram. He lighted each candle in turn with a long stick which was burning at one end, being careful at no time to cross the outer pentagram. Then, stepping back, he proceeded to draw the same design around himself as around the other two, so that he was equidistant from them and facing them. He checked everything visually to make sure it was all to his satisfaction, nodded, and took a deep breath.

"It is a simple spell. Child's play, really. But you get to be an old sorcerer not only from long study but also because you never take even the easy ones for granted. Now, don't be startled by anything that happens from now on. Take it as a show, a magic trick, but for the sake of your souls, do not break your own pentagrams!"

"You gonna conjure a demon?" Joe asked uneasily.

"That's about it," Ruddygore agreed. "A very minor one of little importance, but it owes me. It will appear between us, so I warn you about that right now. It may look fearsome; but as long as you remain totally within your pentagrams, it can not touch you, let alone harm you. It may also sound very decent and civilized, but don't let that fool you, either. At this level, the demons are more raw emotion than intellect and have just about no self-control. If you break your pentagram, it will almost certainly eat you and carry your soul to Hell as its eternal slave. There would be nothing I could do about that—understand?"

They both nodded, and Marge couldn't help thinking over and over, *My god, this isn't a dream or a joke—it's real!* As for Joe, he'd had no doubts from the beginning.

"All right," Ruddygore said, taking a deep breath. "Here we go."

With that he closed his eyes and began chanting, softly, in a language neither of the other two could comprehend. It was an ancient tongue, though, seemingly of some race that far predated humanity, and it was not designed for the human vocal system.

It's no wonder sorcerers also go in for all sorts of potions,

Marge thought, hearing it. *They all have to have chronic sore throats.*

For a while, nothing happened, and the newcomers began to think that nothing would occur. Then, quite slowly, they both realized that the light level was sinking ever so gradually, the torches and lamp flames shrinking in intensity. It was growing, abruptly, quite dark; within four or five minutes, all light sources in the lab were out, except the five candles at the outer pentagram points. Again a minute or two passed with nothing else happening, but the air grew thick with expectancy.

Suddenly, in the space between Ruddygore and themselves, there was a disturbance in the air. It began as a few silver and gold sparkles, but slowly, about three feet from the floor, the sparkles increased in number and intensity and started to swirl, forming after a time a sparkling whirlpool or galaxy shape which quickly widened, took a new shape, and outlined a grotesque figure in its tiny flashing pattern. The sparkles suddenly vanished, and the shape became solid and real before them.

It was a terribly ugly creature, round and squat, in some ways resembling a toad but with a face that was more piglike than anything else, complete with two big, curved, boarlike tusks and lots and lots of teeth. It was hairless, naked, and stood on two birdlike feet. Its eyes were round and bright yellow with black dots in the center, like the eyes of a fish, and, like them, seemed lidless. The skin itself was mottled, gray and greenish, the color of death and mold—and it stank up the place to high heaven.

It looked up at Ruddygore—being only three feet high—and gave a nasty grin. "You don't mind if I check you out?" it rasped in an unpleasant, grating voice. "Even the best slip up now and then."

"Be my guest," the sorcerer responded.

With that the creature waddled around, checking the designs around each of the three humans, then walking the length of the outer pentagram. Finally satisfied, it returned to the middle of the three and again looked at Ruddygore. "They're good enough to restrain me," the demon admitted without sounding in any way surprised. "Wouldn't hold an elemental or anything stronger, though. You're slipping in your old age."

Ruddygore smiled. "It doesn't need to hold anything stronger. You still owe me, Ratzfahr. You know that."

"Yeah, yeah. Damn. Ask a little favor just one time and they never let you forget it," the demon grumped.

"One! You want the list?"

"Aw, okay, okay." Ratzfahr turned his head completely around without moving his body and looked at the other two, then swiveled back to Ruddygore. "They smell funny," the demon noted.

"So do you," the sorcerer retorted, "but I've never let that come between us."

"This is some nutty language you got us talkin', too," the demon went on. "Where'd you get these two, anyway?"

"Earth Prime," Ruddygore told him. "Where else?"

The head swiveled again. "Well, I'll be a cherub! Earth Prime! Been a long time. You figurin' on screwing up the neighborhood?"

"No, but I have need of them," Ruddygore said. "So don't you try any tricks on them, Ratzfahr. They're my guests."

"Guests." The demon chuckled evilly. "I'll bet. Still, what's your pleasure?"

"Acclimatization. The works. Physical. Language. No soul, though. That stays Prime."

"Aw, for cryin' out loud!" the demon protested. "C'mon, you old windbag! That's a hell of a lot! You ask too much."

"No matter what, you must return to Hell," Ruddygore reminded the creature menacingly. "It wouldn't do for everyone down there to know the Profane Name by which you were formed!"

The demon looked genuinely shocked. "You *wouldn't*!"

"You bet I would! And you know it!"

The demon sighed. "All right, all right, you got me where it hurts. You sure about the soul, though? They'll stand out like magnets to them that got the Power."

"I have my reasons," the wizard told him. "Just do as instructed."

"Okay, okay. What language you want?"

"*Makti*, of course. Unless you'd like to give them the Gift of Tongues."

"You gotta be kiddin'," Ratzfahr scoffed. "You know what that would take out of me."

"I do, which is why I ask rather than demand. *Makti* it is, then."

The demon suddenly floated up two feet in the air, turned, and looked at the man and woman critically. "Yeah, I can see they need work," he commented idly.

Both Joe and Marge were tempted to return the insults, but were a little leery about saying much of anything. The demon was certainly not what either of them had expected, but Ruddygore's warning had been seriously taken.

Ratzfahr gave a low whistle. "Wow. They really have high opinions of themselves, don't they? Oh, well. Here goes nothin'! *Raddis on the frabbis! Freebix on the Clive!*" And with those cryptic remarks he started spinning, picking up speed very fast until he was only a whirling blur of motion in the near darkness. Suddenly from him emanated two columns of gold and silver sparkling rays that touched and then seemed to engulf the two humans' pentagrams.

They both felt a sudden falling sensation, as in a fast-descending elevator, and a tingling, like electric shock, only all over their bodies. For a moment, it was all either could do to remain standing in the pentagrams, and each had a fear of falling out and into the clutches of the demon; but while both wavered a bit, they held steady.

There was sound all around, too, now: the cacophony of thousands of discordant voices shouting and competing with what seemed like ten symphony orchestras all playing nonsense and out of tune. It grew and grew inside their heads and all around them until they thought they could stand no more.

And then, quite suddenly, it was over.

Marge shook her head a little as if to clear it, and Joe let out a big "Whew!" Both looked back at Ruddygore, who was again facing the now stationary demon.

Ruddygore said something to them, and it sounded like nonsense. Idiot syllables that hardly seemed like a language at all, but more like the magical chanting he'd done at the beginning. They both just looked at him in confusion, and Marge, at least, worried that the demon had played some sort of nasty trick on them.

Ruddygore, however, seemed satisfied. "How's this?" he called to them. "Do you understand me now? By all means, speak up and tell me."

"Yeah, that's fine," Joe called back.

Marge said, "I thought for a minute something awful had happened."

Ruddygore nodded, mostly to himself. "Good job, Ratty. Now, go! I banish thee back to the realm whence thou didst come! In the name of Hagoth and Morloch, I do send thee to thy world and charge thee remain until called once more! Go!" Ruddygore paused for a moment. "A case of cigars will be sent to you. Enjoy."

"Thanks, T. R.!" the demon responded—and vanished.

"Hold up!" Ruddygore called to the two humans. "Don't go yet. He sometimes likes to pull a fast one!" With that, the sorcerer commenced a long, unintelligible chant.

Suddenly in the air very near them, the demon's voice came. "Aw, *shit!*" it said, and the sense of presence vanished.

All at once, all the lights, flames, and torches in the room flared back into life. There was no sign of the demon. Still, Ruddygore completed the chant, then looked around and seemed to relax visibly. "It's all right now. Let's take a look at you!"

But they were already looking somewhat awestruck, staring at each other.

"Come!" the sorcerer invited them both. "Stop staring and walk with me back here to where the mirror is."

Both hesitantly waited until the sorcerer had walked from his pentagram and crossed the outer one before following, but that didn't keep them from rushing to the mirror once they were assured in their own minds that they were safe.

They stood there, next to each other, gaping at their own reflections as they had gaped at each other.

Joe had been a big man, but now he was even larger. Six foot six, perhaps, in bare feet, and built like a man of iron, muscles rippling with every movement, his skin a smooth, metallic bronze. His face was strongly chiseled, an Indian warrior's face, rugged yet strong and handsome. A young Geronimo, perhaps, or Cochise, with a great mane of shoulder-length, jet-black hair.

Marge, too, had thought taller, but she barely came to his shoulders. Still, she was a vision of her mind—long, pure, strawberry-blond hair, enormous, deep green eyes, with an angelic face and perfectly proportioned supple, athletic, and definitely sensual body.

Joe's voice was now a deep, rich baritone; Marge's, a strong but inviting soprano. It was Joe, after perhaps four or five minutes, who spoke first.

"Hey! We're stark naked!" he exclaimed.

Ruddygore summoned Poquah while he cleaned up his lab, and the Imir took them back to two wardrobes, one with a vast assortment for men, the other for women. The extensive clothing, in a wide range of sizes, told a little more about the land of Husaquahr. Jerkins, tights, and other fashions more at home in a medieval costume epic seemed the rule, although there were hundreds of variations, including elaborate robes, long, satiny dresses, and very ornate male and female clothing. Everything was well made but obviously hand-done in all respects. Poquah told them to select whatever from the wardrobes they would feel most comfortable wearing and assured them that later on they would be allowed to pick more extensively. Right now, this was just to get them started.

Both discovered that undergarments either were not the fashion or hadn't been discovered here. Oh, there were *underclothes*—more or less full-body types—but they seemed to go with the fancy and uncomfortable-looking royal garb.

Marge finished first, then made her way back to the library, where Poquah had coffee, tea, and pastries waiting. "It is best to eat something, although lightly," he told her. "Your digestive system will need a little help in starting up again without your getting ill."

She accepted his advice, pouring some lightly sugared tea and nibbling on a small croissant. She looked around for a mirror, but there were only books about the place. *Too bad,* she thought. *I still can't believe that that image in the mirror back there is really me.* Still, she had to admit she felt—well, different. Lighter, more agile, more nubile and nimble, and disgustingly healthy.

"Almost feel like a kid again, eh?" came Ruddygore's voice behind her, and she jumped slightly in surprise and turned to him.

"Yes, that's really it," she answered. "I don't think I've *ever* felt this good. And—do you read minds, too?"

"When I have to, but it took no sorcerous turns to guess your thoughts this time," the wizard responded lightly. "I assume Poquah has cautioned you against overindulging for a while?"

She nodded. "That's all right. I don't really feel hungry. Just a bit dry."

"That's natural," he assured her. "Drink anything you want, but stay away from ales and other heavy stuff until you have a few meals in you. I might warn you, too, as a matter of general principle, not to drink any water you haven't boiled, here or anywhere. Fermented stuff, boiled hot drinks, and fresh fruit juices, though, are all right."

"I'll remember," she promised. At that moment Joe entered, and she turned to look at him. She couldn't suppress a chuckle. "Well! Look at *you!*"

"Look at you, too," he retorted, and seemed to mean it.

"What do you mean by *that?*"

Ruddygore decided it was time to step in, although he was vastly amused by the reaction. "Welcome to the Rules," he told them. "Come—sit down and I'll explain what this is all about."

Poquah hastened to give Joe the same cautions he'd given Marge. Joe, though, seemed more disturbed by the exchange than by any cautions.

Marge continued to stare at him. She had hardly gotten used to the rough, burly, dark truck driver, and now here was this young, muscular—savage? No, that wasn't the right word. But Joe had gone along with the body and the image. First he'd chosen a crimson headband to keep his unaccustomed long hair in place, and beyond that a wide leather belt—perhaps four inches or more—with small bronze studs or rivets going evenly around near top and bottom. Aside from the belt, though, he'd chosen a long, thick cotton loincloth, leather sandals—and that was it.

As for Joe, this new, strangely beautiful woman didn't bother him much, either—after all, it had been probably no more than a day and a half since they'd met for the first time—but he could hardly understand why a woman wearing a pretty revealing cotton-lined leather halter and a "skirt" apparently made up of thousands of strands of individually strung red and purple beads that showed practically everything every time she moved had any right to comment on *his* garb.

Ruddygore, still wearing his golden robe, took a couple of

large, fat pastries and sat back down in his chair. Marge sat in a chair to his right, legs slightly crossed, and Joe sat facing them, noting that, from almost any angle, the woman might as well have nothing on at all as that "skirt," whose strands fell away to reveal all, being connected only by a slim and nearly invisible waistband.

"Your reactions to each other's choices are natural, but I can explain it," the sorcerer assured them between bites. "First of all, Marge, you're surprised that Joe chose what he did, so let's take care of that. Joe—why *did* you choose the sword belt, loincloth, and sandals over all the rest?"

Joe looked blankly back at them. "Why, I dunno, really . . . It just seemed . . . *right*, somehow."

Ruddygore nodded. "Volume 46, page 293, section 103(c)—the Books of Rules." He gestured back at the wall of red-bound volumes. "Your mental image, Joe, was, in the parlance of this world, the classical barbarian hero. Now, don't get mad at that word 'barbarian.' It's simply a word applied by a culture to anybody who obviously comes from a different one, one they feel superior to—and which may well be superior to theirs. Get used to it."

"I kinda like it," Joe responded. "Barbarian. Yeah. That's about right. But what was all that volume and page stuff?"

"That particular section, Joe, says, *'Barbarian male heroes in southern temperate climes shall wear their hair long, nor shall they shave their beards, and will dress appropriately in sword belt, loins, and sandals.'* And that's what you did. Of course, since you chose an Oriental barbarian, basically, you won't have a beard or much body hair. But, you see, that's how the Rules work. They don't order you to do something. They just make it so you naturally want to do it."

Joe chuckled. "So *that* explains it. Still, it *feels* right. I don't mind." He had a sudden thought. "But what if I have to go where it's cold?"

"Don't worry about it. Section 103(b) covers it. You don't have to know it. You'll just do it when the time comes. You'll *know*. That's the most positive thing about this land, Joe. You *know*. And if you meet someone similarly dressed, you'll know what he is, too."

"Fair enough. And her?"

Ruddygore turned to Marge. "You realize, of course, that

you're almost more in a state of undress than dress. That's what Joe was talking about."

"Well, yeah, but . . . Oh, those books again."

Ruddygore nodded. "Volume 46 is mostly concerned with appearances. Page 119, section 34(a)—*'Weather and climate permitting, all beautiful young women will be scantily clad.'* It's as simple as that."

She just stared at him.

"Don't blame *me*," the sorcerer responded, reaching for another pastry. "I *told* you they were petty—and in great detail. The current Council is overdoing it quite a bit, I admit, but the basics have been here for thousands of years. They lend stability to the land. In a way, you have to sympathize with the Councils of the past. They were faced with imposing sanity on a world based upon magic. And, truthfully, does your current garb bother you?"

She thought for a moment. "Well . . ."

"Truthfully, now. You didn't even realize it until it was pointed out to you, did you?"

"No, I didn't," she admitted. "It's just that, spelled out like that, there's something that offends me, deep down."

"Both of you may find yourselves compromising some of your principles from your old world, but you have to accept the Rules. It isn't like changing the mind of a legislature or something. In a way, it's close to repealing the law of gravity to change the Rules in any substantive manner. And, by the way, gravity isn't locked in concrete here, either. The universe still operates in pretty standard ways, but don't assume that local conditions do. They most assuredly do not."

She got up and walked over to the wall of red books, pulled one out, and opened it at random. She found it a mess of black, blue, and red squiggles and she couldn't read a word of it. She shook her head and put it back. "I guess we're both back to being illiterate here. That brings up a point, by the way. Just as these books are in some other language, people around here aren't going to speak English, either. Do we have to take language lessons?"

Ruddygore chuckled. "Oh, my, no! That was part of the acclimatization process. You remember just after it was all done I yelled something at you? Something neither of you could understand?"

They both nodded.

"I was yelling in English. Look." He proceeded to give off what sounded like a strange and inhuman series of sounds, then smiled. "*That* was English. Neither of you speaks it any more, nor understands it, either. We are right now conversing in a language called *Makti*. It's the trading language of the river. Although there are dozens of tongues spoken just on and around the river, there is one—a sort of simplified amalgam of them all with its own grammar and syntax—that developed because of the need for it. It's locked in the Rules—Volume 306 is a dictionary, 305 gives the Rules governing it. No matter where you are in Husaquahr, there will be those who understand it and speak it fluently."

"Yeah, but what about words not *in* the language?" Marge asked him. "I mean, I still am a Texan, and that's not a likely word."

"Nor is it one," the sorcerer agreed. "But that word, and similar words, are provided for. They remain in a mental *secondary* vocabulary, still as they were in English, and understandable to a speaker of English. *Makti* is a very flexible tongue, you see, and accommodates local idiom. Otherwise it would be of little use as a trading language. However, with its six tones and shorthand basics, it's not transliteratable into English at all. The language as written is also ideographic, I fear, with a basic alphabet of more than two thousand characters and sixteen accent and tone marks. It takes years to learn if you weren't raised with it, and a full vocabulary, capable of complex writing and reading, say, the Rules, is tens of thousands of symbols. The bottom line is that, yes, you're illiterate—like the vast majority of this world—and probably going to stay that way."

"It sounds pretty complicated to me," she told him. "You mean the other languages are even *more* complicated?"

"Vastly so," the sorcerer assured her. "So much so that *Corabun*, for example, spoken in the area of the Fire Hills and Lake Zahias far to the west of here, has never had a successful written language. Or *Hruja*, spoken in parts of Leander, which is so ridiculous that you *have* to know some ideograms because you have to draw in the air just to talk unambiguously to one another."

"Ideograms," Joe put in. "That's picture writing? Like the Chinese and Japanese back home?"

"Something like that," Ruddygore replied. "But it's not the same language by far."

"It seems this would lock in the hierarchy," Marge noted. "I mean, if you can't read or write, you can't be a trader or businessman, or get a top spot in government. So most of the people can't read those Rules, either, which leaves the magic up to those who can."

"I'll admit to that, in a general way," Ruddygore responded, "but not totally. Remember, here most trades, skills, and positions are passed down from one generation to the next. And whatever literacy is required gets passed along, too. Occasionally somebody with a real knack for it comes along who is, say, a peasant farmer, and then he—or she—rises in society and power if he wants."

"So the farmer's kid *can* be king—if he's somehow able to learn the language on his own, with nobody to teach him, and then get access to all the books he needs. Clever. You hold open the hope to the lowest that their kids *might* rise all the way, while conditions make it just about impossible for them really to do so. It's neat," Marge said sourly.

Ruddygore shrugged. "It works. What can I say? And everybody knows some example somewhere. However, whatever gave you the idea that a king has to be skilled or literate? Most of them are blithering idiots, really. Figureheads for their advisors, councilors, and bureaucracy."

"Pretty cynical, aren't you?" Marge retorted. "But since we can't read or write this stuff, we're stuck on the low rung. Some new world!"

"Oh, my, no!" The sorcerer chuckled. "Barbarians can rarely read—but one or two have seized and held kingdoms. Your wits are your best assets, I assure you. That and training and working at needed skills—and keeping those bodies of yours in peak physical shape. I have a great deal of hope for the two of you and a great set of missions. You are very important to me. You see, right now I have remade you to this world and its laws and rules. Almost all of you. But your souls are still of your native world, and that is important. The forces of Hell must work through agents here, but their magic is far different from any here. They attune themselves to the souls of our world. You are totally vulnerable to the considerable magic of this world and this land—but you will find yourselves invulnerable to the direct sorcery of Hell. It may be of small difference to you, but it may be of great consequence to me."

"I'm not sure I understand anything you just said, but it doesn't sound like either of us is gonna have a long and happy life," Joe grumped. "Seems to me like a pretty high price just to get out of alimony and child support."

Ruddygore smiled. "Long or short? Who knows? You were minutes from death when I pulled you away, Joe."

"So *you* say. I ain't real sure I believe all that stuff."

"Believe it or not as you will, it *is* true. But it is also beside the point now, anyway, and that's the way you should think of it. You are here. You can't get back. Even if I were to let you, you are so changed from who you were that you'd be a strange barbarian in your old world speaking a language nobody could understand. They'd lock you up in a little room and throw the key away. Walk out of here now and you will be in a world you know nothing of and are ill-prepared to live in. Stick it out, Joe. Remember, I said I needed a *hero*, not a martyr. You're no good to me dead, and I'm going to spend a lot of time and effort to keep you alive. Take it like that. I need you, and, at least for now, you need me. Fair?"

Joe considered it. "Yeah, I guess so. For now, anyway. But what comes next?"

"I've been wondering that, too," Marge put in.

"Time is not on my side," the sorcerer told them. "Right now the enemy is slowing to a halt far south of here because it is flood season, and the lower river is one vast flood plain. After that will come the monsoons, which make movements unpredictable. Still, the enemy will be fully on the march again in three or four months, and that means we have six months at best before we either act or fight him at our gates. Not a lot of time, but with a bit of magical help and a lot of experience—and the cooperation of you both—I think we can use that time to good advantage. You'll be seeing little of each other from this point until you are ready. Each of you is now going to school. A most unusual school. One pupil each. If and when you finish, you will be well prepared for the hardships and challenges you might face—and more than able to exist in Husaquahr or anywhere else on our world." He turned to the

Imir, who stood nearby as always. "Poquah, show them to their quarters and notify Huspeth and Gorodo."

"When do you wish them to begin?" the Imir asked him.

"As soon as possible. This evening, if practical or convenient. We have no time to spare."

<hr>

CHAPTER 5

ANSWERING THE MUNCHKINS' QUESTION

A witch is the term given to any practitioner of potion magic and/or spells whose practice is based upon a system of religious beliefs.

—IX, 318, 201(a)

LATE THAT AFTERNOON POQUAH CALLED ON MARGE, WHO had been relaxing on a feather bed in the small room the Imir had brought to her earlier. She had mostly been just lying there, thinking of how good it was to be alive and anticipating, perhaps, romantic adventures to come. That and examining her new body in minute detail.

I was dead inside, she realized, *and now through an impossible miracle I'm more alive than ever.* Having come so close to death, she wasn't bothered by risk. In a sense, she was already living on borrowed time—and each precious minute was wonderful. The only thing she truly feared and could not entirely shake from her thoughts was that this new life, still so dreamlike and unreal to her practical mind, might end as suddenly as it began. True, total insanity might be like this—and, certainly, she was now living in her fantasies and dreams. *What if I'm somewhere inside a rubber room?* Somehow, deep down, she wondered if she would ever really be rid of that one fear, if she would ever really know. And, even more of a question, did she fear knowing?

"You will come with me now," the Imir told her. "It is time for you to begin your instruction."

She arose and nodded to him. "Where are we going?"

"It was decided that your best potential would be realized by Huspeth in the Glen Dinig," Poquah replied, explaining nothing. "As you know, we were expecting only the man.

Huspeth, however, is willing, and is better equipped than we. Can you ride a horse?"

"Yes, I've ridden horses. At least I can manage. Why? Is this Glen Whatsis far?"

"Not far," he said. "But too far to walk. Come with me. We should make haste to get you there before dark." With that he turned and walked out of the room and down the hall. She followed, hurrying to catch up.

They went back down, across the drawbridge, and through the outer ring. Just at the start of the road, two beautiful horses, one coal black and the other snow white, waited, being held by an elf groom.

She approached the horses excitedly. "How perfect they are! But—no saddles, huh?" It was true. The horses were fitted only with bridles and a smooth blanket tied about their midsections.

"Saddles are a luxury. It is best you learn horsemanship without them. Then a saddle will be a convenience, not a necessity."

She looked dubious. "Well, okay, but I hope I can hold on."

With the Imir's aid, she boosted herself up on the white horse, grabbed the reins, and tried to get as comfortable as she could. It felt a little strange being up, and she felt some muscles being stretched in unaccustomed places.

The Imir mounted the black horse effortlessly and looked over at her. "Shall we ride?"

She nodded. "Take it easy, though, at the start, will you? I'm a little wobbly."

"Slow and easy," Poquah assured her. Giving his mount a little nudge with his foot, he started off. Her horse, apparently very well trained, followed the black one at a slow, comfortable pace.

Riding down the slope from the castle was fairly easy, although they were following no trail. Still, Marge's horse swayed and twisted with the land, and it took her several minutes and a few near spills to get anything approaching steadiness without saddle or stirrups.

"Who is this Huspeth?" she called to Poquah when they closed ranks.

"She is a witch who lives in the Glen Dinig," the Imir told

her. "She is very old and very wise and very powerful. She is a great one, but she never leaves her forest glades these days."

"Is she a friend of Ruddygore's?"

"Hardly. Huspeth has little use for people in general and for sorcerers in particular. She is greatly feared by many, liked by none."

"Thanks a lot," Marge said sourly. "And I'm being handed over to her? Is it safe?"

"Nothing in life is safe," the Imir responded philosophically. "However, she has her own reasons for wanting this task, which was asked of her but could not be forced upon her. She will do it, not because of the Master, nor for any cause, although our enemy is also her enemy, but because she chooses to do it. We did not expect her to accept, but we chanced to ask."

They went on as the sun sank lower in the fields; with this description of her prospective tutor, Marge's high spirits sank a bit lower, as well.

After more than an hour's ride, out of sight of the castle but just barely, they came over a rise and Poquah stopped. Below, the plain gave way to thick forest, a distinct grove perhaps two miles square between the rolling hills and the River of Dancing Gods.

The Imir pointed. "The Glen Dinig," he told her. "Please dismount." With that he jumped from his horse with a cat's balance and turned to her. She found it difficult to move her numbing legs, which throbbed with pain from the unaccustomed ride, but she managed with his help to get one leg over the other and sort of slide down to the ground. Relief shot through her legs, although she staggered a bit from the painful stiffness.

"Wow! I thought I was a better horsewoman than *this*!"

"Your old body's muscles were so conditioned, probably," he said, "but everything is new to you now. This body is drawn from the energies that are around us and those which made up your old self; it is a new body and it will need conditioning."

She whistled low and nodded, trying to shake the kinks out of her legs. "Yeah. I keep forgetting that." She looked down at the thick forest. "What now?"

"Huspeth never emerges from the Glen Dinig, and I can not

enter it. My instructions were to bring you to this point, then direct you to walk down and into the wood. I will return to Terindell."

Again she looked uncertainly down at the forest, which was fast becoming a place of great shadow as the sun sank almost to the horizon. "You're going to leave me to walk into those woods at dusk alone?"

The Imir did not reply. Demonstrating his little trick once more, he was gone, taking the horses. She looked around but could see no sign of him or the mounts, nor hear anything except a slight whistling of a warm wind. She was alone.

She sighed and shook her head. "Well, on your own again, with not even a highway to bail you out." She considered walking back to the castle, but it *was* a fair distance—several miles, anyway—and most of it would be in the dark. She sighed again. "Well, I've trusted old Ruddygore this far. May as well keep doing it now." With this she walked down the hill toward the woods.

It was much cooler in the Glen Dinig, and there was the smell of the damp, with moss and rotting limbs giving it an even eerier look in the gathering gloom. Insects and occasional squirrellike creatures scampered here and there, startling her.

Having no other instructions, she just continued walking, the forest getting thicker and darker as she went. She began to grow nervous, fearing that she might be trapped alone in total dark for the night, and she started having second thoughts about going blindly through the place. She turned to make her way back, but soon realized that back looked the same as forward now. She had no idea how far she had come, nor exactly from which direction. That being the case, and considering the small size of the forest, she finally decided that the best thing to do was to press on in one straight line. Eventually she'd have to reach the edge of the forest or, at worst, the river.

In a few minutes, when things had just turned to a dangerous, nearly pitch-blackness, she came upon a small clearing; in the middle of the clearing was an earthen hut. It was a very primitive affair, looking much like a wood and straw igloo, but there was a fire burning in a pit in front of the little hut—and some sort of cauldron sat on an improvised stand above the fire, smoke rising from it.

Relieved to see *any* sign of life, she hurried forward.

"Hold, girl!" came a voice, high-pitched and raspy, so grating that it almost sent chills up her spine. She stopped, turned, and looked for the first time on Huspeth.

The woman was not merely old, she was ancient, mostly stretched and wrinkled skin over a bare skeleton. The face was scarcely human, with a long, pointed jaw and a tremendous beaklike nose, and her eyes were like two huge, perfectly round cat's eyes set in a yellow sea that literally glowed. She was medium-sized, but bent over and leaning on a crooked stick. She looked like everybody's bad dream of what a witch might look like, down to the black, full-length robe, scraggly white hair, and small, pointed black cap.

Huspeth looked Marge over critically, head twisting slightly first one way and then the other, as a bird might examine something before pouncing upon it. Finally she said, "So thou art the one they send. Good! Good! Thou fairly *burnest*! What is thy name, girl?"

"M-Marge, m'am. You are—Huspeth?"

The old woman cackled. "Sometimes. Sometimes. But come! Sit by my fire! We shall get to know each other well over what time is given to us. And stop that cowering! Art thou afraid of an old woman like me?"

"I'm told you are a witch of great power," Marge responded carefully. "Power is to be respected, and one mark of this respect is fear."

The old woman roared with laughter. "Fairly said! Oh, truly thou art a goodly one, and clever, too. If thou hast the will, I will take thee farther than thou hast ever *dreamed*." She hobbled up to the cauldron, sniffed, and looked a little quizzical. "Hmmm . . . I don't know. Come, girl. Smell and see if thou canst decide if it is ready."

Expecting some foul witch's brew, Marge approached hesitantly, took a deep breath, let it out, then leaned over and sniffed.

"It smells absolutely wonderful!" she exclaimed in surprise. "What is it?"

"A recipe of mine. An old one, but a good one. I will teach it to thee, and many others. Come! Get a bowl there, and a spoon."

There were two wooden bowls and two small, hand-carved

wooden spoons beside the fire, and the old woman used one spoon to fill first one bowl, then the other that Marge held up.

The food had the consistency of porridge, but had various pieces of unknown fruits and vegetables—and perhaps other substances—in it more like a stew. It smelled of all the good tastes Marge could remember rolled up into one, and it tasted even better, at least once it cooled slightly. Suddenly aware of her hunger, she ate unhesitatingly, feeling more relaxed.

Huspeth, too, ate, but said nothing more. Still, she kept looking at Marge with an almost hungry gaze, as if she saw, somehow, something in the younger woman that was of the elder's own distant past, something lost forever but never from the mind.

Only when they both had finished and the bowls and spoons were put to one side did Huspeth decide to speak again.

"I'm sure they told thee a little about me," she began. "Probably not the half of it. They think I do them a favor by taking thee, but I do no one favors, and that is something thou must remember."

"I'll remember," Marge assured her. "Actually, they said very little. But they know you're not their friend."

The witch cackled. "*That* is certainly true! Still, when I first knew of thee, before even they came to me as I already knew they would, I knew that we had a destiny, thou and I. Thou art unique. Virginal and with the soul of another world inside."

"Another world, yes," Marge agreed, "but virginal? Hardly."

"Virginal, yes!" the old woman snapped. "Hast thou still not understood what Bakadur, who calls himself Ruddygore, has done for thee? Thou hast cast off thine old body and with it thy taints and sins. Thou art the one thing that all believe is impossible. Thou art truly a virgin for the second time! Were it not so, we would not be meeting here thus."

Marge just shook her head slowly. "I'm sorry—this is all so new and so sudden. It takes time to accept something like this."

"Time! Aye, time. Tell me, girl, what wilt thou do with thy new life? More properly, what wouldst thou do with it if the choice were entirely thine?"

Marge thought a moment. "I—I guess I really haven't thought that much about it. Right now I'm just going where I'm pointed."

The old woman nodded. "And yet that is the first thing thou must decide, and quickly. Think on it now with me. Dost thou have any skills? How wilt thou earn thy bread and board?"

Marge thought some more. "No skills, I guess. I've been a flop at most things, and my education wasn't good for anything back home and is of even less use here."

"Then thou hast the choices narrowed," Huspeth pointed out. "Even the most base of peasants has great skills in plowing, husbandry, and a thousand sundry other things that assure his bread and board. There are no repair shops here. If thy roof leaks, thou must patch it. If thou art cold, thou alone must know the arts of sewing, weaving, and suchlike, and the uses of tools and devices *here*, not in that odd land whence thou dost come. Thou must see now that, alone in this world, thou hast but one great and fragile asset, and that is thy great beauty."

Marge sighed. "Here, too, I guess, I'm reduced to that. I'm even a total washout in my fantasies."

"Nay. There are two paths. One is easy and comfortable. One such as thou can have many years as a dancer or courtesan, perhaps finally finding a man to serve in marriage."

"I tried that. I wasn't very good there, either."

"There is a second way, though, for thee, but it involves great work, nor is it easy to attain, nor comfortable, nor for the weak in spirit. It will involve pain and great sacrifice, but it has much reward as well, the greatest being freedom, that thou needst do but as thou wilt. But the path is hard."

By the flickering firelight, the young woman turned in a mixture of apprehension and hope to the older. "What path is this?"

"The path of witchcraft, for which Bakadur has uniquely prepared thy body and soul, whether from design or caprice, I know not."

"Witchcraft!" Visions of dark and evil deeds, devil worship, and women who looked like Huspeth filled her mind. "I—I don't know about that."

"Bah! Prejudice! I see the prejudice inside thee! That same foolish, superstitious fear that marks all thy kind! Thinkest thou of witches as servants of Hell? Thinkest thou that all witches look like *this*?"

"Why, I—"

"Some witches," Huspeth continued angrily, getting to her feet, "look like *this*." With that, the entire area around her body began to glow, enveloping her wizened, shrunken form, whirling and dancing as if alive. And out of the brightness stepped a new form, a young woman of stunning beauty and elegance—possibly the most beautiful woman Marge had ever seen. She was beyond mere description, the distillation of all past visions of female grace, beauty, and form.

Stunned by the vision, Marge opened her mouth both in awe and wonder and sat transfixed.

A perfect hand reached out and gestured toward the seated woman. "Arise, child," the vision said in a voice that was the perfection of every woman's voice, sensual, musical, yet compelling. Marge got up without even realizing it, feeling inside that her new body, in which she'd so reveled up to now, was like the old witch Huspeth compared with the one who now stood before her.

"Why dost thou gape?" the vision asked. "Nothing has changed except thy perception of me. I was, am, and remain Huspeth, at least to thee now this night."

Marge managed to find a semblance of her voice. "You— you are the same?"

"The same. It is thy first lesson. Judge not by appearance in any manner. Yet since others *do* judge by thy visage, the one who controls that visage holds power in and of the self. Great beauty and youth yield one set of results, age and infirmity quite another. Such a power, to make others see as thou dost wish, is of the greatest use. Male, female, child, adult—all have their purposes."

"Wh-which are you?"

The vision smiled. "*That* would be telling. But thou must put away thy prejudices here. Hell is as much my enemy as it is Bakadur's. Not that there are not witches bound to Hell. There most certainly are—and they are the most attractive of the lot and the most seductive. But that is not a prerequisite for witchcraft. Witchcraft is a methodology that may be applied to many faiths, but it requires a faith to frame it properly for use."

"I have little faith in much of anything," Marge admitted.

"First, thou must have faith in thyself, and that is the hardest of all. Thou must believe thyself better than the rest, capable of great things, and thou must couple this with the desire and wisdom needed to fulfill thy faith."

"That is the hardest faith of all," she agreed. "How can you know unless you have been tested? How can you have goals when you don't know what is attainable?"

"I will teach thee these things. Think upon it. What wouldst thou do in this world? What is thy desire? Consider well thine answer, for the wrong choices may yet deny thee these things."

She thought about it. Just what *did* she want from this world? "Adventure," she decided and told Huspeth. "Excitement. Challenge. The feeling of doing something *important*."

The beautiful vision smiled. "Ah! Those answers are the ones that bring joy to my heart. Accept my proposition, and I will teach thee faith—and after that power and skill. If thou dost freely join of our order, I will give thee the means to what thou sayest thou cravest. But the way is very hard."

Again Marge thought about it. Freedom. Independence. Adventure. What were the alternatives? Nothing exciting. She suspected, too, that this was what Ruddygore had intended, no matter what the doubts of Huspeth. He didn't seem to do anything randomly—except eat. Still, there were some doubts . . . "You say the way is hard. What do you mean?"

Huspeth considered her reply. "For one thing, the longer thou dost remain virginal, the greater thy powers will grow. They will not vanish when thou dost submit, but they will never increase beyond that point. Dost thou, young and beautiful, consider that too great a price?"

"No," Marge responded quickly. "My life recently has been pretty full of that. Until I can hold my own with the respect of men, I can withhold myself. At least, I *think* I can."

Huspeth nodded. "No man may enter the Glen Dinig, not even Bakadur and his precious Council. Thy testing will come much later and far from here, when thou wilt need thy skills the most. But come! The night is young! Let us begin!"

Huspeth was human once more, but still the figure of angelic beauty. Only those catlike glowing eyes remained, although such perfection was in itself inhuman. She walked over to Marge, unhooked the halter and bead-skirt, and threw them into the fire. "To begin, thou must return to the beginning," the witch said.

She reached down on the ground and picked up a gourd that

had been hollowed and hardened into a drinking vessel. "Drink of this completely and do it now," she instructed Marge, who took it, sniffed at it hesitantly, first cautiously tasted, then drank the whole contents. It was a sweet drink that seemed honey-based, but as it went down, she could feel a tingling begin, first deep within, then slowly outward until her entire body seemed covered with tiny little electric pricklings. Her mind, too, was slightly numbed by it. She was wide awake, but content to stand there, not really thinking at all.

"Thou art an empty vessel into which I will pour great truths," Huspeth almost chanted. "Come! Stand before the fire."

In a trance, Marge moved as instructed and waited patiently, aware but unable to do much of anything.

Huspeth positioned herself opposite the fire and raised her hands. The fire seemed to grow brighter and leap up to her, like a thing alive.

"Listen well," the witch began. "In the dawn of creation were Adam and Eve created in the Garden, and of the sons thou knowest, but of the daughters of the first time thou knowest not. While the sons did quarrel and kill, the daughters did reject those ways and sought to recommune with the Creator. One found special favor of the Creator, and it is she who is at the root of our order. Look! Look into the flames and behold Eden as it was!"

Marge looked. In the flames she saw that which had been so needlessly lost, a garden of impossible beauty; a magic garden that was beyond any earthly experience because it was created in true and absolute perfection. To see such total peace and such absolute beauty and perfection fairly tore at her mind, but within her, too, was a great sadness that such a place had been lost forever.

"Feel thy sins, thy doubts, thy fears, leaving thee," Huspeth intoned. "Feel them being drawn out when thou art faced with the vision of the one perfect Garden. Feel them as they fall into the flames and are so consumed. Feel thy past consumed, thy guilt consumed, all consumed and gone in cleansing flames. Thou art the daughter of perfection incarnate. Thou art but one step from the Garden, a daughter of Eve, free of all save the one sin that denies thee entrance."

As Huspeth spoke, Marge felt something drain from her,

pour out from every part of her mind and body. Heavy, dark feelings, things which she had lived with so long that she had never even known they were there. Things from the dark corners where no human looked and where all things of Hell and darkness dwelt. And as each poured out, unseen yet as tangible as tumors excised from the body by a surgeon, she felt an increasing lightness, a total sense of well-being.

"Thou daughter of Eve, dost thou accept they wedding to the First and Perfect One and acknowledge her primacy?"

"I do, I do," Marge responded, meaning it.

"Then, thou daughter of Eve, closest to perfection, linked to thy world and ours, know now the curse of our holy order. Know that, having seen perfection, thou canst never attain it, nor can any whom thou dost know or love. For only in knowing what was forever lost canst thou know how truly cursed is all humankind."

Tears welled up inside Marge and spilled out as she realized the meaning of Huspeth's words. To have known perfection and now to know that one might never attain it . . .

"Gather you, daughters of Eve, about this place and time to see this child," Huspeth commanded. And all around the fire Marge sensed but could not see a host of women, all of great power.

"Do you approve this union?" the witch asked the unseen host.

"We do, we do," came a hundred whispers from the dark beyond the fire.

"Who is our Holy Mother?"

"Eve, who was first and created in perfection," came the response from the unseen host.

"Who is our enemy?"

"Hell, who carried corruption to our Holy Mother's bosom," came the response.

"Who is now the mother of this child?"

"Eve, who was first created in perfection."

"Who shall her mother be among the daughters?"

"Thou, who bringest her forward."

"Child—dost thou accept this covenant and this sisterhood, now and forevermore? Wilt thou be my daughter in covenant?"

"I will," Marge responded.

"She will. She will!" the host echoed.

"As a sign of this, child, place thy hand in mine!" With that the witch reached her hand directly into the flame.

Marge was aware that this was a critical choice and that she was free to make it or not to make it. To put her hand in the fire . . .

She reached forward, feeling the heat of the flames, and grasped the hand of Huspeth. There was a searing sensation, then a sharp pain, and she knew that a razor-sharp cut had been made in her hand. Blood, not just hers but Huspeth's, dripped from their clasped hands into the flames and hissed.

"Witness the bonding of blood, you daughters," Huspeth intoned. "Witness the act of trust in placing her hand in the flame. She is truly flesh of my flesh, blood of my blood, and is bound over into our holy order and subject to all its strictures and commands."

"Let it be so," the chorus intoned.

The hands were unclasped and withdrawn, and Marge somehow had enough control to glance briefly at hers. It was unburned, but there was a crosslike incision on the wrist which was just starting to clot.

Slowly the fire died down to its original strength, and the sense of presences all around diminished and was gone. They were alone once more. Huspeth reached down and picked up a second gourd and walked over to her. "Drink and rest," she instructed gently.

Hardly aware of the pain in her wrist, Marge took the gourd and drank from it unthinkingly, then allowed herself to be led to a soft clump of grass in the small meadow, where she lay down and was soon fast asleep.

Huspeth stood there a moment, then said, "Arise thou by moonlight."

Marge's sleeping form did not stir, but from her body rose a mistlike substance that congealed and solidified into a human form. It was the form of a girl-child, perhaps six or seven, and it bore little resemblance to the sleeping woman as she now was, but a great deal of resemblance, had anyone there been able to know it, to the little child Marge herself had once been.

Huspeth reached out her hand to the child and smiled, and the child-spirit approached and took it, smiling back.

"Didst thou see the pretty Garden, my daughter?" the witch asked.

"Oh, yes, Mommy! It was *so* beautiful!"

"Well, it's not completely gone. Look around thee here, at this glade and this forest. See its beauty and its magic, for it is alive."

The little girl looked around with a little girl's eyes and a little girl's mind—and saw.

The weeks sped by quickly, and Huspeth proved a good teacher indeed. Marge was aware that she was getting a lot of information indirectly, somehow, but she didn't discover how. Still, she found many of her old fears and attitudes changing, and within her grew a new sense of self-confidence.

The forest and glade of the Glen Dinig, which had seemed so lonely and fearsome not long before, became a familiar friend in both day and darkness. It was certainly a magical wood, filled with wonders, yet its most magical quality was its utter peacefulness and tranquility. Not even the insects would bite. The deer and marmots and other natural inhabitants had no fear of her, nor she of them, although they were not tame. There was a balance, a perfect balance, and carnivores were not allowed.

Much of the instruction was rote memory, since she had no means of recording or reading over anything, but Huspeth was a good teacher with a lot of aids for problems. The lessons ranged from the simple—how, in fact, to prepare wondrous meals merely from what was around one, and all vegetarian—to the making of potions from the same plants and the recognition of them. There was magic, too—not only in the potions but in how to sensitize oneself to the energies around one, and to sense the life energy in the trees and grasses, the blaze of a deer in full flight, even the furies of nature.

One day there was a great thunderstorm with enormous bolts of lightning all around. Soaked completely, both of them stood in the middle of the glen, and Marge watched as Huspeth called down the bolts, directed them, and bent the terrible forces to her will. Training mind and will, Marge learned a little of wielding such natural power herself and found, later, that one who could deflect the lightning could deflect other things as well.

There was physical training, too. The use and throw of the dagger, and how to conceal it while wearing only the flimsiest of garments. The sword and saber also had their uses, particularly when one could subtly influence the thrust or direction of an opponent's blade.

Her muscles were hardened and strengthened through long runs and severe exercise including the use of weights. She learned, too, to know her own body, to control its every movement and action. Aided by potions, her physical and mental control slowly jelled into almost absolute mastery. Even Huspeth was impressed. "Daughter," she said, "thou art truly superior to most mortals thou wilt meet."

The training advanced, but it never let up. There were times when there was no sleep at all, and she learned to draw on the life energies around her to sustain her.

Eventually, concealed by spells, they went forth out of the Glen Dinig to observe the ways of fairies and men. It took some getting used to, for at the start Marge was almost overwhelmed by the sense of corruption within all of them, but she learned their ways and their powers, their strengths and weaknesses, as best Huspeth could teach. And she felt more and more remote from them all.

"That is because thou art becoming more than human," the witch told her. "It will mark thee. But thou wilt never forget who thou art or whence thou hast come, O daughter."

Of Huspeth she learned only the very little the witch was willing to impart. She knew, though, that the witch was thousands of years old at the very least, that her power was as great as any on the Council, but that she had become so much more than human that she could no longer abide living in the world among the corruption she felt so dearly. For all that Huspeth had imparted to her, Marge knew that the power and wisdom her teacher contained were as an ocean to her thimbleful.

One day, while out on their look at the world the witch had forsworn but to which Marge knew she would have to return too soon, they saw their first unicorns.

They were fully as beautiful and as grand as legend had made them, far more than horses with curved, pointy horns. Their eyes, too, were very different—almost human. And yet, looking at them, Marge felt a disturbance within the magnificent creatures that shouldn't be there.

The source of that was revealed rather quickly as a deer wandered out from the edge of a wood. The unicorn herd, perhaps ten or eleven, took off after the deer, cut it off from retreat, surrounded it, and began a cruel game of torture for the poor deer.

Tiring, finally, of running the deer almost into exhaustion, sticking it with their horns, and allowing it an escape route only to block it and trip it up, the unicorns moved in—and began eating the deer alive.

"How disgusting!" Marge exclaimed. "Those magnificent animals!"

"The way of the world, as it must be to balance nature. The unicorns are a relative to the horses, but they took a far different path. Their teeth are many and are sharp and pointed, as are the wolf's. They play with the cruelty that children exhibit, for that is what they always are, but then they eat. They did not choose their way, nor did the wolf choose his; they just *are*. But, unlike their brethren, there is great magic within them. Shall we go down and see?"

Marge hesitated. "Considering their eating habits, is it safe?"

"For thee, perfectly. The virgin alone is one with the unicorn. All others they will flee from or, if need be, destroy."

They walked down to the herd, which had finished its grisly feeding and was now relaxing, some standing, some lying down as horses never did. The unicorns eyed the two women warily but did not flee.

"Call one," Huspeth prompted. "Go ahead."

Marge shrugged. "Ah, here, unicorn. Come here, unicorn."

"Not exactly the approved way of summoning, but it works," the witch noted as the nearest unicorn glanced up at the call, looked at both of them, and then trotted right over to Marge.

Hesitantly, Marge put out her hand and petted the unicorn on the neck, as she would a horse. The skin was quite different from what she expected, with the feel and texture of velvet. The unicorn seemed to like her touch, though, and the skin certainly felt nice to her.

"Mount him," Huspeth told her. "Let him take you for a ride."

With her tremendous muscle tone and practiced athletic ability, she had no trouble jumping to the back of the beast, although there was nothing to hold onto but mane.

Still, the beast started off at a trot and quickly accelerated.

Marge found that, far from being uncomfortable or badly mounted, she seemed to merge with the unicorn, to become one with the creature, more and more so as it increased speed and sped around the great meadow.

It was a magical and most wonderful transformation, with all of the unicorn's enormous vitality and, yes, sexual energy flowing into and through every fiber of her being. It was a tremendously pleasurable, orgasmic experience that the unicorn gave, and so wonderful that it was Huspeth who had to bring it to an end.

"Thou seest now why the unicorn and the virgin always go hand in hand in legend," she said. "But beware, for just as thou dost take from it, so it takes from thee, and the energy it removes from thee takes many days to replenish, longer if thou hast not the will to stop it in time."

"I'll remember," Marge assured her teacher, still feeling as if she had received a lot more than she had given.

"Now that the two of you are chosen, the unicorn Koriku is wed to thee so long as thou shalt take no man. He will come upon the call of his name by your lips, no matter where thou art, to give pleasure or to rout thine enemies. His strength should be used sparingly, for there is always a cost, but it is there when needed. Beware, too, that Koriku, like thyself, is a mortal creature, and should he die while in thy service, thou, too, wilt die."

Marge shivered slightly at that. "I will remember."

The time flew by. In many ways Marge hoped it would never end. Huspeth was the wisest and most wonderful person she'd ever known, and she loved the witch who was the key to all things wonderful and magical as she had loved no other.

But one day there was a cloud in Huspeth's soul as she emerged from her hut, and a great foreboding filled Marge as she saw it.

"It has come time for the trivial that now becomes the paramount," the witch said enigmatically. "Come, sit beside me, and I will tell thee of this world and its enemies."

"Something's wrong," Marge said nervously.

"The forces of Hell are again on the march. Great battles are taking shape as we speak, and the war advances. The bulk of Marquewood between the River of Sorrows and the Rossignol itself is at stake. If it goes, then the enemy is at our front door, demanding entrance, and there will be few to stop him."

"Who is the enemy, my mother?"

"The same who defiled lost Eden. This time he works, as always, through others, in the guise of armies and wars and philosophies and great promises. Many who march to his tune are willing, many more are unknowing servants, but it makes no difference to him. The Dark Baron himself may be deluded, although he certainly knows for whom he fights, since the gates of Hell must be unlocked to create such a force. All the wizards and sorcerers of Husaquahr traffic to some degree with the demons of Hell, as thou well knowest. But such traffic, which I abhor in all cases, for it involves compromise with the ultimate evil, is the temptation to greater and greater evil. If Hell can wield such powers to the wizard's tune, it can corrupt a wizard's heart as well, and they have got themselves a master wizard totally on their side, self-deluded and thoroughly corrupted by the enemy."

"Who, my mother? Which wizard is it?"

Huspeth shook her head. "I know not at this time. Many of the chief demons of Hell were once the angelic agents charged with the making of our own world. Their power here is as great as in thine own world, and they know all the counters for our magic. The Baron's identity is hidden from all of us, until discovered by other than magical means. But this continual cancer is nothing new to our world. It is an incurable disease that worms its way into every corner and must be continually fought. When it grows too large to control, as it seems it has now, it must be beaten down. The enemy can afford ten thousand defeats, but we can not have one."

"This is not the first time, then?"

"Not even the first time in Husaquahr. But this is a big world, much larger than the one from which thou comest. There are many other continents and many other lands. One, called simply The Land, is so fouled up no one from thy world will believe it's real, even though he be there. Another once put down a dark force under a great wizard, and now that wizard's son, Alateen, refights his father's battles. From Lan Kemar to Lemoria, all the lands that make up our world are continually threatened. Now it is Husaquahr's turn."

"But what can they win, even if they capture the land?"

"Ah, once captured, it will never be freed. But, worse, the Dark Baron's plan is clearly diabolical. He hopes to seize or destroy the lands, castles, and, if possible, persons of a majority of the Council. If he accomplishes this, and he is already a quarter there, he will be able to rewrite, suspend, or even abolish the Books of Rules. Hell will rewrite the Rules and will then have a world of its very own to rule and dominate. *This* will become Hell, and will provide, too, a second front for an assault on the Creator Himself. If Hell wins here, it can devote all its time to thine own world. Armageddon, then, will be fought by Hell from both worlds toward the Creator in the middle. None truly knows the outcome, since Hell rebelled once before and knows what it is up against, should it try again."

"You mean—God could *lose*?"

"It is by no means certain. Sooner or later thou wilt find thyself in the clutches of Hell, and thou wilt know a sample of what waits for all creation if we lose. That is why, now, thou must go."

"No! I mean, not yet. I still have so much to learn!"

"Time later for that, if victory is ours. If not, we all are better dead than what we *will* be. Thou must be a soldier in this battle. There is the adventure and challenge thou didst wish for and the important things to do. No woman of Husaquahr is better equipped than thou to do great things, but all thy studies and training will be for naught if not used. Thou must follow the direction of Ruddygore, who is far more worldly than I, in this matter. He traffics with Hell even as he fights it, and I find him powerful but unworthy of such power—but he *is* powerful, and he is fighting for his very life and so will not waste thee or thy companion."

"Companion . . ." She'd almost completely forgotten about Joe. After all, she'd known him such a short while.

"As for me, I have fought too many of these things. Yet should all fail, and Terindell be besieged, Glen Dinig will fight with Terindell against the common foe. I hope and pray it does not come to that, for it would be Bakadur and I against the Dark Baron and the demons of Hell itself. Thou mayest aid in preventing that from happening, my daughter, if thou keepest thyself as thou art now and if thou dost remember all I have taught. So long as thou dost remain as thou art, thy powers will increase by the day, infinitely so, and new ones will develop as needs arise. Thy true trials and tests lie ahead of thee. Remember well who thou art and what thou hast become."

Marge took Huspeth's hand and kissed it tenderly. "I will, my mother."

Huspeth got up, went into her hut, and emerged with her hands full of various items. "Some parting things, to aid thee in thy future endeavors."

The first was a one-piece garment, both legless and sleeveless, of bright forest green, which had a stretchy clinginess to it yet gave breast support. It was woven out of an unknown soft material that nonetheless was almost silkenly comfortable. Its tightness, though, left nothing to the imagination about the shape beneath, becoming almost a green second skin. It satisfied decency—and the Rules. Also, there was a headband much like a laurel wreath. It held firmly and smelled of forest pine.

"Both wreath and garment are of the forest, of living things magically transformed and transfixed. They will be a reminder of Glen Dinig and the daughters of Eve."

"As if I could ever forget. A part of me will be here forever."

Next came a small green belt that blended with the garment and hung on the hips, but was strong enough for a scabbard shaped like leaves. Into it Huspeth placed a small but ornate dagger.

"The dagger is of faërie metal," she told Marge. "It will penetrate all save iron, which is very scarce here. The blade is fused into the handle of pure dwarf jade. It is the truest and most balanced of all blades, and was once mine when I went forth as thou now goest. In the rear of the scabbard is a small pocket which can be useful."

Next was a little case made out of the purest dwarf jade. Inside was what Huspeth called Marge's "kit"—basic herbs and hard-to-find materials for many potions, plus a small mortar and pestle more or less carved into it. It, too, was designed to be held by a thin belt and was not at all bulky. Finally came a small gourd, useful for all practical purposes and also designed for belt carry, leaving both hands free.

"With those thou canst travel the whole of this world and

need no more, with thine own knowledge of the land and its bounty."

"I believe I can now, my mother," Marge responded, meaning it.

"Come. Let us see thee reflected in the pool."

They walked over to the small, mirror-smooth pond at the edge of the glen that had been their water supply. In it Marge saw a far different person—yet a third self. She was dark now; the sun and wind had weathered her and toughened her without in any way lessening her striking beauty. And, as she had discovered shortly after her initiation into the order, her new strawberry-blond hair had changed to a brilliant white, with the exception of a streak of reddish brown running straight down the center from forehead to back—the mark of the order. She had trimmed the hair into something of a pageboy and, with the forest-green garment she wore, it was a perfect complement.

Her legs revealed that she now had the strength of the long-distance runner and more, and her arms, still smooth-looking, took on an almost bizarre quality when tensed, revealing their tremendous muscles. Her brows, of the same reddish brown as the streak, were long, thick, and sloping inward, setting off her large blue eyes; she looked less human than like some great warrior elf. Her appearance was unique and striking, yet her movements still contained the catlike grace and form of the woman she had been.

"All I need is a bow and a quiver of arrows to make it perfect," she mused, more to herself than to Huspeth, but the witch nodded.

"I agree, and thy skill with the bow warrants it." She left and returned with a small quiver made of some plant's green skin, and a bow of true professional beauty.

"Oh, no, I *can't*. You've given me so much already!" Marge protested.

"I insist, daughter of mine. And I expect that which has been given thee to be freely used in the fight against true evil."

"I promise I will not fail you, my mother!"

Huspeth now showed the only real emotion of the day, hugging Marge and holding her close. "I know thou wilt. Now—go. 'Tis time."

Marge went with the utmost reluctance but knowing her

duty. She was supremely confident now, both of herself and of her abilities, and ready to prove that she had, at last, found her place. Nothing would ever surprise her again.

But she was not only surprised but almost shocked to find an impassive Poquah waiting atop the hill with the same two horses they'd ridden when coming here.

Poquah did not greet her, but his red eyes looked her over critically for a moment, and then he said, "Ah, yes. A proper heroine indeed. It is well. Come. We must make the castle by dinner."

This time *she* led *him*—at a gallop.

CHAPTER 6

BEING A BARBARIAN TAKES PRACTICE

No physical art may be achieved by magic, nor magical art by physical means.

—VI, 79, 101(b)

GORODO PROVED TO BE ABOUT NINE FEET TALL AND MUST have weighed five hundred pounds, with lots of hair and absolutely no fat. He also happened to be a bright blue color with dark blue hair and had a nose that looked like a blue grapefruit, not to mention a pair of very nasty-looking fangs that stuck out of both sides of his mouth. He grinned when he first caught sight of Joe, and the effect was less a real grin than the kind of playful look a cat would give a mouse just before pouncing.

Joe, who was just beginning to feel really macho in his new muscles, stopped, stared, and gulped.

"So this is the big, bad barbarian they want to train to be a big-shot hero," Gorodo said sarcastically, looking down at his new charge. "Boy! They really demand miracles of a tired, weak old man."

Joe tried to find the tired, weak old man he was talking about.

"What's your name, boy?" the blue giant asked.

He gulped slightly. "Joe."

"Joe? That's a pretty stupid name for a barbarian. Barbari-

ans should have fancy names, or funny-sounding ones, like
Conan or Cormac, things like that. Usually with a 'C' sound to
start." He sighed. "Well, there's nothin' in the Rules about that,
I don't think. Not yet, anyway. Still, a name like Joe doesn't
exactly inspire fear and respect. We got to get you a second
name, one with real command."

"I already have a second name," Joe told him, confidence
coming back slowly with the reasonableness of the giant's
tone. "In fact, I have lots of names."

"Indeed. Like what?"

"José San Pedro Antonio Luis Francisco Joaquin Esteban
Martinez de Oro, if you must know," Joe responded a bit
glumly.

Gorodo whistled. "How in the Nine Hells do you remember
all that? Anyway, that sounds just as ridiculous. I mean something strong, like Joe Thunderer or Joe Stormhold or something like that. Well, we'll leave that for now. The Master
wants us to get a start today, even though there's little left of
it. I'd rather just tell you what we're gonna do and let you get
one last night's decent sleep."

"Fine with me," Joe agreed. "I'm not exactly a volunteer.
More like a draftee."

Gorodo laughed. "Listen, boy. In the days and weeks to
come, I'm gonna put you through a living hell. Bet on it.
You're gonna curse me and yell at me and you're gonna hurt
something awful. But when I get through with you, ain't
nothin' made of solid stuff gonna give you trouble. You're
gonna be prepared like nobody's *ever* been prepared. Know
why? Not because I was ordered to, and not because I like it,
but I would consider your death a personal insult after all I'm
gonna do. Understand? You're gonna be the best damned barbarian in this whole crazy world because *my* honor depends on
it. Now, go eat decent and get your beauty sleep. Tomorrow's
gonna be one busy day."

Joe gladly went and discovered the main dining room almost by accident. The food was good, although the only uten-
sils they seemed to use here were a sharp knife and a wooden
spoon.

Few gave him much of a glance at dinner or after, but some
elves in plain livery did tell him where he was to stay within
the outer castle. The room turned out to be of bare stone, fur-

nished with a straw mattress, a single candle, and not much else.

He lay there for some time, feeling more and more depressed and moody. *Barbarian hero*, he thought sourly. *I'm Joe, from South Philly, that's all, lost somewhere in a land of freaks.* He thought of his ex-wife and his young son, who now had even less chance of ever knowing his real papa. He thought, too, of that girl who was more of a loser than he was. Marge. He'd known her only a short time, and now she was God knew where. He couldn't even really get a clear picture of her in his mind just now, which bothered him, but, though it was crazy, he missed her. She was his one link with what was real and comfortable.

He was lonely as hell, and it took a long time for him to slip into a fitful doze.

The routine didn't vary much. Gorodo got him up at dawn, and he began running—first a mile, increasing as his muscles built up to two, then three. Only then did Gorodo permit a large breakfast, after which Joe was expected to run one more mile just to work it down. Next came weight training, along with general physical exercise to tone up a few muscles.

These extensive workouts hurt a lot, and early one morning he'd protested and refused to do more. That was when Gorodo had exploded, growling and snarling, his veneer of civilization dropping instantly.

Very early in the training, Joe discovered that the blue giant was an expert at beating the living daylights out of one without doing any permanent damage whatsoever. The early choice was pretty simple: it was painful torture to do what Gorodo demanded, but it was even more painful to refuse.

It didn't take long for Joe to get both frustrated with and hateful of the huge blue man, whose only redeeming feature was that he did everything he asked Joe to do. Even that was infuriating, though, since Gorodo showed absolutely no stress, strain, or pain doing what was really awful to Joe.

After a big midday dinner, they would go down to a great stone hall where a number of muscular types, human, non-human, semihuman, and a few inhuman, were practicing with one or another weapon. Here instructors in various types of weaponry worked with him, and at least from them he felt he was getting something useful. Broadsword use. Balance. Timing. Dagger and spear-throwing. Mace and pike. All different, all requiring a special set of skills and a lot of practice. Some were also frustrating in their own right. The broadsword seemed to weigh a ton when he was first introduced to it, and he particularly resented the fact that the instructor was a thin, wiry human a head smaller and a hundred pounds lighter than he—who wielded the sword as if it were made of paper.

But he paid attention, and he *did* seem to have a natural flair for it.

After a heavy supper, he was back to running and weights once more and, by the time Gorodo gave him his freedom for the night, he was so hurting and so tired he could do nothing but head for bed.

Day after day, almost without a break, this schedule was kept, varying only in that, as he seemed really to get the hang of one weapon, a new one was introduced.

After a few weeks of this, the pain lessened but never really went away, though he found himself able to lift increasingly greater weights and run longer distances. The broadsword, which had seemed so leaden at first, now felt as light as a rapier. His body was becoming hard, lean, and even more tremendously muscular from the regular hard workouts, which never let up.

Still, a month or so into the course, the weaponry was relegated to the evenings, and the afternoons were taken up with more practical classes by a variety of humans and creatures. Weeks were spent on horsemanship, and there were even lectures and problems on warfare with the weaponry at hand, and also a good deal of hand-to-hand combat. How to disable. How to kill. Where the nerves were, those critical pressure points. There were classes, too, in primitive first aid—what roots and herbs did what, as well as the basics of tourniquets, setting broken bones, and the like. He was acutely aware, thanks to Gorodo's less than subtle methods of persuasion, of the lack of any decent medical care in Husaquahr, and so he paid particular attention to these practical lessons.

As he progressed in skills, particularly with the sword, he was forced into fighting left-handed with it. It was tough going, and for a while Gorodo gnashed and foamed and growled;

but while Joe never quite got as good with the left as with the right, he became at least adequate.

The horsemanship also came very hard; even though he got pretty good at it, he felt he would never be a hundred percent comfortable with any animals. For a man who believed firmly that steaks and milk were created magically at the chain stores, he wasn't as bad as he thought he was.

Time ran on without any real feeling. The weeks stretched to months, and he had no true concept of time or even duration any more. Gorodo was his whole life and his whole world.

The blue giant, for his part, seemed to soften up as things went along, though, not being nearly the hot-tempered beast of those first few weeks. Joe never lost his intense dislike of his tormentor, but he nonetheless developed a grudging respect for what was being done—or at least attempted—by the trainer. He suspected that Gorodo might be a lot smarter and a lot less bestial than the blue man wanted everybody to believe.

Still, Gorodo pushed him and pushed him and pushed some more. Every time Joe felt he had reached his absolute limit in something, the blue man would literally force him to continue. Finally, one day, resentment boiled over so much in Joe that he took a swing at Gorodo—and connected.

The blue giant was surprised, and then was the great man-beast once again—but this time Joe didn't back down.

It was one hell of a fight—furniture smashed all over the place as two bodies, one large and one larger, tumbled and tossed each other about. It lasted the better part of an hour and a half, a total brawl that brought just about everybody within earshot to gawk at them—elves ran through the crowd taking bets at one point—but ultimately Gorodo, winded, bruised, and bleeding from a number of cuts and abrasions, won out by knocking Joe cold.

Joe awoke in his room with a really nasty headache and a lot of sore spots and abrasions, but all his wounds had been well tended. Gorodo, looking pretty beat up, was there as well, and he didn't even look that mean.

"How're you feeling?" the giant asked, and if Joe didn't know better, he'd have sworn there was real concern in the trainer's voice.

"Lousy," Joe responded.

"Me, too," Gorodo said, sighing and sinking into a chair he

or somebody had brought in. He gave a low whistle. "That was one hell of a fight you put up. I'm proud of you, boy. I think you just graduated."

There was still a little ringing in Joe's head, and he was sure he hadn't heard what he thought he heard. "Graduated? But—you won."

The giant laughed. "Yeah. And I always will, too, sonny boy. At least for quite a while. You're good, though, boy. Real good. Best I ever trained, I'll tell you. Don't get too bigheaded, though, 'cause I said that. As I say, I got one thing you ain't got—and it will be a long time comin'."

"Yeah? What?"

"Experience. I been in a couple of armies. I been a pirate, a raider and sacker, you name it. Fifty years' experience, boy, and I'm still here and still in one piece. It's the one thing I can't give you. But I *will* say that the more experience you get, the better you'll be. There ain't but a few dozen in Husaquahr coulda given me the fight you did. What about you? You think you're ready for the real thing?"

Joe nodded, even though it hurt. "I think so."

"Good. I been talkin' things over with everybody else training you here, and we're pretty well agreed. When you're good enough to take me on and hold your own, it's exam time."

"Exam time?"

"Yep. The acid test. Look, you get some rest. You need anything, you call out and somebody will be here on the double to get it for you. Next day or two, when we're both back up to snuff, we'll go into town and raise a little hell. Drink. Wench, maybe. *Then* you'll be ready."

The river town of Terdiera was fairly small—perhaps seven or eight hundred people—but it was civilization itself to Joe after so long in Terindell. The buildings were mostly of straw and mud but were well engineered, and here and there were buildings of stone or brick. The main bazaar was a wooden structure half a block long fronting on a square, with merchants displaying their wares in stalls opening onto the street, and all calling out to every passerby.

"Hoi! Love charms and potions! The strongest of the strong!"

"Hoi! The finest in mystic herbs and spices! More pleasurable than a harem without all the talking!"

"Hoi! The finest in jewels imported from far-off dwarf mines in the mountains of Corimere! Mystic jade said to belong once to the dwarf king Zakar himself!"

It was a bewildering array of products, most of them strange and unusual to Joe's experience. Still, here were leather merchants and stalls with the finest of swords, shields, knives, and daggers. Women were measured and fitted in pretty patterned costumes, and everybody from cobblers to coopers was very busy.

There was money of many sorts, of various sizes, shapes, and designs—possibly from many different lands. Still, all appeared made out of gold or silver, and were worth what the metal was worth rather than what the governments claimed; gems, too, were often taken and given as if they were money.

Gorodo, for all his promises, did not come on this first trip. He begged off, saying he had other work, and something in Joe secretly hoped it was an injury very slow to heal.

Instead, his companion was the grim and humorless Poquah, not much of an improvement over Gorodo in his own way. Poquah, however, was a good lecturer.

"Much of the commerce of Husaquahr is barter, but there is a banking system—and coin, as you can see. Since most of Valisandra's people are farmers and work at a subsistence level, they trade their goods for the products of these merchants. The merchants, of course, totally depend on the farmers for their food and much of their raw materials. It works out rather well."

The bulk of the inhabitants in the town were human, but here and there an occasional other would walk or scamper by, given little notice. The two riders coming into town drew interested glances, but it was Joe, rather than the Imir, who attracted stares. He found he rather liked it, too—that glint of nervousness or hesitant fear in the eyes of many of the men and far different sorts of looks from the women. He knew he not only looked exotic, even by barbarian standards, but could hardly hide the tremendous muscles that made him look like some sort of idealized bronze god. He knew, too, that this was the first reward for all the pain and agony he'd undergone in getting to this point.

The Imir gave him a small sack of gold nuggets, not a lot of currency by Husaquahr standards, but more than enough to buy a few things, should he be inclined, and perhaps a meal and drinks in the town tavern.

He enjoyed the afternoon by taking advantage of that, and he knew he was being scandalously cheated by the merchants he dealt with—but it took some time to get the measure of how much a few grams of gold would actually buy.

At the cobbler's, he traded in his worn sandals for a pair of short, comfortable leather boots with a thin, soft fur lining. The poor cobbler, of course, had nothing in stock for feet like Joe's, but he was both fast and skillful and made a pair to order while Joe went elsewhere.

The leather merchant was handy for buying a thick, comfortable, all-purpose belt with solid brass hooks and rings. To this belt he could attach a scabbard with little trouble, as well as other useful things, and it had a hidden money-purse. The buckle, of intricately worked bronze, was a forest scene, but he bought it because the shape between the trees seemed to form the outline of a diesel truck cab. It was the closest to home he could come.

The hatter was a bit taken aback by what he was looking for; but after some pictures were drawn, she agreed to make it if she could. He was satisfied and, after seeing some intricate and presumably magical designs on some of the more Husaquahr-conventional hats, he also gave her a design he wanted on the front of his own.

By the time he'd finished an adequate but not great dinner and returned, he had what he wanted. It was, possibly, the only such hat in Husaquahr, but to another from his own world it would be instantly recognizable. It was a pretty good imitation of a comfortable cowboy hat of some brown feltlike fur, and right on the front was an outline of a design he knew well, one that here would mean nothing. But he found he could certainly still remember how to write, and on the front, in that mystic symbol, was the alien word "Peterbilt."

He had to admit that the hatter was tremendously skillful, considering she had never seen, let alone made, anything like this in her life.

Feeling more comfortable than he had since reaching this land, the great muscular barbarian, in loincloth, trucker's cowboy hat, and reinforced fur-lined boots—and nothing else—went to the tavern.

People stared when he entered, and continued to stare out of the corners of their eyes as he took a seat at a small table in the back. A barmaid, looking timid, approached and took his order for ale, brought it quickly, and went away. Nobody tried to talk to him, approach him, or in any way make him feel like a human being.

The tavern itself was primitive and basic, with a straw-covered floor and hand-hewn crude furnishings, yet it had much in common with all the bars and taverns he'd ever been in. There was a kindred sort of feeling evoked by the place, with its relaxing men, fresh from travels or the fields, and its rough, worldly-wise women—the kind of place he as a trucker had called home from strange town to strange town throughout a large and distant country he'd once roamed. He could see himself as one of these men, playing a little cards or just swapping tall stories, with very little trouble.

Only, as he was uncomfortably aware, this sort of place was no longer a haven for him, the kind of place where strangers were fast friends. Most strangers, perhaps, but not Joe de Oro. He was far too different-looking and far too potentially dangerous to be invited into any of these groups. That depressed him more, perhaps, than anything up to now and brought back his searing sense of loneliness with crushing force. He wondered what they'd all say here, these strange dark men and women, if they knew that inside that bronze god was a man who desperately wanted to cry but could not.

And so he drank prodigiously, feeling it only a little, and sat in his silent corner and watched the rest of them come and go. After a while he also noticed that, occasionally, burly men and tough barmaids would talk and then leave together, and it wasn't hard to figure out why. Finally, the strong ale lowering his inhibitions a bit, he propositioned the woman who was serving him, more with few words and many gestures than outright, and she thought a moment, looked at his purse, then at him, nodded, and turned. He followed her out, not at all worried about being mugged or rolled.

And he enjoyed it, too, feeling it more strongly and on a more emotional level than he ever had before. The barmaid, too, seemed to have a far more than businesslike good time. It went on and on and on through the evening, as months of frustration and loneliness gushed out of his soul and into the act. When finally done, both he and she fell into an exhausted sleep.

He awoke with the dawn, while she still slept, and he felt a little sense of ego buildup that she slept with a wisp of a smile on her face. He weighed the purse. Not enough for the sword he wanted, but a considerable amount all the same still remained. He knew her intent was to take it all at the end, but he was in better condition than she. He paused a moment, then decided, *What the hell, it's not my money*, and left the purse on the small table near the bed when he departed.

It had been worth every penny, but he knew he could never stand to go this long without sex again.

When he emerged from the little hut down the street from the tavern, he was surprised to find Poquah waiting placidly with the horses. The Imir irritated him with his seeming omniscience and cool manner. They said nothing that was not necessary to each other on the way back.

"Now that you have passed the preliminaries, boy, 'tis time to become a man," Gorodo told Joe. "The final exam. Pass it and you're off to fame, fortune, and glory. Flunk it and I'll kill you myself."

Joe looked at him. "I believe you would at that. If you could. I guess this is some sort of big test of ability and skill. I'm willing to give it a try."

"It's a test of that, all right, but a pretty simple one," Gorodo agreed. "It's real simple but real effective. What we do is this. First, you drink a little potion that kinda knocks you out real gentle. Makes you feel great, though. When you wake up, you'll be stark naked, without stitch, weapon, money, horse, anything at all. We don't tell you where. Just that it's no more than fifty miles from here. Your job is to get back inside the inner wall of Terindell without us catchin' you. No time limit to get back here, really, but one day to the minute after you wake up, Poquah and me and some of the boys will start tracking you down. If we catch you, at any point, you'll wish you never was born."

Joe frowned. "And I'm not gonna have nothing at all? Where the hell do I get what I need?"

"Up to you," the blue giant told him. "Steal it. Make it. Improvise. You been shown the way."

Joe nodded, more to himself than to the trainer. "And what do *I* get if I make it?"

Gorodo grinned. "What kinda question is that?"

"I mean it. You want me to risk my neck on this fool test. What do I win? A gold star for bein' a good boy?"

"It is a fair question," Poquah's voice said, and Joe and Gorodo both whirled reflexively. "It deserves an answer that Gorodo can not give. I, however, can."

"Wish you wouldn't pull that act, ya bastard," Gorodo grumbled.

The Imir ignored the comment. "The first thing you will receive is the satisfaction of knowing you have beaten the best. That is good enough for some. But you will also be awarded an elfsword, a magic blade that is almost alive and is not only one of the best magic swords around but effective even against some magical beasts. Finally, you will have a job with great honor and rich rewards. Those are worthy prizes, are they not?"

Joe thought about it. "Yeah. Not bad, I guess. But you don't sound like you expect me to win 'em."

"We are trained and experienced. We also will know where you started from and exactly what you look like. We will know the lay of the land. Using no sorcery, only our skills and foreknowledge, we will get you. It's that simple."

Once more the Imir's tone rankled him, and he saw the challenge in a different light. If he lost, he was no worse off, really, than if he refused. But if he won'. . . Beating Gorodo at his own game and puncturing that enormous self-centered egomaniac of an Imir's pride would be more than worth it. And Gorodo put the icing on the cake.

"Every hunter of you in this test will be one who has passed a similar or identical test," the blue giant told him. "I don't know about that sword crap, but you win the respect of the few who've done it."

"When do we start?" he asked them, getting interested.

The Imir reached down to a small flask on his belt, poured a little golden liquid into a tiny field cup, and handed it to him.

He sniffed it, and it smelled honey-sweet and quite pleasant.

"Cheers!" he exclaimed and downed the potion.

CHAPTER 7

GETTING IN AND OUT OF SHAPE

Barbarian luck will not prevail without barbarian intelligence.
—XL, 401, 306(b)

HE AWOKE IN A SMALL CLUMP OF TREES, ITCHING ALL OVER. Jumping up, he looked back and cursed whoever it was, probably Gorodo, who had put him so near that damned anthill.

They were true to their word—he was stark naked and without anything except a lot of ant bites. It was cool and damp, the sun off in the east barely clearing the horizon. *One full day,* he reminded himself. *Then the chase begins.* Still, now was not the time to go running all over the unfamiliar countryside. His training and his common sense told him otherwise. So, moving away from the unfriendly insects, he walked from the trees to the top of a nearby hill, the highest ground within easy reach, already thinking about what he had to do.

First he needed information. The sun told him his directions, so that wasn't a problem. But—in which direction from the castle had they brought him?

The hilltop afforded a nice view for fifteen or twenty miles around. Not a lot of habitation, from the looks of things, but to the left—west—of where he stood, about four miles, was a river. That was all right, but which river? Well, he decided, time to cheat a little. He'd seen more than one map of the region around Terindell, and even maps of the entire Dancing Gods river system. He was certainly no more than fifty miles if their word was good—and it would be an inconclusive test if they had lied—and Terindell was in a little pocket of Valisandra between two other countries.

Truck drivers paid good attention to any maps they saw.

He sat down on the cool grass and thought it out. The odds were that they hadn't put so much time and energy into his training just to kill him off. They'd play it safe, put him where they could control all the factors in the game. That meant keeping him in Valisandra. That being the case, he was either north or west-northwest of the castle. But that river down there was to the west. If it were the west-northwest direction, the Rossignol should be in the east or southeast. That river over there, then, was most likely the River of Dancing Gods—and that meant he had only to follow it down to Terindell.

It was too easy. He could *run* that before twenty-four hours had passed and the chase began. But then, how would they know he'd seen and interpreted the maps? They knew he couldn't read them, but one didn't have to read the words or the legend if one was told that the black block was where one was—Terindell—and what the two rivers were. He decided to make his way first to the river, with the idea that its current flow would either confirm or deny his idea as to where he was.

Running the four miles was easy for him, and he found his natural state no real problem at all. At least, as long as there were only birds and animals around, he couldn't care less. It was kind of fun, as in the old days. He remembered from somewhere that the early Olympics, back in Greece or wherever it was, were run in the buff. All he needed was a torch.

Pacing himself and enjoying it, he took about half an hour to reach the trees lining the riverbank—and he felt only slightly winded. After Gorodo, a free run at his own pace was easy as pie.

The river, indeed, ran to the south—actually, southeast—as it should. He stopped and looked at it for a few minutes, relaxing after his run. It was a muddy river with a fast current, but nothing spectacular at this point—certainly no more than a quarter of a mile across. An easy swim. He considered the idea. Across there was Hypboreya, a different country that wouldn't march to Ruddygore's tune. Not friendly to him, certainly, but not friendly to Gorodo or, particularly, to Poquah, either, the Imir being a somewhat official servant of the sorcerer and the government. If there were any jokers in the pack—and surely there must be—and Joe didn't make it before the chase began, he would swim to the other side. He decided that quickly, as something of an equalizer.

It occurred to him that if he *did* make that swim, he would also no longer be under anybody's thumb. With a few clothes and some honest work in that country he'd be truly free. That might be the ultimate joke on all of them—to have their prize pigeon not make for Terindell at all. He wondered if they had considered that.

He put the idea aside for now, but left it as another option.

A large bird flew down, skimming the surface of the water, and as it did, suddenly the water erupted and a thin, slimy, black, whiplike tentacle shot up and caught the bird, dragging it quickly under. It was all so sudden he was totally shocked and stunned, but it was a reminder of an alien world. This wasn't the Mississippi, nor his old Earth, and things existed, deadly things, that could kill in a flash. If he'd decided to swim the river at that point ...

He needed a few things as quickly as possible, he knew. He needed clothing of some sort, so he wouldn't have to skulk, and he definitely needed some kind of weapon.

He searched around in the thin forest that hugged the river, looking at deadwood, and finally found a nice, long stick that was more or less straight, looked pretty strong, and, even better, had a rough point at one end and a pretty solid other end. Pointed weapon or club. It would do until something better came along.

He glanced around. Fifty miles. Not much. But, considering that thing in the river, he didn't really want to spend a night out here.

Suddenly, above and behind him came the sound of laughter, as if from some very small children. He whirled, but nobody was there. He stood silently, trying to catch whoever or whatever it was. As he was beginning to feel it had just been his imagination, the laughter came again—and again, above and behind him. He whirled once more, seeing nothing, then stood there gaping for a moment. On impulse, he whirled around again, waiting for the sound—and saw them.

They were about the size of four- or five-month-old babies and looked very chubbily babyish, but their eyes were large and old, and they hovered there, a few feet above his head, on tiny, rapidly beating, white wings.

"Oooo—look! He's naked!" one of them squealed in a playful child's voice.

He relaxed and felt a little rush of anger. "So are you," he retorted.

"Yeah, but it don't bother us none," the small creature said. "It kinda bothers you, though, don't it?"

"Not for the likes of *you*," he shot back, then paused a moment. "Uh, just who and what *are* you, anyway?"

"Gosh, ain't you never heard of cherubs before?" one of them asked, sounding genuinely surprised.

He thought a moment. "Little angels or something, if I remember. You two look like Cupid."

They both giggled. "That's sorta right. I dunno 'bout the angel part, though. Cupids, though, we been called before."

A sudden fright seized him. "You're not gonna shoot me with love arrows, are you?"

They both giggled again. "Love arrows? That's rich. That's a good one! We don't need no arrows to play with you mortals." The speaking cherub paused, thought a moment, then said, a playful smile on his lips, "You're such a big, strong guy. Bet you ain't scared of *nothin'*!"

He frowned. As a matter of fact, he *did* feel a sudden wrongness, a sudden, nameless fear. Trusting his instincts, he looked around, the feeling getting stronger and stronger. He felt suddenly trapped between the river and ... what? The trees! The trees were something else! Something plotting to snare him! He had to get out fast.

Without a second thought, propelled only by the rising, unreasoning fear, he bolted through the thin line of trees back onto the open plain. Once in the clear, away from those menacing trees, he collapsed on the ground, sweating hard and shaking slightly.

The two cherubs flew out from the trees, laughing uproariously, and approached him. He needed only the smallest glance at them and at their expressions to know he'd been had.

"*You* did that to me!" he accused.

"Awwww ... Big, bad barbarian scared of a couple of trees," one of the sprites jeered mockingly.

He leaped angrily to his feet, wishing he had some kind of weapon. A stone, *anything*. Common sense told him that these two, flitting around like hummingbirds, would just play with him if he tried to nab them bare-handed.

Suddenly he remembered his big stick, and was almost surprised to see that he was still carrying it. Taking aim, trying to get control of himself and not telegraph his intent, he looked at the two.

"Wow!" one of the cherubs exclaimed. "You're real brave,

mister, if you keep holding on to that *thing* there. It will eat your arm off in a minute!"

Abruptly the unreasoning fear filled him once again, and with a yell he flung away the stick, which was, indeed, still a stick. They had outguessed him.

Frustration overcame anger. Less than an hour into the contest, he was already defeated by two sorcerous sprites. "What are you going to do? Torture me all day?"

"Gosh, no," one of them replied. "It's just kinda, well, you know, *irresistible.*"

A sudden suspicion hit him. "Did somebody from Terindell send you?"

They both giggled. "Naw. Nobody sends us no place. But we did kinda get the word that you'd be around."

He sighed. "I should have known. I suppose everybody between here and there will be on the lookout for me. I *knew* it was too easy."

"Probably, if *we* got the word," one of the sprites agreed. They looked identical, and it was impossible to tell one from the other. "So you're in a lotta deep mud, huh?"

He thought about it. "Could be. But if you'll let me go, at least I'll have a crack at it."

"*Let* you go?" One giggled, then flexed a tiny arm. "How are *we* gonna stop you?"

"You know how," he grumbled. "Don't rub it in. I'm a match for any other man, I think, but I can't fight magic."

"Hey! Well, then, maybe we should go along with you for a while," one said. "Maybe help you out on that score."

"Um. Thanks—but no, thanks. Nothing personal, you understand, but you might just get it into your little heads to play some more with me, too."

"Hmph! Just for that we *will* come along. How're you gonna stop us?"

"Yeah," the other one agreed. "We could make you want us, but it's more fun this way."

He sighed. "All right, all right. Maybe you can help at that. That *is* the River of Dancing Gods over there?"

"Oh, yeah. That's what all the mortals call it, anyway," a cherub told him.

"So Terindell is about fifty miles downstream, then, as I figured," he said, thinking out loud. "All right. Let's get going."

He hesitated a moment. "I can't keep calling you 'hey, you' if you're tagging along. You have names?"

"Oh, yeah. I'm Ba'el. He's Lo'al."

Joe gave the trees a nervous glance, then started back for them, not going in but walking along on the plains side. "Okay, Ba'el. You called me a mortal. Does that mean you're immortal?"

"Sorta," Ba'el admitted, sounding uncomfortable. "If you mean growin' old and croakin', nope. But if we're not careful, we can get zapped by somethin' hungry or by sorcery."

"You're both males?"

They giggled. "That don't mean nothin' to us. We got no sex. That's probably why we find it so much fun to watch you folks."

Joe stopped a moment. "If that's true, how do you reproduce?"

"*We* don't," Lo'al told him. "Gee, you're awful ignorant. Everybody knows we come from the egg of the *tardris* flower. Where you from, anyway, barbarian?"

He sighed. "Another world," he replied. "Another time."

Once they decided to tag along, he was almost glad of them, although a bit wary. They seemed intellectually adult but emotionally infantile and easily distracted. He worried mostly about their getting bored enough to start playing tricks with his emotions again. Still, it made sense, particularly when he got out of them that a *tardris* laid just one egg and then sheltered the cherub at night. A new cherub was born only to replace one that did not return in the evening, thus keeping the population stable. The plant itself was almost immortal, it seemed, and it was well known that anyone cutting or harming one would die as it did, so the plants were tolerated where they grew, along lakes and rivers.

The cherubs' tie to their parent flower also heartened him a bit. He wasn't sure of their range, but he was pretty sure they wouldn't go *that* far from their home, particularly when Lo'al let slip that they ate only inside the flower, fed by a fluid it manufactured. They were far too chubby to go long between meals.

The day grew warmer as the sun rose in the sky; within a couple of hours, it was really hot. So far he'd seen or heard no other intelligent beings save his two cherubs, although occasionally in the distance, either from the river or from across the plains, he could hear the sounds of humans calling or yelling or doing something or other.

It occurred to him, though, that going right along the river was exactly what they'd expect him to do. The cherubs were merely a small nuisance, but they'd already shown how impotent he was against such as they. Certainly Terindell's nasty little minds had more challenges ahead, particularly if he kept to the course he was now taking.

Still, if he were to leave the river, he'd need something as a guide. Remembering the map, he recalled that the main road that led from the provincial capital of Machang to Terdiera and Terindell ran down the middle of the little "neck" of Valisandra. The road, he decided, would be much safer until he was closer to the castle.

The cherubs were unhappy at his decision, but didn't put up as much of a fuss as he'd anticipated. He got the distinct feeling that they were already bored with him.

He headed southeast across the plain, glad to be rid of the threat his two companions had posed, and began an easy run. He knew it might be a long distance before he sighted the road, maybe fifteen or twenty miles, but the detour would be worth it. Still, he hoped that he would find some place where he could beg, borrow, or steal at least something to use for a loincloth and some food. It had been a long time since he'd eaten. He also found himself wondering how perfect Eden could have been if Adam had to go to the bathroom the same way as he did. He felt grubby, hungry, and thirsty, and he was ready to do about anything to solve those problems.

About a half hour inland, he came upon a small lake with some bushes but no tree cover. There were a few birds about, but no animals that he could see, save a couple of long-horned cows drinking by the far side.

He looked at the water suspiciously, but there didn't seem to be much of a film and it looked pretty clear. Certainly it looked worth risking a drink and, perhaps, a cleansing swim.

He knelt down by the side of the pond, noting that things were so perfect he was almost looking directly into a mirror. He studied his reflection for a moment, still unable to get used to it, then leaned down to sip. The water tasted fresh and clear, amazingly so for such a small pond in such an isolated plain.

The water rippled where he'd broken it, then slowly settled and re-formed once more into his image. But it was not only his image he saw.

He turned, both startled and embarrassed, to see a beautiful woman standing behind him, fully one of the most beautiful and voluptuous women he'd ever seen. She was also as totally naked as he, which didn't stave off his initial embarrassed feelings one bit.

"Oh, I'm sorry I startled you," she said in a soft, musical voice. "I so seldom get visitors here that I often forget politeness."

He gulped. "Uh, um, I'm sorry myself. I didn't know this was anybody's land."

She laughed. "Oh, it's not my land. It is my pond. I am Irium."

He hesitated a moment, trying to sort it out. For the first time it penetrated that her skin was a pale bluish green, much like the waters of the pond itself. Aside from that and a bit of webbing between her fingers and toes, though, she looked extremely human.

"Uh—your *pond*?" he said questioningly. Something inside him rejected all considerations of her color, webbing, or anything else. She was beautiful . . . gorgeous . . . nothing else in the world mattered but her. Considering his nakedness, his emotions were pretty hard to hide from her.

She smiled at him, and he melted completely. "It's so nice to see someone again. Few ever venture this way these days except cows, and they are poor company."

With that she moved in and closed with him, and all he could think of was her. He didn't even realize that, as she clung to him, she was also edging him close to and then into the cool pond. Waist-deep, then still going in, now neck-deep.

"Hold!" The shout was a woman's voice, icy, cutting, and commanding. "Bring him to me or, by Sathanas and Doharic, you shall have no pond at all!"

The threat caused the blue-green beauty to hesitate; then slowly, still without his realizing what was happening, they rose to the surface and moved as if on currents of force back toward the shore.

He was aware only that somebody was butting in, coming between him and consummation with Irium, and this angered

him. He let loose his grip from his lady love and turned to see
a handsome, striking woman, dressed in long slit skirt and
faded brown blouse, standing there, holding a crooked stick of
some kind out toward them. "Go away!" he shouted at her.
"We don't need you!"

"*We* don't, but *you* do," the stranger responded coldly. Her
brow furrowed, and she seemed to be looking beyond just his
physical appearance. It was done in a flash, but she nodded to
herself. "You have been victimized by some mischievous cherubs who almost killed you." She made a sign in the air, and he
felt a sudden deep chill shoot through him. He turned again to
his newfound lady love and screamed in horror, pushing away
from her and scrambling, splashing all the way, to the nearby
land.

The beauty who had so smitten him was a beauty no more,
but an ugly, hideous thing, the stuff of long-rotted corpses.

"Flee, wicked sprite of the water, for you shall not have
him!" his rescuer called, and the rotting thing gave a gurgling
cry and vanished beneath the waters of the pond.

Satisfied, the newcomer approached him as he lay gasping
on the beach and looked down on him with a mixture of scorn
and contempt. Although a beauty herself, she exuded a strong,
confident, powerful aura that was unmistakable. This was a
woman used to command.

"Wha—what was it?" he gasped.

"A water sprite. She got trapped in here during a major hur-
ricane and flood, and there's been no getting rid of her. She's
really pretty much of an incompetent, anyway—she was rushing to drown you without even the preliminaries. You wouldn't
have been such an easy mark if you didn't have that spell cast
on you."

He sighed. "Those bastards. Couldn't resist a parting shot."

She shrugged. "It is their nature. They are so childlike they
probably don't even remember you now." She looked down
and sighed. "Well, you're a real mess. Pick yourself up and
come with me. You look as if you could use a meal."

He got up, suddenly conscious of some aches and bruises,
and followed her meekly.

Her farm wasn't far away, and it looked very pretty and well
tended.

The farmhouse itself was set in an isolated grove of trees,

but all around, the land had been cleared and tilled. Over in the far fields he could see large animals, perhaps oxen, pulling plows—apparently by themselves. Other animals turned irrigation wheels, while over in an uncultivated pasture cows grazed.

Animals, he realized, didn't work without supervision under normal circumstances, but this strange woman had already proved herself a witch or sorceress of some sort. He owed her his life, so he decided not to comment or pry.

The farmhouse was a simple wooden affair with a thatched roof, but it had a good hardwood floor and seemed pretty cozy inside. It was clear, though, that the woman lived alone.

He was acutely aware of his nakedness once more and apologized for it, but she just laughed it away. "Don't worry. I've seen a lot in my life, and it doesn't bother me in the slightest. If it bothers *you*, I suppose I could rig up something, but it would take time. Just sit over there, relax, and I'll see about getting you something to eat."

He sank wearily into the wooden chair offered, finally feeling a little bit more human again. She went into another room and returned with a bunch of home-baked pastries, bread, fresh butter, and a jug of cold milk. "This will at least get you started," she told him, sitting down opposite. He noticed that she never let go of the strange, crooked walking stick she carried, although she didn't seem to need it and hadn't used it at all to support herself. "So," she asked, "how'd you happen to be around the old pond, anyway?"

He sighed. "I'm a little new to everything around here, it seems." Quickly, as he wolfed down the bread and pastries, he told her of having been brought from his own world by Ruddygore, then trained and tested. She nodded, taking it all in.

When he'd finished, she said, "The old boy's off his block, bringing in outsiders. Nothing personal, but from what you've told me just today, you're no match for Husaquahr. Here most humans fall into two classes: the majority—the bulk, really— who do all the work in exchange for protection from all the magical forces around them; and the few who are smart enough or lucky enough to have the power, so they don't fear those forces. The few others like you, adventurers and misfits, mostly, who wander around getting into trouble, were born into this world and know their way around the magic and the politics. You can't be taught that kind of thing—you have to grow up with all this. And even if it's true that Hell can't handle you—which I most sincerely doubt—it makes no difference. The sorcery of Husaquahr alone is enough to do you in, in ten minutes on your own."

"After this morning, I have to agree with you," he admitted. "Still, what choice do I have? I go along with it or I don't— and if I can't make it on my own in a simple thing like this, how could I make it on my own anyplace around here?" He sighed. "Brawn and common sense, they told me. Well, my brawn hasn't done me much good, and I've shown very little common sense today, for all the good it will do me."

"I think you know you could be of little use to Ruddygore, for all I care of his troubles, but you might be just what I need right now. Come with me—outside for a moment." She got up and went out the door, and he followed, curious.

She gestured with the crooked stick. "You see the farm here. It runs itself, pretty much. Animals are my field of study and my life. Everything I require is produced right here. The locals steer clear of this place, which is why our friend in the pond over there has so few victims. But there are certain husbandry problems I have. Chickens need roosters to lay regular eggs. Cows need a bull to keep the milk flowing. I lost my prize bull the other day to a stupid accident."

He nodded, wondering where she was leading.

"Tell me—have you ever heard of Circe?"

He thought a moment, then slowly shook his head. "I don't think so."

"The legends have Circe as a person, a sorceress. Actually, it is a place. An island, far from Husaquahr. An enchanted island, inhabited entirely by a race of women."

"I seem to remember some old stories of places where only women lived," he told her. "Seems to me they'd die out after a while."

"That would be true," she admitted, "but men are occasionally lured there in collusion with sirens and other allies of the sea. They usually act as expected, waking up on an island of women, and the Circeans let them. In that way the population is renewed."

"Sounds like a fun place to be shipwrecked," he murmured.

"Think you so? I said it was an enchanted isle. After the

people are done with the men, the enchantment is brought into play. A piece of sacred wood, like this, is brought out, and the man is touched *so*." She touched him with the stick. "Then the man is useful in other ways, and Circe is all female once more."

He felt suddenly dizzy and dropped to all fours. "Hey! What—?" he exclaimed, but his talk turned into an outlandish bellow.

She stepped back and looked at him with satisfaction. "I am from that island," she told him. "Exiled for reasons that do not concern anyone but me. Eventually I came here with my enchanted wand and built this place from barren fields. I transform few, for sorcerers such as your Ruddygore could do as they willed with me. But you owe me your life. And you have no future here, as we both agreed. So now you are what you reminded me of the moment I saw you. You are my new bull, bound by my powers to do my bidding and bound, too, to the limits of my land. Your power and your horns will guard the land and herds from unseen interlopers, and you will keep my cows in milk. It's not so much to ask. No petty magic or sprites need you fear ever again, for you are under my protection." With that she turned and went back into her house, leaving him there.

Vision and balance cleared in a bit, and he found what she said was impossibly true. He could turn his massive head enough to see his huge black body, and he could wag his barely seen tail. His vision, he discovered, was poor—after twenty feet or so, things started to blur—and he was totally color-blind, but his powers of hearing and smell were increased tremendously.

He turned and looked back at the house, but knew he could never fit through that door in any case. He needed time to think, he decided, and wandered off toward the fields where the cows were grazing, following—scent? Yes, that seemed to be it.

Almost without thinking, he found himself lowering his massive head and munching the tall grass, which tasted extremely good. But all he could think of was that he'd been suckered again.

* * *

He sulked most of the afternoon, munching grass and feeling rotten, and wandered across the farm without really realizing it. He was both shocked and startled late in the day to hear somebody addressing him.

"So you're the new bully boy," a thin, reedy, male voice said casually. "Welcome to the club."

His massive head came up, and he looked around with all the concentration his weak eyes could muster but saw no one.

"Not there, bright eyes," came the voice. "Down here. And watch where you're stepping!"

He looked down and saw in front of him a handsome, strutting rooster.

"So what d'ya want, big boy? A bear?"

"But—you're a rooster!" he exclaimed in a deep series of snorts and grunts.

"And you're a bull. You wanna make something of it?"

"But—you can talk!"

"To you, anyway," the rooster admitted. "And to any of the other former men who are around here. Maybe a couple of dozen. The rest are real animals."

He hadn't considered this. Just the opportunity for two-way communication excited him. "I'm Joe. How long have you been here?"

"Macore's the name," the rooster responded. "Been here forever, it seems. You lose your sense of time, though. Don't much matter, anyway. We're all stuck here."

He didn't like the sound of that. "Nobody ever tries to escape?"

The rooster crowed derisively. "Escape? Man, you're bound to this land by that stick she's got. No need for fences. It's like hitting a stone wall."

"I'll take your word for it." Joe thought a moment. "Say—you say it's the stick that does it?"

"Yep. From her native land. She never is without it."

His mind was suddenly racing with even this tiny glimmer of hope. "But surely she sleeps?"

"Oh, sure. Oh, I see where you're headed. You figure to swipe the stick, maybe hide it or break it up, right?"

"Something like that," he admitted.

"Well, don't think it hasn't been thought of before. You want to risk her catching you and turning you into a snail or

worm or something, that's fine with me. Bein' a rooster maybe
ain't so much, but it's a lot better than the alternatives."

"I wonder. I wonder if everybody's as content as you are to
be an animal slave for the rest of his life."

"Hey! Wait a minute! Now, don't get me wrong. If there
was a real chance, I'd grab it for sure. But take it all the way.
Say we snatch the stick and get away with it. Her hold is gone.
We can leave. Hoo-ray! But you'll still be a bull and I'll still
be a rooster. The spell's worked *through* the charm, as with all
spells. It will hold even if she don't have the stick—and without the stick not even she could undo it. Think about it. You'd
be steaks in the Machang markets before long, and I'd be
chicken salad. Even if we escaped that, what kind of life
would it be? Worse off than here, I'd say. Now do you see
why nobody tries?"

Joe nodded, but didn't really accept it all. Something the
woman had said kept rattling around in the back of his head,
something he couldn't quite pin down.

"You all right?" Macore asked, concerned about the silence.
"I know it's tough to accept, but—"

"*Quiet!* I'm trying to think!" he snapped. Something she had
said . . . Yeah! That was it!

*"I transform few, for sorcerers such as your Ruddygore
could do as they willed with me . . ."*

"How's that?" the rooster asked, sounding concerned.

"Ruddygore! Sure! You've heard of him, haven't you?"

"Oh, sure. Everybody has, I guess. One of the most powerful sorcerers in the world, it's said. Also nuttier than a squirrel's hoard, by all accounts."

"I think you're right on both counts. But what she said, just
after she got me, was that Ruddygore was tremendously more
powerful than she. She's scared of him. Don't you see? If
Ruddygore personally took over, he could break her spell in a
minute. He could restore us—and protect us from her!"

Macore thought it over. "I dunno. Maybe you're right. But
what good does that do us? These necromancers don't give one
small damn about folks like us."

"This one cares about me, for some reason," Joe said, hope
returning full within him, and with it a sense of self-confidence.
"He suckered me from another world to this one, gave me a
new body, then trained me with the best trainers around. If I

could get to him and make him know it was me, he'd change me back for sure. And as long as he broke the one spell, he'd do it for everybody. I think I know him well enough to promise that."

The rooster looked and sounded interested. "So Ruddygore's a buddy, huh? How do I know you're not just putting me on?"

Joe sighed. "The best I can do is tell you the whole story." And he proceeded to do so.

The rooster listened attentively, then finally said, "Well, *I* believe you, for what this's worth. But I'm not the one you got to convince. I couldn't possibly lift that stick, even though I could get into the house, and you wouldn't fit through the door. Uh-uh. We need help. I think it's time you met the rest of the boys."

The rest of the boys proved to be a couple of magnificent-looking stallions, two pigs, a gander, four oxen, a ram, and a billy goat. They were harder to convince than Macore had been. Many had been there so long they barely remembered being anything else, and a strong undercurrent of fear of their mistress ran through all of them. In the past, there had been examples made that several remembered clearly. There were a lot of unpleasant things the Circean could turn somebody into, and Joe heard the whole catalog.

"It's not a bad life we have here," argued Posti, one of the horses. "Plenty to eat. Security. An easy job."

Joe just couldn't see it. "Is that all being a man meant to you? I mean, really, is that all *life* means to you? *Agh!* Better she turned you into a carrot! Then you wouldn't even have to think!"

"If you wasn't so damned big and mean-lookin', bull, I'd tear you apart for that," Posti shot back. "What does *anybody* want outta life 'cept food, sex, and security?" There were several murmurs of agreement.

"If that's all being alive means, then you *are* better off here," Joe told them. "If being human means something more—maybe doing some great thing, or maybe being a part of some great enterprise—then you're wrong. Maybe love, kids, learning something new, and teaching it to others count for something, too, though."

"Listen, buddy," Houma the goat broke in, sounding more

sheepish than goatish, "what you say may be true for *you*, but not for most of us. I mean, how many people ever can do them great things you talk about? Most of us are just plain, simple folk. Me, I was stuck on a farm workin' my ass off for some duke I never even seen, married off young to a gal who looked worse than Grogha here—" He meant one of the pigs. "—and saddled with a half-dozen kids, all of which looked like her and acted like demons. Hell, wanderin' on this place one day was pretty good luck for me."

Joe looked from one to the other, understanding the problem while not being able to understand fully how people could be like that. He was conscious, though, that he was losing ground in the debate and had little to offer. What kind of men were these, who'd rather stay draft animals? He looked at Grogha the pig. "You, too, hog? You like your life here?"

"It's not bad," Grogha grunted. "Not like what you people seem to think it is."

It was Macore who came to Joe's rescue a little. "I can give you a couple of arguments for going along with the bull here," he said. "The best reason, Grogha, is how you'd like your life if the old bag got a sudden yen for pork chops."

The entire group gave a shocked gasp.

"Yeah," the rooster persisted. "Pork chops. Bacon. Sausage. That's what you'll wind up, you know, when you're too old to produce the little piglets. Same goes for me. I don't like being somebody's chicken dinner. How long do we live in this form? A few years for me at best. Maybe five, six for pigs. Longer for horses and oxen, shorter for sheep and goats, but not very long. How long we been here? Anybody really know?"

"Ten or fifteen years is fine with me," the stubborn Posti responded. "How long was I gonna live back home?"

"Yeah, but you been here the longest, I think," a hesitant-sounding Houma said thoughtfully. "How long has it been, Posti? You ain't as young as you used to be, I know that."

Mentally thanking Macore for the opening, Joe pressed the advantage while it held. "Yeah, Posti. And what happens if you break a leg? All you got to do is make one slip, break down once, and you're nothing but several hundred pounds of dog food."

"Hey! Now wait a minute!" the horse responded defensively, but neither Joe nor Macore was willing to let him off the hook.

"Yeah," the rooster pressed. "What happens to a man with a broken leg? You get an adept in the healer's art, rest a couple of weeks, and you got it. And how old *might* you grow? To sit around the alehouses and swap the old yarns and be the object of respect—or to that certain fate our new friend here predicts if you remain the same? As for me, I do not look forward to my certain slaughter, but even if, as a man, I were then to die, I would rather die a *man* than live this kind of life."

As with any group of basically pedestrian, unimaginative minds, sentiment shifted with the latest decent argument. Now heads were nodding in favor of Macore's words. Joe decided not to let anybody else swing things the other way.

"A vote!" he called. "Let's have a vote! Those with us will try it. Those not with us can go back to their ways for a while, until fate takes them, or until they are overrun and enslaved by the Dark Baron's forces because they were not there to fight him like men!"

That last, said in the heat of passion, shocked them a little more. He'd forgotten how out of touch they'd be—and he hoped he hadn't gone too far. Macore's rooster head cocked and looked at him a bit dubiously, but there was nothing to be done. "Yes," the rooster agreed. "Let us vote now. In turn, I will call your names and you tell me aye or nay."

"I think—" Posti began, but Macore cut him off by starting the roll call. The early vote was clearly for escape, but beginning with Posti it seemed to go the other way. In the end, it was Joe, Macore, Grogha, Houma, and the other horse, whose name was Dacaro, who voted to escape. The others, the majority of the group, decided against.

"Very well," Macore told the dissenters. "Go back to your stables and fields and vegetate. We will be gone soon."

"Or turned to maggots," one of the oxen snorted. Slowly the nay votes drifted away into the gathering darkness.

Macore sighed. "Okay. Sorry if I have problems, but I have no night vision at all. I make it five of us. We'll need a plan."

Joe looked at the odd barnyard assortment. "I'd say our roles are pretty clear. Macore, you absolutely guarantee we can get off this farm if she doesn't have the stick?"

"If she doesn't have *ownership*, then yes," the rooster assured him. "That means it must be in the possession of one of us or hidden where only we, not she, know about it."

"I have no intention of chancing her getting it back again," Joe said flatly. "Who knows what she might do? So once we have it, I'll take the stick. But I can't get inside her house to get it. Our friends the pig and the goat must be the actual burglars."

"I figured something like that," Grogha grumped. "Hell, she's a light sleeper. She's lasted a long time. Our hooves will clatter on that stone floor of hers."

"Then you must go silently and slowly," Joe told them. "But once one of you has the stick securely in your mouth, both run like hell. I'll be waiting outside and I'll grab it. Then we all start running."

"Damn! Wish I could see in this," Macore swore in frustration. "Well, let's work it out as best we can. First the burglary, then the getaway. We can't afford to get separated once we're clear of here."

"Then let's get to details," Joe responded anxiously.

"When do you want to do this?" Houma asked uneasily.

"Frankly, I'd like to do it right now," Joe told him, "but none of us have had any rest and we'd better be at our best for this. There's no reason for waiting, though. There's just as much chance of getting caught if we rehearse it as if we do it. I'd say tomorrow, at mid-eve, about halfway through her sleep. Macore—you seem to know a lot of her habits. When does she usually go to bed?"

"She's asleep now," the rooster told the bull. "She eats her meal shortly after sunset, makes a final check of the outbuildings, then turns in. There's one help, too—she snores."

"How do you know so much?" the goat asked.

Macore laughed. "I been dreaming of this for a long, long time. But I'm not strong enough to lift that stick, and no good at night. Believe me, though—I've worked it out again and again . . ."

The company gathered in the dark away from the house about an hour after moonrise. Joe didn't like the clear, moonlit night much—it would make them very easy to spot—but Macore liked it just fine. Although his vision was bad, there was light enough for him at least to see what was going on.

They were surprised to find an addition to the night's work—Posti, the leader of the opposition. "I just keep dreamin' and dreamin' about dogs," he grumbled. "Besides, if you pull this off, it might get lonesome around here."

"Glad to have you," Macore said, "but there's little for you to do. Just stand out here with Joe and Dacaro and be ready to run interference if you get the chance."

"When I get the stick, run like hell in any direction except the one *I* take until you're out of sight, then double back to the west gate." Joe looked around, his vision not so hot, either. Finally he saw a small stick—actually the broken handle of a shovel or something similar. "Hey! There's a thought. Find one more like this. Then all three of us tearing off will have something in our mouth. She won't know *which* one to chase."

They scouted around and finally found an old piece of fence. Joe sighed, looked at the company, said, "All right—we all know what we're going to do. If we do it, we're free and clear. If not, well, I'd rather try than sit and say I never did."

They moved slowly, singly or by twos, to the cottage. All was dark inside, and they could hear that Macore had spoken the truth when he said she snored, although it was soft and low and would not mask much in the way of sounds.

Macore perched on Joe's back. "I can't get far alone and I don't want to miss this," he explained. Joe just nodded, then turned to the two smallest members of the team.

Grogha and Houma had been very hesitant about this from the start; but once they had made up their minds, there was no second-guessing.

"I figured we needed a small one or two," Macore explained to Joe. "That's why I got the roll call in that order. The sure ones first, then Grogha and, finally, Houma. I figured, if it looked at first like everybody was going to make the break, Houma'd come in. When it turned out different, he was too stubborn and too proud to back down."

"I never could have gotten this far without you, Macore. I owe you one," Joe told him.

"Maybe," Macore replied, almost to himself. "But maybe I owe you one, Joe."

The pig and the goat had already disappeared inside the house.

The fact was that the witch had little to fear and so had

taken few precautions. As long as the spell of her staff was on the farm, anyone could get onto the property, but never off. Her reputation alone was enough to keep most everybody away, but any who came, perhaps to do her harm, would have raised enough of an alarm among the animals, compelled to defend the place, to result in her awakening in plenty of time to deal with that intruder. She had no reason to fear the animals themselves, she'd thought. A few examples and long domestication had made them fearful and complacent, she was sure. Nor was she concerned with the possibility of a rebel in the newcomer. He was far too large to fit through her door.

But the newcomer was not a rebel, but a rebel leader. Now came the revolution—if that pig and that goat could pull it off.

Inside the cottage, Grogha and Houma were moving slowly in the near total darkness, almost too scared to breathe. They were both well aware of how impossible it all seemed—and that they would be the ones to bear the consequences of failure.

The snores were somewhat reassuring, but then Grogha brushed against a chair, which scraped slightly, and both he and Houma froze as the snoring abruptly stopped. Their hearts felt as if they were about to leap from their chests while there was total silence; but finally they heard her turn slightly and begin to snore once more.

Cautiously, Houma the goat approached the bed. He had the best night eyesight of the bunch, and the strongest jaws. Grogha was backup and support only, one who considered his presence in the room mostly for the purpose of moral support.

They feared that the magic stick might be in a holder, or sequestered away in some secret place, but it was not. It was right there, on the floor beside the bed as Macore had assured them, ready to be grabbed in an instant should the woman wake. Had it been smoother and straighter, she might have slept with it.

Houma opened his mouth wide and gingerly wrapped it around the stick, then clamped down tight. Slowly, cautiously, he turned his head to bring the stick horizontal—and there was a crash. The woman hadn't been all *that* trusting—she'd tied a thread to it that brought down the pots and pans!

She was up and turning in a flash as Grogha screamed, "Too late now! *Run like hell!*"

Houma hadn't waited for the advice, but had kicked off on his hind legs and made for the door, stick in mouth. The thread hadn't broken, though, and trailing him came a large iron frying pan, making all sorts of clatter. Unable to get to the goat, the woman grabbed the frying pan and pulled, hard, at almost the same instant Grogha decided that it was act or die. Leaping forward, the hog ran right for her legs and into them, toppling her backward.

Houma jerked around on the line, falling as the woman on the other end of the string fell backward and pulled; but in a flash the pan came free of her hand as she screamed and hit the floor.

"Hurry!" Grogha yelled. "Get out of here! I'm right behind you!" And, with that, pan still clattering behind, both went out the doorway. Feeling lucky even to be alive, Houma dropped the stick at Joe's feet and took off, followed as fast as he could by the porcine Grogha.

The witch had recovered quickly and was now also coming out the door, yelling and cursing at the top of her lungs. Joe seized the stick, and she again made to grab the frying pan, jumping on it and holding tight, but this time the force at the other end was no scrawny goat but a huge bull. The string snapped, and she fell backward once more, still grasping the frying pan.

Macore yelled, "Move it!" from atop Joe's back, and Joe and the two horses took off as agreed.

Now the moonlit night helped rather than hindered, and Joe was able, even with his poor vision, to follow the route Macore had mapped out for him, getting him in a roundabout way to the west gate. He clutched the magic stick in his mouth for all it was worth and feared only that he was going to trip and break a leg or at least lose the stick. In the dim light of the moon, it was unlikely that he or his passenger could find it again.

Ultimately they reached the gate, where the others could already be heard waiting nervously. At the sight of Joe, they gave an irresistible cheer.

The gate was just that—a wooden gate, barred with a simple wood latch that was incorporated into the long fence line. Joe decided not to wait for the niceties—he lowered his head and charged, hardly feeling it as his massive head hit the gate, shattered the wood, and broke him into the open.

The others followed, and they were off on the barren dirt road. Once away a bit, Joe slowed, allowing the others to catch up. The two horses made it almost on his heels, but it took a little longer for the smaller goat and particularly for Grogha the pig to reach the gathering.

Macore crowed in spite of himself. "Whoopee! We did it! We're *out*!"

Suddenly Joe, who'd been running mostly on emotion, realized it, too. "We're free! We're really free . . ."

"Not for long if the old bag catches up to us," a breathless Houma reminded them. "Let's put a little distance between us and the farm—and ditch that stick where she'll never find it."

They made their way down the road, Joe and the horses valiantly trying to be slow enough to accommodate the goat and the pig. Finally the road turned sharply southward, and they realized that they were coming upon the junction of the main road to Terdiera.

Joe stopped. "Any of you with better eyes see a place where we can rest for a while?"

"There's a grove of trees over there that will give us some protection," Houma said. "To your right—near the little pond."

Joe looked up. "Little pond? How little? Does it look deep?"

"Hard to say," the goat replied. "Why?"

"Well, it wouldn't be a bad place to toss this stick, now, would it?"

"Say! You're right at that!"

Macore was more cautious. "I wonder if we might not try to break it, at least in two, first. That won't help us, but it might make it hard for her to go back into business if she ever *does* find the pieces."

They nodded and made for the pond.

Joe, Posti, and Dacaro took turns trying to break the thing, but finally it was a combination of Houma's goat jaws and Joe's weight that did it. Joe didn't know what he'd expected—some weird magical lights, something—but it seemed just like any other old stick. Somehow, the lack of a reaction at its breaking was disappointing.

Still, having broken it, they tossed one piece in the pond, not knowing if the water was inches or yards deep. The other piece

Joe chewed on for a while, then finally dropped in an area in the woods where there was much deadwood on the ground. "No use in making it easy to put the thing back together again, if she can," he noted.

With that they decided on a schedule of guards and tried to get some rest. It was hard, coming after the excitement, and they soon started talking.

"Posti, you were the one who kept the others from coming," Joe noted. "Now you're here. Don't you feel any regrets?"

"Naw. Not really. I just never really figured you could do it. Fact is, I'm still kinda happy bein' a horse. It just makes it easier to be free of that old witch. Besides, if you think on it, the others are free, too, if they wanna be. So I'll string along and see how this goes."

Joe looked over at Dacaro. The sleek black stallion had said barely a word, from the initial debate through now, although he'd done his part and had, at least, said enough to vote for the plan. "What's with him?" Joe asked Posti.

"He don't talk much, but he's a good man," Posti responded. "I dunno much about him, but I got the impression he's not too unhappy bein' a horse, either. You wonder what *he's* runnin' from—or to. Me, you know about."

Joe nodded. After a while, conversation petered out, and they did get a little fitful sleep.

The next day was cloudy and humid, with occasional light rain in the air, which suited them all just fine. The poor weather would reduce commerce on the main road and perhaps give them a little edge in avoiding trouble.

They decided to parallel the road rather than follow it, as much as the land and fencing would allow, avoiding any complications. By midday, Terdiera was in sight, looking a little less than festive in the gloomy weather. They gave the town a rather wide berth to the north, then returned to the road connecting the village with the castle. By midafternoon, the familiar walls of Terindell were in sight.

Joe stood there looking at the great castle and shook his head in wonder. "I can hardly believe it. We made it!"

"Yeah, with no real fuss, too," Posti responded, a little awed by the luck.

"So far, so good," Grogha agreed, "but now what? Are they

just gonna let us barnyard animals wander in? And if we *do* get in—how the hell are we gonna tell 'em who we really are and what we need?"

"We spell it out for 'em," Dacaro said, startling them all. Every head turned to the taciturn stallion.

"He talks!" Houma said with some surprise.

"Shut up and listen!" Joe snapped, then looked back at Dacaro. "How do we do this? Anybody here know how to read and write this stuff?"

"I do," Dacaro told them. "As to the how, we just scratch it with hooves or spell it out with a stick in the dirt. I don't know how much will be necessary, though. I think in *that* castle they will be able to *see* an enchantment."

"Can you show us the marks to make—just in case?" Grogha asked cautiously.

"Just one will probably do in a pinch," Dacaro responded. "Look." With his right front hoof he scratched a simple pattern. "Like this."

They all stared at it. "What does it mean?" Macore asked.

"Basically, the few lines inside indicate an enchantment or spell," the stallion told them. "The shape of the border, with its six sides, says that the sign refers to us. No animal would or could make that sign. Can you all remember it?"

It *was* simple, and all agreed that they could. With that Joe said, "Well, let's get on down there."

They went down from the hill to the road itself, now something of a sea of mud. The great outer castle wall loomed ahead, and the drawbridge inside was down, as usual. It wasn't a real problem, considering the magical reputation.

Dacaro continued to puzzle Joe. "Where'd you learn to read?" he asked.

"Long ago, and in this very place. I am no friend of the one you call Ruddygore, nor is he a friend of mine."

"But you came with us."

Dacaro's proud head nodded. "Yes. I came. But not for the reasons you think. It was not any problems back there, but what you said at the last that made up my mind. About the Dark Baron."

"Yeah, I *did* say something. At the time I thought I shouldn't have."

"It was well that you did." Dacaro looked around as they

passed through the outer castle gate. "Ah, what memories I have. Not good memories."

None of the usual elf gardeners or other staff seemed about, although it wasn't that surprising, considering the weather. There was inside activity, though—fires glowed through windows, and the master kitchen's chimney flowed with white smoke and good odors.

They stopped in the middle of the courtyard, feeling a bit nervous and dwarfed by it all.

"Well? So where's the welcoming committee?" Grogha wanted to know.

Across the courtyard a door suddenly opened, and a tall, lean figure emerged. Joe recognized Poquah the Imir instantly, but, for once, the Imir did not recognize him. In fact, at first Poquah seemed not to notice them standing there as he walked across the courtyard. Suddenly he stopped, turned, and began to frown as he looked at them. Finally he came over to them, without any apparent apprehension.

"Draw the sign! Somebody draw the sign!" Grogha prompted.

"I thought as much," the Imir said. "Enchantments. A Circean spell, if I'm not mistaken. Why do you come here?"

"How the hell can we tell him?" Macore grumped.

"Well, you could just tell me," the Imir responded. "Do you think so simple a spell would be a barrier to *me*?"

"We've come asking for the aid of Terindell," Dacaro said smoothly. "Obviously, those who would receive aid will serve in payment."

The Imir's arrowlike brows rose. "Indeed? And why should we have need of such as you? Go on your way. Fate and your own unwariness have cast your lot. You must accept that. Such spells as we would give you here would be worse than any you might suffer as you are."

"I *told* you it was all for nothin'," Posti grumped.

"Listen, you hawk-faced overgrown elf!" Joe snapped. "I'm Joe de Oro, damn it, and I don't think Ruddygore wants me to stay like this!"

The Imir seemed thunderstruck for a moment. Then, suddenly, his granitelike face began to quiver, as unaccustomed muscles were brought into play. And, slowly, Poquah did the one thing none who had ever known him would believe possible.

Poquah laughed.

Suddenly aware of how his demeanor had broken down, he got himself under quick control and stared at the bull. *"Really?"* he managed.

"Yeah. Really, damn it."

"I must admit we never expected *this*," the Imir said. "We had the whole river region staked out as well as the Valisandra Road. Gorodo must be having fits out there right now." He stood back and shook his head wonderingly. "Actually, you are much improved this way in all except disposition. I assume you decided to cut cross-country and ran into that old witch with her shaping-stick. Yes. It makes sense. Stupid, but it makes sense in your context."

"Well, save your opinions and get Ruddygore!" Joe snapped. "I want release. My friends here, too. I couldn't have busted out without 'em and I owe them."

"That will be up to the Master," Poquah responded. "Remain here and I will see if he's in and prepared to receive you."

"You can also tell him that I won. Fair's fair. I passed your little test."

That, too, seemed to rock the Imir. "You *won*?"

Joe was starting to enjoy this. "Sure. I was to get back here, inside the castle, with no time limit, before anybody from the castle caught me. Well—here I am!"

"A highly unprecedented method," Poquah said, "but you may have a point."

"Just go see about Ruddygore."

"As you wish. I am not quite certain how he is going to take this." He turned to go, then paused and turned back to them. "The Master may not be in, or he may be otherwise occupied. Just stand around and munch grass, or whatever it is you do. He will attend to you in his own good time."

"Thanks a lot," Joe muttered, absent-mindedly munching grass.

CHAPTER 8

BUILDING A COMPANY IDENTITY

*Companies must be composed of no less than seven individuals, at
least one of whom should not be fully trusted.*
—XXXIV, 363, 244(a)

THE DARK HOST WAS IMPRESSIVE IN ITS ORDERED MARCH AND
fairly dripped of evil. Ruddygore, in astral form, looked down
upon the enemy forces from his high vantage point and was
amazed at their number and organization. How many? Ten
thousand, surely, if there was one. The multitude of races, both
from Husaquahr and from realms far beyond, was also startling. When the Dark Baron conquered, he gained forces and
additional loot with which to hire the best from afar.

They were a sinister bunch, but even evil had its beauty,
which was one reason it was so attractive. Huge, beaked *tarfur*
in their great flowing robes of black and gold perched atop
swift, multiwinged suggoths. Behind were the bat-winged
gofahr and at least two small legions of hoglike *uorku* and the
horned riders of far Halizar. There were elves and men as well
down there, the elves biologically identical with the gardeners
of Terindell, yet were somehow rough, hard, and ugly, with
eyes either burning or empty. The humans ran the gamut from
tall, fierce-looking barbarian mercenaries to professional soldiers, opportunists, and obvious conscripts.

The Dark Baron had doubled his forces since the start of the
flood season, and more were coming day after day, Ruddygore
knew. Everybody feared a winner, and the Baron certainly
looked like one. Queasy leaders in a dozen places were making
very certain that they would be positively remembered if the
Baron's forces conquered all of Husaquahr—and beyond. He
knew that many of those far-off leaders, with their own evil
forces and marching armies to face, understood that the Baron
was merely an agent for the same dark powers that moved all
of the others on this huge world of sorcery. Across the mighty
oceans, on far-away continents and in countries unknown in
Husaquahr, other dark and powerful leaders were also pressing,

as they always were; in many cases, the leaders of those forces were the only ones who fooled themselves that they were not tools of a greater master of evil, one forbidden for the past two thousand years to vie directly for control of the worlds, who instead had to use the egomania and greed and lust for power of more worldly agents to do his evil work.

And he and they did it very well indeed.

In the great tent city that was in the process of being struck, the generals plotted their strategies and awaited orders from their supreme commander, whose identity even they did not know, as to where to march next.

Yet already here in Zhimbombe, the legitimate authorities had been reduced to living in caves in the eastern mountains, those who had not broken and caved in to the dark power.

But even those still defiant were refugees. They had been beaten, and the enemy spent the flood season in and around the Zhafqua and in the ruins of the formerly beautiful capital of Morikay.

With the flood plain now drying, the enemy forces were preparing to march, certainly to the River of Sorrows and the border of Marquewood. Would they now flank to the east, or perhaps attempt a second line by crossing the River of Dancing Gods?

They had a hundred miles to the River of Sorrows, which would buy Ruddygore some time. Some, but not much. A bit more time to construct some sort of temporary bridge across the receding but still swollen Sorrows, or work out some way to cross the Dancing Gods in force. *That* would be some trick—between the Sorrows and the Dabasar, the Dancing Gods was already two miles or more wide and over forty feet deep in mid-channel.

East? West? North? East was slow, mountainous, and would leave their supply lines long and ugly, while they would be fighting in the best areas for Marquewood to defend. North lay the Valley of Decision, named for an earlier great war's climactic battle, when the invader of that time was forced to channel his forces through a narrow and uneven valley with gorges at two points. Sorcery or not, anybody at the bottom was going to have a pretty nasty time, and those hills and ledges were hollowed-out castles and fortifications, running for miles and built right into the hillsides. But west he had to cross the River of Dancing Gods. Easy going all the way to Stormhold that way, but—how to cross? And how to supply his armies if they crossed? The wealth and booty of Leander was far to the west, and High Pothique was poor and treacherous.

Still, the sorcerer who called himself Ruddygore reflected, the Baron would *have* to cross the Dancing Gods and count on supplies by river from the City-States.

The time to hit was during that crossing, when the Baron would be weakest and most vulnerable. Either that or abandon all until Stormhold and equal turf were reached. Valisandra and Marquewood, he decided, needed a navy and an air force.

He was about to withdraw from the scene when he felt a presence, a crimson force, in the headquarters tent. Drawn to this strong feeling of power, he peered down and saw the Dark Baron himself.

The crimson aura was incredibly strong and visible only to those well versed in the Arts, yet it was not a distinctive, personal aura as much as part of the mask; had it not blotted out the Baron's true aura, Ruddygore could have instantly identified the evil leader.

His temporal disguise was also impressive, cloaked as he was in shining black armor from head to foot, his head masked by a demon's-head helmet whose eyes burned with an inhuman yellow light.

The defenses, both magical and temporal, were perfect, as always. Although the figure towered at far greater than seven feet, it was impossible to guess the true height or build of the sorcerer inside, or even the gender. More than once, Ruddygore had suspected that the disguise hid far more than mere aura and features, but there was no way to know for sure.

Ruddygore stared down at the massive, giant figure and thought, angrily, *I know you. I have eaten and drunk with you, perhaps exchanged jokes and tricks of the craft. You have been my guest, my friend, my rival in the world we both pledged to serve, not destroy. Which one are you? Who are you, who has sold his body and soul to Hell? In whose name do you rationalize the violation of your most sacred trusts? Damn you! I will know you one day! I will know you and be present to witness and participate in your total destruction—I swear it!*

The force of his hatred and his will seemed to penetrate to

the huge dark figure standing below. The demon's mask looked upward, as if searching him out. A right hand came up, and a gloved index finger traced a searing orange pattern in the air, a pattern which, when completed, suddenly sped up toward Ruddygore, growing and blazing intently as it approached.

Unwilling to face the Baron with a strictly astral form, and not wanting to give that evil one the satisfaction of knowing that there was somebody really watching, Ruddygore rapidly withdrew, making sufficient countersigns to divert the blazing pattern. Nothing clear, nothing obvious. A quick retreat. Let the Baron wonder if it was real or only nerves, the sorcerer decided.

He was quickly back at Terindell. After a brief glance around to make certain he was not followed by anything, he floated over the castle walls. The center quad looked like a barnyard, he noted curiously. He would have to see what was going on. Still, one horse there—an aura of pale greenish blue in a pattern that was vaguely familiar to him. A horse with an aura?

He decided not to investigate until back in human form once more. Some animals could see astral bodies, and he didn't trust that horse with the aura at all.

His own body lay on his bed in his inner chamber, protected by the strongest of spells, apparently asleep. Quickly he approached and merged with it. The body yawned and stretched; the eyes opened. He was starving, he realized. Astral projections always did that to him. He looked around, found a couple of pounds of chocolate-topped butter cookies, and tore into them. They would be just about right as a snack while he undid enough of the door spell to get out.

It was a little more than half an hour before Ruddygore emerged from his building inside the compound and approached the animals there. The ever-attentive Poquah followed slightly behind, and had obviously briefed the sorcerer of Terindell. For his part, Ruddygore seemed somewhat amused.

He looked them over critically. "Hmm . . . Not a bad spell for the old bat. Still, she probably had to use some of that stinkwood. She's going to be very unhappy and vulnerable without it." He turned to Joe. "So—you claim you have won?"

Joe looked up at him and tried to see him clearly with his poor vision. "Sure I did. Nothing about shape or form was in the rules one way or the other."

The sorcerer nodded. "That's true. But nothing said we had to change you back, either. Still, you're right. I didn't go through all this to have you go out making cows happy, and your very survival and return here show that you have the three qualities I counted on you to have. The first is luck— blind, dumb luck that gets you out of jams. Don't sneer at it. It's essential, to be anybody around here. The second is self-confidence, which you have aplenty, it seems, or you wouldn't have returned here no matter what. Finally, you use your head—when it would have been easy to accept your new lot in life meekly, you wasted no time in planning and organizing the opposition and carrying your escape off. I approve. I think, too, you've learned a valuable lesson here—that you can trust nothing and no one, and that almost everyone is out to get you in one way or another." He sighed and looked thoughtful. "I'm tempted to leave you a reminder of all that. The tail, perhaps, or the horns. But—no. This is too serious a business."

Ruddygore's hand came up, and he made a series of apparently random signs in the air. Joe suddenly felt himself restored. He was there in the pasture, on his hands and knees, a clump of grass still in his mouth. He spat it out, sputtered, and got to his feet, looking down at himself and feeling all over just to make sure. "Hey! I'm really back!" he couldn't help exclaiming.

Ruddygore nodded and smiled. "We'll get you some food and clothes and a good night's sleep. After that, we'll talk."

Joe made no move to go, but instead just stood there, looking at the sorcerer and the remaining animals. "Uh—what about them? They helped me. I couldn't have done it without 'em." He cleared his throat a little embarrassedly. "I, uh, kind of promised . . ."

The sorcerer nodded. "You promised what you couldn't deliver and suckered them into helping you, and now you want me to bail you out. That's about it, isn't it?"

"That's about it," Joe agreed a little sheepishly.

"I knew it," Houma sighed. "He's going to leave us stuck."

"Not necessarily, my horny friend. Who might you be?" Ruddygore asked.

"Houma. Formerly a farmer on the lands of Cohorn."

"Uh-huh. And how did a farmer from Cohorn happen to wander onto that farm and get turned into a goat? That's a hundred miles or more from Cohorn."

"Um. Well, sir, we broke a plow, and Cohorn village had no spares, since it was very old, and they sent me to get a new bracing custom-made for it."

"Hmmm . . . A good liar, too. Come, now—what was it, really? Women? Drink? Dishonesty? Or just plain oath-breaking?"

The goat sighed. "Not as bad as all that. We was out workin' in the fields, and a friend of mine, Druka, got caught up in a runaway plow team. Got pretty tore up. Well, this highborn son of a bitch rides over, jumps off his fancy horse, and starts screaming that we've screwed up the production schedule and loused up a good master plow. Loused up a good master plow! With Druka there all cut and bleeding to death! So I slugged the bastard. Felt good. He looked real surprised and went down like a sack of meal. Then I dragged Druka out. Finally I saw he was dead. Chain had broken and snapped back, probably broke his neck. Well, sir, I knew what would happen if that fellow came to, him more concerned about plows than men and all. I figured I either had to kill him or cut and run. He wasn't worth killin' like that, and I'd hardly get a fair fight, so I cut and ran. Bummed around for a while, took odd jobs, and finally applied for work at the old bat's place."

Ruddygore nodded. "I see. And now you want—what? To be restored and returned to Cohorn?"

"Oh, no, sir! There's no time limit on hittin' a highborn. Uh-uh. I'll be happy to join up, work for you or whatever, but if you're gonna send me back or turn me in, you might as well leave me a goat."

The sorcerer laughed. "Well said, sir!" He turned to Joe. "He meets with your approval?"

Joe nodded. "He has real guts, I'll say that. I don't know what you two have been saying, but this fellow sneaked in, got that wand, and didn't panic. I think I'd trust him at my back."

"Then that is where he should be," Ruddygore replied. Again he made a series of signs in the air; suddenly a spindly, knock-kneed fellow with a light beard appeared, on hands and knees. He looked uncertain, almost wondrous, as he made his way unaccustomedly to his two feet. *He looks like a young Uncle Sam,* Joe thought.

Next the sorcerer looked at Macore the rooster. "And you, sir?"

"A tradesman. I sharpened and serviced household gadgets door-to-door and farm-to-farm. I picked the wrong customer, that's all."

Ruddygore turned again to Joe questioningly.

"Macore was the first to agree to the plan and talked the others into it," Joe explained. "He also had almost all the information we needed."

"Hmmm . . . Macore, huh? Seems to me I heard of a Macore a few years back from someplace in Leander. Funny. He was in the same business you were. Only he had a reputation for leaving with more things from the various farms than he should have. You wouldn't be any relation to him, would you?"

"No comment until I've seen a lawyer," the rooster responded.

Ruddygore laughed and turned back to Joe. "What the fellow was, actually, was a common thief. Not even a fancy one. Pretty good, though. He would have valuable skills for us—but I wouldn't trust him too far. He is too clever to have to steal for a living—he did it because he liked the work."

"I'll take the chance," Joe answered. "Besides, I owe him that much."

Again the sign, and now Macore was revealed—a small, slightly built man with a large hawk nose and tiny, deep-set black eyes. For once Joe wondered about the choice of animal the Circean had made. Macore looked more like a weasel than a rooster.

Next was Grogha. That pig looked up expectantly at the sorcerer and eventually told his story about the shrewish wife and mean kids. Like Houma, he was willing to do anything in the service of Terindell, but, rather than go home, he'd remain a pig.

Ruddygore had no problem with him, and the Circean pattern was once again revealed to be fairly consistent. He was a middle-aged, fat man, short and stocky, with a round face and an enormously wide mouth.

Next came Posti. Joe told Ruddygore about the hesitant

horse, but emphasized that Posti, once committed, had acquitted himself well indeed.

"So you would like to be restored and join our Company?" the sorcerer asked. "I detect some hesitancy in you."

"I—I'm not really sure *what* I want," Posti admitted. "I know I was a pain back on the farm, and I know, too, that I came along mostly because I was damned bored. I wanted to see more of the world, get in a little more real living. But I ain't too keen on bein' *me* again, either. I wasn't no beauty. I had a club foot and a cleft chin and I mostly did the haulin' and dirty work, anyway. So y'see, sir, why I was torn. On the one hand I wanted to feel like I saw *something* of this life, more'n most folks, but, hell, sir, I mean, I'm a really *pretty* horse. Strong, too."

Ruddygore thought a moment. "Do you understand what we are doing here? We are fighting a war."

"Aye, sir. I'm willin' to do my duty."

"Suppose . . . Just suppose . . . Suppose we keep you a horse? A horse for one of these men? We'd have a horse with your courage and the intelligence of a man, and you would participate and do your part. You would also get the travel and adventure you seem to crave. How about that?"

"I was kind of thinkin' along them lines myself," Posti admitted. "But I sorta thought it would sound crazy."

The sorcerer grew thoughtful once again. "Still, we must have a way for you to speak, and you just don't have the equipment for it—nor can I really give it to you without changing your nature. However, I think perhaps I have a spell for it." Again the mystic patterns in the air. "There. Now you will be able to communicate with anyone who sits upon your back—and only that person under that circumstance. You will, of course, retain your present ability to talk to others similarly bewitched and to some of the fairies. What about it?"

"I think that will do fine, sir," Posti answered.

Ruddygore turned at last to Dacaro. The sleek black stallion with the odd aura had remained silent and apparently disinterested in the proceedings until now. The head came up, looked down at Ruddygore, and Dacaro said, "Hello again, Ruddygore."

Ruddygore frowned. "Well, I'll be damned! No *wonder* that aura was familiar. Dacaro, isn't it?"

"You know it is."

"I had clean forgotten that you were exiled to the Circean's care! But I have not forgotten why," Ruddygore added darkly.

"I did not think you had," the horse responded.

Ruddygore turned to the others, who, except for Posti, could follow only the sorcerer's part of the conversation. All knew, though, that something was wrong. "This man did me a great disservice once," the sorcerer told them. "He alone was there by force, not by accident."

"He was helpful to us, though," Joe said.

"Yeah, and he could read, too," Grogha added.

"Still, this presents a problem," Ruddygore told them. "Dacaro was an adept here at Terindell several years ago. I'm afraid he had the talent but not the self-discipline for the arts. On his own, he opened the gates of Hell and almost destroyed this place—and me. I was faced with a deep breach of trust and faith and also with the fact that he knew far too much of the darker side of necromancy to be allowed simply to go. He was too ambitious and too easily seduced. He would right now be with the Dark Baron, had I let him leave."

"That's not true!" Dacaro shot back. "In fact, that is the only reason I joined in on this breakout, and certainly the only reason I returned *here*, to you of all people. You forget I have looked into the face of the ultimate evil that sponsors the Dark Baron. Were you right about me, I could have easily cut and run to him after the escape."

Ruddygore thought about it. "What you say has merit, I admit. But I look inside you, Dacaro, and see your tragedy. It is a tragedy I do not think you yourself understand—or, at least, will admit to yourself. What you say is true—but there is inside you something that draws you wrong. You have the makings of a Dark Baron yourself, Dacaro. *He* really doesn't think he's evil, or controlled from Hell. He has fallen completely into self-delusion, which the seduction of ultimate power brings. It's inside you, too."

"I disagree."

"Obviously. And yet my original judgment stands. In your present condition, your powers are somewhat limited, although still there—as is your considerable knowledge. But I simply can't take the chance of restoring you. Not now, particularly. After this is over, perhaps. But not now."

"I thought as much."

"Still, I'm not about to throw you into the arms of the Dark Baron, either," the sorcerer continued. "What say you to the same deal I gave Posti there? Joe can use your magical knowledge and your language abilities. The whole Company can. Will you join the Company of your own free will?"

"As a horse?"

"As a horse. For now, anyway."

Dacaro thought it over for a moment. "All right. For now, anyway. But I do not wish to die a horse."

"You have my word. Prove yourself once more, and perhaps something can be worked out. Deal?"

The black stallion sighed. "Deal."

Ruddygore again made some signs, this time showing obvious concentration.

"What are you doing?" Dacaro asked nervously. "I need no spells from you to communicate!"

Ruddygore kept on, and Dacaro saw ribbons of gold and blue and yellow flow from the finger of the sorcerer and weave the signs in the air—the only one there, other than the sorcerer himself and Poquah, who could see such things.

"You are bound by a stronger spell than the old one, which was so easily broken," Ruddygore told him. "I wish you to face your choices squarely. None but one of the Council could undo my spell."

Dacaro thought about it. "I see. You expect me to run to the Baron in the end."

"Self-discipline is the key to your growth or corruption," Ruddygore said. "Let's see who is right." He sighed and turned to the others. "Now we are almost complete. Joe, Dacaro will be your mount, and you will be able to communicate with him. Listen to him. He has enough of the art to keep you out of some trouble or advise you on the rest."

"Glad to have him," Joe responded.

"Posti, I'm going to give you the last member of the Company as your rider."

"Last member?" both Joe and Posti said.

Ruddygore nodded. "Have you forgotten, Joe, that you didn't arrive here alone?"

The big man snapped his fingers. "Damn! I really *had* just about forgotten! How *is* she?"

"Changed. In some ways greatly changed. In others still the same. We will all dine together tomorrow evening. At that time we will do the last things that must be done, and then I have a job for you. All of you, in fact."

"So soon?"

"Time does not wait. Already the Dark Baron's forces strike camp. In ten days, perhaps a little more, they will be at the River of Sorrows to the south with nothing to stop them. In four weeks or so, we will know where he is going and, therefore, the best point to make our stand. There will be a great battle. I have no time to waste, nor do any of you."

"Four weeks . . ." Houma repeated. "You mean we're that close to a fight?"

"Closer. You see, I have a far different but no less vital task for you. There is a possibility, at least, that the outcome of that battle and perhaps the war turns on your mission. Now go with Poquah. Relax. Those of you who are again humans, enjoy it. Tomorrow those of you who need it will be outfitted and equipped, select horses, and the like. At dinner tomorrow you will know your task. The morning after that, you will be riding far from here. Some of you may not return again."

CHAPTER 9

ALL THE INGREDIENTS FOR A QUEST

Magic swords for quests must be named.
—XVII, 167, 2(c)

RUDDYGORE LOOKED MARGE OVER KEENLY AS SHE ENTERED the room and he liked what he saw. "You have progressed beyond my wildest hopes," he told her.

"I had a good teacher," Marge replied. "No fan of yours, though."

The sorcerer chuckled. "I daresay not. Think of us as members of the same family who went in different directions. Both were of equal potential and inclined, say, to, painting pictures—but one saw the old school as outdated and uninteresting and became an abstractionist and cubist; the other painter saw all that newfangled abstract stuff as nonsense and painted realistic portraits. Neither of them could discuss the other without each one's philosophies of art getting in the way. But even though they disagreed on the nature of art, they saw in each other a sincere belief in art itself. That's roughly the analogy between Huspeth and me."

"But she said she would be with you if the Baron reached Terindell, I remember."

He gave a soft smile and nodded. "Indeed. We disagree on just about everything concerning our own, ah, art, and we can't say three civil words to each other without getting into a fighting and clawing match. Just like our realist and our cubist. But both of those painters would be on the same barricade fighting together the forces of those who would wish to burn all pretty pictures. You see?"

She smiled and relaxed. "Now that you put it that way . . ."

"I had hoped she would see you as I did—the potential there. Tell me—can you perceive and read auras?"

"I can *see* them—sort of. You're a fuzzy purple and yellow pattern. But I can't really tell much from them."

"That comes with experience. You're already much further along than I would have expected. Enough to be considered an adept, at least, at the lower levels. If you wish, as time goes on, I can add to your knowledge and instruction."

"I'd like that," she told him. "I find the whole thing fascinating. But sooner or later I'm going to have to learn to read to go anywhere."

"There are ways around just about everything here," he assured her. "If you have the will, the way will open. But nothing's for free. Not even the training you've had so far. And Huspeth's developmental pattern for you contains a number of potential future problems, too."

Her eyebrows rose, and she waited for him to continue.

"First of all, have you looked at yourself—really looked at yourself—in the past few days?"

"In the pond. Why?"

He pulled himself out of his chair and beckoned her to follow him back into the lab. Again he pulled out the full-length mirror. "Look there and tell me what you see," he said softly.

"A well-stacked Peter Pan," she responded dryly; except for her obviously feminine, well-proportioned figure, she *did* have very much the Peter Pan look, even to the hair, particularly in the clothing Huspeth had given her.

"Nothing else?"

She looked hard. "The ears look a little funny," she decided.

He nodded. "Slightly pointed and angled back against the head. That and the streak in your hair. They are marks of the fairy folk. In order to get as much into you as the time allowed, Huspeth took some shortcuts, I'm afraid. To sensitize you to magic, she infused into you a measure of fairy blood, and it tells. The more you use this new magic art, the more dominant that fairy strain, that changeling strain, will become—and it will show."

"You're telling me, then, that the more magic I use, the less human I'll become. Is that it?"

He nodded.

"But she never told—"

"I know. You think of Huspeth as a kind and powerful teacher. But the philosophical differences with her run a lot deeper than you suspect. She idolizes the fairy folk. Always has. With that bent, she has come, wrongly, to believe that humans are the source of the world's corruption—the gate through which Hell must work. In a sense, she thought she was giving you a gift that would guard you from corruption later. There's no undoing it, either. There isn't time, for one thing, and also, those qualities will be more than useful. But the more of fairy you become, the more those restrictions applying to fairies will also apply, and things you wouldn't think twice about could be dangerous."

Marge looked worried. "Like what?"

"Well, for one thing, even now I would stay away from iron of any kind. There's no natural iron in Husaquahr, by the way, but some of the mercenaries from other lands have iron weapons. The dwarves, whose power derives from their ability alone in faërie to handle iron, always have access to it. Magic swords, too, often have an iron alloy in them. Right now iron will burn and make you a little sick. If you progress, it could kill you with a touch."

She whistled low. "Any other nasty little things like that?"

"The nineteen volumes of Rules covering basic faërie powers and limitations are a bit much to go into now. Let's say that the general restrictions will be self-evident; the specifics can be boiled down to an old Rule that applies to folks like Huspeth and me, too—the more on the magic side you are, the more vulnerable you are to magic as well. Just keep it in mind—if you're tempted, or need to use any powers you might have."

"Not much chance of that," she assured him. "Most of my powers are chemical, not signs and spells. We didn't have much time to get into that."

"More will come to you, with the temptation to use it, as time goes on," he cautioned. "Just remember what I say."

They walked back out into his library. "Say—what would happen if I *did* change all the way over to fairy?" she asked. "Would I wind up looking like Poquah or something?"

He chuckled. "Oh, no. Actually, it's pretty hard to say. But the nonhuman blood would force out the human all the way, eventually. No matter what you became, you'd lose your mortality to age and time."

"That sounds like a good deal."

"Perhaps. Perhaps not. The difference between the fairies and us is that our mystical part, our souls, is hidden from each other—and often from ourselves. With the fairies, what you appear is what you are. Thus, humans may die—and yet not die. There are other planes and other paths. If a fairy dies, though, it is gone."

She considered that, but decided that the concept was too abstract for her right now. This was a new world and a new life—and she wanted to get started in it.

"Let us go to the banquet hall," Ruddygore said. "It's time you met the rest of the Company—at least that part of it that is human. Afterward, I'll tell you what this was all about."

Joe was stunned at the change in Marge's appearance, and she at his, but both still felt inside themselves a certain comfort and kinship with each other that they did not share with the people of Husaquahr. They hardly knew each other, it was true, but both knew where New York and Paris were, and the best Polish jokes—and why one shouldn't tell them. They were from the same world; the others knew it not.

They had a fine meal with the convivial Ruddygore as host. He talked between mouthfuls of this and that and practically everything—except what he had in mind for them. Joe, at least, couldn't shake the uneasy feeling that the condemned were eating a last hearty meal.

Finally all was cleared away, and only Ruddygore appeared to be still capable of eating anything. He passed around cigars, which were mostly declined, then settled back in his big chair and looked them over.

"Well, we've all had a nice evening," he began, "and now it's time for business. I trust that there was something here for everyone. I made it heavily vegetarian, I'm afraid, to accommodate the lady here."

"No problem," Macore responded. "I'm gonna have trouble eating chicken ever again, and I'd guess the rest of 'em have the same kind of problems."

The sorcerer nodded. "That's what I figured. You'll work into it, though. Ah, as you know, the two animal members of our company did not join us, but Poquah is briefing them as we sit—and they have been well tended." He looked at each face in turn. "Are you ready to go to work now?"

"Not particularly," the portly Grogha replied honestly. "But that don't mean we won't."

"Fair enough. First, let me tell you what is going on. The Dark Baron has raised an army of at least ten thousand from a dozen or more races and, now that the floods have subsided, they are preparing to move northward."

Macore whistled. "Ten thousand!"

"And growing more by the day. Valisandra, Marquewood, and Leander are preparing a master conference to decide strategy. We still don't know which way they are going to move, or how, but there's a battle, possibly decisive, in the works about a month or two from now."

"You mean we're enlisted?" Houma said.

"Drafted, you mean," Grogha put in grumpily.

"Well, we can certainly use all hands at the right time," Ruddygore admitted. "If we fail to hold them this time, the next battle will be right outside those walls there. But I don't propose that you all trot off and join the army. Not right now, anyway. There is a side errand that must be run, and it is of vital importance. If anything, it must be completed *before* the decisive battle, so time is also of the essence." He looked at them, "Anybody ever been to High Pothique?"

"I have," Macore told him. "Cruddy place. Not a real country at all. Just a lot of small holdings. Why?"

"In Starmount, just beyond the Vale of Kashogi, a thing of great value has just been discovered, something believed lost to Husaquahr for all time—and better left lost. But now that it's been found, it must be returned to its rightful owner. If the Baron gets his slimy hands on it, he may win a major objective of his war without firing an arrow or raising a sword. It is nothing less than the Lakash Lamp."

"Long ago, in the ancient fires that birthed the world, a greater demon cheated on the laws agreed upon to govern the world," Ruddygore told them. "It was not so much a cheat, really, as a shortcut, a solution to a problem that the demon found no other way to solve. In order to establish certain of the laws of magic, it was necessary to have a safety valve, a wild card, an exception to those very laws. And so, out of those early fires was fashioned the Lamp of Lakash, named for its demon creator.

"To make certain that such a dangerous thing as the Lamp would never fall into the hands of one fully prepared to use it, the Lamp was not left in the world but transferred, taken to the other Earth whence Joe and Marge have come. There, up until roughly two thousand years ago, it remained—occasionally falling into the hands of a person who used it and causing a great many stories and legends about evil genies and magic lamps. But then new rules were placed upon both Heaven and Hell, and all matter which had been displaced from one world to the other was instantly returned to its world of origin, the Lamp included. Thus, the Lamp came to Husaquahr.

"It went through many owners here, but all were eventually trapped and defeated by its curses and limitations. Still, attention was drawn to it, and it came into the hands of my predecessor, Jorgasnovara of Astaroth. When it came time for him to pass on to the next level, he left the Lamp in my care, here in Terindell, where I'd already set up shop. And here it remained for a very long time—until, eventually, an error was made. An inevitable error, considering the time involved, I suppose, but an error all the same.

"There was an adept at that same time named Sugasto—a very talented adept, who was on his way to becoming a great sorcerer someday. Sugasto was so good that I was blinded somewhat to his great character faults and, as a result, I stupidly told him one day of the Lamp's existence. He was seduced by its potential, particularly since it could be wielded only by mortals using magical arts—and were he to attain full wizard status, he could not directly use it. He begged me to show it to him, but I refused again and again, regretting I'd ever brought it up. Jorgasnovara, after all, only told *me* about it some weeks after he died. But somehow, Sugasto found out where the Lamp was. It took him several months, but it had become an obsession with him.

"I said he was good at the art—and he was. *Very* good. To get at it, he undid spells that would have defeated some very good sorcerers and he stole the Lamp while I was away on the other Earth plane. Knowing that I would sense the undoing of those spells and hurry back, he ran from here, ran south and west. We pursued, of course, and nearly caught him near Stormhold—but he fooled us by going up into High Pothique, and there vanished forever from our knowledge. All we knew was that the Lamp was no longer in mortal hands and we could not sense or trace where it was. That was more than two centuries ago.

"But now, just recently, we have found the ending of that story. Piecing together legends and old documents and working with the Xota People, who've consented to talk to anybody human only in the last few years and then just slightly, an explorer and trader named Vaghast discovered that my wayward apprentice had fallen straight into the hands of the Xota, who were upon him before he could use the Lamp. I suspect that he was so reluctant to *use* the thing—waste it, to his mind—that he died of his own greed and lust for power. At any rate, the Xota sensed the tremendous power of the thing, even if they didn't know what it was, and they put it in their god-cave, a sacrificial place, and their own shamans placed protections upon it. Supposedly the cave is guarded by a horrible monster of unknown shape, size, and nature, held there by spells and bound to destroy all who would enter the cave.

"We know the general location of the cave and we know now for certain that the Lamp is still there. Unfortunately, the Dark Baron knows this as well. I am quite certain that the Baron is one of the Council, and it was to the Council that all this was reported not two days ago. It's a sure thing that even now some of his forces ride to the cave. We must beat them to it."

Macore whistled again. "That's pretty wild—and pretty hairy. First of all, last I heard, the Xota were still as nasty as ever, even if they did talk to this guy, and that high mountain country is theirs for sure. Even if they were friendly as pet dogs now, they'd still be savages when it comes to anybody disturbing their god-cave."

Ruddygore nodded. "That's true. They'll be fairly noncommittal now, but once the *first* group to get there betrays its goal, they'll be ferocious."

"I'm more concerned with that horrible monster part," Houma put in. "So we fight or sneak our way through this horde—and once we go in, this thing just gobbles us up."

"That's a possibility," Ruddygore agreed. "But I didn't form this Company for an easy job."

"All the while the Baron sends a small army," Macore added. "Less and less do I like this."

"*That* is not a concern—at least the army part," the sorcerer assured him. "First of all, it's no mean trick to cross the Dancing Gods below the River Tasqom, particularly with a large force. Second, such a force would be set upon by Marquewood and would have a hard fight through Stormhold, only to have to climb and pass through the Vale. Not likely. No. He will send a small company, somewhat under cover. They won't be pleasant folk, but they, too, will know they have to get there by stealth, not a fight."

"Okay, so that puts 'em in the same shape as us." Joe said. "It still don't sound like a picnic."

"Neither was the Circean, and you managed," Ruddygore noted. "You, Joe, and you, Marge, are particularly well prepared. Dacaro has a great deal of knowledge to aid you, should it be necessary, and Marge has the means to use that knowledge."

"Okay, so we won't be completely disarmed," Joe responded. "Still, the odds look pretty bleak."

"As bleak as escaping from Circe's grasp and regaining humanity?" the wizard teased. "Joe—all of you—trust me a bit. We are not alone in this fight, you know. The Baron has the forces of Hell, but the other side is pretty effective, too. They told me that you were the one, Joe. They sent me over to get you. I did—and at the time, I didn't even know why. Frankly, I *still* don't—but I know you're their choice. Your very survival the past few days proves it. You know you were very, very lucky, Joe. Lucky the Circean came along just when she did to save you from the water sprite. Lucky to have succeeded in your crazy scheme to steal the rod and escape. Well, Joe, there's no such thing as luck. Not really. Good luck and bad luck are the terms we lesser ones give to angelic and demonic forces. For some reason, Joe, you have friends in high places. They'll help you out."

Joe chuckled dryly. "Friends in high places. Guardian angels. Man! I sure ain't no saint!"

"There's no way to understand them—they are beyond us and very alien from anything we know or understand. But they're real. It's how they've operated the past two millennia. Why they choose one over the other, why they let good men be tortured and killed and evil ones march, I can't begin to understand. But I go with the flow, Joe, because it's also in *my* best interest. And you're it."

Joe sat back, trying to accept what he'd been told and having trouble with it. "Well, I'll be damned—uh, I guess if you're right, maybe I won't be, huh?"

Ruddygore laughed. "Maybe you will, maybe you won't. Dante put most of the popes in Hell, remember. So don't let it go to your head. And don't count on it. They can drop you, or make you a sacrifice, as easily as they can take you all the way. But they have forearmed you a bit."

"Huh?"

"You have a Company of brave men. You picked up this young woman on the road, and she has proved a talented adept. You have—by chance?—Dacaro's knowledge and understanding of the magical arts. And these three men know the territory, more or less. One has been near there; the other two still are more accustomed to *this* world and are valuable as, say, native guides. And I'll add one additional factor before we leave here tonight. For now—any more questions?"

"I think I have a bundle," Marge said. "For one thing, why is this Lamp so vital?"

"Surely you recall the legends of magic lamps," the sorcerer replied. "What were those magic lamps like in the old stories?"

"Grant wishes," Grogha said brightly.

Ruddygore nodded. "Yes. Grant wishes. With this Lamp you can more or less suspend both Laws and Rules, magical or physical. Within limits, of course, or the Lamp could destroy the structure of the universe. Still, whatever mortal holds the Lamp of Lakash has the wishing power. And contrary to all those stories you may have heard, one wish and one wish only is what you get."

Marge frowned. "Only one? Isn't it always three?"

The sorcerer smiled. "*That* is the curse of the Lamp. Almost everyone believes it that way, and there are few to tell you different. And so, consumed by power, you make a second wish, secure in the old tales that you will get it."

"And what happens?" Houma asked, breathless and fascinated.

"Interestingly, you get it. But you get something else as well. Come! Come! What is the other thing that comes with the Lamp?"

Marge thought a moment. "A genie?"

"Exactly!" Ruddygore cried. "A genie! But what is the nature of this genie? What sort of being is he, and whence does he come? The answer is rather simple—*the genie is the last person to use the Lamp more than once!*"

"But they always called the genie the slave of the lamp in my old stories," Grogha noted. "What does he do, anyway?"

"He is, in every respect, the slave of the Lamp, bound to serve whatever mortal next possesses it. And I *do* mean slave. You must do *whatever* the possessor commands. And you're stuck that way until somebody else makes the same stupid mistake you did and replaces you. Now you see the greatest curse of the Lamp. If you don't get rid of it—literally give it to somebody else—you'll eventually be trapped. And if you do, then *they* will have a wish—so you had better trust them absolutely, since you no longer may use the Lamp. Of course, no matter what, the Lamp's possessors eventually run out of a chain of people they can trust. And that's why it's best in the hands of somebody like me. I can not use it and, therefore, can not be cursed by it. And I will seal it away so that no one will get to it unless there is dire need—and under my control."

"Hey, now! Wait a minute!" Joe jumped in. "If *you* can't use it, then neither can this Baron, right?"

Ruddygore nodded. "That's correct."

"So what harm is it just to let him have it?"

The sorcerer sighed. "Joe, surely your own experiences show that mortals can be placed under a *ton* of spells and told to do just about anything at all. Remember your cherubs? The Baron wouldn't need to use it himself—but he has an endless supply of people he owns and controls body and soul to make wish after wish *for* him."

"Yeah, I guess he could just wish he'd win the war and that'd be that," Houma speculated.

"No," the wizard assured him. "I said the Lamp was quite limited—and it is. First, the wish must be personalized, and confined to a specific localized magical event. So all right, he could wish for a fog before the battle, or that our horses take sick. Even for an earthquake, if he were losing. But a battle has too many people, human and nonhuman, with too many variables for the Lamp to handle it properly. He couldn't even wish for the enemy army to turn to stone, since that wish would affect only the mortals in the army and would be limited to his specific area of battle. It would allow him to escape a desperate situation, but not to win or lose. It could, however, tip the balance in his favor."

"If it works only on mortals, does that mean we can't wish this monster somewhere else?"

The sorcerer shrugged. "Probably you could. I doubt if you could wish it dead, though. And you can never be sure if you've properly phrased your wish. That's another little curse. For example, saying 'I wish we didn't have that monster to worry about any more' gives the Lamp a lot of leeway. It could allow you to die—and then you wouldn't worry. If *I* wanted a sure thing, I would wish that the monster was friendly toward me and my companions and would not bother us in any way. *That* would be pretty sure."

"*I* see," Marge nodded. "Make the wish about *us* and our relationship to the threat."

"Man! You could still wish yourself filthy rich! Or maybe immortal!"

" 'Filthy rich' is an interesting term," Ruddygore noted. "Knowing the Lamp, I imagine it would probably put your gold at the bottom of a great cesspool. Yes, you could wish for wealth—but even there you must be careful. Being rich or noble does you no good if your riches and title are in some far-off land. As for immortality—I suspect that that wish would be a real curse, particularly if you could never remove it. And once you make that wish, beware of any loopholes you leave, such as about whether or not you'd age. The rules are basic. Keep it simple, very specific, and very personal. And be careful about random wishes. The possessor of the Lamp has only to preface a statement with 'I wish' and it is one. So, saying 'I wish I had a drink' or something like 'I wish I were dead' can at best be wasteful and surprising—at worst, fatal. Even something as simple as 'I wish I knew' would do it."

"You seem pretty confident of us," Macore noted. "What makes you think *we* won't be corrupted by that power?"

"Oh, some of you probably will," he responded cheerfully. "However, I have laid a *geas* on you that will require you to get the Lamp back to me."

Marge thought a moment. "Can't we just wish us all back here as soon as we have the Lamp?"

Ruddygore sighed. "I wish it were that simple. Unfortunately, the Lamp's transportability is somewhat limited. A rule of thumb would be that, if you can't see it, you probably can't reach it. Actually, the possessor alone could wish himself anywhere at all and probably get there—but only the possessor. For a group, its power is limited—more or less to line of sight. Say, fifty miles."

Joe sighed. "Oh, great. One of us can escape, but we'd leave the others stuck. So we have to make a run for it, anyway."

"That's about it," the sorcerer agreed. "In and out. Unless, of course, there is only one of you left."

That thought sobered them. "I wish you were coming with us," Grogha said. "Then it would be easy."

"Not so easy, with me or not, for there are some things beyond my powers," he replied. "In any event, I am needed to aid and coordinate the battle that must come, no matter who wins the Lamp—if anyone does. But regardless of what else may happen, I must be assured that the Lamp either is in friendly hands or is impossible to get by either side. If the Baron gets it, we may fail. I think we have forces that are a match for him. It is much better to defend than attack. But if

I must spend all my time negating the Lamp, the Baron will be free to aid the battle. The Lamp's power is considerable, no matter what I've said. I *think* I can cancel or negate anything it does, if I work fast and furiously—but I can not handle the Baron *and* the Lamp. Better *we* have the Lamp and the Baron have the problem. See?"

"Negate . . ." Marge repeated, thinking. "You mean we might get the Lamp and then find the Baron lousing us up?"

"You could. And a negated wish still counts. Remember that." He sighed and got up. "Well, I have done what I could. Dacaro can help with advice, although he can't use the Lamp himself." Again he paused. "You understand now why I had to be so harsh with Dacaro? He was—is—very, very much like Sugasto. I simply could not take the chance with him after he, too, violated a sacred trust. Come."

They walked out into the darkness and to Ruddygore's library. He went over to a wall, pressed a hidden stud, and the bookcase moved back and then to one side, revealing a small chamber. He entered, then returned with a long, heavy object wrapped in silk cloth. He went to the table as they all watched and carefully unwrapped it.

They crowded around and gasped when they saw what the silk masked. It was a sword—a great, magnificent sword. Its fancy hilt looked like polished gold, and its blade was sharp and shone with an unbelievable brightness. The blade, however, was totally encased in a solid block of what looked like transparent amber.

"Long ago I did a service for one incredibly high," Ruddygore told them. "This was a reward, of sorts. A true magic sword, forged by the ancient dwarf kings thousands of years ago. It's one of a number of such swords, all made during that time and all given only through supernatural will. It's rare, though, in that it remains as it was when forged. It has never been used. I had no need of it, and nobody before was worthy enough of it. Now, I think, Joe, it is time to put it to use."

Joe looked down at the sword. "It's beautiful," he breathed. "But why is it magic?"

"First, the blade is an alloy of steel better than any ever seen. Most blades here are bronze, as you know. Steel contains iron, which means the blade is fatal to most fairy folk except dwarves. Just a wound, the merest prick, would do it." He turned to Marge. "Don't *you* touch it, either! Even if it's necessary!"

"I'll remember," she assured him, looking at the beautiful sword nervously.

"Additionally, such swords as these are harder than diamonds. They will cut through rock, metal—you name it—amazingly easily. And they have something of a life of their own. No one, save the owner, so long as he lives, will be able to wield the blade—and the sword itself will pick its next owner, so it can not be stolen. It may have other powers that will manifest themselves—it's hard to say."

Joe looked at it hungrily. "It's great. Just what I needed. I didn't have enough to buy a sword at the market." He frowned. "But it's stuck in this plastic or whatever."

"The amber prevents anyone from using it but the right one," the sorcerer told him. "There! Take the hilt. Raise it high. Let's see if it will accept you."

Joe reached out and took the sword in his hand. It felt extremely heavy, but he managed to lift it, even raise it over his head.

There was a strange humming sound, and a moment passed before they all realized it was coming from the sword itself. The humming grew louder and louder as he held it—and finally the vibration from the sword cracked, then shattered the amber casing, which fell to the floor as so much dust.

"Hey! It's suddenly real light! Almost like a fencing foil!" Joe exclaimed.

"To you," Ruddygore told him. "Only to you, Joe. Nobody else will even be able to pick it up. It accepts you. It is yours—one with you. Use it well. Its relative strength is unknown—but it is very possible that it could even kill the Dark Baron himself if you gave it a chance."

That thought pleased Joe. "Wouldn't that be somethin'!" He lowered the sword, which seemed to have taken on a glow, and placed it in the scabbard on his newly purchased sword belt. The glow subsided and was gone when he let go of the hilt.

"You must name it, Joe," the sorcerer told him. "It is a virgin sword. You will name it for all times."

"Uh—name it?"

The sorcerer nodded. "Just take it out once again, hold it in front of you, and give it a name with real meaning. You should be honored—few have the opportunity, and this may be the last unnamed magic sword anywhere."

Joe did as instructed. The sword glowed and hummed softly in front of him. He thought for a moment, then seemed to brighten. "Okay. Uh, let me know if I'm doing this wrong. I name this sword, my sword—Irving."

"WHAT!" It was Marge who screamed. "Irving? That's ridiculous! Joe—haven't you ever read *anything*? Magic swords are named things like Stormbringer or Excalibur. Fancy, exotic names."

Joe looked puzzled. "But I *like* the name Irving. That's the name I gave my son. I never could have him, but at least I got somethin' here named in his honor so I don't forget him."

Marge looked frantically at Ruddygore, who shrugged. "The sword has accepted the name," the wizard noted. "Irving it is. Somehow it is fitting that a barbarian named Joe has a sword named Irving. I don't know *why*, but it is."

Marge shook her head, started mumbling to herself, and went over and sat down in a chair, still shaking her head and saying all sorts of unintelligible things.

"I kinda like the name," Grogha said, trying to be cheerful. "I mean, it's *different*."

"It sure is," Ruddygore muttered, but Joe beamed at the comment and sheathed the sword once more.

"Now, then," the sorcerer continued, "let me show you a couple of tricks. Joe, remove the sword again and place it back on the table there. Go ahead—do it."

Joe looked uncertain, but did as instructed.

"Now move back—over by that chair. Ten feet or so, I'd say."

Again the trucker turned barbarian complied.

"Grogha, pick up the sword and bring it to Joe."

The portly man went over, took hold, and tried. He tried very hard, until sweat rolled off his brow. Finally he gave up and turned to Ruddygore. "Man! That *is* a heavy blade!"

"Anybody else?" the sorcerer invited.

Each in turn, except for the unconsolable Marge, also gave it a try—and failed. "That thing's nailed there," Macore grumbled.

"All right—now, everybody over by Marge, out of the way

of Joe," the sorcerer instructed. "Ah. That's fine. Remember, Joe, try this only when nobody you like is in the way. Call the sword. Put out your hand."

Joe put his hand forward.

"No. Not like that. As if you were going to catch the hilt."

Joe looked puzzled, but did as instructed.

"All right. Now call it. By name."

"Uh—heeere, Irving!"

"It's a sword, Joe! Not a dog!"

Joe cleared his throat. "Irving! To me!" he shouted. In an instant the sword flew threw the air and right into his raised hand. The movement was so sudden and startling that he almost fell over from the shock and surprise—but he didn't drop the sword. Recovering, he looked down at it. "I'll be damned!" He turned to Ruddygore. "How far is that effective?"

"If it can hear you, it will come—no matter what's in the way. Farther than that, if you have a clear line of sight from it to you."

"Wow! That's really neat!"

Marge looked up at him sourly. "Really neat. I don't *believe* you."

He looked back at her, frowning again. "But it is."

She sighed. "If you say so. Jesus! Irving!"

"And now, my friends, you should all get some sleep," Ruddygore told them. "Tomorrow you begin—and very early. Macore, you remain. Since you've been in Pothique, I'll give you the terrain and trail maps. Before you leave tomorrow, Poquah will brief you on the basic route, although he's already briefed Dacaro and Posti. The rest of you will have more conventional horses, but Dacaro will have power over them. Oh, by the way. Rather than my original idea, I think I'll let Marge have Dacaro, and you, Joe, will ride Posti. It makes more sense to have the magic application and the magic knowledge together."

"Whatever you say," Joe told him. "Hell, I'm ready to go now. If I'm stuck here with all this, I guess I'd better get into the spirit."

Marge sighed. "Think of it, Joe," she prompted. "Don't you remember Ruddygore once saying that the fantasies of our world are the truths of this one? This could be the start of an epic! *The Chronicles of Marge and Joe!* Think about *that*!"

He thought about it. "Not bad. *The Chronicles of Joe and Marge.* It has a ring to it, I guess. I doubt if I'd ever read it, though."

"You make light of that possibility, yet you may regret labeling your adventures an epic in times to come," Ruddygore warned them.

"Huh? Why?"

"Oh, we'll cross that bridge when we come to it. For now, don't dream too much of immortality in legend. First you have to earn it. And I might as well tell you, the odds of any of you surviving this mission are beyond those any bookmaker would give or take."

CHAPTER 10

OF TROLLBRIDGES AND FAIRYBOATS

Unlike all other forms of energy, magical energy may be created and destroyed by applications of positive and/or negative spells.
                                        —II, 139, 68.2(a)

JOE, MOUNTED ON POSTI, LOOKED AROUND AT THE REST OF the Company and found the group somewhat imposing. Marge seemed almost dwarfed on the sleek black Dacaro, but the other three looked well matched to their more normal steeds. Ruddygore had said that seven was the proper number for a Company, according to the Rules, but this Company included five humans and two transformed ones upon whom he and Marge rode. He had to trust it to Ruddygore that the number worked out.

Macore rode up beside him and pulled out the map of the region. "We'll have to cross the Rossignol east of Terdiera," he pointed out. "That's the only bridge for a hundred miles, and it wouldn't do to backtrack any more than we have to."

Joe shrugged. "So? What's the problem?"

"Trolls," the little thief replied, a sense of distaste in his tone. "Damn them. Only really decent bridge builders in Husaquahr."

Joe gave another shrug, and they started off, enjoying the early morning air. As they rode through a not-yet-open

Terdiera, Joe looked around for familiar places and faces and saw more of the former than the latter. Early risers stopped to gape at the five riding through the town center, and particularly at their leader, who thought he looked pretty good in his loincloth and trucker's hat.

On the other side of town they departed from the main road, down a narrow side street that quickly became a dirt track when it left the town behind, going down to the river. It was a fairly well traveled path, to judge from the deep ruts and gouges in the road, but there was nobody on it this early in the day.

The bridge was nothing fancy, but still was impressive engineering for the technology of Husaquahr. A wooden structure supported by thick pylons made from the trunks of hardwood trees, it stretched the thousand yards or more from shore to shore and even curved up in the center to allow barges to pass under. The channel was not wide but was fairly deep. The bridge, also, wasn't very wide—they would have to pass single file to feel safe, since there were no guardrails or other safety devices or guides.

"Whew! I'd hate to have to drive a wagon and team across that thing," Grogha noted. "I'm not too sure I feel thrilled riding it now."

"The bridge is perfectly safe if you don't panic but just go straight," Macore assured them. "However, this is no free ride. See!" He pointed and they all looked.

The sign contained a series of pictographs and accompanying very formal-looking text, the former for the mostly illiterate locals, the latter for the unwary traveler who, being most likely a trade or political figure, would be able to read and needed a more detailed explanation. The sign's pictures fascinated them:

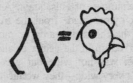

Joe frowned. "Now what the *hell* does *that* mean?"

"Dacaro is reading the sign to me now," Marge told him, but it was Macore who spoke up first.

"That's standard picture writing," he explained. "It says, 'STOP! PAY TROLL! Pedestrians one chicken each, horse and rider one pig, wagons and drivers one pig per axle or one cow for the whole load.' What did you expect? It *is* a trollbridge, after all."

Joe looked quizzically at Marge, who nodded. "That's what the writing says, according to Dacaro, except that the text adds, 'Or equivalent.' "

"Pretty steep," Grogha noted.

Joe looked at Macore. "So what do we do? We don't exactly have a barnyard handy."

"I'm not sure I like that live pig business," Grogha added nervously.

"Oh, you're not a pig any more," Houma scolded. "You'd probably be worth a whole wagon as you are."

Macore looked back at Marge. "You're the keeper of the treasury. You have those silver coins Ruddygore gave us?"

She nodded, reached down on her saddle pack, and removed a heavy sack. "How much will we need?"

"Well, if a pig's the fare, we need five pigs. That'd be about eleven of those coins at today's prices, I think—but I'm a little out of touch. May as well go down and find out." He turned to Joe. "Now don't panic or start swingin' that sword when the troll comes up," he warned. "They're liars and crooks and really nasty, but even if we took the one or two on this side, they'd have us on the bridge. Better to pay."

Joe just shook his head sadly. "Yeah, I know. I'm used to these things."

They went down to the bridge itself. There was no structure or sign of life or authority anywhere around, which puzzled Joe. "What's the matter? They not up yet?"

At that moment there was a great roaring sound from beneath the bridge, and the water erupted. A gigantic blue creature climbed out, covered in woolly hair, with two enormous eyes and a teeth-filled mouth that went the two-foot width of the eerie, vicious face.

The creature looked at the Company hungrily for a moment, then said, in a voice much like an angry bear's, "You wanna cross?"

"Why else would we be here at this ungodly hour?" Macore

shot back, sounding totally unintimidated. "Five horses and riders. How much in coin?"

The creature looked over the people waiting and licked its lips with a huge purple tongue. "I'll take two of the horses and you can all go," it suggested.

"Uh-uh. No horses. We have a long way to go. Coin. How much?"

"Twenty-five for the lot."

Macore sounded shocked and hurt. "Twenty-five! That's robbery! We'll go back up to the village and buy five pigs when the markets open and save a bundle."

"Yeah, but that's three hours from now." The creature smirked. "You want special service, you pay the extra freight."

Macore sighed. "C'mon. We can kill three hours." He made as if to turn.

"Wait!" the creature called to him. "All right. Special. Twenty."

"Ten."

"You rob me! I tell you, little one—how about I just eat *you* and the others go free? What about it, the rest of you? You should be happy to be rid of such a robber and thief as this."

"Sorry," Joe told the troll. "But I think ten *is* too low for such a fine bridge. How about twelve?"

The troll roared and splashed the water in very real-looking mock anger. Finally he said, "Eighteen! Low as I go!"

"Split the difference," Macore suggested. "Fifteen. It's a good profit. Either that or we wait for the markets to open—which won't be very much longer if we keep this up, anyway."

The troll growled and gnashed his teeth and somehow managed to foam at the mouth. They all thought he was going to attack them in rage, and Joe's hand went to his sword hilt, but finally the great troll calmed down. "Pay me!" he snarled.

Macore reached back, got the fifteen coins from Marge, and flung them at the troll, who frantically grabbed for them with massive clawed hands. He missed a bunch, and they went into the water.

"All right, gang," Macore said. "Now—listen closely and I'll tell you the rules. We go single file and keep a fair distance apart. Take it *real* slow. We've met his price, so he and his kin can't molest us in any way—that's the Rule—but they may try some funny stuff to panic us or our horses. If any of us fall in, we're fair game and they can eat us. Understand? So keep real control of your horses, and ignore *anything* that happens on either side of the bridge. You all understand?"

They nodded but looked slightly uneasy. "I'll lead," the little thief told them and guided his mount onto the bridge past the fuming troll.

Joe went next, then Marge, then Houma, with Grogha nervously bringing up the rear.

All went well until Macore reached the point at which the bridge arched sharply upward over the main channel. At just that point the water erupted on both sides of them, with giant trolls growling and screaming menacingly. There seemed to be a dozen or more, all as repulsively ugly and nasty-looking as the gate troll.

Posti gave a start but held, and Macore had firm control of his mount, while Dacaro ignored the commotion, but Houma's mount reared in shock and he almost toppled in. Grogha, having the same problems, was just a little more in control than his friend in front.

Macore turned angrily and screamed above the noise, "Get these mounts under control, you two! As soon as you get 'em calmed, everybody dismount. Let's *lead* the horses from this point!"

Both Joe and Marge found it difficult to ignore the roaring and screaming trolls, but Houma got his horse calmed a bit and slid off, followed by the rest.

Macore turned to the nearest foaming troll. "Ah! Your mother was a fairy princess!" he yelled derisively.

The troll roared and foamed all the more and slapped the water.

"Your father was a fairy princess, too, pumpkin-nose!" Macore taunted.

While this made the troll all the more furious, it had a different effect on the other huge creatures, who stopped their panic acts and started laughing uproariously at the obvious discomfort of the target of Macore's insults. This, of course, infuriated the target all the more, and it took a swing at the nearest fellow troll. In a few moments, they were all oblivious to the travelers and swinging away at one another.

Looking smug, Macore led his mount up the center span and

down, followed at prudent intervals by the other four. They crossed the rest of the bridge without further incident, the sounds of the fight still clear behind them.

"Trolls are good engineers and savvy bargainers, but outside of that, they ain't so bright," the little man said, chuckling. The Company mounted once more and followed the dirt track on the other shore for a quarter of a mile or so until it hit a main road. At the junction was a large sign. "Welcome to Marquewood. Obey local ordinances," Marge repeated Dacaro's reading of it.

"Well, onward and upward," Joe called. "I'm beginning to feel as if I'm back on the road again!"

About a mile farther down, the road split into three directions, and there was a roadhouse and inn. Joe looked at the place hungrily, but Macore cut his impulse short. "I think we better make time today. We got seventy miles to the Dancing Gods, and that's a good two, three days. Best we stop when we *have* to or we'll *never* get there."

Reluctantly, Joe nodded, and they rode past to the junction itself, well marked but totally unintelligible to them.

Marge rode up to the signpost, letting Dacaro do what he wanted, and the black stallion looked at the signs. "The extreme right road is the one," his voice came into her mind.

Although they'd talked a bit before, it was still startling to her to hear the horse speak to her. Dacaro was no conversationalist, and she hadn't had time to get used to the fact that her mount was more than a beautiful, sleek, intelligent animal.

Marge pointed to the road. "Dacaro says this way. Any objections?"

Macore looked at his map. "Nope. That should be right."

They traveled most of the day, and it was past dark when they reached a small inn on the road. Macore cautioned them to say as little as possible about their origin, mission, or destination, "because you never know who's gonna sell you out, particularly in places like this."

Joe nodded. "We better have some kind of cover story, though," he suggested. "Just to keep it straight."

"Hmm . . . All right. You two—" Macore indicated Houma and Grogha. "—are merchants. Get it?"

"What kind?" the practical Grogha asked.

"Anybody asks you, you tell 'em it's none of their business," Macore replied. "But you're picking up some raw materials for clients in Valisandra. We're your associates, see? You say that and everybody will figure we're your guards, anyway. Don't pick fights or start conversations. Let me do the talking. The less we say the better. Got it?"

They all nodded.

"And, lady, you get Dacaro to give you a neat little spell for that money, huh? We need it bad, and they'll lift it at the first opportunity."

Marge nodded and then paused, as if listening to something none of the others could hear. Finally she said, "We'll take out what we need ahead of time and leave the rest in the saddlebag. He's got a pretty fair spell for it, and it will be right there in the stable, where he can protect it and raise the alarm if the spell fails."

"Good enough," Macore said. "Take out—oh, a dozen, I suppose. I don't think we'll need more; if we do, we can always come out and get it. Right?"

Marge paused again. "He says twenty and forget coming back. It's a pretty strong spell to undo just to make change."

"I'll go along with that," the little man told her, and soon they were at the inn and settled down.

The roadhouse was almost deserted, and the family that ran the place seemed willing to ask no questions of paying guests. The night passed uneventfully, which was fine with them all. It had been at best a tiring day.

The next morning Macore was enthusiastic. "We have a little more than thirty miles today, according to the innkeeper, to reach the River of Dancing Gods," he told them. "Looks like we might be in High Pothique by this evening."

"I understand that this High Pothique isn't really a country at all," Marge said between bites of breakfast. "Will we have any trouble on the roads there?"

"Oh, I wouldn't worry about the roads," the little man assured her. "They're pretty well traveled. But there isn't much of a central government in High Pothique—too many magical domains and freeholds under minor sorcerers and the like. Right along the river are a few villages that will be okay. It's when we cross the low mountains into Stormhold that things might start getting a little dicey. It's kind of a magical free-for-all, if you know what I mean."

"I'm not sure I do," she replied, but pressed no further. She began to wonder, though, as had Joe, who had appointed the little thief as leader of this expedition. Still, they were helpless without him—his knowledge of the country had already proved itself out with the trolls. Marge just hoped he was as widely traveled as he pretended to be.

On the trail later that day, she decided to press him a bit on her doubts. "Have you ever actually been to this Stormhold?" she asked him.

"On the edges," he replied. "At the limits of navigation on the Sik, a tributary of the River of the Sad Virgin, which forms the southern border of High Pothique, there's a town called Kidim. It's something of a trade center for the interior—at the river limit and also at the foot of the Vale of Kashogi, which is the only real way into the interior, considering that the mountains are two miles high on both sides. I once got to Kidim." He looked suddenly thoughtful, then shook his head. "Naw. They'd have forgotten about that by now." That last was said mostly to himself, but in the same loud tone which he used normally. "At least, I hope so," he added, sounding a little nervous.

Joe, who was following the conversation, gave a chuckle. "Returning to the scene of the crime, huh?"

"Aw, it was nothing, really. They're a bunch of hicks up there. Close-knit little community, never go anywhere or do anything—solid burgher types. Nice-looking gals, though. Still and all, they make all this money brokering among the races and rulers of High Pothique and the rest of the world and they don't do anything with it. Who can figure them? So I figured I'd liberate some of that dough." He sighed. "Well, I found out that the one thing they *do* spend money on is burglar prevention. Those spells were so good I doubt if *they* can get their hands on it."

They rode on to the south, approaching the great river that was the life of Husaquahr. As Macore had hoped, they reached it in late afternoon.

"How do we cross this one?" Houma wanted to know. "More trolls?"

Macore laughed. "You couldn't build a bridge over the Dancing Gods. Too wide and too deep, that's for sure. The only way you can cross is by boat. See? There's the river. I don't see the fairyboat, though."

"Another ferry," Joe muttered. "I'm still not too thrilled about the last one I took."

They made their way down to a landing, actually nothing more than a cleared area of hard dirt, and looked out. Anchored to a piece of solid rock a few feet from the river's edge was a thick cable that went out into, then dipped under, the river.

Joe got off, went over, and looked at the cable. "Damn! Looks like *steel*!"

Macore came over and examined it. "Well, I'm not really sure what steel is, but I can tell you what *that* is. It's fairy-spun rope, from the forest elves of Marquewood. It's incredibly strong and waterproof to boot. You can tell it's fairy—see how it's actually fused with the rock, not tied to it?"

Joe nodded, then turned and gazed out at the river. It had been extremely wide around Terindell, but now it was positively huge. Two other rivers, the Rossignol and the River of Sighs, had merged with it at this point, along with a hundred minor creeks and streams, and the extra volume had added a mile to the width of the Dancing Gods. Across on the opposite shore, little beyond a green smear could be made out, although behind that smear rose a series of imposing and barren, domelike mountains.

"Where's the ferry?" Joe asked nervously. "And why the cable?"

"Oh, it's probably on the other side or on its way back," Macore told him. "Don't worry about it. They'll be making trips, even at night. As for the cable—it holds the boat, of course. If it didn't, we'd wind up forty miles downstream with this current."

They settled back and relaxed a bit, aware that this was the last really calm moment they could expect for some time. Once across the Dancing Gods, with the great river to their backs, they would be in hostile territory.

"We'll put up at a coastal inn tonight, I think," Macore said. "It will probably be dark or a little after when we get across, anyway."

"Sounds good to me," Joe responded. "Say—about this boat. Who runs it? Some more nasty critters?"

Macore laughed. "Fairies run it. Why else would they call 'em fairyboats?"

"Um, yeah, uh-huh," was all Joe could manage.

Grogha stared out at the broad expanse of the river, then frowned and shaded his eyes for a moment against the glare off the water. "Yep! Here she comes!"

They all got to their feet and looked out. Still far off, they could now make out a dark shape against the waters, approaching with agonizing slowness. Try as he might, Joe couldn't get a good idea of what the boat looked like.

It wasn't until it was very close that he realized why. It was a large flat made of wooden planks, with big log bulkheads on both sides. The cable went through a long tube on the right side of the boat, keeping it in position but doing little else. The motive power, however, was rather startling.

The motive power for the huge skid was eight small forms on each side of the boat, all wearing harnesses that were attached by cables to the boat and all of whom were flying their hearts out. This was no mean feat for the sixteen of them—they were quite small, perhaps two or three feet tall. Obviously, Joe reflected, they had a lot more strength relative to their size than people.

The boat was not empty; a very heavy-looking wagon loaded with something and pulled by four draft horses was on board, as well as a few individual horse-and-rider combinations.

The tiny fliers pulled the glorified raft right up onto the hard landing; then the forward pair dipped down to the ground and tied off their pulling cables to studs set in the ground.

The wagon lost no time coming off and headed away. Two of the riders did likewise, but the third approached the Company, waiting its turn to board.

"Good afternoon," he said in a sonorous voice. "Might I inquire how far it is to the nearest inn up the road?"

Macore studied the rider. He was tall and gaunt, possibly of mixed human and elvish ancestry, with a gray goatee and wide-set, reddish eyes. He wore a totally black riding outfit, with cape and broad-brimmed black hat.

"About nine miles north," the little thief told him. "What is the situation on the other side?"

The stranger paused to think. "The situation, sir, is unpleasant. All sorts of strangers flooding into Pothique's river towns, looking very secretive. I fear the war is approaching."

Macore nodded seriously. "I suspected as much. But what of inns along the river? We'll need to stay over tonight."

"Try the village of Jaghri a mile south of the landing," the stranger suggested. "There should be reasonable rooms there—but watch your valuables and keep on guard." He looked at the trail. "Well, I must be going. I don't like to be on strange roads after dark."

"I don't blame you. Have a good journey, sir, and a successful one!"

"And you the same," the stranger responded and rode off down the road.

Joe approached Macore with a quizzical look. "What *was that* all about?"

"Either he's a spy for the Barony—which I doubt, since he's so incredibly obvious—or he's running scared. More likely scared. I think we take his advice and be on extra guard tonight—and every day and night after."

"Hey! You two! They're waving us on!" Grogha called, and they turned and got on their mounts.

Dwarfed by the riders and the wagon, one of the fairies they hadn't noticed until now stood on the deck, acting as loadmaster. He was a curious sight as they passed him and stopped where directed. He looked something like a tiny man—about two feet high and very well proportioned, much like a Greek statue—with a crop of purple hair between two overlarge pointed ears; from his back sprouted a set of transparent wings that were configured much like a butterfly's and were as large as the rest of him. Around his waist he wore a pair of leaves as a loincloth, and around his head was a garland of what looked like seaweed.

He both walked and flew—*flittered* was the word that came to Marge's mind—from spot to spot, showing each of them where to leave their horses, apparently trying to balance the load. Still, the raft could take far more than five horses and riders, and it wasn't much of a problem.

Once positioned, the fairy got a series of stakes that seemed to fit into holes in the deck and lock there and placed them so that all five horses could be tethered.

Then the fairy rose straight into the air and gave a high-pitched whistle; the crew on each side of the boat rose with the paddles, kicked off to the boatswain's chant, and got in unison. The boat began to move.

Once it was under way, the loadmaster fairy settled down, so that he hovered about five feet off the deck, making him roughly equal in height to the humans, now dismounted and stretching once again. The tiny creature approached Joe, and there was no mistaking his intent, so the big man gestured back to Marge.

More of the precious silver pieces were eked out, more than for the trollbridge, but it wasn't the same, somehow. Hearing and seeing the effort put into moving them and the craft across the broad expanse of water, they all felt that this money was well earned.

The crossing took about an hour and forty minutes, and the sun was almost behind the rounded granite domes to the west when they pulled up on the opposite shore and disembarked. There were no signs of either direction or welcome, but they had sighted the lights of a small town just a bit downriver as they crossed, pretty much as the stranger had told them, and they headed there at a moderate pace.

Still, as the fairyboat pulled out once more for its last run of the day, they all felt a certain additional loneliness. The great river now lay as not only a physical but a mental barrier to the land they'd known, and they were heading into unknown realms with that water barrier at their backs. For the first time, all of them felt truly on their own.

The village of Jaghri was a ramshackle collection of wooden shacks and a warehouselike inn around a boat landing. The design was slapdash and primitive when compared with what they'd been used to, and the whole thing looked weathered. Clearly it had seen better days.

The stableman was a little hunchback with the face of a prune and the disposition of sour milk. His round eyes were offset, so he looked as if his face were at an angle when it was not, and he drooled and spat with no regard for people or property.

Dacaro and Posti, however, assured the others that they'd be fine, even if they had to take care of themselves, and Dacaro suggested this time that the saddlebags be taken inside with the group and kept under close guard. He reminded Marge of the spell that would safeguard them.

The inn itself was a stinking waterfront dive. Where the past night's roadhouse had been clean, modern, well kept, and not very crowded, this place was in every way an opposite. It was crowded and it stank.

Those inside were also a rough-looking lot, and a minority was human. Even those who were human, though, didn't look very friendly—or too human themselves. All eyes were on the five as they entered, and there was a slight drop in the noise level, but it quickly rose back to normal.

Macore looked around, spotted a bartender, and went over to him. "You got any rooms to rent tonight?"

The barman, who apparently had never bathed, gave a grin that revealed yellowish, rotten teeth and said, "Yeah, we got a couple upstairs and more in back. What d'ya need?"

Macore thought for a moment. He was about to suggest the same as the night before—a quad for the men and a single for the lady—but he decided that nobody had better sleep alone around here. "Two rooms," he told the barman. "One for three, one for two."

"Eight grains in advance," the bartender grunted. "Pit toilet's in the back."

Macore nodded and counted out the money, which vanished even faster than the fairy had made the boat fare vanish. "Show me the rooms."

The bartender gave an evil grin. "Rooms? You want rooms? Sorry. Just rented the last two."

The little man stared at the bartender for a moment. "I play no games and give few warnings," he said matter-of-factly. "Either you stop this game now and give us our rooms, or you are dead. I will count to five. If your life is worth eight grains, let me count down."

The bartender laughed. "Who's gonna do it? You, little squirt?"

The thief was swift, drawing his shortsword and leaping at one and the same time, pushing the bartender right in the face and landing on top of the bigger man, sword at his throat. *"Five,"* Macore said icily and made a small cut on the man's throat. Blood trickled.

There was dead silence in the room, and the other four, who had remained to one side, placed their hands on their weapons.

"Upstairs, first two on the left," the barman rasped. "Let me be now!"

"Not until you give us our change," the little man responded, as cold as before. "Ten grains I have coming. *Now!*" The sword hand moved slightly once more.

"You bastard!" the barman snarled. "I only charged you eight!"

"That's true. And I charged you ten. Shall I count to five again? Don't worry. If we have a decent sleep and are unmolested, I might give you a big tip tomorrow. Perhaps ten grains' worth. Understand?"

"You win." The bartender sighed. "Let me up."

Macore backed off with an athlete's grace, sword still at the ready.

"I'm gonna have to reach under the counter here to get your money," the bartender told him. "Just take it easy, friend." He reached into a small compartment, brought out some coin, and took out a ten piece, putting it on the counter. "There. See?"

Macore nodded, picked up the piece with his free hand, and relaxed a moment.

"I'm beginning to feel useless around here," Joe muttered.

Macore grinned, sheathed his sword, and turned back to them.

"Macore!" Houma yelled as the barman reached back under his counter and took out a menacing-looking dagger. The little man dropped and rolled, pulling out his shortsword as he did so, and Joe brought his great sword from its sheath and leaped over the thief to the barman with a yell.

Taken off-guard, the barman, who'd been ready to throw the dagger or plunge it into Macore's back, instead tried to shield himself with it against Joe's attack. Not really wanting to kill the man despite his manner, Joe ignored the dagger and brought the flat of the sword down on the barman's head.

Sparks flew from the point of contact; as a startled Joe yelled, there was a sudden flash of smoke, heat, and light—and the barman was gone.

The would-be barbarian stood there, getting his breath, looking stunned at the spot where the barman had stood. "What the hell . . . ?"

Macore got to his feet and put his sword away once more. "He wasn't human, Joe. He *looked* it—sort of—but he wasn't. You touched him with iron."

Joe whistled. "Well, I'll be damned . . . I never really killed anybody before."

"Well, if it's any comfort, you probably still haven't," the thief responded sourly. "He was sure a nobody if there ever was one." He looked around. The crowd had stopped to watch the show, but was now slowly returning to drinking and gaming once more. Nobody seemed the least upset at the fight, and particularly at the fate of the bartender.

Macore let out a breath. "I must be getting old. Houma— Joe. I owe you both one, that's for sure."

"That's why we're a Company," the lanky Houma responded modestly. "You'd do the same for us."

Macore gave a slight shrug, but did not otherwise reply. Instead he said, "Well, let's take our rooms—at least see if there really *are* two vacancies upstairs."

There were. They weren't much—the linen was stained and the whole place could have stood a fumigation, but it would have to do for the night. "Joe, you and Marge take the first room. The rest of us will take the second," Macore said. "That way the numbers and experience are on one side, the power on the other. Good enough?"

They all nodded. Joe went over to the door and saw that it could be barred by a large board. There was a small window with just a piece of burlap for a curtain, but there was no balcony, and it was a good thirty feet to the ground. The room would do.

Marge looked at the door and the window thoughtfully. Finally she said, "You know, the same security spell Dacaro taught me for the money would also work on the rooms, I think. But you'd be stuck here until we came and got you."

"That might not be a bad idea, anyway," Macore replied and looked at the other two. "Any objections?"

"Nope," Grogha said. "Might help me actually get some sleep."

"I'll second that," Houma added.

"It's settled, then—if you're up to it," Macore told her. "But first let's put the spell on the bag and go down and get something to eat. If anything this place serves can be eaten without eating us, that is."

"Let's just hope the cook isn't related to the bartender," Joe responded nervously.

CHAPTER 11

A COMPANY PICNIC

Energy for minor magicks is transformed from the practitioner's own energies.

—I, 346, 89(b)

MARGE PREPARED ONCE MORE TO PERFORM THE SPELL ON THE saddlebag, after first removing a few coins for use and giving them to the other four. She was acutely aware of her powers and her lacks in the process. To work magic required three things—an inborn sixth sense that was the ability to see the forces, the training to recognize and control what you could see, and the ability to understand and, if necessary, solve complex mathematical equations. For, of course, that was what all spells were—equations involving the magical energies and forces. The more complex the spell, the more complex the math involved.

She certainly had the ability to see the forces, at least after Huspeth had finished with her. In fact, the witch had probably not given her the talent at all. She had the strong feeling that she had always been able to see and sense those forces—but failed to recognize them for what they were. Huspeth, too, had shown her how to recognize those forces and spells; the meanings of colors and auras—not just for people but for everything. To work the forces was also simple for Marge, although she was aware that none of the others in the Company save Dacaro—and possibly Macore—could see what she could see. But the equations were beyond her, at least for now. She had been good in literature, the arts, and social sciences like history. Math had never been her big subject, not since she'd barely limped through high school algebra. Thus, she was dependent on Dacaro. Prevented by his equine form from shaping the forces, he yet knew from his training the necessary math and could pass it along. Neither was powerful individually; as a team, they were a complete minor sorcerer.

Most of the chants used in spells were mere devices, either to aid in concentration, as memory tricks to bring forth the equations, or simply to confuse onlookers. The actual practice was quite simple—you just concentrated on the person, place, or thing you were working the spell upon, then moved your finger or hand and let the energy flow from you into the object itself.

This spell consisted of yellow lines, glowing yellow strings that looked like paint on air. She looked at the saddlebag, repeated the little mnemonic Dacaro had given her as a memory aid, then pointed at the bag with her finger and drew the yellow lines, as if with crayon or marker. When she had finished, the saddlebag looked normal to the rest of them, but to her it was covered with a complex child's scribble of yellow lines. At least, it looked like a child's scribble—in actuality, it was an equation expressed that way. Anyone meddling with the saddlebag would find the results extremely unpleasant; anyone wanting it now would have to undo that yellow stringy mess exactly the opposite from the way she'd done it, with no slips.

Such a task would be child's play for a sorcerer like Ruddygore or a powerful sorceress witch like Huspeth, but the spell was more than adequate for average men and fairies. In a sense, it was like a good burglar alarm system—it wouldn't keep out the competent pro, but it certainly discouraged the amateurs, who were ninety-nine percent of any threat.

She rejoined the others, and they went downstairs. The same motley crew was still there—and there was a plump, middle-aged woman now behind the bar—but the only notice taken of them was that folks tended to move away from them as they took a table. They had gained a measure of respect, if nothing else.

They were briskly attended to, though, by a small, sad-faced waiter who gave them no trouble and no extra words. They had some problems finding a proper vegetarian dish for Marge—the others' repugnance to eating animal flesh had lasted only until the first roadhouse—and when the food came, it was greasy, overcooked, and tasted like an unwashed stove, but it *was* filling and there wasn't any more to be said. They talked little while eating, except about the quality of the food.

Afterward Marge excused herself to go out to the stable and see Dacaro. "I want to be sure of the spells," she told them, and they agreed.

"Want me to come along?" Joe asked her. "You never know whom you're going to meet."

"If I can't manage that much, I have no business being here," she responded and left.

It was quite dark out and humid now. The smell of the river was rich in the air, but she had no trouble walking the block to the stables and finding the stableman. He was a little amazed that all she wanted was to sit on the horse, but he simply muttered about having seen everything in this business and left her.

Once she was upon the black stallion, rapport was instantaneous.

"Anything wrong?"

"No," she assured him, "but it's not the world's nicest inn." Quickly she told him about the evening's exploits and the kind of spell she wanted.

Dacaro thought a moment. "I think it is time you received some instruction. Perhaps it will be a good way to while away the miles from here on out. You seem determined to practice the art."

"Of necessity," she responded, "although I admit it fascinates me. I know I'll never be great at it, but it is something unusual that I can do."

"Ruddygore explained to you the price of such dabblings? The fact that you are a witch's changeling?"

"Something like that. I'm not sure I understand it and I'm certainly not going to let it bother me."

"The principle is simple. Only the masters of the art may create magical energies. All else must come from the practitioner. The more difficult spells can literally take a lot out of you, energy that must be replenished slowly. In your case, the replenishment is not of flesh and blood but of the nature of faërie. The more energy you expend—send from yourself—the more faërie will replace it. If you lost blood, your body would eventually replace it with new blood. But if you lose the plasma of magic, it must be replaced from magical sources. Your sources are attuned to faërie. If you continue, your entire body will eventually be so replaced. You will *be* of faërie."

"Is that necessarily—bad?"

He considered this. "It depends on how you look at it. The more you are of faërie, the more magic of the minor sort will be instinctive, requiring no training. But you will be subject to the magic of mortals and the rules of faërie. Never having been of faërie, I can not say if this is good, bad, or indifferent. But it is certainly *different*."

"We'll cross that bridge when we come to it," she told him. "For now, the protection spell for the rooms."

"Simple. You have a good memory. Remember this spell and do it so." He sketched out in her mind a pattern and a rhythmic chant to aid the pattern's symmetry. "Try it. Just a bit. Just in the air here."

She concentrated and tried it, going just a little ways. The color of the bands was orange, and they were a little thicker and harder to manage, but not much. "How's that?"

"It will do. Go now. Get some rest. We have a busy day tomorrow."

She left him and returned to the inn, where the rest of the Company was still at the table drinking ale. Joe and the portly Grogha seemed in the best of spirits.

After a while, they went upstairs. She first checked the saddlebag and found it undisturbed. That didn't mean that no one had tried, but certainly the spell had worked. After bidding the other three good night, she stood back and worked the protection spell, first on the window and then, from outside, on the door. It looked really pretty, she decided.

She and Joe went one door down to their room. From inside this time, she traced the spell once more on door and window. Joe watched her, fascinated, seeing only a chanting woman waving her right hand about, but he knew that something was indeed taking place.

She felt a little tired when she finished and sat down on the bed of straw.

"I just happened to think of something," Joe said.

"Huh?"

"We had a lot to drink. What if I have to go to the can?"

She smiled and pointed under the window. "See that pot there? That's a chamber pot, as in the old days."

He went over, looked at it, and frowned. "Umph. Some privacy! But I suppose if you gotta go you gotta go."

She nodded and lay back on the bed. "I really am starting to feel worn out. I think maybe I'll just go right to sleep."

He came over and knelt down beside her. "Sure ain't Texas, is it? Or South Philly, either."

She smiled. "No, it sure isn't. And I'm glad it isn't. I wouldn't go back for anything now, I think. We have something everybody dreams about at one time or another but almost nobody ever gets, Joe. A new life. A second chance. It's funny. Here we are, in a dirty roadhouse in an ugly foreign country, about to put ourselves into real danger—and I've never been happier in my whole life. Never. You understand that?"

He nodded. "In a way. But only in a way. Me, I'm still on the road for somebody else, stopping at flea traps and risking my neck for not much. And I got nobody, really, to be doin' it for—just like back home. This stuff ain't so glamorous, either, when you bean somebody with a sword and electrocute him or something like that. I got a feeling that the only thing that's really changed about me is that now I'm gonna get paid for killin' folks instead of haulin' their stuff."

She thought about it a moment. "Maybe you're right, Joe. But it's the only life we've got now. Let's play it out. It could be fun, too."

He sighed. "I dunno. Maybe—maybe you and me will be a team, huh? We're different, you and me, from any of them. We're from someplace else. Someplace different, if you know what I mean."

She leaned over and patted his arm. "I think so. We'll see."

She snuffed out the lantern. It was an eerie scene for her after that, with the orange bands of the window and door and the yellow on the saddlebag aglow, yet reflecting not at all the rest of the room. To Joe, of course, it was pitch-darkness.

"Marge?"

"Yes, Joe?"

"I'm just lonesome, is all. I have been for a long, long time. Long before comin' here, I mean."

"I know."

"Marge?"

"Yes, Joe?"

"I'm horny, too."

"I figured as much. Not now, Joe. Not for a while. Not between you and me, that is. Let's just be—friends for a while, huh? Companions from another world."

He sighed once again. "What's the matter? Afraid it will louse us up?"

"No, it's not that. Look, Joe, I can't be as strong as you. And this is even more of a man's world than ours is. My only chance to be independent—to be free—here is through the magic. The place Ruddygore sent me, well, it was sort of like a convent. I joined their order."

"You mean you're a nun?" He sounded genuinely shocked.

"Think of it that way, if you can. It's not to say that— someday—I might not bend. When I think the time is right. When I'm ready. But as for now, the longer I stay celibate, the stronger my magic power gets. Once I break it, I can never get any stronger. I just told you what the magic means to me, Joe. So I have to pay the price."

He was silent for a minute, then finally said, "You ain't the only one payin' a price." But then he rolled over and was soon snoring. She had no trouble joining him in that endeavor.

It was Joe who was up first, shortly after dawn, and he tired rather quickly of just lying there and waiting for her so he could leave. He gently shook her awake.

"Hope you don't mind—but I'm trapped," he said apologetically.

"No, I don't mind at all," she told him. "In fact, the lack of clocks and wake-up calls is a real pain around here. How come you got up? Trouble sleeping?"

"Nope. When you're on the road and time is money, you get so you can mentally set yourself to wake up at a particular time. It's no big trick—just a practical necessity."

She got up, yawned, and stretched. "I always heard about people who could do that, but I never could." She rubbed her eyes and blinked a few times. "Right now I wish we had some running water. I'd like to wash my face off and get the sleep out."

He laughed. "And you were the one who really loved this place."

"I didn't say it couldn't stand a few improvements." She laughed back. She got up, yawned once more, then turned to the saddlebag. "Easy stuff first."

Having made the pattern in the first place, she knew exactly where to start and how to retrace the pattern backward. It was so quick and effortless that even Joe was surprised. "You're learning that stuff pretty good," he told her.

She nodded, then sighed and looked up at the window. "Seems almost a waste to undo the window, but somebody may have to jump out of this firetrap someday." The orange bands were still a bit bulkier to manage but no real trouble. The door was a bit slower, because of the greater complexity and sheer size of the pattern, but it took only a couple of minutes. Finally she said, "Okay, Joe. Lift the latch and let's go spring the rest."

He did so, and the door opened without trouble. She grabbed the saddlebag and they went to the next door, where another two or three minutes was spent undoing the spell. Joe then pounded on the door, and was greeted by a sleepy "Who's that?"

"It's us!" he called. "You can open your door now! Time to hit the road!"

There was the sound of grumbling on the other side, then the sound of the board being removed, and the door opened. All three were sleepy and grumbling, but were ready to go by the time Marge had removed the window spell from their room. She looked around at them. "I suppose it's too much to ask for there to be a bath in this place, but let's at least wash up and get breakfast."

Grogha yawned and scratched. "You ain't got no spell for fleas, have you?"

"Maybe we can find something," she replied. "A bath would be best—but I'm not too sure I want to expose myself around here."

"Bath?" the portly man repeated, as if it were a totally alien word.

"Yeah, you might try one sometime," Macore prodded playfully. "You should do everything at least once in your life."

Marge washed herself off at the outside pump, as did Joe and the others. Then they went back inside the inn, almost deserted at this early hour. Strong coffee was available, though, and some fruit and pastries, which suited them all just fine. When they had eaten, the stout woman who'd taken over the bar the night before came over to them.

"You owe eight for the rooms and two for the breakfast. Jajur is on the house. Skimmin' like that's not proper. At least not so up front."

"Jajur?" Joe asked.

"The bartender. Though I should charge you for me havin' to work extra hours last night."

Marge thought a moment. "How about twelve and call it even?"

"Fair enough."

The money was counted out and paid, and they headed for the stables. The five-grain charge there seemed a bit stiff, but they paid it without complaint. Macore looked over at the moneybag. "How much more we got in there anyway?"

Marge shrugged. "About a hundred grains in various denominations, plus some gems."

"Let's see some of the gems."

She reached in, took out a few, and gave them to him. He looked them over with an appraiser's eye, then whistled. "Not bad. These three ought to be enough." He kept them and handed her back the rest. Then he sought out the stablehand to ask about outfitting, and they went further into town, leading the horses, until they came to a weathered store. It wasn't open yet, but the owner was inside setting up, and it didn't take much to get him to start business a bit early.

By the time the little thief was done, they had a mule, pack, and harness, bedrolls, canteens, and a small camping outfit. There was a lot of haggling, but, as Macore had predicted, the three stones proved sufficient.

Joe and Marge were impressed. "All that for three of *those*?" Joe asked incredulously.

Macore nodded. "And he got the best of the bargain. One thing, our master Ruddygore is not stingy, I'll say that for him."

Marge looked at the overloaded mule. "Is all this really necessary?"

Macore took out the map. "I think so. I doubt if we'll make it more than halfway today to Kidim, and that means a campout in the wastes. Tomorrow we'll be climbing and maybe we'll make it, maybe not. Besides, *after* Kidim we'll be fresh out of stores, anyway, so we had to buy some of this sooner or later. Why not now? It will only be a lot more expensive as we go further inland."

The next step was letting the horses and the mule drink and filling the canteens. By that time, the first of the open-air markets was open, and they were able to buy a fair amount of fruit and some dried meat, as well as coffee and tea. Checking the map once more and getting information from the fruitseller, Macore was able to lead them on the proper path, first back to the ferry junction road, then a bit north, where the shore road forked, one way following the river, the other turning first west, then south, into the mountains.

That road was clear, but it was obvious that it was not widely used, particularly from the approach to the Bald Mountains themselves. The mountains weren't high, but they were barren granite domes of some ancient volcanic origin, and a natural climatological barrier.

The trail led up to them, then began a series of switchbacks, taking the Company up a thousand feet or so in slow stages. The summit was only thirteen or fourteen hundred feet high, but that was a lot when one was starting from the bottom.

Once the travelers were through the pass, the trail descended much as it had brought them up, but the landscape had changed dramatically. Almost up to the foot of the Bald Mountains, the river-fed earth had been green and lush. Now it was mostly desert, a desolate yellow, purple, and orange landscape of dry beauty, marked with mesas and buttes wind-carved into fantastic shapes.

"Looks like the Badlands," Joe commented.

At the bottom of the descending trail, they hit another junction, unmarked as had been all the others in High Pothique.

"Inland route," Macore told them. "Used mostly by caravan traders who don't want to be that obvious. We go straight, though. Through *that*." He pointed at the desolation. "See those mountains in the distance, almost blending with the sky? Well, they're the really big mother mountains, and that's where we're heading."

"Lead on," Houma called to him. "You got the map."

The hot sun bore down on all of them as they went, and Joe cracked that he should have brought his suntan lotion from the truck, but he knew, somehow, that he would not burn. By the evening, though, he was already several shades darker than when he began, and all their faces and hands showed weathering.

Dacaro was as good as his word to Marge. "If you are determined to master the art, then I will help you," he told her.

The theory of it was not all that esoteric—since they were talking applied rather than theoretical magic—but to move from doing presupplied spells to creating one's own to suit whatever purpose one wished was something else again, something not mastered in a day.

It was with some inward fascination that she couldn't help but think of it as being much the same as learning computer programming—something she'd once taken a course in at one of those fly-by-night business schools back when she was still looking for a job. Up to now she had been using pre-prepared "software"—the spells furnished by Huspeth or Dacaro. Now she was being taught, in slow steps, how to build them herself. Of course, she'd graduated from the course, but not with any decent handle on programming. Her math was just a bit too slow—and so it was here, with no pocket calculators to help her out.

Still, Dacaro was patient and reassuring and seemed delighted to be able to do something finally with the knowledge he'd gained over his years as an adept.

At one point she asked him point-blank what he'd done to incur Ruddygore's wrath.

"I went on a trip with him—to your world," he told her. "A most smelly and confusing place, I must say, but one with a lot of things I thought would improve our situation here."

She was surprised at this. "Does he go to our world often?"

"Fairly often. Two or three times a year, perhaps, for a week or so each time. He sees shows at theaters, mostly, and buys horrendous souvenirs of places—tacky stuff even by your world's standards. He did not show you his collection?"

"No."

"He will. You will be appalled. I argued with him that bringing back some of the technology of your world would ease a lot of misery here. He adamantly refused, even though he admitted it. He talked about intangibles, values this world had that had been bred out of yours by your technology. I did not agree with him then and I do not now. So I disobeyed him.

I brought back something which I thought could be useful here in our eternal fight against the enemy. I brought it back mostly to study and have copied. But he discovered it, sensing the iron in its construction, and so we had our bitter falling out that left me in this state."

She grew curious. "What was it you brought back?"

"A—revolver, I think you call it. Or is the word 'gun'? And five hundred rounds of ammunition."

She whistled. "Why a gun?"

"I argued with him. I asked him to imagine our brave forces lined up against those of the Baron, armed with these or more efficient versions of these, instead of swords and spears and arrows."

"Sounds reasonable to me," she agreed. "What did he object to?"

"He told me that I was looking at the problem the wrong way. I was to imagine the Baron with such weapons. But *we* would have them first—and we could always improve upon them. It would end war as we know it!"

"Yes, it would, Dacaro," she said sadly. First one side would have pistols. Then some would be inevitably captured by the other side, and *they* would copy the design and make their own—only better. Maybe scale them up. What was a revolver but a miniature cannon? And then the other side would . . . Was there uranium here?

She knew too much about that sort of pattern to be on any side but Ruddygore's, and she could understand why Dacaro so frightened him—and why poor Dacaro would never understand the reason. She gently changed the subject back to magical spells and did not refer to his problems again.

Although the sun was still up, they made camp at a small water hole right in the middle of nowhere. The horses and the mule had no hesitancy drinking from the stuff, even though it looked a little stale, so they didn't, either. It tasted odd, but they suffered no ill effects.

The watering hole hardly qualified as an oasis—the pool was barely ten feet around and looked to be a place where the bedrock had weathered away at a soft spot, allowing an underground river a small outlet. There were some bushes, but no trees, and it looked as if it were used, but seldom.

"As far as I know, this is the only water between here and

Kidim," Macore told them. "Of course, all I know is the map. I never actually crossed this way before." He frowned and looked southward. "Still, I'd say we should make the town before dark tomorrow." He sighed. "Man, I'm hot and tired!"

"We all are," Houma replied. "It is desolate country indeed. Still, it is open country, too. Less likely to bump into funny things."

"Don't get too confident!" Macore shot back. "The last time I was real self-confident, I tried to sell sharpeners to a nice lady who ran a farm all by herself—remember?"

There seemed no way to reply to that. Joe looked around. "We should build a small fire. I doubt if it will attract much attention, but it might make anything that lives out there think twice about us, not to mention keeping us from stumbling in the dark and drowning in the pool. It's gonna be mighty dark here soon."

"Good idea," Grogha said. "I think we can use some of this dead stuff in the thicket and maybe spare a couple of frame boards from the pack mule."

"Or you could use the wood in the gray pack in the middle there, as I intended when I bought it," Macore said laconically. They all glared at him, but they had their fire going before darkness fell, as it did with amazing suddenness.

Grogha proved a pretty good field cook, considering the limited makings he had to work with. After cleaning up and putting everything away, Marge looked at the packs, and the mule. "Do you think I should put a spell on them—just in case?" she asked.

"Better to be safe than sorry," Joe responded. "Go ahead. Be kinda hard to protect *us*, though, so we'll have to stand turns at watch."

"Yeah, but how will we know when to change watch?" Houma asked worriedly. "Not town clocks in sight."

"Candles," Macore said. "Actually, I can't take credit for this. The merchant suggested them." He got them out of the pack and lighted one in the fire. "They take two hours to burn down. Simple, huh?"

"Good enough for me," Joe told him. "Who's first?"

"Me," Marge said. "I'd like a little time more or less to myself."

They started to protest, since none of them had even thought of her for the duty, but she silenced them, and they knew better than to press it.

Another hour or so was spent sitting around, talking about nothing in particular and watching the spectacular stars that appeared in the desert sky, then most were ready for bed. Marge helped them get their bedrolls settled, and Joe suggested a semicircular arrangement around the fire. Within two hours, all were asleep except her.

She first made the spell on the mule pack—removed, of course, from the mule—and on the all-important saddlebag, finding it easier and easier. Like writing her name with a pencil, she thought, pleased. Dacaro had told her that the more she practiced any magic, the easier it would all become.

It was deathly quiet, without any sort of breeze, and the air had not cooled off much at all. Idly, she started practicing some of the simple exercises Dacaro had taught her. So simple . . . She could draw faces with the spell light, twirl it around like a lasso, and hurl the energies where she willed, at least within her line of sight.

She pointed her finger at the ground from a standing position and traced a pattern. Once the pattern, in light blue, was established, her index finger became a stylus, allowing her to carve shallow designs in the rock itself.

The world is pure mathematics. Know the proportions and the relationships of any given thing and you have the potential of doing anything with it. That was the key, Dacaro had said. *And when you can look at a tree, a rock, a bush, or a person and see the pattern in their auras, then you will take the final step to sorcery.*

She concentrated on a nearby bush. *Pattern . . . pattern . . . find the pattern . . .*

And, to her surprise, she saw it. Thin, impossibly complex spiderwebs of white plasma. She turned to the fire, which was getting dangerously low. There was still a lot of combustible material there, but it had not caught for some reason. She concentrated on the fire and the unburned wood and saw, after a while, the magenta pattern of the fire and the white of the wood. *Tie one to the other,* she thought, *and maybe . . .*

She found an end on the magenta strand and another on the white and willed them to move, move toward each other, touching, combining . . .

The fire suddenly roared up, looking like a Roman candle, and she laughed aloud in delight. Suddenly conscious that she might wake someone, she stopped and willed the fire back to normal levels. It went obediently, as she knew it would. She had the pattern. Still, she could make it dance, rise up and down, gyrate—until the wood was completely burned, anyway.

She turned to the water and saw its golden weave. In a sense, it was simpler than the fire pattern, which was in turn simpler than that for the wood or the bush. So simple to ripple it, or cause a small eddy . . .

Suddenly she tensed, sensing something else where she looked. There was certainly something other than water there, something alive. It was not close, but it was down there, somewhere. She could feel it, knew it with absolute certainty.

She stood at the edge of the pool and made a decision. It was a huge job to work the room preservation spell over the mouth of the underground water hole, and took her quite some time, but she made it doubly strong and extra tight, blue bands forming a virtual net over the opening.

Whatever was down there might be able to break it, but at least the thing would have a hard time, if indeed it was a threat at all. But she somehow knew it was a threat, something ancient and repulsive that fed on those who used the water hole. Not us, she decided determinedly. Not without a fight.

She went back over to a rock near her bedroll and sat, feeling suddenly tired and a bit drained. Parts of her face hurt—too much sun, she decided, now taking its toll. She looked over and saw that the candle had burned out. How long she had been watching she didn't know, but she was certainly ready for sleep now. As gently as possible, she shook Joe awake.

He yawned and groaned. "Anything?"

She shook her head. "But there's something living at the bottom of that pond. Something nasty," she told him. "I put a protection spell over the whole thing. Whether it will try and come out I don't know. If it does, I don't know either whether or not the spell will hold it, but keep an eye on it."

"I will," he assured her. "You get some sleep."

She needed no urging.

It was still dark on Houma's watch when there was a sudden roar from the pond that awakened them all and startled the horses as well. A roar and a lot of splashing. They were quickly on their feet, adrenaline racing, and Joe pulled a burning ember from the fire to use as a torch, grabbing his sword in the other hand.

They approached the fuming water cautiously, not knowing what to expect. What they saw in the water was a sort of face—a huge, incredibly old, demonic face, full of hatred. It exuded a sense of terror none of them had ever known before, but the hatred was only partly directed at them. It was straining, struggling against the surface of the pond, and Marge understood that, at least for the moment, the spell was holding.

She felt a nuzzle at her back and almost jumped a foot, but then realized it was Dacaro. She understood what he meant immediately and quickly jumped upon his back.

"Dacaro! What is it?"

"I have no idea," he replied, "but it's sure a good idea you put that spell there. It's not going to hold, though. You can see it unraveling around the edges. This thing isn't very bright, but it has a hell of a lot of sheer power. Ask Joe if he can stick his sword into the water and hit the face. Let's see if iron does anything."

"Joe! Can you stab it without losing your sword or falling in?" she called.

"We'll see!" he shouted back, revolted by that hideous face, yet unable to tear his eyes from it. The sword hummed and glowed in his hand. He poised, waiting for the face, which filled most of the pool, to get a part of itself in a no-miss spot against the edge, then plunged the blade into the water and quickly withdrew it.

The face roared its pain and hatred, but only redoubled its efforts to break its bonds.

"Well, scratch that," Dacaro told her. "I really doubted it was that easy, anyway. This is going to test us both, woman." He thought furiously for a moment. "Okay, we'll try something, but it's damned complicated. I'll feed it to you slowly, and you do it as I tell you. Got it?"

"I'm ready." She looked at the men near the pool. "Hey! Everyone get back! We're going to try some sorcery on it! Keep your weapons ready, though! Be prepared to strike, but not until I tell you!"

Slowly, cautiously, the four men backed off, giving both Marge and Dacaro a clear field.

"Here goes," Dacaro said and began feeding the spell to her. It was enormously complex, far beyond her ability to understand or comprehend, at least at her level. She had begun mastering arithmetic, she realized, upon seeing this thing; now Dacaro was feeding her incomprehensible calculus. She had no choice but to follow through.

The energy field that formed like a wall in front of them was of all the primary colors and perhaps a hundred shades. She had never seen anything like it, nor did she have any chance to appreciate it, but she could feel its awesome power.

"Joe!" she called, relaying Dacaro's orders. "We're going to let that thing come out! When it does, it will run headlong into the damnedest spell you ever saw, like a net that will close on it. When you hear me yell again, get in on the side and hack that whole damned head off *behind* the face! Understand?"

"Got ya!" Joe called back, too charged up to feel afraid right now.

Quickly, Marge, using a Dacaro shortcut, removed the blue bands from the pool. "What if *this* doesn't work?" she asked worriedly.

"Then we run like hell," the equine adept replied.

Freed of the protection spell, the face roared up and out of the water and onto the rock.

"I'll be damned! It's some kind of worm!" Grogha shouted. "Yuk! Look at that slime!"

The demon worm was six feet out of the pool when it hit the new and more powerful shield. It reacted to the great net of force much as it had done to the blue—pushing into it with a terrible rage.

"Good . . . good . . ." Dacaro said, mostly to himself. "It really can't see the spells, as I figured. It's just so big and strong it's used to pushing its way through anything."

Marge watched as the thing plunged directly into the net of force, which gave a bit in the middle, enveloping the evil face.

"It's giving way!" she called nervously.

"No!" Dacaro shot back. "It's designed to do that. Tell Joe to be ready."

She did, and Joe brought his sword up. Grogha and Houma

also brought their bronze swords up, ready to tear into the demon worm from the other side.

The face was now completely enclosed in a bulge in the magical netting, and Dacaro gave the word. "Now!" Marge shouted.

Coming in behind both net and face, all three started swinging and hacking at the wormlike flesh in back. The face howled in rage, but seemed unable to understand what was happening to it, or where. Pieces of giant worm flew as they hacked away and finally severed it. The severing was so sudden that both Joe and Grogha almost fell into the mess and barely backed away.

The remainder of the body flailed around for a moment, then slid with astonishing speed back into the pool. The head, apparently suspended in air to the human onlookers, continued to snarl and snap for a while.

"We've won," Dacaro told her. "Now do this." He fed her a small set of instructions, and she translated them into a huge mental shove at the face in the net. It flew back, rolled, flopped a bit, then rolled again into the pool, where it sank rapidly.

Again following Dacaro's instructions, Marge pushed back the net, at one point having to shout Houma out of the way, then laid it, like a tabletop, across the width of the pool. Only after attaching it to the pattern of the bedrock did she relax and realize that she was sweating like mad. She felt suddenly very, very tired indeed. Before she knew it, she fell off the horse.

CHAPTER 12

ALL THE CIVILIZED COMFORTS

Virgins are uniquely useful for certain magicks, yet they have drawbacks beyond the obvious.

—CX, Introduction

WHEN MARGE AWOKE, SHE FOUND HERSELF ON A MAKESHIFT litter being pulled by Dacaro. They were on the move again, that was for sure. A worried Joe rode an equally worried Posti behind the litter. When her eyes opened, he gave a shout that brought the party to a halt.

Joe jumped down and went to her. "How do you feel?"

"Lousy, but I'll live," she replied. She looked around. "What hit me? Where are we?"

"You just keeled over," he said. "Luckily for you, one of the bedrolls was underneath. I don't think anything's broken."

"I feel good enough to ride," she told him, not sure if that was really the truth. "Untie me from this thing."

With Macore's help, Joe did as instructed and lifted her to her feet.

"Woosh! A little dizzy, and I have a couple of bruises in places I never had 'em before, but I think I'm okay." She looked around again. The tall mountains loomed ahead, not more than ten miles away. "So where's the pool?"

"Way, way back there," Joe told her. "We talked it over and figured it was better to move with you this way than to risk another night with our slimy friend back there."

She nodded. "I agree with that. But—didn't you kill it?"

He shook his head negatively. "I doubt it, and so does Dacaro. What brains the thing had weren't in its head at all. It will probably nurse its wounds down there, regenerate a new face, and be ready for the next suckers."

She thought of that hideous face and shivered. "You know, up to now, I've believed in good and bad and in between, but that thing was true *evil*. Could you feel it?"

They all nodded. "Something from the dawn of the world," Macore said. "Some terrible force in that form. Maybe it once thought, but now it's nothing but pure hatred and rage."

"And appetite," Grogha added.

"That, too," Macore agreed. "You want to try riding now?"

She nodded. "I'll manage. But help me up on Dacaro. He may have some spell that can relieve me."

They helped her up, then disassembled the litter and packed it on the long-suffering mule.

"Glad to find you back among the living," Dacaro told her.

"So am I," she responded honestly. "I don't know what came over me."

"That spell. It was far too complex and draining for a novice—but it was necessary. It took all your reserve. Hurt much?"

"A lot of bruises. I feel as if I had been run over by a truck."

"Didn't you say you had a witch's kit? Isn't there something you could brew up for yourself?"

She felt foolish. "Sure there is. Damn. I almost completely forgot. Uh—if we have any water."

"The water from the pool was all right—in the morning," he told her. "The canteen's full."

"How long was I out?"

He thought a moment. "Hard to say. Several hours. It's past midday. But better whip up your witchery before we push on again."

She called out to the others, and they obliged, watching as she mixed certain herbs together from her kit, then brewed them into a tea and drank it all, even eating the mixture.

"Taste good?" Grogha wanted to know.

"Terrible," she told him. "But I can already feel it starting to work." She folded up her kit and put it on her belt. "Let's get moving."

Back on the trail, Dacaro explained to her his correct guess about the nature of the evil worm. "It was all rage and hate," he said. "When I saw how it simply tried to bully its way through your spell, I knew it was pure emotion. Its sensory apparatus was all in its head, while its brain was protected back in the tail someplace. But it seemed to have no way of telling anything without the information that head provided—and it just pushed on straight ahead. I gambled it wouldn't even know where it was being chopped—and I won. Once the head was severed, it was blind, deaf, and dumb."

"I think I've had enough of monsters for a while," she remarked. She suddenly had a thought. "Uh—Dacaro. That big spell took a *lot* out of me, right?"

"Yes. All you had, really."

"And—it's being replaced slowly out of faërie?"

"Um, yes. I was wondering when you'd think of that."

"Have I—changed?"

"A little," he answered honestly. "But it will be gradual in any event."

"Will it be—enough? To push me over the edge, that is?"

"I can't say. The external changes first, though, that much I know. But you won't be beyond mortality until your wings grow out, so you can at least tell from that."

She thought about it. "Wings. You mean like those the little fairies had on the boat?"

"Perhaps. There are lots of wings. I don't expect you to shrink much, since that would have been among the first things to notice. So the wings would have to be different—they have to support a different mass. Why? Having second thoughts? Nervous?"

"Nervous? Yeah. Because I don't know what to expect, what price I'm paying. Sort of like selling your soul to the devil. At the time you don't even realize it's gone, but when the time comes, you sure miss it."

"Perhaps, when this is over, you can talk with some of the fairies," he suggested. "But, regardless, you either stop or go on."

"It's not that much of a choice, really. Like last night. It was me or nobody."

"I think I might have done it—differently—through Macore. He has the sense of the art, but absolutely no knowledge or training. It might have killed him, but I could have done it."

She sighed. "Some choice. But that's not the only factor, Magic's my edge. It's what I *do* here. If I give it up, I might as well open a stall and sell potions."

"Suit yourself. I wouldn't get so worked up about this changeling business, anyway. We'll probably all die in this mission."

She chuckled. "Optimistic, aren't you?"

"We'll see."

The pass through the mountains showed clearly now. The slope was steep, but gentle enough for horses and perhaps a wagon team if need be. The pass itself was quite wide, although it looked to be a very slow and relaxed climb of a couple of thousand feet, at least. They started up and were soon surrounded by high mountain walls.

Within the first couple of hours the temperature had dropped considerably, and they all were feeling chilled. Although there was no snow evident in the pass, it was all around not too far above them.

"We're going to have to buy some warmer clothes for this place, if we don't freeze to death right here," Joe muttered.

"Near naked's all right for the hot stuff, but it's nothin' to be in a snowstorm."

The others, who were dressed better than he but not for this, could only nod in agreement. Making matters worse, the sun was already low enough to be masked by the surrounding mountains. Marge shivered and called to Macore, "How much longer to this town of yours? Will we make it before nightfall?"

"Hard to say," the little thief called back. "Remember, I never came in this way before. But I do know that it's in a glacial valley just below this pass on the other side. It will be touch and go between us and night, but we'll have to do what we can."

It was early evening, and there were flecks of snow in the air when they finally made the summit of the pass and could look out to the other side. There was little sun left, but it was still light enough for them to see, and the village just below was as Macore had promised.

Kidim was set inside a U-shaped glacial valley carved out long ago. The valley was almost a bowl set in the mountain, not terribly deep but about a mile and a half wide. Its water was glacial melt, which formed a formidable lake in about half the depression; but while it was fed by mountain snows, it overflowed away from the village part of the bowl, over in an imposing, tall waterfall that dropped into another bowllike lake several hundred feet below. That lower lake was in turn the source of the River Sik—incredibly, navigable from that point all the way down to the River of the Sad Virgin and eventually to the great Dancing Gods itself. The lower pool was fed not only from the waterfall but also from countless rivulets and small streams, some gushing right out of the mountain.

Kidim, however, was above all that, in the best defensive position. It reminded Marge of nothing so much as a Swiss village, the kind they used for the Olympics or bobsled runs. It was a town of perhaps seven or eight thousand living in elaborately painted and decorated clapboard and gingerbread-style houses, and it was alight with life.

Joe looked around. "Not bad. They could hold that pass back there with a relatively small force; nobody would be safe charging up here from down there. It's almost a perfect natural fortress."

Macore nodded. "And those walls are heavily fortified. They can close it off in a moment and withstand a tremendously long siege. It is said, too, that caves in the mountain itself, known only to the townspeople, are stocked with food and weapons—and even offer escape routes. Their treasures are stored somewhere back there, which makes them so hard to get at."

Cold and miserable, they anxiously headed for the town gates, the pillars of which were carved out of the natural granite. The gates were open. Although there were guards atop the walls looking down on them, there was no challenge or attempt to stop them.

The town was busy at dusk. Sidewalk cafes were filled, and from the various brightly lighted buildings that so resembled chalets could be heard the sounds of entertainment, eating, dining, and general merrymaking.

"Now *this* is more like it!" Marge exclaimed. "I'd begun to give up on High Pothique!"

"It varies widely," Macore responded. "This little City-State is extremely rich and fat. But it gets that way because of its position here. Anyone who wants the valued raw materials of High Pothique's interior deals through here. Anybody wanting to sell anything to the remote tribes and nomads of the interior has to go through here. This is a classic case of geographic greed in action!"

First they found the stables and, for a very high charge, got the horses and mule taken care of and the supplies stored in a bonded and guarded storage area. It was clear from the almost ten grains they were charged, though, that Kidim knew it had travelers where it wanted them.

At Macore's urging, they decided they would splurge for this one night, staying in the highest-class inn—actually called a hotel—in the town. Each would have a separate bed this night—a soft, down-filled, luxurious one with silken sheets and fine wool blankets. Again they took two rooms, using the same arrangement as before.

They skipped the hotel dining room, though—it looked a bit too posh for such burned and unwashed travelers as they—and opted instead for a small, friendly restaurant down the street. The food was wonderful, the wine choice, and when Macore got the bill and told them what it was, they could only wonder what the hotel dining room would have cost.

Afterward, since they wanted to walk off their stuffed feelings, Macore counted out some money to each of them so they could wander about and perhaps pick up some warmer clothing.

They walked around together for a while, but Marge got interested in a clothing store with exotic fashions, Macore wanted to check out some old haunts, and that left three. Grogha and Houma were soon at home in a bar with the promise of live female fairies performing erotic, unnatural acts on stage, and that left Joe.

He wandered down the street, stopped in a clothing store for men, and finally found a wool jacket and high-top, fur-lined boots that would be good in mountain country. Feeling warmer and much, much poorer, he just ambled around for a bit. He was feeling lonely again, and there wasn't much he could do about it.

A young woman—she couldn't have been more than sixteen or a few months older—approached him coyly. She looked too clean and well dressed to be a prostitute, but here one never knew.

"Sir?" she whispered conspiratorially.

Well, maybe they *were* clean and well dressed here. "Yes?"

"Sir—you look like a gentleman. Would you care to seduce and abandon me tonight?"

He chuckled over the phrasing. "Sed—how much?"

She looked shocked. "I'm not a common whore!" she snapped. "I would not dream of charging!"

He was immediately suspicious in the extreme. It sounded like one of those too-good-to-be-true offers—which they always were. *Sure, honey. Go with you, then get waylaid by thugs, robbed, and maybe murdered.*

"Uh-uh, honey. Not tonight," he told her regretfully and walked on.

He hadn't gone another block when a totally different woman, perhaps even younger than the first, beckoned and made the same offer. Again he refused, although she almost pleaded with him.

Finally he said, "All right—what's this all about? Why does

every young girl in this town want to be—seduced and abandoned—tonight?"

She looked a little apprehensive, then pulled him gently into an alleyway right off the street. "You have been propositioned before tonight?"

He nodded.

She sighed. "We're all trying it on every stranger we meet. It is impossible to get anyone local to do it. They would insist on marriage or we'd be dishonored because it would be found out. But a stranger could do it—and no one would know. Lots of girls have done it. What's wrong with *me*?" She pouted almost like a small child.

He stepped back a moment, still confused. "Let me get this straight. Are you telling me you're a virgin?"

"Of course!" she came back proudly. "Otherwise, what would be the point of this?"

He coughed and swallowed back a snappy reply to that one. Only a virgin would make that kind of a comment.

"What is it—some kind of bet? Or maybe some magic spell?"

"Oh, of course not! It's the dragon!"

That stopped him. "Dragon? What dragon?"

"You *are* new here. Just a little over four weeks ago a dragon was spotted flying to and from a new eyrie in the high mountains just behind us. It's been seen almost every night since, flying to and fro, probably establishing its nest. Once it does, it will—hunt." She looked up at him desperately, and there were actually tears in her eyes. "Don't you see? Dragons are attracted to virgins!"

He leaned back against the building wall, feeling the need for support, an expression of utter disbelief on his face. "Let me get this straight," he said again. "There's a dragon in the area?"

She nodded. "First one in more than a century in these parts."

"And dragons eat virgins?"

"*Everybody* knows that."

Well, everybody didn't, but . . . "Are you trying to tell me that every virginal girl past puberty is sneaking out at night in this town and begging to be—" He groped for a word she'd understand instead of the ten that came immediately to mind. "—*violated* by every strange man she meets?"

"Well, of course! Why else would we be doing this?"

He broke into a big grin. "And about how many of you virgins are there?"

"A couple of hundred a month ago," she told him. "Maybe half that now. It's kind of—hard—to bring yourself to do it. But the Books of Rules state that the dragon could start hunting any time after establishing its eyrie, and that takes thirty days. So you see why . . ."

He shook his head in wonder. *A trucker's paradise,* he thought. *As if you died and went to heaven* . . . Not, he told himself, that he didn't feel sorry for the poor girls. He understood their fears—he thought. But—a town full of willing virgins whose honor would force them never to tell? It was the most absurd thing he'd ever heard. Funny, too. He no longer felt very tired at all . . .

It was quite late when Marge got back to the hotel room, and she was surprised to find none of the men there as yet. She sighed and shook her head. She felt really done in and about as grimy as she ever had.

She spread out the garments she'd bought with almost all her money. They were practical ones, good for mountain work, but the fur was soft and fitted snugly about her. She couldn't be certain what the fur was—the term used by the saleswoman had been unfamiliar to her—but she decided it was probably better not to know. Still, with these clothes, she'd be extremely warm; and with the small, pointed-toe boots and tight-fitting gloves, she'd look almost like an elf.

Like an elf? She wondered about that. Casually she undressed and went to the full-length mirror in the luxury room and looked at herself once more. *Had* she changed?

The image looking back at her from the mirror was not really a familiar one, of course, but it *had* changed since she'd last examined it. Her ears, for example, which Ruddygore had noted were turning back and changing, had changed more. They were fully pointed now and sharply back on her head. Elflike ears that looked fine, even exotic, with her streaked hair—but were definitely not human in the slightest. Her eyes, too, seemed huge, sad, and teardrop-shaped, with unnaturally long lashes. They were beautiful, erotic eyes—but they were not human eyes.

She thought of the fairies on the boat two days earlier. They had all been male—sort of, anyway—but they had this sort of ear and something subtly similar about their faces. Not the eyes, though, or the general facial shape she was developing. It was not *their* kind that she was becoming.

She went back to the clothes on the bed and just lay there for a few moments, fingering them. Suddenly she stopped and looked at her hands, then sat up and looked closer. There was no doubt about it. Some sort of—webbing—was growing from the points between each of the fingers. It was only a tiny extra mass of very thin skin now, perhaps an eighth of an inch from the base of the hand, but there it was. Her fingernails, too, seemed extra hard, somewhat silvery in appearance, and were taking on a different nature, perhaps more—animallike? She couldn't decide.

Before she could think on it further, though, there was an officious knock at the door. Acutely aware, suddenly, of her nakedness, she called out, "Who's there?"

"Concierge, madam," came an equally officious reply. "You had asked at the desk if a bath could be arranged?"

She frowned. "Yes—but they told me it was too late in the day."

"A clerk checked with me, and I discovered that there was more than sufficient hot water. It won't keep, so we thought you might wish to use it tonight."

She smiled. A bath! A real bath! "Hold on, let me get something on," she called back and quickly got back into her dirty jerkin. Picking up the new clothes and a large towel, she walked to the door and opened it. Only then did she think how trusting she had been—how she had only his word that he was the concierge.

But he *was* the concierge. She had seen him at his desk in the lobby. "Follow me, please, madam," the little man said, and she followed him down the hall, down to the lobby level, and then below. The bathhouse was small—not even the well-to-do took many baths in Husaquahr, it seemed—but surprisingly modern. The sunken tub was steaming with clear, hot water brought in from coal-fired tanks that also provided some heat for the main floor, and there was a large bar of soap, a full supply of bath linen, and even a white towel-robe, imprinted with the symbol of the hotel.

"I will see that no one disturbs you, madam," the concierge assured her. "When finished, please stop by my desk in the lobby and let me know, so that we may drain the tub."

"I'll do that," she promised him, eager for the water. "And thanks!"

He left and shut the door behind him. She quickly laid out all her stuff, got undressed, and slipped into the tub. The water was quite hot, but that didn't matter at all. It wasn't *too* hot, and the warmth penetrated her body, eased her bruises and muscle tension, and just felt absolutely wonderful.

It was in the wee hours of the morning, after the last bar had closed, that Joe returned to the hotel. He felt tremendous, despite the long day, but he was really tired now. All he wanted was sleep.

He knocked on the door of the room, softly, just to warn Marge of his impending entrance, but then didn't hesitate to open the door and walk in.

He stood there for a moment, puzzled. She wasn't there. The oil lamps were still on, and there were signs that she'd been lying on top of the bed at one time—but that was all. Idly wondering if the Rules also specified boy virgins, he looked around for a clue. He dismissed his thought about the boy virgins in a minute. That wouldn't make sense. She had that celibacy thing. He stopped and thought a moment. Everything was closed now, he knew, so there was no place she could have gone to, except maybe to the wall to look at the night view—but that was unlikely. She'd had a hard day, and even her potions weren't a hundred percent effective. She'd been tired and achy when they'd first hit town, and she'd said after dinner that she was going to get some mountain clothes and then try for a bath and go to bed.

He snapped his fingers. A bath! Sure! He looked around, saw that the big towel was missing, and nodded to himself. Then he stopped for a moment, puzzled. A bath at three in the morning? This wasn't like back home, where one just went into the bathroom . . .

He turned and walked back down to the lobby. He didn't immediately check with the desk, but saw a pictograph indicating baths on a floor below. The desk clerk and the concierge watched him but did not say or do anything as he went down the stairs.

He checked both the small bathrooms. Nothing in the first, but the second showed signs that somebody had used it recently. He went over and tested the water temperature of the bath. Cool, like the other—but the other had been clear. This was soapy and still messed up. He glanced anxiously around, then found in a small pile her old clothes and the new ones she must have bought. Only the towel had been used.

Knowing now that something was terribly wrong, he bounded back up the stairs to the lobby and approached the night clerk first. The clerk smiled and looked up at the big man, nodding. "Yes?"

"The woman who checked in with me—do you know where she is?"

The clerk shrugged. "Sorry. I haven't been on very long. Try the concierge."

Joe went over to the little man at the concierge's desk, who also looked up expectantly. Joe noticed he seemed abnormally nervous and couldn't quite sit still.

"The young woman who checked in with me," Joe repeated. "Have you seen her tonight?"

The concierge frowned and pretended to look thoughtful. "Young woman? Sir, we have many. I can't be expected to remember *everyone*."

"Streaked hair, big eyes, pointy ears," Joe responded, getting a little steamed up.

The man seemed to think hard again, and was about to speak when Joe added, "She took a bath tonight—downstairs."

Sensing that he couldn't conceal obvious facts without sounding worse, the concierge brightened. "Ah, yes! But I *do* remember her! She went down to the baths *hours* ago. Why, is something wrong!"

"She's missing, that's what. You been here all night?"

"Except for a couple of calls, yes."

"Do you remember her coming back up from the baths?"

The concierge thought a moment more. Sweat was breaking out on his brow. "Uh—yes, I believe I do."

Joe reached out, temper flaring, and literally picked the little man out of his chair with one hand. *"Liar!* You forgot to remove her clothes! They're still down there! *What have you done with her?*" With one mighty move, he pulled the man across his desk so that they were face to face, all the while keeping him suspended off the floor by the grip on his clothing.

The concierge, deathly afraid and sweating like mad, yelled "Codoary! Help me!"

With an angry shove, Joe threw the concierge halfway across the lobby, where he struck a stuffed chair and toppled over. In the same moment the big man whirled, his face a fury, to see, not just the desk clerk, but two other men, all with swords, coming at him.

In an instant his great sword leaped to his right hand and hummed brightly. "I hope none of you got any fairy blood," he growled at them, " 'cause I got to leave one of you alive to torture!"

The three advanced in a semicircle, threateningly but not very professionally. It was obvious that none of these men were hired thugs or assassins. They looked like shopkeepers, hotel clerks, accountants, that sort of thing—and they looked mighty uncomfortable facing a barbarian warrior.

He didn't wait for them to make up their minds. With a mighty yell, he leaped at them, and his sword hand moved with swift and terrible precision. He didn't even have time to think about it—it was as if the sword itself were alive and doing all the right things.

In an instant's time, or so it seemed, the humming sword slashed off the nearest assailant's sword hand at the wrist, then came back up under the next and knocked the sword away and into the air. With his left hand he punched the disarmed middle man in the stomach, and he fell back and collapsed on the floor.

This left only the desk clerk, who was aghast and scared to death. The shock of what had happened to the first two totally unnerved him. With a squeal, he dropped his sword, raised his hands, and cried, "Please! Don't hurt me!"

Joe approached him, then pushed him rudely against a pillar and brought the sword up to the frightened man's throat. The clerk made a noise and looked so close to pure terror that, for a moment, the big barbarian was afraid the fellow was having a heart attack. Still, he was the most conscious of the four, so it was best to start with him.

"You see my friend here? His name's Irving." Joe pushed the point to the throat so the clerk could really feel it.

Even so, the clerk managed to gasp back, *"Irving?"* in a disbelieving tone.

The big man nodded. "Think it's a funny name, huh? He don't like it when he thinks people are makin' fun of his name." Joe paused a moment, genuinely angry but thinking. "All right—you know what my friend Irving's good at? *Cuttin'!* How about it? Shall I let him cut off a hand, maybe, like your friend's there? Then another hand? Then maybe the legs—and what's between 'em?"

The clerk whimpered.

"All right, you tell me what they've done with the girl, and *now*! I'm not a patient man!"

"Please! You got to understand!" The clerk was almost gibbering. "The dragon. It had to be appeased. Our daughters—"

"Dragon!" Joe stormed. "What the hell does this have to do with the dragon?"

"W-we saw that she was a virgin. Duoqua, who's the town elder, can see the magic. She was the first virgin stranger we'd seen! Honest! You gotta understand! My own sister's pregnant by some outland stranger because she was so scared! We *had* to!"

"What did you do with her—scumball?" Joe roared. "Where is she?"

"C-castle rock! They took her to castle rock! The altar there!"

"Where is it? How do I get to it?"

"I—I *can't*!"

"Either you can or you're dead," Joe snapped coldly, and he meant it. "I have no time for you to think about it. Your friends are coming around!"

"I'll take you! Let me loose!"

Joe let the clerk lead the way—down again towards the baths. "If there's any trickery, just a little, *anything,* not only will you regret it but, I swear by all that's holy, so will your whole stinking town. Forget that she's an agent of the sorcerer Ruddygore! Forget that she's sister to the great sorceress Huspeth! She's my rider, damn it!"

At hearing the first two names, the clerk swallowed hard and muttered, "Oh, my god!" They were apparently sufficient to strike in the man the realization that, while armies could never conquer Kidim, enemies like those could cause terrible desolation and hardly feel it. The clerk gave Joe no more trouble.

Through a service door they went, then down again, into a maze of well-lighted tunnels with steps and railings, past rooms with symbols for various Kidim banks and merchants on them, others with pictographs for various kinds of foodstuffs, and even a whole chamber full of wine. Joe knew that this was the labyrinth in the mountain of which Macore had spoken. For a moment he regretted not rousing the other three, but there wasn't time, really. Right now Marge could be staked out, with a horrible monster circling to strike . . .

"I'm surprised you don't have guards all over the place," Joe remarked as they went.

"Don't need 'em," the clerk told him. "There are spells and magic guardian beasts all over those rooms—and as for the labyrinth, once in—how would anybody find his way out? It's booby-trapped, too."

"It better hadn't spring any traps on me," Joe warned.

"It won't!" the clerk cried nervously. "Ruddygore . . . Huspeth . . . God! Did we pick the wrong one! But you gotta understand . . ."

"Cut the moral justifications! Just get me there as quick as you can!" Joe snapped. He was becoming increasingly irritated by both the time it was taking to get where they were going—if the clerk was playing fair with him—and the growing knowledge that *labyrinth* was the right word and that he had very little idea of where they were and less of how to get out of there.

Suddenly they emerged outside. The cold wind hit them in the face, and they were on a stone walkway along a mountain ledge. Joe had not been conscious of much upward movement in their walk, yet they were either above the town or on a different side of the mountain at about its level.

Someone had lighted torches all along the way, their flames whipped by the wind, but they showed the path. It wound sharply up, around a curve, then out to a lookout station that seemed suspended in space.

"Anybody guarding this path?" he asked nervously.

"With a dragon around? Are you kidding?"

The sounded reasonable enough. "All right—stop. She's out there—on that ledge?"

The clerk nodded. Suddenly he gave a sharp cry. "The dragon!"

Joe didn't wait for anything more. He slugged the clerk hard, knocking him cold and thus preventing him from easy escape or raising an alarm, then started running up the stone walk at full speed.

Something suddenly flew over and quite near him, raising a wind so large it almost bowled him over. He stopped and turned, sword at the ready, and saw the dragon. He could not get a clear look at it in the dark beyond the torches, but it was a *big* sucker, he kept thinking. He stopped to get his bearings on it, knowing timing would be crucial, and saw that the creature seemed fascinated by the lookout and was, in fact, slowly and warily circling it.

Joe took off again, knowing that this probably meant that the dragon had not yet taken its sacrifice, but that it could and would at any moment. The trail took a sudden slight and unexpected dip, and he stumbled and cursed, then got up and took up the chase once more. The trail wound around now, putting him for just a moment out of sight of the lookout itself. But the dragon's huge, dark shape was too great to be hidden, and it descended, just in front of him, where the overlook would be. *I'm too late!* he thought frantically.

At that moment the mountains echoed with the most terrified, horrible scream of fear he had ever heard. Crying out in frustration, Joe rounded the bend to the overlook, determined that he and Irving were going to avenge Marge, at least, or die in the attempt.

CHAPTER 13

A BATTLE IN THE VALE

Dragon motives are inscrutable.
—C, 228, 167(a)

JOE WAS PURE EMOTION AS HE ROUNDED THE BEND AND SAW clearly the scene on the lookout. He was so charged up that what he saw only penetrated his consciousness when he was halfway to the makeshift altar to which Marge had been tied. Only then did he realize that, although tied down stark naked on the altar stone, she was unharmed.

Just beyond, on a huge stone ledge overlooking the lookout, the dragon perched, gazing down upon the scene below with unconcealed terror in its great crimson eyes.

"You all right?" Joe called anxiously to Marge.

She managed to turn her head slightly. "Yeah, I think so. If my heart's started again."

"When I heard you scream . . ."

"But I *didn't* scream," she told him. "*He* did." She gestured with her head toward the dragon.

Joe kept one eye on the great beast while he edged closer to Marge. Once there, he started to cut the ropes with his sword, but she cautioned, "Watch it! If that sword touches me, it could kill me!"

Joe risked looking down at her, then carefully cut the arm and leg ropes binding her to the structure. She sat up, massaging her wrists and ankles, all of which bore discolorations and minor rope burns. Finally, though, she felt well enough to stand and joined Joe, who was staring at the dragon.

It was a magnificent-looking beast. The old legends had never done the dragon proper justice. It was sea green except on its underside, where it was a dull rust-red, with massive scales protecting its vulnerable points. Its great, leathery wings were a curious mixture of silver and black in a pattern. The piercing crimson eyes seemed aglow with a light of their own, neither reptilian nor mammalian, but filled, somehow, with a great alien power. There did, indeed, seem to be little puffs of smoke coming from the large, flared nostrils at the end of its perfect reptilian snout, and Joe suddenly grew nervous that it might breathe fire on the overlook and cook them both.

At that moment the dragon opened its great mouth . . .

And whimpered.

Joe frowned. "The damned thing acts as if it's scared to death."

"Maybe it thinks you're Saint George," she suggested.

He shook his head. "No. It screamed and backed off while I was still out of sight. I don't get it. I thought they were supposed to *love* virgins."

"Well, I, for one, am sure glad things aren't that cut-and-dried around here," she responded. "I thought I was a goner for sure."

"Snarfle," added the dragon, which sounded as if it had to blow its nose.

"For my part, I'm all for getting the hell out of here before somebody rushes up and reads in the Books of Rules on dragon preferences," Joe muttered. "Besides, you must be half frozen."

"I'm still too scared to be cold. Later I'll get frostbite."

Joe started edging Marge and himself back from the altar, at all times facing the dragon, Irving still in hand and at the ready. The dragon's eyes followed them, but it still looked as nervous as they were. They were almost to the path when a gruff voice yelled, "How *dare* you! How *dare* you! Six weeks' work, down the drain!"

Joe risked a turn and saw, coming toward them from farther up the trail, a medium-sized figure that looked at first to be a walking bush. It was running, though, on what seemed to be enormous, bare human feet. Out of the mass, two thick arms, raised high in fists, gestured angrily at them.

Joe pushed Marge behind him and made ready to meet this new threat. The creature or whatever approached fairly closely, oblivious of the sword, and they could see that it was a man-like figure completely covered with thick, matted black hair. Other than the arms and legs, the only things visible were two huge, yellow, oval-shaped eyes peering from beneath the brush.

It went past them and out to the altar. Joe let it go, still aware of his precarious position on the trail but too curious to run.

The hairball, as Joe thought of it, reached the altar, turned, saw the cowering dragon, and stopped. "Oh, poor Vercertorix! What have those nasty people *done* to you?" he called out, in a tone one would use to a small child.

The dragon snarfled some more, then sniffed and seemed about to break into tears.

"I think I've had about enough of this," Joe muttered to Marge. "Hey! You!" he called out. "On the overlook there! What in hell is going on here?"

The hairball turned. "Ruining a month and a half of hard work!" the creature snapped angrily. "Not to mention scaring the poor thing half to death."

"*We* didn't do anything!" Joe told him. "The villagers kidnapped this woman and stuck her out here as a sacrifice to that 'poor thing' there!"

"Bah! Ignorant, superstitious fools! I'd have Vercertorix here destroy that pesthole if his nerves were up to it!"

"They think he made a nest up here—that he was going to attack the town, anyway," Joe called out. "That's why the sacrifice of this innocent stranger."

Naked and cold though she was, Marge was madder than anything. "Don't you snap at *us*! Who the hell are you, anyway?" she demanded.

At the sound of her voice, the dragon whimpered and tried to press himself back into the rock, causing no small landslide.

"Nest, indeed!" the hairball scoffed. "Why any self-respecting dragon would want to nest in this hole, I can't tell you. But will you *please* stop scaring him, woman? You're only making him worse!"

"How am *I* scaring him?"

The dragon had another minor fit. "Don't *do* that!" the hairball screamed angrily.

"Do *what*?"

"Talk. Remind him of your presence. He's got enough problems without being tortured. Have you no humanity?"

"But he's *not* human," Joe noted. "He's a dragon."

"Semantics! Bah! That's why I went up high into these mountains seventy years ago and why I haven't had any truck with human civilization since. Stupidity, greed, war, superstition, bureaucracy, and semantics. Stupid ills for stupid people!"

Joe thought it over for a minute. "This dragon's been visiting you each night, then. Why?"

The hairball sighed. "Isn't it obvious? We may as well shout it now. The damage is done. Everybody will know, and his shame will be such that we'll probably have one less dragon. They breed only once every thousand years, you know!" He sighed, calming down slightly. "I've been treating him for his neurosis, of course. He has a complex. Isn't that obvious?"

All Joe could see was the fairy stories of his childhood collapsing like houses of cards. "You don't mean . . ."

"Certainly! He has a morbid fear of fair maidens! And *now* look at what you've done!"

"*We* didn't do *anything*," Joe retorted. "Besides, if he's scared of pretty women, why'd he come this close to begin with?"

The hairball took a tone of utter impatience with such stupidity. "If you had a brain, barbarian, you'd figure it out. Dragons are as curious as cats. Sensing something alive staked out here and seeing the torches, he *had* to investigate and find out what it was. That's his nature. And as you see, he wasn't ready yet."

"Thank heaven!" Marge breathed.

Aware of how cold it was, Joe took off his jacket and put it around the freezing Marge. She was thankful, despite the fact that it fitted like an army tent.

"And who are you?" Joe asked the hairball.

The strange man cackled. "They call me the Old Man of the Mountains, I'm told. I'm a scientist, of course. I specialize in dragons and other endangered species."

"Well, see to your patient, Doc. I think we'll go back down now."

"Wait!"

"What now?"

"I see that the lady is a halfling," the Old Man of the Mountains noted, sounding friendlier. "And I recognize that sword. It was given a thousand years ago to a man I once knew. How did you come by it?"

"It got it from the sorcerer Ruddygore," Joe told the hairy one. "If that's any business of yours."

"Ruddygore? The name is unfamiliar. Huge, fat man with a beard? Always eating?"

"That's him."

The mass of hair seemed to bend in a nod. "I thought so. So he's still alive, huh? Come on up the trail a bit. I have a cave nearby with a warm fire and some strong drink where I was waiting for Vercertorix here. I would like to talk to you."

"No, thanks," Joe told him. "We have to get back to town."

The Old Man of the Mountains chuckled. "And how are you going to do that? Could you find your way back through that rabbit warren of theirs? Come to think of it, how'd you find your way here?"

"There's a clerk from the hotel down there. I knocked him cold. He'll get us back."

"Oh, yes? Well, go on down for a moment, if you will—but you will find, I think, that you did not hit him hard enough. He is gone."

Joe didn't have to go down. He figured that the hairball was telling the truth.

"Come up to my cave," the Old Man invited again. "I'll get you back."

"Won't we—scare that friend of yours?"

The two big, yellow eyes glanced over at Vercertorix. "You just stay there and get calmed down," he soothed the dragon. "When you're confident, go to your nearest den and sleep it off. It will all be better in the morning. Then see me tomorrow night as usual. We'll get this straight. And I'm sure these nice people will not spread your problem around."

The dragon whined a bit, and there was a huge tear in its left eye. Having no choice, but not relaxing his guard or his sword grip, Joe followed Marge and the Old Man of the Mountains up the trail.

"Dragons are unusually intelligent," the hairy one, who introduced himself as Algongua, or just plain Doc for short, told them. "Almost as smart as the average person. And they're a lot more powerful and mobile. Of course, they get a bad reputation, but any carnivore that has to eat a minimum of five hundred pounds of meat a day just to keep up strength is not going to be exactly beloved. They aren't hostile to people—not really. They kill people only when those people are a threat to them. Actually, they prefer cattle most of all, or aurochs."

"But that thing in the Rules about virgins . . ." Marge interjected.

"Ah, that thing's caused more problems than it's solved. Basically, it was intended to *protect* humans. If a dragon must eat a human for food, he'll choose a virgin every time. That's the Rule. And why? To give the rest of us a chance. Somehow it's gotten all twisted by superstitious folk into a demand for sacrifice. Stupid. Dragons want as little to do with human folk as possible."

They reached his cave, which was well concealed, and then they still had to squeeze through a narrow, twisting corridor in the rock to get to the main cavern.

It was surprisingly luxurious inside. There was a roaring fire in a large, conventional fireplace and a thick rug on the floor. There was also a wall of books, including some—perhaps ten or fifteen—of the Books of Rules.

It was, in fact, rather warm and cheerful. Joe wondered idly where the chimney came out.

The drink was strong, but it tasted good to both Joe and Marge after the chill on the ledge, and the fire was particularly welcome.

Finally feeling relaxed, Algongua took a stiff drink and sat in front of them. "Now, then—what's this all about? You're not here for your health. Not from Malthasor."

"Who?" Joe responded.

"Ah—Ruddygore, I think you said he was calling himself now."

Marge grew interested. "I've heard another name for him, too, but it wasn't that one. How many names does he have?"

"Probably hundreds," the hairy man responded, cackling a bit. "None of them his real one, of course. Sorcerers never tell their real names to anybody—it can cost them. But he's basically a good man and a strong wizard as well."

"You knew him well?" she pressed.

"Long ago, as I said, we both had the same—er—employer, let's say. That was long ago and far from here. So—if I may be so bold—where are you headed in his service?"

Joe thought about his answer. He didn't want to alienate the strange man, but he had only Algongua's word that they were on the same side—and, come to think of it, the Old Man had never as much as said *that*, either. Only that he knew Ruddygore. "We go up the Vale of Kashogi," Joe said at last. "There is something in Starmount that was stolen from Ruddygore and which he wants us to retrieve."

The hairy man whistled. "Starmount! I'm sure the Xota will not be pleased. I wouldn't like to take an army into there!"

"The Dark Baron might—he wants what we want," Marge put in, sensing Joe's caution and understanding it. "We are a small Company—we hope to sneak in."

Algongua laughed. "Sneak in! Well, perhaps it can be done. But this Baron, you say, may march on it? That should be most interesting."

It was obvious he had no idea who the Dark Baron was, and Marge decided to tell him, giving as much detail as she herself knew.

The strange man sighed. "Always another archvillain! The Dark This and the Black That and the Prince of Something Else. They're all the same. Ridiculous. No sooner do you beat one than another comes along. I long ago gave that up as non-productive. I am beyond these petty temporal battles and wars." He sighed. "But that doesn't help you, does it? Here— let me think a moment. Starmount . . . hmmm . . . Yes, I think I can remember a few things."

"Can you tell us what the Xota people are?" Marge asked him. "That alone would be a great help."

"They're a degenerate race of fairies. Ugly brutes, with bat's wings. More animal than anything else. Expect no mercy or quarter from them! They'll eat people, other fairies, even themselves. They sacrifice to primitive, bloody gods. Still, my dear, I'd kill myself if I were you, rather than let them capture me. *You* they won't kill. You're a halfling, and they'll just complete the process and keep you as a slave—and they do terrible things to women slaves."

"I'll keep that in mind," she assured him. "Still—since we're on the subject, you said they'd 'complete the process.' I'm a little curious and nervous as to what I'm turning into even now. Can you tell?"

He looked at her with his big eyes and cackled again. "Too soon to tell, really. Depends on what your fairy parent was. I gather you don't know."

She decided not to go into her true origins—or Joe's. "No, I have no idea. It began when I served an apprenticeship with the witch queen Huspeth."

"Huspeth!" He made a sound that was definitely derisive and sounded something like *bleah*. "Who knows, indeed? But, I assure you, she didn't start the process. Halflings are born, not created—and remain human, and occasionally ignorant of their nature, unless heavily exposed to faërie or given to dabbling in sorcery. Since I see you're well along and *he* certainly is human enough, I assume you're an adept of some sort."

"A rank beginner. Otherwise I wouldn't have been surprised in the hotel tub, knocked out, and carried out to that overlook."

"Still—enough. From your looks, I'd say you were probably in the nymph family, which is common for changelings, but there are a hundred types and tribes of nymphs, all different. Well, you'll find out soon enough." He thought a moment. "Starmount. Hmm . . ." He got up, went over to the bookshelves, opened an old book and took out a small piece of yellowed paper, then returned to them. "This is, if memory serves, a map of the Vale and the Starmount Gateway." He unfolded it. "Yep. As I thought. There's an old high trail. Real narrow—single file for horses a lot of the way, and a long way down if you slip—but at the three-thousand-foot level most of the way. See?"

He laid it out for them and they looked at it. They couldn't read the script, but the trail and many natural features were well marked.

"Once you're in Starmount you're on your own, but this should get you there—if you're plucky enough to use it. Also, I can't vouch that the trail's maintained at all. This map's two hundred years old. But you have a fighting chance if it is."

Joe felt a sense of excitement rising within him. What was it Ruddygore had said? *Luck rode with the barbarian hero.* And here was just what they needed—handed to them.

"I don't want to be ungrateful, but we'd better be getting back," he told the strange hairy man. "We've had a long travel day and a longer night—and no sleep as yet."

"Of course, of course. I was just enjoying conversation again. But—how well will those meddling fools receive you down there?"

Joe thought about it. "I don't know. They can't be too

friendly—after all, I *did* beat up two of 'em and take one's hand off right in the hotel lobby. But they kidnapped Marge. I figure they better *hadn't* do anything."

"Come, then. I have a small complex of caves here that tie into theirs. I'll get you back."

He was as good as his word, although the route was even more tortuous and confusing than Joe's had been on the way out. Still, once more they stepped into the bath level of the hotel. When they turned around to thank Algongua, he was already gone.

"Wait a minute," Marge told Joe. "Let's see if they left me my clothes." They checked the bath room, but it had been drained and cleaned. There wasn't a sign of anything that was hers. It wasn't just the clothes—her kit had been there as well.

"So they even steal my stuff!" she stormed, sounding really angry. She took off Joe's coat, which had almost reached the ground on her, and gave it back to him. "Well, I hope they're easily shocked!" And with that, stark naked, she marched up their stairs into the lobby, Joe following, curious to see what she was going to do. He was by no means certain of their reception and put his hand on his sword.

There was a new clerk and a new concierge on duty when they came up, and the mess from the fight had been cleaned up completely, but there was no question from the shock both men on duty showed at the sight of them that they knew full well whom they were facing.

She marched up to the concierge. "You! You'll get me my clothes and have them cleaned, neat, and ready when I call for them in the morning!" she commanded, then whirled on the clerk. "And you—we will be staying one more night. All five of us. On this hotel. That's just for starters. If you don't agree, I will cast a spell on this place that will make it fit only for worms like those miserable creatures who run it!" And with that, she stormed up the stairs.

Joe looked around, noted that neither man had so much as breathed during that, grinned, and said, "If anything is out of place while we're here, this hotel and all who work for it will be destroyed. Even so, I assure you its reputation for what was done tonight will be spread the length and breadth of Husaquahr." He sniffed. "First-class, indeed!" Then he followed Marge upstairs.

There were snores coming from the room of the other three, so they didn't disturb them, but Marge insisted on putting a full protection spell on the room she and Joe were in. She collapsed on her bed and sighed. "Oh, god! I feel as if that dragon *did* eat me! Don't wake me, no matter *what* you do."

"Don't worry—I won't," he assured her and blew out the light.

The events of the previous evening were the talk of the town by morning. After the fight in the hotel lobby, there had been no real way to keep anything secret. Most of Kidim sympathized completely with the men who'd done the deed, but were now acutely embarrassed by it, particularly since it hadn't worked. A merchant and trade city like Kidim fed on reputation, and its reputation was for honorable transactions and a totally safe and secure haven in the midst of a barbaric country.

Thus, while Macore, Houma, and Grogha had no idea what had gone on when they awakened, dressed, and went down to a late breakfast, they were more than pleasantly surprised to discover they could not pay for anything at all—whatever they wanted was theirs, with hopes that the "incident" would not be held against the whole town. They were so pleased by the reception that they took full advantage of it for several hours before they could find somebody to tell them what it was all about.

Joe and Marge did not appear until midday. Marge was delighted to find outside the door both sets of clothes—the old ones laundered and neatly folded—and all her belongings from the bath. She donned the brown skin outfit and packed away the skimpy green one for better weather.

Grogha had come up every hour or so to check on them, and so they were just about ready to go out when the portly man, seeing the clothing taken in, had pounded on the door. He quickly told them of their treatment by the town, which pleased Marge no end.

"Just remember, they're only being this way because they aren't sure they could kill all of us," Joe warned. "But I think they know it won't bottle up forever, regardless."

They had a large brunch on the hotel and noted that they were being stared at again and again by various townsfolk. This would be one those people would tell their grandchildren.

They decided to spend one more night, simply to get their systems back in order, and they supplemented their supplies and weapons—on the house, of course. Marge even had another bath the next night—although with full protection spells around this time. Joe, too, took advantage of the bath and got his meager regular clothing cleaned as well. The other three couldn't see the sense of it.

Still and all, the town was mighty happy to see them go the next morning.

"Maybe we should have told them that the dragon was no threat to them before we left," Marge suggested.

"No!" all four men responded in unison, then looked sheepish. "Ah, that is," Macore added, "they don't deserve it. Let 'em worry. I doubt if they'll try this kind of trick again."

"Besides, finding out it was no threat might lose us our status—which is pretty nice—while increasing their sense of guilt," Joe continued smoothly. "They deserve to sweat." He was, however, amused by the frantic reactions of the other three. So he hadn't been the only one to have a full night, it seemed.

They reached the point where Algongua's map said that the higher trail branched off, but it took them a half hour to find what they hoped was it. It was overgrown, worn, and weathered and only hinted that it was a trail—but it went west at roughly the three-thousand-foot level, and that was what the map claimed.

There were several rocky stretches where any semblance of a trail just gave out, and they spent some time hunting to pick it up again, but it did not prove in the early going too difficult to follow. As it thinned and hugged the granite sides of the mountains, it became more definite. But a trail that was no more than three or four feet wide on the side of a sheer cliff and that had a drop on the other side of more than fifteen hundred feet at the minimum was by no means comforting, and parts of it had been weathered uncertainly, while small streams and waterfalls crossed it and wore deep grooves in the face.

There were actually some clouds below them, but after a while they disappeared, and the main road up the Vale of Kashogi to Starmount and beyond could be clearly seen. It looked pretty deserted, but Macore thought at one time he saw the dust of some riders far ahead. It might have been a wisp of cloud or some optical illusion, he admitted both to them and to himself. But the enemy forces had been conspicuous by their absence so far, and there had been no real sign in Kidim, although even Ruddygore had thought they would be thickly represented there.

"Perhaps they were," Dacaro suggested to Marge. "Those are merchants and bankers, and most are educated men. Who stirred up the dragon fears? Who could read the Rules—and only those parts on dragons guaranteed to scare the hell out of people? And who suggested they do what they did to you? I suspect more than meets the eye there. Evil is often best when it is the most subtle, reasonable, and invisible."

"But they failed—if in fact it was them at all," she noted. "That means we have to expect another try."

"Yes. More of a brute-force one, I would suspect. They won't have any easier time with the Xota than we, if that's any comfort. And they may not know about this trail—although they'll draw some conclusions when we fail to show up down there. We will have to take things as they come. The enemy may even be at the cave already."

She didn't like to think of that. Not after all this. She did, however, tell Dacaro about the Old Man of the Mountains and his comments on her.

"I don't know who—or what—he is," the equine adept told her, "but he is certainly correct in that halflings and changelings are not made. Not by Huspeth, anyway. It is something that, considering your unique origins, I did not take into account before. But, yes, Ruddygore himself must have cast you like this—and let Huspeth take the heat for it."

"But why?"

"Only a guess. He saw that you had an aptitude for the art, but also understood that you had not the time, nor the ability, perhaps, to learn the complexities of the spells. And certainly your lack of reading ability as an adult is also limiting. So he took the path of best advantage—for him. As one of the fairy folk, you would have natural, instinctive uses of magic and total sensitivity to it."

"Algongua said I would be a—nymph, I think he called it. I know what the old legends are on nymphs, but not what that means here. Can you tell me?"

"Well—yes and no. Basically, a nymph is a race of faërie,

all members of whom are female. They are closest to human in size and general form and are quite often extremely over-sexed in all senses of the word. A nymph has the ability to mate with *any* male of *any* species, whether fairy, human, or animal—you name it. Her progeny, then, are always halflings themselves, generally human in form, but if they become in-volved with fairies or in the art, as you are, then they will change into their fairy form. The results can be quite bizarre. Satyrs. Centaurs. The small winged ones. Strange amphibians. Depends on who—and what—the father was. Whole new races of faërie have been created in that way. Of course, if the child is female, it has a fifty-fifty chance of being another nymph, so the race doesn't die out. As to kind, there are wood nymphs who live in and are linked to trees, field nymphs, water nymphs, all sorts. You name it. But I still sense the potential for wings in you, so you may be an aerial of some sort. We will see, won't we? It should be interesting to discover what happens if the transformation is completed."

"Huh? What do you mean?"

"As primarily human, your powers gain with celibacy. As those of a full nymph, your powers will gain with the opposite type of conduct."

"What! You mean . . ."

"Precisely. Since the magic of faërie is innate—the potential is there and develops automatically under certain circum-stances rather than having to be learned—the more times you do it with anybody, the stronger you will become."

She was silent for a while. Finally she said, "You're amused by that, aren't you?"

"I'm sorry, but I must admit I am. Don't be too angry. Would you rather have *your* problem or mine?"

There really wasn't much of a comeback to that.

They camped out early in the evening, at the first area they came upon, with enough room, not wanting to chance being on this trail after dark with no place to turn into. It was damned cold, but a small waterfall provided water, and there were some scrub bushes for the horses. It was still a cramped eve-ning and a nervous one that high up and in the cold.

The next day dawned cloudy, but they were anxious to get going. During the morning they made good time. Early in the afternoon the clouds descended to the trail level, and travel became something of a nightmare. With so little tolerance, they soon were chilled, wet, and unable to see the tail of the horse ahead of them. It was sheer luck that they came upon another wide place—narrower and even less comfortable than the previous night's, but enough—and found themselves having to stay the afternoon and through the night. Quarters were really close then, and they had to be careful simply not to step in and slip on the horse droppings, but they had to stick it out and remain through the second night.

The third day showed not much improvement, and they feared that they would be stuck yet another full day in that cramped space. But after a couple of hours, the sun broke through and burned off the fog. Not all the way—still, the cloud level was a hundred feet or more below the low points of the trail. While there was no guarantee of safety, they were all willing to chance it. Dacaro, with his bulk, was particularly uncomfortable and offered a fog dispeller spell if need be rather than remain there any longer. He didn't normally want to risk any spells until he had to—the enemy below might be sensitized to such things.

On the fourth day, about midmorning, the trail started down in a series of hairy switchbacks that left no margin for error. They almost lost Grogha when his horse came close to losing its footing, but he was able to keep control in the nick of time.

Macore and Joe consulted Algongua's map and decided that they were coming down to join the main trail—which was rising to meet them. The Starmount Gateway, then, would be only a few miles ahead of them—and where, again, they would be on their own. Still, it was supposedly only eight or nine miles from the Gateway—actually a natural pass that opened onto the great Starmount Plateau—to the cave they sought. That brought another sobering realization—the Xota could be anywhere, starting now. As fliers, they could leap down from hiding places above, or swoop in in aerial attacks. The Company was suddenly acutely aware of how exposed it was on the high trail.

The junction was certainly not far, perhaps just around the next bend, from the looks of it, when Macore put up his hand, halting them, and turned and put a finger to his lips.

Joe, just behind him, frowned and whispered, "What's the matter?"

"They're ahead of us. Probably laying for us," the little thief whispered back. "I can almost smell 'em. But I heard a horse snort and shuffle."

As quietly as possible, Joe relayed the message back.

"Horses!" Marge exclaimed to Dacaro. "Then this won't be the Xota."

"No. These are the ones we have feared. Obviously they got here ahead of us and set ambushes at this end of both trails."

Macore slipped off his horse, aware that he had very little room on the trail. He drew his sword and made his way forward, in front of his horse. Slowly, with a thief's skill and practice, he crept ahead and soon more or less *oozed* around the bend in the trail.

They all drew their own weapons, but aside from Joe's getting in front to hold Macore's horse, there was little he could do. They waited anxiously, fearful that the little man had been taken.

Finally, though, Macore slipped back around as quietly as he'd gone. "There are six of them," he whispered softly to Joe. "They picked a nice position, too. We would have been exposed at least three hundred yards on the trail. They may have been there for some time. They're all dismounted and seem to be mostly sitting around looking bored. That will change the moment we appear, though."

Joe thought about it. "No way to sneak up on them?"

"Not unless you can fly," the thief told him. "Three hundred yards to a broad, flat rocky area with some trees and bushes where we join the main road. It ain't much when you just gotta walk it, but it's ten miles when you're fighting. And this drop is all the way to the junction, almost. There's a mighty big hole until the trails join."

Joe nodded and looked down. He could see the other trail, only forty yards or so away on the other side, but in between was about a four-hundred-foot-deep gap. He thought furiously. "All downhill?"

"You said it. *Real* grade, too."

"I wonder—considering none of us can fly, and we'd be suckers for crossbows . . ."

"So? So?"

"How about a charge? You sure they don't know we're here?"

"Pretty sure. Did you say a charge?"

"Uh-huh. As soon as we round the bend, go for a gallop. Full charge, yelling and screaming, weapons brandished and ready."

"Are you crazy? The horses will probably lose their footing and fall into the ravine!"

"Yeah—but if they don't, it will sure surprise the hell out of those men, won't it? They'll have to pick up and aim their weapons; maybe some of 'em will have to mount up. Three hundred straight downhill yards ... I figure maybe twenty, thirty seconds at full gallop at the worst. Maybe even ten."

Macore shook his head wonderingly. "It's impossible."

Joe grinned. "That's what *they* think, sure. You go tell the others." He looked back and sighed. "I wish Posti was in front, but you'll have to do as the leader," he said to Macore's brown horse.

Macore went back, talked to the others, then made his way forward again. "They all think you're nuts, too."

"Anybody got another idea? We can't back up—not enough room. We can't fly over that ravine. We don't have any way of climbing down, even if we were willing to desert Posti and Dacaro. And the longer we stay here, the more likely it is that one of us or one of the horses is going to give us away."

Macore nodded glumly. "I know, I know. But if we must commit suicide, why do you have to be so logical about it?" He looked at his horse. "Who leads?"

"You take Posti—and brief him. He'll come through. I'll take yours."

"*That* I won't argue about," Macore responded honestly and made his way back once more.

"When I raise my sword, be ready to follow," Joe called after him. "When I drop it, we start."

They all drew their weapons and waited tensely, eyes on Joe. Both Marge and Houma had small crossbows with a supply of bolts conveniently in front of them; the other three held swords at the ready. It wasn't much of an attack force, but it would have to do.

Macore glanced nervously around. "I hope he's as good a rider as he thinks he is," he muttered aloud.

"I hope we're all better fighters than I think we are," Grogha responded worriedly.

Joe raised his great sword, positioned himself, and was ready to begin when he heard Marge say, "Wait!" in a loud whisper. As tense as he was, it was almost enough to start him off, anyway, but instead they all turned and looked questioningly back at her.

"I can call a friend," she told them. "One who will cause one hell of a ruckus. That will give us the diversion we need to go in."

"A friend?" Macore repeated, frowning. *"Here?"*

"A unicorn," she told them. "My—protector." *I hope*, she added silently to herself. "I don't know why I didn't think of him earlier."

Joe was skeptical. "How the hell can a unicorn get here in time?"

"I don't know, but it all just came back to me. What have we got to lose?"

He thought it over and knew the answer was "Not much." He nodded and said, "Okay, give out the call. The rest of the plan stays the same, though. If this unicorn comes thundering by, it's the ball game, so as soon as we're sure they've seen or heard it, in we go. Got it?"

They nodded, but none, not even Marge, really believed in any sort of unicorn savior.

"Stay away from the unicorn no matter what," Marge warned. "He's friendly only to me." With that she sat back, tried to concentrate, and said, more mentally than physically, "Koriku—come! I am in great danger and need your help!"

For a moment nothing happened, and Joe relaxed, turned, and raised his great sword once more. Then abruptly there was a roll like thunder and the sound of hooves, and they saw the great magical white beast coming toward them, riding the air above the ravine, level with their road. Marge smiled, then gestured for the creature to move to the opposite, main road and continue. The signal was taken and heeded.

Around the bend, there were sudden shouts as the men in the ambush both heard and saw the creature charging in upon them. At that moment Joe dropped his sword and kicked his horse in the ribs. The time for thinking was done. The others quickly followed, yelling, as was Joe, to add to the confusion.

Posti kept Macore almost in the rear end of Joe's mount, showing the guts he had displayed so long ago at the Circean's farm. Next came Marge and then Houma, who released their initial crossbow bolts as soon as they could see the men in the wooded clump. Grogha brought up the rear, his horse pretty much taking him along, and tried mightily not to fall off.

The sight of the great unicorn bearing down on them was a complete shock to the defenders, who had been very lax up to now. They looked up and saw the charging white, single-horned apparition and were frozen for a moment; then they moved as one to counter it, toward the main road and away from the high path.

At that moment, the riders came around the bend with their yells, and the defenders were caught, divided in their attention and ducking the first bolts sent their way, even though those were far short of any mark.

Two, though, were clearly pros, archers who jumped up, bows ready, and let loose two wild shots in the direction of the exposed party. While neither hit the mark, the archers were shooting and reloading with a fluidity that seemed almost inhuman.

Koriku sensed the immediate threat in the archers and lunged for them with a snort that became something of a roar, landing on both and knocking them down. Suddenly he was the enraged carnivorous beast Marge had seen in the fields, spearing men with his great horn and rending flesh with row upon row of sharp, pointed teeth set in powerful equine jaws.

By this time Joe had reached the guardpost itself. In maneuvering around the unicorn, he exposed himself to the no longer dazzled defenders. He felt an arrow pierce his side and he whirled and bore down on a crossbowman who was now trying to reload, running over the hapless man and trampling him. Joe's horse went down, rolling on top of a swordsman who screamed in agony, but Joe managed to jump off and come up on his feet, the arrow in his side now causing some bleeding he was too charged up to notice.

Between Joe and the unicorn, the defenders were turned inward, allowing the rest of the party to make it in relative safety. Posti hit the ledge with his hind legs, kicked off, and landed full on top of another archer, who also went down—as did Macore, who flew from Posti's saddle and spilled onto the rocky ground, losing his sword for a moment.

Marge and Houma had managed to reload, and each took

out a swordsman, one of whom was running for his horse, which was tied up in the rear. Another soldier leaped from a rocky bluff and carried Grogha over onto the ground. The portly man struggled with his larger assailant for a while, but blood was trickling from his mouth and he was in great pain. When it was clear that Grogha was out of the fight, the soldier abandoned him to writhe and moan there and turned to Macore, just now getting groggily to his feet. The soldier, a huge, bearded man in black uniform and chain mail, towered over the little thief, and the first blow of the soldier knocked Macore's sword away; a second, with the flat striking Macore's head, sent the little man reeling backward, coming to rest in a bush where he groaned once, then fell back, still.

Now the soldier smelled victory and turned on Marge. Koriku, finished with his archers, saw the move, turned, and in a great leap was upon the bearded man, first pushing him down, then knocking the sword from the man's hand with his great horn. As the huge equine head came down and the gaping, blood-soaked jaws filled the soldier's vision, all confidence vanished and he screamed in terror.

Joe, for his part, took on another swordsman. It was quite a duel, since the soldier was extremely good and obviously well trained, but Irving's magic always seemed to provide the proper counterblow and move into every opening. Finally gaining the upper hand, Joe flung the sword from the other's grasp and then plunged his own into the soldier's abdomen. The man gave a terrible cry, bent over backward, then collapsed in a heap.

Marge saw another uniformed shape come from behind a rock, sword in hand, toward Joe's back. She let loose a bolt that penetrated the attacker's chain mail, and the man gave a horrible cry that brought Joe quickly around. Irving wasted no time in finishing the man off.

Houma looked around, saw the bleeding and broken Grogha, and cried out the man's name, riding swiftly to him. Joe spotted Macore's limp form in the bush and ran to him. Marge leaped off Dacaro and ran first to Macore, examining him for vital signs.

"Is he dead?" Joe asked worriedly.

She shook her head. "Not yet. But he's in a bad way, I can

tell. Help me get him down here on the grass and keep him still. I'll see about Grogha."

Houma was leaning over the portly man, and there were tears in his eyes. "Grogha, you filthy pig, don't you dare die on me!" he shouted. Marge had some trouble getting him away, but then she bent down and examined the fallen man's wounds. Her moderate powers of witchcraft came to the fore, for they included diagnostic and healing arts. She tried to soothe Grogha, who was conscious but in terrible pain, while she probed his body.

Finally she sighed, got up, and went back to Joe, who asked her, "How is he?"

"Beyond my powers," she responded sadly. "So is Macore, although he's not nearly so bad off. Macore's got at least a nasty concussion and a broken rib or two; Grogha's got bad internal bleeding. I'm afraid a rib may have punctured a lung."

Joe thought frantically. "Wait a minute! Magic's gotten us out of a number of scrapes. Don't they use it instead of doctors here?"

She looked up at him, suddenly a little cheerier. "I'll ask Dacaro," she said and jumped up on the horse. "Can you do anything?"

"Perhaps," the adept replied. "Perhaps not. It will depend on the nature of the injuries. But there is no good way for me to treat them as it stands. It's not like spoon-feeding you a spell. I will have to project myself inside each and effect whatever repairs, major and minor, are needed as I go." He paused a moment, thinking hard. "There *might* be one way, though. Do you trust me enough to let me take over your mind?"

The question startled her. "Can you do that? If so, why should I object if you can help them?"

"Because if you consent and assist, I *can*. But consider—I do not have to reverse it once it is done. You will have to trust that I will do so."

She understood what he was saying now, but she looked at the unconscious Macore and the limp form of Grogha, which, even now, had only the most tenuous of threads to life, and made her decision. "What do I do?"

"I'm certain Huspeth taught you the trance state. Clear your mind. Make it as blank as possible. You will feel me enter—

but do not resist, for that will simply seal me off. Let it happen. Understand?"

"I can do it. Let's hurry, though. I'm afraid we're already too late."

"That is up to the gods," the adept responded fatalistically. "Let us do what we can."

One of the archers was badly wounded but still alive. Joe checked all the soldiers' bodies out, finding little or nothing on them, and then went to the archer on whom his horse had fallen. The horse itself was in bad shape, he could see, and would probably have to be destroyed. Posti, at least, had come through with nothing more than a bruise.

Like the others, the injured soldier was dressed in a silver-trimmed black uniform of some kind, chain mail, and a partial helmet, and was ruddy-faced and bearded. The man writhed and groaned in agony, but stopped when Joe approached and just stared with eyes blazing hatred at the man who'd done him in.

"How many did the Baron send to the cave with you?" Joe asked coldly.

"Barbarian!" the soldier gasped defiantly. "I die, but I tell you nothing!"

"You die slowly, friend," Joe noted and looked up, then back at him. "Already the buzzards and other scavengers are gathering. You could last a long time here—picked alive by beak and claw. It's a pretty unpleasant way to go."

"Do what you will," the man responded.

"I'll pull you out from that horse and give you swift release," Joe offered. "Swift release and burial from those that eat the dead. I'm not asking for a betrayal. Only the answers to a couple of questions."

The man seemed to think it over, and Joe knew he'd hit a nerve. "What does it matter, anyway?" the soldier asked mostly himself. "What questions?"

"How many in the Baron's party?"

"Thirty-six of his best fighters."

Joe felt uncomfortable. If that was the truth, there were still thirty like this man ahead.

"How far ahead are they?"

"More than half a day," the soldier told him. "They left at dawn."

That, too, was disturbing—but if it was only a few miles to the cave, why hadn't they returned by now? Joe wasn't sure whether he should feel better or worse that they hadn't returned. The fact that they hadn't meant they'd walked into some big trouble—and they were thirty seasoned army men. As of now, he had Marge, himself, and Houma in any shape to go on.

"One more question. They went up the main road here?"

The dying soldier nodded. "Yes. There really is no other way."

That was enough. He looked down at the man and drew his sword. "Too bad you're with the bad guys," he said softly, "but you're a good soldier, a gallant fighter, and you die with honor."

The man looked genuinely pleased and touched by that. "Hold, barbarian, one moment. That sword is a magic one that will slay me. Which great name does it bear?"

"Irving," Joe replied.

The man looked aghast. "Irving?" he repeated unbelievingly.

Irving came down and severed his head from his body at that moment. Then Joe tried to get the body out from under the horse, and almost made it, when he suddenly felt dizzy and collapsed over the horse's torso.

CHAPTER 14

THE GENIE WITH
THE LIGHT BROWN HARE

All magic lamps, charms, etc., shall be guarded well.
                                        —LXXX, 494, 361(b)

HE WAS ROLLING DOWN INTERSTATE 80, A BUXOM BLONDE *at his side, a beer in his hand, and Merle Haggard on the tape deck as the miles flashed by. It was a wonderful, satisfying life, and it was good to be alive . . .*

"He's coming 'round!" a voice called out from somewhere, somewhere far from I-80 and the blonde and the beer.

"Clean towel!" another voice ordered, wrenching him farther and farther away. Something was wrong, really wrong, and even Merle Haggard was singing English madrigals in a foreign tongue . . .

He opened his eyes and looked around. It took a minute or so for him to remember where he was, and who these people were, and the details of the day. He could see that it was dark now, and there was a small fire in the wooded glade. He saw Marge come to him with a towel soaked in hot water, bend down, and wipe his face.

"Wh—what happened!" he managed, his voice sounding like a croak.

"You had an arrow in you. Went almost through you, too. You're very lucky, Joe. Dacaro says a one-inch difference and you'd be dead now. As it is, the wound's already healing, although you might feel it for a few days yet."

"Macore? Grogha?"

"Much worse off, I'm afraid. Macore will recover, but he'll need a couple of days before he's up to riding. Grogha, however—he was real bad, Joe. His back is broken. I've given him a potion that's knocked him out, but even the magic's no good unless you know exactly what to do. Dacaro's a good sorcerer, but he's no healer. He was able to repair your hole pretty well and fix up Macore's leg and ribs, but Grogha lost a lot of blood, mostly internal, and he's too cracked up for anybody but a specialist. The nearest specialist would be in Kidim. I doubt if he could stand the ride."

Joe whistled, coming out of it now. "I don't know. Until today it still was something like fun and games. That bartender, it didn't seem real somehow, and none of the rest made much difference. No matter what *we* did, no matter what scrape we got into, we always got out of it. Now this." He suddenly grew tense. "The rest of the Baron's men—any sign?"

She shook her head from side to side. "We've been watching. Nothing. Not a sign."

He sighed. "Well, keep a watch. But, somehow, I don't think we have to worry about them. Just a feeling. Still—we'll know soon enough." He pulled off the moist towel and brought himself to a sitting position. It hurt like hell in his side when he did, but it was bearable. "I'll be okay. Just whip me up something to dull the pain a bit, give me the night, and I'll be ready to ride tomorrow."

"Tomorrow! How can we possibly go tomorrow?"

"We have to," he told her. "For one thing, either those nasties *are* going to come back, in which case we're dead if we stay, or they aren't—in which case the reason why they aren't is going to come sometime to see who else might be in the neighborhood. We're too close to stay put. Besides—we got a wishing lamp to get, huh? Maybe one of those wishes can be used on Grogha."

She thought about it. "Yeah! You're right! It may be the only way. But if thirty hardened soldiers couldn't do it . . ."

"We have no choice. And we have to know what's going on in advance." He looked up. "That's almost a full moon up there. Where's Houma?"

"By Grogha."

"Get him."

She did as instructed, and soon the lanky farmer and former goat was by Joe's side. It was clear he'd been crying some, and Joe didn't hold it against him at all.

"Houma, I'm sorry I got you both into this mess," he said sincerely.

"Oh, hell, you didn't exactly torture us," the other replied. "We did our share today, didn't we?" There was a certain pride in his sad tone.

"You sure did. But you know we're going to lose Grogha unless we get the Lamp."

Houma brightened. "Sure! The Lamp! I damn near forgot! Then there's a chance!"

"A slim one," Joe said. "Look, not too far ahead, the road reaches Starmount Plateau. It's a clear, moon-bright night, so it should give a good view of where we're going. If these Xota are fliers, and if the Baron's men were trapped by them in daylight, chances are they're day folk themselves and will be licking their own wounds tonight."

"I getcha," Houma said. "You want me to go up and find out what we're up against."

Joe nodded. "This wound's pretty painful, but I think I can live with it. I'd rather get a night's sleep, but if things look good, I'm all for trying it tonight."

"Are you out of your mind?" Marge practically screamed at him. "You're too banged up!"

But Houma was game. "I'll take Posti. That way, if anything happens to me, he might be able to get back with the word."

"Good. But don't take any chances—and get back as soon as you know anything."

With that, Houma was off. Marge sat down beside Joe and shook her head in wonder. "I don't know what I'm going to do with you. You're crazy."

He chuckled. "Well, you were the one who wanted adventure, right? I'm going to keep going with my impulses. They've been pretty good so far."

Marge looked over at the two motionless forms across the fire. "Yeah. Real good."

"We're all still alive. That's more than anybody would have figured at this point. This close to our goal, I don't want to lose now." He sighed. "It's not a simple world any more, though."

She looked at him strangely. "Yeah. You and those close to you can die here."

"No, not even that. That soldier I talked to. He wasn't some nasty, evil, menacing Baron or supernatural wart on the world. He wasn't evil at all, I don't think. Just an honorable man doing the job he was best at. That makes it a lot tougher, really. It's easy to fight and hate your enemies when you think of them as some kind of supernatural monsters. I dunno. I just figured the kind of folks that would ride with the Baron would be more like, well, Nazis or something, at least. Now I find out they're the same kind of folks we are."

Marge sighed and leaned back for a moment. "Yeah, I think I know what you mean. This *should* be a kind of romantic world—you know, knights, dragons, that sort of thing. But it's a real place, not some fairy tale. It's a place where most of the people are owned by feudal lords, where the garbage is still tossed out the back window, and the same kind of people still die for the wrong causes. Even the supernatural side isn't all that glamorous, with these silly Rules and hung-up dragons seeing psychiatrists. I wonder if maybe it's the price we pay when and if our fantasies ever do become real?"

"These aren't *my* fantasies," he grumbled.

She smiled. "Are you sorry you came?"

He thought about it. "I'm not sure. Even now I'm not sure. Ask me when this heals and this stuff is over and done with." He paused a moment. "Where's your friend the unicorn, by the way?"

"Gone. I don't know where. I'm not even sure just *what* he is. Until recently, I thought of unicorns as just, well, pretty animals. Now I'm not sure what they are. I'm not even sure if whatever they are is good, frankly, or whether that's a proper question. You see, there's a price I must pay for that. It was much too busy here for me to pay it now, but Koriku will remember the bill and collect. Oh, don't look so upset. It's not that bad—but I'm not sure what it is, either. Don't worry about it for now." She sighed. "I want to look at Macore and Grogha. Then we all better get some rest—you in particular."

She left him there to ponder all that had been said, and he managed to drift off to sleep without the aid of Marge's potions.

He was awakened gently about four hours later, in the dead of night, by Houma. He was so glad to see the lanky man that he didn't even grumble at being awakened.

"I got almost to the cave itself," Houma told Joe. "Had to make the last part on foot, though, to keep close to the rocks. Posti would have stuck out."

"Any sign of the Baron's forces?"

Houma nodded grimly. "They're all over the place. It was pretty ugly, Joe. Their bodies, and the bodies of their horses, were spread out all over the flat about four miles up. Most of 'em were badly torn up, and a lot of the bodies of both the men and the horses looked—*gnawed*, if you can believe it." He shuddered. "It was the worst thing I've ever seen."

Joe sighed. "Did you count the bodies?"

The farmer nodded. "I think it's all thirty. Couldn't be positive, since I didn't really want to go out there too far, and there were some—things—working on a couple of the corpses."

"Xota?"

"Naw. Don't think so. Looked like animals. I didn't see any signs of them Xota people."

Joe struggled to his feet. "That settles it, then." He got up, staggered a bit, then winced and stretched. "I'll do." He looked at the two sleeping forms. "Marge—you stay with them. Houma and I are going to take a little trip."

She looked stubbornly at them. "Oh, no! Even if you manage somehow to get by and in that cave, which I doubt, don't forget there's some kind of monster in there. You need me, Joe. Dacaro gave me a number of spells that may or may not do any good, but I know enough to know that you shouldn't go in there without me."

"But somebody's got to stay here with them," Joe pointed out.

She nodded. "Houma will stay. He's done enough tonight."

Houma's expression was a cross between protest and relief. Still, he said, "I can give a good fight."

"No, she's right," Joe told him. "This is as far as the Company can go for now, and you might have to protect them and this camp. Marge and I will go. If we're not back by tomorrow evening, though, don't come after us. Do what you can for those two and get back. Ruddygore must know what happened to both expeditions."

Houma sighed. "I guess you're right. If you ain't back by this time tomorrow, poor Grogha will be dead, anyway, and I guess me on Posti and Macore on Dacaro—tied down if need be—could make it on the low road." He paused, then suddenly leaned over, kissed Marge, and gripped Joe's hand hard. "You two be careful. I already lost Grogha, I figure. I don't want to lose you, too."

"Neither do I, my friend," Joe answered sincerely, then looked around. "Where's Irving?"

The road went up through the pass, then down onto what appeared to be a wide plain. They knew that this was Starmount, the great plateau at twenty-eight hundred feet that stretched for almost seventeen miles westward into the interior of High Pothique. It was aptly named, with a full view of the sky and a great moon now far lower than it had been earlier in the night, but still bright enough to see by. The cave was supposed to be against the mountains to the right of the road, and they turned their horses northwest to hug the rocky side of Starmount.

In a short while they came upon the scene of an earlier battle. It was much as Houma had said, but they did not try to get close to see the grisly details. There were dark, four-footed animal shapes out there, and some snarling could be heard. Best to leave them alone, they decided.

And then, at last, they came upon the point where the mountain wall became smooth and sheer. They dismounted and looked across the way—a clear stretch of perhaps a quarter mile, with no cover whatsoever, to a dark spot at the base of the mountain wall.

"Right where it should be," he muttered, and she nodded. "That moon's getting awful low. Shall we ride or leave the horses here?"

"I think leave them," she told him. "I feel more confident on that open flat on foot—and without cover, there's no point to taking the horses, anyway."

"Speed," he pointed out.

"Yeah—and noise. They'll attract whoever killed those soldiers. And we'll have to tether them right outside the cave. We couldn't advertise better."

"You convinced me," He sighed, thinking of his aching side.

She thought of it, too, and handed him a gourd off her belt. "Here. Drink this. It will deaden the pain a little and give you some extra energy."

He took it gratefully, sipped it, almost spat it out, and said, "Yuck! This is as foul as sewage water!"

"Most of 'em taste awful, but they work. Drink it down."

He held his nose and finally managed it, making a terrible face afterward. But he had to admit that within two or three minutes he felt far better, with less pain and less tiredness. They gave a light tether to the horses, hoping it would keep them there but allowing them to pull free and run if spooked. There was nothing else they could do.

"Let's go—slowly and carefully—while we still have some moon," he said, and they were off.

There was an eerie stillness about the whole place, one that was more than a little unnerving, and they moved toward the cave, weapons drawn, looking in all directions, expecting something or someone to rise against them at any moment. But nothing did, and after a suspense-filled fifteen minutes, they were at the mouth of the cave itself.

Now that they were there, facing it, they could see that there was light inside. Torches flickered, not right near the entrance, but farther in, giving enough light for them to see but not to betray the cave to any distant onlooker.

"Looks as if we were expected," Marge whispered.

"Or our monster is scared of the dark," Joe replied. "Well, it's now or never."

She nodded. "I just wish somebody knew what this monster was."

They entered, Joe first, and kept cautiously to the walls of the cave. It was a narrow and winding entrance, but shortly it opened up, until they were on the edge of a huge chamber, perhaps half a mile across and almost that wide. It was here the torches were set against a far wall. There was a huge altar, and before it were stacked an enormous number of bodies of black, winged creatures. They stared at the scene, and Marge absently counted.

"There are more than fifty bodies there," she whispered to Joe. "No wonder the Xota are off licking their wounds somewhere. Those soldiers made them pay for the attack."

He nodded, looking at the altar itself. "That carved altar there. See the larger shape carved around it? Remind you of anything?"

She stared, then frowned. "A rabbit?"

"Yeah. A rabbit god. I'll be damned. Never heard of *that* one before."

At that moment they heard a fierce, screaming noise, like a beast in a terrible rage. There was no way to tell where it came from—the echoes in the cavern masked any source. Both of them tensed at the sound. "The monster," Marge breathed.

Joe looked around what he could see of the cave. "Say! Look—out there in the middle! Those are two of the soldiers' bodies! Some *did* get this far!"

Marge stared at the two forms. "They look squashed flat."

"Yeah . . . squashed." He looked around once more. "Where would you say they'd keep the Lamp?"

She shrugged. "The altar's the only place I can see that looks used."

He nodded. "And that's where the two soldiers lie—between here and the altar. But what kind of monster could do that? It looks as if they were swatted with a giant flyswatter."

Marge thought a minute. "Listen! You hear heavy breathing?"

"My heart's too loud," he responded. But now that she mentioned it, he *did* hear it. It sounded as if the whole cavern were breathing. "Still can't put a handle on where it is. But anything that big—we ought to be able to *see* it."

She sighed. "Maybe it's invisible. Well, I guess it's time to use one of those spells. I want to see what we're up against before going out there."

"What are you gonna do?"

"Dacaro figured we might be able to confuse a monster. If this spell works as advertised, you and I are going to walk across that cave in a couple of minutes—while we're both here."

"Huh?"

"Just shut up and watch." She turned to the cave, put her hands to her temples, and concentrated on the spell Dacaro had made her memorize. It had been easy to get a number of such spells while he'd been inside her head, and she had taken full advantage of the opportunity. The only trouble was, of course, that neither she nor Dacaro knew what spells would come in handy in an unknown situation—they had to guess.

The air shimmered in front of her, and slowly the images of two people faded in before them. As the images grew clearer, Joe could see that they were taking on the shapes of him and Marge.

In another minute the visions had solidified to the point where he could almost swear he was looking at himself and Marge. The illusion was, in fact, uncannily real. She sighed, looked up at them, and said, "Walk to the altar."

The two simulacra turned stiffly and started walking out onto the cavern floor toward the two squashed soldiers. Marge kept looking directly at them, which Joe understood was necessary to preserve the illusion, but he was under no such compulsion. He started looking around for the monster once more, hoping that it could be fooled by this trick.

Suddenly there was a roaring sound, the same as they'd heard before, followed by a sharp and sustained odd sound that reminded Joe of nothing more than a giant's fart. And down on the two replicas fell the great monster of the cave from its hiding place above.

"My god! It's a giant bunny rabbit!" Joe said, amazed.

"It's the biggest damn Texas hare I've ever seen," she ad-

mitted. The thing was *enormous*—twenty feet high, not counting the ears, and terribly muscular, the Mr. Hyde of hares. Its
face, too, was not the passive hare's face, but an ugly, contorted version; its large, yellow eyes were burning with fierce
hatred, and its two great buckteeth were flanked by saber-
toothed fangs.

Its giant legs struck the two replicas full, then did a dance
on top of them. Had they been real, it would have flattened
them for sure.

Marge wasted no more time keeping up the illusion, but
couldn't help staring at the rabbit, then up. "There are no
ledges up there for something that size," she noted. "Where
did it come from?"

The great hare god roared its conquest, then quieted and
glanced around. They ducked back for a moment into the cave
mouth and were certain they hadn't been seen. Joe peered out
again, just as the hare roared and screeched once more, looked
at the altar, roared at it, then did something that neither Joe nor
Marge expected.

Its great mouth opened, and it inhaled—and kept inhaling.
As it did, its great brown body seemed to fill up and stretch
like a balloon, until it was as big around as it was tall. And
with that, the enormous hare floated up the sixty feet or more
to the roof of the cave, becoming almost invisible in the darkness, its brown hair blending with the weathered limestone.

"So *that's* it," Joe breathed. "This is crazy. How can it float
up there like a helium balloon on just plain old air?"

"Because it's not a normal monster," she responded. "It's
some sort of magical creature, a demon, perhaps, in the form
of a hare. I was taught that true demons have no form. Their
form is made for them by the ones who bring them into the
world, and can be almost anything. Somebody, long ago, decided that the Xota people needed a god. Who knows? Perhaps
one of their most powerful magicians once tried to control a
demon, or accidentally let one in, and it took on the form of
the common hares that might be all over these parts. If it were
trapped here, this might be the result."

"That's all well and good, but how do we get this gasball
demon out of the way? Got any spells for that?"

She thought a moment, then looked up at the cave ceiling.
"I can see where it is now that I know what I'm looking for.

Hmmm . . . Well, disguising ourselves as Xota is out. I don't know how to do that one." She unhooked her crossbow from her belt and loaded a bolt. "But I think I can shoot it."

He whistled. "Man! If you miss—or if you only wound the thing—it will go nuts."

She nodded. "Don't I know it. But that's a chance we have to take. I'm pretty sure it's too big to get at us in here."

"Yeah—but it's loud enough maybe to bring the neighbors at our backs," he responded nervously. "Still, I don't have any better idea." He stopped a moment, thinking furiously. "Or do I?"

She turned to him. "Got something?"

"I doubt if an ordinary bolt would do it," he told her. "But if we could shoot Irving . . ."

She looked at him thoughtfully. "Yes. I think I *could* jury-rig it so that we could shoot the sword. But it would be terribly unbalanced, and so heavy it might not make the distance."

"I can always call it back to me," he assured her, then caught her frown. "What's wrong?"

"Joe—I can't touch that sword. You know that."

"That's all right. I've had training with the crossbow. Have I ever! Hand it to me—hey! Uncock it first! Yeah. There. Now—stand back."

He drew the sword and tried loading it in the simple cross-bow. He failed several times, and Marge felt frustrated that she dared not reach out and show him how to adjust it; but finally, with her coaching, he managed to load it and cock it. Still, it looked ridiculous and unwieldy. "I don't think it's going to work," Marge said worriedly. "The bow just wasn't designed for this."

"All it has to do is give Irv a boost," Joe assured her confidently. "This sword has a mind of its own. It won't fail." *I hope*, he added mentally. "Irving, speed true to your target and puncture it."

The sword seemed to glow slightly and hummed in response. Joe took a deep breath. "Well, here goes."

He stepped out into the cavern, looked up, spotted the quivering ball above, and took aim. "Hey! Gasball! Come and get it!" he yelled.

The hare god roared and started its drop. At that moment Joe lifted the bow and shot the sword right at the descending mass. The sword flew from the crossbow and, as Joe had said, seemed to take on a life of its own, flying straight and true. It was helped by the fact that the hare god was descending toward it, and the sword struck and penetrated the flesh of the horrible creature.

There was a loud bang, like a cannon shot, that almost broke their eardrums, and they yelled in pain. Joe was sure he was deaf. All around the cavern, however, bits and chunks of flesh fell in a grisly rain.

Ears still numb and ringing, Joe stepped into the cavern again, shouted, "Irving! To me!" and held out his hand.

From somewhere far across the cavern, the great sword hummed and flew like iron to magnet right into his hand.

Their sense of hearing returned slowly. "It burst like a balloon!" Marge laughed.

He nodded and grinned. "Yeah. That's all it really was. A big bag of air. Come on. That noise is bound to bring somebody curious. Let's get to the altar." They made it on the run.

The bodies of the gargoylelike Xota were grisly even without their gaping wounds and injuries, and they smelled as all decomposing flesh did, but Marge and Joe went around the large bier of dead to the stone hare itself, carved into the solid rock. Behind the bier were a lot of things, many of which looked quite valuable, but it was on the stone hare's "lap" that they saw what had to be what they sought.

"It looks just like Aladdin's Lamp in the old fairy tales," Marge noted. She bent over and picked it up. "I wonder if it currently has a genie? And, if so, how you get him—or her?"

"Rub it—right?" Joe suggested, remembering the stories.

"Yeah. Here. Let's see." She rubbed the Lamp—and, almost immediately, from the spout flowed an ethereal shape that took form as a young man dressed in odd, baggy clothes. He looked around and smiled.

"Well, I'll be damned! Somebody finally got it!" he exclaimed.

"You're the slave of the Lamp?" Marge asked. "This is the Lamp of Lakash?"

"Yes and yes," the man responded.

"And who are you?"

"I am Sugasto," he told her. "If that means anything to you after so long a time."

"Sugasto! Ruddygore's adept!" Marge cried. "So you *didn't* die!"

He sighed. "Hardly. I made a very stupid wish on it for power and wealth—and wound up having to travel to High Pothique to claim both. I got cornered by the Xota. They killed my horse, my companions, and their horses as well—it was pretty absolute—and they had me totally trapped. There was only one thing I could do, and that was to use the Lamp again. I wished that I would be safe from harm from the Xota—and got my wish, as you see. As the slave of the Lamp, I can not be harmed, because I'm basically a spirit, not solid at all. I just look that way. The second wish made me the genie, freeing a most unpleasant old woman who was immediately torn apart by the Xota. Of course, since they saw the old bag emerge from the Lamp and me flow into it, they knew it was magic—and so they brought it to their all-too-real god. I've been stuck in this damned hole ever since."

Marge thought a moment. "You've got to do whatever the possessor says, right?"

He nodded. "That's about it. Not much I *can* do, though, being a spirit."

"And I'm the possessor?"

"As of now. I can not tell a lie or fail to answer a question—to you."

She hooked the Lamp on her belt. "Well, come on, then. We have to get out of here—and fast."

"I go where the Lamp goes," Sugasto noted. "I have no choice."

They made their way across the cavern floor once more and around the narrow, winding entrance until they reached the cave mouth.

"Uh-oh. It's gotten to be daylight," Joe muttered. "That's bad. Even if the Xota didn't hear all that commotion, they're probably back now."

Marge turned to Sugasto. "How about it? Can you reconnoiter for us?"

"I can."

"Okay, do it. That's not a wish, now. Just an order."

"That's the way you play the game," he agreed and sped from the cave mouth out into the early morning. It didn't take him long to return.

"Well?" Marge demanded.

"You've got troubles," He sighed. "Half the Xota nation's out there right now. There are forty or fifty directly above the cave, ready to pounce on whoever comes out, and maybe six or seven hundred staked out along the two miles from here to the road."

She thought a moment. "We couldn't wish both of us back to our camp, could we?"

"You could," the genie replied, "if your camp's not more than forty or fifty miles from here. I can check. It would have to be within my range from the Lamp."

"It's at the trail junction outside the Gate," she told him. "Go."

In a flash he was off once more, and back within twenty or thirty seconds. "Yes, you can transport out. But as much as I would like you to overwish and free me, I don't want to suffer the fate of my predecessor—particularly not now that I'm out. You've got a small army of black and silver uniforms not ten miles farther on. Maybe a hundred pretty tough-looking soldiers. If you transport out, you'll be a sandwich between the Xota and the soldiers—who, I assume, are not your friends, considering the dead bodies around here."

"You're right about that," Joe agreed. "We'll fill you in on the political news later, though. Hmmm . . . What about sorcery? Anything we can do to trick those people conventionally? You were supposed to be an adept of some kind."

"I was pretty good," Sugasto huffed with pride. "But I'm way out of practice, and in this form I can't do anything, anyway."

"I can carry out your spells," Marge told him.

He looked surprised. "Can you, indeed?" He thought a moment. "Still and all, this isn't exactly a situation I can spell us out of. If I could, I wouldn't *be* here in the first place."

He had a point there. "That means the Lamp or nothing," Marge said, thinking furiously. "But I'll have to get the wish exactly right."

"And fast," Joe noted. "They won't wait all day without coming in to see if we got smashed by their god." He had to chuckle. "Wonder what they're gonna do for a religion when they find we popped him?"

"Quiet! I'm trying to think!" she snapped. She looked back up at the genie. "I don't suppose they left us our horses."

"Breakfast, I think," Sugasto replied ruefully. "Sorry."

She sighed. "Well, so much for that. Hmmm ... Wait a minute. How compound can this wish be?"

"Not too much," Sugasto told her. "One magical event, that's it. You can't wish yourself invincible, immortal, and rich all at the same time."

"All right. But could I wish for a *single* solution to the problem of *both* armed forces?"

Sugasto thought that one over. "Maybe. Depends on how you put it."

"I think I've got it. If not—Joe, it will be your turn."

"Go ahead," he invited. "I'm a little uncomfortable around that thing."

She held the Lamp tightly in both hands. "I wish that our entire Company would be rescued from all our enemies this day by a powerful force friendly to us."

"Done!" Sugasto shouted.

Outside, there was a sudden, tremendous roaring sound.

CHAPTER 15

FROM THE JAWS OF VICTORY

Companies must break up before an objective can be truly secured.
—XXXIV, 319, 251(b)

JOE HAD NO PARTICULAR TRUST IN WISHING LAMPS, BUT HE had to see what was going on out there regardless. Sword held at the ready, he approached the cave mouth from where he could see the plains of Starmount clearly. Marge came close behind him.

Just then a huge, dark shadow flew over the cave, and they heard another mighty roar and felt the heat of great flames not far away. Joe jumped back a bit. "Jeez! Did we get the Marines with napalm?" he wondered.

"No! We got Vercertorix!" Marge replied, pointing. Joe crept again to the cave mouth as a number of flaming bodies fell from atop the cave to the area just in front of them. Off in the distance, they saw the great form of the enormous dragon, wings spread, looking both noble and magnificent as it made pass after pass at the cave walls, occasionally bumping rock and starting landslides, but more often barbecueing the Xota with tremendous blasts of flame from its great mouth.

Some of the Xota, who were flying creatures themselves, took to the air and managed to get into a reasonable attack formation after the dragon had passed. Bows and spears at the ready, the Xota, perhaps fifty or sixty of them, waited almost suspended in midair for the great beast to turn once more and come swooping back in. The flying force could hardly hide themselves from the dragon, but they stood their ground and waited until they could almost feel the dragon's breath before letting loose their weapons.

"The little bastards have guts, I'll give 'em that," Joe muttered, fascinated. "It's like pygmies against an armored tank."

For a moment it almost seemed as if Vercertorix were going to fly directly into the formation, but at the last minute he pulled up and beat several times with his massive wings. The Xota tried to get off their arrows and throw their spears, but the downdraft the dragon caused was so tremendous that their formation was suddenly broken, sending them tumbling. Vercertorix, who'd expected that and planned it, did a magnificent loop-the-loop in the air and came back again on the same tack, now letting loose his flaming breath at the broken Xota formation. It was no contest, and more small bodies fell burning from the sky.

"How can something that huge fly that gracefully?" Marge asked, awestruck.

Joe was more pragmatic. "I couldn't care less—just so long as the Xota don't have a fair maiden to drag in front of him."

The dragon made one more sweep of the terrain, scattering the last of the Xota and making sure that no major force remained, then came in for a pinpoint landing near the cave.

"Hey! My friends! Are you still alive in there?" they heard a familiar voice call to them. "If so, come out by all means!"

Even Sugasto was impressed. "There's somebody *riding* that thing!"

"Algongua!" Marge cried. "It's the Doc, Joe!" She was ready to run to him, but Joe put out a hand and restrained her.

"Hey, Doc!" he called. "Won't Marge cause—problems?"

"I think not!" the hairy man called back. "Come and see!"

That was all they needed, and out they came. The dragon glanced over at them as they emerged, and looked a little dubiously at the woman but did not flee or yell.

"It worked! It worked!" Algongua exulted.

They came up beside the dragon and regarded the hairy man on its back. "*What* worked, Doc?" Joe asked.

"Therapy! We owe it all to you two, really. After six weeks of my treating him, it took only one look at the lovely lady here to cause a complete relapse. I was angry at the time, remember, but the more I thought about it, the more I was sure I'd been on the wrong track. You see, his fear stemmed from an encounter a few months ago with a powerful sorceress—young and beautiful-looking, too. She caused him some great pain, and that set up his problem. It really wasn't a fear of fair maidens at all—that was just a symptom. It was a loss of self-confidence! So, I reasoned, if I went with him and we eased into a battle, with me shouting encouragement and sharing the risk, it might restore him. And see? It worked!"

"Snarfle," the dragon agreed, nodding.

Marge frowned. "But now I *am* confused. Did my wish cause this to happen—or would it have happened, anyway, in which case I wasted it?"

"The Lamp is like that," Sugasto told her. "It's always a little perverse if it gets the chance. My guess is that reality was subtly altered with minimum—perhaps no—damage by your wish, which made this rescue possible, even inevitable. But we'll never really know."

Joe was more concerned with the reality of the dragon and the hairy scientist. "I thought you were the hermit, beyond battles and such."

Doc shrugged. "Maybe that's been my problem. I can divorce *myself* from the miserable world, but I can't divorce my patients and studies from it. Oh, well, it was fun, anyway."

"Marumph!" Vercertorix agreed.

Marge snapped her fingers. "I'd almost forgotten! This is only half the battle. A company of the Dark Baron's soldiers is almost to our camp now. Poor Houma's there with two very injured men!" She looked up at Algongua. "Can you stop them, too?"

The scientist thought a moment. "How about it, Vercertorix? Want to try some soldiers? The ones we saw on the way in?"

"Grausch!" the dragon responded, nodding slightly.

"All right. Why don't you three hop on—I think you can hang on here—and we'll drop you at your camp. Then we'll take care of those soldiers."

Marge turned to Sugasto. "Why not get back in the Lamp until we reach the camp?"

"Whatever you say," he responded, sounding a little regretful—and flowed back into the Lamp on her belt.

Algongua was fascinated. "A real genie! How *about* that! So that's what the old boy sent you for!"

"We'll talk later," Joe told him. "Give you the whole story. Let's get those soldiers first."

They linked up, Marge grabbing Algongua and Joe grabbing Marge. It was pretty nerve-racking when the dragon began to move and spread its massive wings, and even worse when the great head suddenly came up and they lifted, but in a matter of no more than two minutes they were level and headed at great speed toward Starmount Gateway.

In another minute, no more, the dragon reached the Gateway, circled once, and landed just down the trail from the junction camp. Joe and Marge wasted no time jumping off and getting away from the great beast, and Doc waited only long enough to assure Vercertorix clearance before taking off once again. Joe and Marge had to brace themselves to keep from being blown over by the backwash, but the dragon was soon up and out of sight.

They were less than half a mile from the camp and reached it quickly. Houma was both astonished and overjoyed to see them, and they were pleasantly surprised to find Macore sitting on a rock, smiling and waving to them.

"It will take more than a cracked skull to get me," the little thief told them. "Now if it had been any place other than my *head* . . ."

Marge was bubbling over to tell Houma and Macore about their adventures and reassure them about the dragon, and she was halfway through before she suddenly stopped and said, alarmed, "How's Grogha?"

Both the others' faces fell. "He's gone, lady," Houma said sadly.

"It was all for the best. He was in such great pain . . ."

She got up and walked over to the other side of the camp, where Grogha's body had been carefully wrapped in his bed-roll, and looked down at it. Tears welled up in her big eyes, not only for Grogha but also for her failure to remember him right from the start. Most of all, she was frustrated by the fact that she had the Lamp, but too late, too late . . .

"Damn!" she swore aloud. "I wish we'd been in time to save him!"

Suddenly she heard Sugasto cry exuberantly, "I'm free!" Then things happened too fast and too confusedly to be sorted out properly.

There was a blurring, a dizziness that overtook not only Marge but each of them, and then they were all there again, in the same places—but Grogha was no longer dead and wrapped, but lying there pretty much as they had left him, moaning and groaning in pain.

The Lamp fell from Marge's belt as if the loop had broken. She bent down, still confused, to pick it up and found that her hand went right through it. "What's happening?" she cried, in something of a panic.

A very solid Sugasto stood near her. "You made a second wish and it was granted," he told her. "Now you've paid the price for it. *You* are the slave of the Lamp."

Joe was over checking the supplies and, except for the slight dizziness, which he put down to lack of sleep, didn't seem aware that anything was wrong. Houma and Macore, however, *had* seen it and, while confused, went over to her and to the stranger now suddenly in their midst.

Sugasto pointed to the Lamp. "If you want to save your friend, pick up that Lamp, one of you, and wish him whole and healthy once more. I'd do it quickly—he won't last long, And since I can't use it or touch it ever again, it's only fitting that the lady's sacrifice not be in vain."

There was a greedy gleam in Macore's eyes as he realized what the Lamp was, but it was Houma who picked it up first, held it, turned to Grogha, and said, rubbing the Lamp, "I wish Grogha was whole and well, healed of all ailments and afflictions."

The bloody, broken body of Grogha shimmered, then solidified, and all traces of the illness, loss of blood, wounds, and lacerations were gone. He opened his eyes, looked confused, saw them all, shook his head, and said, "I—I had the most *horrible* dream . . ."

Houma was so pleased and excited that he dropped the Lamp and rushed to embrace Grogha, tears of joy in his eyes.

Seeing his opening, Macore grabbed up the Lamp, smiled, then turned to Marge. "Inside the Lamp until I call you out!" he commanded.

Suddenly she felt a tremendous force drawing her, like a vacuum cleaner, into the Lamp's mouth. It was a strange, eerie sensation, and the limbo in which she found herself was neither dark nor light, but an odd, formless land that went on and on. She could hear no sounds at all. No—wait. There *was* something. A voice. Macore's. He was talking to somebody— but she could not hear any response, none at all. She was attuned to his voice and his voice only. But something *was* happening to her . . .

Forms, concepts, and a great deal of information poured into her mind from out of nowhere, almost as if they had been there all along, but unknown and untapped until now. She knew everything there was to know about the Lamp of Lakash, its powers and limitations, and her own nature, bonds, and powers. She also suddenly knew the plane of existence she was now on and understood that it was not empty at all . . .

Macore stared suspiciously at Sugasto. "You were the genie?"

"But no more," The adept replied. "Nevermore. After a thousand years!" He sighed. "It's good to be alive once more, particularly with the new knowledge I've gained from the Lamp."

Macore looked crafty and thoughtful. "She was telling us before that wish that you were the guy who stole it in the first place. That true?"

Sugasto shrugged and bowed.

"You're some kind of adept, right?"

"Something like that," Sugasto agreed.

"Well, we're workin' for the guy you took it from. If you don't fancy meetin' up with him again, you better use what powers you got to get that guy Joe and these two off your back."

The adept thought about it. "And off yours?"

Macore grinned. At that moment Joe finished checking the supplies and walked back to them, looking confused. He didn't think Sugasto's appearance was unusual, since he didn't think of him as flesh and blood, but he glanced around. "Where's Marge?"

Sugasto smiled and made a few signs in the air in Joe's direction. Joe suddenly froze, then looked even more confused. "I forgot my train of thought! Damn!"

"You asked about Marge," Sugasto reminded him.

The big man frowned. "Marge? Who's that?"

"Nobody important," the adept responded smoothly, then turned and made the identical gestures in the direction of Houma and Grogha, who hardly noticed. "Why don't you see about Grogha?"

Joe nodded. "Yeah. Good idea." He walked over and bent down beside Grogha.

Macore looked impressed. "That's some trick."

"A simple one. It won't last long, you know. When the dragon returns, Vercertorix and Algongua will know, and it would take a lot more work to make them forget. The dragon is only here because of her—and so their return will precipitate a return of memory."

"But that could be any minute!" Macore protested. "Some trick!"

"There are other tricks," Sugasto bragged.

"Yes, there are," Macore agreed, touching the Lamp. He suddenly became stiff and glassy-eyed. "I wish Sugasto and Dacaro would exchange bodies, curses, and *geases*, and that Sugasto would then be subject to and obedient to Dacaro in all matters."

Nothing seemed to happen at all, but Sugasto's look of astonishment suddenly changed into a broad grin. He flexed his arms for a moment, then reached out and took the Lamp from the still-stiffened Macore. "Thank you, Macore," he said, his voice and inflection subtly altered. "I knew I could count on your greed to get this Lamp sooner or later."

He turned to the three men now excitedly talking to one another, oblivious of the little drama that had just taken place, bowed his head, and concentrated for a moment. Grogha, who was just getting to his feet, slumped down again, and Joe and

Houma fell into a heap on top of him, unconscious. The adept then turned back to Macore, pointed to the ground, and snapped his fingers, and Macore, too, collapsed.

Feeling satisfied, he walked over to the two remaining horses, the gray spotted Posti and the black stallion that was Dacaro, but who now looked at him with frightened and puzzled eyes. He carefully saddled Dacaro, then placed the Lamp in the saddlebag, got up on the horse, and turned to Posti, who stared back at him.

"Don't look so shocked, Posti, old friend. You can explain it all to them when they come to, which won't be very long from now. But tell them not to look for me. Warn them. I wish none of them harm, for they are good people, but I will do whatever I have to to protect myself—and I am now *very* powerful."

"Who are you?" the gray horse challenged. "And who's now inside Dacaro?"

The man sighed. "You never *were* too bright, were you? While in the mind of Marge to heal Macore, I was able to cast spells—and I cast one on Macore, certain that the opportunistic little thief wouldn't rest until he'd gotten his hands on the Lamp. I triggered it, and dictated his wish, from my own mind. I'm your old friend Dacaro, Posti, and I have no intention of letting that bastard Ruddygore keep me a horse." With that he reined around, then urged the horse forward, riding off on the upper trail.

Posti was still confused, and tried to sort it out in his mind. For a moment he considered chase, but realized that, alone, the way he was, he had little chance of it. He remembered that upper trail, though. There was no way off until almost to Kidim. Dacaro might think he was smart, but he was trapped.

Joe, Grogha, and Houma came out of it rather quickly, as did Macore. Of them all, only Macore realized what had been done, and he was none too anxious to tell anybody about it.

Doc Algongua had brought them around when he returned and found them out. He was no slouch on practical magic, either, it seemed. Sorting it out, even with Posti's help, wasn't quite so easy.

"So Dacaro planned all along to steal the Lamp," Joe said, shaking his head. "Ruddygore never *did* trust him. But Marge did—more and more. We needed his knowledge. And all he did was lead us on until he had what he wanted. But—where will he go now?"

Algongua thought a moment. "Not back to Ruddygore, that's for sure. You remember he added that bit about transferring *geases*?"

They all nodded.

"That means he's freed from any obligation to get that Lamp back to Ruddygore. Sugasto—the real one—now has the *geas*, much to his discomfort, probably, but he's totally subject to Dacaro's orders. I would say that Dacaro has no intention of using his wish any time soon, and he's got enough power and self-control not to waste it. That means he's got some greater game in mind."

Joe thought a minute. "Marge said the whole thing between him and Ruddygore was over his trying to smuggle a gun into this world." Briefly he explained what a gun was, and Algongua seemed to get the general idea. "That means either he's going to use his wish to open up the route between my old world and this one to him, or he's going to the Dark Baron."

"Probably both," Doc replied. "He can't ally himself with Ruddygore or with anybody who's a friend of Ruddygore's. Any member of the Council he might turn to would demand the Lamp and would then have him. That leaves the Baron. He's got a lot to offer. His own considerable powers, the Lamp, and the way to the other world, a world he knows and has been to."

"Poor Marge," Joe sighed. "Trapped in that Lamp as a genie. Slave to his wishes." As Sugasto had predicted, memory had returned with the dragon's arrival.

"Well, she can't help us—or herself," Doc noted. "Looks as if I'm going to be involved more than I figured. Vercertorix and I will go the length of the upper trail and see if we can pick them up. His powers will be few against a true dragon."

They all brightened. "Yeah! He wouldn't have figured on the dragon! He thinks he's left us here with one horse!"

"Well, he's got several surprises," Algongua told them. "First of all, you ought to be able to pick up a soldier's horse or two or three not too far down from here. We finished them, but a number of horses escaped unharmed." He sighed. "I'm afraid I may have made another mistake about Vercertorix. Now that he's had two battles, he wants more. It's like eating peanuts—he just doesn't want to stop. I'm afraid he wants to get into the war itself now."

They searched what they believed to be every inch of the upper trail, and the lower one, too, but found no trace of the elusive Dacaro. He was incredibly powerful in the magical arts, that was clear—so much so that Ruddygore had not trusted him with the human form to operate his skills. Now he was joined with an adept of additional great powers subject to his command—Sugasto, in the body of the horse, whose skills and knowledge could be called upon when needed, as Marge had used Dacaro.

About the only solace Joe took from any of it was that Sugasto had thought he'd been freed and now he was captive and slave once more. He certainly deserved it, as much as Dacaro did, but there was little real comfort in that knowledge. Marge was still captive, and Dacaro had all the high cards in his favor.

After getting Vercertorix to scare a few of the runaway horses toward them, Joe bade Algongua fly to Terindell with the news, taking Macore with him. What was left of the Company would return by trail and, hopefully, pick up Dacaro's tracks somewhere.

For Dacaro's part, the spells of concealment and invisibility had been simplicity itself. He was confident that, while they might follow him, even chase him, he was more than a match for the lot of them. His only fear was that Ruddygore would get personally involved.

The first night, he rubbed the Lamp and brought forth Marge, mostly to have conversation with somebody other than the seething Sugasto. He saw, somewhat to his surprise, that she had changed more physically. She was somehow less human-looking, more exotic than ever; her complexion was becoming a light brown, and the webbing between her fingers and toes was nearly complete. Her nails, too, were becoming harder, thicker, more animallike, and sharp. All of which meant nothing as long as she was in spirit form, unable physically to manipulate any material thing in the real world, but it fascinated him nonetheless that the process continued even in this state.

She was, of course, by no means very happy with him, and he finally got tired of her cracks and ordered her to speak only when spoken to. Ever obedient as required, she shut up, but couldn't disguise her contempt for him regardless.

"Sugasto tells me that those of the Lamp don't live inside it, but rather on a different plane," he said. "Is that true?"

"It is," she told him. "The land of the djinn. It is fascinating."

"Tell me about it. Describe it."

"What you ask is not possible. There aren't any words for it. The frame of reference is different. It's like trying to describe our three-dimensional universe to a one-dimensional being. It took me a while just to be able to perceive it myself. Even now, I'm not sure what it is or what I'm perceiving, and I certainly have no way of describing it. There is no way to relate it to anything we know or experience."

"So even the command of the master of the Lamp has limits," he muttered. "You can't tell about what you have no frame of reference to relate to. Still, there is intelligence there—and knowledge?"

She nodded. "Vast knowledge. Since the realm has no physical existence at all, as we know it, it is a realm of pure magic. But the Lords of the Djinn impart little they don't wish to impart."

"The Lords of the Djinn . . ." he repeated thoughtfully. "I wonder. I have heard of their realm and of them, but I had no idea that the Lamp was a gateway to it. In the end, the entire Council studied there before becoming the most powerful. Yet I find Sugasto's added knowledge from that realm to be mostly petty or useless. Is it so with you?"

"It's not much," she admitted. "They are mostly concerned with my triple nature—from another universe and a changeling. Still, I find my mind much clearer on magical principles and procedures, and my understanding of spells and incantations is far greater, even for the short time I've been there. It's like learning a foreign language, I think. The best way to learn one is total immersion—going into an environment in which only that language you wish to learn is spoken. Substitute magic for language and you get the idea. When magic is everything, learning is easier—and you learn or you go nuts."

He nodded. "Do they have a sense of what is going on here?" he asked her. "The battle between the Dark Baron and the rest?"

"They know of the battles between the greater forces, Heaven and Hell, and that's all that concerns them. They take no sides because they feel no threat from either side. Nor will they deliberately help, hurt, or in any way interfere with events here. That's in the laws of magic they obey."

He shook his head in satisfaction. "That's good enough for me. I would like to go there sometime and see and learn for myself. But, as of now, I know of only one way to do that— and I am not willing to make *that* kind of sacrifice. There is another way later. Perhaps the Baron will complete my training to the point where I can go on my own."

He ordered her back into the Lamp and got some sleep.

Even a man with Dacaro's considerable powers was still a physical and mortal being. As such, he required the same three days back that he'd needed getting to the Gateway, and he also required food, shelter, and rest. He risked Kidim because he had to, but used a spell to alter his features subtly so that they might not betray him to later inquisitors.

Kidim, however, was more crowded than usual, he found. More of the black-liveried soldiers were about, mostly relaxing as they waited for the rest of their parties to return from Starmount, still ignorant that those parties would never return.

After a day or so in the town, he had a good idea of who was who among the Baron's forces, and had overheard a hundred conversations. He was satisfied and confident enough to approach an officer of the rear guard.

"I'm an adept, formerly with Ruddygore," he told the man, a Captain Thymir. "We have had a falling-out. In the meantime, I have acquired something that your master wishes very much."

The captain was distrustful. "How do we know you're not a spy or double agent?"

Dacaro chuckled and, in the privacy of his room, showed the captain the Lamp and brought forth its increasingly exotic and beautiful genie. The captain was convinced and very impressed, but discovered quickly that Dacaro was no pushover.

If the Lamp were to be taken from the adept, it would have to be by one far more powerful in sorcery than Dacaro himself.

"All right," the captain said, after being forced within a hair-breadth of spitting himself on his own sword, "what is it you wish?"

"Safe and rapid passage from here to your lines," Dacaro told him. "After that, as soon as practical, an audience with the Baron himself."

The captain thought a moment. "All right. I think it can be arranged. We'll take one of the boats downriver tomorrow. All I can promise, though, is to get you to somebody higher up. I've never even seen the Baron myself, so I haven't the slightest idea of how to go any further."

Dacaro nodded. "That is satisfactory. But I remind you of my own powers. Any attempt on me will bring a most unpleasant slow death. Do you understand me?"

The captain looked at his sword, on which he was so recently almost impaled against his will, and shivered. "Don't worry. As much as we want that Lamp—who wouldn't?—I'm not about to go after it. But I'd suggest you keep it hidden. I'll tell no one else until I report to my superiors, understand?"

"Agreed," Dacaro said. "Oh—my horse must go along. Can you manage that?"

"If you speak the truth about our men, I can," the captain responded. "The way you tell it, we won't have nearly so many goin' back."

A day before Joe and the remaining Company reached Kidim by the lower road, Vercertorix returned—but the rider was not Algongua.

"Poquah!" Joe shouted. "Are we glad to see *you*!"

The impassive Imir looked his usual grim self. "Had we time, it should have been and would have been the Master himself. But there is a great battle shaping up, perhaps only days away, possibly only hours. If he were here tracking down the traitor, he would get satisfaction, and probably the Lamp, but it might cost the war."

"You'll do," Joe told him. "Where do we start?"

"First I'm sending Vercertorix back to Dr. Algongua, who is still at Terindell," the Imir said. "Although I have never heard of a dragon of Husaquahr taking part in the wars of men and fairy folk before, this one seems most eager, and we are happy to get him. Then we four will go into Kidim. It is certain that our man stopped there, although probably in good disguise. I think I can penetrate it, even if he has already flown."

Their return to the town was hardly welcome news to the townspeople, but was final confirmation to the soldiers, too, that what Dacaro had told their captain had been correct. They were too far from their forces to cause trouble in Kidim now, though, and so they made preparations to leave and return. They, too, had gotten word of an impending battle.

Joe, Grogha, and Houma let the Imir do all the detective work. It was magic they needed to penetrate, and magic was Poquah's game. It didn't take him long, either. They were never certain of his methods, but he was most thorough and positive.

"Dacaro is here, and he and the horse are on one of the transports in the lake below," Poquah told them.

Joe jumped up and grabbed his sword hilt. "Well, let's get down and find him then!"

Poquah sighed. "Your heart and spirit are commendable, but your common sense is addled. There are still seventy of the enemy against us four. Dacaro, being of mortal stock, also has the edge in any magical confrontation with me, our relative powers being equal. And he has the Lamp, against which even the Master might have problems if the wish were suitably nasty and well phrased, as it would be. I know this Dacaro. He is a terribly dangerous man, all the more so for being sincere. He believes the modernization of Husaquahr is a cause, a way to lift the people into a better life. As a result, he sees himself as the good side in this contest and is willing to go to any lengths to achieve his goal. In this he is much like the Baron, who is also self-deluded yet quite sincere."

"I like things simple. You're complicatin' everything up too much," Houma grumbled. "The bastard's an evil traitor. If I get the chance, I'm gonna cut his throat."

"Me, too," Grogha added.

The Imir shrugged. "Have it your own way. I agree he must die. But don't confuse what I say with what must be done. He *is* evil, and he flees to an evil master, but no evil leader ever thinks he is evil. The subtleness of Hell in this world or any other is that it is always built on good intentions. That is why it is so pervasive."

Joe understood him, but the other two remained unconvinced. "Still," the big man asked, "if we can't go after him now, what *can* we do?"

"We must take him when he is least prepared," the Imir responded. "Therefore, we must first find out on what boat he sails, and follow that boat and its occupants. If we have no opportunity before to get at him, we must continue to follow him—all the way to the Dark Baron himself, if need be." He looked at Houma and Grogha. "But not all of us. The two of you—with Posti—should join our forces. This is not a job for all of us—our chance of discovery and betrayal is too great."

Both men protested vigorously, but Poquah was adamant, and they accepted his decision with a lot of grumbling. The Company had been dissolved. Now Joe and Poquah must go with the enemy to catch a powerful fish.

CHAPTER 16

THE DARK BARON

Those aligned with evil may cheat, but must always leave an opening, however tenuous, for the virtuous.

—II, 112

POQUAH'S MAGIC MADE THE SOLUTION TO THEIR PROBLEM OBvious. Knowing that a force of this size probably would have been put together only for this mission, and thus not everybody would know everybody, the Imir cast a spell on both him and Joe so that they appeared to be common soldiers to everyone who looked at them. And, with that, they simply joined formation and marched onto one of the boats when the main force was withdrawn.

It was not the boat with Dacaro aboard, but Poquah was relieved at that. "These disguises are more than sufficient for man or fairy," he told Joe, "but a good adept would see through them in an instant. Best we do not get too close to him until we are ready to strike."

"It's lucky that most folks aren't magical, or I'd feel down-right uncomfortable," Joe noted.

"You would feel more than that, my otherworldly friend," the Imir responded. "This place would be an insane asylum. It almost is now."

They sailed down the Sik and joined the River of the Sad Virgin, still pretty much in neutral territory. But the four boats pulled in before they reached the Dancing Gods, and crews busily changed the appearance of two, adding camouflaging, redistributing and adding masts, and repainting. It was clear that the boats were designed and the crews were trained for this sort of thing. By the end of the day, they looked like two merchant freighters, exactly what they should be in this kind of commerce, and flew the Kidim flag and sail markings.

Neutral merchants.

The soldiers, too, changed their uniforms for civilian clothes, those of merchants, sailors, and the like, causing Poquah to have to alter his spells as well. Particularly interesting was the fact that the soldiers' beards were shaved and their hair trimmed short. Now they hardly matched any description of the soldiers seen at Kidim.

Poquah had used his powers of persuasion to find out as much information as was known. Of the four boats, they were on the third in the convoy, while he was quite certain from the crew's comments that Dacaro was on the boat directly in front of them. Joe, in fact, was certain that he spotted the black stallion with the others in the rear tethering area. But their boat was not one of the ones changed.

Four boats had left, but now crews and passengers consolidated into the two that looked like Kidim's. With over a hundred and fifty of the company missing, it was no real crowd—and it made their progress down the river less conspicuous. The other two, including the one they'd been on, were scuttled.

Now they found themselves on the suspect boat and had to be careful. It took Poquah no time at all to establish that there was, indeed, a very special passenger none had seen, staying in the captain's cabin. It was all very mysterious, but the troops were good soldiers who asked few questions and started lots of wild rumors.

"Maybe we'll get lucky," Joe said hopefully to the Imir. "I mean, maybe we'll get overhauled and taken."

"I doubt it. First of all, our side has a weak navy with little experience. I suspect these two crews are more than a match for any on the other side. But in any event, I hope not. That would simply force him in to the open, and he still has his wish. That's his insurance policy in case the Baron proves less than accommodating."

"But Ruddygore said either he *or* the Baron could probably negate the Lamp," Joe pointed out. "Some insurance."

"That's true if it is used against them," the Imir agreed. "But it need not be so. It can be used to elevate Dacaro's status."

"I just wish there was some way to get to him."

"He never leaves the cabin. His meals are brought in. Yesterday I volunteered for galley duty, with the thought of poisoning the food he eats."

"And?"

"I succeeded. But there is no report of any problems, so he apparently has a routine cleansing spell in use, as I feared. So far he has made no mistakes. The spells on the cabin are so strong he would have a lot of warning, even if a member of the Council went to work on them, and I am far lower than that. We will have to wait. Sometime, somewhere, he *must* make a mistake."

Joe understood that this was more a hope than a certainty. Where was his great luck now, all of a sudden? So far it had saved his neck, but had mostly aided the wrong side.

It was another three days of hazardous travel downriver once they reached the Dancing Gods. Below the Sad Virgin, the river meandered all over the place and had countless bars, eddies, and islands. It took a tremendous amount of skill, experience, and flawless navigation to get through the extremely long stretch, and Joe's admiration for the crew transcended his loyalties.

Now they passed the Dabasar, and the River of Dancing Gods was more than three miles wide and tremendously deep but, if anything, even more treacherous, since they were now within the flood plain, and the annual great flooding always changed the river's course and nature.

Poquah was a little concerned in the later stretches. They were deep within the enemy's area of control, and he was afraid that, on horse detail, he had been penetrated by the equine Sugasto. He did not tell Joe, who was worried enough, and hoped that, if true, the ancient adept either would think nothing of someone with a disguise spell or would keep quiet. Sugasto had no love for Dacaro, certainly, and although he was bound to do his bidding, there was no need to volunteer information.

Before nightfall they made their landing. Joe and Poquah were both relieved—at least now their quarry would have to reveal himself.

Their patience did not go unrewarded. Late in the evening, the captain came on deck, followed by a mysterious-looking stranger in dark clothing. He didn't look quite like Sugasto, whose body Dacaro wore, but Poquah was no more easily fooled than Dacaro would have been in spotting him. He did not allow that spotting to occur, though, and Dacaro certainly had no reason to be suspicious of enemies from Ruddygore at this stage. The adept would be much more concerned with treachery by the Dark Baron and his men.

Joe and Poquah ducked out of sight as the two men walked back, selected their horses, then led them off the gangplank to shore.

"If they're going far, we'll have to steal some horses," Joe noted. "And it's gonna be hard not to get pressed into duty around here."

"Has my magic failed you yet?" the Imir asked him, and together they slipped off the boat.

The two men made no move to mount their horses, but continued to follow a road from the river landing for a few hundred yards, leading their mounts. Soon they were in the midst of a huge tent city, flags of many nations and peoples flying before them, and a lot of hectic activity that actually helped conceal the pursuers' true nature.

The captain and the dark stranger reached one particular tent, not very distinguishable from the others but flying no flag, and tethered their horses in front. The captain walked over to the guard at the entrance and whispered a few words. The guard nodded, and the two men entered the tent.

"The captain has already sent runners on ahead," Poquah told Joe. "It is certain that they wait here for the Baron himself, when he can spare the time from battle preparation. I think we must move before the Baron gets here—or we will be totally outgunned."

They turned off the main path to the tent and walked casually around in back, making their way closer and closer by a circuitous route. So far, nobody had paid them the slightest attention, and they were able to reach the rear of the tent they sought without problems. They bent down to see if they could perhaps get a piece of tent up and crawl under, but as they did so, something fell on both their heads and they went out like a light.

They came to in the tent. Both Joe and Poquah had been stripped naked, and hung from a support beam by thick ropes tied to their wrists.

In the center of the tent was a plain oak table and a few chairs. The captain from the boat stood near the doorway opposite them, putting down a large bundle of stuff on the tent floor—Joe saw that it was their clothing and swords, Irving included.

The other man, whom they now recognized as Sugasto—at least in body—looked at them and smiled. The precious Lamp of Lakash hung on his belt.

"I see you're awake," Dacaro said cheerfully. "You went to so much trouble that I thought you should not be denied meeting the Dark Baron. And you, Imir—you'll find your magic nullified quite handily. I've learned a few new tricks since we studied together at Terindell."

The Imir's face contorted with rage and contempt, the first display of pure emotion Joe had ever seen on the creature, and he spat in Dacaro's direction. "You bastard! The Master was too kindhearted, but most certainly correct about you. You are unworthy to lick his shoes!"

Dacaro shrugged. "New ways are coming, Poquah. The best of the old with the new technology from the other world. Neither you nor Ruddygore can cling to your power much longer and you know it. The new ways we will introduce will break your feudal hold on the oppressed people of this land."

"And replace them with a newer and even more bitter oppression," Poquah shot back.

"We'll see. Or, at least, *I'll* see. I doubt if you two will have to worry about things one way or the other. Oh, by the way—I spotted you the first night you came aboard our boat. Or, rather, Sugasto did. He doesn't like me very much, for some reason, but he fears the wrath of Ruddygore far more. That's why he's where he is and I am where I am. I am neither fearful nor in awe of Ruddygore. He represents a dying and bankrupt way of life."

At that moment there was a commotion outside, and into the tent burst an awesome figure. He was enormous, towering over the others—but still below the suspended captives. He wore a full set of shiny black armor covering every part of his body, including gloves and a fighting helmet, visor down, whose aspect was cast in the shape of a terrible demon. He had the kind of commanding presence that seemed inborn, that of regal bearing and total self-confidence. Even masked and featureless, the Dark Baron captured everyone's immediate attention. Dacaro seemed slightly awestruck by the presence, which was a far cry from the fat and slovenly Ruddygore.

The Baron wasted no time getting to the point. "You have the Lamp of Lakash," he said to Dacaro in a deep, commanding voice that Joe couldn't help comparing to one electronically disguised—although that was obviously impossible. "I am here to receive it."

Dacaro was certainly awestruck and totally aware that he was facing someone as far beyond him as Ruddygore was beyond Joe, but not so awestruck as to buckle under. The stakes were too high here. "I have the Lamp, my lord, here. It is my intent to present it to you—but I must have certain assurances of my own before I do."

The Baron seemed slightly amused. "You propose to *bargain* with me? I do not drive bargains to receive what is mine by right. And, since you are here in my camp and in my presence, you are in a poor position to bargain."

"I am Dacaro, formerly adept to Ruddygore," he began, but the Baron cut him off.

"I know exactly who you are and what you are. I have no time to dawdle or dicker. The battle begins with the dawn and I must be there. You will hand me the Lamp *now*."

Dacaro gave a slight smile. "I wish you would accept my terms and conditions for handing it over," he said mildly.

The Baron started a bit. "So you have not yet used the Lamp. Very well—what terms do you suggest?"

"I wish to have my training completed so that I may be elevated to full rank and initiated as a true sorcerer. Then I would aid you as, say, sorcerer to one of the armies, in the balance of the war. After we are victorious, I would like to be installed at Terindell."

The Dark Baron chuckled. "Only that, huh? You wish to be elevated to the Council and replace Ruddygore. Well, my treacherous friend, we see no reason for trusting traitors. The man who would so willingly betray Ruddygore for such power has no honor, and without honor he would as lief betray any lord and all oaths of fealty and allegiance. *I will take that Lamp now!*"

The veneer of self-confidence Dacaro had worn now crumbled in total confusion. "But—but I *wished*! You can't go against the *wish*!" He took a step backward and looked about nervously. "Slave of the Lamp! Attend me!"

Smoke poured out of the Lamp and congealed into the figure of Marge. Joe was struck by how much she'd changed, but he was too concerned with the drama being played out in front of him to think much about that right now.

Dacaro looked at Marge. "Why didn't it give me my wish?" he demanded.

Marge seemed to take some satisfaction in her answer. "Because this is not the Dark Baron," she told him, "but another in his armor. And the other within is not of this earth, nor of any earthly kingdom, and, as such, is not bound by the Lamp at all."

The Baron's hands went to the demonic helmet, unfastened it, and lifted it off, showing the head beneath. It was the same as the mask—a terrible, demonic face, only not fashioned by craft of metal but in a blue-black, leathery skin. "I am Hiccarph, Prince Regent of Hell," the creature told him. "The Baron sends his regrets, but he has a war to fight," And then the demon prince laughed.

Dacaro screamed. "No! No! I wish you back to Hell! Begone!"

"Free!" Marge, breathed and stepped back from the two now facing each other.

Dacaro gave a laugh. "You haven't won me, Prince of Hell! I go to the land of the djinn!" And, with that, he faded into smoke and poured back into the Lamp, which had dropped on the floor of the tent with his second wish.

The demon just stood there a minute, thinking. He moved, then, to get the Lamp and picked it up.

Joe realized that, because he was hanging so high, the demon's head was now between his hand and Irving. Held painfully by the wrist, he nonetheless managed to open his hand. The magic sword was on the floor, with Poquah's weapon and their clothing. The idea had come into his head from the start, and now was the first and perhaps only time it might work. With a little silent prayer he yelled, "Irving! To me!"

The sword flew from the bundle of clothes right at the demonic head, striking it and knocking the creature back, then continued onto Joe's hand. With a flip of the wrist that was tremendously painful, he brought the blade around and it sliced neatly through the rope. One arm free, he brought the blade up and cut through the other rope, falling to the floor.

The demon had been knocked over, losing the Lamp, but now the terrible creature rose to its feet. Its face was the face of nightmare, its power something that could be felt by all in the room.

Marge dived, scooped up the Lamp, and pitched it to Joe.

The demon got to his feet, smiled, and said, "Now feel the powers of Hell, mortal!" He threw out his hand and Joe instinctively drew back—but nothing happened.

The demon looked puzzled. "What in . . . ?"

Joe gave him no more time. "I wish all in this room and its contents were now with Ruddygore!" he yelled, holding the Lamp.

In a moment, they all winked out of the tent.

To say that Ruddygore was shocked and surprised was an understatement. One moment he had been alone in his tent thirty miles across the Valley of Decision from the enemy army, meditating for added powers, when suddenly in popped Joe, Marge, Poquah, a strange soldier looking scared to death, and a full suit of the Dark Baron's armor.

Joe whooped and hollered, waved his sword in the air, then tossed the Lamp to the astonished Ruddygore. "It worked! We did it!"

It was Marge's and Poquah's turn to be astonished. "But—how?" they both asked at the same time.

The black-clad captain, still in a state of shock, looked around fearfully and squeaked, "I surrender! Won't somebody accept my surrender?"

Ruddygore was the first to regain some sense of self-control. He walked over to the fearsome armor, kicked it, and frowned. It was empty. He turned to the captain. "Just put your sword over there and sit down like a good fellow," he told the frightened soldier. "We'll get around to you when everything's sorted out." The captain complied.

"Now, then," the sorcerer continued, "Just what *is* going on here?"

As quickly as possible, the three sketched the events in the tent. Ruddygore listened attentively. Finally he nodded his head affirmatively and sighed. "Well, I think I can at least explain it. The Baron, knowing that he was vulnerable to a well-stated wish even if he could block moves against himself with the Lamp, drew upon his ultimate power and raised Hiccarph. Now, Hiccarph's powers are quite limited on this plane—he has, in fact, no more real existence than the genies of the Lamp—but he could move that suit of armor and, most important, he was totally invulnerable to any magic of Husaquahr. Using the armor, he could pick up the Lamp and take it to his ally. When you summoned Irving, Joe, the sword struck the upper part of the armor. In the summons it was an irresistible force—so the armor went sprawling. That was quick thinking, by the way."

"I'd hoped it would run the Dark Baron through, damn it," Joe muttered.

"Be content. This was a major victory from the very brink of total defeat. It's a good thing I wasn't in Terindell, though—or you and the Lamp would have gotten there, but not the rest. I shudder to think what might have happened to you."

Marge frowned. "But the Lamp was completely powerless against this demon! And he seemed amazed to be powerless against *us*!"

Ruddygore nodded. "The forces of Hell would not be directly subject to any of the Laws or Rules, because they have no physical existence on this plane. They must work through humans—in this case the will of the Baron that placed

Hiccarph in that armor. But as to why Hiccarph had no power over you, Joe—it was because you are not a native of this world. Your soul is still your soul, and it is of a different place. Hiccarph was summoned by a native of this world and, as such, he was attuned totally to the things of this world. Since he had no physical being beyond the armor, he could only reach out for your soul—but he was wrongly attuned. That's the best way I can put it. On your native world he would have plucked your soul from your body and carried it with him back to Hell itself. But *here*—let's just say he was on the wrong frequency. That's what I counted on. It is the extra edge you and Marge have over anyone else." He paused a moment. "I fear it will also mean both of you are now marked. Hiccarph and his bosses will never rest until they know why they failed against you. They will be after you."

Joe grinned. "Let 'em come! We faced down the Prince Regent of Hell a few minutes ago." He leaned over, grabbed a startled Marge, and kissed her on the lips. "We're ready for *anything* now." He paused and looked at her and smiled. "Welcome back to the land of the living."

She smiled and patted his hand. "What of Dacaro?" she asked. "He's now in the land of the djinn."

"And there he'll stay," Ruddygore assured her. "Nor will he get what he seeks there. They will string him along, but give him nothing of substance. And one day I will pay him a visit there, and he will learn that the Lords of the Djinn may be disinterested in our affairs but *do* value old friendships."

A military officer entered, bowed slightly, and said, "Sir—it will be dawn in less than half an hour. Lord Kasura awaits your pleasure."

Ruddygore turned and looked suddenly very tired. "Tell him I will be there straightaway." He turned back to Joe, Marge, and Poquah. "The three of you have done what you can, and it is more than any man had a right to expect. Get something to eat at the mess tent—anyone will be able to tell you where it is—and then get some rest. The outcome of this day will no longer depend on your labors, but our cause has certainly been fortified by your deeds."

Poquah, who was pulling on his clothes, said, "Master, I will be with you. My place is not to rest during a battle."

"As you wish, old friend. But ours is a different sort of battle from what those brave ones will face."

"I can still fight," Joe told him, and Marge nodded as well.

"No. It is time for the professionals now. A battle requires planning and discipline, and you were not a part of the training. Remain here, or go up the heights nearby at the command post and watch it unfold as best you can. But fight not today—unless we are lost and overrun." And, with that, he turned and left, Poquah following, trying to get his pants fastened.

The captain stirred in the corner. "Won't somebody take my surrender?" he pleaded.

Joe looked at him. "Go. On your word of honor, go to the river and join your own forces, but do not fight us until you are with your own."

The captain shook his head from side to side. "Oh, no. I'm going to surrender. *I looked into that thing's eyes.*"

Joe sighed. "Then turn yourself in to the captain of the guard. I'm sure they'll have a place to accommodate you." Then they, too, walked out, leaving the prisoner alone.

The found the officers' mess tent with no trouble. They filled plates from a cauldron of scrambled eggs, and Joe, at least, took slices from the roast of pork on a spit as well. Both sipped abnormally strong black coffee.

After a while they felt somewhat themselves again and began to relax a bit, although the tension throughout the camp was too thick to ignore. Still, in the moments before things broke loose, Joe took advantage of the little time remaining. "Well—you sure have changed, that I'll say."

She looked a little embarrassed. "The djinn accelerated the process. It was only a few days, but time there didn't pass like time here."

He nodded, although he didn't quite understand. Certainly her short pageboy hair was now down to her shoulders, and was a true silver color except for the ever-present streak in the middle, now a burnt orange. Her elfin ears stuck out cutely, and it seemed that her whole face and figure radiated an unnatural sexuality. Her figure had become so exaggerated that the clothes she wore bulged and pulled, and he knew they wouldn't last long. "You're going to have a hard time with that nun's vow," he noted playfully.

She sighed. "I know. But maybe that's for the best. Huspeth will never understand, though."

His brows went up. "Then she didn't do this?"

"No. Ruddygore lies when it's convenient. It's his sort of practical joke on Huspeth, I think. I can see why people get irritated with him."

"So you're still glad you hitched a ride?"

She smiled. "Very glad, Joe. Very glad. And you?"

"I'm beginning to get the hang of this place. I think maybe I'll stay a while. Have you thought of what you're going to do—after today? Assuming we win, of course, and we aren't on the run."

She shrugged. "I don't know. I'd like to go to the realm of faërie for a bit, to complete this and to learn more about what I am and what it all means. That will determine the future, more or less, I guess. But I haven't had my fill of this land. I'd like to see all of it someday. What about you?"

He shook his head. "I don't know. I think I can hold my own here now. I guess maybe I'd like to travel, too. Just sort of let things take me along, like that river out there. Go with the current and the flow and see where I wind up."

"Still—we made a hell of a good team, didn't we, Joe?"

He grinned. "We sure did, Marge."

Trumpets sounded across a broad area outside and seemed to echo and go on forever. Officers still in the mess grabbed their weapons and ran out, while the cooks started frantically cleaning up the place. Drums began to beat, and there was the sound of massive numbers of horses and men moving into positions.

Joe sighed. "I think I'd like to see this battle."

She nodded. "Me, too."

With that, they got up and walked out into the breaking dawn.

CHAPTER 17

THE BATTLE OF SORROWS GORGE

*Although magic may play a significant part in any battle, victory
must be secured by soldiers supported by sound strategy.*
                                                    —XIX, 301, 2

"NOW IS THE TIME FOR SWORDS AND SORCERY!"

With that ritualistic exhortation required by the Rules, the
commanders of both forces urged their men into battle.

From the heights overlooking the great battlefield, the leaders of the northern countries watched and plotted. Behind
them, apart from the rushing messengers and great birds and
winged fairy folk bringing reports and taking out orders to the
field, Ruddygore stood alone, dressed now in his robes of gold
and looking quite imposing. He sat in a large wooden chair
that seemed almost like a throne, and his arms rested on the
arms of the chair, while his eyes were closed.

Poquah saw Joe and Marge and came over to them. "The
Master is right, as usual," he sighed. "I am far too weakened
to do more than assist." His slitted eyes seemed to burn,
though, and they knew he wanted to be out there with the
moving armies.

The sight was imposing. Huge masses of men and equipment marched in formations, while the nonhumans and people
of faërie formed their own ranks, covering the human foot soldiers. Ahead, almost a thousand massed cavalry stood, barely
holding back their mounts.

"Looks like a Roman epic from the late show," Marge
noted. "Only this is for real."

"I don't understand why they waited for dawn," Joe said to
Poquah. "This looks all too set for a guy with a reputation like
his."

"Crossing the River of Sorrows is no mean feat," the Imir
told him. "Our own forces harassed but could not prevent it.
We didn't have the time to get sufficient armies south. By the
time our troops were gathered, most of his were across, and so
it was better to take up defensive positions and wait. The

Baron has a real problem, you see—he's in Sorrows Gorge, his entire force with its back to the River of Sorrows and the Dancing Gods. If he loses, he could lose a lot of his main force. But if he wins, he can break through the mountains there and have a clear plain for hundreds of miles and an unimpeded run to Terindell."

Joe shook his head wonderingly. "I'd have used all that to cross the Dancing Gods. From the map, it's much easier going on the other side."

"True—but he would telegraph his move weeks in advance and he would be in essentially the same position at the Sad Virgin. That is why the Valley of Decision has always been the place would-be conquerors have come, and why none have yet breached it."

Marge gazed out nervously at the assembling forces. "How good a chance does he have to win?"

"About even, with the Master here," Poquah told her. "But if he punches through here, there is nothing much to stop him."

The defenders had dug trenches and built effective-looking earthworks, and Joe didn't envy anybody having to come against them. There were also large catapults and other less familiar machinery of war, but no permanent fortifications in the area.

The sky was suddenly alight with hundreds of fireballs, rushing in toward them, landing, and bursting, spilling their fiery death in a random manner. Poquah watched them come in. "It has begun," he said softly.

The defenders took cover and generally weathered the storm of fireballs, the catapult equivalent of heavy artillery. It was merely a softening-up measure, for all its spectacle. While the fireballs did little damage, they made certain that the main field was clear for the attacker.

Now, across the field, perhaps ten miles from the command post, a huge thing like a black snake moved across the length of the battlefield. It took a little thinking to realize that what they were seeing was a line of men almost a mile long and perhaps ten or fifteen deep. It was not merely impressive—it was downright awesome.

From defensive earthworks, a similar line began to march out from the defenders' side. It was not quite so deep or so wide, but *they* didn't have to march over a mile or more of open ground. These were the elfin *hacrist*, master bowmen, and they took their positions and stood their ground, waiting for the approaching line to get within range. Behind them formed cavalry, so many horsemen it was impossible to count them from the command post. They formed into company-sized detachments and waited, about a hundred yards behind the *hacrist*.

When the two forces were within range of each other, the bowmen let loose with a tremendous hail of arrows that nearly blackened the sky. They concentrated on the center of the attacking line, which suddenly seemed to turn into a solid wall as the soldiers held their shields horizontal, forming something of a roof. The closer they were and the better the discipline, the more absolute that roof would be.

Soon there were holes in that roof, as such a concentration of arrows and bolts as none there had ever seen struck with great force. Without exception, the men who fell were left, with those behind falling in and taking their place in the relentless advance.

From behind the bowmen, the catapults of the defenders went off in perfect series. Some were firebombs, but most contained as much as a quarter of a ton of junk, rock, and scrap metal that would tear into or crush flesh.

The catapults took their toll on the advancing marchers, whose roof was certainly caving in at a number of key spots—spots on which the bowmen now concentrated.

Joe frowned. "They're not going to get here *that* way," he noted.

Poquah nodded. "Yes. They have something up their sleeves, that is certain."

In his great chair, Ruddygore, too, was thinking the same thing. A frontal attack was useless unless supported by a flank; if this kept up very long, the edges of the force would be the only attackers and could be disposed of long before they could close the vise. He rose up into the air, his astral shape taking in the entire battle scene, but he could see nothing—and he determined that the great mass of the Baron's troops was, in fact, committed. They looked to be about the numbers and types of beings he'd seen in his earlier reconnaissance. Something was definitely wrong here . . . But what?

On a hunch, he swung over his own forces, jubilant in their easy victory, and beyond, in back of them, to the ox bows near the River of Dancing Gods. He saw almost immediately that his hunch was correct. Four thousand infantry together with flying *cosirs*—perhaps several hundred, in nine flying companies, all wearing the colors of Marquewood—approached. They were now less than two miles from the rear camp of the defenders. They flew traditional Marquewood colors, but the *cosirs* gave them away.

Abruptly, Ruddygore's physical body stood up from his chair and he screamed, "We are attacked from the rear by men in our colors!"

Two of the generals turned and frowned. "How?" one asked.

"They must have been carried in small groups up the river and stayed dispersed until last night," the sorcerer told them. "They wear the colors of Marquewood, but who of Marquewood would be supported by nine companies of *cosirs*?"

As suddenly as that, the Baron's true strategy was revealed, along with the fact that there were far more of the enemy than believed. The fight was no longer one-sided, but at least even. Even if the new enemy were exposed, a large percentage of the defenders would have to shift to open field fighting in their rear, weakening the frontal assault. Now, instead of the defenders having the Baron with his back to Sorrows Gorge, they were caught in a vise themselves with no place to run to.

Either the Baron or some other sorcerer with the rear force must have sensed Ruddygore's astral presence; from behind, even as orders were being issued for a defense of the rear positions, committing the reserves to that fight, the *cosirs* came silently out of the sky directly at the command post and reserves.

The creatures were as large as men, with folds of skin between arms and legs, yet they were also feathered and taloned and had tails that were vertical, acting almost like aircraft rudders. Their orange and blue coloring made them things of lethal beauty, and their faces, a curious blend of bird and elf, were triumphant as they swooped down in well-disciplined columns. The early ones carried cauldrons of some thin, foul-smelling liquid which they poured on the ground, the tents, and whatever forces they could reach. The latter ones carried only torches, and it was clear why, without thinking much about it.

The reserve bowmen took a good toll of *cosirs* as they swooped in; perhaps one in three was struck, and more than half of those were knocked right out of the air, but that was not enough.

Joe drew his great sword and swung around, ready to help the reserves. Then, at that moment, he saw that Ruddygore had chosen to ignore all this and was sitting calmly back down in his chair, eyes closed once again.

The archers started aiming specifically at the *cosirs* with torches, preferring to smell like oil rather than boil in it, but many of the torchbearers made it through and dropped their loads. Suddenly the entire command post and reserve center were on fire, and men and fairy folk screamed and scattered, writhing in pain.

Joe ran past the flaming holocaust to the rear, where he could see that the approaching enemy force was moving with astonishing speed for infantry toward their positions. Officers tried to regroup their troops and set up some sort of defensive line in all the confusion.

Marge looked at Ruddygore, then at Poquah, with alarm. "How can he just sit there like that? They'll get him for sure!"

"No, he is well protected," the Imir assured her, "although I can not for the life of me understand what he is doing right now."

At that moment Ruddygore came out of it once again, rose, and looked around in anger. "No!" he shouted to the generals. "Continue concentrating on the frontal assault! Frontal attack! Forget the rear guard! Press them back against the river!"

One general, a very noble-looking man with experience in his eyes, frowned. "But we must defend the rear!"

"No! *I* will defend the rear! Trust in me as you have trusted no one since weaned from your mother's milk, but do as I say, Prince! Do what I say or we are lost!"

With most of the fires out or burning tents beyond redemption, Joe saw officers rounding up men and pulling them back toward the original attack. He frowned, but followed, determined to see this out no matter what. Still, he spotted Marge and Poquah and ran to them, confused. "If they're all fighting forward, who's gonna take out the thousands that are about a quarter mile back?"

Marge looked at him, then past him, and broke into a big grin. "That's who!"

Joe turned and saw, coming in low over the flats, the dragon Vercertorix.

The dragon had practiced on smaller numbers back in High Pothique, but now it faced a formidable array and it did not seem too worried by the greater number, even announcing its presence with a monstrous roar. It was obvious from the start that Algongua or someone else was telling the dragon what to do—or, at least, making suggestions—because Vercertorix approached the columns with careful precision, carving zigzag paths of flaming breath through the ranks, forcing the breakup of the columns and general disorganization.

After doing as much initial damage as possible, the dragon then concentrated on keeping the main force back. The object wasn't so much to fry all four thousand—that would have been next to impossible—but to keep them scattered and falling back toward the relative protection of the silt mounds around the ox-bow lake. Heartened by the sight of the great dragon routing their enemies, what was left of the reserves and support troops on the command post hill began cheering, which let those below, who were fighting the main battle, know that something good was happening at their backs and taking the pressure off.

Cavalry moved forward into the wrecked ranks of the Baron's main force with a vengeance, breaking the attack column into smaller units which infantry moved to mop up. The Baron's officers and field commanders, realizing that their rear attack had at least stalled, if not failed, tried valiantly to regroup and fall back to defensive positions against the river gorge.

Ruddygore stood on the hill overlooking the battle, suddenly grim-faced even despite near certain victory. Marge looked and saw what few others could see—a tremendous field of magical force embodying every color imaginable and in such a tight pattern that its complexity was beyond her abilities to follow. The source of the magic flow was clearly from the Gorge area, and she understood that the Dark Baron was making himself felt.

Now the field of force congealed and took on a new and more animated pattern, becoming a gigantic, three-headed monster, all jaws, teeth, and claws. Although outlined in the near unreality of the magical lines of force, it was truly the most horrible and loathsome creature she had ever seen, and she gave a gasp at both its terrible visage and its enormous size—it seemed to encompass the entire battlefield.

Joe turned to her. "What's the matter?"

She pointed. "Can't you see it? It's—horrible!"

He looked, and saw only victory in the making.

"The Baron's trying to reach Vercetorix!" Poquah told them. "It must be black for him indeed to take such a chance. Now we'll see the Master in action!"

Joe just turned and looked at them, then at the battlefield, and shrugged.

To those who could see magic, many things were happening. Ruddygore, who'd stood there watching the approaching monstrous shape, suddenly flared and changed into a shining giant being of near blinding white light. As huge as the monstrous creation now approaching, this was far different in color, texture, and form, almost as unbearable in its beauty as the Baron's monster was in its hideousness. It floated eerily out to meet the monster, and the two met over the battlefield. So great was the force of their meeting that clouds came in from all directions, rumbling and shooting thunder, congealing around the spot where the two great creatures of powerful sorcery grappled. Even Joe could see this phenomenon, and stared at it, fascinated.

The clouds, turning all sorts of colors and rumbling threateningly, began to swirl about them, kicking up a wind and bringing the smell of ozone and a deadly sort of chill. They swirled around the battlefield at an unnatural speed, as if being pulled into some sort of drain, but in the center of the drain—the hole—where the great beasts fought, the invisible battle was clear and eerily sunlit.

The patterns in the mixing of the two beasts were almost beyond endurance. Merely watching them started to give Marge a terrible headache and a sense of disorientation. This was power—pure, unadulterated power, both of magic and of will, between two whose powers were greater than the sum of all magical powers she had witnessed in the past.

The soldiers on the battlefield seemed aware of what was going on above and around them. The forces of Marquewood and Valisandra did not break, but took advantage of the swirling winds and terrible lightning and thunder. They were going to press the enemy to the Gorge, and the hell with the weather.

The sight to the attackers, however, was simply one last terror that had been visited on their proud forces this day, and they retreated steadily before the advancing Marquewood-Valisandran infantry.

Commanders still at the command post pulled back all surviving rear-guard troops, those not actually engaged in the press, and sent them immediately rearward. While this was little more than a thousand soldiers of mixed specialties, Vercertorix was having the time of his incredibly long life evening the odds. In fact, the dragon seemed to be making a game out of how he could split up, chase, and panic groups of soldiers. One entire company of the Baron's rear troops fled before the fiery breath of the dragon straight into the ox-bow lake itself. Unfortunately for them, most were wearing full battle armor, and the lake was about ten feet deep.

The intense power generated by the fight of the two sorcerers over the battlefield finally became too great for those onlookers who could see it to bear. Marge felt dizzy, then swooned and collapsed, and even Poquah had to turn away, looking sick and weak. Joe demanded to know what was going on.

"The Master and the Baron are directly engaged—out there," the Imir managed. "It is the greatest confluence of magical forces I have ever seen, and is too much for those of us of faërie to bear, though we live in magic constantly."

Joe thought about it. "If they're evenly matched, though, it's a draw. And that means the Baron can't get to us. Ruddygore only has to hold, not win—our boys on the ground are doing that."

From the vortex in the center of the battlefield, suddenly a voice rang out; a cold, mechanical voice that all could hear, not only those of the art but everyone on the battlefield.

"Hiccarph! Rally your forces to me or we are lost! Forces of Hell, attend me now, for I have served you well!"

And behind the great beast on the field, the Princes of Hell appeared to those who could see them; great, giant, ghostly outlines of creatures too horrible to look upon, mounted on vicious black creatures forged from the fires of Hell itself.

And from the opposite forces, another great voice spoke. "You have failed, Baron, because of your *own* overconfidence, your *own* tactical errors. We will allow a withdrawal, but we will help you not, for it is beyond redemption. Another day, another time, another battle . . ."

The Baron's voice, so cold and mechanical, broke, and he cried out in anguish, "Noooooo . . . !"

The storm that swirled around the warring sorcerers broke suddenly, the rain coming in so great a torrent that it was almost a physical force. The battlefield turned quickly to slippery mud, spilling horses and men and knocking the flying fairy folk out of the air. Lightning struck constantly, creating with the tremendous rain a huge wall that flowed out of the storm and into a great barrier between the forces.

The Baron's terrible three-headed monster broke from its fight and faded into the wall of water and lightning, quickly becoming one with it and then vanishing entirely.

To Joe, who watched the storm become the wall, it was merely very impressive and a little frustrating. "Damn! They're going to get away behind it!"

"Yes, a withdrawal will be possible," Poquah responded, "but not without great cost, more to them than to us. We have won. The Baron failed to anticipate the dragon, and now he pays for it. But such a cost to us as well! Such a cost . . ."

Joe turned and gently picked up Marge, taking her back to one of the few tents still standing. Poquah ran to the spot where Ruddygore had stood before the great battle and found his Master there, sprawled out on the grass. When the Imir turned him over, it could be seen that the sorcerer was still alive, but looked as if someone had tied him down and beaten him severely.

"Master!" Poquah cried. "Master! Do not desert us now in your triumph!"

The body of the fat man seemed to shudder slightly, and his breathing became more regular. With an effort, Ruddygore opened his eyes, groaned, and looked up at the anguished Poquah. "Don't worry, old friend," he gasped, his voice cracking and weak. "You shoulda seen the other guy . . ."

The Battle of Sorrows Gorge was over, and the defenders had held, but the mopping-up operation took several days. The sight of the battlefield the day after was sobering to the most romantic in the group. Bodies littered the field, wearing all sorts of colors, many human but many not. Joe was both shocked and sobered at the sight; it made him feel a bit sick.

The Dark Baron had sent eleven thousand across Sorrows Gorge and another forty-six hundred in the rearward force. Of that number, he managed eventually to extricate slightly more than half. Fewer than eight hundred, almost all from the rear force, had been taken prisoner. The rest lay dead upon the field.

Roughly ten thousand total had defended. Of that number, only a bit over fifty-one hundred remained, many of those wounded or maimed. It had been a costly battle indeed.

Ruddygore was taken to Terindell by boat, along with Joe, Marge, Poquah, and a number of others associated with that castle. Of Grogha and Houma, who had been in the fighting force, there was, as yet, no word, although things were still extremely disorganized. Macore, however, who was still recovering from his wounds suffered in High Pothique—or so he claimed, anyway—had remained behind at Terindell and greeted them upon their return, wanting to know all the details.

It was clear Ruddygore was in very bad shape, and they all relaxed and waited at Terindell until there was some word on him, some sort of reassurance about his condition. Unlike physical wounds, the wounds on Ruddygore's body had been physical stigmata of the inner spiritual wounds he had suffered in the fight with the Dark Baron.

During the next three weeks they saw the sorcerer not at all, although there was a steady stream of visitors and dignitaries to the great castle and lots of gifts and well-wishes.

Joe and Marge again talked of what they might do now, but all was put off until Ruddygore was well. It would be unthinkable to leave him without knowing, without a parting word.

Near the end of the third week, two weary knights appeared on horseback, one on a gray spotted horse, and there was great rejoicing all around. Both Grogha and Houma looked very much as if they'd been in a terrible experience, and both had suffered many wounds, yet they were cheerful enough to start telling and embellishing their battlefield exploits until only a few days later they told how they'd won the war.

Algongua, too, arrived, although not on Vercertorix, to say

his farewells. He was going back to High Pothique, more convinced than ever that people weren't worth it. Still, he was more worried about Vercertorix. "I'm afraid he'll never be happy with an occasional cow again," he sighed. "Oh, where have I failed!"

Four weeks after the Battle of Sorrows Gorge, word came that the Baron's forces were regrouping and re-forming and that a new alignment of commanders had been established to the south. Lacking forces sufficient to counterattack and retake the southern areas, the north knew that it had indeed won a great battle victory—but no war.

And, too, on the same day as that word came, Poquah went first to Joe, then Marge, and asked them to come to Ruddygore's library that evening. The sorcerer wanted to see them.

They went anxiously, not knowing what to expect, but the sorcerer received them, looking fairly fit if still a bit gray and weak. He'd certainly lost a good deal of weight and was, possibly, down to a mere three hundred pounds. But the bruises and lacerations had faded, and he moved with far less stiffness and discomfort.

They dined with him that evening and felt secure and relaxed, now that the sorcerer not only was going to make it but was his old self again.

"I've been back to your world, you know," he told them.

"Oh?" Joe responded. "Why?"

The sorcerer laughed. "I like it—for a visit. Besides, there was a Gilbert and Sullivan theater festival in San Francisco." His eyes twinkled slightly. "I could hardly pass that up. It was good therapy, too." He relaxed in his plush chair and lighted a cigar, then grew a bit more serious. "Have you two thought of what you'd like to do now? Seriously?"

"Nothing definite," Joe told him, "but I do have sort of the wanderlust."

"I'd like to find my exact tribe and go to them for a bit," Marge said. "I'd like to know more about myself and what I'm becoming."

"I can tell you the who, what, and where of that," Ruddygore assured her. "I'm afraid I played something of a cruel trick on you, but I couldn't resist doing it to Huspeth."

"I don't mind. Not any more," she told him. "I'd like to go

to Huspeth one last time, though, and explain the situation. I'd feel better about it."

He nodded. "You can do that any time. Poquah will arrange for a proper horse and give you the route. It's not far." He sighed. "But I think now, considering how much your service has meant to me, that I'll play completely fair with the two of you. I'd like to give you a series of options and let you pick."

"Go ahead," Joe urged, interested. "But I don't see that we did all that much for the big picture."

"What you did was incalculable! With that Lamp, the Baron would not have had to engage me. He could have knocked Vercertorix into the ground, even masked that entire rear-attack force until it was upon us! Getting that Lamp was the difference between victory and defeat. You can be very proud. It is because of you that so many of our brave people did not die a vain death. Control of the Dancing Gods is still not the Baron's, and the bulk of Husaquahr is still free. It was the job you were summoned here to do—and you did it well."

They both smiled. "I'd like to believe that, anyway," Marge told him.

"Well, it's the truth. And because of it, I'll lay out *all* your options. First, you can remain in the service of Terindell as honored folk. We have won a battle but not a war, and there will be much more to do in the future. The Baron will not be so overconfident again. Of course, I'd give you both whatever time you wanted or needed, and transport you anywhere you wanted to go, before sending you on any more missions. That is option number one."

He paused, puffed a few times on the cigar, then continued. "Now, option number two is that you both go your own way. Find your own lives here. I won't hold you. But I *do* think the two of you make a good team, a near unbeatable combination of beauty and magic on the one hand and quick-thinking brawn on the other. That business in the Baron's tent, Joe, was sheer brilliance." Again he paused, looking thoughtful. "There is a third alternative, of course."

"Huh? What?" Joe wanted to know.

"You could go back. I could send you back. Your souls still belong elsewhere, and so you could return—as you are, in fact. New lives. Marge, you could have every male eating out of your hand back there. A little cosmetic alteration on the ears, perhaps, and you'd be the most exotic and erotic woman since Helen of Troy—and she was vastly overrated. And, Joe, with that body and quick mind of yours—and some quantity of gold I could give you—you could be or do almost anything you want."

They were thunderstruck by this last option, since both of them had abandoned any hope of ever returning. Joe had often thought of it, of course, but he'd never expected to have the choice offered to him.

Marge smiled at Ruddygore. "No, I don't think I want to return. Maybe someday for a visit, but never for good. I've been in this world perhaps only a year, but I've lived more than I have in all my previous life. It's not the wondrous, romantic world of my fantasies, true, but it *is* a wonderful place nonetheless." Both she and Ruddygore looked at Joe.

"You know, ever since I met you, I've been aching to go back. It's all I dreamed about. But—I don't know. Call it inscrutable Indian perversity, or maybe just an old trucker's whim, but there really *is* nothin' there for me. The funny thing is, I might have still taken you up on it until we got back here. Just seein' folks like Macore, Houma, and Grogha—you know, I got more friends in this world than I have in the other? And I'm still my own boss here, still on the move, only here one place ain't so much like another."

Ruddygore sighed and nodded. "All right, then, that's settled. As for the other, perhaps I wasn't playing *quite* fair with you."

Both of their heads snapped up and looked at him suspiciously.

He sighed. "Remember back at the start of this thing? Remember, Marge, when you labeled it the start of an epic?"

She chuckled. "Yes, I remember. I didn't know how true that was when I joked about it."

"You still don't," he told her. "The Books of Rules, Volume 16, page 103, section 12(d)."

"Yeah? So what's that crazy set say about us?" Joe wanted to know.

"All epics must be at least trilogies," Ruddygore replied, and laughed and laughed and laughed . . .

DEMONS OF THE
DANCING GODS

For Ken Moore, Dan Caldwell,
and the rest of that crazy bunch,
along with a gift certificate for
a presmoked cigar.

TABLE OF CONTENTS

CHAPTER 1

ENCOUNTER ON A LONELY ROAD

The road to Hell is sometimes paved with good intentions.
            —The Books of Rules, CVI, Introduction

IF HE HAD TO GO TO HELL, WELL, IT WAS BETTER TO GO dressed in expensive clothes, drinking good wine, and smoking a fine cigar.

The small figure walking slowly down the road was hardly visible in the darkness, and any who might have come along would probably not even see, let alone notice, him. He stopped for a moment, as if trying to get his bearings from the stars, and sighed. Well, he thought to himself, the clothes weren't bad for being nondescript, and the wine was long gone, but he did have one last cigar. He took it out, sniffed it, bit off the end, and stood there for a moment, as if hesitant to light and consume this one last vestige of wealth. Finally he lighted it, simply by making a few small signs in the air and pointing his finger at the tip. A pale yellow beam emanated from the finger, and the cigar glowed. Such pranks were really pretty petty for a master sorcerer, but he had always enjoyed them, taking an almost childlike pleasure in their simplicity and basic utility.

He found a rock and sat down to enjoy the smoke, looking out at the bleak landscape before him, invisible in the darkness of the new moon to his eyes, but not to his other, paranormal senses.

The darkness was in itself a living thing to him, a thing that he sensed, touched, caressed, and tried to befriend. He found it indifferent to him, interested instead in its own lowly subjects—the lizards, the snakes, the tiny voles, and other creatures that inhabited the desolation and knew it as home. For these and all the nameless citizens of its domain, the night was life itself, allowing them access to food and water under cooling temperatures, sheltered from greater enemies by the cool, caring dark.

The road seemed empty, lonely, desolate as the landscape itself, a track forlorn and forgotten in the shelter of deep night; but as he sat there, nursing the last cigar, he extended his senses and saw that *this* road was different, *this* road was for those with beyond normal senses and training. *This* road was inhabited, used in the night; as he let himself go, he could hear the groans and lamentations of those who used it now in the depths of night.

Even he could not see them, not now, but he could hear them, hear the crack of the whip and the cries of hopelessness and despair from those who moved slowly, mournfully, down that lonely road.

For in the dark, at the time of the new moon, he knew—perhaps he alone knew—that this road had a dark and despairing purpose beyond its utility to the travelers of day and full moon.

They were walking, crawling, along that lonely road, he knew, going toward the destination they dreaded yet had richly earned.

The month's quota of damned souls was a bumper crop, judging from the sounds.

One night, he knew, he'd be there, reduced to the same level as all the rest, walking or crawling down that road himself. One night, he, too, would be brought as low as the lowest of those now moving down that road, paying a due bill he had willingly run up. Perhaps, just perhaps, it would be this night, if his tongue and quick mind failed him for once. He was willing to go, he tried to convince himself, but not yet, not just yet. He had surrendered much to travel that road one day, not the least of which was his honor, and he certainly was loath to pay without at least attaining the goal for which he'd sold his soul.

The cigar was almost finished now, but he continued to nurse it along almost to the point of burning his fingers, as if the end of the cigar would also be the end of his hopes, his dreams, his life, and his power. For the first time, in the dark, with the sounds of the damned filling his bargained soul to its core, he had doubts and fears about his course and his own well-being. Was the great goal worth this sort of ultimate price? Did it really matter one way or the other what he did or didn't do, or was he, like the cigar, a momentary brilliance turned to ash and of no more consequence than that in the scheme of things?

He got up, dropped the stub, and crushed it angrily with his right foot. Such melancholy was for fools and failures, he scolded himself. He had not failed yet, and in his setbacks he had learned a great deal. Now was not the time for self-deprecation, self-doubt, and inner fears to consume him—no, that was what *they* would want, not merely his enemies but his unhuman allies as well. They, his allies, were the cause of this, for they dealt in such matters, traded in doubt and fear, sowed the seeds of turmoil inside you, and, in that way, they fed and grew stronger.

He began to walk along the dark, lonely road in the wastes, conscious now of being among the milling throng of the damned on their way to perdition, and conscious, too, that they knew he was there, a living, breathing man of power. He could feel their envy, their hatred of him for still cheating what they now faced; he could feel, too, the pity in many of them, not merely for their own sorry fates but for him as well.

Turn back, he could hear them crying. *Do not walk this path with us, as we have walked. You still live! For you, there is still time* . . .

Still time . . . Until his corpse rotted as theirs now did, until his cold and silent soul received their summons, there was always time. Time to set things right. Time not to repent, nor turn back—never!—but time, instead, to complete the work.

Within the hour he had passed through the slow-moving throng and stood at a point in the road where, in the light of day, it went through a narrow pass and emerged in greener, more beauteous regions beyond. Any who dared this path on a night so dark would still pass through to that other side, oblivious to that which lay before them, only slightly out of phase with the world they knew. But he—he was a sorcerer and he saw the many plains in his mind's eye and in the magical energies that flowed through all the world.

The colors of the valley's magic were crimson and lavender, the colors of its district prince, and they flowed along the road with its great traffic of once-human misery, flowed with a curious and subtle beauty to the head of the pass, then seemed to pause a moment before beginning a swirl in the air before him, as if, somehow, these great colors were some sort of liquid, here reaching a great drain.

And, in fact, it was so, for through him passed the souls of

the damned, screaming in terror, unable not to press forward, **reaching** the great swirling mass of magical energy and falling **in,** their cries and pleas for a mercy now forever denied them cut terribly short as they were sucked down the great outlet from the real world in which they had forged their fate to Hell itself.

Not that Hell was actually so terrible. He had visited there on two occasions and found it more a place of curious fascination than the abject horror of the old tales and mystic religions. Yet it was still an unhappy place, fueled with hatred and revenge, its most terrible punishment a constantly available vision of the glory and beauty of absolute perfection that could always be seen but never experienced. They walked in Hell, always avoiding the vision, their eyes averting from it as men's eyes averted from the sun; yet they were always aware it was there, a place of indescribable joy and beauty that was held tantalizingly before them, just out of reach—always out of reach. It was this vision that had been denied him on his visits, for no living being was permitted to see such a sight as Paradise, lest, it was said, he be consumed in the light and desire nothing else. This did not really bother him; everybody in his past whom he knew, liked, or admired was in Hell anyway, along with all the other interesting people.

The swirl was changing now, becoming more irregular, as if disturbed by some great power or form arising within it, going, as it were, against the flow of the thing. It was less a drain now than a spiral. He saw the four arms of the turning swirl break from the main mass and fly upward above it, then form in a diamond. The light of these four shapes was no longer nebulous, but instead took on the form of wraithlike faces, demon faces, looking down upon him with cold interest. Now from the center of the magical mass shot two more bright lights, out and up into the diamond-shaped phalanx of faces, the demonic captain and the equally demonic sergeant of the guard.

Finally, out of the mass, so large it almost *was* the mass, walked a vaguely humanoid form. The creature was terrible to behold, one who had once been a creature of near perfection, an angel, distorted by hatred and an unquenchable thirst for revenge into a vaguely manlike thing that oozed the rot of long-dead corpses and whose face, twisted in an expression of permanent hatred, was set off by two huge pupilless eyes glowing a bright red.

The creature was dressed in royal robes of lavender, set off by a crimson cape, boots, and gloves. It halted in front of him and looked down menacingly. He bowed low and said, "How is my lord Prince Hiccarph?"

The demon prince gave a bull-like snort. "You really blew it, didn't you, Baron Asshole?"

"*We* blew it," he responded calmly. "Despite that cursed dragon and the very considerable powers of Ruddygore, it was the lack of the Lamp that did us in. We had it in our grasp—and, in your august presence, a brainless hulk and a slip of a halfling girl stole it right out from under your nose. All that when one wish would have carried the day and the war for us. You can't make me take all the credit, not *this* time."

"I can make you take whatever I wish," the demon prince hissed. "You're mine, Baron. I own you, not merely when you get here but right now. I think this fact bears reminding."

He smiled. "If that is true, my lord, and I am your abject slave, then the fault is truly yours for the loss, for you chose the instrument and you played its string."

"You *are* an impudent bastard," Hiccarph commented, his tone softening. "Perhaps that's why I like you. Perhaps that is why I just don't strike you down and take you with me tonight."

Inwardly, the Baron relaxed a bit at the comment. Still time . . . still time . . . Aloud, he asked, "Have you determined why those two were able to ignore your powers? At first I thought it was the Lamp, but I soon realized that the magic Lamp of the djinn would have little authority over you."

"I have done much research on the matter," the demon prince told him, "and still I have not the answer that is true. Dozens of explanations have occurred to me, but which one is the right one? Unless I know the exact means by which Ruddygore accomplished this, I can take no measures to counter it. We know very little about them, after all; and, if I peer too deeply into it from my side, it will certainly alert his Majesty, and I would prefer *he* in particular learn nothing of our little project, at least not yet, for understandable reasons. Since they worked so well for Ruddygore, though, it is likely he will continue to use them, and in that we might ultimately learn the secret through your offices. Remember, Baron, that we are in a sense kindred in this matter. Neither of us can afford to fail, and both of us will suffer terribly if we do."

The Dark Baron nodded. The harsh and rugged land of Husaquahr, dominated by the great River of Dancing Gods, had never been totally conquered by force of arms and, as such, it was the key to the domination of the entire continent. The continent, in turn, was the key to the entire world, since a bare majority of the Council of Thirteen, the most powerful necromancers in the world, lived on it—including, of course, himself. Control of the Council meant the ability to rewrite the Books of Rules, which governed the lives and powers of all who lived on the world, and that meant absolute control. From this world, formed by angels in the backwash of the Great Creation, Hiccarph and the minions of Hell could launch an invasion of Earth Prime, an Armageddon that might well have a different ending from the one everybody and every holy book of both worlds predicted.

Of course, there was more to it on a personal level than merely giving Hell a great advantage. Hiccarph might be a prince, but as his sphere of influence was Husaquahr and not any place on Earth Prime, he was a decidedly minor one in the Hellish hierarchy. If Hiccarph could deliver *this* world to his Satanic Majesty free and clear, his standing in the royal pecking order would be second only to great Lucifer himself.

But Hiccarph was taking a terrible gamble himself. For over two thousand years there had existed a compact between Heaven and Hell, a reordering of the rules of their great war. No longer would angels and demons walk directly upon the planes of the worlds, but would, instead, act through intermediaries native to those planes exclusively. Thus balanced, the minds and souls of the worlds would themselves choose sides and do the work freely and for their own motives. To break the compact would be tantamount to a formal declaration of war, the second War of Heaven called Armageddon, a war Hell did not wish to fight unless it believed it could win.

And yet Hiccarph had in fact broken the compact and directly intervened in Husaquahr. With his powers, unconstrained by the man-made Books of Rules, he had built and backed the forces of the Dark Baron and conquered over a quarter of the entire land. They had been stopped, though, in a great battle in which Hiccarph's powers were blunted by his inability to act against the two from the other plane at a key point in the battle, and by the subsequent skill of opposing sorcery and swords. Because of that defeat, the Dark Baron's forces had had to withdraw, and both the Baron and Hiccarph were in pretty deep trouble.

The longer it took, and the more direct involvement by the demon prince, the more likely his activities would be discovered by his own king, who might not approve of such a premature and unilateral breaking of the compact by a comparatively minor underling. But the more open and direct Hiccarph's involvement, the more the enemies of the Baron would be strengthened, since those opposing Hell would be able to rally all the most powerful sorcerers to their side—a combined power Hiccarph alone could not block. Worse, proof that the compact was being violated would raise even the hands of evil against the Baron—for who, living in decadent splendor and enjoying the power and possessions that evil brought, would like to take a risk on Armageddon, at which point their wonderful wickedness might be destroyed for all time, when they had sure things in the here and now?

"Those two saw you," the Baron pointed out. "Live witnesses now exist that know you personally intervened."

"They are of no consequence," the demon prince assured him. "After all, Ruddygore already knew. But the others— particularly those who are already in the service of Hell—will not want to believe. They will find the idea that any might violate the compact unthinkable. Only if faced with proof so clear and incontrovertible that they can not help but believe will they do so. That's the only thing that's saving our collective asses, Baron, but it's a big thing."

He nodded. "So what do we do about these two you can't control?"

"They are no longer any threat, now that we know their looks and boss. Remember, while they are immune to me, they are vulnerable to the Rules of Husaquahr; thus, they can be easily handled by such as you. It is ironic, my dear Baron, that, had you actually gone to attend to them instead of me, we would have won. While my far greater magic was powerless against them, you could have frozen them to statues or turned them to toads with a flick of your wrist. Ruddygore is clever—he foresaw in the Mazes of Probabilities that such a situation might occur and prepared for it—but his advantage is now known. Once known, his schemes are of no consequence. I think we have seen Ruddygore's bag of tricks. He will not expect us to act again so soon, and we will not give him the time to prepare more tricks and traps."

"You have a plan, then?"

"You still control a quarter of Husaquahr. Your army is a good army, perhaps the greatest ever raised here, and it retired from the field intact and in good order. In the end, it was geography that defeated us, as it has defeated all past conquering armies here. Even without the Lamp, we almost carried the day, nor could our enemies mount a credible counterattack. They won in the end because geography told them where we must meet and they were there, well fortified and in the defensive positions of their choice. Eliminate the geographical factors and we will carry any battle."

"But how do you eliminate geography?" the Baron asked, fascinated but skeptical.

"With me, you are the equal of six of the Council," Hiccarph told him. "We have the power. Now listen, my impudent instrument, as to how it will be used."

CHAPTER 2

VISITS WITH OLD FRIENDS

The fairies may belong fully to no human orders, nor their political parties.

—The Books of Rules, LXIV, 36(b)

THE GLEN DINIG WAS A PLACE OF MAGIC AND MYSTERY. THE sacred grove of trees along the banks of the River of Dancing Gods was but a few hours north of the great castle Terindell at the confluence of the Rossignol and the Dancing Gods, yet it might as well be on another planet. Legends abounded concerning it, but few had actually seen it and fewer still dared to penetrate its depths. Even those who scoffed at the legends and tall tales nonetheless admitted that there was a strong spell on the place; no human male could enter it, no matter from what direction or means, nor male fairy, either. Only a few steps into the tree-covered area and a man felt his breath become labored and hard; in a few steps more, he would be gasping for air, with the choice of suffocation or fleeing outside the invisible but tangible boundaries.

Legend said that a great witch, a virgin power who was the daughter of Adam and Lilith, had finally tired of the world and its struggles and created this place, perhaps on the spot where, a world away, Eden had once stood; and here she remained to this day, never aging, never changing, in some strange and wondrous world of her own creation, echoing imperfectly the Garden she once actually saw so long ago. Exiled, as her mother had been, to this new and alternate Earth, unable to die and unable to forget, she was in a state where, at least, she might not go mad.

Some said she *was* mad, of course, while others said she had transformed herself, and that she was not in the Glen Dinig but rather was the magical forest now. All that was agreed upon was that she was there, that her name was Huspeth, and that even those who really didn't believe in her still feared and respected the name.

The woman who rode into the forest confidently had a great deal of the respect and awe that Huspeth and the Glen Dinig radiated within herself, but she did not fear either the witch of Glen Dinig or the forest itself. She knew them well, as old friends and great teachers, and she owed them much. She *did* have fears and concerns, though, and she dreaded this trip for what to the superstitious outsiders would seem amazing reasons. She was coming to ask of them that they separate her from this wonder and magic forever, because she had no choice.

The woman had a strange appearance, both human and fairy, with a beautiful, almost unnatural face and figure set off by enormous, deep, sensuous eyes that no human ever had. Her skin, too, was a soft orange, and her hands and feet, with their length and clawlike nails, were pure fairy.

Huspeth met her warmly at the small glen in the center of the forest and tried her best to put the newcomer at ease. The cauldron outside the hut where the white witch lived was bubbling with grand smells, and Huspeth would hear nothing serious from her visitor until both had supped and the sun had vanished far beyond the trees.

Finally, by fireglow, the legendary witch gazed sadly at her strange-looking visitor and sighed. "Well, my daughter, time has caught up with thee, and thine anguish I share."

Marge smiled a sad smile and nodded. "I owe you everything," she said sincerely, "and I'm pained by this—but I can put it off no longer. It's—well, it's driving me crazy!"

Huspeth nodded sympathetically and gave her hand a motherly squeeze. "Already thou art burdened with living in two worlds, not truly a part of either yet very much a part of both," the witch said soothingly. "That is a far greater burden than any should bear, yet to live in three is impossible."

Marge stifled a tear, knowing that at least one other understood. Two worlds and not truly a part of either, she thought sourly. A Texas girl who'd failed at a career, failed at marriage, even failed as a hooker and as a waitress, who'd hitched a ride on her way to Hell with a crazy trucker drafted by a sorcerer to fight a war in another world. Joe was *supposed* to be here in Husaquahr, at least, although he might argue the point. Ruddygore had needed a hero not born of this world and thus immune to the demons of this place and he'd plucked Joe from Earth just before Joe was to die in a crash. She'd hitched a ride with Joe that dark night, thinking of suicide and expecting to make El Paso. Instead, here she was, in the land where fantasy was real, the origins of all human fantasies and myths, across the Sea of Dreams. And here the sorcerer with the impossible fictitious name of Throckmorton P. Ruddygore—Huspeth had taught her that none of the Council of Thirteen used their real names, since knowing the real name of someone in their class gave an equal opponent some kind of advantage—had sent the hitchhiking Marge to Huspeth in the Glen Dinig, to be trained as a healer and white witch. After the training, she had done her job well and contributed to keeping the powerful magic Lamp out of the hands of the marching Dark Baron, but there had been a catch. The order of white witches to which Huspeth and she belonged drew power from their virginity and celibacy—and Marge had once again been virginal in Husaquahr—but the more magic she had used or been subjected to, the more she changed.

"Aye, thou art a changeling sure," Huspeth told her, echoing her thoughts. "It is he whom thou dost call Ruddygore who did this knowingly. Is there hatred in thy soul for him for this?"

She thought a moment. "No, not really. Not at all. Just for a moment there, I was back on that lonely west Texas highway, not caring if I lived or died. Without him I'd be dead, either in that wreck or not too long after by my own hand. Whatever he did, he had a right to do. I've got no kick coming."

Huspeth smiled and nodded. "Thou hast learned much, my daughter, and thy wisdom becomes thee. I do not much like him, as thou knowest, for he trafficks in demons, yet his heart is good even if his soul be impure. He had very good reasons for bringing thee and thy companion to this world, and his skill at the art placed you both in the place where you were most needed. It may seem cruel to send thee to a celibate order and then make thee a changeling, but I divine strong purpose in it. Thy string is complex and far from played out. At first I thought him taking a subtle jest at me, but now I see it is not so. He needed thee as a witch of the order, but the clouds of Probability change with events. The first act is done, the curtain is down, but the play is far from completed."

Marge felt a little better on hearing this. "Then—whatever I'm becoming—is what is needed next?"

The ancient witch nodded. "It is clear now."

"Then—why? What must I face?"

"That is unknown to all save the Creator," Huspeth told her. "The future is not fixed but is all probabilities. One highly skilled in the art may see that a thing is needed while not knowing why, or when, or how. But it is now clear that the curtain must rise on the next act of our play. A conference of the Sisterhood was already held. Thy vows are lifted, as they must be. Thou art free."

Marge frowned. "Just like that?"

Huspeth laughed softly. "Just like that. And why not? For all the magic of the initiation which confers the power, a vow is a vow and not a spell. It is not a command but a contract. Thou hast not broken thy vow, so there is no dishonor. Release is needed and granted freely and willingly. The war against the forces of Hell needs thee." She sighed. "But stay the night with me. Enjoy the Glen Dinig. In the morning, perhaps, we shall visit the unicorn and say thy farewells. Then shalt thou ride forth to a new destiny."

Marge was almost overcome with emotion, and tears welled up in her eyes. "May I still—return? For a visit?"

"At any time, my daughter, for my daughter thou shalt remain always. The Glen Dinig shall sing whenever thou dost approach, and here thou mayest always find rest and comfort."

That made it much better, much more bearable. "Mother— what shall I do now?"

"Travel to the east along the Rossignol," Huspeth told her. "Ten days' comfortable journey will bring thee to the tributary called the Bird's Breath, and so thou shalt follow it to a forest called Mohr Jerahl, a place much like this one. There shalt thou find the fairy folk called the Kauri, who will complete the process and instruct thee in thy nature. Thou art bright, and so it will take some doing inside thee to trust thy feelings at all times, even over thy head, but this is the way of fairy folk, and they live lives far longer than humankind."

"What about Joe?" Marge asked. "Can he come with me? I think I'd like some moral support."

Huspeth gazed off into space for a moment, seeming not to hear, then turned back to her visitor. "He may accompany thee to the edge of Mohr Jerahl, but he must wait there for thee. There is mortal peril for a human to enter the home of fairy folk; should he enter, he will almost certainly have to kill many Kauri or be consumed by their power. It would not be good to begin thy relationship with thy new people with death, for the fairies do not age as humans do, but exist in their soul-state, and death for any fairy, including thyself, is the true death, not the transition of the humans. If he must come, then make him wait. Time to the fairy folk in their own land is not like time elsewhere, so his wait will not be long, no matter how long dost thou tarry."

"These—Kauri. What are they like?"

"An ancient folk of great power over mortal flesh, which is needed to safeguard their fragility. Their nature is quite elemental and is best experienced firsthand. Don't worry. *Thou* wilt find peace and confidence as one of them."

CHAPTER 3

A NICE LITTLE BUSINESS TRIP

For a barbarian, image is the most important thing.
        —Rules, LXXXII, 306(b)

THE MAN WALKING ACROSS THE CASTLE'S INNER COURTYARD
would have stood out in any crowd. He was a huge man, well
over six feet and so totally muscled that those looking at him
generally expected him to crash through stone walls rather than
be bothered to walk around them. His face, which he himself
described as vaguely Oriental—a meaningless term in Husaquahr but not back in his native Philadelphia—was handsome
and strong, with piercing eyes that seemed almost jet-black,
the whole thing set off by a thick crop of truly jet-black hair
that hung halfway between his shoulders and waist. His skin
was tanned a magnificent bronze and looked tough enough to
deflect spears. He wore only a flimsy white loincloth, hung
from an ornate hand-tooled leather belt, and a hat, made to his
specifications by the milliner in the nearby town of Terdiera. It
was a cowboy hat, brim sides turning up in starched salute,
and on the front was a strange symbol and word, in English:
"Peterbilt." The hat, which had shown great utility in deflect-
ing the elements, had been widely imitated in the land around
Castle Terindell.

He approached a low building separated from the castle
proper and knocked at the wooden door. It opened, revealing a
tall, sinister-looking elf whose thin-lined face, penetrating eyes
in perpetual scowl, and cold manner were in stark contrast to
the small, happy groundskeepers always working on the castle
itself. This was a warrior elf, an Imir, a professional soldier
and deadly fighter.

"Hello, Poquah," the big man said cheerily. "Is he in?"

"Downstairs, working on cataloguing his sculpture collection," the Imir responded. "Come in—the lady is already waiting inside. You can go down together."

Joe entered, having to bend his head slightly to clear the

door, and looked around the familiar study of the sorcerer Ruddygore, its sumptuous furnishings complementing the walls of red-bound volumes that seemed to go on forever—the Books of Rules, which governed this entire crazy world and were constantly being amended.

Marge was standing there, just looking at the huge books as she always did, probably wishing she could read them. Although the trading language they now used routinely as a first language bore an amazing resemblance to English, at least in many of the nouns, adjectives, and adverbs, its written form was pictographic, like the Chinese of their old world, with over forty thousand characters representing words and ideas rather than letters. It took an exceptional mind to learn it, starting from childhood. Total literacy meant power and position, no matter from what origins one came; but there was far too little time to learn it, once one was an adult.

She looked around as he entered and gave him a mild wave, then turned back to the books. "You know," she said, "they still remind me of the U.S. Tax Code. Thousands of years of petty, sorcerous minds constantly making Rules on just about everything they can think of. And every time there's a Council meeting, there's another volume of additions, deletions, and revisions. I bet nobody knows or understands it all, not even Ruddygore."

He just nodded and shrugged. The whole world was nuts, but people still acted like people, and that meant nutty, too. He'd long since stopped being amazed at much of anything in this world and just accepted whatever came. "So how are you doing?" he asked her, trying to start a more normal conversation.

She turned and shrugged, and he couldn't help but reflect how she seemed to get more beautiful and sexy every time he saw her. "Not bad. You?"

"Bored," he said honestly. "The first time I bent a three-inch iron bar into a pretzel, I was like a little kid and I went around bending all sorts of stuff, lifting horses, wagons, you name it. But now it's all just nothin'. I mean, it's no big deal any more."

Nothing, in fact, was any big deal any more. He was used to stares and people scrambling out of his way—so used to it that he pretty well took it for granted now. Just going into a town was an experience only for those with him for the first time—the women all gaga over him, no problems with service, conquests, you name it. There wasn't even any fun in claiming that he could outdrink and outfight anybody in the town. Hell, he *could* and he knew it. In the two months since the battle, he'd become totally bored, jaded, and itchy for anything new, even if it was risky. Just a couple of days before, two thieves from out of the area had attacked him in a back alley. One had hit him over the head with a club while the other had swung a board into his stomach. Both the club and the board had broken on impact—and so had the two thieves.

Just now he'd come from the practice field down by the river where several trainees had tried to shoot arrows into him. Without even thinking about it he'd twisted and turned, and knocked those arrows that still would have hit him down in midair. Gorodo, the huge, nine-foot, blue, apelike trainer of heroes and military men, had asked him for permission to have trainees try to kill him any time. So far, none had shown the least promise. He feared no man and no physical threat; only against sorcery was he powerless and, even in that department, he'd used his brains and quick reflexes to dodge most of it.

That had been the plan, anyway, since the start of all this. He would be the brawn and Marge would deal with the magic, aided by this Huspeth she always talked about and by Ruddygore, of course. They made a near-perfect team. But since the Dark Baron's defeat, there had been little to do.

Poquah appeared—he had the habit of doing that, without any sound or sign until he spoke up—and said, "The Master says to come down. He's in the middle of the catalog and he doesn't want to lose his place."

Marge joined them, and they walked out a back door and down a corridor which led to the sorcerer's magical laboratory. They were not going there, though, but to a basement beneath the main hall and study, where Ruddygore kept many of his more personal valuables. She looked up at Joe and whispered, "Ever seen this collection?"

He shook his head negatively.

"Don't crack up or make jokes when you see it," she warned him. "He's pretty sensitive about it."

Before he could ask any questions, they were in the basement and surrounded by what she was talking about. For a moment he looked around, trying to sort out the collection from the junk—but it didn't take him long to realize that the junk *was* the collection.

There were thousands, perhaps tens of thousands of them—in every size, shape, color combination, and in just about every style. It was, he had to admit, the largest grouping in one spot of tacky plaster sculptures short of a Hong Kong factory. Here they were—the monkey contemplating the human skull while sitting on a plaster book labeled "Aristotle," plaster dogs, plaster cats, pink flamingos, lawn jockeys, and just about every other expression of the tacky art ever "won" by contestants at Beat-the-Guesser stands and fire carnivals the world over. The souvenirs were there, too—the plaster Statues of Liberty, the U.S. Capitols, even ones with a foreign flavor like the seven Eiffel Towers, half a dozen Big Bens, and three different Mannekin Piss statues from Brussels, one of which had a definitely obscene corkscrew imbedded in its painted plaster.

He was about to say something when a shaggy head popped up from the midst of the statuary that virtually filled the room, looked at them, and beamed. "Marge! Joe! How good of you to drop in! How do you like the collection? I daresay it's the finest of its type on any world!"

Joe was about to make a comment on just what he really thought of the junk when Marge kicked his shin. "Um, I'll agree that nobody else has a collection like this one," he managed, trying to sound diplomatic.

Throckmorton P. Ruddygore got up slowly from the floor, where he'd been working, then started looking for a way to get out of the pile that surrounded him without breaking anything. This was no mean task for him, since the sorcerer looked like nothing so much as the classical depiction of Santa Claus, although, at a height of more than six feet, his proportionate bulk was certainly over four hundred pounds.

Joe and Marge carefully helped to make a path for him by moving statuary where they could, and at last the sorcerer was able to reach the entryway. Usually dressed in fine clothes or majestic robes, he allowed few people to see him in the gigantic T-shirt and Bermuda shorts he was now wearing.

After greeting them warmly, he looked at Marge with his piercing blue eyes and asked, "What is it you want, my child?"

"I think you know," she responded. "At least, you'd *better* know."

"Well, I don't know," Joe grumbled.

Ruddygore just nodded. "I think it's best you go and do it as soon as possible. Events are moving at a far faster pace than I had anticipated. Something very odd is going on in the Baron's lands, and that spells trouble. I may need you both at any time."

That interested the big man. "You mean another battle?"

"Not like the old one, Joe. I think the Baron has learned his lesson on that one. But there are disturbing reports from the south. Whole military units seem to have vanished or been broken up and re-formed elsewhere. Boundary defenses have been strengthened, although obviously we can't possibly mount a successful counterattack, and it's getting tougher to get in and out of his areas. Something's up, something new, and we can't get a handle on it; but it's certain that the only reason for such ironclad border control, other than to repel invasion, is either to keep your own people in—and he has other means to do that—or to keep the flow of information to a minimum. Our usual spies have been next to useless, I'm afraid, so I'm hoping to learn something at the convention."

"Convention?" Marge prompted.

The sorcerer nodded. "Yes, the annual meeting of the sorcerers, magicians, and adepts of Husaquahr. It's a rather large, elaborate affair lasting five days, and it's only three weeks away. This year it's in Sachalin, Marquewood's capital. I leave in ten days for it, since it's a long way. Everybody will be there, though—the entire Council, as a courtesy, including those members, both greater and lesser, from the Baron's lands. I might learn something useful."

"Wait a minute," Joe put in. "You mean to tell me that even the Baron's side will be there? In a country they just tried to conquer?"

Ruddygore smiled. "Yes, it *does* sound odd, but the Society is above politics, and politics often intrudes but never interferes. They'll all be there—but on their best nonpolitical behavior, I assure you. The guarantee is that there will be so much magical power and skill present that any side in a dispute will be in the minority—and the majority will act decisively and ruthlessly, I assure you, if the bond of the Society is violated."

"The Dark Baron—he'll be there, too?" Marge asked, temporarily forgetting her purpose.

"Oh, yes, but not under that guise. He'll be his usual self and impossible to detect by normal means. It's interesting. He may greet me warmly, then buy me a drink—or I might buy him one. All the time he'll know, while I'll just wonder at each and every one of them. But, no matter, some slip, some slight thing, might be betrayed in such an atmosphere, and we must be on the watch for it."

"We?" both of them echoed.

"Oh, yes. I certainly want you there as my guests and part of my entourage. Poquah will also be there, along with other interested members of the household, but they'll all have been there before. You two will be fresh, unknown to other attendees and they to you; you might pick up something that familiarity misses. If you leave tomorrow, you can make Mohr Jerahl, then take the old road through the Firehills and get there in plenty of time."

Joe frowned. "Now, one of you want to tell me what this is all about?"

Marge laughed and turned to the big man. "Poor Joe! I'm sorry! I'm going to the home of—well, my people, I guess I could say. I want to complete the transformation quickly, just get it over with."

"The way is possibly dangerous, Joe," the sorcerer added, "although probably no more than any place else in Husaquahr. The perils are more likely thieves and the like than any really magical dangers, though there might be some. You must remember by experience what sort of things might lurk off every trail. Going, Marge will be extremely vulnerable to such dangers, which is why I'm asking you to go. Once you get there, *you'll* be in more danger than she, so when you reach the edge of Mohr Jerahl you'll have to camp and wait for her. The kind of magic the fairy folk have on their own home turf is beyond you or most others, Joe, and I don't want to lose you. I'm going to need you when the time comes again for sword and spear."

"Well, I don't know . . ."

"Trust me, Joe," Ruddygore urged sincerely. "Even I would

think twice about going in there without all the armaments of the magical art, and you have none. The Kauri are particularly powerful, which is why, once the transformation is completed, you and Marge will make the perfect team. You will complement each other almost absolutely, and that will make the two of you among the most dangerous pair in all of Husaquahr."

Joe thought that over. "The most dangerous pair ... I kind of like that. And I've been bored stiff, anyway."

"Then go with my blessings and heed my warnings," the sorcerer told them. "We will meet again three weeks hence at the Imperial Grand Hotel in Sachalin."

Much to Joe's disgust, the journey was without incident and through rolling farm country. They decided to skip the long and treacherous trollbridge near Terdiera and made their way along the Rossignol and its good trading road to the much larger town of Machang, which, being at a particularly sharp and inward angle of the river, was a convergence of many roads and trade routes and had a bridge there built and run by the government.

The Rossignol at this point was barely a hundred yards wide, but the channel was still more than ten feet deep, hardly fordable. The falls to the east of the town offered too risky and slippery a crossing on horseback; beyond that, the river was heavily patrolled and the border strongly fenced, as the water was shallow enough for anybody to walk across.

The formalities on the Valisandran side of the border were few; a small shack contained an official and a sorry-looking soldier who barely seemed interested in checking anybody going out. On the other side, though, was the tiny Marquewood town of Zabeet, a poor and rundown little place that seemed to subsist on cheap tourist trinkets sold to those who, coming along the trade routes for one reason or another, wanted to say they'd been to Marquewood without actually having to go there. The people were poor and dressed in rags; many of the children weren't dressed at all, and everybody seemed anxious to sell travelers something petty and crude that they had no desire for.

Still, for such a forgotten part of the country, it had one hell of an official entry station—a gigantic building entrants actually had to ride through, complete with officious clerks who were dressed in uniforms that suggested they were chief generals in some big army. The little man with the ten stars on each shoulder and the fourteen stripes down his blue uniform's sleeves was at least thorough.

"Names?"

"Joseph the Golden and Marge of Mohr Jerahl," Marge responded, already a little bit annoyed.

The eyebrows went up. "Mohr Jerahl? Then you are a citizen of Marquewood?"

"In a way, I guess I am," she admitted.

"Documents, then?"

"The fairy folk need none, as you know."

"And if you were truly of Mohr Jerahl, you wouldn't need this bridge, either," the clerk responded coldly. "Insufficient documentation. Entry refused. And you?"

Joe was growing a little irritated at the man's manner and drew his sword. It was an impressive weapon, being one of the last of the legendary dwarf-swords and thus magical, with a mind and personality of its own. To the consternation of all, Joe had named it Irving, after his small son a world away; but looking at the thing induced only respect, not derision.

The clerk was unfazed. "Striking a customs and immigration official with a sword, magical or not, is an offense punishable by not less than ten years at hard labor and/or a fine not to exceed fifty thousand marques," he said casually. "Undocumented and threatening. Entry refused." He turned to go back to his station, and Joe roared.

"How are you gonna impose that punishment if you're dead?"

The clerk stopped, turned, and looked at the big man as if he were a small child or an idiot. "I am only a small cog in a great bureaucratic machine. What happens to me will not alter things one bit. It will simply trigger the crossbows now aimed at you both and, if you survive them by some miracle, will make you wanted fugitives. It is not my job to bring you in or punish you. We have police and army units to do that."

"Why, you cold little—machine!" Marge snapped, and started for him.

"Wait!" Joe shouted, sheathing his sword. "As an old trucker, I should have realized that you don't fight his type with weapons." He saw Marge stop and look hesitant and he turned back to the little man.

"Tell me, Mr. Official, what is the penalty for bribing an officer of the government at an official entry station?"

The clerk thought a moment. "It would depend on the amount."

Joe reached into his saddlebag, found a small pouch, opened it, and removed two medium-sized diamonds. He dismounted and walked over to the little man and handed him the two stones. "How about for this amount?"

The clerk reached into a shirt pocket, pulled out a jeweler's magnifier, and looked them both over critically. He placed both the stones and the magnifier back in his pocket, then took out a small pad and scribbled something on it that neither of them could read, handing two sheets to Joe. "Documentation all in order. Have a pleasant and enjoyable stay in our beautiful country," he said. He turned and went back inside.

Joe grinned, looked at Marge, and said, "Let's mount up."

They were through the little, shabby town and out onto the Eastern Road before they slowed and pulled alongside each other. Joe was still grinning. "No doubt about it," he said. "People really are the same all over."

She shook her head wonderingly. "You know, he wasn't kidding about those crossbows. I spotted them all over, on some kind of lever and spring mechanism. Either he or a buddy could have made pincushions of us. What made you sure he'd take the bribe and not just arrest us for violating some rule thus-and-so?"

The big man chuckled. "Because people *are* the same. The more straightlaced and officious they are, the more corrupt they wind up being. That fellow had no flexibility at all, yet here he is at the only major border crossing to a town dependent on tourists. He wouldn't last long there if he was for real— the people in that poor little town would have lynched him. No, he's an old pro. He spotted us for people likely to have money and tried the good old shakedown. I've seen his type many times, usually at seldom-used border stations."

She was still shaking her head. "But what if he was wrong? What if we didn't have the money or never caught on? I notice he never asked for a bribe, and you never actually offered one."

"Well, if we hadn't gone across, we'd have gone back and stayed in Machang long enough to gripe about him. Somebody would cue us in—bet on it. Somebody working with him, most likely. And that same somebody would find out if we had no money and offer to get us across for something—say one of the horses. Don't worry—that fellow will spend the end of his days either a very rich and comfortable man or in jail. Bet on his being rich. Don't believe what they told you in school—crime pays real good. That's why so many people are in the business."

She thought about that for a minute. "Uh—were *you* ever in that business?"

He laughed. "At one time or another, I think most everybody is. For truckers, it's maybe half the time. Not even the most honest, flag-waving Jesus man doesn't run an overloaded rig once in a while and skip the coops—weigh stations—or maybe run at ten or twenty over the speed limit. About a quarter of us haul stuff we shouldn't in addition to what's on the waybill, to make a few bucks. You talk as if you never did anything illegal, either."

"Let's not talk about that," she responded, and they rode on.

Again the road followed the river for a long way; but midway through the second day out from the border crossing, the main road diverged into three branches, one heading west, one south, and one southeast. Joe looked at Marge quizzically. "Which one?"

She didn't hesitate. "None of them. We go due east now. That way." She pointed.

He looked in the indicated direction and could make out a not-very-worn dirt path that went out over the meadows and toward a wild forested area far to the east. "You sure?"

She nodded. "Forget the maps and road markers now. I can—well, I can *feel* it. It's kind of like a—magnet, is the best way I can say it."

He shrugged, and they set off on the primitive path.

And yet it wasn't so much a magnet as a presence, she decided. There was something there, something warm and alive, something that she could feel with every step now. It was an odd, indescribable feeling, and she could only hope that Joe would trust her.

Joe really had no choice. He let her take the lead, although the path was still clear enough to follow, and just relaxed.

They camped well into the forest that night. It was a pretty peaceful place, but he didn't want to take any chances; he suggested they alternate sleeping, with Marge going first. She tried it, but soon was back by the small fire.

"Trouble?"

She shrugged. "I don't know. We're very close now, Joe. We'll reach it easily tomorrow with time to spare."

"Cold feet, huh?"

"Something like that. I mean, I don't know what to say, what to do. I really don't know what's going to happen to me—what I'm really turning into, if that makes any sense."

He nodded sympathetically. "Yeah, I think I know. It's been pretty rough on you here."

"Oh, no, not really. Remember, I was a total washout back home. I was on my way to kill myself when I ran into you, you know. No, it's the other side. I've been *happy* here. For the first time in my life since I was a kid, I've been happy. I really like this place. And now, somehow, I'm afraid again. This—whatever it is—is forever. What if I don't like it? Or what if *they* don't accept *me*? What if I change into somebody you and all my other friends don't like or can't relate to? It seems that every time I have something right, it goes wrong."

He squeezed her hand tightly. "Don't worry so much. You'll have a real home here, with people you can call your own. None of the people of faërie I've met are any kind of holy terrors if you just treat 'em as people. Besides, Ruddygore said we were gonna be a super team, and he wouldn't say that if we couldn't stand each other, right?"

She smiled and kissed him lightly. "You're right, I guess. But I can't help worrying."

She was able to go to sleep after that, but she started him thinking in odd directions, some of which he didn't like. He wished for one thing that he were as confident of this changeling thing as he made out. He really cared for her, and that made her special in more than one way. He also valued her because she was his only link back to Earth, to the world in which both of them had been born and raised. Oh, sure, Ruddygore went back and forth all the time, but he was still a man of this world, not of the other, and he was hardly around all the time. Joe needed Marge, he knew—she was the one link he had to all that had been his world. He couldn't help but fear that she would have no such need of him—not after this.

No matter how he sliced it, after tomorrow she *would* be at least as much of this world as of their native land, and she would have roots, family, tribe, grounding. Not he. Even here he was the outcast, the outsider, the barbarian from a far-off land that didn't really exist.

The Kauri would be her new roots, her anchor, he knew—but she was the only family he'd ever have here. He wasn't like her. He'd never read all those books, dreamed those fancy romantic dreams, the way she had. He hadn't wanted to be here and had never felt at home here.

He wondered what all those trainees who watched him knock their arrows from the air and all those people who cleared the streets for him would say if they knew that this big, hulking brute of a muscleman was scared to death.

CHAPTER 4

BECOMING AN ELEMENTAL SUBJECT

Faërie seats of power may not be invaded by mortals without permission without exacting severe penalties.

—Rules, XIX, 106(c)

THEY REACHED THE BIRD'S BREATH, LITTLE MORE THAN A creek at this point, about midday. The air was hot and thick and insects buzzed around them in constant frenzy, setting up a cacophony of buzzing sounds. Marge halted and turned to Joe.

"This is where we split up," she said a bit nervously. "Make camp somewhere along here and wait for me." She turned back and pointed to a dark grove of trees beyond the small river. "That is the start of Mohr Jerahl."

He stared at it, but could tell no difference between the forest they'd been traveling through and the one on the other side. Still, he knew, there was little to distinguish the Glen Dinig from the surrounding countryside, either, and it was certainly a real and, for him, deadly place. "I still think I should go with you, at least as far as I can," he argued. "You don't know what's there, really."

"No. Absolutely not. First of all, you remember Ruddygore's warning. That's magic over there, Joe—a place of enchantment."

"If you remember, Irving and I have done pretty good against enchanted places and things. As for Ruddygore—he's not my father, whom I never listened to, anyway. I paid my dues to the fat man; he don't own me any more—just rents me for a bit."

She grew alarmed at his stubbornness, remembering Huspeth's very dark scenario. As best she could, she tried to explain the position to him. It was possibly true that Joe could survive, even triumph, but not without dire cost to her. "For *my* sake, Joe, stay here. Promise me. Give me your solemn word."

He sensed her genuine concern and, although he put up something of a front, he knew from that point on that he'd lost the argument. He glanced around. "Okay. Two days from right now—then I'm coming looking for you."

"Two days! Joe, I don't know how long this is going to take! It could be going just right and then you'll come in and screw it all up!"

"Thanks for the confidence," he grumbled. "but two days is it."

She thought a moment. "How about this, then? If I'm delayed for any reason, I'll send a message somehow. One that could only come from me. Fair enough?"

He considered it. "Maybe. But remember, we've got a hard way to go to that wizard's convention yet. We'll see. That's the best I'll do for now."

And, in fact, it was the most she could get out of him, and she decided it would have to do. She realized that his attitude was entirely based on his concern for her safety, and that made it really impossible to go farther. She got down from her horse and turned toward Mohr Jerahl.

"You gonna walk?" he called out, surprised.

She nodded. "I think it's best. I *know* it is, somehow."

"No weapons or food or stuff?"

"No. Joe. This one I walk into clean. You take care of yourself. You're going to be a sitting duck out here for a couple of days, and this kind of place holds who knows what kind of dangers."

"I can take care of myself," he assured her. "Just make sure *you* can."

She blew him a kiss. "I think I'll be pretty safe once I get across the creek." With that, she walked down to the riverbank and into the water. It wasn't very deep; even at the center, it did not come up beyond her waist, and the current was weak and lazy. She had no trouble making the other side. Emerging, she turned and saw him, still there atop his horse, staring after her. She waved at him, then turned and disappeared into the forest.

That feeling that she'd had since they diverged from the road less than two days earlier was tremendous now. She'd felt its overpowering influence from the first time she'd looked at the place across the river, but now she was in it and the feeling was all around her. For the first time she sensed, at least, what the nature of that strange sensation was.

It was raw power.

Mohr Jerahl was in some ways an analog to the Glen Dinig; it was a place of enormous magical power, power that could be seen, touched, felt. But while Huspeth's small realm was under tight and absolute control, Mohr Jerahl was not. The term "raw power" was literally correct—this was no tame and obedient magic, neatly tied into complex spells, but a force of supernature, an unbridled power that just *was*. It was incredibly strong, yet it had a single defined center, a locus, that she instinctively headed for. There, at that central radiation point, would be Kauri. There she would meet what she must become.

It seemed to take forever to get anywhere in the forest, and the sun was passing out of sight and influence by the time she was sure of any real progress, yet she felt neither hunger nor thirst, nor did she feel the least bit tired. The tremendous magical radiation went through her, tickling and even slightly burning not only her skin but *inside* as well, yet she knew it could not harm her. How she knew this, she wasn't sure, but it was a certainty that she was feeding off the radiation, drawing strength and whatever else she needed from it.

Darkness fell, in a land where the trees were so thick they would block the sun in daylight, yet she had no problem with that darkness. In fact, fed by the radiation she could now see as a bright, bluish glow that illuminated everything and bathed it in its eerie light, she saw every object distinctly and without shadow. In many ways it was a clearer vision than normal sight, although a more colorless one.

She knew that, somehow, she'd been delayed until darkness fell, that the magic was strongest then, and that the Kauri, as was the case with a majority of the fairy races, were more in their element.

She heard all sorts of stirrings in the trees; once or twice, she thought she caught girlish laughter from above and sensed the sudden shift of mysterious bodies, but they kept too far away for her to tell who or what was making the sounds. She was beginning to regret leaving her bronze dagger and bow back at the river, though.

And then, with a suddenness that startled her, she broke through the trees and saw the locus of Kauri power.

The clearing was enormous, composed entirely of some gray lava base that seemed permanently rippled, as if built of a frozen river rather than a hard-rock base. It rose slightly for perhaps a half mile, forming a cone-shaped structure, and at its center was a perfectly circular opening through which bubbling, roaring sounds and heavy, sulfurous smoke billowed upward. The crater was not only the source of the radiation but also a source of tremendous heat, and she knew that, somehow, this was a perfect miniature volcano.

Again she heard the girlish laughter, this time behind her, and she whirled and faced five of the Kauri.

The thing that struck her first was that they were absolutely identical; some fantastic, fairy quintuplets. Their basic form was human; all were female and might be called by many voluptuous. Their rounded, cute, sexy faces were marked with large, sensuous lips and huge, playful brown eyes. Yet the faces had a quality that could only be described as elfin, and through short-cropped hair that was a steely blue-black color, slightly more blue than black, protruded two cute, pointed elfin ears.

They were under five feet tall, but not by more than an inch or so. Their skins were a deep orange in color. Looking closer, though, she could see some familiar yet quite nonhuman differences. Their fingers were abnormally long and ended in clawlike nails; their toes, too, were a bit longer and more regular than human toes and ended in similar sharp, pointed, animallike nails, pointing slightly downward. Between digits on both hands and feet was the webbing that had first appeared on Marge back in the mountain town of Kidim. But their most distinctive feature was their wings, sinister and batlike, yet somehow less threatening in deep crimson than in demonic black, although, she saw, the crimson was only on one side; the back of the wings was a deep purple color. The wings were not merely attached to their backs but seemed to be woven into and between their arms and their bodies, so that, when an arm moved out or forward, the membranes fluttered and acted something like a natural cape. The Kauri just stood there, watching her, not so much with hostility, but with a sort of playful puzzlement on their interminably cute faces, and she sensed she was supposed to make the first move.

"Are you the Kauri?" she asked.

"We better be, dearie, to be here," one of them responded in a voice that was soft and somewhat childlike. "So what's it to you?"

"I was told to come here," she explained lamely, trying to decide how best to put all this. First meetings were always a problem for her. "The sorcerer Ruddygore of Terindell said I was a Kauri changeling. I am supposed to complete the change here, rather than let it go in little bits and pieces."

"A changeling!" another exclaimed, sounding exactly like the first. "Well, I'll be damned! Been a long time since we had one of *them* for a Kauri!"

Suddenly there was a tremendous babble of voices—or, as it seemed, the same voice repeated hundreds, perhaps thousands, of times, all at once, and saying different things. She whirled around and saw that the crater was filled with Kauri, all looking and sounding the same and talking at one another. There was nothing to do but let them run down; nobody could ever get them quiet any other way.

One of the original five broke away from a conversation and came over to her. "Well, I sure hope you *are* a Kauri changeling," she almost shouted over the din.

Marge frowned. "Why's that?"

The Kauri took her hand and led her back toward the wood for a bit. The grip was feather-light, and the fairy creature moved as if she had almost no weight at all. She still had the moves, though—they *all* did. If there were fairy hookers, this was their convention.

The combination of forest and the slowly diminishing din, as Kauri ran out of things to say, helped a bit.

"Whew! It's always like that around here," the fairy woman told her. "I'm Aislee, by the way."

"I'm Marge," she responded, glad to find some kind of friend. "This is all pretty new to me, so thanks."

"Oh, no problem. You got to learn how to cope around here, anyway. I was *born* around here and it still drives me nuts sometimes."

"I'm afraid I don't know enough even to comment on that. In fact, you five were the first Kauri I'd ever seen."

"Yeah? Well, I guess that's natural. Most of us stay around here or in the Firehills region and east. It's kinda the pledge, y'know; keeps us pretty bored most of the time."

"The pledge?"

Aislee nodded. "Yeah. You know—we won't do to others if they don't do to us, that kind of thing. They're scared of us and we're scared of them, so we take it easy."

"You mean nobody ever goes far from Mohr Jerahl?"

"Oh, some go a long way. We're always in demand, y'know. Conventions, banquets, troop entertainment, that sort of thing. But it's strictly temporary and real limited, y'know."

No, Marge *didn't* know, but in fits and starts she began to get a picture of just who and what the Kauri were.

The Kauri flew, of course, like many other fairy folk, and were very light and hollow-boned. Still, they were tough—their skin was covered with a substance that had the feeling and texture of felt, while their wings were soft and satiny. This covering protected them from almost everything—it was waterproof, even fireproof, and it somehow acted like a major shock absorber. The Kauri were also extremely fluid in internal construction, so they could bear almost crushing weights without problem—yet they themselves were so light that they had trouble staying grounded in a strong breeze.

While hard to damage or kill—except with iron, of course—they were by nature quite passive and found it impossible to cause permanent injury, let alone to kill anyone or anything. Although without any magic powers or spells themselves, they were controlled empaths in both directions. The emotions of any human were an open book to them, and they could instantly tell fear, love, sincerity, or falsehood. This had its drawbacks—sorrow would flood into them and they would find themselves crying uncontrollably; hilarity or joy around them would make them so manic they'd be higher than kites. They could, however, project desired feelings to others—humans, certainly, but also many of the fairy folk, particularly the most dangerous. It could be conscious, especially in a one-on-one situation, but it could also be instinctive. If a threat were perceived—and it usually could be from the empathic input—then they became impossible to harm or kill. The more intense the negative emotion, the more the counter was radiated.

As Marge and Aislee talked, a couple of other Kauri found them and joined in, like excited schoolgirls.

It was obvious that the Kauri had no self-control over their emotions whatsoever. Emotional seven-year-olds, Marge decided, with the brains and physiques of very adult women.

Naturally, they were in great demand as courtesans, exotic dancers, and everything else that adult physique implied. They could and did mate with practically any male of any species, human, fairy, or animal, and the occasional issue of such matings was an unpredictable hybrid in half the cases, or, of course, a Kauri in the other half. All Kauri were absolutely identical, it seemed, because all descended from an initial mother Kauri back at the start of the world. The laws of genetics often went wild in the magical Kauri world. The Kauri, at least, believed that many of the hybrid races of their world were their children—the centaur, the satyr, the medusae, and just about all other hybrid forms. Changelings, too—those born of one race who turned into another, such as Marge—were their doing, although it was extremely rare that a changeling would become a Kauri.

Marge sat down and relaxed with them, not sure if it was the fairy empathic powers that made her feel at ease or that it seemed she was back with a group of barely post-pubescent girlfriends in junior high school, but not really caring, either. They giggled, they played, and they seemed incapable of staying on a single train of thought for any length of time; but as the hours passed, she did get most of the information she wanted.

In many ways, each of the fairy races embodied some basic, elemental force of nature, and it seemed that these elf-nymphs represented a curious blend of childlike enthusiasm and raw sexuality.

They had no government, no ruling class or council. They could never have gotten organized enough for that, nor could any of them for long follow another's lead. Their lives, in the main, seemed the classic fairy ideal—they awoke, they played, they sang, they danced, they spent all the time having childish fun. Occasionally an emissary from some far-off place would appear at a clearly defined "gate" to Mohr Jerahl and make them a proposition. In exchange for their limited services at some great occasion or function, they would get—well, nice things. Their wing structure precluded clothing, but they loved jewels and jewelry—the more finely crafted and the prettier the better. New songs, dances, games, toys, and puzzles for the whole tribe were also highly prized. There was no order or system—whoever happened to be around and felt like going for whatever offering was tendered just went.

Although they had no active powers of their own—save projecting emotion, and that was best done one-on-one—their passivity was no problem in a violent and magical world. Without their knowing how, any spell or physical overpowering was somehow countered. They *absorbed* the strength, whether physical, mental, or magical, from the one trying it on them and retained its power for some time—from a few hours to a day or more. They had no idea of the nature of any of their attributes; they were too elemental to have a science. They had not reached their current point through evolution—they had always been as they were now and would always be so—and, therefore, had no interest in the matter. Marge began to realize what Huspeth had meant by saying she must put reason and logic aside and do things instinctively, unthinkingly.

A top-grade sorcerer, of course, could negate their powers, since the very nature of long studies in sorcery was the scientific investigation of magic and its application. Ruddygore knew how the Kauri's incredible defenses worked and so he could methodically prepare a counter to them—but few others could, and only the best would block all the magical loopholes.

Still, the Kauri were as much feared as prized. If they

wanted, they could overload a man's emotional centers so much that they could turn him into a virtual love slave, sapping all self-control and free will. At the same time, that strength or power taken from someone was in a way vampiric; the one from whom it was taken lost it, perhaps for good.

There was danger outside, too, even for such as these. Their power was strong only against or with males; with women they had, at best, a localized and temporary effect. The emotional projection still worked, but little else, and that meant that women, particularly those skilled in magic, could harm them.

Marge began to see at least part of Ruddygore's thinking, particularly when she considered only the sorcerer's interests. And why consider more, for that matter? After all, Joe and she had both been very close to death back home and, no matter how much they might resent the sorcerer's machinations concerning them, it was, at least so far, much better than the alternative.

As a team, they had what Ruddygore would be interested in most. As a passive shield, she could protect against much of the magic of this world they were likely to encounter; Joe could certainly handle the rest of the problems. What concerned her was just how much of what was truly her would survive in that partnership.

She was still full of questions, though. "If you all look identical, then how do you tell each other apart?" she wanted to know.

They laughed at the question. "It's easy. You just *know*, that's all," one answered.

You just know, *that's all . . .*

The basic schism between human and fairy.

"But come," Aislee—at least Marge thought it was Aislee—said to her. "We can solve this a lot easier by making you totally one of us." They all got up, and the Kauri added, "Uh, you are *sure* you're Kauri, aren't you?"

Marge frowned. "As far as I know. At least, that's what the sorcerer told me, and he should know. You should, too, if you can read me as you say."

"Oh, yeah, we can tell *you* believe it, but not whether it's so. There's only one way to find out; and if your wizard slipped up, it will be real trouble."

"How do we—do it?"

"The last mortal part of you has to be taken off, of course. Come on—this should be interesting."

Marge didn't like the tone or the implication here, realizing that to these creatures she was a game, a diversion, a bit of fun and no more.

The crowd of Kauri was still out there, but now they sensed that the big moment had come and lapsed into near-total silence. They were the spectators in the coliseum now, waiting to see the show.

Aislee and the others led her up the gentle cone to the very rim of the crater. The heat and smoke coming from the mass bubbling not far below were secondary to the tremendous, blinding magical radiation at this point.

"Well," one of the Kauri prompted, "go ahead. Jump in."

She felt doubt and panic flood into her. "You mean—jump in *there*?"

"That's the only way to do it."

She swallowed hard, and her mind swirled with tremendous doubts. What if they were testing her? What if they were trying to get rid of her? What if this were some grisly practical joke of bored fairies?

Behind her, she could hear the crowd shouting, "Jump! Jump! Go on! Jump!" It sounded like some ghoulish cheerleader squad for a virgin sacrificial ceremony and—uh-oh. She'd forgotten that *she* was biologically virgin now. Virgin plus volcano equals sacrifice . . .

"Jump in, jump in! Rah! Rah! Rah!"

She just stood there, petrified with fright, knowing she could not move a step in any direction, not even to run.

"Oh, the hell with it. This is getting boring," one of the Kauri next to her muttered. The next thing Marge knew, she felt a violent shove and she was falling, falling right into the boiling, bubbling magma . . .

There was a shock as she hit the red, bubbling mass that might have a temperature of perhaps two thousand degrees, and an all-encompassing but very brief pain, much like that which an electric shock would give.

And then she was floating, swimming, flying, suspended in the mass but no longer sensitive to it. There was no up, no down, no east, west, north, or south. There was however, a presence. It was in there with her, all around her and coursing not only through the molten magma but right through her as well. She did not know what it was, but it was undeniably the locus, the source of the magic.

"Be at peace," came a powerful, all embracing, motherly voice in her head. She realized that no words had been spoken, since none could be, under these conditions; but the voice was so commanding, so authoritative, yet so friendly and reassuring that it could not be denied.

It was her long-dead mother's voice.

"Mother?" her mind shot out, trying to reach it.

"I am indeed the mother of the Kauri, of which you are almost one," the voice responded.

"Who? What . . . ?"

"You are troubled, child. The Kauri are not troubled, for were one to be troubled, the race would be troubled. To be troubled is for threats to person or the race, not otherwise. Mohr Jerahl is a place of peace, of art and dance and fun. The Kauri are the creatures of Mohr Jerahl, and so they must reflect its nature. Come to me in the fire, as all those who venture outside our homeland must, and let me ease your trouble. Relax and think not; come unto me and give me your mind."

The creature, whatever it was, hesitated a moment, as if waiting for her, but she did not, could not, yield to it.

"You hesitate. You close your mind to me. Why?"

"I—I'm afraid," she admitted. "A change in form is one thing, but I don't want to be not me any longer!"

"But you will always be you and no other," the voice of her mother soothed. "You come from the world of the Creator. He alone fashioned your soul and its nature, and He alone can refashion it. But the shape of that soul is Kauri, deep down. Your sorcerer knew this when he directed your destiny so."

"But the Kauri are of this world, not mine!" she protested. "How can I have a Kauri soul?"

"Child, the soul is insubstantial, mystical. It exists on the magical plane and on no other. The fairies—all of faërie—are souls bared, souls distilled, unencumbered by human form and fears, for they exist only in the world of supernature. They exist on the plane of pre-creation, before the universes were formed, at the level of elemental, basic magic. Humanity was made by imposing natural law on the soul; natural form, pain, toil, suffering, mortality—these came later, when the Rebels caused the violation of Eden's perfection. All that is now taken from you. All that was mortal and natural in you was borne away when you entered here. The nature of the soul determines the nature of the person.

"The fairies exist in all humankind and are not bound by any world or its rules, only by those rules imposed upon the race by the Creator. We were the models and the overseers in the grand design. Humans who go against their own natures—as many do for a variety of reasons, not all under their control—suffer all the more for it. For, you see, that is the true curse laid upon man after Eden—that he will turn his back on supernature and will fight his own soul. In such a way do misery, unhappiness, and evil breed."

She was startled by this information and its implications. "What you are saying, then, is that we are *all* changelings."

"Yes, all. But when death comes to the mortal and frees the soul, and that soul is purged of its sin, it lives apart from us, within the Sea of Dreams, in a world that is wholly supernatural. Fairies, being of the world, do not have an afterlife. The price is paid—we may achieve the true balance of our natures only by remaining alive until the end of all time, when Creation shall be undone. That is our curse for being lax and allowing the chief Rebel to slip unnoticed into Eden. That is the curse you now share, a fair exchange for shedding your mortality. But a cleansing is needed to make you truly of faërie and allow your full supernature to come out. To do that, you must surrender to me."

Marge understood now the logic of it all, understood the nature of the fairies and the soul as few had understood before her, yet she could not bring herself to yield. Most of her wanted what was offered, but there was still that corner of her that was afraid, that feared tampering with her mind as this world had tampered with her body.

"Or, to put it another way," the goddess of the volcano added, "if you don't yield to me, you'll swim around in this hot muck, frying your little buns off for all eternity." For emphasis, the pain began, and slowly increased.

A Kauri goddess might be somewhat intellectual, but she was the mold of the race and not much more patient than her children. The vision, the sensation, of the classical hell of

Marge's Christian upbringing was a really persuasive argument. As the pain continued to rise, she could stand it no longer. "All right! Take me!" her mind screamed.

The pain ceased, and the entity, whatever it was, assumed complete control. Marge was aware and fully conscious, yet not in control of even her own thoughts. Her memory was triggered and read out in reverse order, every moment of her past flowing from her and into the creature. Her mind was incapable of digesting the minutiae that were stored in her own brain, and she tended to seize upon and partially relive only brief scenes of major events.

She was outside the volcano. She was walking through the forest. She was leaving Joe. She was at the entry station, now back at Terindell, then in the Glen Dinig. In fits and starts and in a sort of backward review, she relived the great battle, the Land of the Djinn, the fight for the Lamp, and the battle at the pass. Backward, ever backward.

She crossed the Sea of Dreams once more and found herself totally shorn of hope, direction, or self-interest, walking along a lonely west Texas road.

His face was a furious red with anger, hatred, and frustration, and he was beating her repeatedly, all the while shouting, "What the hell good are you? Can't even make a damned kid in this Godforsaken hellhole!"

"I, Marge, take thee, Roger . . ."

"I'm sorry, but less kids means less teachers and lower budgets. You know how it is. Now if you'd been in math or science . . ."

She stood on the steps outside the administration building, still in cap and gown, holding the diploma up to the bright, blue Texas sky. "See, Momma? I did it!"

"Mommy! Guess what! Tommy Woodard asked me to the prom! Tommy Woodard!"

It was blood! She was bleeding from *there*! Oh, God! *"Mommy!"*

"There, there! It's just a skinned knee. Mommy'll put a little stuff on it and kiss it and make it all better . . ."

She didn't like playing hide-and-seek when there were *boys* playing. They always cheated or ganged up on the girls. "Eight . . . nine . . . ten! Ready or not, here I come!" She could hear the squeals of laughter and see just a corner of somebody's foot behind the bush. She ran for the hider, who, suddenly knowing she'd been spotted, broke from her hiding place and started heading for the tree base. Marge felt a thrill and whirled, trying to beat Mary Frances to the . . .

Sufficient, a voice said from somewhere. *Freeze.*

Quickly, methodically, she began to come back toward the present. All of the events were there, all the traumas, all the heartbreak, but it wasn't quite the same as it had been. It was real, it was hers, it was even totally comprehensible, but somehow it just didn't matter so much any more. The dark times that had formed her were there, all right, but the good times, the happy times, the fun times stood out. She could reach out and touch any of those dark spots at any time, but, left alone, it was the good times, the fun times, the *innocent* times that seemed somehow forward, filling in the empty spaces.

The goodness of the Kauri had in fact been truthful, honest, and correct. Marge *understood* now, understood the nature of the Kauri and the reason for it. She had recaptured it, with the goddess' help—that essence of childhood that adults could fondly and wistfully remember but never really reexperience, except vicariously through watching their own children. She realized, with a tremendous surge of excitement, that she had indeed buried the horrors of her past, even though she was still and would always be shaped by them. She was new, reborn, free . . .

Free!

She burst out of the top of the volcano and flew up, up into the night, with a feeling of incredible energy and joy. She spread out her arms and let her wings catch the air currents she could easily see. Not even thinking about what she was doing, or how, she did whirls and flips and laughed and giggled at everything like a drunken flyer on a real tear. The world looked subtly different, and very, very beautiful, with every single object, every single substance, in clear focus as far as she could see; yet, unlike her earlier experience, it was also a riot of colors. She began to shift through all the levels she could see, and the world changed dramatically each time.

The colors, the rainbow of colors—*why, the whole world was magic!* She saw below, above, all around, the world of faërie, and it was more beautiful than she could have ever dreamed.

And now others were joining her, playing, looping around in

the air. She knew them without having to think at all; her sisters, the Kauri, each radiating a subtly different magical pattern and emotional register. They greeted her, welcomed her, by drawing from her the tremendous feelings she was having, and they played, chased, showed off, and generally had a really good time themselves.

They soared together beneath the stars, protected in the glow of the Earth Mother's radiant embrace, skimming the treetops, then rising upward, ever upward, until the whole magical land was spread out before and beneath them. With no cares, no worries, they soared like superchildren, everything new, everything a wonder.

She saw the treasures of the Kauri and plucked a beautiful, gem-encrusted tiara out of the pile and crowned herself queen of the air; others scrambled for even grander headwear and challenged her reign, laughing and giggling all the while, flittering about and snatching crowns, tiaras, and all sorts of other regal stuff from one another. There were forty or fifty queens crowned that night, all self-anointed—and the same number dethroned by playful, giggling subjects with ambitions of their own.

There were toys and games and maddening puzzles, and all sorts of fun things. And never once was there hatred, malice, anger, or fear.

They plucked ripe fruits from trees and bushes and ate them, often throwing them at one another, and walked on the waters of a deep volcanic lake without sinking in. And they were *all* queen of this mystical, magical, happy place.

When the sun came up, turning the land a new set of colors, they went to the trees, high up and far beyond any ground-dwelling things, and settled into happy, dreaming sleep. For Marge, it was a sleep filled with the happy experiences of childhood and the best and deepest sleep she had had in many long years.

The next night was more of the same. There was total acceptance of her by the native Kauri; like her, they could see and feel inside one another, and she was one with them. This time they ranged far, almost to the Firehills, great ridges in the earth that seemed to hiss and glow from long fissures in their sides—mountains that were at once solid and yet continually on fire.

She did wonder that they never ventured forth by day, but she was told that the brightness of the sun hurt their eyes and could actually blind them for a while. Paradoxically, the Kauri were attracted to light, or, at least, to open flames, and great fires could have a near-hypnotic effect on them. While it could not harm them, it induced an odd sort of catatonia of mind and body, and this, in turn, left them defenseless. It was a hard thing to explain, being more related to brightness than to the size or shape of the light; but, they assured her, she would know the first time she left the protection of Mohr Jerahl. That comment for the first time brought her thoughts back to Joe, who would be waiting for her only this one more night. Tomorrow he would enter Mohr Jerahl in search of her, committing the ultimate sacrilege of bringing iron into the enchanted land.

"I must go to him while the dark still holds," she told them with much sadness and regret. "He must not be allowed to enter here."

"But you'll get rid of him and return soon enough," Coasu, one of her new friends, responded.

She thought about it. "No, not right away. I think I must leave for a time, my sisters. Something pulls me that I can not explain, something that is still important. I am Kauri for a reason, and that reason pulls me away, but only for a time."

They could read her sincerity, but they could not understand it. "Then we will go with you, too," Coasu said. "Aislee, me, and perhaps others. If this matter is so important, then if one Kauri can help, perhaps many can help more. You are sad to leave, and one must never leave Mohr Jerahl in sadness."

Her deep affection for them and their offer reached out to them, so that no words were needed, but she shook her head. "No, I am sad to leave only because I love this place and you all so much. But once I looked in the face of Hell, and I know that somehow I must help defeat it here and now. They all knew this—the Earth Mother, Ruddygore, Huspeth."

"This is getting heavy," Aislee noted grumbling. "We have nothing to do with that kind of thing."

The thought came, unbidden and from elsewhere, into Marge's mind. "The Earth Mother knows. We have no dealings with the affairs of politics, but this is beyond that. All of the faërie is involved in this. Ask the Earth Mother."

They knew instantly that it was not Marge who had spoken, and they became quiet and almost reverential. Marge smiled and kissed them all in turn. "I'll be back," she promised them. "I am a Kauri now, and a Kauri forever, until the end of time. Besides," she added, part seriously, "it could be a lot of fun being a Kauri out there." She laughed. "And I'll bring back a new present and let you drool all over it."

That broke the mood. "Yes! Something really good!" one cried in anticipation. "Make them pay well for your services! It is a Kauri tradition."

Visions of tacky plaster sculptures came into her mind and gave her a mild case of the giggles, but, she promised herself, there would be none of *that* here.

It was an emotional farewell, a party of sorts that got enough out of hand in the Kauri's usual anarchistic way so that she finally just slipped out on it and flew to the Bird's Breath.

Crossing the little creek and leaving Mohr Jerahl gave her a cold, eerie feeling—a feeling of being somehow cut off from a warm and friendly glow.

She flew down the river a bit, until she saw Joe's camp. It's fire was just a few glowing embers, and both the big man and the horses were fast asleep. It was easy to find him, though—the iron in the sword, deadly to her even in the early stages of her transformation here, was now a tangible and terrible, cold darkness that she would simply have to adjust to. She knew that it gave these sensations to all fairies, save only the dwarfs, whose special power it was to handle iron and its deadly magic, and in that alone was there some comfort. Although all iron threatened her, this was as close as she could come to "friendly iron," and she knew Joe had been well trained and was accustomed to shielding fairies on his side from its power.

She flittered down near the fire, just across from him, with the unnatural silence that only a fairy could have, and stood there a moment, looking at the sleeping man.

The sword began to hum softly but irritatingly. She took a single step forward and the noise became a terrible, grating sound. In that same instant Joe rolled, grabbed the sword, and was on his feet, at the ready. As with all dwarf things, Irving was far more than a mere sword of iron alloy. Now, unsheathed, it seemed almost to burn her with a cold, deadly radiation all its own, a flow that ebbed and pulsed with the humming sound.

"Who are you?" the big man challenged menacingly.

"Put the sword away, Joe," she almost pleaded with him. "It's hurting me."

He made no move to do so. "How do you know my name?"

"It's Marge, Joe. This is the way I look now. All the Kauri look like this."

He frowned a moment. The creature was incredibly, voluptuously beautiful, but it was not reminiscent of Marge in any definitive physical feature. "Can you prove it? I've had some bad experience with good-looking nymphs and sprites that didn't mean me any good." He thought a moment. "What's the capital of Pennsylvania?"

"Oh, good grief." She sighed. "I don't know. Philadelphia?"

"I was thinking Philadelphia, but it's really Harrisburg," he snapped back. "You're just reading my mind!"

She could feel his anger and suspicion flowing out of him and into her, and it was an ugly feeling indeed. She could counter it, of course, even bring him down, but the empathic projection might not have much power over that damned sword, which had a mind of its own and could protect against some spells as well. Instead she countered, "Joe—what's the capital city of Missouri?"

He was startled. "Huh? St. Louis?" She shook her head. "Columbia? Kansas City?"

"Jefferson City," she told him. "See all that proves? But I'll describe every inch of every truck stop in Ozona, Texas, for you and even describe all the damned tacky sculptures I can remember being in Ruddygore's basement."

He relaxed, and so did the sword, as his face reflected an unthreatened but incredulous feeling. "Marge? Is it *really* you?"

She nodded. "Now put that damned pig-sticker away. Feed it a bone and tell it to be a good dog or something."

He sheathed the weapon, which lapsed back into silence, reading his conviction, but he still could hardly believe it. He walked over to her and examined her closely, dwelling, she noted, on some rather interesting parts. "Damn!" he swore. "This is like coming out of Ruddygore's lab, way back when, all over again. You're—smaller."

That was true enough. Not only was she the four-foot-ten that was the height of all adult Kauri, but her exaggerated shapes and curves gave her an even more elfin appearance.

"But I've grown my wings," she pointed out.

He cleared his throat. "Yeah—and other things, too."

"You called me a nymph, and that's right. In fact, we're the prototype for all nymphs. They say this is my true nature coming through." She chuckled. "No wonder I kind of fell into prostitution back in Texas for a while. But back there I had so many problems and hang-ups, they drove me crazy. Over here, like this, I'm free of all that."

He grinned at the implications of that. They had a long way to go, after all. That did, however, bring him back to the future. "We should be going in the morning. Ruddygore's convention is still a rough ride from here, and it's all paths rather than roads."

That brought her up short a bit. "That could be a problem," she told him. "I'm nocturnal. The sun kind of saps my strength, puts me to sleep."

He laughed and walked over to the packs, then rooted through them for a moment before coming up with an object. "That explains this, then. I didn't have much to do, so I decided to look at what Ruddygore had put in here. Among the things was this." He brought the object over and handed it to her.

It was a pair of sunglasses, a wraparound sort that hugged the face, with cupped lenses that blocked all light not coming through them, almost like goggles. She put them on and was not surprised to find that they were a perfect fit, even adjusted properly for her pointed, elfin ears and the new shape of her face. She took them off again and looked at them, then giggled. "See the printing down here on the frame?"

He shook his head. "It's too dark for me."

"It says, 'Made in Taiwan'!"

CHAPTER 5

A FEW MINOR OBSTACLES

It is best to avoid volcanoes whenever possible.
—Rules, XXII, 196(c)

THE GLASSES PROVED SUFFICIENT FOR MARGE TO ENDURE daylight, but did nothing to restore needed sleep. She fitted on the horse fine, though, despite the membranous wings and her smaller size, and found no trouble keeping an almost effortless balance. Finally she just told Joe that she had to nod out, and he told her to do so. Although the fearsome Firehills loomed in front of them, they would not reach them until late in the day, and the land was pretty much a flat semidesert, requiring no real riding skills. Her horse was well trained, although Joe wished often for Posti, the gray mare who was really a transformed dirt farmer. Posti had returned safely to Terindell, but was not allowed to make this trip to Sachalin. Ruddygore had been more than worried about a transformed horse in the midst of a bunch of drunken sorcerers.

Things went smoothly for several hours. Joe was a little bored, but he'd made his living in the old days driving a truck, and this was a lot easier to handle than a fully loaded semi. He *did* wish now, as he had often wished, that saddles came with tape decks, but he compensated by singing his favorite old Ferlin Husky and Waylon Jennings tunes. He had a lousy voice, but it was always impossible to convince him of that fact in this world or the one from which he'd come; as he belted out tune after tune, he hardly took notice of the hordes of insects, small animals, and birds fleeing in all directions before him as if from a forest fire. As for Marge, when she was out, she was *out*, it seemed, which suited him just fine right now. He needed some time to think.

She definitely took some getting used to, he reflected. She'd been okay before; Ruddygore had given her a pretty good figure. But, particularly after that witch in the wood got hold of her, she'd been less of a looker and more like a female jock.

319

This new Marge—or new, new Marge—was something else again. Small, petite, cute, sexy as all hell, and naked to boot. The batlike wings were so beautifully colored that they seemed more like some precious butterfly's than anything negative. She was definitely no longer human—no real person had ever been put together so absolutely perfectly, except maybe in some artist's dreams—but the old Marge personality and an incongruous trace of a Texas accent still came through.

Those wings, they were funny things, he decided. He'd seen her fly and knew that she just lifted off effortlessly, like Peter Pan or something, often hovering as if gravity didn't exist for her, and quite often without spreading those wings at all. They weren't necessary for her to fly, that was for sure, and he wondered if they were just decorative or whether they had some different kind of function. They definitely made wearing clothes impossible, so her unnatural endowments were out there for the world to see. That, too, would take some getting used to. He wanted her, and he knew that any other man who was the least bit turned on by women would want her, too. He wasn't sure how he'd take that. He'd gone crazy during her whole celibacy period, but at least it had been the same for every other man she knew. Now, though—well, creatures weren't put together that way just for the hell of it. Every fairy he'd run into since being in Husaquahr had a particular role to play and was more or less designed for the part. It didn't take a lecture in fairy lore to tell him what the Kauri's obvious role in the supernatural scheme of things was.

In a sense, it made him feel even more alone, since he knew that there was now a gulf separating them forever. She was no longer human, nor could she be expected to be human again. The fairies always did what they had to do, what they were supposed to do, his teachers back at Terindell had assured him. While that made them somewhat predictable, it made Marge and him more than a world apart.

He continued to brood as they slowly approached the Firehills, alternately cursing Ruddygore for bringing him here and himself for feeling weaknesses inside himself he never really knew were there.

The Firehills looked more intimidating the closer he got to them. Less a mountain chain than a whole line of continuous small volcanoes, their tops were shrouded in white smoke, through which occasional flashes of fire were visible now. He was worried about that fire, and by the fact that there seemed no break as far as the eye could see in that solid, if fairly low, black wall. They had been following the now tiny Bird's Breath all the way, but soon it petered out into a not-very-wet marsh, while the path continued right toward the barrier ahead, with no pass in sight.

There were bushes and many odd-looking groves of trees, but now in the air there was the unmistakable smell of sulfur and the rotten-egg odor of hydrogen sulfide. The path led through brilliantly colored mud pots, some of which occasionally gurgled and bubbled and steamed their foul odors. Here and there were pools of very clear water, but he could see within the pools the discolorations from the settling out of minerals and the steam rising off their surfaces. Clearly the Bird's Breath had its origins in volcanic waters, and probably should have been named Dragon's Breath. It sure smelled like it, anyway.

Off in the distance, a geyser spouted a hundred feet or more into the air with a great rush and roar, and he stopped momentarily to watch it, then became acutely aware that there were a lot of geyser holes all around him. He sighed and pressed on, trying to reassure himself that it had been Ruddygore who had recommended this route. It didn't reassure him all that much, though, since Ruddygore had always been more certain to get them in trouble than out of it in the past.

The sun was low in the sky when, threading his way through a virtual mine field of volcanic manifestations, not to mention leading Marge's horse through it, he finally reached the base of the Firehills themselves. The horses were getting jumpy and acting uncomfortable from all the hissing, roaring, bubbling, smoke, and smells, but they didn't feel anything he didn't feel double. He decided that it was time Marge woke up, no matter how much beauty sleep she needed.

After finding that yelling and shaking her produced only a dreamy reaction and shifting, he finally got fed up and did some obscene and not-very-gentle things to her. She gave a big, dreamy smile and sighed; her fairy eyelashes fluttered a bit, and those great, sensuous eyes opened a crack. Under any other circumstances, he would have been delighted at the reaction, but the fear of being roasted alive had a tendency to drive all other impulses from his head.

"Marge! Wake up!" he screamed as the lids started to flutter back, and he reached over, cursing, and dropped the dark glasses back into place.

From Marge's vantage point, it was at first like being awakened from a pleasant sleep filled with erotic dreams to a disorienting confusion; but when the glasses slid down, she suddenly saw perfectly and sat bolt upright. "Wha—what's happened?" She looked up at the blackish cinder wall rising just ahead of them and the strange and violent landscape behind and grew instantly alert. "How'd we get *here*?"

"We rode," he responded sourly. "The map says there's a path over this damned hill. Not only do I not see one, but darkness is coming on, and I sure don't want to spend the night here!"

She glanced around. "Looks okay to me. Real pretty, in fact." She stopped short for a moment, realizing her reaction and comparing it with her memories. The Kauri were creatures of this earth-fire, but others were not. The land posed no problems for her, yet she could sense Joe's fear and discomfort with that empathic ability and she grew concerned for his safety. She looked up at the Firehills, so dark and featureless to their smoke-covered tops, and she could indeed see the flashes of molten fire through that smoke. It looked as if the whole ridge had a crack most of the way to the top, a crack running horizontally as far as the eye could see. "Let me have the map," she said, suddenly serious. She looked at it for a moment, frowning. "Let me go up and see what's what."

Without waiting for his reply, she rose effortlessly off the horse and into the air, moving straight up until she was out of sight. All he could do was wait there, calming the horses and starting to worry more and more.

She was gone for what seemed like ages; then, as silently as she'd left, she returned and quickly settled, standing daintily atop her horse's saddle. He could see by her expression that things were at least as bad as he'd imagined.

"Trouble," she told him needlessly. "I've been all over the area, and finally I figured out that we took a wrong turn. There's something of a break in the Firehills about twenty miles northwest of here, in a place where they're not very active, and there's an old path to it and across. There's a second branch of the Bird's Breath we were supposed to take and didn't."

He sighed and shrugged. "The thing was so small I never saw any junction. That damned map doesn't show which is which, so I followed what looked like the main course all the way here."

"Yeah, this *is* the source, but it's not the stream we were supposed to follow."

He looked toward the darkening, nightmare landscape to the northwest. "So I guess we'll have to detour."

She shook her head. "Uh-uh. You don't want to go through that mess, I'll tell you. This is a calm and stable part. I'll swear. You could never be sure of the ground elsewhere. It's a good twenty miles back to the fork, then another thirty to the pass. That's two, maybe three days, and I don't think the horses could take it. They're straining now."

He sighed. "So what else can I do? *You* can fly over and be safe and comfortable in bed tomorrow, but I sure as hell can't, and I'm not going to abandon the horses and supplies unless I have to. In this stuff, it would be their death warrant."

She nodded. "Then the only way is to go up. If we can cross over, the horses can get a good rest and watering on the other side." She paused. "You, too."

He wiped sweat from his forehead and looked up at the ominous hill. "So how do we do it?"

"First let me go up and check it out, see if there's any place we can cross. Then we'll risk my horse, with me leading. If the stuff underfoot holds her, it will hold you and yours."

He nodded. "Fair enough. But be careful—I don't want you melted down."

She laughed. "No danger of that. I can swim in the stuff, Joe. I *have* done it." She sighed and looked up at the swirling smoke. "Well—here goes!" And with that, she was gone, flying up the side and into the dense cloud at the top.

This time she was gone for only a couple of minutes, reappearing and setting down in front of her horse. "There's a way, I think," she told him, "but it's going to be a real hairy time for you and the horses. It's cinder most of the way, but I think it will hold. Up just into the smoke, though, the heat comes and goes. There are real nasty cracks all over the place." She pointed. "But in one spot, just over there, it seems fairly cool. It's been hot, though, and the heat has melted and remelted the stuff up there. The surface is almost like glass, and it's bound to be slippery. If you slip, it's pretty nasty on either side."

He looked up swallowed hard. "Well, let's try it. *Anything* to get out of spending a night around here. I want to get it over with while there's still some light."

She nodded. Taking her horse's bridle, she stepped out onto the cinders. The horse resisted for a moment, then went along when she saw Marge being supported. Then the horse sank a bit into the cinders and ash and thrashed for a moment in confusion. It took precious minutes of Joe's daylight to calm her down and get her to go on.

Beyond, the cinders and ash were so dense that they gave a surprisingly solid footing. Joe decided to lead his horse as well and was relieved to find that the hill felt, at least at the beginning, cool. He was, however, really beginning to wish he could trade his thick sandals for some even thicker boots. Asbestos boots, preferably.

The slope was rather gentle, and they took it at an angle, but it was slow going, and several times the material gave way, causing a momentary loss of footing. The horses were a big problem here, but, fortunately, none were sufficiently unbalanced by the occasional loss of footing to go tumbling over and back down.

Almost before Joe realized it, they were up to the smoke level and into it. The stuff stank and stung his eyes, causing even more problems with the horses, but the gases weren't very dense, once he was in them, and he could, at least, see ahead to the rear of Marge's horse. One thing for sure, though—the air was getting really hot, and he was sweating as he never had before. The volcanic surface, too, was getting pretty damned warm, although not bad enough to cause burning.

And then they hit the remelted area. He had imagined a smooth slope. In fact, it was rough and irregular, but it *was* shiny and slippery. Only the irregularities in its surface, almost like a frozen sea, allowed them any chance of footing. The stuff was *hot*, too—he felt as if he were in somebody's giant oven, and the bottom of his sandals were becoming very, very warm.

He soon saw why. Only ten feet or so on either side, the glassy surface dropped away to reveal a bubbling, hissing pit.

"I'm already well done!" he called out, coughing at the smoke and miserable from the intense heat. "How much farther is it?"

"Not far," she called back. "Just ten more minutes and we're home free!"

He groaned. He wasn't sure he or the horses could last that long. Right about then he was so miserable he didn't give a damn about the horses.

Suddenly Marge stopped, and he almost screamed out in agony. "*Now* what?"

"We're not alone up here," she responded, sounding worried. "I think you better draw Irving."

"He's so damned hot I can't even *touch* him," Joe called back in disgust, but he did try the sword hilt—and found he wasn't kidding.

A series of small, dark shapes that looked like moving globs of obsidian formed around them on the peak. Joe couldn't get a good look at them, but Marge had no trouble at all. They did, in fact, appear to be made out of the same stuff as the melted material on which they all stood, but these creatures had definite form. They looked like funny little men—or, rather, statues of funny-looking little men, she decided, with short, stocky bodies, stubby limbs, and huge balloonlike noses. She couldn't help thinking of Grumpy from *Snow White* as she stared at them, and that certainly fitted their expressions and mean-looking gazes.

"Are you union or scabs?" the lead one rasped out in a stern, deep, gruff voice.

The question took her aback. "What do you mean? All we're trying to do is cross this mountain before the man with me and the horses die. *Please* let us past!"

"Are you union or scabs?" the creature repeated, unmoved.

"I am Kauri, and no scab!" she responded angrily. "You should know we have no need of a union!"

"Hah! Sexual exploitation without love or involvement and all for some cheap bauble," another of the creatures muttered. "And they're so dumb they don't even see how they're exploited."

Marge was acutely aware that time was running out, but she

decided she had to play their game before they forgot their challenge and started debating among themselves. She'd had enough of that with the Kauri. "We're independent, yet collective! You know that! It's in our nature to be so! What sort of creatures are you that you don't know this?"

"We're kobolds, of course," the leader snapped.

"And we're on strike," another piped up. Joe felt his horse shudder, and began to feel that he was going to pass out on his feet, as well. He couldn't take much more of this.

"Aye," another kobold responded. "No more of them fairy rings and stuff until we get our contract!" The rest of them cheered.

"Your dispute is none of our affair," Marge argued pleadingly. "Please—this man will die if we're delayed even a few moments longer."

The leader looked over at Joe. "How do you stand on unions?"

Right then Joe was not feeling in a fraternal mood. He decided that, if he weren't about to die, he'd like to chop these bastards up into little pieces. He tried to snarl a reply, but only inhaled more of the acrid smoke and started coughing.

"He *is* a union man!" Marge told them, thinking furiously. "He's a Teamster."

The kobolds all looked at Joe critically. "Indeed? He don't look like no wagon driver to me," the leader noted. "Let's see your union card!"

At that moment, Joe's horse gave another great shudder and this time collapsed onto the hot surface. Joe whirled, then fell almost completely over the horse.

Marge yelled in a mixture of anger and panic, "In the name of the Earth Mother, help me get him off this place before he dies and quickly!"

"Religion is the opiate of the masses," one of the kobolds muttered, seemingly unmoved.

"Still," the leader mused, "we can't have a popular workingmen's movement—"

"And women," another added.

"—sullied at its great beginnings by a lack of compassion . . . Hmm . . . You! Imli! Zimlich! Grab his head and feet! You, Kauri—get going! We'll follow!"

Quickly the little men snapped to action. They were extremely strong and powerful, despite their small size. It took only two of them to lift Joe as if he weighed next to nothing, and four more actually lifted the horse and started after Marge and the others at what was close to a trot.

The obsidian bridge thinned appreciably as they went, and it was none too clear just how much longer it could support weight, but Marge's horse needed no urging. They were across, followed by the kobolds, in a few brief minutes. The weight of Joe's horse, though, was the final straw for the weakened bridge; just as they cleared the last of it, the entire center shuddered and collapsed with a rumble back into the volcano.

Joe awoke slowly in the darkness. He had been nearly comatose for several hours, often delirious and out of his head. He felt a cold compress being applied to his forehead and groaned, although it felt really good.

"Joe?" Marge asked tentatively, and he could hear the concern in her voice.

"Yeah," he croaked, his voice a dry rasp. "I *guess* I'm here."

Her joy at his coming out of it was such that not only was it evident in her physical reactions but also was radiated from her into him. It was a strange, warm sensation, unlike anything he'd experienced before, and he was deeply moved by it.

"How bad am I hurt?" he asked her, trying not to show what he was receiving. To his relief, the joyous emotions didn't change.

"You're not bad. A little scorched around the edges, but mostly it was dehydration. I've been feeding you water in small doses all night and getting compresses on you to bring the temperature down." She handed him a canteen, and he drank from it so greedily that she had to pull it away. "Uh-uh. I know something about dehydration, and you take water in slow doses," she cautioned. "Here. Take a little of this."

She handed him a small, crumbly ball of gray-white stuff, and he put it in his mouth, then almost sat up and spat. "That's *salt*!"

"Yeah. I got it from a salt lick. You need it to replace what you lost and help keep in the water."

He took a little more water, forcing himself to go slow, and did feel a bit better. "What about those bastards on the mountain?"

"They finally carried you most of the way here," she told him. "They're a very funny sort, but not bad really, once you get to know them."

"I know what *I'd* like to do to them," he grumbled.

"You couldn't if you wanted to. They're as hard as rocks; and since they're related to the dwarfs, iron has little effect on them. Besides, they could melt your sword before it ever got to them, anyway."

"Where'd they get all that militant labor crap, though? They sounded more like *our* world than this one."

She nodded. "I wondered about that, too. Apparently there's been a movement going around to organize all the fairy workers, particularly the heavy-labor types like the kobolds. Nobody's sure where the idea came from, but it's going around and it's catching on with some like the kobolds. I think we better tell Ruddygore about it when we get there, though. There was one thing that really puzzles me."

"Huh? Only one?"

"Well, in this instance, anyway. One of the kobolds quoted Lenin, word for word. Lenin, Joe! Here! Where nobody ever heard of him!"

"You mean the Russians are invading?"

"No, of course not. Don't be silly. But somebody over here is bringing in ideas wholesale from over *there*, that's for sure. That bothers me, Joe. Remember that Ruddygore was worried about the plot to bring guns into Husaquahr?"

He nodded. "I remember. He had that rat Dacaro turned into a horse for suggesting it."

"Well, maybe—but it doesn't add up. Ideas are stronger even than guns, Joe, and somebody's importing ideas. Trouble is, who's the only guy we know who can make the trip between our world and this one any time he wants to?"

Joe, although still dizzy and weak, saw her point. The base of Ruddygore's power was his unique ability to travel between the worlds across the Sea of Dreams. They had never been really sure about the big sorcerer, and this compounded the doubts beyond measure. Ruddygore had fought the forces of Hell head on, yet he conjured up and used demons from the same place for his own purposes. He had fought the Dark Baron to a standoff, which had put him with the good guys, yet—had he fought for the same reasons as the rest of them?

Or was he, in fact, taking on a rival challenger to his ambition of ruling the Council and the world? Certainly there were depths and layers to the sorcerer far beyond the funny fat man in opera clothes, depths and layers hidden by his wild personality.

"Let's let it rest for now," Joe suggested. "I'm tired, weak, and dizzy and I feel that I could sleep for a month. But let's remember that we're only doing some work for the old boy. He doesn't own us, and we'll work for ourselves first. Okay?"

She smiled at him. "Okay. You know, though, I—" She stopped in mid-thought, seeing that he had sunk back down into a more normal but very deep sleep. She got up and sighed, looking around. Let him sleep—he certainly needed it.

Joe slept through most of the next day, and it was early evening by the time he woke up. He was sore and stiff and still felt terribly dry, but he managed to go through a series of exercises without doing too badly.

His horse, he found, was dead and already stinking up the place. Marge or the kobolds had managed to get the saddlebags off, though, and he found some salted fish and the few cakes remaining of the hard, extra-sweet Terdieran candy. It wasn't enough, but it would have to do for now.

Marge's horse seemed to have come through the mountain crossing reasonably well, but he thought it best not to push her for another day or so. For now he'd repack the supplies into one load and let the horse carry that. He felt he could walk.

He found what he could of dry wood and, with the flint from the packs, made a small fire. There was a rustling in the trees behind him and he turned warily, but it was only Marge, who'd apparently been asleep up in the tree.

"How are you feeling?" she asked him, settling to the ground. "You look a mess!"

He chuckled. "Oh, I'm okay. I think we ought to press on, even though it's dark. You can see pretty well around here, and my night vision's not all that bad. I've been looking at the map and I figure it's about forty miles to the main road, if we can go due west, then maybe another fifty to the city. It's a long, tough walk, but I can make it."

She nodded. "The land's not bad. I went up and took a look at it. While it's all overland, no good roads or clear paths, it's mostly farmland and forest. Maybe we can hitch a ride when we hit the main road. They might have some kind of coach service or something. At least maybe we can buy another horse."

He frowned. "Do we have enough money left for that?"

"We do now. The kobolds decided it was their fault the horse died, so they gave us compensation." She went over to her own pack and rummaged through it for a moment, then reached in and pulled out a large, blackish rock. She seemed to have trouble with it, so he went over and took it from her, then almost dropped it. It was incredibly heavy.

"What *is* that?"

"Raw fairy gold," she told him. "Worth a hundred horses."

"Well, then, let's get started, now that we're on the same clock."

She laughed. "I think maybe you ought to go down to the riverbank first—it's really a creek, but the water's fine. You're coal black from soot and ash."

He didn't feel much like it, but he went, and he *did* feel a little better after he immersed himself in the cool waters for a while. Coming back out, he checked over his clothing. The belt with his great sword had come through pretty much untouched, but the thick loincloth he'd been wearing was stained and singed. He had spare loincloths, so that was no trouble. The sandals, though, were his only pair, and they were cracked and worn almost beyond belief. He decided to go barefoot until he could buy some new ones.

His cowboy hat, much to his relief, was virtually unscathed, and he stuck it on his still wet hair, fastened the loincloth to the belt and strapped it on, checked to see that his sword was easily drawn, then nodded to himself. "Okay, faithful scout," he called to Marge. "Let's pack up and get on the trail."

"Ugh! Kemo sabe!" she responded playfully, and they went to work. Somehow they managed to get everything of importance onto the horse.

Using Marge's incredible night sight as the pathfinder, they had little trouble going for most of the night. By early morning, although it was impossible to tell for certain, they thought they had made it at least fifteen miles. Joe let Marge sleep then on the horse, in front of the pack—since she seemed to weigh virtually nothing, the horse never noticed—and, taking frequent breaks for both his and the horse's benefit, he managed to add over five miles before deciding to camp out in a small wooded grove.

Marge had been correct—the rough land had given way quickly to rolling farmland, with lots of herd animals idly grazing and, here and there, red-roofed farmhouses and fields of neatly planted wheat, corn, and other grains. He remembered somebody telling him once, after some big eruption down in South America or some place, that the reason people lived so close to volcanoes was that they only went off once in a lifetime, while the stuff they spewed out was the best farm dirt in the world, and he could see that, at least here, it was true.

Occasionally they stopped at a farmhouse along the way. But, while there were a few draft animals available, there were no horses. Finally giving up, they settled for a mule and loaded most of the supplies onto it, allowing Joe to ride Marge's horse, while she sat atop the packs on the mule. Now they would make better time.

He kept to his modified schedule, remaining awake through most of the night and into the morning, then joining Marge in sleep for the afternoon. He didn't really need as much sleep as she seemed to, and certainly this was the most peaceful and uneventful part of any of their journeys in Husaquahr.

They reached a farm road which, they were assured, led to the main highway, and it was in the early morning, with Marge barely dozing on the mule's back, that they met their first odd or unusual experience.

Joe stopped both animals, reached over, flipped down the dark glasses, and shook her awake.

"Hmph? Uh? Something the matter?" she muttered drowsily, still mostly asleep.

"I'm not really sure," he responded a bit cautiously, "but unless I've gone nuts, the road ahead is being blocked by a pig."

"So? Shoo it away."

"Uh—this pig is standing up like a human on its hind legs and is holding a cutlass, and I really don't like the mean glint in its eye."

CHAPTER 6

THE TROUBLE WITH MAGICIANS

Once a thief has committed himself or herself to that vocation by deed rather than by inclination, the thief is bound by that nature, regardless of consequences, and the Rules apply for life.
—Rules, VIII, 41(b)

MARGE SUDDENLY SAT BOLT UPRIGHT AND STARED AHEAD OF them. Sure enough, there in the middle of the farm road was the biggest pig she'd ever seen, impossibly standing on its hind legs. The creature was easily Joe's height that way and must have weighed in at half a ton or more. Around its middle was a belt of some sort, its only clothing, and again impossibly, in its right foreleg it gripped a menacing-looking cutlass, apparently held mittenlike between the two parts of the unnaturally pliable split hooves.

"Halt! Stand and deliver!" the pig grunted menacingly.

Joe sat back and shook his head in wonder. Of all the sights in Husaquahr, this was certainly the most ridiculous he'd ever encountered. "So, pork chops, what do you need with money?" he called back.

"You think I *like* being like this?" the giant pig retorted. "It takes money to hire somebody good enough to break a spell like this."

Joe reached down and took hold of the hilt of his great sword, which hummed in anticipation of action. "Well, porker, it will take more than a pig with a pig-sticker to get anything from us. Stand aside and pick an easier victim."

"Your choice," the pig grunted back. "We take what you have from you now and you escape with your lives, or we pick over your bodies."

"We?"

There was a rustling from the underbrush on either side of the road ahead of them, and there appeared the most incredible trio of creatures they could imagine. One had the head and torso of a chimpanzee that blended into the body of a large snake. The second had a giant duck's head on a cow, udder and all, while the third looked like nothing so much as a human-sized catfish whose fishy body merged into that of a crab, complete with pincers. The monkey-thing had a broadsword, while the cow-thing held a bow. The fish-crab needed no other weapons than those pincers.

It was hard to take such monstrosities seriously. "What in *hell* happened to you?" Joe asked them, as Marge just gaped, open-mouthed.

"We were lying in wait for the Sachalin night coach, which was late as usual," the cow-duck quacked, "when we saw this guy coming, all alone, decked out as if he was king of the gem mines. It just got the better of us, I guess. The sight of all that wealth made us forget about the sorcerer's convention."

Joe nodded. "I see. And when you jumped him, he turned out to be somebody powerful and he zapped you. I must say he had a real sense of humor."

"Hilarious," the pig snorted. "Now that we've had our introductions, can we get back to business?"

Joe sighed and sat back a bit in the saddle, positioning himself. "Your bad luck continues, my odd thieves. As you can see, neither my fairy companion nor I have much to hide, and we are going to that same convention. I think, again, you'd better wait for safer game."

"Says you," the monkey-snake retorted. "You don't look like a sorcerer to me, and it's clear *her* magic powers, whatever they are, aren't for fighting." It chuckled. "Care to kiss me, honey?"

"It's true, we're not magicians, although we serve Ruddygore of Terindell, whose power will find you no matter where you are—and you look to be pretty easy to find in any case. But I *do* have one bit of magic, and it is of the most fatal kind." Joe paused and whispered so low he could only hope Marge could hear. "Be ready to charge when I do."

"Yeah? And what kind of magic's that?" the pig sneered.

Joe drew his sword, which began to hum even louder. Its blade seemed like something alive, pulsing a glowing bronze. "This," he told them, "is my very good friend Irving."

"Irving!" They all started laughing and sniggering. "What sort of name is *that* for a sword?"

The great sword's hum rose in pitch, as if it were angry and insulted by the remarks. The sword was, in fact, a semi-living thing of sorcery and iron, as only the dwarfs could make it.

"Irving doesn't like to be laughed at," Joe said quietly, then suddenly kicked his horse and sprang forward with a yell. The attack took the thieves by surprise, and he was on the pig before any of them could react, bringing Irving down on the cutlass and slicing through the thief's weapon as if it were butter. With his foot, he kicked out and sent the great pig sprawling on all fours.

The monkey-snake screamed in anger and launched itself at Joe, but he whirled around and this time was not so gentle, slicing off not only the sword but the arm that held it.

Needing no more of a cue, Marge charged on her mule right through the mêlée, the mule jumping over the pig.

Joe reined in his horse, reared back, and looked at the other two creatures. The duck-cow had seen enough, dropped its bow and stepped back. The fish-crab, however, looked uncertain.

"Well, fish-face? Do we see what Irving does to those claws?"

"Uh—I think Irving is a real nice name for a sword," the fish-crab blurbled and backed off.

By this time, though, the pig had gotten back up behind Joe and now reached to unhorse the big man. Joe saw the move from the corner of his eye and pulled back on the reins, causing his horse to rear up on its hind legs. The pig, startled, fell backward and Joe came down and had his sword at the creature's throat before it could recover. "Be thankful I spare your lives," he told them. "If I meet the man who did this to you all, though, I'm going to buy him one hell of a good drink." With that, he whirled and rode off, following Marge, who'd stopped to watch about a hundred feet farther on. He passed her, slowed, and called out, "Well? What are you waiting for? Run for it before they get their wits back!" Then he was off.

She shrugged and kicked the mule, proceeding forward at a lesser pace.

They kept it up for almost a mile before Joe slowed to a walk and relaxed, allowing her to catch up. "Close one," he commented. "If they'd had any guts at all, they'd have had us, Irving or not."

She burst out laughing. "Somehow I don't think they'll *ever* have the guts. A pretty poor lot of robbers they are, even as monsters."

"Don't laugh too long, though. Remember, we're riding into a whole city just crammed with magicians, and most of 'em with the power won't think any more of us than they would of bugs."

"That's more your worry than mine, I think. I'm not really sure of my powers, but they seem made for a situation like that."

He cleared his throat. "Um, yeah. I've been meaning to ask you about that. I kind of assumed that your powers were in the ah, lovemaking area."

She laughed. "Well, so I'm told. But that's only the lesser part. Supposedly, I can cancel out magic, even redirect it. I'm not sure how that works, and they weren't very good at explanations. It's just supposed to come when I need it, more or less."

He thought about that. "It makes sense, sort of. No great powers, like a lot of the fairy folk are supposed to have, but you'll have the power of whatever is used against you. Seems to me, they'll think twice about using you for a subject with that in mind."

She nodded. "If they know it. Kauri are better known for the other thing we do best, and I don't think it would work well against somebody like Ruddygore or the Dark Baron or even Huspeth. Still, most magicians aren't on that level, so I feel fairly safe. Truth is, I might not have much offense, but I'm a catalog of defenses, which is what I think Ruddygore had in mind. You're the offense and I'm the defense." She saw him frown at that. "What's wrong?"

"The old bastard hasn't done anything for us or to us, unless it's for some reason of his own. That magic Lamp business was big, but I don't think it's what he really brought us here for and made us what we are today, whatever that is. He's got something big planned for us, and I don't like the smell of it."

"You were the one who was bored," she reminded him. "I would think you'd like a real challenge."

"Challenge, yeah, but if that Lamp business was just practice, what's he *really* got in mind, and can we survive it?"

"You're unusually gloomy today! Huspeth said Ruddygore could see the direction of the future and planned accordingly, and those silly Rules said we were destined for at least three great adventures. Me, I'm not going to worry until the third one. Instead, I'm going back to sleep."

And she did.

The main road was wide and well traveled, as they expected one of the primary routes between the capital of Marquewood and the rest of the nation to be. Not only were there the usual wagon trains of goods going to and from Sachalin, but there was much traffic by individuals and small groups. Joe noticed that most of the people going away from the city looked rather ordinary—merchants, deliverymen, carpenters, all the people a capital would be expected to have. The traffic in the city's direction, though, beyond the commercial trade, seemed a different sort. Old women in black cloaks and hoods, small groups dressed in varicolored robes, and mysterious, mystical, even sinister folk were the rule.

Joe stopped at a roadside inn that was doing a large business and went inside. He was getting really tired and he figured that they would most likely have a room available at midday. Few landlords could resist the possibility of renting a room twice in one day, and he could use a bed after so long on the road.

The innkeeper, a big, burly man named Isinsson, didn't disappoint him, although a large eyebrow was raised at the sight of a groggy Marge wearing only dark glasses.

The price was reasonable, and Joe agreed readily to leave by eight in the evening. The room was small but adequate, and the double bed had a genuine feather mattress. They looked at it groggily, and Joe said, "Too bad. If we weren't both so dead, we could make real use of it, as the landlord thinks we will."

"Maybe we'll wake up early," she muttered and lay face down on the bed. Joe looked at the velvety wings sticking out from her back and, with a silent wish that she didn't toss and turn in her sleep, he secured the door and joined her in slumber.

When he awoke, to his great disappointment, it was after seven. Marge, he saw, had already arisen and gone from the room. For a second, he was worried about that, remembering the last time she'd disappeared from a hotel, but she hadn't been fairy then. He was pretty sure she could take care of herself. At least, he hoped so. The next dragon they met might not have a neurotic fear of fair maidens.

He packed up and went down to the main floor, which was

fairly crowded with traffic. He didn't see Marge anyplace, but he decided not to get really worried until it was time to leave.

There were no empty tables; but with such a crowd, any empty chair belonged to the first person to sit in it, and he picked one with a small group of ordinary-looking people and ordered a heavy meal.

The people at the table were a little taken aback by the giant barbarian in their company, but they soon relaxed and warmed to him as the place filled with those more mysterious sorts and various kinds of not very pleasant-appearing fairies.

The squat, middle-aged man with a light beard and no mustache was Jeklir the grainer; the pudgy, middle-aged woman with him was his wife Asarak; and the teen-ager with them who looked every bit their progeny was their son Takgis.

"So you're from Sachalin," Joe noted. "On your way home from a trip?"

"Going on one, rather," Jeklir responded. "Time to visit the wife's relatives in Mobadan, at least for a week or two."

Joe's eyebrows raised a bit. "I would think this would be your busy season. I came through a good bit of farmland, and it looked as if the harvest was just coming up."

Jeklir's eyes darted nervously at the crowd around the inn. "Um, usually you would be right, barbarian, but ordinarily merchants would welcome a convention, not close up shop and leave as it dawned, if you get my meaning."

Joe did. "I guess the ones coming will be a pretty scary group, if what we've seen is any indication. My—partner—and I ran into some unlucky thieves this past morning who had run afoul of a sorcerer."

"You have no idea," Asarak assured him. "Every time this convention comes to a town, horrible things happen. Be just a trifle slow with the ale, and they turn you into who knows what; and the adepts—they're the worst, practicing spells on all the honest people with abandon. If you're going into the city, watch your step, young man. They pour love potions in the punch, make people bark like dogs, and worse, just for the fun of it. The authorities can't do a thing, either."

"I'm surprised anybody will have them, if what you say is true," Joe noted between bites of the first really good, solid food in a week.

"What choice do they have?" Jeklir responded. "I mean, it's

always sponsored by a master sorcerer, and if your local sorcerer decides to host it, what can anybody, even the government, do?"

Joe nodded sympathetically. "Yeah, I can see that. But you mean the whole town will be closed up?"

"Oh, no. First of all, the government can't close, so all those people have to stay and they have to have their services. The hotels can't close—they're booked. And the bars, restaurants, and shows will be open, of course. Many of the owners will keep a low profile and send their families out of town, but they hire a lot of farmers and contract for a lot of serf labor to be out front. There are always the ones who do so good they get special favors, too, and some of it can be put right after, particularly the stuff done by the adepts. That doesn't help the embarrassment and degradation while it's happening to you, though."

Joe understood. Like all conventioneers, these magical ones would let their inhibitions down and have a totally good time—for them. In the process, they'd drive the town nuts, but there was always a cleanup crew of powerful sorcerers around to fix things. He wondered how long it took and whether everything ever got fixed, but he suspected that, within the confines of the host town or city, anyway, things were under more careful watch than they seemed to be. In the end, it was mental anguish applied to ordinary people that was the real price—but the rewards, too, were great. Few groups had conventions this large, and while some might get stuck a hundred times with phony money or gems that vanished, others found overly generous rewards. It really meant millions to the city, too.

Not, however, for a grain merchant. Joe couldn't blame the family for getting out for a while.

He finished his meal and settled his accounts. But after saying good luck and farewell to the temporary refugee family, he still hadn't caught sight of Marge and he began to grow a little worried. He found the innkeeper and asked if he'd seen her.

"The sexy fairy lady? Yeah, I seen her. Don't worry. She'll be back down in a little while, like she has been."

Joe stared at the man. "Like she has been?"

Quickly and a little bit nervously, the innkeeper described Marge's activities of the past couple of hours. Joe was incredulous and more than a little hurt. He stalked outside to the stable area, got the horse and mule, saddled them, and reset the packs, brooding all the time.

Marge came out of the inn entrance and spotted him, then walked over to him with a very light and sassy manner. She stopped short, though, about ten feet from him, and the smile faded as she sensed his emotional turmoil. She instantly understood the problem, but couldn't really sympathize all that much. "Well? What did you expect?" she asked him. "You just kept lying there, snoring like mad."

"Yeah, but . . ." he tried lamely. "It's so . . . *cheap.*"

"It's not that," she told him, stepping more into the light and putting out her hand. He looked at it and saw two large and obviously very valuable rings on her fingers. He saw, too, that she wore a very expensive-looking gold necklace. In her left hand she held a small velvet case. "I found out a lot of things already tonight, and one of them is that you *must* give a gift to a Kauri or she owns your soul. The first man practically fell all over himself finding something to give me."

"Well, at least you'll always be able to buy what you need," he grumped.

"Oh, Joe—it's just in my nature. It's one of the things I *do.*"

"Yeah, but—so many?"

She shrugged and got on the mule. "It was like eating peanuts. Once I got started, I just couldn't stop."

He sighed and mounted his horse. "Well, you ought to have real fun in convention city up ahead."

"I intend to," she told him. "But don't be so damned sanctimonious about it all. I heard Houma and Grogha talking in little-kid whispers about the virgins of Kidim. It didn't matter when it was you men against scared, defenseless girls, now did it?"

"But that was different!" he protested.

"How?"

"Well, um, the damned town deserved it, that's all. They staked you out for the dragon, remember!"

"Even if that were a good excuse for the seduction of innocent kids, which I doubt, it certainly wasn't true that first night. You didn't know about it."

"But you were celibate then! A virgin witch!"

"And you weren't then and aren't now. The only difference is that I'm not now, either. Deep down you're just like all men, you know. It's okay when *you* do it, but women—uh-uh. And I'm even more of a threat—a woman who can control the emotions of men. A woman in command, you might say. No, Joe, don't pull that hurt act on me. Not until you can explain to me why I'm an immoral prostitute while you're just having a boy's night of fun out on the town." With that she kicked the mule and started out onto the darkened road.

He waited a moment, not at all agreeing with her position but unable at the moment to figure out why she was wrong, then followed her.

It took two more days' ride to reach the city, and during that time he still hadn't really figured it out, but he'd partially come to accept it. He did more or less understand why he took it so personally, though. It was one thing for him, say, to meet a woman he didn't know and have a fling in the hay, but Marge was something else, somebody special and important to him. People he knew and cared about just didn't do things like that.

Except, of course, once he'd known and cared about a very special young woman, who'd even borne him a son, but now, in another world and in another life, she was living with another guy and probably griping about never getting any more alimony. And he'd tried more than once to pick up truck-stop waitresses and lady truckers, some of whom he knew very well indeed, and sometimes he succeeded. In a sense, he realized, he'd taken refuge in Marge's former self. She'd been safe, dependable, nobody else's, even if not his.

But, irrational or not, he couldn't shake his sense of hurt and perhaps jealousy, at least not yet, and he consistently refused her advances as if, somehow, at least that could be preserved between them. She would remain, then, somehow, his partner and his friend and nothing more, in the same way that, were she a male and a womanizer, he might accept but not approve.

It was, damn it, just that she was so damned *desirable* . . .

Sachalin was truly deserving of the term city, rather than the less important designation of town. It spread out for miles along the shores of Lake Zahias, a lake so huge that it resembled an ocean or, at least, one of the Great Lakes, and had tides.

The city was built up against a series of low hills that were, perhaps, the moraines of the great glacier that carved and became Lake Zahias. Also deep, the lake actually made Sachalin a major port, since at its southern end the River of Sorrows be-· gan, winding its way through deep gorges to Lake Bragha, then slowly between the mountain ranges to Lake Ogome, until finally, as a great river, it reached the Dancing Gods itself. A parallel canal had been built between Zahias and Bragha, but two great falls prevented full access to the sea. Still, it was a simple transfer of goods from ship to barge to ship to get materials easily into the interior of Husaquahr, and this made Sachalin a rich and important city indeed.

The volcanic soil from the Firehills covered hundreds of square miles to the north and west of the city and lake, meaning that a tremendous amount of food, principally grains, was sent back down from the port all the way to the City-States and beyond.

Sachalin was set only slightly inland from the port and the white, sandy beaches, and it seemed to be constructed of uniformly blocky buildings, two to six storeys high, built of some white stone and masonry materials, topped with characteristic red shingle roofs. Unlike most cities and towns in Husaquahr, it was not walled, being far too large and sprawling for that, but it did have big, open arches at its entrance that served a strictly decorative function. The road led along the lakeshore after that, where Marge and Joe could see countless fishing vessels tied up in neat rows for the night, as well as occasional yachts and luxury vessels. The heavy-goods commercial port was north of the city, leaving the center for public beaches and pleasure use and not spoiling the view.

They arrived in early evening. The city did not die after dark as most towns did, but took on a whole new character. Uniformed men of the watch, as they were called, walked every street, lighting lamps with long lamplighter torches. The glass containers for the streetlamps were irregular and often multicolored, their bright flames inside producing not only more than ample light but also colorful, dancing patterns against the white stucco buildings. It was, in a sense, fairyland by engineering rather than by magic, but it was no less effective.

Although neither Joe nor Marge could read the language, the pictograms on the signs were easy enough to follow. When they reached a broad park with beach on one side and town on the other, the road formed a circle around a huge monument to some very odd-looking creature. Leading into the circle from town was a tremendously wide avenue, paved with tiny little bricks and lined with trees the entire way. It seemed to have a series of circles through the town to the hills in back, each one with a small park and monument in the middle, but far back, against and seemingly either carved out of or sitting on a ledge in the hills, was the great capitol building itself, looking less like any capitol building they had seen than a huge, columnar, Grecian-style temple to some ancient gods, bathed in great lights.

They turned toward the capitol and started into the city proper, following directions on the small map Ruddygore had sketched for them of the city center. The large buildings behind the trees on either side seemed to be mostly banks and offices—shipping brokers, the grain exchange, and other such institutions. This was the financial heart of the city, it was clear.

"It's *beautiful*," Marge said, mostly to herself. "And everything's so *clean*."

Joe understood what she meant. Even the best of towns they'd seen in Husaquahr had been straight out of the Middle Ages, with sanitation to match. Here, though, it looked as if an entire crew of workmen came out each night and scrubbed the place clean, removing trash, droppings, and just about everything else, then even polishing the brick and scrubbing the building facades. The air was crisp and clean-smelling, with no hints of garbage or even horse droppings.

At that moment, Joe's horse relieved herself on the bright roadway, and he felt suddenly very guilty for her doing so. He hurried on a bit, and they were a couple of blocks up and at the next circle before he halted at Marge's call. "Hey, Joe—look back!"

He looked and saw dozens of tiny fairy gnomes emerge from the trees up and down the whole block where his horse had violated the scenery. They hurried quickly to the center of the street, swept up the droppings and took them away, then scrubbed the whole area and vanished once more into the tree-lined sides of the boulevard. "It figures," he muttered, then turned and continued on.

Although the hotel and entertainment district was in the dead center of the city, the fancy hotels for the business clientele who would be visiting those financial centers were all directly on this main, wide boulevard, and the grandest of them was the Imperial Grand, a huge, fancy structure that took up more than a square block. Like all the buildings, it wasn't really very high—though at eight storeys it was one of the tallest buildings in the city—but it was fancy.

The front, in fact, was almost entirely of glass, rising from street level up four full storeys, creating a massive atrium and lobby which was like a glass-covered right angle viewed from the side. This connected to a solid four-storey stone and stucco block with balconies sculpted on its face, so that anyone coming out of any room would have a free view of the open space area. On top of this were three four-storey cubes, giving the whole building a distinctive look. It reminded Joe of some fancy American hotels, as if designed by Mayan temple designers. There was even a parking entrance on the side, which led down below the hotel to an underground stable that looked fancy indeed. Liveried attendants helped Marge and Joe off their animals, unloaded saddle and packs, put small collars on both horse and mule and a sticker on the saddle, then handed Joe three embossed leather claim checks. Another packed up their meager luggage in an odd-looking cart, and they followed him to a wide, beltlike structure rising at a steep angle. Strong, thin boards were spaced about eight feet apart going up. They were instructed to sit down, and the attendant then went over and rang a large bell.

"A real bellman," Marge noted dryly.

Suddenly the belt started moving slowly upward. It so startled them, despite the obvious intent of the gadget, that both almost fell off. The bellman, as soon as they were clear, rolled his cart onto the next plank below them and hopped on himself. Joe looked nervously around and saw that they were going to be raised just above lobby level, followed by a steep drop. The ascent wasn't very fast, but they were traveling backward.

When they were most of the way up, the bellman reached over and grabbed another rope, ringing the bell below once more; just as Joe rose up so that his feet were clear of the floor level, the device stopped and he and Marge jumped off. It then moved again, and the bellman and his load were lifted up.

Joe looked at the bellman with unconcealed curiosity. "How does it work?"

The bellman smiled, telling them both that this was his most asked question. "There's a treadmill down there. Put some mules on it every once in a while and it winds up a tremendous spring. When we need to run it, we just take the brake off and it goes up until we hit the brake. During the busy periods, we just keep the treadmill going all the time. Smart, huh? Wait till you see what else this place has. There's no other hotel like it anywhere."

They looked around the broad, glass-enclosed atrium, but there were few people about, and Marge remarked on it. "Oh, they'll start coming in big tomorrow," the bellman assured her. "We're full up the next seven days. Tonight we'd normally be about half full, but with most of the business down the boulevard taking a holiday during the convention, there are only some early arrivers like you now. Ah, you *are* here for the convention, right?"

They nodded. "We thought we were late. I guess we made better time than we expected," Marge commented.

They followed him to the registration desk, a massive horseshoe-shaped affair of stained and polished oak. The desk clerk, dressed in almost regal splendor, eyed both of them with some suspicion and a nose high in the air. "Yesssss . . ." he virtually hissed at them, trying to avoid any sort of eye contact.

"We may be a little early, but we're supposed to have rooms reserved for us here," Joe told him.

Now the beady little eyes focused first on Joe, then on Marge. "Are you certain you have the correct hotel?"

"This is the Imperial Grand Hotel, I presume."

"It most certainly is."

"Well, we're in the right place, then."

The clerk gave a bored sigh. "Very well, then. Name?"

"Joseph the Golden, Castle Terindell, Valisandra."

"How original," the clerk muttered patronizingly. "A barbarian with a mailing address." He checked through his large card file, then checked again, and finally said, "As I suspected, there is nothing, and our hotel is booked for the next week."

Joe thought a moment. "We are with Ruddygore of Terindell," he told the clerk. "We are a part of his party."

The clerk was unimpressed and yet he dutifully checked and

cross-checked his file cards once more. Finally he nodded to himself. "Ah, yes. Ruddygore, Throckmorton P., party of seven. Let's see . . . Yes, an Imir is already in as the advance man for the party. I will send a runner up to approve you." He turned and tapped a small bell on the desk. From a place somewhere beneath him, a tiny pixie, no more than two or three inches high, popped up and waited for further instructions, its transparent multiple wings beating so fast they were virtually invisible. The clerk jotted something on a pad, tore off the top sheet, folded it in quarters, and handed it to the little creature. "Lake Suite," he told it.

The creature was off in a flash, flying into one of a number of round tubes that seemed to go into the wall in back of the clerk.

"Those tubes go to every room in the place?" Joe asked a little suspiciously. If pixie's could use them, so could other things, and they made nice sound conductors as well.

"Oh, my no!" the clerk huffed. "They go to each floor of each wing, and the messenger then rings a bell."

Joe nodded, feeling a little better. He didn't trust hotels at all, and his experience with any of the larger ones in Husaquahr had been less than pleasant.

"Madam," the clerk said as they waited, "we would appreciate it if you would, ah, cover up while in the public areas. The Portside, down at Lake Boulevard and Pier Six, is more, ah, suited to your sort."

Marge got mad fast. "And what exactly is my sort? Do you discriminate against fairies? Are we not good enough for you?"

"Oh, of course not! That's not what I meant at all."

"Then make your meaning plain. I am a Kauri, and we have very short tempers."

"Exactly my point. I mean, with the convention coming in, it's very bad for the hotel's image."

Joe, too, got a little rankled. "With what I hear about this convention, you'll be lucky to have a hotel left when it's over. Are you going to be working through the next week?"

"Why, uh, I expect to. Whatever do you mean?" The clerk was uncomfortable when the topic got personal and forced him to the defensive.

"When the adepts get through with you, you might wish

you'd gone on vacation with an attitude like that. Now you've insulted my partner and friend, and we weren't doing anything but following your rules and making no trouble." He put his hand to his sword hilt, but Marge stopped him.

"No, Joe. Just stand to one side for a moment. This is *my* little problem."

Curious, the big man moved over and just watched. Marge stared hard at the clerk, then brought her two arms up over her head, fully extending her magnificent, soft wings. The clerk started to say something, then stopped and became suddenly dull and glassy-eyed. She smiled at him, and he smiled back, although Joe was surprised that it didn't crack his face. She rose, floated over the desk, and landed just in front of the transfixed man, whose gaze never left her. Marge nodded, still smiling, put down her arms, and began systematically to undress the clerk. Joe—and, he couldn't help noticing, the bellman and other employees in the lobby area—watched with a mixture of awe and amusement. Within two or three minutes, the clerk was completely nude.

At that moment, the pixie shot back through the tube, flew up to the clerk, and stopped short, the look on its face one of total incredulousness. Marge reached out and took the small paper from the pixie and glanced at it, then turned and handed it to Joe. It was a scrawled mess, but they recognized Poquah's distinctive calligraphy and guessed what it said. "Well, we can go up now," Joe suggested a bit nervously.

"Awww . . ." Marge pouted, sounding disappointed. She leaned over, kissed the clerk lightly, and said, "You'll wait right here just like that until I get back, though, won't you?"

The clerk nodded dreamily.

Marge smiled, floated back to the other side of the desk, and looked at the bellman. "Let's go."

The bellman led them around the big registration area to a hallway and into the main building in the back. On one side was an opening in the wall, revealing a small, gondolalike car. They could see a second about halfway down the hall, and guess a third at the end.

The thing proved to be something like a ferris wheel, but very, very slow and driven, apparently, by the same sort of treadmill-gear-spring device as the escalator from the stables. They went to the top, then had to transfer to a smaller, similar device and do the whole thing all over again. "Uh—you *do* have stairs," Joe said to the bellman hopefully.

"Oh, sure. This is mostly for the bigwigs and the luggage. The top two floors of each tower are suites only, and the kind of people who have 'em not only usually have tons of baggage but they don't walk no place."

"Um—just out of curiosity, what do you think of that little scene down there?" Joe wanted to know as they reached the top floor of the south tower.

The bellman chuckled. "Some people, they run outta town when this convention hits. Me, I love to stick around. I mean, I gotta work under guys like that for most of the year."

Both Joe and Marge grinned. "And you're not scared of something happening to you?" she asked him, trying to sound nonthreatening.

"Naw. I been around magicians and stuff a lot, and overall they're a pretty fair lot. Mostly they stick it to people who really need it, and, I mean, most of us can't, right? This convention's the payoff to all them types who do the same to everybody, and I love it."

They both chuckled and followed the little man to a large and ornately carved set of double doors. The bellman pulled on a satin rope that dangled from a small recess. In a few seconds, the door opened, and the familiar face of the warrior elf Poquah looked out at them. The Imir was as outwardly impassive as always; but when he saw Marge, his thick, ruler-straight eyebrows that flanked his cat-shaped eyes at a forty-five-degree angle went up about an inch. It was as much of a rise from him as either of them could remember. He looked at Joe, nodded, then turned back to her. "And this is our old Marge?"

She grinned. "No, it's the new one. Hello, Imir."

"Hello, Kauri. Come in, both of you."

They entered, and the bellman followed. Marge stopped short when she saw the suite and gave a low gasp.

It *was* impressive. The walls were entirely of some sort of tinted glass, apparently going all the way around the top of the tower. There were drapes, controlled by long, thin ropes, that could be lowered from recesses in the ceiling to cover them, but Poquah had left them open in this large parlor.

It was furnished with thick sofas, ottomans, and luxuriously padded chairs. The tables were of carved and beautifully stained hardwoods, each one a handmade work of art. The entire suite was carpeted in thick, soft wool, dyed in patterns of reds, yellows, blues, and greens. Facing the inside of the parlor, against the wall parallel with the hall, was a huge bar on one side and a mini-kitchen on the other, complete with a small stove, wood for that stove, and a chimney leading up.

The bellman looked questioningly at Poquah, who simply said, "Just set them down here. We will put them away when we arrange who's to go where."

The bellman did as instructed and turned to go. Joe fished in the pack, brought out a small chunk of Firehills fairy gold left over from their road transactions, and called after him, "Here—catch!"

The bellman did so and realized almost instantly that he had more than an ounce of fairy gold in his hands. It was certainly a bigger tip than he was used to, but he suppressed his surprise and joy and tucked it in a pocket. "Thank *you*, sir and madam, and if you need anything, just go to the middle of the hall and call the messenger." With that he was gone, shutting the door after him.

"That was an abnormal tip," Poquah noted. "It sets a bad precedent."

"Well, it was mine, not Ruddygore's, and I liked that little guy," Joe told him. "Besides," he added a little sharply, looking at Marge, "he's going to have to clean up a bit after us, isn't he?"

She gave him a "Who, me?" sort of innocent look, and Poquah was quick to sense that there was something he'd better know. "What have you two done already?" he asked suspiciously.

"We had a little run-in with a stuffed shirt at the front desk, and Marge got mad," Joe told him.

"What did you do?"

"He told me to get out of his hotel and go down to the docks, as if I were some kind of tramp," she responded defensively. "I just gave his libido a nudge so he only had eyes for me, that's all."

The Imir sighed. "And I suppose he's standing there behind the desk right now, stark naked, just pining for your return."

"Why, yeah. How'd you guess?"

"As hard as it might be for even me to believe, the Imir and Kauri are rather closely related, and I have had some experience around you as well. Combining your rather odd sense of humor with the Kauri's almost total lack of self-control, it was obvious. Is it permanent?"

"Oh, no. Oh, he'll still have a thing for me, but he'll snap out of it in an hour or so, get real embarrassed, and put his pants on again."

The Imir nodded. "Ah, yes, you Kauri *do* have that nice little trick, don't you?" He looked over at Joe. "You see, her victim will still have 'a thing,' as she put it, for her even after it's over, so he'll take it out on the staff, on everybody else, even on himself, but he'll *never* be mad at, let alone blame, her. Hmph! Totally useless in a fight, but with those defenses nobody ever lays a glove on them." He thought for a moment. "The Master and the others will be in sometime tomorrow. The master bedroom, with the harbor view, is through there, so that will be his. The room on the other side will be shared by myself and Durin, his personal chef. There are two more rooms down the hall that interconnect with each other but not with this apartment, and we have Macore and Tiana to take care of as well as the two of you."

"Macore! It will be good to see him again!" Joe cried. "But what's he doing here?"

"The Master has his reasons," the Imir replied enigmatically.

"And who's Tiana?" Marge wanted to know.

"Tiana—oh, yes, you might not have met her. She fled from Morikay and has been under the protection of the Master for years. He sent for her to meet him here. You'll learn more, perhaps, when you see her." He looked thoughtful again. "I assume the best course is to put you, Marge, and Tiana in one of the rooms, with Joe and Macore in the other. I regret that, but I do not think Macore is the correct sort of person for many reasons to put in with the young lady."

Joe looked a little sourly at Marge. "Suits me," he said. "Why not just give each of us a key now?"

Poquah nodded, walked into his own room by sliding back a door, and soon returned with two large brass keys. Each key had a small leather tag attached with a welded brass ring. "If you use any of the hotel's amenities, the key will be all you need for payment," he explained. "Outside, use what money you have. From the bellman's tip, I assume you do not require any more at this time."

"I think we're okay for now," Joe told him. "At least, I am."

"I have no need of money," Marge said, "but I'm going to have problems carrying this key around. I'll leave it either at the desk or with you when I'm going to be gone for any length of time."

The Imir nodded. "Very well, then. Come over here." He walked to the wide windows that looked out on the town. "Below there, and for several square blocks on either side, you see the entertainment district, which usually goes all night. The restaurants and bars are quite expensive, but all of high quality. There are also stage shows, strolling entertainment, and other amusements down there. On the other side, opposite this hotel, is the central market, which is quite extensive and has some of the finest craftspeople in all Husaquahr, and which also has for sale almost anything you might wish. Please keep your expenses down if possible. Prices always double or more when a convention is in town, and our coffers are not unlimited."

Both of them knew that this was more of the Imir's nature speaking than any policy or problem from Ruddygore. The fact was, to somebody on the Council with his own castle and more, wealth was virtually limitless. Poquah, though, was not only the sorcerer's chief bodyguard but also the manager of Castle Terindell, and he took every expense personally. He was also, contrary to the traditions of his race, an accomplished sorcerer himself and, because of that, was somewhat in exile from his own people. Being of faërie, he could never gain the power and control of a human sorcerer, but he was nonetheless a very, very dangerous man in all respects.

Joe picked up the bags, and he and Marge walked out of the suite and down the hall. Poquah shut the door behind them. Joe realized almost immediately that the Imir had failed to tell him which room was which, and the pictogram on the keys was very little help, so he tried his on the first door they came to; naturally, it didn't work. Marge unlocked the door with hers, and they stepped inside.

The room was large and comfortable and had a huge bed and a mini-parlor with sofa, but it was nothing like the master suite. It was still better than either of them had seen in a long,

long time, though. Marge turned and looked at Joe questioningly. "Sure you don't want to sleep here tonight?"

He sighed. "No. Not yet. Let's let things go a bit, huh? Besides, you ought to enjoy a solo room for one night. What do you want from the packs?"

She thought a moment. "The glasses, I guess, and my trinkets from the last couple of nights." He put the packs down, and she rummaged through and got the few items. "That's it," she told him.

He shrugged. "Okay. Well, let me get settled in next door. After that, I guess I'll find a restaurant and then hit the sack. I think I want to move myself back to a little more of a day schedule."

"Suit yourself," she told him. "The night's still young." He turned to go, but just as he cleared her door, she called out, "Joe?"

He stopped and actually hesitated for a moment, but shook it off. "Look—that stuff you did with the clerk. Never do anything like that to me. Never. Promise?"

She nodded, looking suddenly serious. "I promise, Joe. You know I'd never do anything like that to you."

"I don't know anything about anything any more," he responded and walked down the hall.

His room proved to be a mirror image of hers, but with two slightly smaller but still plush beds. He put the packs down and looked around, for the first time noticing a small sink in one corner, with a pipe coming out of the back and angling down like a spigot. Looking a little closer, he discovered a rod and handle on the floor next to the sink that actually went through the floor. Curious, he pushed down on it, finding it something like a bicycle pump. Pumping it a bit harder, he saw water coming out of the spigot and into the basin. He checked and found it cool but not cold and marveled anew at how clever the people who designed and built this place were. The pump took very little effort, so he wasn't bringing water up from anywhere. Probably there were tanks on the roof, he decided, so the pump only opened some sort of valve when it was pushed—it *had* turned halfway around when he'd pushed it down the first time, and twisted back at rest—and the pump's suction just drew water a short distance into the sink line. It was clever. More than likely there were huge cisterns up there catching rain off the lake, supplemented when necessary by hauling water up to the top.

The water closets were at either end of the hall, and he was tempted to find out if they had flush toilets, but that would wait. He'd know soon enough.

Using the water and towels, he gave himself something of a sponge bath and turned two bright white towels almost black doing so, then changed into his last clean breechclout. He reminded himself to find out about laundry services here and that he had to get over to that market the next day and buy a new pair of sandals, or, perhaps, boots. Maybe both, he thought after a moment. After all, he was here on Ruddygore's expense account, and to hell with Poquah.

Satisfied as he could be, and with his hair combed and fastened by a headband, he left the room and went down the hall, stopping at Marge's room. He knocked. When there was no answer, he tried the door. It opened, and he peered inside, but the room was empty.

Well, he thought, so much for company for dinner. That brought him up short for a moment, and he frowned. Come to think of it, in the days since she'd come out of that forest with wings, he'd never seen her eat. He wondered if she did, and, if so, what.

CHAPTER 7

ON THE CONVENTIONS OF UNCONVENTIONAL CONVENTIONS

It is permissible for a white magician to buy a black magician a drink, or vice versa, openly at convention, without poisoning it.
—Rules, VI, 201(b)

RUDDYGORE ARRIVED IN THE MIDDLE OF THE AFTERNOON OF the next day, accompanied by Durin and Macore and also by an extremely large retinue. He made a grand sort of entrance, being carried in in an ornate, gold-embossed sedan chair on the backs of four dark, burly men wearing loincloths and turbans. They brought him right up in the chair on the lifting stairs from the stables, so that the proper impression was actually enhanced as he rose into view. Besides, the whole thing wouldn't have fitted through the front doors.

The sedan chair was the immediate object of interest for all in the lobby area, and there was quite a crowd by this time. Joe had been sitting in the lobby bar for about an hour, waiting for this, having been awakened by Poquah, and even he had to admit it was really impressive. The rest of the people checking in had been a pretty weird lot, with robes and strange chants and bizarre animals and birds accompanying the costumed magicians, but this one had real style.

A clearly prompted Macore, looking resplendent in scarlet and silver noble's dress and leading the parade, walked solemnly back to the door and opened it. After a dramatic pause, the huge sorcerer got out, looking imperiously neither to the right nor to the left, instead just standing there waiting to be admired. He wore formal opera clothes best suited to the nineteenth century on Joe's own world, including a full opera cape, and carried a brilliantly polished mahogany walking stick with its handle a magnificently carved, solid gold lion's head in full roar. He snapped his fingers and Macore scampered around him, reached inside the sedan chair, and brought out a flat disk which he then shook with his wrist, causing the disk to form into a great top hat matching the formal outfit. The little thief, playing the part to the hilt, handed the hat to Ruddygore, who idly placed it on his head, then snapped his fingers once more.

Durin, his fairy chef, a very round and cherubic figure, who looked like a five-foot-tall version of a Disney dwarf, was attired in splendid white fur. He walked from behind the sedan chair and around Ruddygore and Macore to the front desk. The uniformed desk crew, already accustomed to serving all manner of humans and creatures, nonetheless was gathered together awaiting what came next. "Throckmorton P. Ruddygore, Master of Castle Terindell, Vice Chairman of the Council of Thirteen, Grand Master of the Society of Thaumaturgists, Keeper of the Threshold of Worlds, Th.D., Ph.D., M.D., and D.O.G." Ruddygore smiled and bowed.

The desk clerk was not officious but also not all that impressed. A hand went down and he called out, "Front, please!" Several bellmen engaged in a pushing and tripping contest to see who could make it first to what was obviously a big tipper.

"Show Dr. Ruddygore and his party to the Lake Suite," the clerk instructed the winning bellman.

That one grinned, went over, and bowed to the master sorcerer. "If you will follow me, sir," the bellman intoned and started off with his body militarily erect, aware that he was leading a parade.

Macore followed, adapting the same manner of walk, then Ruddygore, and finally the little chef, obviously having the time of his considerable fairy life. Joe chugged down the remains of his tankard—it was full of straight hypercaffeinated tea, anyway—and decided he'd take the stairs. Even if he didn't hurry, he knew that, by the time they all took that set of elevator contraptions, he'd be ten minutes ahead of them. As he made for the stairs, he heard the clerk snap, "You muscle guys! Get that rig back down where it belongs!"

Joe was certainly ahead of the game as he knocked on the suite's large door. Poquah answered, looked at the big man's face, and said sourly, "I assume he's arrived?"

"And how! Did he come all the way here with that outfit?"

"No, actually he had me rent it a couple of days ago here in the city, and they picked him up on the edge of town. Cost a fortune, too, not to mention a lot of my time. Do you know how hard it is to find four men who not only can bear that kind of weight but also are about the same size?"

"I can guess," Joe sympathized. "Whoops! I think I hear them coming now!"

It was pretty unmistakable, hearing the clanging and clattering of the car arriving and then the bunch of them getting out of it. Joe chuckled. "I hope they have a really heavy-duty set of springs on that gadget."

Poquah went over, opened the double doors wide, then did a double check of the bar stock and of several large trays of pastries sitting on the kitchenette counter. Satisfied, he waited. Soon the batch of them walked in, led by the bellman. They stood there a moment while the sorcerer looked over the place. When he nodded, Poquah went over to the bellman. "Arrange for the bags to be delivered as soon as possible," he instructed, "and do not touch or disturb the seals on them if you value your life."

The bellman, not easily intimidated, just stood there. Finally, out of the corner of his mouth, Ruddygore ordered, "Tip him, you idiot!"

The Imir sighed, took a pouch from his belt, and gave the bellman three gold coins. Joe didn't know how much it was, but it certainly was less than the hotel man had expected, judging by his expression. "More if the bags arrive quickly and in perfect condition," Poquah told him. "Now—go!"

The bellman nodded glumly, turned, and left, and Poquah shut the doors behind him. At that moment they all relaxed, and Ruddygore broke into hearty laughter. The big man went over, grabbed a pastry, and plopped into one of the plush chairs, which groaned and sagged noticeably. "God!" he exclaimed. "I've been wanting to make an entrance like that ever since I saw *The Thief of Baghdad*!"

Joe was the only one who even slightly understood the comment, although he'd never seen the movie. Ruddygore, with his ability to go between the worlds, was equally at home in either one.

"So what's a D.O.G.?" he asked with a smile.

Ruddygore's eyebrows rose. "Why, hello, Joe! A pleasant, successful, and uneventful trip, I trust?"

"Not exactly," he responded, "but that will wait."

"Yes, I *do* want to talk to you in a bit, after we're settled in and I find out what godawful stuff they have me doing at the convention. Poquah, did you get a program?"

"They were late, as usual," the Imir replied. "They only finished carving the plates the night before last. Naturally, they had lots of last-minute changes."

The sorcerer sighed. "I suppose we ought to give them the idea of the Gutenberg press, eh? I think movable type's time has come for Husaquahr. It's almost impossible to have anything accurate when it takes a team of scribes a month to carve out each page." He turned back to Joe. "A D.O.G., if you must know, is a Doctor of Oddball Gimmickry. It's irritating at times, but a lot of titles, particularly in academia and the Society, have rather unfortunate initials. Try not to laugh at them when you hear them if you don't want to be turned into a toad."

"I'll remember," Joe assured the wizard.

Ruddygore reached into his inside jacket pocket and took out a cigar, lighting it by pointing his index finger at the tip.

A tiny spark jumped, and he was puffing away. He sighed. "It's been a wearing trip, I fear. With a week to go, I really should just take it easy today and get a decent night's sleep, but I probably won't. That was one of the reasons for the grand entrance down there, though. If I just walked through the door, I'd run into three dozen people, all of whom are either old friends not seen in a long time or people who have to talk to me or to whom I have to talk. I'd be hours just getting across the lobby."

"It *was* effective," Joe told him. "You overawed everybody except the desk clerks."

Ruddygore shrugged. "Can't win 'em all. I assume Marge is sleeping during this pretty day?"

"I guess," Joe answered. "I don't know. We had private rooms last night."

The sorcerer frowned and looked thoughtful for a moment. Finally, he sighed and got up. "I think perhaps we'd better have our little talk now. Come on into my room." He looked questioningly at Poquah, who indicated which door, then grabbed several more of the gooier pastries, opened the side door to his bedroom, and walked in. Joe followed, deciding he might grab one of the pastries himself on the way.

The master bedroom was truly huge, with a massive bed, a full parlor area, its own water closet, and a mini-bar. Ruddygore slipped off his coat and boots and tossed the hat on the bed. Almost as an afterthought, he turned back and stuck his head into the parlor. "Poquah, when the bags come, prepare some of what's in the red canister," he instructed. "Then have it brought in." He then slid the door closed, indicated a chair to Joe, and took one himself, sprawling comfortably. For a while he said nothing, just looked at the big man across from him. Then he sighed. "I gather you do not approve of the new Marge."

Joe shrugged. "What can I say?"

"Just to be honest, that's all, particularly with me. Joe, before I started this operation, I consulted a series of oracles who are pretty good at seeing future trends. Trends only—I've yet to find a reliable perfect predictor, and I'm not sure I'd like the implications of one if I found him or her. The trend was entirely the Dark Baron's way, and it was highly unpleasant in the extreme. The threat went far beyond Husaquahr to the entire world and from it even to yours. It's an end-around to millennia of darkness, even if it fails beyond this world. At the very least, millions of lives were at stake, their children's lives, and their children's children's, not to mention my own ancient hide. Most of what I organized to fight them—and it's a vast and complex system—is better for you not to know, but in all those predictors I kept hitting a blind spot, an irregularity that skewed anything that might be in my favor and reinforced the Baron. It took no great deduction to see that he was being backed by forces from Hell itself, directly, on stage, in violation of every agreement between Heaven and Hell ever made, but it was so clever, so subtle, I couldn't get the proof I needed."

Joe nodded. "I met that demon, remember."

"Indeed you did and you escaped when none should have. That's what I saw as well. If the Baron had a joker, a real demon prince, to help him, then I needed a wild card of my own. That wild card, Joe, is you."

"So you've said. But I'm not magic, and I'm no match for demons."

"Oh, but you *are*, Joe," the sorcerer told him. "You are indeed. And so is Marge. I couldn't stand up to a demon prince, Joe—but you not only could, you did. He had no power over you, and, if you had been able to strike at him, you might have actually wounded him. That's because any demon prince coming through to Husaquahr is attuned to Husaquahr. Things, people, even souls are very subtly different between worlds, Joe, and they must be on the right frequency, so to speak. The demons of your world could harm you, but not one here. That's what I was looking for when I went shopping, as it were, over Earth way."

"But magic works on me here," Joe pointed out. "I'm as vulnerable as anybody else."

"No, Joe. Your body is vulnerable, since flesh is flesh. But if the flesh were all that mattered, then the Baron would have no need of a demon prince, would he? No, Joe—the demon can't even perceive flesh, believe it or not. He sees that permanent part of you, your soul, your true self. It's on that level that demons get you, twist you, corrupt you, often in spite of yourself. Not you, though, Joe—or Marge, either, for that matter. That doesn't mean you can't be corrupted, but you can't be reached on that level against your conscious will here, and that's a vital but very fine point. When that demon saw you both, it reached out to command your souls—and it couldn't. Thus, you were able to break free, use the Lamp, and escape. And, because of that, the Baron was deprived of the Lamp and its powers, and we were able to win the battle. All because *you* were there, Joe, as predicted—you and not one of this world."

"Yeah—but why me?"

"You fitted the bill. You were a big man with a strong ego, an independent with no real ties, and the probabilities said you would be killed in an accident that very night we met. I set up the conditions to divert you to me, and you were diverted. Somehow, inadvertently, those conditions also brought Marge first to you and then to me as well. I didn't expect her, but I couldn't complain, either. But I was prepared for you, not for her, and that caused some problems. Unlike you, her ego, her self-esteem, and her self-image were extremely weak, and never so weak as at the point when we crossed over. Forces that are too complex to explain operated, and while you, with a little help from me, were able to shrug them off, they took hold of her. This is a world of magic, and magical forces are strongest on the nonintellectual level, on the emotional line, as you can see in your own world, in the example of religious fervor. To Marge, back then, the intellect had failed. Her college availed her nothing, her knowledge and skills went unneeded or unappreciated, and the only thing she'd done, once she'd sunk very low, that worked was selling herself, turning herself into an object, a thing for the momentary gratification of strangers. This was the pattern she brought with her as she crossed the Sea of Dreams."

Joe nodded, following him on at least the intellectual level, although finding it impossible to see how somebody so bright and capable could have sunk so low. He said as much to Ruddygore. "I sure had everything thrown at me and I just kept fighting."

"That's true, but you already had a profession, a skill, and the tools to get by. You were also older, more experienced, and had . traveled all over the country. She'd never been out of Texas."

"Yeah, maybe, but I never got to college, either. In fact, the army was the only reason I got my high school equivalency."

The sorcerer sighed. "Joe, you're like a lot of smart but un-educated people. You always had that little glimmer of inferi-ority when you met somebody with all that education. I can tell you right now that most people with degrees, even doctor-ates, are dumber and less qualified to make their way than peo-ple like you. Consider the fact that I have been educated up the rear end, and a lot of it was interesting but very little was use-ful. One of my degrees is in music, for example, although I'm only adequate at the piano. It gives me a better appreciation of opera, for example, and opens up new entertainment pleasures to me, but it's just that—pleasures. It's not worth a damn in the real world, not even as entertainment, since I lack the inborn talents that would require. My talents lay in a different direc-tion, and the way I learned how to use those and master the in-timate secrets of magic was not by any university experience but by a lot of hard, degrading, and backbreaking toil as an apprentice—read that as a virtual slave—to somebody who'd learned it the same way."

Ruddygore could see that Joe wasn't quite accepting this, and knew the man never really would, but it would have to do.

"All right," the sorcerer continued, "let's just say she blew it both because of her own wrong choices and because of things beyond her control. The fact was, the forces that played on her played on those parts of her that were the most primal, the most basic. They reinforced those elements, while every-thing else about her was weakened. As a result, despite my ef-forts to keep her human, she entered here a changeling, and there was nothing I could do about it."

That was interesting, not only because it implied that Ruddygore's powers had real, clearly defined limits but also because Marge and everybody else believed it was hardly nat-ural. "Everybody thinks you caused it. Even the witch she likes so much."

Ruddygore chuckled. "She would. No, I had no idea at the time—since I neither knew nor expected Marge, and knew nothing about her. When I realized it, after acclimating you to this world, I tried to block it by sending her to Huspeth and her witch order, which are, as you well know, celibate."

"Yeah, I know," Joe said glumly.

"Well, that only slowed the changes a bit, and the time she spent among the djinn broke the last restrictions. That's why I decided to get her to Mohr Jerahl to complete the process as quickly as possible. Otherwise she might have gone quite a long time, perhaps years, with a Kauri nature and a basically human body bound by that celibacy oath. She would have either gone nuts or had her newly established self-esteem crushed. By completing the process, it's all right for her to be that way, you see. It's the Kauri nature. And so her self-esteem is intact, her confidence actually strengthened, and she's whole and healthy. She *belongs*. Now do you understand what happened?"

"I guess so," Joe responded hesitantly. "I think I follow you, anyway. You're saying that, if this hadn't happened, she'd have gone nuts or killed herself, and I can follow that, but it's really not my problem. She belongs, sure, but *I don't*. I dunno, maybe it was mean and rotten of me. I guess it was. Sort of misery loves company, I guess. As long as she was, well, somebody else who didn't fit ... Oh, I like Macore, and Grogha, and Houma, and even Poquah—although I'd never tell him that. But they've never seen a football game, don't know Pittsburgh from Peoria, and think Clint Eastwood's a magic spell for curing warts."

The sorcerer nodded. "Joe, you may find this hard to believe, but I do understand. Yet I think you're missing the point yourself here. Let me ask you something, and I want you to be absolutely honest with me."

"Shoot."

"Are you in love with Marge? I mean, really in love with her?"

Joe thought a moment, searching his feelings, and he had to admit that he'd never really thought about it before. *Was* he? The fact was, he hardly knew her. He'd picked her up, at least partly with the idea of maybe making it with her, and he'd wound up feeling sorry for her. That was—how long? A couple of hours' drive between Ozona and Fort Stockton, and she'd been asleep half of that. Then they'd gotten waylaid by Ruddygore, slept most of the way across, gone through his magic stuff, then separated. He'd spent many long weeks in training; she'd spent them off with Huspeth learning to be witchy or whatever. In fact, the only real time he'd had to get to know her, and this was the new her, so to speak, was on the expedition to Stormhold, and off and on after the battle.

They'd had maybe two or three serious talks during that whole time. Once back, she'd taken off again for the Glen Dinig, returning only for what they'd just gone through.

He didn't really know her at all, and she didn't really know him, either. Yet he'd treated her as wife, girl friend, consort, whatever, in his own mind at least. But—love?

"No, not love. At least I don't think so. I'm all mixed up about that," he answered truthfully. "I guess it was more that I needed her, particularly here, and she needed me."

Ruddygore nodded. "And now you still feel a need for her, but she no longer needs you. That's what it's all about, Joe. It gripes your independent trucker's soul that you need somebody and it gripes you even more that they don't need you. But it's not Marge you're really mad at, Joe—it's yourself."

Joe sighed. "I guess you're right as usual, Ruddygore."

"Not guess, Joe, and you know it. I *am* right, and you'd better face that fact, if only for your own sake. Don't let your ego, your self-esteem, get low, Joe, or you'll sink into that same pit she did way back when. I need you, Joe. This world needs you—and you have a real opportunity here to carve out anything you want. Anything, Joe! Pirate or king, merchant or adventurer—you have the potential for all of it. The only one who can stop you is you."

There was a knock at the door, and the sorcerer called out for whomever it was to come in. It proved to be Durin with a pot of something on a silver tray and two mugs. Joe sniffed it, and his face showed total amazement. "That's *coffee!*"

Ruddygore grinned. "Yep. Good stuff, too. A private blend. I had to duck over to New York a couple of weeks ago; while there, I picked it up just for you. I bought a twenty-pound sack and I brought five pounds here."

It was the perfect gesture and it was well timed. Although it was possible to grow coffee in this world—in fact, it was supposedly grown on other continents—it was not native to Husaquahr, and there was nothing Joe had missed more. He savored the mug as if it were filled with some fine, expensive wine, and his morale was lifted accordingly. Ruddygore was able to resume the talk after a bit with the atmosphere much relaxed.

"Joe, we're having this talk because I have some important work for you to do," the big man told him.

Joe nodded. "I figured as much."

"Let's wrap up our discussion of the lay of the land, though, first. You ever wonder why the fairy folk exist?"

"No. I haven't given it much thought. Kind of like why everything else exists. Just the way things turned out, I suppose."

"Nope. When things were set up, evolution was supposed to be the perfecting mechanism, such as it was, but some hedges were included. Intelligently directed redevelopment, it's called in my trade. To ensure that vital pollination was carried out, there were more than a hundred and sixty different races of pixies, each ensuring that certain types of plants grew and dominated in certain areas. The land was protected, particularly in the key areas, by the kobolds, who control vital volcanic areas and can make certain that soil is renewed, especially in areas where there is heavy erosion. I could go through the catalog of thousands of fairy types, but you get the idea. I admit that sometimes it's tough to figure out the vital service of a particular race; in a few cases, like the Imir, they are the guardians and protectors of other races performing essential services, but they all have their niches. That's their primary function—one thing each that guarantees that things will develop in certain ways."

"Seems to me, bees pollinate things pretty good," Joe commented.

"But that's the way things were *supposed* to work. In the early days, though, they needed a nudge. That's what the original fairies were for on your own world. Of course, they weren't that needed, and now those who are left are hunted, oppressed, or hiding out and coping. That's part of my job—finding them and bringing them over here, where we still need them. You see, Joe, this world wasn't as thoroughly planned out or carefully formed as yours, so compromises had to be made. Not only are the fairies vital, but the wild card is magic, which fills in the holes, so to speak. It's actually a more awkward system, but it's worked out pretty well so far."

"This is all leading somewhere."

"Smart lad. First, I want you to remember and accept what I've just said. Marge is still culturally and intellectually of your world, so there's still somebody around to talk to. However, she's also of faërie, an elemental, and that controls her actions and attitudes from here on in."

"You talk as if she's some kind of smart bee or something."

"Well, that's close. Faërie nature and function is instinctive. It's in the genes, if you will. The intellect is imposed over that, and is subservient to it. Not that fairies are any dumber than humans—many are far smarter—but they have less control. Instinctive behavior, of which we have almost none, comes first. That's why you're going to have to be both patient and understanding with her, Joe. I don't want you two at each other's throat or mad or upset at one another. I can't afford it."

"I'll try. But I notice you keep dancing around the subject without actually coming to it. Don't you think it's about time you stopped discussing the troubles I have and start telling me about the troubles you're going to give me?"

Ruddygore grinned, but the grin faded quickly. "I'm after the end game, Joe. The *coup de grâce*. The Baron's planning something and we don't know what it is. Whole armies have simply vanished, and we don't think they've been disbanded or used internally—he has far too many troops and far too much magic for that."

"And, somehow, you want me and Marge to find out what's going on."

"If you could, it would be a bonus, but I have others working on that. No, Joe, if all goes as planned here this week, I'm going to play my own end game, my separate table. Even if we find out what's up and stop it, it will only be another short victory before something else is tried, then another thing and another. But if I can take out the chief player in this game, I can set these demonic plans back for a generation or more, until they find a new Dark Baron and properly corrupt, train, and position him or her. It's the Baron I want, son—nothing else matters as much."

Joe nodded. "So you're going to try and smoke him out here, then send us against him. The demon can't interfere, so Marge vamps him and Irving runs him through, huh?"

The sorcerer chuckled. "I wish it were that simple. I really do. But Marge would be powerless against somebody of the Baron's strength. In fact, that's her biggest danger. Right now she's feeling her powers and she's cocky and overconfident, which is to be expected. But her powers are really quite limited and easily muted—probably by half or more of the delegates arriving here."

That worried Joe. "Uh—I've seen the results already of what one of you boys can do when you get irritated."

"I'll talk to her. Hmmm . . . No, that wouldn't do it. I know—I'll set her up."

"Huh?"

"I'll have a couple of old friends get to know her. Either one will become as nasty or obnoxious as the situation permits, and she'll find herself powerless to defend herself. Maybe we'll stick a harmless spell on her, like compulsive singing and dancing or something like that. It will take her down a peg, make her more cautious."

"Well, I'll leave that to you. But if she's powerless against the Baron—and I *know* he could turn me into a toad before I got close—then what are we going to do?"

"During the convention, I, along with Poquah, Macore, and several others not obviously with me, will pursue various lines of investigation. With any luck, we're going to be able to narrow down the Baron's probable identity."

"Good trick. How many real high-class magicians are here? Two thousand?"

"Closer to ten thousand, but that doesn't matter. The Baron cannot conceal the fact that he is one of the top masters of the art in the world. I took him on, you remember, and I *know*. He fought me to a draw, and you get where I am today by going head to head in some very serious contests of wills and magical talent. More importantly, all the talent in the world won't help you achieve true command unless you have these contests with the masters. Why, here I'll probably take on a dozen challengers for my Council seat. It's the only way they learn and, eventually, the only way they get on the Council. The Baron got his skills through such sorcerers' battles, since there is no other way to get them. Consider—he became that good, good enough to tie me, without ever having taken me on before. I'd know if he had, believe me. A battle technique's like a fingerprint. And since the only truly powerful wizards I've never taken on are those on the Council who have made the Council *after* me, I deduce that our Baron is not only a councillor but one of the newer ones."

"All right, that makes sense, I guess. So it's one of thir—ah, twelve people."

"Uh-huh. And it's easier than that, since six of the twelve do not live in Husaquahr, and I'm certain that the Baron must. We have pretty good records of where the others were, considering the distances involved and magical transportation means, while the Baron was active here. He simply *must* be on top of things through his expanding empire, and that means a Husaquahrian. So now it is one of six, and we shall try to narrow that down further as we go here."

"Uh-huh. And if you do?"

"Then it's your turn. I need proof, Joe. I need absolute, incontrovertible proof that the Baron is a tool of a demon prince. Only with that proof will the Council act against one of its own, and only the Council can do the job."

"Are you sure even of that? I mean, there are several of the Council working with him, aren't there? Don't a bunch live in lands he controls?"

"Quite true, but you misunderstand the seriousness of the affair. The more truly evil and corrupt a sorcerer is, the more stake he has in making certain that the covenant between Heaven and Hell remains unbroken. If Hell breaks the covenant, then the Creator's forces are free to do the same, and that means total war to the finish between the two sides. Armageddon. The end of all the universes. And on whose side will those evil and corrupt ones find themselves?"

Joe's Sunday school was a little weak, but he thought he had the idea. "Uh-huh. So they've got their cushy evilness here, kinda like the Wicked Witch in Oz. They have their own crazy idea of Heaven now, and they won't be anxious to pay the bill."

"You have it. I'm convinced Hell, too, doesn't really know about this. I don't think they're ready for the final battle, which, of course, they intend to win by picking their own time and place. Last I checked, old Lucifer's still got his heart set on nuclear war over on your side. But since he started his whole career on disloyalty and treachery, it's little wonder that his underlings echo that, even to him. He's so busy spreading his little bombs all over Earth, he's not paying any attention to our side, and that's his mistake. So you see, Joe, the odds aren't totally stacked against you. It's few people who have both God and the devil on their side. Maybe you can also now appreciate the real stake. You have a son, I recall?"

Joe nodded. "Yeah. In Philadelphia. I think about him a lot. That's why I named my sword after him."

"So don't let your emotions get the better of you. A lot hangs on you and Marge getting along and working together. I'll have a little chat with her later on in the convention, perhaps after she's learned her lesson."

Joe knew it was a dismissal and he was glad for it. Besides, the coffee was all gone here, but there was more in the parlor, he was sure. Still, one thing bothered him. As he got up and turned to go, he suddenly turned back to the big sorcerer. "Uh—you say you're gonna have to fight a bunch of up-and-coming sorcerers here?"

Ruddygore nodded. "That's the way it is."

"Any chance you'll lose?"

"There's always a chance, but I've already looked over this group and it looks like a pretty lean crop this season. Not that some of 'em don't have potential—maybe in twenty or thirty years they'll be up to it, but not now."

"Now, don't you get cocky, either."

"Point taken, swordsman to magician." Ruddygore snapped his fingers. "Oh, I almost forgot. Has Tiana arrived yet?"

Joe shrugged. "I don't know. I wouldn't know her if I bumped into her."

"Oh, if you bump into her, you'll know, Joe, I promise you. You two should get along very well, actually. Ask Poquah for her background when you get a moment."

"Okay, I'll do that. See you later?"

"Perhaps. Perhaps not for some time. Relax and enjoy yourself here. Consider it a vacation with pay and relax. In another week you're going back to work."

"I'm going to do just that," Joe assured him and left.

"This your first one of these things?" Joe asked Macore over coffee and pastry in the parlor.

The little thief nodded. "You better believe it. Man, I wouldn't try to hustle any of *these* babies. Their rooms and belongings have magical guardians. You run a con on 'em, even if it works, and they send out the spirit world to get you wherever you are. Uh-uh. This is *one* convention that's safe as a holy temple."

"So how come you're here?"

Macore grinned. "I was asked. Well, more than asked. Better you don't know any more, for your own sake as well as mine. If the old boy wants to tell you, then we'll talk."

"I think I get the idea." Ruddygore was at least the equal of any of the top sorcerers here, so he could offer major protection to a thief—and a master thief, able to tap magical powers through his boss, would be quite an asset here. Looking for— what? Joe wondered. A suit of ghostly armor? Certainly something, anything, that would lead to the identity of the Dark Baron, probably through the adepts. They wouldn't have as good protection, and they'd be overconfident here. Any adepts working directly for the Baron had to know, and, if they did, there might be something telltale somewhere. Joe didn't envy the little thief his job, but he appreciated the risks involved. For some of these more-than-human sorcerers, death wasn't the worst thing to fear.

They had begun talking about old times when there was a sudden, sharp pounding on the door, and all conversation ceased. Poquah emerged from his own room and went to the door, opening it. After a glance, he admitted the newcomer.

At first sight of her, all other topics were forgotten by Joe. As Ruddygore had said, if he ever bumped into Tiana, he'd know.

She was, quite simply, the most beautiful woman Joe had ever seen; from the expressions on the faces of the others, he wasn't alone in that assessment. It was hard to go beyond that. Everything about her was absolutely perfect—perfect figure, perfect proportions, and a beautiful, sensuous face. Her skin was tanned a deep and very dark brown, matching her eyes, but her lips were curiously light and very enticing. Her jet-black hair hung down almost to her narrow, perfect waist, while her skin was as smooth and blemish-free as polished ebony. She looked, Joe thought, like some stunning Italian movie star; there was a Mediterranean cast to her features, as if she belonged somewhere romping on the beaches of the Riviera, and that thought was enhanced by the fact that she was wearing only a breechclout made of the hide of some furry brown animal and a halter of the same material that did nothing to hide her obvious attributes, as well as a necklace of what looked like gold chain to which small, carved pieces of bone had been attached. From a sword belt, a broadsword nearly the size of Joe's hung in a leather scabbard. The belt was worn loosely, emphasizing the curve of her hips.

Probably the most outstanding thing about her was that she was barefoot, yet stood well over six feet tall. In fact, when Joe stood up, transfixed, he found her to be perhaps a half inch shorter than his own six-six—and he was wearing new sandals.

For a moment, nobody said anything, so she walked briskly into the room and looked around. "Well? Is everyone struck dumb?" she said irritably, her voice deep and rich. She spoke with a trace of what sounded like a German accent to Joe; but, considering the fact that this was a world with languages different from his, it might only seem that way.

Poquah was quick to recover. "Tiana, I presume. I am Poquah, the Master's chief associate. These gentlemen here are Macore, Joseph, and Durin, respectively."

She looked them all over, then settled on Joe and frowned. "That is an unusual name here, Joseph. Where are you from?"

"Philadelphia," he told her.

"Oh, that is in the United States of America, I believe," she responded, literally shocking the hell out of him.

"Uh, yeah, it is, but how . . . ?"

"I was never there, but for seven years I was in hiding in Basel, Switzerland."

This was too much at one time. "Switzerland! How?" But instantly he knew the answer. Only one person he knew could hide a Husaquahrian in Europe, and that person was in the next room.

"I was the oldest daughter of Hapandur of Morikay. When I was but nine years old, he was defeated at a gathering just like this one by that pig Kaladon, whom my father had befriended and treated as a son." She went over, looked at the pastries, took one, then sat down on the couch and sprawled out.

Joe sank back into his chair. Suddenly the coffee didn't seem a strong enough drink right about then. He'd once described Marge's moves as catlike; Tiana was a tigress.

"So you had to make a run for it, huh?" Macore prompted. Barely five foot five and perhaps a hundred and twenty pounds, he couldn't help feeling like a little child who'd just come across a ten-thousand-gallon chocolate sundae.

She nodded. "Yes. Kaladon had dreams that he would marry

me as soon as I was old enough, thus legitimizing his rule, since everyone knew the bastard won only by cheating. He actually made advances to me, an innocent of nine!"

Joe just followed along, but couldn't help wondering how Tiana could ever have been an innocent nine-year-old.

"Well, with the help of some fairies loyal to my poor father, I escaped, but Kaladon pursued. Fortunately, the faërie network got me to Ruddygore, one of my father's few very close friends who could be trusted, and he took me out of reach for a while."

"But you came back," Joe noted. "Why?"

"I was discovered. Kaladon is in league with Hell itself; in exchange for certain favors here, ones which involved aiding the Dark Baron, the demons of Earth sought me out and attacked. It seemed pointless to remain there when this was my native land, so I was returned. I have been in hiding since, these past eight years, moving with the wild tribes and studying and training when I could in both the magical and the combat arts. I have grown quite good." That last was said without any trace of boasting, and they believed it.

"But now you're back, and in the same hotel as this Kaladon," Macore pointed out. "Why? Are you ready to take him on?"

"No, I do not believe that I am ready for him yet. One day I will be and I will reclaim what is mine by rights. I was summoned here by Dr. Ruddygore, and, considering what I owe him, I could not refuse. It makes no difference. Kaladon had found me out, anyway, and killed many of those who were closest to me."

"Then you are in great danger here," Macore suggested. "Kaladon will know you are here."

"He dares do nothing at the convention unless he wishes to challenge Dr. Ruddygore," she told him. "And that he is not up to doing under any circumstances."

"Quite true," came a voice behind her, and they all turned to see the great sorcerer enter the room, resplendent now in his golden robes. "He has already been informed that any move against Tiana will make in me an enemy he can not avoid in this public place."

"Ruddy!" Tiana cried out joyfully. In a flash she'd gotten up, turned, and actually jumped over her chair, finally reaching and embracing the sorcerer, who, if he'd been of lesser size and bulk, would certainly have been bowled over.

Joe looked at Macore. "Ruddy?"

The little thief tried to suppress a laugh, and it was clear that Ruddygore was not amused. Still, he tolerated the display and attempted to pass it off. "Tiana, it is good to see you once again. I must be going downstairs to find out my schedule, but I can spare a moment. Come—sit just a bit."

She moved obediently back to her chair and settled there. Joe bet a bundle to himself that nobody else could ever get such meek obedience from her. Ruddygore did not sit, but stood facing them all. "That spell I sent you—I gather it worked?"

She smiled and nodded. "Very well indeed. In fact, I passed the usurper in the lobby here and he never recognized me."

Macore looked crestfallen. "You mean she really doesn't look like that?"

Ruddygore chuckled both at the question and at the mean look Tiana gave the little thief. "Oh, my, yes," the sorcerer assured them all. "The spell is particularly powerful and undetectable one, since it's tailored strictly to Kaladon and affects no one else. To him, and to him alone, Tiana looks quite different, although still rather striking. Basically a blond, blue-eyed, and fair-skinned priestess from the northern wastes, if I remember correctly. It's just enough of a change so that she is definitely not Tiana to him in looks, voice, or habit, but close enough that the reactions of those around him will be consistent with what he sees. It's a thin disguise at best, but I don't expect him to crack it easily, since he's very confident that no one can put an undetectable spell over on him. Don't rely on it too heavily, my dear."

"I am not worried about him," she said confidently. "Not with you around, anyway."

He just shrugged. "Well, I must get down there. Tiana, I've had you preregistered as Uma of the Golden Lakes, just as an extra precaution. Why make it any easier on him, after all? I'm also curious to see how long it's going to take him to find you out."

"That is fine with me," she told him. "I will see you later, then."

With that, Ruddygore turned and, accompanied by Poquah, left the suite.

"Have you any luggage coming?" Joe asked her.

She shook her head. "None. I travel as light as I possibly can. You learn that most of all after eight years in hiding. Always I carry my sword with me, and in the belt is a hidden compartment in which there are some coins and gems. The only thing I don't have with me is my bullwhip. I was forced to abandon it a few weeks ago, so I will have to get another here."

"The market is excellent for just about anything," Joe told her. "And, right now, we're on Ruddygore's expense account."

She nodded. "Good, then. I am also starved. Will you show me this market? Then we can perhaps get something to eat."

Joe got up and she did, as well. Again there was an eerie sensation in him at her size. "Delighted," he responded, trying to sound as Continental as possible. "Shall we go?"

They walked out the door, leaving Macore sitting there. Durin chuckled from the kitchenette. "Left you alone, huh? I guess you're just not big enough for her."

Macore got up, walked over, took some of the fabulously rich iced pastry from the tray, and, without a word or a wasted motion, pushed it into the fairy cook's face.

Joe was absolutely delighted with Tiana. Although of this world, she had some knowledge of a different corner of his and she was certainly a fascinating person indeed. It was also a relief, after all this time of putting up with Marge's vegetarianism, to find a woman who obviously enjoyed real meat.

Slowly, over the meal, he told her more about himself and about his doings since arriving in Husaquahr. Gradually, the rest of her story came out, as well.

Her father had been of royal blood, but a third son with no chance of inheriting position or title. His obvious talent for the magical arts, however, had taken him in the direction of the Society in the same way that second and third sons of European nobility during the Middle Ages had gone into the Catholic church. He also married a wealthy noblewoman he'd known since childhood, and they were very much in love. In due course, they had a daughter, Torea, but she died mysteriously in infancy of some disease or spell her father was powerless to do anything about. They tried again, of course, at about the time Hapandur won the Council seat and became ranking sorcerer in Zhimbombe, but the pregnancy was well along before he discovered that his first daughter's death had been due to a strange and powerful curse laid on his children by someone unknown who hated him very much. Just who was unknown.

The curse was so well constructed that he could not dissolve it, nor find its key, but he did manage to unravel it "at the corners," as Tiana cryptically put it. The result was that her mother was able to make the decision—either her life or her child's—and she made it. The distraught wizard pleaded with her, but she had taken the death of their first daughter very hard and she was adamant.

"What my father did was complex," Tiana told Joe. "Basically, though, my birth was a magical event of sorts. The soul, I am told, enters at the first commands to the body to give birth. My father, or so it is said, blocked that process, against my mother's strong wishes, so that I might be stillborn, but so strong was her resolve that she died at the moment of my birth. My father would never speak of it, but others have told me that her soul, because of her will to bear me, entered me instead of another."

Joe was startled. "You mean you're your *mother*?"

She shrugged. "I do not know. But it is certain that I have always had strange dreams, and memories of people and places that I have never seen, and I have always been told by those of Morikay that I have my mother's mannerisms, habits, and even turns of phrase. Physically, I resemble more others on both sides of the family than her, but it does seem, sometimes, when I look into a mirror, that another, different face should be there."

Still, her father never remarried, nor, as far as anyone knew, ever even looked at another woman sexually; but he doted on his daughter, to whom he gave his dead wife's name. She had a very spoiled and pampered childhood, she freely admitted, and was totally unprepared for what came after.

Kaladon, a handsome young man with a great deal of talent, became apprenticed to her father and proved a more-than-worthy adept. He was treated as a member of the family—in fact, as the son the old man had never had. She liked him at the time, considering him an older brother, and she had no idea that, even back then, he was arranging for her to get as little education or training as possible, particularly in the magical arts.

"Then came the great convention, at Coditz Green in Leander, where we knew Kaladon would challenge for a leadership position. How proud we were of him—the son of a pig! He was so trusted and so close that it was a shock when he challenged my father, and an even greater shock that he won."

"You mentioned that he cheated," Joe noted.

She nodded. "Later I was told how it was done. He had drugged some of the food my father was served. He could easily do this, because he was a household member and very trusted. It was also a very light drug, one that you would not even know you had taken, but it was enough to slow my father's thinking and speed of action and reaction. After he won, while still at the convention, the usurper's true nature came out, and we knew that we were in the hands of and at the mercy of the blackest of black magicians."

Joe hesitated a moment before asking the obvious question, but he really was interested in the story and anxious to know. "Uh—what happens to the losers of these challenges?"

She gave a slight shudder. "Horrible things. That is why even very powerful magicians do not challenge for the Council. True adepts, not going for a position but simply testing themselves, are prevented by the umpires of such matches from going too far, and so there is no penalty; but if a councillor is deposed, he or she must be utterly reduced so that no rechallenge is possible."

"Your father is dead, then."

She nodded sadly. "Yes, but not by Kaladon's hand. They do not work like that, particularly the black magicians who dominate the white, nor, in fact, the white who dominate the black, but my father had many friends and one was merciful."

He whistled. "Are these contests open to the public?"

"If you mean can you see one, the answer is that you can see as many as you wish here, but it can be a very dangerous thing to watch. The forces involved are tremendous."

He could understand that. "Still, I think I'll see one of Ruddygore's matches if I can. I should know everything I can about the kind of people I'm actually facing here. The fact is, except for some of Ruddygore's stuff with me, the fairies, and the magic Lamp, I've seen very little real magic here. Not the kind they talk of the sorcerers having, anyway."

"Then you should see one, in fact," she agreed.

After the *coup* she was returned, a pampered prisoner, to Morikay, entirely in the hands of her father's betrayer. Kaladon began a purge of all those, human and fairy, loyal to the deposed sorcerer, but some had gotten the word and arranged for escape routes. Two winged elves from Marquewood, who had worked at landscaping in Morikay, managed to flee with Tiana, as well.

It was a harrowing, risky escape, the material for an epic or two, but finally she was passed along from fairy race to fairy race until she reached Castle Terindell. It was Ruddygore who took her in; when he realized that she would be a virtual lifetime prisoner inside the castle as long as Kaladon lived, he took her across to Earth. Ruddygore, it seemed, had a major interest in a bank in Switzerland, and, since that was where he was heading, that was where she wound up, with loyal guardians in his employ taking her in and providing an identity for her as the daughter of deposed Romanian royalty killed later by the communists there. Having been magically prepared by Ruddygore, she took to languages easily, quickly acquiring a fluency in German, French, Italian, and even Romansch. Her tutors were both of Earth and of Husaquahr, imported for the occasion by Ruddygore on frequent visits, and it was during those years that she threw herself into her studies with but one long-term object in mine—revenge.

By this time, though, Kaladon had fallen in league with the Dark Baron, whose demonic master could talk to and deal with the demons of Earth, and it was as a bribe to Kaladon that the Baron had the demonic forces seek her out and find her. A well-financed Satanist organization in western Europe then was called in for the actual deed, and again she barely escaped back to Husaquahr.

"Ruddy decided that, if they could find me once, they could certainly find me anywhere, now that my appearance was known. As you might have guessed, I had grown and turned from girl into woman."

She had, in fact, been a fairly normal-sized girl, but with puberty came tremendous growth, far beyond anything in her ancestry. "Ruddy has a theory that it was the diet, eating such a different balance of things in Switzerland from what our bodies are used to here. I believe it was probably a spell of some kind put on me before I left Husaquahr, although by whom I am not sure. It might have been my father, of course, or any one of the fairy races who aided me, or a combination of those things. It does not matter, because this is how I am and this is how I like being."

"*I* certainly see nothing to complain about," Joe told her honestly. "You are certainly the most beautiful woman I've ever seen."

She smiled. "That's very nice of you."

"I mean it, too."

She sat back a moment, holding a slight grin. "You know, because of my size I have been very intimidating to men. I wonder if perhaps Ruddy is not engaging in a bit of match-making."

He wondered that himself. If so, he hoped that she had the same attraction for him that he felt for her. It certainly was a very convenient meeting, just after his troubles with Marge, and it *had* been arranged by the sorcerer. Well, if so, it was the best thing the old boy had done for him, even if it didn't work.

Tiana's history for the past eight years had been far different from her earlier life. It was only among the barbarous nomadic tribes of the far reaches of Husaquahr that she could blend in, somewhat, with the large, burly denizens of those places, and it was only among them that she could feel relatively safe from Kaladon's spies and the threats of civilization in general.

At first, she had rebelled at the primitive, hard existence, and there had been a period of tremendous adjustment until she'd learned to accept it. It was a kind of existence that Morikay and Basel has not prepared her for, and she was flung into it much as Joe had been flung into his existence. She had been taken under the wing of some very powerful warriors who owed Ruddygore a favor. She became, however, strong, powerful, and athletic and, because of her size and condition-ing, she trained with swords and took the tests of a warrior usually, but not exclusively, reserved for the men. She had ex-celled at all of it in the end, particularly when she saw the value of it in having some personal freedom in Husaquahr and, perhaps, one day leading a rebellion in the south.

She also trained in, and worked on, the magical arts with the help of Ruddygore and knowledgeable ones he sent to her, first in Basel and later in the northern wastes. She had her father's talent, of that there was no doubt, but she began formal training very late in the game and on an intermittent basis. "It gives me an edge, but not more," she told Joe. "It means, also, that I can often ward off or undo some spells, but the more complex spells are still beyond me, for I have not had the mental training for it." She could, however, read the pictographic language fairly well, and with the proper volume and section of the Books of Rules open in front of her, she could probably do very well indeed. "It is, you might say, the difference between being a good cook and being a chef. A great chef does not need recipes."

They finished, he paid the bill, and they made their way back into the market. There were several leather shops selling whips, and she tried one after the other, impressing the hell out of him, the proprietors, and the passers-by with her skill, but rejecting whip after whip until, at last, in a small second-hand store, she found one that seemed just right to her. "With the others I can do many things," she explained, "but with a whip of perfect balance such as this one, I can work miracles."

She looped it on her belt, on the same side as the sword, in a clasp apparently designed for the weapon, and they walked back to the hotel.

"No shoes or other clothing?" he asked her.

She laughed. "It is odd, but I have been with the barbarians so long that most of those things feel unnatural. If I need furs, I will buy them, but for now I am enjoying for the first time in a long while a comfortable climate. It is not easy to explain, but in order to survive in the wastes, something had to be killed inside me, and that was my sense of civilization, you might say. I find myself preferring to be a barbarian woman, thinking like one, acting like one. All this which was once my own sort of world seems now so soft and decadent. The sword, the whip, and a good horse are all that are really needed, and all that I have or intend to have."

"You seem pretty cultured and civilized to me."

"Because I want to be. That is my veneer, my coat which allows me to go anywhere and do anything. It is the inside that matters, and I have proof of my conversion, as it were. The applicable parts of the Books of Rules that apply to me now are those governing barbarian women; before, they were of the civilized classes. Even the Rules recognize my change, you see."

"But if you depose Kaladon, you'll have to rule Zhimbombe," he pointed out. "That will take more of a change."

"I think they deserve a barbarian queen. We will face that if it comes about."

He noted that she had used the word "if" instead of "when" and nodded to himself. Just how realistic her dream was, even in her own mind, was in question. She had as much as admitted that she could never be the equal of Kaladon and, unless he was finished off, she had little hope of having any kind of control over the country. Kaladon, of course, had probably intended just that—she would be his puppet queen and consort, by which he would consolidate the country and its popular old families and his own rule as both sorcerer and temporal ruler. Joe decided that he'd like to meet, or at least see, this fellow at close range. Certainly, if nothing else, Kaladon would be one of Ruddygore's prime suspects for the Baron's true identity. How easy it would be to pretend to ally with the Baron for favors when actually he *was* the Baron—and Zhimbombe was the first nation of Husaquahr to fall prey to the Baron's forces. A prime suspect indeed. If Joe's suspicions were so, there was a chance through Kaladon's elimination to give Tiana a crack at control by clever politics, sword, and whip.

They reentered the hotel, which was teeming with crowds of people of all shapes and sizes, garbed in every imaginable way. "Shall we register?" Tiana asked him.

He nodded. "Might as well."

She thought a moment. "You are called 'the Golden,' is that not correct?"

"Yeah. Mostly because my last name's de Oro."

"And I am Uma of the Golden Lakes. It gives me a thought. We are both dark-skinned giants, you might say, and we certainly look as if we belong together."

He wondered what she was driving at and just nodded.

"Kaladon will not expect a pair. Let us, at least for disguise purposes, register as mates."

"Huh?" It took him aback, mainly because he'd love it that way, but he hardly wanted to risk alienating her by suggesting it. He just wasn't used to women *this* aggressive.

"You don't wish it?"

"Oh, sure. I think it'll be fun," he answered hopefully. "Let's go."

It was like waking up from some really strange dream, although she knew it was no dream at all. She wasn't physically tired, but she'd come back up to the room for a little break and found herself just sitting back, relaxing and thinking, and she realized thinking was something distasteful. She certainly hadn't been doing much of it over the last few days, that was for sure.

It was funny how this reaction had hit her, like something out of the blue, but suddenly, after being almost frantically active, she no longer felt the desire. She walked over to the mirror in the room and looked at herself. It was still strange to see the fairy reflection there, to understand that this unnaturally sexy, kittenish, winged figure was herself. But it wasn't the exterior that was troubling her; it was what had happened inside to her head and heart.

She'd been to every bar and bistro in the city, she felt certain, but they all blended into one. And the men—so many of them—all blended into a faceless crowd as well. Not a single one stood out as a real human being. Instead, they were objects, things, nothing more. She went over to a dresser and pulled out the top drawer. It was crammed with junk—small items of jewelry, ornaments, little carvings, even toys. She was afraid to count them and slammed the drawer shut and went back to the bed to think.

Had she enjoyed acting that way? Yeah, she had, she had to admit to herself, but it wasn't really *her*; at least, not the way she always saw herself. Her whole body still tingled, and on that level she had never felt better in her whole life. But was this what she was to be for the rest of her life? How long did a fairy live if not killed? Until Judgment Day, it was said, and nobody knew how long that could be. Hundreds of years, perhaps. Maybe thousands. All like—this?

She remembered the magic time when she had emerged from the volcanic fires as a Kauri and she remembered her sisters of faërie. At the time, they had seemed radiant, magical children at play, but they didn't seem quite so exciting or magical any more. Instead, they now seemed like what they must be—permanent fourteen-year-old girls, locked forever in the state of irresponsible and irrepressible adolescence and freed of all inhibitions; a female version of the Lost Boys, without even Peter Pan, let alone Wendy, to give them any sort of control or direction, and each one more or less exactly like the others. Even she had become exactly like them, and that bothered her only because the Kauri didn't know any other existence or any other way, had never faced or understood responsibility or had a single serious thought in their playfully empty heads. She had, and that alone set her apart from them.

But she *had* been that age once and had been frustratingly restricted by her mother, the school, and the rest of those forces that kept folks in line. Still, life had been unhappy enough since adulthood that she had grabbed on to the chance to return to that state of not-so-innocent grace, to become again that giggly adolescent without any rules or restrictions whatsoever. Who wouldn't love that sort of chance—but as a chance, a lark. It was only now that she realized that this wasn't some second chance but rather a permanent condition.

Already she had hurt poor Joe, the first man in years to be a real friend, the one whose kindness and pity gave her this second chance in the first place. She'd not only hurt him, she'd mocked him, and that was far more painful. Her practical jokes and funny exercises of her strange powers had frightened rather than amused or reassured him. Worse, she knew deep down that she might not have the self-control or willpower to keep those impulses from dominating her again and that each cycle would make them even easier and more natural to accept. The more she lived as a Kauri, the more she would become one inside as well as out. This she knew, although not really from any faërie insight, but just from knowing herself. Conditioning *did* work—as Pavlov's dogs had proved—particularly when there were no alternatives and an endless future of such conditioning. The Earth Mother knew this, and counted on it.

Kauri awoke with the setting sun. Kauri played games, danced, sang, flew around, and soared through the skies playing tag, then went to their toy box and played pretend with their pretty toys. At sunrise, Kauri went to sleep and dreamed only happy dreams, awakening again to do the same thing with minor variations the next day and the next. If they felt like it, on impulse or whatever, they ventured out of their faërie Never-Neverland and played with the boys in the real world that was still nothing more than an extended playland to them, with the inhabitants merely toys like those on the scrap heap.

Kauri didn't need to think. In fact, thinking was something that was an absolutely bad thing for them. Oh, they needed to talk—but innocuously and as vacuously as possible. That, in fact, was an advantage among the kind of men they liked to play with. Marge wondered how long she would be able to have this level of introspection, or even remember words like innocuous, vacuous, or introspection. Certainly her spoken vocabulary already seemed to switch to something more childlike and basic. Following the period of her binge, she now realized, she was speaking in a sexy variation of little-girl speech without even thinking about it.

Without even thinking . . .

At that moment, she heard a commotion in the hallway and went over to her door. To her surprise, she heard Ruddygore's booming baritone and then the sound of the door of the adjacent room opening and closing.

The old Marge would have hesitated to disturb him and would have just sat and brooded, but she literally didn't think about it in this case. She opened her door, went down to the big double doors of the parlor suite, and just turned the handle and walked in without knocking.

Both Ruddygore and Poquah turned in puzzled surprise at her entrance; but when the big sorcerer saw her, he broke into a grin and sat down in the chair. He looked very tired, but he said, "That's all right, Poquah—leave us alone."

The Imir looked a bit concerned for his boss, but bowed slightly and did as he was instructed, sliding his own door shut behind him.

Ruddygore beckoned her over with his hand. "Pardon me for not rising, my dear, but I'm about done in."

"That's all right," she told him. "I guess I should have set up some better time to see you, but I don't seem much in control of myself any more."

"I think I understand," he said sympathetically. "Don't

worry about me. Although I hadn't intended to seek you out until another day or two, this is fine, since I'm not getting any younger and this pace is telling."

"I just want to know why."

"Huh?" The comment took him by surprise. "Why what?"

"Why am I a Kauri? I was happy the way I was, after coming here. Why did I have to change?"

"Those are two different questions, my dear. You seem to imply that I had something to do with it."

"Well? Didn't you?"

"Not a thing, I assure you." As quickly and as clearly as possible, but with more detail on the fine points, he explained to her, as he had to Joe, why she had been made a changeling from the moment they crossed the Sea of Dreams. "I made you neither changeling nor Kauri. You did that to yourself."

"Me!"

He nodded. "Oh, with your mental state, I should have known from the start that you would be a changeling—but what sort was really up to you." He thought a moment. "My dear, what is your vision of Heaven and Hell?"

She shrugged. "Harps on the one side, fires on the other, I guess."

"Uh-uh. Would it shock you to learn that Heaven and Hell are actually the same place?"

"Huh?"

He nodded. "That's why Hell is such a curse. You can look around and *see*, with little difficulty, just what you missed, but you're stuck as you are, permanently. And the way you are is what you built for yourself. Let's see if I can explain it. If Joe should die, his soul would be re-formed according to the chain he forged in life, with his own mind, conscious and subconscious, creating his own Heaven or Hell. Most folks, as you might expect, wind up somewhere in between. Then, at the end of time, there will be a Judgment. Those of Hell will at that time suffer the true and total death, while those judged worthy will be able to perfect their own existences and live happily ever after in total communion with the Creator. That's the way it works."

"But not for me?"

"Not quite. As a changeling, your physical form was burned off in the fires; and because you, as a fairy, exist in the physical world, you became what your mind said it should become within the limits of our world. You never wished to harm anyone, so you became something that can not consciously harm anyone. You felt that the world was out to do *you* harm, so you became something that can defend itself against the evil, cruelty, and malice of the world."

She sighed sadly. "I see. With a bad world all around, I wanted only to give and get pleasure," She stopped for a moment, suddenly feeling stunned. "And since I ran down my education as getting me nowhere and nothing and being a real waste, I became something that didn't need any of that. Sweet Mother! I *did* do it to myself, sort of. But this wasn't what I had in mind!"

"It seldom is," he told her, "for anybody, and not just changelings. It's wonderful to see some of those Holy Joes permanently sitting on clouds, forever singing hymns and hosannahs, bored out of their skulls. You very seldom get what you really want, but you usually get what you deserve, based on your own life and thoughts and desires, both expressed and suppressed."

"Then that's it, I guess. I'm stuck until Judgment, and by that time I'll be as empty and bubble-headed as my sisters and probably just keep on going, like somebody with a lobotomy."

He looked serious. "So that's what it is. I should have guessed as much." And he *did* see. The Kauri form was exactly what that lonely loser on her way to suicide in Texas would have wanted; and, since it was from that woman that the forces of magic took their cue, that was what she'd become. But now Marge was not that woman; Husaquahr had given her a whole new life and outlook, and she was no longer a perfect match for what she now was.

"The best I can offer," he told her, "is some hope, with work on your part, for something a little more than that. You are Kauri and you will remain Kauri. There is nothing anyone can do, since you of faërie may be destroyed but not transformed. But the fact that you're talking to me, here and now, shows that there's still *you* inside there."

"Yeah, but me, the Marge that's talking, is losing. I mean, I think I figured out that Kauri are elementals, not like the elves and gnomes and other creatures. There are water elementals, and wood elementals, even fire elementals, but we're a different kind, since we're out of Earth, Air, and Fire. I don't know about Water."

"You swim like a fish," he told her. "Go on."

"We're—emotion elementals. Only certain kinds of emotions, though. The good ones, I guess. Singing, dancing, playing, even sex."

"That's close enough." Briefly he told her the function of fairies in the scheme of things, as he had told Joe. "Now, Kauri, they have a very important place in the scheme of things. You may not know it, but each and every man you were with so far had some sort of problem. You're attracted to them without realizing it. They're not evil or nasty or anything like that, not in the main, but they have totally lost touch with that sense of childlike innocence and wonder. They're troubled by all sorts of things—business pressures, deadlines, deep depression, that kind of psychiatric illness—and you, believe it or not, help restore to them a sense of fun, of life worth living. That's the Kauri function."

"All I can say is there are a lot of men with hang-ups," she noted acidly. "That and the fact that never have I felt less like a shrink and more like a homebreaker."

Ruddygore chuckled. "Homebreaker? No. You leave no guilt. That's part of the magic. Those men, like all who receive fairy gifts, take with them only the positive. They become better husbands, better fathers, better in their work for it. Believe me when I say that *Kauri can do harm to no one* unless that person attempts to harm them. *Any* kind of harm. The magic knows.

"Look, Marge—don't downplay your importance. Maybe if they had Kauri on Earth, they would have a lot fewer problems, although there are—counterparts—for the other side as well, you know. Incubi and succubi, they're usually called, and their purpose is the opposite of yours. They are elementals of a far different sort and they are your sole true enemies."

She considered that. "Then is there a male form of Kauri? It seems only fair."

He nodded. "Yes, there is such a race, the Zamir. But let's get back to the Kauri. Tell me—what have you eaten in the past few days?"

She thought a moment, then realized that, while things were

a blur, she was pretty sure of this answer. "Nothing. Nothing at all."

"Feel hungry?"

"Not in the slightest."

"Because what you eat is the collective terrors, insecurities, and nightmares of the men you serve. In an ironic way, they power you, as the succubus devours the good and leaves corruption. That's why you feel both physically wonderful and mentally down right now. In time you will transform that spiritual decay and it will lessen, but often it gets too much to bear. Then you *must* return to Mohr Jerahl and cleanse yourself in the fires of the Earth Mother. Otherwise it will tire you terribly and weaken you to a tremendous degree. You see the system now? I always thought it was rather nice."

She *did* see the system, and that made her feel better, to a degree. It explained the very substance of Mohr Jerahl and the reason for the uninhibited innocence they all had there, as well as why they were concerned about her going outside it the first time.

She gave a dry chuckle. "So what you're saying is that I do my job, then revert to this adolescent level, only to build it up again. And because I've eaten my fill, so to speak, and because ol' Marge is really a collection of hang-ups, I'm only me when I'm carrying around everybody else's burdens."

"If you want to put it that way, yes," he told her. "And the longer you go without eating, let's say, the more you will revert. It's actually a tough job, since you, the mistress of emotion, will be on an emotional roller coaster. That's why so many Kauri stay at Mohr Jerahl as long as they can, until their instincts force them out. No, Marge, you don't have to worry about forgetting yourself. Your big problem, particularly if you overdo it, will be carrying the extra weight of depression, neuroses, and anxiety."

She thought about it, and it did make life sound a little better. "Does Joe know this?"

"No, not specifically, but I'll make certain he's instructed. Tiana will probably explain it all to him."

"Tiana?" Very oddly, she felt a slight tinge of jealousy at the name. That made her feel a little guilty, considering how she'd chided him for that sort of feeling.

Ruddygore nodded. "They've hit it off very well." He

smiled. "You see? You just felt jealousy and guilt—I can tell. They're inside you now, until you transform them into energy as needed, but they are familiar to you from your past experience. In fact, I'd say that you can handle a far heavier load than a born Kauri, because you have experienced such things firsthand and know how to deal with them. No, Marge—you're not going to lose yourself, just take on a new set of problems. I'm counting on you to be able to handle a great deal in the weeks ahead, more than I'd ever ask a born Kauri to handle."

She got interested in spite of herself and lost some of her self-pity in the process. "So this *isn't* just a vacation or a shakedown for me."

He shook his head wearily. "No, hardly. I hesitate to say this, Marge, but the odds are you might be the only one left at the end of this to tell the tale."

CHAPTER 8

THICKENING PLOTS

The convention shall be limited to members of the Society and their authorized guests.

—Rules, VI, 29(a)

TIANA WAS PROVING A GOOD GUIDE TO THE COMPLEXITIES OF the convention, but it was still a confusing blur to Joe. He felt like a truck driver at a convention of nuclear engineers celebrating Halloween.

Registration proved to be no problem. Their names were on file, their single room number raised no eyebrows, and both were suddenly handed large bags full of written material and silver necklaces from which hung a bronze rectangular pendant with various cuneiformlike letters on it, some large and some small. When they were away from registration, he got Tiana to translate.

"Well, the top row gives the name of the Society and says it is their four thousand two hundred and thirty-first meeting, which is abbreviated as Sach-con Nine Hundred and Two. Below that it says, 'Hello, my name is Joseph the Golden.' "

He looked at the last little figures. "So that's my name in

this chicken-scratch writing. I'll have to remember it, or keep this as a reference, in case I have to sign my name and pretend I know it all."

She laughed. "Keep that thing on whenever you are in the convention areas," she warned him. "Each one has a spell personalized to the first wearer that admits you to all public areas. Try and get in without it and you will get a nasty shock."

"I'll remember," he promised. "Where to now?"

"Let us go back into the exhibition hall. I want to see how much has changed since I was a child."

They went back, both clutching their bags, and Joe felt a little absurd. *Mr. and Mrs. Barbarian go shopping,* he thought. "Any reason why I should lug all this stuff around when I can't read a word of it?" he asked her.

"It is hard to say, but probably not. Why not just put it over in that coat room there and get it on the way back, if it is still there?"

He did just that and felt at least a little less foolish. They then entered the exhibition hall, and Joe was surprised to feel it comfortably air-conditioned. "A minor housekeeping spell," Tiana told him.

So this was more of the magic of Husaquahr. "Pretty tame magic," he noted. "I kinda figured that magic lands like this one had all sorts of stuff going all the time."

"Oh, of course not. It is true that magic is all around us all the time here, but it is not intrusive. In fact, the less it is used or has to be used, the better. It is sort of like a balance of power. Earth is a world dominated by nuclear bombs, yet I would say you have seen more magic in this world than nuclear bombs in yours."

She had a point there, so he let it pass. The exhibition hall was huge and filled with large numbers of creatures, both human and fairy—and some he wasn't quite sure about—all in booths or behind long display tables. There was no logic or order to the arrangement, so the old crone selling the latest chemical advances in aphrodisiacs was right next to the bright young fellow selling the Handy Miracle Pocket Indexer, which was apparently less hype than a description of a portable quick-file system that could be clipped onto a belt or carried in a shoulder bag and that allowed the average magician to access and classify spells by all sorts of cross-indexing methods.

They went on, passing a group of salesmen peddling a condensed Books of Rules—only three hundred volumes—complete with the magical Codex, a cross-indexed compendium allowing anything needed in the three hundred volumes to be found easily. Tiana tried to beat off one of the salesmen and finally got rid of him by commenting, "You are already four years out of date, and by the time I received my volume a month on your plan, you would be twenty-nine years out of date." Arguments that a new edition was in preparation fell on deaf ears.

Some of the exhibits were downright disgusting, like the demonstrations by the Entrail-of-the-Month Club. Another service offered fresh bat's blood and monkey's eyes. There were also countless protective gadgets and amulets being sold—all worthless, Tiana assured Joe, since any value they might have had was compromised by their being so commercially available.

Some of the salespeople were disconcerting, too. He didn't really mind the centaurs and their variations so much, nor the Panlike satyrs, and certainly not the nubile nymphs, but some of the creatures selling various artifacts and substances, the purposes of which could only be guessed at, were like nothing he'd ever seen before. There was that creepy blue creature, for example, with the wiry hair and buzzardlike beak whose huge, unhuman eyes kept following them, and the things that looked like giant swamp logs with eyes at the tip of each branch.

There were also memory and concentration aids for sale, voodoo dolls and substances to make more—"free demonstration on request"—and much, much more. Small fairy elves were hawking clothing spun in the fairy way out of fairy gold, "for the wizard who truly wants to look the part."

There were booths representing specific interest groups as well. At one booth an old black-clad hag straight out of *Snow White* was apparently representing the Wicked Witches Anti-Defamation League; at another an extremely fat sort of pixie in a blue Keystone Kops-type outfit offered membership to qualified individuals in the Elves, Gnomes, and Little Men's Chowder and Marching Society; while at a third a tough-looking mermaid was half sunk in a tank of water, smoking a big cigar, and representing something called the City-States' Benevolent Protective Organization. Tiana explained that traders bought insurance from them or their ships mysteriously sank somewhere.

Joe could only shake his head in wonder and say, "Gee, I always thought mermaids were real pretty and lovely and all that."

"Oh, many are, particularly the sirens who lure ships onto the rocks by bewitching the sailors. She is just one of the sirens' minor godmothers."

It also took a little adjusting to get used to some of the titles, whose stated acronyms were more than a little disconcerting. Tiana was in a nostalgic mood and kept pointing out luminaries with a disquieting lack of understanding for the way his own mind worked. He decided that maybe it was the similarity of the common trade language to English that was doing it for him.

"Oh, there is Sargash!" she breathed excitedly and pointed. "She is a famous idiot."

Joe looked at the red-robed woman and frowned. "She doesn't look like an idiot to me. She looks pretty smart."

"Oh, you *are* strange, Joseph! I meant she is a famous I.D.I.O.T.—Inconological Doctor of Incantations, Obturations, and Transudations."

"Oh. Yeah, sure."

"And there is Mathala, ogre."

"Actually, she's sort of distinguished."

"No, no. She is head of the Order of Geomorphic Reification and Exuviation."

"If you say so," was all he could respond. Even though he was getting the idea, he *still* didn't know what those words meant.

"Ah, and that man all in black over there is a world-renowned nutcase."

"Do I want to ask questions about that one?"

"Notater of Ultravires, Transubstantiations, Casuistry, Alchemy, Soporophics, and Ephemerides," she explained. "He will be one of the referees in the sorcerers' matches."

"First get me a dictionary—one that I can read," he grumped.

She stopped and gasped. "There—there is the evil bastard himself!"

He waited, noting a tall, distinguished-looking sorcerer in red and green velvet garb, catching up to and talking with Mr.

Nutcase. "Well?" he said after a moment. "Aren't you going to tell me what evil bastard stands for?"

"It stands for usurper, cheat, murderer, and harlot," she spat out.

Joe was trying to figure out how that fitted the title when she added, "That is Kaladon."

He looked again with new interest. "He's a lot older than I thought he was."

"He is five years my senior. The aging that you see is the wages of his art. He is in fact still the youngest of all the Council members by more than three hundred years."

"Spell or not, I think we'd better be on our way out of here," Joe suggested. "As I understand it, everybody else can see you normally, and you stand out in any crowd."

"As do you," she responded and squeezed his hand playfully, but she also wasted no time heading for the nearest exit.

Back out in the corridor, he looked at her and asked, "Now where?"

She shrugged. "Let us go up to the room and sort through this material. Somewhere in there is a program that will tell us what is going on with whom and where."

He nodded and retrieved his untouched bag from the cloakroom. They headed out into the now jam-packed lobby and up the long series of stairs.

As they walked down the hall, the door to the suite opened and a small figure stepped out. They both halted as the figure turned and looked up, first at Joe, then at Tiana.

"Hello, Joe," she said.

"Hello, Marge. Uh—this is Tiana."

"So I gather," the Kuari answered a little coolly.

"Joseph has told me much about you," Tiana said, trying to break the ice a little. "You have had many great adventures."

"You don't look like much of a slouch in my sort of adventures yourself," Marge responded cattily.

"Uh, Marge—you'll be sharing with Macore," Joe put in.

She looked up at him strangely. "I thought as much."

He shrugged. "*You* called the tune, remember. I'm just playing along."

"Yeah. Well, have fun, you two," she replied, then turned and walked back into her own room.

Tiana didn't quite know what to say, so Joe just moved forward down the hall, unlocked his door, and the two went inside and closed the door after them.

Finally Joe said, "You know, I'm really going to hate myself for that tomorrow, but right now I just have that feeling that there *is* justice in the world."

"She looked so hurt and lonely."

He nodded. "Yeah. She looked, somehow, almost like that scared, lonely kid I picked up back in Texas. Funny. If she'd been like that the last couple of days . . ."

The big woman thought a moment. "Joe, I think I can explain it. I was just sort of putting myself in her position now." Briefly she described the true nature and function of the Kauri and their strong shifts in mood.

He nodded, understanding to a point. "Well, that explains it, I guess."

"No, Joe, not completely, judging by your expression. You and I, we feel grumpy sometimes, happy other times, as all people do, and as she used to. Now, though, she has no control over it. She can fix the souls of others, but only by taking the hurt inside herself."

"Yeah, but you said the effect wears off—she eats it or something, or she can take the cure back home. That's more than *I* can do."

"That is true—as far as it goes. But tell me, what do you do when you feel very mad about something, perhaps about something you yourself did that you wish now to take back and can not?"

He thought a moment. "Smash my fist into a wall, I guess, or pick a fight."

She nodded. "But the Kauri, they have no release. There is no Kauri to clean *them* up, and they can not harm anyone, not even themselves. It must be particularly difficult for someone with a long human past, I would think. And you should be flattered rather than upset that she did not make love to you."

"Huh?"

"It means you do not have as many problems as you think you do. The only opening she had to help you was your feeling of loneliness, and now that, too, is gone, I think. I hope."

"You're making me feel like a heel right now."

She smiled. "No, you are human, and that is a wonderful thing to be. She is not human, but she is still your friend. I think perhaps she needs you more than you think, and you need her far less than you think, if that makes any sense."

"Yeah, I guess so. Think I ought to go over and try to smooth it out?"

"It might not be a bad idea, particularly if, as Ruddy implies, we three must go a long way together. I will look through this mass of material we have collected while you are gone."

He smiled, got up, kissed her, then turned and walked out of the room and down the hall, stopping at and knocking on Marge's door.

For a moment he was afraid she was gone; but finally the door opened a crack, then wide, and he entered.

"Hey, look, I just want to say I'm sorry for the smart remark," he told her honestly.

"Yes, I know," Marge replied. "I don't really hold anything against you, Joe—I couldn't! Not after what we've been through. I deserved it and I know it."

He sat down on the side of the bed. "Hey, look—I've had this whole thing explained to me. You're going to find this hard to believe, but Tiana understands the problem and she was a pretty good explainer."

"Oh, I know she's probably a wonderful person and everything, but it's deeper than that. I mean—oh, I don't know what I mean!"

"You mean you'd rather be her than you. *The Chronicles of Joe and Marge,* right?"

She said nothing, but he knew he'd pretty much hit it on the head.

"Well, you're not—and you never were," he went on. "You're you, that's all. Hell, I'm still not sure I like this crazy world much and I'm really not sure I like this barbarian business at all, but I'm stuck with it."

She looked at him curiously. "What would you rather be, assuming you'd still be in Husaquahr and not back home?"

"No thinking there. One of these wizards. Somebody with magic at his fingertips. Swordplay skills are handy here, but all that fighting's like being in the infantry. Cannon fodder for the magic boys—and no match for magic, but a hell of a lot of work, all the same, not only to get the skills but to keep 'em."

She slowly shook her head. "You don't want any magic,

Joe. It's not power—it's a curse. For anybody under the master sorcerer rank, it is, anyway—*it* controls *you*, really, and it costs too much. And even the masters—well, every one I've met has been more than slightly nuts."

"Ruddygore?" He paused a moment. "Hmmm . . . Yeah, I see what you mean. And your witch, Huspeth, has sealed herself off from the world. The more I hear about the others here, the more I think we've met the nicest and sanest of 'em all, too."

"It's the power, Joe. It corrupts most of them, makes them evil beyond redemption, even if they don't think of themselves that way. I can feel it, just walking these halls. Those very few who were so strong it didn't corrupt them, like Ruddygore and Huspeth, it drove into tremendous loneliness. The responsibility's so *huge,* Joe! And as for the fairies—I know now that we are imprisoned by our powers, not free. Like bees and ants, deer and wolves, we're programmed like robots to do one job each and we have to do that job just like the animals. The only difference is, we can think, so we know we're not free. I always used to wonder why those European elves of legend always drank so much. Now maybe I understand."

"Well, maybe. But a little magic might be nice, anyway. It doesn't matter—I'm not magical, that's all, except through Irving. Tiana's an adept. Daughter of a big-shot sorcerer who got killed by another one."

"Yes, Kaladon. Ruddygore told me the background. You know he's the prime suspect for the Dark Baron."

Joe nodded. "Yeah, I know. I'm not sure if I'm hoping he is or he isn't, though, for Tiana's sake."

"What do you mean?"

"If he is, and we manage to polish him off, then she's bound and determined to take over Zhimbombe. That may be her birthright, but it's not her style. On the other hand, if he isn't the Baron, he's just a superpowerful, evil black magician she can never hope to get rid of, so it will eat at her until she tries it, anyway."

"You really like her, don't you?"

He nodded. "A lot. And I think it's mutual, at least so far. Hell, we've just met. We'll see how it goes."

"I'll try and be nicer to her then, Joe, I promise, if you'll be a little understanding with me." She paused a moment. "Still partners?"

He grinned and stood up. "Still partners—and still friends. Uh—I'd give you a hug if I didn't think I'd crush your pretty wings."

"You won't. They're kind of funny, but they have no bones in 'em. I can lie right on them face up if I want to."

So he did hug her and kissed her, too; then he winked. "Three adventures—remember?"

She thought of Ruddygore's gloomy assessment and forced a smile. "Yes, Joe. *At least* three."

Macore sat in Ruddygore's room, still wearing the one-piece black cloth outfit he'd used in his work, his face and hands black as pitch from the material he'd smeared on them.

Ruddygore studied the various papers and objects before him and frowned. "This is pretty tough, I'm afraid. Two are definite servants of Hell and the third must be, to keep his own holdings. Hmph! I always thought of Boquillas as a hothead, but an idealist. I wonder what his price was?"

"Well, we know for sure that this Kaladon is a head man with the whole Barony movement," the thief noted. "I'm positive the units in that report were all involved in the battle at the Valley of Decision."

Ruddygore nodded. "They were. There's no question he's a leading figure in this, but he makes little secret of it. Still, I find it hard to believe."

"He's incredibly young, or so he says. Much too young to have won a Council seat on his own and just the sort to fall into this kind of campaign."

"That's true, but it makes him so bloody obvious. I don't see him as a leader, somehow, with the skills to keep an alliance like this together. He's also pretty weak, really—there are any number of adepts here who could challenge him for position. The only reason they don't this time is that they fear the Baron's wrath, and that bastard can marshal three others of Council rank to back him up in this. The one I fought over the plains of the Valley was as strong as I am, and that's strong indeed. I'm pretty sure Kaladon cheated to win his spot, and he's dependent on the Dark Baron to keep his position. If the Baron loses, he's done in. He has no choice."

"Unless he's diabolically clever," the thief responded. "He's a smart one, I think, and real ambitious. Hell, you know you can become a hawk or a wolf or anything else you want to be. Maybe this Kaladon's not any spring chicken but really an old pro."

The sorcerer considered it. "You mean he created Kaladon as a *persona*, lived as Kaladon those years in Morikay, then made it seem as if he beat the old man, huh? What a fascinating idea! Diabolical! Why didn't it occur to me before?"

Macore grinned. "Because you're a square, that's why. Oh, you can be pretty devious, but only in response to evil. Who do you listen to? A puffed-up, straight-arrow Imir who thinks the only way to get something is to fight your way through a mob? A muscle-bound ex-Teamster? A fairy who used to teach kids?"

Ruddygore thought about it. "Well, more than that, but your point is well taken. Maybe I have been neglecting my true education and perspective of late. Perhaps I should talk more often with thieves and politicians."

"There's a difference? Oh, well, let's look at the others."

Ruddygore nodded. "Esmerada. I had just about written her off because she was a woman, but now, with your new perspective, I see that I can hardly do that. Any of us could be anything we wanted to be at almost any time, so having a male Baron would be a near-perfect red herring."

"I thought the same way. And she's well positioned, too, with a long history in the black arts. She's got tremendous power, even if she is a little kinky about the ways she uses it. Certainly that stuff I found in her adepts' rooms is interesting, if only because it's in no language I've ever seen before."

Ruddygore reached over and picked up the two books. "But I have. You'll have to get these back later tonight."

"No problem. They secured the important stuff real solid, but you sometimes learn more from the stuff they don't consider important. Those books—what are they?"

"An interesting set. This one is a condensed version of a major theoretical work by V. I. Lenin. This other one is almost an opposite, in one sense. *My Battle*, by Adolph Hitler. This fits in some ways with information I've been getting from all over. Even Marge, earlier this evening, told me about a kobold quoting Lenin."

"Never heard of either of 'em."

"And you shouldn't have. Neither should the adepts, for that matter." He studied the books. "Not originals. These are of Husaquahrian manufacture. From one of the City-States, I'd say. Fascinating. I wonder how the original text made its way from one world to the other, where it's certainly not appropriate."

"You mean those things are from the place Joe and Marge came from? Huh. I thought only you could get over there and bring things back."

"So did I, my little friend. So did I. But both angels and demons can dictate, and have done so in the past to a variety of people. This is more diabolical than I thought possible! That damned demon is to blame for this!" He calmed down and sighed. "Well, at least I know part of the plan now. That much is clear."

"Well, *I* don't."

"And you don't have to. That's a separate problem to be attended to besides the one on the table. What of Count Boquillas?"

"He never showed. In fact, word around is that he hasn't showed in the last six months just about anywhere. Rumors in his home district of Marahbar say that he left for his castle hideaway on Lake Ktahr a couple of months ago and hasn't been seen since. Good suspect, though. Idealistic, ambitious, very powerful, and a City-States man to boot, which ties him in to your books, with a castle in Zhimbombe, which puts him directly in the Baron's lands."

Ruddygore frowned. "Still, I would be a little more inclined to him, had he not vanished. He had reservations here?"

Macore nodded. "Him and a whole entourage. But he didn't show—didn't cancel, either, according to the hotel records."

"I don't like this at all. Esmilio Boquillas is an old and valued friend of long standing and a most unusual one among our fraternity. He has a strong conscience and he is an idealist, if somewhat hotheaded. He has been appalled by the carnage of the Baron's conquests—this I know—and has been outspoken against them. He *is* the sort of fellow who might well be influenced by such books as these, if he had a way to know about them in the first place; but, although he was an excellent fencer in his youth for strictly sporting goals, he can't even bring himself to kill a deer or fowl for sport. He is extremely powerful, but not, insofar as I know, a black magician."

"But he's in the Baron's back yard."

The sorcerer agreed. "Indeed he is, and that worries me. He worked out a tacit understanding with the Baron early in the game—indeed, he was the one who negotiated the open-city concept for the City-States, so that trade and commerce could continue—but he's always been disparaging of conquerors. He actually wrote a long dissertation a couple of years back, showing the futility of force in conquering Husaquahr, and it was aptly reasoned out. He is, in effect, our hostage to the Baron to keep the river open."

"Some hostage. Skips out and doesn't even show up here."

"Yes, and that's a worrisome thing. I can't conceive of anything short of defeat and death that would keep him from a meeting of the Society, but he's gone. And I cannot imagine any way that one of his strength could be subdued and taken, unless . . ."

"Unless?"

"Unless the Baron holds him responsible for the defeat in the Valley. Kaladon has often argued, according to my reports, that Boquillas was a dagger in their midst, a spy to those of us in the north, despite his word that he would observe the understanding. With the defeat, Kaladon's paranoia might be taken more seriously."

"But what could they do to him?"

"Individually, very little. Collectively, they could destroy him, but the rest of the Council would know of that. They and their pet demon prince might imprison him, perhaps, as they intend to do to me. Together they could have tricked him into a conference and then created a Null Zone. Inside there, no magic of any sort would function. If that Zone were also a prison cell, he would be helpless. It appears that our young friends will be asked to do double duty, then. I must think on it. Summon them here tomorrow evening, after the matches. I'll talk to them then. By that time the Council will have convened, and we'll see if Boquillas is still among the missing."

CHAPTER 9

THE MISSING MAGICIAN AND OTHER WERE TAILS

Even one who is very good and says his prayers by night, can become a werething when the full moon is bright.

—Rules, XC, 106(a)

"HELP ME GET HIM ON THE BED HERE!" TIANA SHOUTED, AND Poquah, Macore, and even Durin rushed out to see the large woman supporting a Joe in pain and bleeding from one calf. His leg was obviously too painful to stand on, not to mention dripping blood here and there on the fancy hotel carpet.

Marge opened her own door, looked out, saw the scene, and ran to them. "Get him in on the big bed in my room!"

They did as instructed, but it was Poquah who vanished and then reappeared with what proved to be a small medical kit and tended to the wound. "A nasty thing," the Imir commented. "What sort of creature did this to you? A wolf? Some monster from the exhibitions?"

Joe shook his head wearily. "No, it was a Pekingese, damn it."

"A what?"

"He means a little hairy dog with a pug face and curled-up tail," Marge explained.

"Ah! A tansir dog. From the size and depth of the wound, I would have suspected a much larger dog."

"It was as big as it had to be," Joe grumbled. "Damned thing nearly tore my leg off. I didn't even *see* it—I just stepped on its tail. It yelped, turned, and, the next thing I knew, it took a hunk out of my leg!"

Poquah frowned. "Where did this happen?"

"At the lecture on theriomorphism. I was trying to find out a few things and I'm afraid I dragged Joe into this," Tiana said apologetically.

"*Umph!* I think we were the only humans in the damned place," Joe added as a salve was applied. "Centaurs, mermaids, satyrs, minotaurs, all sorts of creatures."

397

"But that is what theriomorphism is all about," Poquah noted. "All of those you mentioned are half human, half beast, which means they are all theriomorphs."

"Well, how was *I* to know? And since when do those creatures keep fancy pets?"

"They don't," the Imir replied, sounding wary. "Not usually, in any case. Let me examine that wound again." He leaned down and let his curious almond-shaped red eyes focus for a moment, keeping very still. "Hmmmm ... Marge—will you look at this?"

She was startled to be the one he called, but she moved forward and bent down to see what the elf was talking about. At first it looked like a nice, large dog bite—they *did* have big mouths for such little dogs, she noted absently—but then she saw what Poquah was talking about.

Very faintly and very subtly, the entire wound gave off a soft blackish glow, like a negative almost, but not quite, superimposed on a positive picture. It was so faint it was no wonder nobody had noticed it before, but it stood out clearly now. "That's a spell of some kind," she said, puzzled.

Poquah nodded absently. "And in the black band."

The pain had faded, but Joe started to feel a different sort of discomfort. "What's that mean? How the hell can a dog bite be magic?"

"I'm not sure," the Imir told him, "but it most certainly is a black band spell, transmitted *through* the bite."

"He means," Marge explained, "that the dog that bit you wasn't a dog."

"It sure looked like a dog, acted like a dog, and bit like a dog. And what's this black band business?"

Tiana sounded worried and tense. "It is the color of the spell that tells its nature. Magic is a very colorful art, Joe, made up of a tremendous variety of colors. Which colors are combined, and in what fashion, determines its mathematics and thus what it does."

"Okay, I follow that. What's a black band spell, then?"

It was Marge who answered. "It's a curse, Joe. And because it is only in the base color, it is transferable."

Joe sank back on the bed. "Now, let me get this straight. The dog had a curse, and because the dog bit me, I now have the curse, too. Is that about it?"

"That's about it," Marge agreed.

He considered it. "And I suppose if *I* bit somebody, they'd get it, too?"

"Most probably," Poquah said. "I believe the Master should examine this, although he's fast asleep right now, and I'm not going to awaken him. The wound is still a wound, no matter what else, so we will bandage it, and then you should get some sleep yourself. Tomorrow at the dinner hour the Master would like to see all four of you in any case, so that is plenty of time to find out more of this. In the meantime, I will try to learn something about this dog."

"Sounds good to me," Joe told him. With the usual pleasantries, all but Tiana and Marge left him. He looked from one to the other. "Well, if this isn't any trucker's sex fantasy, I don't know what is. Trouble is, it hurts too much in the leg to do anything about it."

They both smiled, but neither could conceal her concern. He had to admit he didn't exactly like the idea of a curse, either—they were always pretty bad things, and in this crazy world—and particularly at this crazy convention—they could mean anything at all.

Joe awoke feeling pretty good. There was still sunlight outside, but from its angle he could tell that the hour was pretty late and he'd slept a good, long time. He looked over and saw Tiana stretched out beside him, still sleeping. All scrunched up in a chair, Marge was out, too. He knew that Marge, at least, would be out until sundown and he quietly brought himself to a sitting position, then examined the bandages. It was odd—the damned thing had been so painful earlier it wasn't funny, yet now he could swear that there was no wound at all. Cautiously, he put his good foot on the floor, then the bandaged one, and stood up. There was no sensation, except the tightness of the bandage. Otherwise, his leg felt and moved just fine.

He went down the hall to the john with no problems and then walked back. When he re-entered the room, Tiana turned and woke up. She saw him standing there and looked surprised. "You all right?"

He nodded and grinned. "No fangs or funny ears, either. The bandage is tight and it itches like hell underneath, but otherwise no problem. Want to go next door and get Durin to make us a pot of real coffee?"

She got up, yawned, and stretched, her hands actually touching the rather high ceiling as she did so. "You go on over. I need to go next door and get myself a little cleaner and brush my hair."

"Okay. Marge'll wake up and join us at sundown." He went over to Tiana, nuzzled her, then kissed her. "Good morning or afternoon or evening, whatever."

She smiled. "Conventions do that sort of thing."

"Being partners with a Kauri does it, too."

She patted him on the rump and went to the door. "See you in a few minutes," she said and left.

He turned, scratched, sighed, then went out and down to the double doors and knocked.

Poquah opened the door, looked at him, and said simply, "You're early."

He shrugged. "No place else to go—unless there's business going on, in which case I can think of a way to pass the time down the hall."

The entendre went unrecognized. "No. In fact, the Master is not even here right now. He's in a Council meeting."

"Um. Then I can get Durin to make—oops! I already smell it brewing." He walked by the Imir into the room, and Durin's elfin face grinned at him from the kitchenette. Joe got a mug of coffee, then sat down comfortably on the couch.

"How is your wound?" Poquah asked him, after checking on things on the bar.

"Good. In fact, the bandage is the only problem."

The Imir pulled up a stool, stretched out Joe's leg, drew a sharp knife from its sheath on his belt, and slit the bandage cleanly. Then he removed the whole thing with a single swift motion.

"Ouch!"

"Just the dried blood. It cemented your leg to the bandage, so to speak. Durin—some hot water and a cloth, please."

The chubby little elf was ready for him and brought the cloth over and handed it to the Imir, then scampered back to the kitchenette.

Poquah carefully washed away the very ugly-looking caked blood, then frowned and rubbed some more.

"Hey!" Joe exclaimed. "Watch it! You're taking leg there!"

The Imir took no notice, but continued until the last of the blood was off. He motioned to the area of the wound with his head. "Most interesting."

Joe looked down and felt sudden amazement. "Hey! There aren't even any teeth marks! That skin's as smooth and unmarked as glass!"

Poquah nodded. "Indeed. That confirms it."

"Huh? Confirms what? Did I get bit or didn't I?"

"Oh, yes, you were bitten, all right, just as you say. The blood alone proves that, does it not? No, it just confirms what I was able to find out from others around and at the meeting where it happened. I would like to get a second opinion, of course."

"Cut the weaseling! What *is* it?"

"Well, last night was the last night of the full moon, which should have alerted me right away. Then, as you said, there is the question of what a dog was doing in the seminar. Now we have the total disappearance of the wound. Tentatively, I would say that you were bitten by some sort of were."

"Were? You mean as in werewolf?"

"And a lot of other things. Weres come in all types, really. It certainly explains why a tansir dog should be sitting in at a seminar on theriomorphism, which means human into beast, does it not?"

Joe sat back, remembering all the werewolf movies he'd ever seen, and this didn't fit the image at all. "You mean every time there's a full moon from now on, I'm going to change into a *Pekingese*?"

"Possibly. Possibly not. Although the spell is totally concealed now, I am positive that it was *strictly* black band—most unique for any sort of werebeast. A werewolf or weredog would also have to have the codex for its particular creature, and this was not at all evident. My tentative diagnosis is that you have become the most rare of all theriomorphs, a true and pure were."

"Huh? A were *what*?"

"A were, period. As there was no codex, it must be externally supplied."

"Plain speech, please. Short words, too, so I can understand what you're saying."

The Imir got up, took the bandage over, and discarded it, then returned and took a seat opposite Joe. "All right. You've been through this before, if I remember. The Circean turned you into a bull."

Joe nodded, recalling the incident with a slight shiver.

"Well, were curses are generalized forms of that sort of thing. Volume Four Sixty-Four of the Rules, if I remember correctly, treats them in some detail but never actually comes to grips with them. Nobody really knows how such curses originate, and the Rules prohibit originating new were curses of a communicable nature. Think of them as diseases, perhaps—not only skin contact, but actual saliva or blood transfer is required."

"But you or Ruddygore can read this volume whatsis and give me the cure, right?"

Poquah shook his head sadly from side to side. "No. Since their origin and exact nature are unknown, so is their cure. They can mostly be arrested through the regular injection of exotic herbs, different ones from different types, but this is unique to me."

"Get to the point."

"Well—" At that moment the door opened and Ruddygore entered. At first he seemed preoccupied, but then he noticed Joe over on the couch.

"So! Feeling better, I hope. Now, what's this about a werewound?" He walked over, bent down, and looked at the area on Joe's leg that was now distinguishable only by the marks left from the bandages. He nodded, then turned to Poquah. "You've told him?"

"No, he hasn't!" Joe snapped. "He's done everything but. Would *you* mind telling me what all this is about?"

"Well, you stepped on a were's tail, it bit you, and you caught the disease. Of them all, I'd say you were the luckiest, Joe. It's incredibly rare."

"That's what Poquah keeps telling me, but nobody tells me what it is I've got a rare case of! You guys are worse than doctors!"

Ruddygore nodded. "I managed to get hold of the woman who bit you. If it's any solace, she's very, very sorry about it, but she just reacted in pain. She's actually a very nice person, and you're the first person she's ever bitten."

"She's a bitch as far as I'm concerned," Joe growled.

"Well, she was last night, or she wouldn't have been able to bite you, but that's beside the point. Joe, you always said you wanted a little taste of magic, and now you have one. A rather unusual one, I admit, effective on only three nights a month on the average, but somewhat controllable. You see, Joe, you are now a were, but you're not a were anything. Just a were."

"Huh?"

"To put it bluntly, for every night of the full moon you will turn into whatever you're closest to at moonrise. It might be a good idea to carry an almanac from now on."

Joe sat bolt upright, a funny feeling growing in the pit of his stomach. "Let me get this straight. Whatever I'm *closest* to?"

Ruddygore nodded. "It's very unusual, but there's only the were curse, no codex attached; so when the curse is activated, it derives its form from whatever is closest."

"So this one who bit me—she was nearest a Pekingese at moonrise last night? And if she'd been nearest a cow, she'd have turned into a cow?"

Ruddygore nodded again. "An exact duplicate, with everything in place. The curse works on a modified fairy pattern, so you won't turn into a tree or grass or anything like that; but if it's animal or fairy and that's closest, you're going to duplicate it from moonrise to sunrise—unless the moon's already out in the daytime, in which case it will be sunset to sunrise. If you remember your lunar calendar, you can usually control what it is, anyway. It's not a good idea to be riding a horse when it happens, for example. The change is pretty well instantaneous."

Joe whistled, not quite believing what he was hearing. "This woman who did it—how'd she get it?"

"Oh, the fellow was a spider and she walked into the web. He felt so guilty about it afterward he courted and married her. That pretty well solved their problem, since most of the time they just turn into each other. They seem to think it's fun. At least it's appealingly kinky. Unfortunately, her husband fell ill yesterday and she had to go get some medication in town. She lost track of the time, there was this fellow with a dog nearby, and, well, you know the rest."

"Oh, great. This is all I needed. Hey—wait! Poquah says there are herbs and stuff to keep it off, right?"

"For most types, yes. But pure weres are so rare, thanks to their conscious control, that nobody has ever done any research on them. I'll put a couple of good people on it right away, though, so we might get lucky. Unfortunately, I can't wait for the results of the research."

"Oh, no! Wait just a minute, here! You're not sending me out on some mission with *this*. I mean, it'll happen in—what?"

"Twenty-seven days, for three nights. So? It might actually come in handy, if you can learn to control and use it. Look on the bright side, Joe. You've just increased your survival factors by a tremendous amount. There's no external sign on a pure were. Even a top sorcerer would have to know exactly what he was looking for to see it at all. But for all practical purposes, you're invulnerable."

Joe brightened a bit. "Oh, yeah. Silver bullets, right? And they don't have bullets here. Hmmm . . . Maybe this thing has possibilities, after all. And this invulnerability works all the time, even when I'm not, ah, you know?"

"All the time. But don't feel totally cocky about it. A truly powerful sorcerer will spot it after a while, or deduce it the first time your invulnerability shows. You're still subject to certain spells from the fairy folk and other sources, too. Silver is the key, not just bullets. Silver of any kind can wound you; if it hits a vital spot, it can kill you. A silver sword or dagger—or the silver hilt of a weapon or walking stick used as a club—will be more dangerous than any blade you've known."

Joe thought about it a moment. "Well, the club might be a problem, but I don't remember seeing any silver swords around here. Silver would make an expensive and pretty lousy blade, except for show stuff."

"True. But total security lies in an enemy's not knowing until it is too late." With that the sorcerer stretched out his hand; there was an electricallike flash, and he held in his hand a broadsword of what appeared to be solid silver. "Otherwise, a transmutator can do this." He lowered the sword, twirled it, and it became a wooden cane.

Joe heard someone coming down the hall. "Uh—listen. Okay, I'll go along with you, at least for now, but promise me you won't tell anyone else, huh? I want to break it to the others myself."

Ruddygore nodded. "That's all right with me, but—be cautious! Telling the wrong person might prove fatal; but if you tell no one, then you're going to have a tough time explaining it when it happens."

"I'll cross that bridge when I come to it. I—"

There was a knock on the door. Poquah sprang to open it, and Tiana walked in. "Hello," she greeted Joe. "How is it?"

"All well," he told her.

She frowned. "All well so soon? And the curse?"

"Some other time," he responded nervously. "Let's relax for now. It's nothing I can't handle."

"As you say." She sounded uncertain and worried, though, and it didn't escape Joe that her mother had died from a curse, one that she feared she carried but did not know for certain.

Marge joined them within another few minutes; last to arrive was Macore. Durin set an excellent table, and all ate, enjoying the truly magical touch of the elfin chef, except, of course, Marge. After Ruddygore's promptings, however, she found she could still enjoy good wines and the taste of fancy desserts, even though she didn't need them and couldn't fully metabolize them. Still, it made her feel a little more human and a part of the social group that a fine dinner formed. She was also inwardly very grateful to Poquah for calling her in for consultation on the wound. It was, she knew, because they were both of faërie and he had known instantly that she could see the fine magical pattern that most could not because of that fact, but that was a very important thing to her.

Although fairy races usually didn't get along very well and were rife with jokes and rivalries, when it came down to practicality, it was *we faërie* in Poquah's mind. It meant a lot to her, although she was sure the Imir hadn't even realized he was doing her such a service. She was Kauri, yes, but she was more. She was a member of an entire family of living, thinking creatures. She was *faërie*.

There was conversation at dinner, of course, but it was of a social nature and generally concerned with the convention. Joe told the sorcerer that he'd seen two of his matches against adepts. "Nothing like that battle over the Valley of Decision, though."

"Oh, no, this was a lot of sound and fury and clever parries and thrusts, but little more," Ruddygore responded. "None of the challengers were very taxing, and all of them have a long way to go to get any real command, if they ever do. In a sense, it's like giving two people a math problem to solve, only one of them has studied and practiced calculus for years, while the other is just learning algebra. That's all magic really is— topological mathematics combined with concentration and willpower. First you must have the talent to be able to understand and construct the complex patterns which we call spells, then the concentration to hold them at all cost against all distractions, and finally the force of will to impose those patterns on a person or object precisely as you wish. An adept can impose such things, usually from the Rules and other references, by memorizing a lot of standard stuff, but that's about it. A true magician can form what he or she needs without references, and tailor it to the specific requirements of the situation. The best can hold and create multiple original patterns. The more you can do at the same time, the stronger you are. One like Kaladon, for example, might be able to create and maintain as many as ten separate temporary and permanent spells at once."

"Kaladon! He is a pig and a usurper!" Tiana spat.

"Sorry to spoil the food with a bad name, but when you consider that he's the weakest on the Council, you see what a poor adept is up against. Kaladon is good at it, but he's not one of the best."

"My father could maintain fifteen or more," the large woman bragged.

"He could indeed, but not on one particular night."

"The food was drugged!"

Ruddygore sighed and signaled for the table to be cleared, which it rapidly was. "I see it's time to get down to business." He lighted a cigar as Durin served coffee for those who wished it. "First of all, Tiana, your father was not drugged that night."

"What! That is a lie!"

"You said it yourself. He was capable of fifteen or more spells. No pro in this business goes into action before doing a static purification spell on himself, not to mention a series of mental tests, even against the weakest of opponents, to ensure he is in his best physical and mental shape. No, Tiana, I'm afraid your father was, in fact, in his usual fine form."

"But it must have been the food! Otherwise that pig would have been ground to dust!"

Ruddygore drew on his cigar, sat back, and relaxed a bit. "Well, that was the story the Council more or less allowed to spread around Zhimbombe. It was a face-saving gesture, really; although it was rather insulting to Kaladon, even he went along with it. You see, after the death of any Council member, there is, shall we say, a psychic post-mortem by the remaining members which includes an examination of the winner and his testimony, those of the referees, and others. It is a matter of concern to all of us when one of us goes, as you might imagine, and we are most interested in seeing that it doesn't happen to us." He paused again, then added, "The official judgment was that your father threw the match."

Tiana stood up and glared angrily at him. "I will not remain and listen to this, not even from you! My father would never commit suicide!"

"Oh, sit down, Tiana. *That's* why you'll never be more than a weak adept. No self-control, no discipline. Even if you know all the magic I know and can handle fifty spells at a time, you'll challenge Kaladon, he'll make some off-the-wall remark about your father, you'll get so mad your concentration will crumble, and he'll have you."

She hesitated a moment, then sat back down, but she continued to glare at him.

"Kaladon was, I'm afraid, your father's weak spot. He considered him his son and heir to his Council seat. You knew that. You remember what it was like—before."

She nodded, but did not seem to mellow.

"He had no reason to suspect treachery. Kaladon was quite clever—he fought the match in such a way that it looked very natural and very accidental that it escalated to that point. He must have spent years planning those exact moves. What happened was that he pushed things just over the edge, so that there was so much psychic energy in that hall that it could not be easily canceled out. Likewise, Kaladon had spent some effort making you look very untalented in the art in your father's eyes. So there he was, faced with the choice of killing Kaladon, letting Kaladon kill him, or hoping the referees would realize the problem and step in. All the evidence suggested that the referees *did* move to cancel; but for some reason, the attempt was not effective. Either the spells were too personalized, or not all the referees were in agreement; but the hesitant ones weren't willing to admit their error later. Regardless, your father weighed all the factors and decided to will his seat to Kaladon."

She shook her head unbelievingly. "I know how he regarded Kaladon, but I can not believe he could do this. He would not do this to *me*."

"If it's any help, Kaladon did cheat. I know how he did it, but I could never prove it."

"What?"

"It would have taken all three referees in tandem to stop the match. All three claimed to have tried and failed. One of them, however, was Esmerada, who is now a close ally of Kaladon and the Baron. The fix was in, and that sort of energy couldn't have been held for long. Your father was backed into a corner and forced into a split-second decision. In a sense, Kaladon's victory was legitimate in that, as I mentioned, his opponent allowed an extraneous factor to divert him. It is entirely possible that your father was simply unable to solve his moral dilemma and thus broke his concentration. The most talented sorcerer in the world can be beaten by a middling-fair magician if his concentration is broken, even for an instant."

She considered it. "You are probably right. But—even with all his deceit and Esmerada's complicity, that means he was the legitimate and legal winner under the Rules! That is terrible!"

"Is it? He still schemed and took advantage of your father and you to get the seat, and he's an even blacker magician than ever now. He must be removed, eliminated—and Esmerada, too. We must stop his cancer of the Barony for all time."

"Can't you just take him on?" Joe asked. "You said he was weak."

"Oh, I could finish him, yes, but he would sense the attack and call upon Esmerada and the Baron for support; and the Baron almost had me last time. As for a challenge in a formal context, the Rules specifically prohibit one Council member from challenging or fighting another within the rules of the Society. Nor can I enter the castle of a fellow Society member without his or her permission, just as none of them can enter Terindell."

"And I guess they aren't too likely to invite you in for tea and cookies," Marge put in.

Ruddygore nodded. "But I've been studying the proper volume of the Rules pretty closely, and there are other ways. It seems that if someone is in my service and is invited in, he may then invite me. That I find most interesting."

"Uh-oh. I just got a funny case of indigestion," Joe grumbled.

"It's not a very easy or pleasant task, but I think you see where I'm leading with this," the sorcerer continued. "We must strike at the heart of the Barony. We must eliminate Esmerada, Kaladon, *and* the Baron. If I can reach the first two, I can take them. That will leave our Baron, if he is indeed not one of those two, alone and out front. I can tell you right now that I cannot take the Baron; but if I can find out who he is, perhaps he can be goaded into trotting out his demon master. If I can get him to do that, with the Council looking on, they will destroy him as a matter of survival."

Joe whistled. "You sure aren't asking much, are you? We're to get into these castles and call you in, somehow, all without getting killed or turned into toads or something; and if we happen to unmask the Baron in the process, we're to get him to trot out a demon prince for us."

Ruddygore shrugged. "I didn't say it was going to be easy. In fact, tricking the first sorcerer should work out because of the element of surprise in the plan. The trouble is, in the inevitable post-mortem, the loophole will be exposed, so the second one will be ready for you. As for bringing out the Baron's demon, I hardly think that will be difficult if you meet him. Remember, his demon couldn't do a thing to either of you, and he's probably just panting and drooling to do a whole set of things to see why and how he can get around it."

"What army are we leading?" Joe wanted to know.

"No army. It would do no good. I'll supply the army if and when it's necessary. You and Marge are involved, not only for your skills and complementary abilities but also because, pardon me, you are perfect demon bait. All that I have been able to teach you, and all that you have become, have been oriented to this purpose. Tiana will join you for several other reasons, although she, too, is well trained and dedicated, with a bit of both your skills to boot as a backup. But, most importantly, she's a native of Zhimbombe, and I've had her traveling in and out of the area for the past month before coming here."

Tiana nodded. "I wondered why you asked, and only hoped it was for an assault on Kaladon. Much has changed, particularly the people and the very atmosphere of the place. It used to be a happy place. But the roads still go where they once did, and the towns and cities are the ones I knew in my youth. It was strange how it all came back to me, although I have traveled those roads ten thousand times in my mind."

Joe was used to Ruddygore by now, and he was thinking ahead of the plan. "Uh—in what order do we tackle these fearsome giants?"

"Geographically. Esmerada's Witchwood is on the way to Morikay, so she is certainly first. She is the stronger magically, which is why she is the best start—the best to take by surprise. And she is the most hidebound and rigid. My, how she loves the old clichés!"

"Uh-huh. And then Kaladon, all forewarned."

The sorcerer nodded. "But in known territory, with a native guide even to the castle passages and entryways."

"He's likely just to have us killed on sight," Marge pointed out.

"No, not all of us," Joe responded, turning back to Ruddygore. "Right?"

"Well, uh, that's true."

"I would have no problem getting invited into *that* castle," Tiana said, stating what the others were thinking. "That is it, is it not?"

"Well, yes, as a last resort," the sorcerer admitted. "However, I hope we won't have to use that method. I'll be with you all the way, in a manner of speaking, anyway."

Poquah got up from the table, went into Ruddygore's room, and returned with a very pedestrian-looking, Earth-style briefcase. Ruddygore made several passes over it with his hands and then went into an almost trancelike state staring at it. In less than a minute, though, he relaxed, then opened the case. They all realized that the case had been guarded by spells so great they might have destroyed anyone trying them other than himself.

He reached inside and pulled out a small jewelry case, set it before him and opened it, then pushed it across the table to Marge. Inside was a necklace of what looked like solid gold chain; from it, a small but distinctive ruby pendant hung. She looked at the chain, then picked it up and stared at it in puzzlement. "Where's the clasp?"

"I had it made without one," he told her. "Don't worry. Allow Poquah to put it on for you."

The Imir reached over, picked it up, and she felt his long fingers on both sides of her throat and the cold of the chain. There was a hissing sound; for a brief moment, the necklace felt very hot, but it cooled quickly.

"The thing is made of fairy gold and a combination of alloys that make it almost impossible to slip off," Ruddygore explained. "As it has no clasp, it's on for good, I hope. While the blend is strictly Husaquahrian, it was created at Cartier's in Paris to my specifications."

She chuckled. "Cartier's at last."

Again he delved into the case, brought out a jewelry box, and opened it, this time pushing it in front of Tiana. She looked, then reached in and picked up one of the two objects inside. They were attractive, if slightly large, earrings of the same fairy blend, and suspended from each was a finely crafted charm in the shape of a gryphon. Except for being oddly thick, the charms looked to be made of the same stuff as the earrings. Again, there was no break or clasp in the earrings themselves. "Think you can stand wearing them more or less permanently?" the sorcerer asked her.

She nodded. "They are beautiful. Also Cartier?"

"Oh, yes. Well, if you're satisfied—Poquah?"

The Imir went behind her, but this time he took one earring in each hand; pulling back her hair, he tugged on the lobes with his fingers. There was a slight hiss and a wisp of smoke, and Tiana exclaimed, "Ouch!" That, too, was quickly over—and the earrings were through the lobes as if she had been born with them. She reached up with her right hand and felt one of the dangling charms. "It feels strange."

"You'll get used to them quickly." Again Ruddygore repeated the process, pushing another open box toward Joe. The ex-trucker frowned and grumbled, "Oh, no. I'm strictly straight!" Inside was a single small earring with a golden gryphon attached, identical to Tiana's.

Ruddygore laughed. "Joe, it doesn't necessarily mean that back on Earth and it definitely doesn't mean that here. Almost all the barbarian tribesmen wear 'em."

"Well, I don't!"

Tiana looked over at him with an amused expression. "Joe, among the Cagrim tribespeople with whom I lived for some time, when a woman and a man mated, they wore matching earrings. Two each."

"I don't care! What's so important about these fancy pieces of jewelry, anyway?"

Ruddygore grinned. "Inside the jewel Marge is wearing, and inside the left gryphon in Tiana's set—and in your lone one—is the latest miracle of Japanese electronics."

"Electronics! Here?"

"Exactly. Oh, I know, I know. I'm the one who has kept guns and other modern ideas out, and I admit it. However, you must understand that, more than anything, that is my advantage, Joe. It's why this plan will work! This sort of technology is as alien and magical to this world as my magic is to yours. The tiny little power cells in those jewels will last a year and, because they broadcast a simple signal, they carry quite far. You will never be out of range of my messengers, Joe. Although the cells will broadcast only a couple of miles at best, that's more than sufficient for signals to be received *outside* any of the castles—far outside. That's Macore's part of the job."

The little thief nodded. "I don't understand it, but I never did understand spells, anyway. All I know is that I'm going to be able to track you with those things and that you can call Ruddygore with them if you need him. The rest of how it's done I think best to keep from you, and he agrees. What you don't know you can't divulge, and that will keep me safe. I'm also your backup, though—if real problems develop, I'll help where I can."

"Those measures are needed because the things were designed to work in connection with directional receivers that would be large and impractical here," Ruddygore explained. "However, their tiny, very inaudible signals will reach Macore and his, uh, messengers, and that's enough."

"And if we want to call you?" Joe asked. "Then what?"

"This may sound odd, but just take the object—jewel or gryphon—in your hand and say my name. It is triggered to change its signal at that, and that will alert us."

"How soon could you reach us after we needed you?" Joe pressed him.

"I will be publicly and visibly here and in Terindell. There must be no suspicion whatsoever. I feel bound to tell you that it might be many hours before the message gets to me. After that, I will use my unique transportation abilities to reach you very quickly. Now, this is important! While my name alone, uttered in that way, will bring me, you must say, 'Ruddygore, please enter castle such-and-so,' wherever you are. I can be summoned through the device, but I will require the invitation to circumvent the Rules."

"Uh-huh. And what are we supposed to do for the hours it takes you to come to the rescue?" Joe asked him.

"The best you can, of course. After the message is off, Macore will be available as an outside party to help, and he will have other resources to draw upon."

"You won't see me after tonight," the little thief warned, "but I'll never be far away. Count on it."

"Do we have a—ouch!" Joe was startled by a burning sensation on his left ear. His hand went up, and he felt the ring already in place there. He whirled, rising at the same time, and faced an impassive Poquah. "Damn you!" the big man cursed.

"Don't blame him, Joe. I expected some, ah, resistance," the sorcerer told him. "Don't worry. I can hardly see it under all that hair, anyway."

Tiana reached over and pushed Joe's dark hair back. "I think it looks very swashbuckling."

Joe sat and fumed. He said nothing, but it was clear what he was thinking.

"Now we'll work out briefings and strategy sessions," Ruddygore told them. "You should be as prepared as possible. And henceforth, by the way, we will *not* mention the radios. That will remain our little secret—and our little advantage."

They talked on through most of the night, the enormity of the task not escaping them in the least. Finally Ruddygore handed Joe a small, round portrait of a distinguished-looking man of middle age with gray hair and a bushy gray mustache.

He had dark, piercing eyes that the artist had caught exactly, and it was clear to look at him that he was one of those lucky ones who aged so well they were even more handsome than they had been in their youth.

"Count Boquillas," the sorcerer told them, explaining the background. "If you happen across him, or can determine his whereabouts, then be sure to tell me. He is the mystery player in this game, in that we don't really know which side he's on or what his game might be. All we know is that a powerful and outspoken critic of the Barony has suddenly vanished, and it would be of great value, not only to find him but to prove how little the Baron's word is worth, if Boquillas is in fact a prisoner."

"So when do we start this death march?" Joe asked.

"I think tomorrow, about sunset," Throckmorton P. Ruddygore replied.

CHAPTER 10

SAILING DOWN THE RIVER

Piracy need not be a dishonorable vocation if bound by the Rules.
— Rules, CLIX, Introduction

THE PORT DISTRICT OF SACHALIN WAS BUSY ALMOST ALL THE time. Although much trade had closed down for the convention, ships kept to schedules as they had to, and that meant those depending on those ships must be ready when they arrived.

Ruddygore had arranged passage for the trio on a merchantman carrying what seemed to be thousands of neatly racked amphoras of whiskey made from the unusually large harvest surplus in the region. Accommodations were not the most gracious or comfortable, but the ship's captain, who was also half owner, was being well paid and neither asked questions nor even raised an eyebrow at the sight of the unlikely-looking group.

Lake Zahias was huge, and by midmorning there was no land in sight as they moved out to the deep center and proceeded south. The ship was close to three hundred feet long and had a slightly rounded hull that accentuated any rough water but allowed it to take full advantage of the wind, which was quite brisk. Twin masts each held a single, enormous square sail, bright orange in color and with the ship's identification symbol inside a round yellow circle in the center of each. Joe had to admire the way the crew seemed to anticipate every little shift in wind and water and do just what was necessary to keep the speed steady and the ship relatively stable. The sight of so much water reminded him of the ocean, although there was no smell of salt in the spray and the large number of sea birds trailing the vessel betrayed land off somewhere within flying distance.

There were long, empty stretches, but other areas seemed filled with small fishing boats trawling for fish, shrimp, and whatever else these waters held; here and there, they passed a ship like theirs headed the other way and watched the semaphores on both send greetings and news of conditions to each other.

One such passing was followed by a sudden flurry of activity from the crew, each sailor hurriedly falling to one or another task. Joe, who'd been getting very bored playing a local version of backgammon with Tiana, grew curious and soon learned that there was word of a major storm ahead. At the time, it was sunny and fairly warm with just a few fleecy clouds in the sky, and both he and Tiana found all this haste hard to justify.

Within an hour, though, a huge front seemed to move in on them. Not long after, the wind picked up until it quickly became a roaring gale, complete with monster waves, thunder, lightning, and tremendously heavy rain. It soon became impossible to walk even below, the ship lurching and turning in what seemed all directions at once, and Joe found himself wishing for boredom once again.

He and Tiana both became violently ill before too long and just strapped themselves to their too-small bunks, trying to hit the chamber pots when they had to.

Marge came in, looking very comfortable and seemingly unaware that she was being tossed about with the ship. She spotted them both and regarded them with some pity. "You should *see* it up there!" she said excitedly. "Waves just about swallow half the ship, then up it comes again. It's real exciting—and the crew is wonderful."

They looked at her with misery and irritation in their eyes. "You don't feel—anything?" Joe managed.

"A little wet, maybe. I'm sorry for you both, but I guess I just don't get seasick. Hell, I've never been out on a body of water this big before and I think it's exciting."

"Well, go enjoy it, then," Tiana groaned. "Return when the sun shines and the water is like a mirror."

Marge took the hint, but the storm did not abate during the night or into the next morning. Through it all, except for trimming sail, the captain kept his ship fairly well on course and seemed reasonably pleased with the speed he was making. "It will take more than a little blow like this to make me run for safe harbor!" he told Marge proudly.

By the next evening the storm had slackened off a bit, but not enough to allow either of the seasick sufferers below any sort of recovery. Joe was more miserable, he believed, than he'd ever been in his whole life and he would have gladly ended it all if it wouldn't take too much effort. Even his great sword Irving, strapped to a handhold, seemed to hum a mixed and discordant series of notes.

Three days out, the storm passed, although the skies remained overcast and the air was a bit chilled. Joe, feeling weak and miserable, nonetheless had the need for fresh air; the small cabin stank of the remnants of two very large people's innards. He managed to pull himself dizzily up the stairs and onto the deck. The cool mist struck him, and it felt very, very good; he luxuriated in it for a few minutes before taking any sort of a look around. When he did, he was surprised to see land off to the left, even a few houses and animals. The ship was, in fact, close in to shore.

Marge spotted him before he could look much farther and came over. "Feeling better?" she asked, sounding genuinely concerned.

He shrugged. "Well, I feel as if I want to live again, but I'm not sure I'm going to."

"How's Tiana?"

"Worse, I think. What's this over here?"

"We'll be in tonight. Zichis is only a few miles up ahead, and that's the end of the line."

"Suits me. Land again," he added, almost dreamily.

"Don't get too comfortable. Tomorrow we just go down and get on another boat, remember."

He groaned. "Don't remind me!"

"Well, at least it's a riverboat."

By the time they berthed, it was well after dark, but both Joe and Tiana showed renewed strength when the idea of setting foot once again on dry land was staring them in the face.

Zichis was a lot smaller than Sachalin and far different, too, in architecture and ambience. This was a working town with no pretensions to anything political and no thoughts of tourism. It was here because, just below the town, at the start of the River of Sorrows, was Zichis Falls, and all commerce heading in either direction had to portage around it. The ships, of course, did no such thing, so all cargo had to be transferred to the next ship in line on the route south. In the meantime, the three were to stay over at one of a dozen or so guest houses, as they were called.

These turned out to be large wooden structures with a hundred or more rooms apiece, all built of the same weathered wood as were the other buildings in the town. The rooms were not much larger than those aboard ship, nor any more comfortable, but they were in solid buildings on solid ground and they neither rocked nor swayed. Marge explored the town while both Joe and Tiana recovered enough to get and keep down a heavy cream seafood chowder at a small restaurant and then to sleep it off.

The next day remained chill and overcast, but the seasickness that had totally immobilized the two humans passed as quickly as it had come upon them, and they both felt cheerful, if weak, and ate heavy breakfasts while Marge slept.

The system for moving cargo down below the falls to a river port consisted of an ingenious series of water-filled locks that lowered the huge crates and racks on large wooden flats a hundred feet or so at a time. The falls were large and highly impressive, although no Niagara, plunging more than eight hundred feet into a whirling mass below.

People, however, were expected to walk down an apparently endless series of wooden stairs. They soon learned that, to get information on their next watercraft, they would have to descend to what the natives called the Lower Port, despite the fact that there seemed to be no guest houses or any other services there.

Joe looked down, sighed, and said, "Well, I need the exercise."

"What of Marge? She is sleeping right now, remember," Tiana responded.

"Well, she knows the schedule, and the guest houses make it their business to see that people make their connections. I don't think we have to worry. It's several hours until sailing time."

After a seemingly endless descent, they found themselves at the Lower Port and quickly located the shipping offices of the line Ruddygore had told them to use. When they got there, though, they discovered only bad news.

"The *Pacah* is delayed at least eighteen hours," the agent told them, "perhaps more. There have been pirates on Lake Bragha, and shipping has been delayed while protection is arranged."

"Pirates? Up here?" Tiana asked, looking puzzled. "I have never heard of pirates on Bragha before."

"These are bad times, lady." The clerk sighed. "The border runs right through the lake, remember, and even the ownership of the falls is in dispute down there. It's impossible to police anything any more."

"But surely both Marquewood and Zhimbombe patrol the area!"

He chuckled dryly. "Patrol? How long has it been since you have been in Zhimbombe?"

"Many years," she admitted. "Why?"

"They invaded us not too many months ago down south, remember. They're not nice or cooperative people—if all of 'em are people, which I doubt. You goin' there?"

"Down the river, anyway," Joe put in smoothly. "Actually, we're headed for the City-States."

"Yeah? Well, you're both big enough to fight it out, I guess. Me, I wouldn't get any nearer the border than this, let alone go through their territory."

Joe gave him a sour smile. "You're implying that they don't exactly mind the pirates?"

"Hell, who could tell the difference? You watch it, though. When the *Pacah* gets here, it's one of ours and a good ship.

You'll be treated well. But from Tochik, you'll be on one of *their* ships, and I wouldn't go to sleep on one of them things if I were you."

Joe looked over at Tiana, but she just shrugged. "We're staying at the Cochis Guest House. Will we be notified when the ship comes in?"

"Oh, sure. No problem there."

They left and walked back to the falls. Joe stared at the huge set of stairs rising up into the mist of the falls and sighed. "Well, I *said* I needed the exercise."

Tiana nodded glumly. "I wish I had a spell for levitation right about now."

They began the long walk up.

It was, in fact, three days before a small group of ships arrived at the Lower Port, four merchantmen and two rough-looking craft manned with archers, bowmen, and even fore and aft catapults.

These were quite different craft from the Lake Zahias freighters—all shallow draft with large single sails and side slots for a dozen oarsmen on either side. In point of fact, the merchantmen were really large rafts with boxy wooden structures fore and aft like small houses and pilothouse atop each. Clearly the helmsman at the rear could not see what was going on and depended on a crew with an elaborate series of signals forward for direction. In contrast, the two warships resembled sleek Viking craft. They reminded Joe of canoes—the biggest canoes he'd ever seen—with a single sail in the middle.

According to those getting off, the voyage had been a rough one, not only from the usual natural hazards but also from pirates, who had actually managed to separate a ship from the convoy near the mouth of the river, take it, and get it across the theoretical border in the middle of the lake. At that point, as usual, an armada of nasty Zhimbombean warships had come virtually out of nowhere to keep the convoy warships from giving chase.

The captain of the *Pacah* was more than happy to see two large, tough-looking barbarians come aboard, although he wasn't so sure about Marge. He neither liked nor trusted fairies very much, it seemed, no matter how small and cute and sexy they were, but he tolerated them.

There was almost a complete crew change at Zichis, but the officers remained aboard, where they lived below the forward pilothouse. The ship was a co-op, with each of the officers owning a share commensurate with his relative rank. The crewmen coming aboard were paid wages and looked large and tough, as they had to be in order to control oars and poles on the river portion. This, however, would be a far easier trip than the northbound had been—they were going with the current.

Navigating such a craft down a winding and not very wide river was a skill that made the crossing of Lake Zahias seem like child's play. It was clear that the pilots depended not only on years of experience but on a certain necessary sixth sense to avoid the eddies, bars, and other hazards of the river, whose current was strong enough to change things just about every trip.

The land, too, changed dramatically as they moved down the river. There were few trees and great expanses of savanna going off in both directions. The yellowish grasslands were broken here and there by isolated groups of trees, and only the area right along the riverbank was overgrown and green. Off on the grassy plains beyond, they could see legions of wild beasts grazing or running about.

Still, the slow, cumbersome craft, built for tonnage rather than for speed or maneuverability, took two days to reach the lake.

By this time Joe and Tiana had gotten to know each other quite a bit; if Ruddygore had been playing matchmaker, his scheme seemed to have taken. By the time they reached Lake Bragha, Joe had to admit to himself that it was already a problem to remember what it had been like before he met her. Marge had the good sense to realize that this was going on and intruded as little as possible. Although she couldn't really bring herself to make friends with the huge, strangely accented woman who had joined them, she managed at least a professional relationship, which seemed enough for now. Joe felt sufficiently secure now to return to a platonic but cordial relationship with Marge, and that made it a little easier, too.

And, of course, ship's personnel had plenty of problems to keep Marge reasonably busy, particularly after she flew over to the nearest military guard ship.

Lake Bragha was only a third the size of Zahias, but it was still a pretty big lake, although quite different from the almost oceanlike parent that fed it. The river here flowed so gently into the lake that there seemed no seam in the transition, and Bragha, shallow and gentle, was virtually mirror-smooth and highly reflective.

It was only forty miles or so across from the river's entrance to its outlet, but that was the danger area. They could have avoided much of the threat by sticking to the coastline of Marquewood, but that added more than a day to the sailing time, and time was money. Still, the first mate admitted, if losses continued to mount, it might be the only alternative. "Either we go bankrupt taking the slow and safe way, or we get captured and killed," he remarked gloomily.

Although they reached the lake in the early morning darkness, they decided to lay over until sunup before crossing. The three hours or so might put them even further behind, but sailing would be a little easier in daylight. "Not that the pirates don't attack in daylight—they do," the mate told Joe. "But at least we and our protection can see what we're fighting."

The day dawned sunny; while there was still a slight chill in the air, it was clear that the sun, unseen for so long, would warm things considerably by midday. They proceeded as soon as they had good, clear visibility, since at the speed of the flatboats it would take almost nine hours to cross, even with a decent wind. There was no current. "A good wind at our back and a lake mist would have been best," the mate told them. "As it is, I feel like a very big target."

The tension mounted as they started across, and both Joe and Tiana could feel the strained nerves of these peaceful merchantmen. Still, they'd be no pushovers—anybody who could row a craft that size could break a neck in two with a flip of the wrist.

At almost the halfway point, a lookout from one of the other merchant vessels called out, and suddenly the tension became so thick that it was almost a tangible, visible thing. Tiana looked over at Joe, who said, "I'm going to get Marge." She just nodded and continued staring where everybody else was looking.

Marge, even with her goggles, was grumpy and irritable when awakened, but all that fell quickly away when he told her that an attack was possible. Both of them rushed back on deck.

The mate, a big, bearded man, was strapping on a weathered old cutlass. He yelled out that this was in fact an attack, and Joe felt a rising sense of excitement within him. Although he knew that many good people might die in the fight to come, he couldn't suppress an almost boyish anticipation of battle. Damn it, it was what he was trained to do in this crazy world.

He climbed up to where Tiana stood atop the crew's quarters and looked at the oncoming enemy, then frowned. There were clearly five ships coming in, but all five were extremely small and shaped much like the two far larger escorts the convoy had. On those escorts he could hear the barking of orders and the sound of battle drums.

Tiana looked over at him. "What is the matter? You look disappointed."

"Yeah, well, I dunno, but when you say pirates, I kind of expect a big galleon or something flying the skull and crossbones, not five big rowboats with sails."

The mate overheard. While he didn't really understand the reference to galleons, he got the idea. "Don't let them fool you, lad. A single big ship would be easy pickings for the navy boys here. But those little things can really move—easily three times our speed, if they're handled right in a fair wind like we're now getting, and perhaps twice the escorts'. They're hard targets to hit, but they have a single catapult apiece that can sure as hell hit *us*. They can turn in a few hundred feet, and three of 'em will engage the escorts while the other two try for one of us."

Joe nodded. "Will they try to board?"

"As soon as they can. Counting you two, there's twenty-two of us, probably about the same in the two that will try for us. Don't hesitate on any of 'em, remember. They're professionals at this sort of thing."

Joe turned and looked out at the approaching small fleet and smiled. "So am I," he said softly. "So am I."

The pattern was pretty much as the mate had predicted, with two of the small boats separating from the group and bearing down on the lead escort vessel. When they were barely in range, both suddenly seemed to catch fire. Tiana gasped at that, but it was quickly clear that what was being lighted were flaming masses attached to the catapults, both of which were launched with a military precision at the lead naval boat, after which both attackers turned hard in opposite directions. Both shots missed, and the larger military boat proceeded full ahead, aimed straight between the two smaller vessels, which now turned back in.

Two more broke off, going unexpectedly right at the warship, creating four closing attackers on the one larger craft. The bigger ship adjusted slightly, then let loose her forward catapult, which was apparently filled with half a ton of small rocks. It was the machine-gun approach, Joe thought. Nobody could hit the broad side of a barn with a machine gun, but it pumped so many bullets in the right general directly that it was impossible to dodge them all.

By choosing one attacker and firing the tremendous onslaught of stone, the navy couldn't miss, and it was clear that the strategy was successful as the target attacker turned desperately to avoid the mass and could not do so.

But at the moment the rocks were striking the craft, the other three all let loose with fireballs. One fell short, one struck the side of the naval craft, rocking it but otherwise sliding back off and into the water with a great hiss, but the third struck against the rail, splintering into a series of small fires. While the bulk fell into the sea, several small fires and some black smoke were visible in the bow of the convoy's protector.

Undaunted, the naval craft swung around and let loose a second volley of stones as the stern lined up with another of the attackers. Clearly the pirates were paying a stiff bill for this one. As the stones rocked the small craft, a cheer went up from the four merchant crews watching the battle.

Suddenly the second naval escort came gliding past the *Pacah*, closing on the attacking boats. As soon as it cleared the merchant convoy, it loosed its own rocky attack.

Joe frowned and looked around. "Where's the fifth one?"

"Huh?" Tiana, like Marge, was entranced by the battle and was startled by the question. "It is right—where *is* it?"

There was a sudden shout from the lookout of the *Tolah*, just behind them, and they turned back to see what was going on. *"There!"* Joe shouted. "They're already boarding the *Tolah*!"

The mate turned, grabbed a megaphone, and shouted at the pilot in the aft wheelhouse, "Bring her around slow! Make fast for collision! Crew at the ready! Prepare to board aft!"

Joe suddenly saw what the mate was doing. He meant to bring the *Pacah* about slowly, causing the *Tolah* to run into their ship's side. At that point, the crew was prepared to jump to the defense of their sister ship before any of the pirates could gain control of the *Tolah*'s wheel and take her out of the convoy or avoid the maneuver.

Joe looked at Tiana and Marge. "I don't know about you, but I'm going over there!" Without waiting for a reply, he went down the ladder to the deck and made his way aft, drawing Irving as he did so. The great sword gleamed in the warm sun and began to hum expectantly.

Tiana followed, drawing her own nonmagical but still lethal bronze blade. They joined the dozen crewmen, armed with a variety of swords and pikes, waiting to jump over.

Certainly the fighting was furious on the *Tolah*, and yells, curses, the sound of clashing metal, and an occasional cry of pain or anguish could be heard.

One burly crewman looked at the two newcomers and grinned. "All right, barbarians—as soon as you hear the bump, over the side we go. We have at best only a few seconds before the force of the collision separates us again."

They nodded and braced for it. It came almost immediately, nearly knocking them off their feet. But in an instant, and with a joint cry, the *Pacah*'s men stood and made for the boat just on the other side of the rail, already moving backward a bit as it recoiled on the placid water from the shock of the collision.

The pirates were not expecting the attack, and three lost their lives just by turning at the wrong time to see what new enemy was screaming so. The rest recovered quickly and arranged to meet the newcomers. The fight was soon joined, and before long it was a mass of people. Joe was painfully and suddenly aware that he could hardly tell the human pirates from the crew of the *Tolah*, but that didn't bother him right away. At least half the pirates were nonhuman, some in the extreme.

A reptilian creature fully as tall as he, with burning yellow eyes and a mouthful of sharp teeth in its lizardlike head, turned and hissed at him. The creature was a rather sickly blue and covered in scales, and Joe had no time to reflect on what the hell the thing might be. The gleaming sword in its humanoid right hand told him his job, and Irving came up to parry a blow. They were joined.

He concentrated on fancy footwork and positioning as usual and let Irving do the work. This thing, whatever it was, was no pushover, though; it was incredibly strong, and he reeled under the force of its blows, even as Irving parried them. Still, he had greater maneuverability and was able to jump once he got the rhythm of the attacker's sword strokes. He leaped sidewise and let Irving sweep out of the way; the creature missed, and its own momentum carried it forward. Joe brought his great sword down quickly and sliced right through the creature's scaly neck. Greenish ichor squirted out from the gaping wound, and the creature roared and reeled backward, dropping its sword. Joe pressed forward, plunging Irving into the creature's abdomen several times and drawing even more green blood.

Satisfied, he turned and saw Tiana taking on a squat, solid humanoid. The thing was a head shorter than she, but totally hairless and built like a tank, with huge, clawed hands grasping a lethal-looking sword. Joe paused to note the expression of sheer joy on her face as she swung her sword again and again, matching the pirate blow for blow. She was *good*, he decided.

At that moment, he felt a sudden, sharp pain in his back and cried out, whirling at the same time; this maneuver brought him face to face with a thing he could only think of as a four-armed creature from the Black Lagoon. Each of its four hands held a weapon, but one held a broken-off staff, telling Joe that he had been pierced with a spear.

Too mad really to feel the wound, he screamed and swung Irving up at the creature, who lifted one of its two swords to parry.

This was a tough adversary, since it could use all four arms separately and had the strength to wield its own broadsword with only one hand. Joe knew that this sort of creature was deadly to most opponents, but he'd been trained by an equally ugly, four-armed monster named Gorodo and he knew the tricks, moves, and weak spots.

The creature, too, was damned good; in the hack, slash, and move attack Joe employed, trying to get position, he suffered a wound for every one he scored—but soon two of the thing's arms were flopping on the deck, and it was roaring in pain and flinging its swords wildly in front of itself in a hopeless defense. Joe easily moved under the swords and struck deeply again and again into the thing's armored chest, so strong his anger and so powerful his sword that the armor proved no protection at all.

The creature howled in agony, dropping both swords, and Joe rushed in, pushed it against the rail, then shoved it over. He heard a thud rather than a splash and took the time to look over the side. The creature had struck the pirate ship and now lay sprawled on the deck.

He turned again and saw Tiana engaging a large, tough-looking human swordsman. Praying that it wasn't a crew member, he looked for more game. His eyes went up to the aft pilothouse, where he saw a hairy man climbing the ladder to the wheel. It was clear that, if the pilot was still up there, he'd been felled by a bolt or an arrow. Using his sword as a passage through the deck fighting, Joe made for the ladder himself.

Any doubt that the man now up on the wheelhouse level was a pirate was dispelled as the fellow shouted down to the pirate craft to pull away, then headed for the wheel.

Joe appeared almost in front of him; for a moment, the two just stared at each other. The pirate, Joe saw, was as cold and nasty-looking a character as he'd ever faced, but the man didn't seem to have any weapon. "Come out from behind that wheel or die there!" Joe challenged.

The pirate chuckled and spat. "Goodbye, barbarian!" he snapped and raised his hand in a motion suggesting he was about to throw something. Joe ducked as a small fireball sped past him, right through the spot where he'd just been standing.

Joe knew now that he was dealing with at least a low-level adept and was at risk, but he couldn't wait for reinforcements. The pirate was already turning the wheel hard, bringing the *Tolah* about and separating it from the convoy. Crouching, Joe made his way around the back of the wheelhouse and prepared to rush the pirate. Taking a deep breath, he stood and moved into the wheelhouse with a cry that stopped in mid-utterance. The wheelhouse was empty.

"Nice try, barbarian. Now it's time to die," the pirate said from behind him. Idly, the man made the tossing motion, and

Irving, with its own life, began to parry the little fireballs as they came.

Joe at the same time eased back to the door on the other side and quickly ducked around, then pressed himself against the cabin wall. He wasn't sure what to do now.

The pirate walked calmly out from behind the wheelhouse and looked at him, grinning. "Nice work. Too bad I can't afford any prisoners. With a little seasoning, you'd be one hell of a pirate yourself."

Joe tensed and turned to face the man standing only a few yards from him, trying to figure out if he could throw Irving with enough speed and force so that the adept would be unable to parry.

Suddenly a figure seemed to appear from nowhere and come to rest between them, facing the adept. It was small enough that the two men could see right over the newcomer.

"Marge!" Joe cried. "Watch it!"

She spread her wings and looked at the pirate adept. "Want to practice on me first?"

"Out of my way, fairy, or you burn!" the pirate snarled.

"Go ahead."

This time both hands went up, and from the pirate's palms came a tremendous surge of yellow energy. It struck Marge fully, and Joe cried out, "No!"

Suddenly the pirate adept stopped and stared at the Kauri, his expression of confidence fading with his magical energy bolts, to be replaced by a look of sheer fright. "No! Don't!" he cried.

Joe was behind Marge and so could not fully see what the adept was seeing, but he *could* see a huge field of yellow energy shoot from her back at the pirate. The man screamed and was suddenly enveloped in crackling flames. He fried on the spot.

Marge put down her wings, turned, and grinned at Joe, who was just gaping at her. "I thought you couldn't fight," he managed.

The grin grew broader. "But I can defend. *He* attacked *me*, and he got exactly what he gave. Gee—that was kinda neat. I didn't even use all of it, you know. Let me see whether I can release the rest of it down below." She walked to the front of the wheelhouse and looked down at the fight, which was certainly now going the merchant's way but was still pretty fierce. Extending her wings again, she picked out those she could who had to be pirates. Little spurts of yellow energy shot from her; down below, humans and nonhumans alike yelled and screamed in pain. It wasn't nearly enough to kill, only to sting or burn, but the shock of getting hit with a bolt was enough to distract the pirates from the people who were cheerfully trying to kill them and who took full advantage of their added worry.

Joe went back to the wheelhouse. He had no idea how to run one of these things, but he saw the rest of the convoy a thousand yards distant and going away. At least, he knew enough to bring the wheel around so that the *Tolah* was heading back toward its friends. He only hoped that somebody was left down there who knew how to find the brakes on the thing.

That proved an easy task to tell, since the sight of many of their people being killed and of Joe in the wheelhouse was too much for the pirates, who began to break off, close in as a group, and make for the rail where their corvette was lashed.

"Marge—you got any juice left?" he yelled.

She turned. "A little, I think. Why?"

"Fly down there and zap the two lines holding their boat to this one! They'll have to swim for it!"

"Gotcha!" With that she was off, over the side and out of his sight. A moment later he felt a bump and, looking over, he could see the mast of the pirate ship begin to move away from the *Tolah*. He grinned. "Good girl!"

Suddenly he saw a thick plume of inky black smoke appear near that pirate mast. Marge flew back up to him and landed, looking very satisfied with herself.

"They're on fire!" he almost shouted.

She nodded. "I wondered how much juice I had, so after I zapped the ropes, I saw all this crap on their deck they use for the fireballs. It was real easy to light."

He looked down again and saw the remaining pirates leaping over the side. "Damn! Too bad we can't get 'em all, or at least one, alive."

"I'm not sure there's much chance of that," Marge replied. "They had to climb to the top of the rail, which is about five feet, then jump clear of the running board or whatever it is. I make it a jump of maybe twelve feet and I think the water here is only two or three feet deep. The way we're still swinging around, they'll all still be stuck headfirst in the mud when we run over them."

CHAPTER 11

ZHIMBOMBE

A percentage of all seats of magic shall be dark towers, said percentage to be not less than twenty percent of all such seats of power at any given time. Practitioners of the black arts shall be given preference for these locations.

—Rules, IV, 203(b) & (c)

BOTH MARGE AND TIANA LOOKED HIM OVER BACK ON THE *Pacah* and did a joint shaking of heads. Joe was almost covered in blood, much of it his own, and Marge swore that she had seen a crewman on the *Tolah* pull the working end of a spear out of his back; yet when the blood was washed off, there seemed not a sign or mark on him, front or back.

"It's a spell, I think," he told them at last, "although just how much I want to push it, I'm not really sure. I don't want to test it by getting my skull crushed or my head lopped off or anything like that, but it seemed to do its job here. Trouble is, a weapon still hurts just as much going in as it always did, damn it."

Both women studied him, skepticism written all over their faces. Finally Marge said, "I've just run through the entire spectrum and I can't see a spell anywhere. Joe—are you holding something back from us?"

He sighed. "Well, you'll find out about it sooner or later, anyway. Um, would it be clearer if I told you that only things made of silver can cause hard wounds or kill me?"

"A werewolf!" Tiana exclaimed, slightly shocked.

"A were Pekingese, more likely, unless I miss my guess," Marge responded. "Is that it?"

He nodded. "Only it's not a werewolf or a weredog." Giving up, he told them what Ruddygore and Poquah had made plain to him. "So, you see, I didn't even want to come on this crazy mission. I've been trying not to think about it since I found out."

"Well, you said you wanted a little magic," Marge reminded him. "Looks as if it's handy magic at that. Either the spear or the sword into your belly might have done you in during that fight back there—or you'd probably be badly infected, at least. As it is, you're sitting here chewing on an apple and feeling fine."

He looked over at Tiana, who seemed very uncertain about this whole business. Aside from a very small nick on the arm, she'd fought through without any problems and without the aid of a magic sword, too. Still, it was she he was most worried about. "Does all this make a difference to you?" he asked her nervously.

She shook her head wonderingly. "I—I do not know. On the face of it, certainly not, but when the moon is full . . . I do not know. The curse is transferable, and who knows how much self-control you might have?"

"A fair amount," he replied. "That's why it's so rare. That Peke wouldn't have bitten me if I hadn't stepped on its tail. I think it's something I'm just going to have to endure, like people with malaria. We'll have to see."

"Maybe it will even come in handy," Marge said thoughtfully. "In a way, it already has done so."

Tochik was another version of Zichis, although it spread on both sides of the falls, which meant on both sides of the border, and each country had its own routing and lift system. The *Pacah* touched port only on the Zhimbombean shore, since all of its passengers and cargo were to be transshipped south.

South Tochik was an immediate contrast to the lands they had known. Entry formalities were officious but correct, although they gave the impression that exiting would be far more difficult. All of the officials, not only at the port of entry but everywhere in the town, wore black military uniforms, and there was a definite impression of being under martial law. The immigration officer asked only routine questions of them, writing in a small book for each; but when all three books were handed to them, he was very stern.

"These are documents necessary for safe passage in the Barony. Keep them with you at all times. It is an offense punishable by imprisonment or death not to have them, and it is an equal infraction not to present them to any uniformed soldier of the Barony, regardless of rank, as well as to innkeepers, transportation officials, or others who might require them. As you are in transit to Marahbar, you will go only to those areas and frequent only those places officials might approve while you are passing through the Barony. Is that understood?"

They all nodded.

"Good. You will proceed now to your hotel. The corporal there will escort you and see that you are properly checked in. As transient passengers, you are restricted to the hotel, its shops, and its restaurants, unless given permission otherwise. Have a nice day."

The corporal was a dour, thin young man with the crispness of a military cadet and the communicativeness of a rock. He was definitely not a native of the region, whose people seemed dark and swarthy, but of some place far away and far different.

They were not fifty feet from the customs station when they saw long lines, not only of men but of various sorts of fairies and creatures from unknown places, all shifting cargo under the watchful gaze of a number of tough-looking military types, some of whom had whips and others with mean-looking crossbows, loaded and held on the workers. It was clear that these were hardly volunteer labor; and this close to the border, with ships from the free north putting in and needing service, the local authorities were taking no chances.

Likewise, it seemed as if there was a uniformed soldier on each street corner, keeping an eye on everything and everybody. The few ordinary citizens on the street looked cowed and terrified and were being stopped every block for some sort of credentials check. The travelers were waved on, since they had an escort. They finally reached their hotel, a small, three-storey structure that badly needed repair and several coats of paint.

In point of fact, the whole town looked as if it needed a great deal of repair. Hitching rails seemed rotted or fallen everywhere, wood sidewalks were dangerous to walk upon, and the shops were dingy and grim-looking.

The hotel was as bad as the rest, inside and out. It stank and looked so rundown that it reminded Joe of more than one bad flophouse he'd seen in the older cities of America. The bathrooms were on the first floor and barely better than holes in the floor, not cleaned or sanitized in ages, and smelling so bad that no one could waste any time in them. The flies, too, were awful, not just in the bathrooms; and everywhere roaches and other insects scampered about. The desk clerk and a few of the people in the lobby looked just like the hotel—dirty, worn out, and hopeless.

Marge shook her head in wonder. "We'd need the entire race of Kauri to do anything here at all. And the soldiers are worse. They all feel so—*dead* inside, beyond all hope."

"You be careful around here, no matter what your impulses," Joe cautioned. "You saw how all those 'dead' soldiers were looking at you out of the corners of their eyes. I can just imagine what would happen if you fell into their hands."

"Worry less about me and more about us," she cautioned. "I wonder how long we'll be stuck in this great pigsty of a town?"

The answer was quite some time, with no way of telling exactly when they would leave. The soldier outside refused permission for them to inquire of the shipping agency, but also could not inquire for them without getting approval from her superiors. No, they couldn't contact her superiors without the proper forms and permissions. No, she couldn't supply the proper forms and permission. It was one of those bureaucratic nightmares and it meant they were kept bottled up.

Tiana, in particular, didn't like it. She was in her home territory now, but there was a pretty good fugitive warrant on her that their simple cover names and stories would not hide for long. How many beautiful and exotic women six feet six inches tall would there be trying to get into the country? They discussed their options, which included fighting their way out, waiting for capture, or just sitting around, and grew itchier and itchier as they did so. Joe, in particular, was not enamored of the enormous prices they were being charged for the stale bread and half-rotten meat they were being served by the hotel.

Finally, though, just as they had decided to force a move, a soldier arrived and informed them that their ship was now in and that it would leave in just one hour. They were to accompany him immediately, or they would be stuck for two more weeks.

The inn, which, it turned out, was owned by the local government, quoted an outrageous room rate and they couldn't afford to haggle. They either disputed the bill, they were told, in which case the dispute would be heard by a local magistrate in "six or seven weeks," or paid up now and got their boat. Snarling, they paid up.

The boat, another shallow draft freighter, was also a patchwork affair, and it was clear that this, more than anything else, had thrown its schedule into disrepair. The oarsmen on this one were chained in place and supervised by tough-looking soldiers; the sail had been patched so many times it was impossible to see anything that looked original on it. But the boat clearly had been built by the same company that had constructed the *Tolah* and the *Pacah*, and the cabins, while not very comfortable, were at least an improvement over the hotel. The smell, however, was overpowering at times, since the entire central flat carried, not standard freight or amphoras, but goats. Hundreds and hundreds of goats.

Still, if a decent place to look could be found and the wind was right for the passengers and wrong for the goats, the scenery was spectacular.

The heights of Sogon Gorge reached almost a thousand feet on both sides, making the travelers feel as if they were moving through a small Grand Canyon. The gorge emptied into the third and last of the lakes leading to the River of Dancing Gods, Lake Ogome, a very deep natural reservoir that looked as if it should be fished as well—but they saw no craft of any sort on their passage southwest. Although there were no falls at its outlet, there were violent and swirling rapids, and a great deal of work had been done to dig an elaborate canal with locks to get the boats around them. It took the better part of a day to clear the locks and rejoin the river once more.

Everywhere now, there was a strong contrast from the opposite shores. To the north was still Marquewood, with small, brightly colored villages and lush farmland; to the south was Zhimbombe, rough, ugly, and overgrown, the few villages in sight looking either deserted or unfit for animal, let alone human, occupancy. Obviously the area along the border, perhaps all the way, had been cleared of people by the Barony and allowed to overgrow into wilderness, but there was no doubt in the minds of the three passengers that the riverbank was heavily patrolled, and it wasn't to keep Marquewooders out, either.

For Joe and Marge, what took place on the boat itself was an education. Neither had ever really experienced slavery and its cruelties firsthand, nor seen human beings chained and beaten as expendable draft animals. It was repulsive—and, worse, it was beyond their abilities to do anything to help the poor wretches. Captain, crew, and military, which were of the mixed races that seemed standard in the Barony, were crisp but not friendly or approachable. They handled their three passengers like carriers of some dread disease and spoke only when necessary.

The boat crossed the joining of the Tofud and the River of Sorrows late in the evening and moved into the mainstream of the now great and powerful river. The trio knew that they soon would be reaching their departure point, which might be more of a problem than it had sounded when Ruddygore sketched it out.

They were to leave at the junction of the River of Sorrows and the Corbi, the closest point to Witchwood and on the main road to Morikay. It would have been along this road that the troops of the Barony had marched for their crossing into Marquewood for the fatal battle not many months past, a battle those troops had almost won.

They passed the spot, still littered with the remnants of temporary bridges and abandoned equipment, late in the day, but decided to ride a bit farther downstream. Darkness would be a better ally here, and it wouldn't do just to jump ship near the road that was probably the most heavily guarded in the entire Barony.

It was still fairly easy to slip over the side, despite all the military aboard. The goats, for once, came in handy, covering any sounds they might make, and nobody really paid the three passengers much heed, anyway. The idea of jumping ship at *this* point was obviously ridiculous.

The water was surprisingly cold and the current rough. Joe cleared the ship and then, half swimming, half drifting with the current, made his way toward shore, with Marge slightly overhead to be sure he made for the right one. She had already scouted the immediate shoreline and found no signs of a patrol.

He reached the bank and pulled himself up onto muddy land and into the brush, then just lay there, getting his breath, while Marge went back to make certain Tiana would not get separated from them. She was gone a fairly long time, and Joe began to get worried, but finally Marge returned. "She's about a hundred yards down from here," the fairy told him.

He nodded, got up, saw how muddy he was, then made his way along the bank. "What was the hang-up?" he asked her.

"The sword belt, apparently. Getting it freed from herself so she could swim, she ran into some brush drifting down and had to get herself untangled."

He nodded understandingly. "Yeah, I had some hairy moments myself with Irving. Lost my new sandals, too, damn it."

Marge chuckled. "Well, she lost more than that."

They soon joined Tiana, and Joe saw that Marge meant. Tiana was sitting there, breathing hard and looking disgusted, wearing only mud.

"What happened to you?" he asked, trying not to chuckle.

"I was not born with three hands, that is what happened," the large woman responded disgustedly. "I tried carrying sword and belt and whip and wound up losing my clothes to a floating bramble. Scrambling for them, I lost the rest. Damn." She got up and walked a little way forward.

"Where are you going?"

"Back in the river. I *have* to get some of this mud off." This she did, taking several minutes, then sighed and came back out again. "I don't really mind losing the clothes, but the sword, belt, and whip are a real loss."

Joe thought a moment. "Well, maybe we can replace some of it, anyway. Let's take advantage of this darkness while we have it and see if we can find that road. Marge?"

"I'm off," the Kauri responded and flew into the night. It was not long before she returned. "I'd say three miles, no more. There's an old village right on the river that's abandoned, except by troops. Nasty-looking bastards, I'll tell you. Big eyes and beaks, of all things."

"Bentar," Tiana said. "They are birdlike humanoids, very large, very fierce. Mercenaries all. Their eyes see like cats in any light, and they are swift and powerful."

"Can they fly?" Joe asked worriedly.

"No. They have arms and four-fingered hands, although their feathers give them protection almost like armor against the elements and even all but the most powerful and true of blows. I would be surprised, though, if they don't have winged scouts out. They have a communion with the birds that is hard to explain; often ravens and condors work with them as their protective shield, as well as several species of owl. You saw no birds?"

Marge shook her head. "At least none that I noticed. A few bats and a lot of insects, that's all."

"Any patrols?" Joe asked.

"Yeah, two that I saw. Parties of five, all on these big mothers of horses.".

"That's too many, particularly with only one weapon," he said, almost as much to himself as to the two women. "Our best bet, I think, would be to parallel the road if possible and wait for a better opportunity."

They both nodded. "I agree," Tiana told him. "Things will have to wait. Still, Witchwood is but fourteen kilometers in from the river. Once we reach it, the risks will be less from the Bentar than from the wood itself, with the Dark Tower in the center."

"Hmmm ... Yes, Esmerada. But won't those troopers be under her control and supervision?" Joe asked.

"They would be. She runs the entire area between the Corbi and Zhafqua, west to the Dancing Gods. However, within Witchwood she will need no troops. In there, she rules by magic."

Joe groaned. "Another magical grove. Is there no end to them?"

Marge grinned. "Probably not. So far, they all seem to be run by women."

Tiana nodded. "It is true, in a general sense. But Witchwood is much more than those you have seen so far. It is a seat of government for a much wider area, for one thing, and it is a place of black magic, not white or fairy."

Joe sighed. "Well, the object wasn't to storm the place, just to get invited inside. Let's get closer to it while we can move, and we'll talk about the fine points when we get there." He paused a moment. "I hope she's home after all this. I think she was still at the conference when we left."

"Oh, she has returned by now. Remember the delay on our part," the big woman assured him. "She has the advantage of fast flight."

"Huh? I caught sight of her back at the hotel and she looked human. Kind of imposing, but human."

"Oh, on her broom, of course. All wicked witches fly on their brooms. Surely you know that much."

"Hmmm . . . I should have known. Time to switch frames of reference," Marge put in. "So long epic fantasy, hello Brothers Grimm."

CHAPTER 12

WITCHWOOD

Since a witch's broomstick is for life, care should be taken to select one that will support not merely current but also future size and weight conditions.

—Rules, XVIII, 27(a)

MYRIAD SMALL SHAPES BROKE THROUGH THE DAWN, FLYING on long, tireless wings. Their leader wore around his neck a small golden charm, although never before had any of his tribe allowed such symbols of subservience to man or those of faërie. He allowed it now because he owed a debt of honor, and he and his would play their part in the drama for no reward other than honor, for that and the free skies that none could chain were all that was of real value in the world.

The magic charm about the leader's neck continued to give off a soft buzz that was not irritating but insistent, so close to his small earholes it was. Suddenly the buzzing sound was diminished, although it did not fade entirely, and over the sound was a very tiny, unnatural voice.

"I am in place on a small plot of what seems to be safe ground about three hundred yards from the side gate of the tower," the tiny voice said. "I have them located roughly at the edge of the wood, just off the road. I hope they have the sense to stay near it."

The leader looked down along the great expanse beneath him and saw the little road the groundlings made and of which the voice spoke. It was relatively straight and paved with loose white granite that made it stand out, even from this altitude, as a white line through the otherwise unbroken greenery. He saw now where it entered the witch's wood and became then only visible in little bits as it made its way in a nearly straight path toward the center of that wood. In the center, he saw, was a perfectly circular clearing in which sat a great structure of dull black stone, a single tower, only slightly tapered to its flat top, surrounded on the ground by a low, star-shaped outer wall. The road was clearly visible there, as it divided at the clearing and circled the Dark Tower before coming together once more and vanishing back into the dense wood.

He cursed the groundling agent mentally. Where was the side to a round structure? Or, for that matter, to a star-shaped one? Still, it would be easy to find the groundling when the need arose, but more difficult once the message had to be carried.

He heard a warning shriek from his point, and looked around to see a small swarm of blackish creatures rising from the village near the river. Clearly they meant to challenge, but just as clearly they could be ignored. Ravens. Was that the best the Bentar could send against the royalty of free eagles?

The flock slowed and circled to meet the oncoming black tide. The ravens approached brazenly and with great confidence, as they always did. When their leader reached hailing range, he called out to the soaring, great white and brown birds who awaited him.

"You trespass, eagles, far from range and eyrie. What seek you here in the land of the Barony?"

"And who are you, crow, to challenge us?" the eagle chieftain shot back. "Will you bind the skies as your foul masters who hold your leashes bind the earth? We recognize no boundaries here, nor any crow authority over our whereabouts." But lower, in the royal language understood only by his fellow eagles, he said softly, "None, not even one, should return alive or dead to the camp."

The ravens seemed so cocky and confident that they didn't even notice the eagle formation fan out and slowly and subtly take up the most advantageous battle positions. The chief raven replied, "The bird crumbles as victim to man. We are shot by the hunters and eaten by all manner of man and beast. We are captured, leashed, enslaved, even set forth by those slavers to catch and kill our own. We follow this cause out of choice, not from bindings, for the air must be liberated and purified as the ground will be."

"And this you propose to do to us here and now?" the eagle chieftain scoffed. "All ten of you against twenty-four eagles?"

By the time the ravens realized the import of that statement, the circle had closed and the eagles were upon them.

"Magic," Marge said, "flows toward you. I should have seen it before, but I never really got into the habit of shifting to the magic bands, particularly after spending so long in a city full of magicians. Now, however, I see it clearly. Bands of black and silver and bright green, they're slowly moving at you as if you were a magnet."

Tiana nodded worriedly. "Can you describe the pattern?"

"If I had pen and paper, maybe I could, but not much longer. As we move inland, more and more pieces are added, forming increasingly complex formulae."

Joe had that look that he always got when magic was being discussed, since he lacked not only the ability to see such things but even the proper frame of reference to imagine them. "In plain words, what are you two talking about?"

"A spell. No, several spells, all coming at me," Tiana told him.

He frowned. "I thought you were supposed to be more or less immune to that sort of thing while under Ruddygore's protection."

"Only fully when I am with him. I fear our little deception at the convention did not last. Kaladon was quite clever about it, though. In a sense, Marge is correct—I was, in a way, magnetized by Kaladon. Since it was not, in and of itself, a spell, it remained totally undetected and undetectable by anyone. Basically, he laid half a spell on me, then randomly scattered the rest through Zhimbombe. Were I never to return here, there would be no problem, but once I did return, the opposite pieces of the spell are attracted to me, and only to me, wherever I am in this country. I see now that the loss of my clothing and weapons was not an unhappy chance, but the workings of the usurper's evil mind."

"Huh? He seems a little nuts, then. All that just to have you disarmed and naked? You can always find something for a weapon; and even if you have to wait a while for good clothing, you weren't exactly inconspicuous to begin with."

She smiled. "Poor Joseph. You are so totally practical. Kaladon is teasing me. What is more demoralizing than to make someone both naked and unarmed in a hostile land? It is his way of telling me who is boss and just what power I am facing. I suspect, too, that bad things will happen should I try clothing or weapons again. The spell is not a one-time thing, like your pirates' fireballs, but a true creation of the mathematical art of sorcery. And, as Marge tells it, I am to be greeted with even more annoyance as we grow closer to Kaladon."

Joe frowned. "Then you should get out of here and let us handle it. Get back out of range."

Tiana leaned over and kissed him gently on the cheek. "That would do no good. Whatever spell I wear, I keep until dissolved by my own resolution, which is unlikely, or by one greater than Kaladon, which means weeks of northward travel without clothing or arms to Terindell, or by the death of Kaladon. Besides, are we not supposed to be targets? The three of us are hardly inconspicuous. All Zhimbombe must know of us by now, I would think. As you yourself said, we are simply to get inside the seats of power, not storm them."

He sighed. "All right. It's kind of like my own, ah, problem. I don't like it, but I can live with it—if you can."

She nodded. "I am committed to this. Did you ever consider that nothing like this has ever been attempted before in the whole history of this world? To assassinate top members of the Council, whose power is just a little less than that of gods?"

"That's probably because they never found any suckers stupid enough to do what we're doing," he shot back.

Marge looked around. "Dawn is coming. Shall we press into the wood or wait for dark again?"

Joe looked over at Tiana quizzically, and she responded, "We may as well press in, at least as far as we can. There are far less dangers in Witchwood in daylight than in darkness."

With that, Marge, who flew and had only one piece of baggage, unclipped her sunglasses from the necklace and put them on. They started into the wood, keeping just to the right of the road in the brush.

The forest was full of the sounds of tens of thousands of birds awakening to meet the new day and of insects changing shifts from night to day, but the road remained deserted. The trees, however, began taking on a sinister appearance as the three travelers pushed deeper into the seat of power, with huge trunks looking like the ghosts of tortured souls. Vines and underbrush, too, grew thicker and harder to navigate. Many seemed to have thorns or brambles that caught and scratched.

"I think we're going to have to risk the road, at least for this part," Tiana said.

Joe shrugged. "It's a little rugged, I agree, but—*what*?" That last was caused by a nearby bush with long, vinelike branches, one of which managed to snake around Joe's foot and start pulling. He found himself suddenly crashing to the forest floor as yet another branch, then another, threw themselves around whatever parts of him they could, and all then began pulling him toward the large plant. With a yell, he managed to draw his sword, but had some trouble keeping enough balance to slash away at the tendrillike branches that held him. Tiana rushed over, trying to keep out of reach of more of the things herself, and grabbed him under his shoulders, creating a tug of war with the plant.

"Hey! Let go and push me up!" he shouted. She did, and Irving came down again and again, slicing through the vines and causing the bush to issue loud, high-pitched screams. Suddenly all vines were withdrawn, and he managed to get to his feet. Only Tiana prevented him from rushing in to take the sword to the bush itself.

"There are too many of them!" she shouted at him, and he calmed down and saw that what she said was true.

"Let's get over to the road," he suggested nervously. "Marge—take the high road as far up as you can without getting into the trees. Better they not see you until they have to."

Marge nodded and rose into the air, then paced her companions there as they limped out to the road. Joe found he had some fairly nasty welts where the vines had grasped him, but they began to fade almost immediately. Tiana looked at them and said, "Perhaps it *is* well after all that you have this curse. The poison those things have is often strong enough to paralyze a horse."

"I'll be all right," he assured her, standing and stretching. "But anybody we meet on the road, I'll face with the sword, I think. I don't like those green uglies."

With Marge softly humming, "We're off to see the Wizard," they started nervously down the road.

Joe felt better after a while and chuckled dryly. "You know, here I am surrounded by sexy naked ladies, and the only thing

I can think of right now is that I haven't eaten anything since we left that damned boat. Must be really getting to me, though—I could swear I smelled something cooking right now."

Tiana sniffed the air. "You are not imagining things. It seems to be coming from just over there. Let us see what this could be."

They walked over and saw a small path through the trees and brush leading back to what looked like a fairly large, two-storey Victorian house. Or, rather, it looked like a cast of one. It was perfect in every detail, but clearly it was a solid block of some dark brown substance. They approached it cautiously; then Joe went up to the front steps, sniffed, and said, puzzled, "Gingerbread?"

Both Tiana and Marge approached and checked it out, then they nodded. "Gingerbread." Marge giggled. "It really *is* a huge gingerbread house."

"Yeah, but for whom? First time I saw two tons of gingerbread in my whole life," Joe noted.

Tiana was the only one who did not find it amusing. "This is one of Esmerada's famous creations. It appeals to her warped sense of humor."

"Huh?"

"She creates these things, then sentences those taken for crimes to work on them. Soon there will be prisoners here, forced to eat according to their offenses."

"Forced to eat? You mean it's not poison or something?"

Tiana shook her head. "No, not poison. But do not take it so lightly. For a major crime, you could be sentenced to eat out an entire living room, parlor, and two bedrooms. With a minor witch inducing a spell of gluttony, you could literally stuff yourself to death. It has been a traditional punishment with her ever since her great-grandmother was killed by a pair of bratty kids."

"Hmmm . . . Well," Joe said, "I don't know about punishment, but I feel hungry enough to eat out a room or two myself. Shall we try it from the back? They'll never miss it."

Tiana shrugged. "We must have something. Why not? Marge, will you watch, just in case the prison gang approaches?"

Marge did, not being able to suppress a bad case of giggles, and they had gingerbread for breakfast. It wasn't very nutritious, but it was filling, and a small creek that ran through the clearing provided a little water with which to wash it down.

"I suppose that somewhere around are the poisoned apple groves," Marge commented when they were done.

"They are to the north," Tiana told her matter-of-factly. "Not all are poisoned, though. There is one, for example, that is the most powerful aphrodisiac known. A fair amount of business is done by selling those throughout the region."

"Sounds like fun," Joe remarked.

"Esmerada has been known to feed them exclusively to people in adjoining cells of the tower dungeon, within sight of each other but just out of reach. They kill themselves trying to get at one another."

"Pleasant character. Was she here when your father was on top?"

Tiana nodded. "Oh, yes. Witchwood was then essentially a buffer, and it was simply regarded as an autonomous region. The road was guaranteed, in exchange for Esmerada's having her own way in the balance of the place. Once this was the seat of power for a great region and the place of learning for all black arts witches, but my father more or less limited her activities. Still, he thought they were as friendly as two great powers ever get, and there was a general compromise. She gained the Council with his help and support, as part of the deal which protected her and her order from others in Husaquahr. And look at how she repaid him!"

"Well, let's see how—oops! Somebody's coming!" Quickly the three of them checked out the brush, picked their spots, and barely got under cover in time. Joe hoped fervently that there were no more nasty vines around or other unpleasant surprises.

The big surprise was what was passing along the road. They had expected an occasional Bentar patrol, but this was a fairly long column of twos, all human and obviously very military, yet all wearing ordinary clothing and carrying standard knapsacks or bedrolls on their saddles. With varying growths of hair and beard, they looked very much like the sort of people who might be met anywhere in this world, despite their bearing.

When they had passed, the trio emerged from hiding. Joe scratched his head and frowned. "Now what the hell was *that*?"

"There is no way to tell," the big woman responded, "but clearly they are heading for the river and are in disguise. Something is going on, I will say that."

"Do you suppose it fits with the shortage of boats on the River of Sorrows?" Marge put in. "The pirates caused the delay upstream, but we had to wait almost a week for ours from Zhimbombe. The Marquewooders just about said that the Barony was in league with the pirates. They have all this, so it's not the cargo they were really after. Maybe it's the riverboats they want."

"Now why would they want riverboats?" Joe asked her. "They'd have to take 'em apart and shove them overland to get them to any place useful to them."

"That may be, but it's still an idea. The Zhimbombean boat looked just like a worn-out Marquewoodian one. Maybe they're using their own boats for something else, huh?"

"Yeah—but for what?" he mused. "Something's funny here."

They pressed on, speculating but unable to add anything to the mystery. They still lacked too many pieces of the puzzle, and that was supposed to be Ruddygore's problem, anyway. They had other jobs.

They finally found a spot concealed from the road that seemed safe enough to use as a camp and got some sleep. Joe stood first watch, then Tiana, and finally, as shadows fell again upon the wood, Marge took her turn. It was well into the night before all were rested enough to continue, and the two humans were feeling very, very hungry.

As they made their way again along the road, Marge suddenly called, "Joe—look out! Above you!"

He stopped, turning and drawing his sword at the same time, and saw a menacing black shape leap at him from the treetops. Marge's warning had been well timed, and the thing missed Joe's dodging form and virtually impaled itself on his sword.

It twitched a few times, then was still, and they all stared at it. "An impaka," Tiana told them. "It is a vicious, meat-eating rodent."

Joe looked around nervously. "Do they hunt in packs?"

"No, they are usually solitary hunters. This one is a male and is probably a forager for a den. We might meet others, but we might not. Still, this is a very good omen for us."

"How's that?"

"They are tough and gamy, but they taste very much like a cross between rabbit and squirrel."

Joe looked at its nasty snout and dirty black hair and wondered just how hungry he was. Still, with Marge's scouting, they found a safe-looking spot and some branches for a crude spit. Tiana, using a spell she called a very simple thing, made a fire and then instructed Joe in the proper skinning and mounting of the beast.

Although they were nervous about the fire being seen and reported, both Joe and Tiana were too hungry to care at that point, and the thing yielded close to eight pounds of meat. Marge found a plant with a bell-like flower that was stiff and permanently open, it seemed, and managed to locate and fill two bells with water and fly them back to the camp.

Satiated, they proceeded along the road once more through the night, occasionally having to dodge an isolated patrol. They were aware of strange sounds within the wood and odd chants. Once in a while, white ball-like things floated through the trees deep inside the forest.

Although they went mostly by night and slept most of the day, Tiana showed an uncanny ability near dawn and sunset to become perfectly still, often for up to an hour, waiting for a small animal or bird to come near, then quickly pounce and capture it. She came up with several rabbits, squirrels, a few unfamiliar but edible small animals, and even two fair-sized birds. When Marge and Joe asked about it, she simply told them to spend several years among the barbarian tribes of the north. There one learned such things or one starved.

After more than three days of this, they reached the center of Witchwood and the Dark Tower. It lived up to its name in every respect and seemed not only ancient but downright sinister.

The fortification surrounding it was shaped like a five-pointed star and rose about ten feet from the ground. There were gates in the wall at each of the inner angles, but it was clear from the paths to them that only two were actually in any sort of use these days. The walls themselves were patrolled by nasty-looking Bentar sentries and by what sounded like a roving pack of equally nasty guard dogs. The tower itself stood in the center of the fort, rising over three hundred feet into the air.

Here and there, windows were occasionally lighted with an inner glow.

Marge tried flying up to the top and approaching the uppermost window, but she found that, as soon as she got to the start of the fortification part, there seemed to be an invisible wall that was impenetrable by living beings of any sort. This, then, was the sorcerous barrier that could be crossed only with the permission of those inside.

Joe sighed when told the news. "So what do we do now? Go up and knock?"

"She is much too clever to fall for that," Tiana responded. "Our identities, or at least our descriptions, must be known to them. She would understand in a moment our objective if we did that."

"That would go for being taken prisoner, too, then," Marge put in. "So what do we do?"

Tiana suddenly had a thought. "Joe—how long has it been since you were bitten? The moon looked almost full last night."

He thought about it. "Let's see . . . Two days later, we were still in Sachalin, then three days down the lake, another three laying over in Zichis, then four down to Tochik . . ."

"Seven more stuck in that hole, then five downriver," Marge continued the count. "How many is that?"

"Twenty-four," Tiana told them. "And we have now been five more in this land. Tonight will be the first night of the full moon, then. Marge—can you not see the curse coming forward?"

Marge looked at Joe, and, sure enough, in the bottommost part of the magic band, there was a faint but discernible black pattern. "Yeah. What have you got in mind?"

"First we spend the day here, within sight of the tower. Let us see who and what goes in and out of those gates. When we know that much, we can better make our plans."

They did as she suggested, finding an uncomfortable but adequate concealment near the gate facing them, while Marge, grumpy about being kept up all day but nonetheless curious, staked out a convenient tree near the other gate. In midafternoon they met to compare notes.

"Well, let's see, not counting the dozen or so witches on broomsticks flying in and out from the top of the tower, we have a half-dozen Bentar, two ogres, five humans, and four fairies of unknown but various types," Marge summed up. "Where does that get us?"

"In, perhaps," Tiana said. "I do wish we knew the exact time of sundown, though. It would be a great help." She looked at the sky. "Perhaps three more hours. The moon is already full, so the transformation will be directly at sundown, which is a help. Marge—more work, I fear. We must pray that the good spirits remain with us and that a target of opportunity presents itself."

They fell back about a quarter of a mile from the tower and waited while Marge continued to scout the area. She returned as sundown was almost upon them and they had just about given up being able to put the plan into operation that night. "Rider coming. Bentar on a big black horse. I think it's one of those that left earlier today."

Tiana nodded. "It will have to do. Joe, get into position. I'm going to lure it your way if possible."

Joe drew his sword and got behind a tree just inside the forest. Tiana and he had gone over this many times, but he was still uncertain about it and still apprehensive about all that could go wrong. The sun was almost gone, and it would be cutting things very close indeed, even if all went well.

The Bentar came along the road, dressed in full armor, a huge, muscular, man-shaped bird with nasty eyes. It was looking pretty well straight ahead, but Tiana made enough of a commotion to attract it by the simple expedient of seeming to trip over a vine and cursing.

The Bentar officer glanced quickly in her direction and did not hesitate. Dismounting and drawing its sword at the same time, it proceeded cautiously into the woods, being as quiet as a creature as large as it was could be.

Tiana had gotten up and taken cover behind a tree, but she was careful to leave just a part of leg exposed to view. The Bentar, after checking the area, suddenly spotted it; while the great birdlike head remained expressionless as always, a tiny forked tongue ran out of its mouth and along its beak in anticipation. Slowly, carefully, the Bentar soldier crept toward the tree that almost concealed her, passing several other trees at the same time. After it passed one particularly large specimen, Joe, still unseen, brought down the flat of his sword on top of the Bentar's bronze helmet, and the creature toppled over, groaned once, then lay still.

Tiana quickly rushed over to the fallen soldier, checked, and nodded to Joe. "Hurry," she told him.

"I'd still rather be the Bentar," he muttered, but he went out to the road all the same. They had gone over and over this, and the way they were doing it was the safest and surest way to do what had to be done.

Marge held and pacified the large horse, but backed off when Joe approached. He looked around nervously, not quite knowing what to expect, or even whether this wasn't something rather stupid. It certainly looked dark enough to him, if this curse thing were really true. He just stood there, petting the horse, and hoped that all would go well.

There was a sudden, odd blurring of vision and the fleeting feeling that he was on fire; then it was over. Marge rushed out, looking very happy, and she and Tiana hurriedly removed the saddle, pack, and bridle from the Bentar's horse—and put them on Joe, who was now that horse's twin.

Only his prior experience as a bull, when he'd had an encounter with a Circean, kept him calm and cool. In point of fact, being a horse felt, well, *right* somehow.

The two women barely got the original horse out of sight before there was a great stamping and cursing in an inhuman language issuing from the brush. Joe turned his horse's head and saw the Bentar, dizzy and rubbing its head, manage to make its way out to the road. It headed for what it believed was its horse. Just before mounting, it turned unexpectedly and shouted, in the universal language, back at the forest, "All right—you have had your little victory! Enjoy it! None of you shall leave Witchwood alive, and your fate will be most unpleasant!" With that the Bentar mounted the horse and urged it slowly forward.

Joe had been uneasy that he wouldn't know how to react, but he found that his duplicate horse's body felt like and reacted just like the original. They approached the gate nearest the ambush spot, and the Bentar reined him in and called out, "Guards! Open the gate! I have important news!" This was followed by several under-the-breath curses in the oddsounding Bentar tongue, but Joe didn't think he needed a translation.

Despite the sorcerous protections, the place was as well guarded as any fort, and two sentries appeared atop the wall with crossbows aimed at the outsider, while a small peephole in the gate itself slid back to reveal a pair of eyes, then slid shut again. There were muffled commands given, dogs barked furiously, and the double gate of bronze and wood opened inward. The Bentar rode into the castle at this, and Joe was relieved to find no barrier to his own passage. He had been worried about what constituted an invitation and had feared that he would be stopped at the entrance while the Bentar sailed through.

They entered a courtyard that was larger than Joe had expected by what could be seen from the forest. Two female grooms ran to take the bridle and halter as the Bentar dismounted. The soldier then went immediately to a nearby tower entrance and stalked inside, while the grooms led Joe to a stable area.

Within a short time, he was unsaddled, given a wipedown and brushing, then taken to a stall where a fresh bale of hay had been prepared. He was mildly annoyed that he'd found that the wipe and brush felt really good, and he started in on the hay without thinking about it. In fact, it wasn't until he'd eaten his fill and relieved himself in true horse fashion that he bothered to think much at all. He tried the welcome invitation, but found that only a contented *neighing* issued forth; that brought a curious groom, who petted his head and fed him a lump of sugar, but nothing else. There seemed little to do but try to catch some sleep and hope both that he awakened before dawn and that the Bentar didn't want to go back out that night on him.

In point of fact, he expected a hue and cry and a full-force patrol to be dispatched and didn't know whether to be relieved or apprehensive that neither occurred. He vaguely guessed, since the Bentar talked to and used birds, that the message was being conveyed by swifter means and that the avenues of escape would soon be closed off in the immediate area, with perhaps a bird search for the strangers in the forest. He hoped that Tiana and Marge could withstand the search until dawn.

Joe awoke and looked nervously around. He was human again, and that was definitely sunlight coming in through the wood slats of the stable. He was stark naked and unarmed, of course—there had been no way to take or transform his sword or breechclout—but definitely in control. Except for stepping in a little horse excrement and reflecting embarrassingly on where it probably came from, he was in fine shape. First business first, he decided, reaching up to his left ear. The device, somewhat to his surprise, had been transformed with him and was now still there. Keeping his voice low to avoid attracting a groom, he took hold of the earring, rubbed it, and said, "Throckmorton P. Ruddygore and any in your service, you are free to enter the Dark Tower of Witchwood and invited to do so."

There was no apparent change, and he only hoped that the message had been heard and that the wording had been sufficient. If so, then Marge could reach him if need be by flying, and whatever the system was of getting word to Ruddygore would go into immediate action. If not, then he was in for a pile of trouble.

He wondered how late it was. The cool dampness he felt told him that it was still quite early, perhaps just beyond sunrise, which was fine with him.

He heard someone enter and ducked down, then crept to the front of the stall, crouching in expectation of an attack.

"Joe?" came a familiar whisper.

He stood up, cautiously looked out, smiled and nodded, then reached over and undid the latch. "Good to see you, Marge," he said, keeping his voice low. "And thanks."

She dropped a bundle at his feet and looked greatly relieved. "That's *heavy*, damn it, and that sword hates me. I hope you appreciate what I did for you just now! *I carried iron!*"

He nodded and quickly re-formed the breechclout and put it on, followed by sword and belt. Marge had taken a great risk carrying Irving, and not just from the terrible weight, even though Tiana had another simple spell to help her for the short haul here. The glorified loincloth, tied around the hilt and scabbard of the sword, was all that had been protecting her from the deadly iron blade. Only the ornate gold and bronze hilt, which covered the true iron base of the sword, had made it possible at all.

He hugged her. "Now I think we better get out of here.

Those grooms or Bird-face and his friends will be here any time."

She nodded gravely. "But where? There are sentries on the wall that I really had a time avoiding to get in here—that sword dragged me down a lot—and every place else is their barracks, the kennels, and the tower."

"The tower, then. We might as well take risks here. If the old boy doesn't come through, I'm done for, and probably Tiana, too." He paused a moment. "She's okay, isn't she?"

"When I left her, anyway. She's dug in within sight of the gate, figuring that's the last place they'll look for her. There were owls everywhere last night, and at dawn a huge flock of ravens lifted off from the top of the tower and fanned out in all directions. I thought I even saw some eagles up there, believe it or not. The hunt's really on, so her best bet is to stay still."

They made their way back to the stable door, and Joe peered nervously out. The sentries were visible on the wall, but they seemed to be looking either out or straight ahead, and the courtyard itself appeared clear.

At that moment there was a wild, maniacal cackling sound from the direction of the tower's upper levels, and the sentries turned and looked up. There was a sudden roar, and then all eyes followed a black figure on a broomstick riding out over the wall to the west.

"I wonder why they always cackle like that?" Marge mused.

"Probably in the Books of Rules," Joe grumbled. "Let's move before this one turns around for another launch."

They made the barely twenty feet to the tower door with no trouble, and Joe was relieved to find that it opened when he tried it. Quickly, both were inside and they shut the door quietly behind them.

Clearly the tower was a complex place, and they had entered on the ground floor. Stairways led around the whole outside, both up and down, and vanished in both directions through cavities in the floor and ceiling. This level in general looked barren. There was, however, illumination from torches around the hall, and a stone altar in the center.

"I don't think we better stop here," Marge said nervously. "That altar's stone, but it has a reddish look. Before long, this might be Grand Central Station."

Joe nodded. "Up or down, though?"

"Well, down's probably either the dungeons or Esmerada's workshop, neither of which I particularly want to visit. I'd say up. If we hit some novice witch, I might be able to deflect some of what she has, although my power's not much against women."

"Up it is," he agreed, and they cautiously crept up the stairs. The next level was a warren of rooms, but they had no desire to find out whose. There were definite snores coming from the darkened level, lots of snores, and some of them sounded decidedly nonhuman.

They went up through several more levels. These contained everything from rooms full of various sorcerous paraphernalia and wardrobes to an entire level in which young women were preparing meals. That one was not as hard to get through as they had feared, since the girls were busy and there were few of them.

"What happens when we get to the top?" Joe whispered to Marge as they climbed and climbed.

"We don't get that far—I hope. I think maybe we ought to find a hiding place and just camp out. The top level's the home of those packs of birds, I'm pretty sure."

"The storerooms would be handy," he suggested. "Shall we go back down?"

"One more level. I'm really curious about this place."

He shrugged and followed. They emerged into a brightly lighted room with a polished and stained oak floor and walls that squared off the chamber, made of some sort of paneling. There were no furnishings, but at the far end of the room, flanked by two floor-to-ceiling red satin curtains, was a huge and hideous multi-armed idol, seated in the lotus position. Its face was a travesty of a human woman's face, and it had eight human arms coming from its somewhat distorted human torso. Each of the hands held a different deadly weapon—dagger, sword, crossbow, garrote, and the like. While it seemed made of some black stone, its eyes were blazing red rubies of nearly impossible size and perfection.

"Looks like something out of *Gunga Din*," Joe noted. He wasn't much on books, but he loved old movies.

"The goddess of death, all right—or what passes for Kali here," she agreed. Together they approached the altar and its statue and examined it. "Look at those stones! Wouldn't Marcore love it?"

"I, for one, wouldn't touch it. It's probably cursed a thousand ways from Sunday."

"Actually, I'm not," the idol responded. "If you looked like this, would you need much in the way of curses?"

They both jumped. Joe started to pull his sword—and found that it would not come out of its scabbard. He pulled and strained at it, but it just wouldn't come. There was a chuckling behind him, and he and Marge whirled to see a tall, attractive woman standing there. She was dressed in a black satin robe and, except for snow-white hair, looked very young and pretty. Both, in fact, had seen that face only weeks before.

"Esmerada," Marge said, feeling trapped.

Joe stopped tugging at Irving and just stared at the witch queen. Swords wouldn't do for somebody like her. It would be like going against an elephant with a peashooter.

"This is all quite amusing and interesting," Esmerada said conversationally. "How in the world did you two get in? Well, never mind that for now. I assume the plot was to get inside somehow, then issue an invitation to Tubby Ruddy for a showdown. How droll. Well, you're here, but old Tubby's nowhere in sight; and since the invitation must pass from inside to outside, I hardly think you'll get the chance." She turned and shouted down the stairs, "All right, boys—bring her up!"

There was a commotion below, and Tiana was brought up, flanked by half a dozen Bentar. She had her hands tied behind her back and her arms lashed with heavy rope around her chest. She looked at her friends, shrugged, and said, "Sorry."

"Since you two were taking the tour, come on up one more flight," Esmerada invited Joe and Marge, still being casual.

They followed her, with the Bentar and Tiana bringing up the rear. The next level proved to be a comfortably appointed apartment, obviously the witch queen's private quarters.

"Untie the woman," Esmerada commanded the Bentar. They hesitated, and she added, "She's no threat—now."

The rope and hand ties were swiftly cut, and Tiana massaged her wrists for a few moments.

"You can go," the witch told the Bentar. "I'll handle things from here on in." They looked uncertain, but left.

"Please, take seats, all of you," the witch urged. "We might as well be as comfortable as possible for a little while."

Figuring that they had no other choice, all three of them took seats. There really wasn't much else to do. Esmerada seated herself in a large, high-backed plush chair opposite them and crossed her legs. "So, now. What shall we talk about?"

"That idol—is it really alive?" Joe asked, genuinely curious.

She chuckled. "Oh, yes. A former adept of mine who got too big for her robes. I changed her into the statue because it was amusing. She's totally frozen except for her mouth. She's a useful object lesson, though, to the newer girls, don't you think?"

"Charming," Tiana muttered.

Esmerada smiled. "So glad you approve. I'll try and make things equally entertaining in this case. You, Kauri, are simple. Just neutralize your therapeutic qualities, remove your ability to think, and give you to the soldier boys. You and they will have a continual ball. Nothing but animalistic sex until the end of time."

Marge shivered but said nothing.

"As for you, big boy—you're more of a challenge. Hmmm . . . Let's see . . . We really shouldn't lose the properties of that magic sword, I think. Maybe a gargoyle. Yes, definitely—a big, lurking, hulking gargoyle with bat's wings to guard the gate and attack any who enter that I wish eliminated. No, too ordinary. Well, I'll think of something." She sighed. "I wish I had the complete set. Too bad I can't play with both you *and* the amazon here."

Joe looked up at her. "What's that mean?"

"She's due on the ten o'clock broom to Morikay. There's a friend of mine there just dying to meet her."

Tiana bristled. "You would not do this!"

"Why not? Then he owes me one." The witch chuckled. "Seeing your reaction, I think it's the absolutely perfect thing to do."

Tiana started to rise, but Esmerada gave an idle flick of her hand, and it was as if a giant's hand pushed the big woman back into the chair. The witch smiled sweetly, then made a few gestures in the air. Marge switched to the magic band and was startled to see just what a riot of color and complex patterns filled the room. Still, she could see the witch's hand actually trace out a basic pattern of new material. It shot out from her rapidly moving fingers like spider's silk, reaching and covering the big woman. "Just stay there for a few minutes, won't you dear? I have to stick these two in storage for a bit."

Tiana struggled, but she was bound tightly and securely to the chair with a pattern so complex that neither she nor Marge could have understood or duplicated it in hours—and the witch had done it almost as an afterthought!

Esmerada got up and gestured to Joe and Marge. "Come with me." She paused. "Oh, take the sword off first and just leave it over there on the floor."

He hesitated, and she gave another seemingly random series of finger motions. Abruptly the sword belt tore on the side opposite the scabbard, and both it and Joe's breechclout were flung against the far wall by a force invisible to him, but all too visible to Marge.

The witch smiled her sweet smile once more. "Now, follow me and don't dawdle, or I'll have to get a little unpleasant," she warned them. It was enough, and they followed her.

To their surprise, they went not down but up. "I put the dungeons up here when I redecorated," Esmerada told them. "In the basement, escape was unlikely but possible. Up here, you not only have to break out but must get down through all the lower levels. Or fly, of course."

The dungeon level, as she called it, was second from the top and contained about two dozen small cells. They walked along and saw some pitiful remnants of humanity and fairy people in them, most certainly no longer sane. All were naked, but one wore on his head a helmet that totally enclosed it. As they passed, he rushed forward, crying, "You *must* listen! I *am* King Louis! I *am*!"

Marge frowned and hesitated, then shook her head and went on.

They finally reached the end of the cell block, and Esmerada opened a cell door. "In here, big man."

Joe hesitated, there was the hand motion, and he felt himself violently shoved inside the cell. The door clanged shut behind him. Marge made no resistance to entering the next cell. The doors, while of metal, bore no clear locks. They were made fast by Esmerada's spell, and that was better than any lock.

The witch looked back at the Kauri and thought a moment, then made a few more motions with her hand. Marge saw long threads of gold and silver emerge and bind her in a pattern even more complex than the one that held Tiana downstairs. "What is that all about?" she asked.

"You're grounded, dearie," Esmerada replied. "In technical terms, I just increased your density and altered your specific gravity. You won't notice it, because I've compensated you for it, but if you try and take off, you'll get nowhere. You now weigh two hundred pounds, you see. I also removed your wings so you wouldn't smash them, although I fear that also removes any power you might have."

Marge gasped and raised her arms; they were totally free once more. She now must look pretty much like a wingless, naked, burnt orange version of Disney's Tinker Bell.

"Well, goodbye for now, darlings!" the witch queen called as she walked away. "I have much to do today, including getting our big beauty off to the city, but I won't forget about you, never fear. Ta-ta!" With that, she was gone down the stairs.

The cells were made of solid stone blocks, bound with some very hard mortarlike substance, and it was clear that escape was all but impossible from them.

Joe looked around his cell. There was a large pile of straw that served as a bed, he supposed, and what looked like a bronze chamber pot. That was about it. The old girl took no chances with her prisoners, that was for sure.

He walked to the only opening, the barred door. It was far too tight for him to do more than get a hand through between the bars, and there was no lock even to try to pick or reach. It was hopeless. "Marge?" he called.

"Yeah, Joe," came her voice, sounding a little far away. "I'm sorry I have to stay back a bit, but those bars are iron."

"I understand." He sighed. "Well, I guess we just pray for rescue before she remembers us again, huh?"

"I guess so," Marge responded dejectedly. "I hope it's a rush job. It wouldn't take more than a few flips of the wrist for her to do to me what she said she would."

"Yeah, I know." He sighed again. "Wonder why she even waited?"

"It's no fun to her unless she lets you stew for a while," came a man's cultured voice from the other side.

Joe was startled. "What? Who's that?"

"A fellow prisoner, I fear," the voice replied sadly. "I've been here quite some time. Months, actually, although it seems like years."

"Huh? How come she hasn't turned you into a toad or something?"

The voice sighed. "She doesn't dare let me out of this box. I am held, my friend, by the strongest, most diabolical set of locks you can imagine, and I'm actually inside an inner box as well. She is very evil and very clever. My inner box is but a scant foot from the outer one, which is only a fraction short of what I can reach. She is diabolical."

"Why two boxes and locks?" Joe asked.

"One finger," the voice said mournfully. "If I could just get one finger a *fraction* outside the cell, all would be changed. She knows that, and she's tortured me with this arrangement."

"Who's that, Joe?" Marge called. "I can hardly hear him."

"Yeah," Joe pressed, "who are you, anyway?"

"I am Count Esmilio Boquillas," the voice replied.

CHAPTER 13

OF FRYING PANS AND FIRES

No thief shall ever travel without all the necessary tools of his or her trade.

—Rules, VIII, 117(b)

"IT WAS THE BARON WHO DID IT," BOQUILLAS TOLD THEM AS the morning passed. "I believe in the necessity of social revolution, but the battle should be for the minds and hearts of the people, not their lives. Yet what could I do? As a theoretician, both of social principles and of the magical arts, I was no threat. I have no vast armies nor great cults. By common agreement, the City-States remain neutral territory, lest all Husaquahr strangle for lack of trade. I gave my word to them. I would be free to speak out against this terrible war, but I would not actively intervene on either side. As neutral, then, as morality would permit me. For a while it was enough."

"The Baron thought you stabbed him in the back, huh?" Joe responded.

"Indeed. The Baron was convinced that his battle plans in the Valley had been betrayed, so that his flanking maneuver was in itself outflanked. He felt, too, that certain of his powers had been neutralized; and since he was facing Ruddygore, the only sorcerer with the guts to defy him openly, he felt that the additional sapping of power had to come from an outside source. He blamed me, but I didn't know it at the time. He was, in fact, quite cordial. He told me he was investigating his own lacks in that affair and, since I was the foremost theoretician in the area, he invited me to what amounted to a magical postmortem of the battle. Naturally, I accepted; even though I opposed the war, the idea of being able to study and analyze this methodology firsthand was a once-in-a-lifetime opportunity. I had no reason to suspect his motives, as we had had many such meetings on a friendly basis before—and I've also met with the other members of the Council from time to time."

"It was three to one, though, and you got trapped," Joe guessed.

"Precisely. This box had been specially prepared for me. I am far too good for them to destroy, even all three, but they did manage to knock me cold for a period. My defensive spells were too much for them to unravel in the short time remaining, so I was carried up here and put inside. It is a bizarre and humiliating experience, and a humbling one. It must have taken them months to construct this cell, but it is tight. Within the inner box not a single spell can be cast, not a single thin strand of magic can penetrate in either direction. I am totally and completely powerless within it. The locks are elaborate and made of dwarf-forged steel, taking three keys that must be moved together and in certain ways to unlock them."

Joe had to chuckle. "Crazy. Here I am in a magic box, and there you are in a nonmagic one. Each of us is helpless where we are, but might do something if our positions were reversed."

"You know the picking of complex locks?"

"No, but nothing mechanical is foolproof, particularly in this world. That's why thieves still do a good business. They're just the local equivalent of truck mechanics."

"What mechanics?"

"Oh, never mind. I—What the hell is *that*?"

From the floor above them came terrible screeches and squawks and a great deal of thumping around. The noise lasted for some minutes while they waited to see what might be coming next. Finally things seem to quiet down once more, and they heard someone slip down the stairs and land on their floor. Who or what it might be they couldn't see, but the upstairs commotion had started the predictable outcry in all the cells, and so it was impossible to do anything but continue to wait.

A few minutes passed. Then finally someone approached the door of Joe's cell and looked inside. "Joe? Is that you?"

The big man was thunderstruck. "Macore? Is that really you or is this some witch's trick?"

"Oh, it's really me. I was just holding down the fort, so to speak, when I saw Tiana come out on that broom, captive of one of those harpies. I figured I better get in here before it was too late."

"But—how?"

"Let's just say I have a lot of fine feathered friends. Hmmm . . . Where's Marge?"

"Next cell—no, the other way."

Macore went over, looked in, then returned. "Fast asleep. Well, we'll wake her up when we have to. Hmph! Spellbound doors. This will be a tough one. Even if I work on the hinges, the damned thing might stay in place."

"Wait a minute! In the cell next to me is Count Boquillas. He's in a nonmagic cell, and that means locks. And here we were, just wishing for a good thief!"

Macore walked over and examined the outer door. "That you in there, Count?"

"Yes, it is me," the cultured voice of Boquillas responded. "Can you do anything?"

"Let me study the situation for a minute. The outer door's pretty standard. I'll get my small pick and jeweler's hammer out and do some probing." For a while there were only small picking and hammering noises, with all comments and questions shrugged off by the thief as distracting. Finally they heard a decisive, hard metallic *tap* and then the sound of creaking hinges.

"You did it!" Boquillas breathed, not really believing it. "But—can you take the inner locks?"

Again Macore set to his work, at one point actually closing the outer door so he could get rid of the annoying other noises from the prison area. He began attaching a series of small magnets around various points in the door, then maneuvering them with his ear to the inner cell door. Finally he seemed satisfied, and out again came the pick and tiny hammer. There were three hard taps, then two more, then one more. "All right—push on the door now, Count."

Boquillas did, and the door swung open. Macore found himself facing a wan, elderly, and very scrawny-looking man with long, matted, white hair and beard and hard lines in his face. He didn't look much like the picture Ruddygore had shown them, except for the eyes, which were the same energetic, almost electric brown eyes of the portrait.

"I can't believe you actually picked the locks so easily," Boquillas said wonderingly. "If you only knew how long I studied them . . ."

"Oh, it's a talent, just as you have talents," the little thief responded modestly. "However, a thorough knowledge of all kinds of lock mechanisms, years of on-and-off practicing on them, and the right tools help. Come on—let's free the other two."

Boquillas nodded and made his way out to the hall. At this point, he stretched and seemed to gain in both strength and stature as Macore watched him. Before the thief's startled eyes, the frame filled out and both face and form appeared to grow younger. Finally all that was left of the old man he had freed was the hair and beard; the rest was unquestionably the Count Boquillas of the portrait, his face full of determined self-confidence. He walked to Joe's cell, looked at the door, chuckled, then began a series of tracing motions with his left index finger. The door creaked and then opened a trifle. Joe went over to it, pushed it, and entered the hall. "You don't know how glad I am to meet you, Count," he said sincerely.

Boquillas nodded, then walked down to the next cell. "Humph! The old girl's getting sloppy. Same damned simple spell." Again the finger traced and again the door unlocked itself.

Marge was still fast asleep, but it was a shock to see her. Without those grand wings, she looked very frail and childlike.

Boquillas stepped inside. "A defrocked Kauri. Amazing."

"Can you restore her?" Joe asked hopefully.

"Certainly, but it will take time. This is a far more complex spell; if I don't get it right, she'll wind up worse than she is now. Best I simply *add* something, which is easy, and take care of the restoration later." Again a few finger gestures. "This will give her a jolt of energy to get going and also rearrange her time sense and eyes to daylight. For the moment, I think we'd best just get the hell out of here. I assume Ruddygore is coming?"

"Yeah," Macore told him, "but it won't be quick. These communicators don't have much of a range, so the message is going north by eagle."

"Then I don't think we dare wait for him. I couldn't protect both of you people, even though I have no worries about myself any more. I think, also, that I want to go to some place that is mine and get myself back in shape before going on with this. Thief, can you handle Ruddygore's amenities?"

"Sure. No problem. But where will you go? And how?"

"Up. Up and over, the same way you came in."

"But eagles can't carry you!"

"No, not eagles. Me. As much as I would like to stick around for the showdown for personal reasons, these two need me to get clear not only of the tower but of Witchwood. We'll go to my retreat on Wolf Island. When Ruddygore is finished here, send one of your eagles to tell us the news, and we can plan from there. Agreed?"

Macore nodded. "Sounds fair to me. Oh—Marge is waking up."

She turned and groaned, then opened her eyes and looked around, puzzled. "Joe? Macore? Am I dreaming?"

Quickly things were explained to her. With Joe carefully holding the door open wide so that she would not contact iron, she walked out and glanced around. "Now what?"

"To the top!" Boquillas said, and they started upstairs.

The rookeries and aviary inside the top level looked like the remnants of a war zone. There were dead birds, feathers, and blood all over the place. "The boys were a little messy," Macore told them.

A ladder and trapdoor brought them to the top of the tower and outside into the midday sun. Marge was startled. "It's been a long time since I could look normally at a day like this."

Macore turned and looked upward, then made a series of motions with his arms. "I just told them everything was fine."

Boquillas nodded. "Good. Let's waste no more time. Stand back against the far wall, all of you."

They did as instructed and watched as the sorcerer went to the very edge of the tower's top, then got up on the narrow ledge. He seemed in intense concentration; then he stretched out his arms, and they all gasped as he apparently plunged off the cornice.

But Boquillas did not fall. Instead, rising back up to the top was an enormous bird, the largest and perhaps the ugliest any of them had ever seen. It had to weigh close to a ton, and it seemed impossible that such a thing could fly. It landed back on the roof, completely blotting out the sky and giving them little room to move. "Get on my back," Boquillas' voice came from the giant, misshappen beak. "I will carry you all to safety. Be quick. A giant roc is bound to cause a great deal of attention below."

They needed no urging, but it was scary getting up on that broad back. They finally did, though. "Now just hold on and do not panic," Boquillas told them. "Grab one another around the waist and dig in hard with your feet—quickly!"

They followed his instructions and then felt a tremendous jolt and bounce. They were airborne.

Boquillas settled down and hovered unnaturally at treetop level. "Hop off now, thief. You should be able to make your way down from here."

Macore let loose and looked nervously at the top limbs. "Yeah, if I don't break my fool neck. Well, here goes." He slid off and managed to grab on to a branch that held, finally pulling himself in. The roc then flew away, gaining altitude and speed as it went. Soon they were high in the warm air and rapidly heading southwest.

"Over to the right, there is Morikay," Boquillas told his passengers. "You can see the great castle directly in the center of town, rising on top of the mesa." They looked and saw a large city spread out along the banks of a river at the junction of the main river branch with what had to be the Zhafqua. The land was quite level; but in the center of the densely populated area, a single reddish hill with a flat top stuck out, and atop it was Castle Morikay.

"It looks like Disneyland," Joe commented. He seemed suddenly struck by other, darker thoughts. "Tiana's in that thing somewhere."

Marge gave him a squeeze. "We'll get her out. Don't worry about that. First things first."

He nodded, but was mostly silent for the rest of the journey.

He had no idea of the speed they were making, but it was in the best tradition of jet airplanes, despite the heavy breeze and lack of comforts. In only a couple of hours the flat land gave way to what appeared to be a seacoast. This was Lake Ktahr, and soon they could see two large islands. The roc banked toward the southernmost of these, a heavily forested wilderness. Near the southern end, though, on a bluff, they could see Boquillas' retreat—a castlelike structure that was not large as castles went but looked very much the part. Boquillas descended toward it, landing just outside the low castle walls.

Joe and Marge slid off quickly, then stood back as the giant bird reared up, stretched out its massive wings, and seemed to dissolve and shrink into human form once more. Soon only the Count himself stood there, looking much as he had looked back at the Dark Tower. He smiled and nodded, then came over to them. For a moment he examined them with a critical eye, then noted Marge's golden necklace and Joe's lone earring. "I assume that these hold the communicators the thief spoke about."

Joe nodded. "So we're told."

Boquillas reached out and took the necklace in two fingers, then pulled. It was still intact, impossibly so, as if it had come right through Marge's neck, but it was off. With a quick motion, he reached up and pulled on Joe's earring as well. It, too, came off. "Hey! What?" Joe managed, but Boquillas silenced him with a nonmagical gesture, holding up his hand.

"A thousand pardons for this, but, you see, although I trust you just fine, I cannot really trust Ruddygore. These will be put in a safe place and returned to you, I promise, when you're ready to leave the retreat. I simply can not afford to have you even inadvertently invite him in without my permission and restrictions. You do understand, I hope."

They didn't really like it, but they had little choice, and it did seem reasonable. Both, though, remembered that Ruddygore had not really trusted Boquillas, even though the two were on good terms with each other. No top sorcerer ever could fully trust another of at least equal and possibly superior powers.

Boquillas turned, said, "Follow me now," and walked up to a small gate which opened inward as he approached. There had been no hue and cry at their arrival—in fact, the place looked deserted—but Boquillas wasn't in need of a lot of servants. He had a large place in the City-State of Marahbar for that, after all. This was his place and his alone.

They entered the courtyard, which looked somewhat overgrown and unused, and headed for the small castle's main door. Marge glanced down at the soft earth and gasped, which caused the other two to stop and turn in puzzlement. "What's the matter?" Joe asked her.

"Look at the prints I'm making in this wet ground! I'm practically sinking in it!"

"That is Esmerada's spell, or part of it," the sorcerer explained to her. "Kauri normal construction is far less dense than that of humans or even most other fairies. The spell is actually a transmuter, altering the atomic structure so that you are made up of much heavier stuff. Don't let it trouble you. I will examine it in more detail tonight and see about unraveling it. Esmerada is quite good, though, at that sort of thing. We may have to wait until Ruddygore does her in before the spell is loosened enough to be worked on. Still and all, it's temporary. Come in and let's get cleaned up and have a decent meal."

They entered. As Boquillas went along the dark castle halls, torches burst spontaneously into light, and even fireplaces began to roar. Marge recalled Ruddygore's comment that Boquillas had a penchant for cheap magic and theatrics. She wondered who was expected to cook this meal and how fresh the food would be. That startled her, too—thoughts of a meal. She was starting to get hungry for real food, she realized, although she hadn't needed to eat since plunging into that molten pit back in Mohr Jerahl.

Boquillas led them to a combination dining hall and study, the walls of which were lined with copies of the Books of

Rules and other volumes. He stopped by one wall briefly, then took them up a flight of stone stairs to a second floor area.

There were only two rooms and a large alcove upstairs. The Count led them to the far room and opened the door. It was a spacious bedroom, with thick carpeting on the floor and carpets of various designs hung on the walls as well. A window looked out on the lake, providing a nice view, once the thick shutters were opened.

"Things are a trifle dusty," the Count said apologetically, "but I'm afraid it's been a while since anyone was here. The small door over there leads to an operable shower and toilet, which you share with my own room. I have begun the fire under the cistern above, so there should be hot water. Soap, shampoo, and all the amenities are there as well, and I will allow you some time to clean yourselves up. A bit of conjuring has permitted me to take a look at you and shape some appropriate clothing, which you'll find in the chest over there. When you're washed, dressed, and relaxed, join me downstairs in the main hall, and we will eat and talk."

With that the Count left them alone. Marge looked up at Joe. "What do you make of all this?"

He shrugged. "I don't know, but it's a damn sight better than a cell in that witch's tower. I do know, though, that I'm in bad need of a cleanup, a good meal, and a nice, long sleep."

"I'll go for that," she agreed.

The shower, which used a rooftop container that apparently caught rain and held it, was ingenious and practical. There was even hot and cold running water, from two separate tanks, although it took a lot of experimentation to get the balance right. The soap was the heavy lard soap so common to Husaquahr, but there was also a liquid soap that made a good shampoo, and both Joe and Marge used it.

The climate here was tropical but damp, and the stone of the castle made things a bit chillier than they normally would have been.

The clothing Boquillas had conjured up for them had to conform to the Rules on such things, of course, so Joe found a clean breechclout and a pair of well-made sandals for himself. Marge, who had not been able to wear clothing since getting her wings, now could once again and found that Boquillas had interesting tastes. He had provided a loose slit skirt of some satiny yellow material that hung on her hips and a halter top of the same material, as well as a pair of matching, open-topped, high-heeled shoes that gave her a couple of inches in height but also quite a wiggle to her walk, due not only to the shoes themselves but also to the excess weight they had to bear.

When Marge had finished dressing, she paraded in front of Joe and asked, "Well? How do I look?"

"Beautiful. I'm turned on already."

She laughed. "At least I come up to your thick neck now." She looked at him playfully. "Sir, may I have your arm?"

"Delighted," he responded, and they went out and down to the main hall.

As far as they knew, there were only the three of them in the castle or on the whole island, yet the table was set with fancy tableware and covered tureens and dishes. Boquillas, sitting in a high-backed chair trimmed with gold, rose and greeted them with a smile, closing a book he'd been consulting. It looked very much like one of the volumes of Rules, but since neither could read the language, they couldn't tell which volume it might be.

"You look wonderful," he told them. "Please be seated."

"You look pretty good yourself," Joe replied, and it was true. Gone were the last vestiges of the scrawny, bearded prisoner of the Dark Tower. Boquillas wore the fine clothes of a civilized gentleman, reminding Marge, at least, of some Spanish don, complete with ruffled shirt. His beard had darkened to black with only a fleck or two of gray here and there, and his hair, now washed, trimmed, and combed, matched that coloration. On each hand he wore several large golden rings in which were set precious stones.

Boquillas took them through the meal, from appetizer to salad to soup to main course, which was a whole roast pheasant perfectly done, all accompanied by very fine wine, but the talk they had was mostly small talk. Marge found herself eating ravenously, as much as or more than Joe, and she had to ask about it.

"When Esmerada took your wings, so to speak, she took with them the powers of Kauri," the Count explained. "That meant your very unusual biochemistry had to be changed, and this was done. With a structure that is three times as heavy as that of a human or earthbound fairy—about the density of a dwarf or a kobold, actually—you require more to fuel it. You see now why these spells are easier put on than taken off, I think. It is not enough just to change one thing. When you change that, you also change thousands of other things as well by sheer necessity. To put on the spell is easy, as much of this follows automatically. Magic runs by natural laws as fixed as any in the world. But to remove the spell, one must decode it. I must crack Esmerada's personal secret code, then undo the spell in such a way so that you aren't killed in the process of restoration."

That seemed to make sense. "Just how—dense—am I?"

"You mean weight? Well, if you were human, someone your size would weigh, perhaps, eighty pounds. She tripled your density without adding to your apparent size, so that would make you about two hundred and forty pounds. It's not as complex as you make it out to be. Just imagine a feather. Light, airy, a floater. Now transmute that feather's atoms by adding a bit here and subtracting a bit there so that those same atoms, the same number, are atoms of lead. That's what was done to you."

She nodded. "But I still feel the same. I still have the same, well, urges and inclinations."

The sorcerer grinned, and Joe looked at her curiously.

"You are still you, that's why," the Count told her. "Why not just relax and take things as they come? It is always best in this crazy world."

They continued to talk after dinner, this time on more substantive topics. Boquillas wanted to know their basic histories, background, and details on the scheme. They decided to keep as close-mouthed as possible, but he had surmised much.

"Of all the sorcerers of this world, Ruddygore is the most complacent and satisfied with things as they are," he told them. "I suspect this comes mostly from his being able to move between the worlds, almost at will. You know—the man who can travel anywhere, see, enjoy, and experience anything he wishes, then comes back to his comfortable, stable home to rest. The trouble is, for the rest of us it's not all that simple. This world is, after all, comfortable only for those with wealth or magical power that brings such wealth. The vast bulk of the population, both human and fairy, toils under a system where muscle is the only thing that matters. It is their labor that makes the comfortable lives of the few possible, yet they share very little of the rewards. Nor can they—for if they stopped their unceasing toil, the whole world would grind to a halt and collapse. It is not the magicians and kings of this world who are essential to it, though—if we all vanished overnight, this world would probably be the better for it."

"You sound as if you feel guilty for being one of the leaders here," Joe noted. "It seems to me that you're talking one side and living the other."

"A fair point," Boquillas conceded, "but any social revolution here will never come from below. It can't, as long as magical talent is the measure of authority. It must be imposed from above by ones who are firmly committed to changing things."

"A benevolent despotism," Marge said.

"If you like. The alternative is either a malevolent despotism or a totally amoral one that doesn't care about anybody and has a stake only in keeping things the same. Esmerada is a good example of a malevolent despot, and your friend Ruddygore is the amoral one. In a way, he's worse than the witch queen."

"Huh?" they both said at once.

"Yes, I know that's a shocking statement, but consider that even the evil ones are committed to change. Not the kind of change we would want, I grant you, but change all the same. It is Ruddygore who stands against change of any sort. Any society whose intelligentsia knows atomic theory and structure, to name just one example, is one with the potential to grow, to create machines to ease people's labor, to produce, in fact, a system whereby everyone profits from his labors according to his contributions. We have a complex, multiracial society here with everything it needs to become a great civilization, yet we find innovation stifled, invention wiped out. Even in the magical arts, which create the elitism and maintain the feudalism, there is room for expansion. Look at those Books of Rules on the walls around me. Absurd, aren't they?"

"From what we've seen, I'll grant you that," Marge admitted.

"With guts, a benevolent Council could eliminate those Rules—wipe 'em out instead of continually adding, deleting, modifying, and changing. That alone would totally liberate society from its stratifications. You could change. Barbarians wouldn't continue to be barbarians unless they wanted to, nor would dwarfs have to toil in the mines, or Bentar be mercenaries. Each might also learn what of the art they could, so that all would have a measure of power, and their collective power would be enormous. The Rules are nothing more than those of the privileged elite keeping things forever static. The steam engine was invented at least eighteen hundred years ago, yet, thanks to one of those Rules, it is nearly instant and horrible death to build one. You see what I mean?"

They thought about it. Finally Joe said, "I don't know. I've seen the other side and it's not so great."

"Oh, you've been to Earth, then? Ruddygore must indeed favor you."

Joe shot a glance at Marge, and she got the look. "Yes, we've both been there. Every time they have a revolution with noble goals, it seems to wind up just the same—dictatorship, the workers working just as hard for just as little, while somebody new gives the orders and lives the good life. The only difference is, those new leaders kid themselves that it's okay, that one day it will all be different. But it never is."

"You sound like Ruddygore, which, I suppose, is to be expected. And, in fact, I agree that things usually work out for the worst in such movements. That's why the Council is so important. If, right at the beginning, it writes the new, simpler, more free and democratic rules, progress *can* work here. I've devoted a good deal of my adult life to determining those ideal rules, and they are very simple and very basic indeed."

"It's an interesting idea, but I'd hate to see all this spoiled if you made one mistake. I guess you've never gotten the rest of the Council to go along?"

Boquillas chuckled. "They're all stick-in-the-muds by the time they reach their positions. It takes decades of work, dedication, endless practice, and stress to get to the top in my profession. By the time most of them reach that position, either they're too old and set in there ways or they feel they are getting their just payment for all the agony they went through getting there. It does tend to give you quite an ego."

"Sounds like doctors," Marge muttered, but he didn't hear her.

"Yeah, but what if it's the Baron who gets to rewrite the rules instead of you?" Joe asked him. "I'm not sure I'd like *those* rules, considering the company he keeps."

The sorcerer shrugged. "In many long conversations with the Baron, I have never been absolutely clear on what he wants. So far, it's just getting control that matters. It was my hope that I could influence him, should he win."

"Could be," Joe said, yawning. "But I doubt it. Sorry about the yawn, but I'm dead tired."

The Count was suddenly all courtliness. "Oh, I beg your pardon! Please—both of you. Go on up and get some rest. Sleep off the whole of your ordeal. Tomorrow we will get down to what happens next."

As much as Marge wanted to keep talking, she, too, was really feeling the exhaustion of the past few days. With a few more words, they excused themselves and went upstairs.

Joe looked around the room. "Well, what do you think of him?"

"I don't really know," she admitted. "On the one hand, I like him. He's got tremendous charm and a real sincerity about him. On the other hand, I don't think I'd trust him too much. I had the feeling he was keeping a lot from us, and I don't like his taking away the transmitters, even if Macore and Ruddygore know where we are."

"We can't worry about it," he told her. "Hmmm . . . Only one bed. I hope we'll both fit on it."

"Oh, we'll fit," she assured him, and they both undressed and got in, after brushing a bit of dust off the sheets. Joe just lay there a moment, thinking, and she knew what the problem was.

"You can't forget Tiana, can you?"

"No. I keep thinking of her in the hands of that bastard and I want to go charging off to the rescue."

Marge sighed. "I wish I still had all my powers. I can feel the hurt inside you, Joe, and I wish I could help."

He turned and pulled her close, then kissed her. "Maybe you still can. Want to try?"

She smiled. "You know I do." They embraced and kissed. *"Damn!"*

She pulled away and stared in confusion at the other in bed

with her. Where Joe had been only a moment before, there was now an exact duplicate of herself.

The duplicate rolled onto her back. "Damn!" she echoed. "It must be sundown."

Marge sighed, remembering the curse. "Well, we might try it anyway."

The transformed Joe shook her head. "No, it's no use. When I was a horse last night, I was every inch a horse. It's an exact physical duplication. Exact."

"Huh? You mean . . . ?"

"Uh-huh. I want it as much as you. I want it from Joe, though, and, hell, *I'm* Joe."

Marge sighed, knowing exactly how Joe felt, and pulled up the sheet. "Well, at least we both fit on the bed."

They awoke at almost the same moment. It was quite dark and all seemed still. Both just lay there, not really aware that the other was awake, lost in thought.

For Joe, it was an interesting experience. Not merely the physical change, but the change from human to fairy. It felt—well, not better or worse, but *different*. Without even realizing it, he shifted his Kauri eyes from the regular band, which saw only darkness, to the magic band, and suddenly all was alight with intricate and colorful patterns. It was all over the place, in, around, and through them and all the objects in the room, as well. For the first time he saw as Marge, Ruddygore, and Boquillas could see, and he understood just what this world was really all about.

He got up from the bed and went to the window, something he couldn't have done under normal circumstances without breaking his neck in the dark, and found it unusual to have to strain on tiptoe to the utmost to see out of it. It had seemed relatively low to him the day before.

There was a storm off in the distance. He could see the night sky occasionally light up, and every once in a while a distant, jagged pencil stab of lightning. A breeze whipped up by the storm made the lake surface rough and caused breakers to smash themselves against the cliffs far below with repeated dull roars.

Marge got up and came over next to him, also looking out. "It's very pretty, a night like this."

He nodded. "This magic band is kinda wild, though. Jeez! It's all over the place! Even the lake has it!"

"Well, it's a little more crowded around here than it is with the usual spells, but, yes, there's magic in everything and everyone here. Both the Laws and the Rules are magic, and they determine just about anything."

"You know, it sort of reminds me of that night in west Texas, except for the water. Same kind of far-off storm, same pitch darkness. We sure have been a long way since that night."

She took his hand and squeezed it hard. "Yeah, we sure have." They both lowered themselves and hugged and kissed each other. "You know, it seems that we should have been a pair rather than just a team. Things never worked out the way we figured."

Joe chuckled. "Yeah. Even tonight. Seems as if something's always working against us, doesn't it?"

There was a tremendous rumbling sound echoing outside, and they turned back to the window and again looked out. As the lightning lighted up the southern skies, Joe said, "Funny."

"What's funny?"

"Those big clouds out there. When the lightning goes off, they almost look like demons' faces."

"Huh? Let's see." She stared out, waiting for the next flash. It seemed as if it would never come, but then it did, and she saw that he was right. "Yeah, I see it. Looks almost like that hideous thing we met in the tent just before the battle." She looked again, making adjustments. "Joe—I don't think this is imagination. Shift back to the magic band."

He did, and looked again. It took a while waiting for the next flash, but then he saw just what she meant. When the face in the cloud was illuminated in the magic band, it seemed framed in shades of crimson and lavender, but there was no pattern. All the other magical things had patterns. "What's it mean?"

"Solid magic, Joe. Pure magic. A pure magical force, not the kind of things we see here. Joe—that isn't a dream. It's real. That *is* the demon we met. The Baron's demon, coming toward us under cover of that storm."

Joe frowned. Although frustrated in one respect, Marge found it fascinating to see herself as everyone else saw her, and she liked what she saw. "What are you thinking of?" she asked.

"Didn't he say the bathroom connected? Want to try a peep and see if he's there?"

"He may have a spell on the door, but let's try. You stay here. I'm more used to this than you are and I'll know what to look for. If I can get a peek into his room, it's going to be tremendously crowded with magic."

He nodded and watched as she entered the bathroom and crept to the door on the other side. After listening for a moment, she tried the door and found to her surprise that it was open. She peered in, then quickly shut the door again and returned. "He's not there."

"It doesn't mean anything. He could be downstairs, anywhere."

"I think maybe we ought to find those little transmitters and turn them on," she said. "Just in case."

Joe thought a moment. "He had 'em in his hand when we came in, but not when we went upstairs. I don't think he dematerialized them or anything, so they're probably downstairs in the den. That's the one place he could have stopped for a moment before coming up."

"Right. Let's go."

Joe sighed. "I don't know how we're going to explain my looking like this if he catches us."

"If he catches us, that will probably be the least of our problems."

"Good point," he conceded and followed her out into the dark hall. The magic gave enough of a glow to the place to guide them to the stairs. The torches were still burning dully below, enabling them to proceed on normal visuals.

They crept down the stairs and peered into the den. Several books were open and scattered around the table, but there was no sign of Boquillas. They walked in and started looking carefully for any place that the Count might have put the jewels, but not discovering any likely one. Joe was also finding it hard to adjust to being far shorter than he'd ever been. Things that had been within easy reach of him before now seemed unattainable. He began to understand why Kauri had the ability to fly.

They looked over the area for the better part of an hour

without finding anything. Then the storm hit outside, and Marge turned to him. "We'd better give it up and get back upstairs. If the storm is here, he's probably finished."

Joe nodded, and they scampered quickly upstairs. The rain was blowing through the windows in great sheets, and only by dragging over a stool could Joe get enough height to close the shutters.

Marge took one of the long sulfur matches from a holder and lighted the lamp, illuminating the room with a ghostly glow.

Joe got down off the stool and sat on it, oblivious of the wetness. He was wet enough anyway. "So what do we do now?"

She shrugged. "Wait it out. I just can't believe he's the Baron. If he's the Baron, then what was he doing in Esmerada's prison?"

Joe suddenly felt a burning sensation once again, and knew now just what that meant. "How about that? Sunrise, I guess. I'm me again."

"Welcome back, Geronimo. Speaking for myself, I like you this way a lot better. But I still can't figure it all out."

"I agree with you. If he's the Baron, then everything that happened yesterday was a sham. It meant they knew we were coming, what we were there for, and that he planted himself in that cell next to us so we'd fall into his hands."

"Yeah, but even if we buy that, how could he possibly know that Macore would be there and the right man to break us out?"

Joe had an uneasy thought. "Maybe it wasn't Macore. Ever think of that? We saw somebody turned into a crazy statue, and I've sure been turned into stuff lately. Even you were turned with a few finger motions, and the Count became a big bird with no trouble. So what's to keep him from turning somebody into an exact copy of Macore, or even Esmerada herself doing it?"

"It just could be. But—why? I'm sure neither she nor Boquillas knew about the transmitters. If that's so, then Ruddygore's still going to get in and find her. Certainly the Count didn't have a chance to tell her."

Joe shook his head sadly. "I don't know. Maybe he just didn't need her any more. Maybe she was even in the way."

"Not quite right, my friend," a familiar voice behind them said. "She was of great use to me." They whirled and saw Boquillas standing in the door to the bathroom.

"Don't look so shocked," he told them. "You think your wanderings of the evening would go undetected here? I left a lot of magical strands to see just where you went. For your information, the transmitters are in a small chest on the top shelf of the den, masked by a few books. If you had had more time, you probably would have discovered them. It was an oversight on my part, but not one that was fatal."

"I have a feeling that the reason you're telling us this is because we won't have a chance to get back there, right?" Marge said uneasily.

Boquillas grinned. "Alas, no. However, as long as those devices remain there, they will give out an all's-well signal to Ruddygore's eagles. Your thief friend, who should arrive nearby in a day or two just on suspicion, will be lulled. I may even trot you out under a spell to tell him how wonderful it is here, if it's still necessary by that time."

"What do you mean, still necessary?" Joe asked. "What the hell is going on here, anyway?"

"A very complicated plot, or series of plots, I fear. My original plan was already under way, but I still lacked a key element. I had to get Ruddygore out of the north. I had to bring him south, the farther south the better. There were any number of ruses, of course, but when he launched his own little plot against the Barony, it all fell neatly into place. Although I still don't know how you got into the tower, I had no doubt you would. Because I had to know the mechanics of Ruddygore's little plot, I contrived that imprisonment scenario. Thanks to it, you not only came willingly here with me but also told me about those interesting little devices. That was what I needed to know."

"Was that really Macore?" Marge wanted to know.

"Oh, yes. It would hardly have the ring of truth, not to mention giving me a nice alibi, if it wasn't. He has quite a—record, I suppose you might say—and is rather well known up and down the rivers of Husaquahr. I had no doubt that he'd come running when he saw Tiana flown off as a prisoner, or that he could pick those locks. If he hadn't, though, I had other rescues arranged. So now, today, Ruddygore enters Witchwood and faces down Esmerada, who is convinced that I will come to her aid. Poor Esmerada. She has style, but she always was a second-rate politician."

"You intend for Ruddygore to kill her, then?" Marge responded, somewhat appalled.

Boquillas shrugged. "I have far more vital things to attend to today and tonight as the Baron. Ruddygore is very powerful, as well I know, and I would prefer to face him on my own terms at a later date. That, however, might be rather soon. You see, Ruddygore will attain the seat in Witchwood, but at the expense of Terindell."

"What!"

The Dark Baron grinned at them. "For the past few months, in small groups and under civilian cover and disguise, a rather large force has been moving north on riverboats. Even now they are beginning to assemble for their individual marches, closing in on Terindell. Another army is north of Lake Zahias, set to strike at Sachalin. Yet a third will besiege Halakahla at the same time. The Sachalin attack will tie down my only sorcerous threat in the region, while I take the key cities and transportation hubs. I personally will take Terindell, then attend to my brother wizard to the east."

"Big talk," Joe told him. "If Ruddygore can't set foot in here, what makes you think you can set foot in Terindell?"

The Baron laughed. "Alone I cannot, but I have a rather powerful ally. You saw him earlier this morning, I would guess."

Marge just shook her head. "So all that talk about the horrors of war and a great moral crusade was just so much wind for another brutal dictatorship."

"Oh, no! All that I told you last night I fully believe, I assure you. I am bringing revolution to this world and I will change it for the better, make it free and great. But I grew weary of trying. I was a voice crying for sanity against a world oppressed by powers who would fight all change. It was obvious that no change was possible except by using the one thing they respect—brute force in all its ways. But come. We must attend to you for a while." He made a few hand gestures, and both Joe and Marge felt their bodies below their necks go completely numb. With no control at all over themselves, they found themselves getting up and walking out into the hall, then down the stairs, the Baron following.

Their heads were still their own, though, and they continued to press the conversation.

"All your allies are evil sorcerers and a demon from Hell," Marge pointed out. "I don't think they have the same visions as you do. You've fooled yourself."

The Dark Baron chuckled. "Well, Esmerada's going to be a vacancy soon, and I will appoint the next candidate, one who thinks as I do, because I will control what's left after all this. There will be other vacancies around as well. In fact, I have a number of friends already on the Council who are simply dubious about my chances. It's been figured out pretty well, my friends."

"You mean Kaladon has your idealism? I doubt it," Joe spat.

"No, Kaladon is playing out a very long game of his own, a game that seems to involve your girl friend in an integral way. He will support me as long as it serves his purposes, then try to dispose of me when I win."

"I thought he was the weakest on the Council," Marge said as they walked down to the cold, damp cellar of the castle.

"He is, but he knows it. Magic is a curious blend of art and science, you know. Sort of like mineralogy and a symphonic composition at the same time. Kaladon is very strong on the science, perhaps the most knowledgeable man in the business, but weak in the artistry. As I understand it, years ago he worked out a very strange plot, partly by duping the girl's father. She was in Kaladon's keeping when she was quite young, and he performed some mental games with her, stuff that her father would never notice unless he really suspected something. When her mother died in childbirth, her considerable powers were transmitted to her daughter, and the old boy continued the process, weakening himself in the bargain to where Kaladon, with a little help from Esmerada, could knock him off. So Tiana has more of the artistic side of magic than any other alive, I'd say. She is potentially the most powerful sorceress in the history of the world, from what I've been able to understand—but, thanks to Kaladon, she suffers from a very minor bit of selective brain damage."

"What!" Joe roared.

"Yes. All that potential is wasted without the ability to form spacial abstracts and complex mathematical formulae. Poor Tiana couldn't count past her fingers and toes, I fear, nor draw even a cube in perspective. You can see Kaladon's problem, can't you? For twenty years and more, he put together his scheme whereby he'd be the only one able to use and in complete control of the most powerful sorceress the world has ever known. And then she went and escaped from him!" Boquillas chuckled. "The man's been paranoid for years, afraid he would be deposed before he found her again. He grasped at my offer for protection in exchange for absolute service like a drowning man clutching at a branch."

"Aren't you afraid that, now that he's got her, he'll turn on you?" Joe asked. "Not that it would be much of an improvement."

The Dark Baron shook his head. "No, Kaladon simply has no idea that there's a demon prince involved in all this, capable of negating the power of three or four Kaladons, even augmented. I intend doing things the same way Ruddygore hit on—one sorcerer at a time, although I must work faster than he. Ah! Here we are!"

In a few moments, deep in the dungeons under the castle, the two captives found themselves actually cooperating in getting into manacles stuck in the wall. Boquillas closed the locks on each of them, then also closed locking waist bars and leg manacles. Both now hung helplessly on a stone wall, about five feet apart. The sorcerer stepped back and looked at them with satisfaction. He then used a small wooden stool to get up next to Marge first, then Joe, and attach something to a small rod which he brought out. In front of each, about two inches from their mouths, hung a loaf of bread and a hunk of smelly cheese.

"I'm sorry. I had hoped this would wait until after breakfast, but at least you won't starve. You can manage the bread and cheese with a little effort and practice. There's a small trough just above you both that's rather sensitive to loud sounds. If you just shout, it will tip over and produce a stream of water for half a minute or so. After the rain last night, it's quite unlikely to run out." Boquillas stepped back, took the stool, and walked to the front of the cell. "I'm doing this only because I can't be here for a long period. However, I'm not like the fool in the stories who takes it for granted that he has his enemies trapped and then ignores them." He walked out and clanged the cell door shut, then locked it with a large key which he put in his pocket. He concentrated for a moment and made a few more gestures with his hands.

"There," he said, satisfied. "I have transmuted the cell floor so that it is now an iron alloy. So is the ceiling, and so are these bars. There are no windows—you are deep within the rock itself. So, if by some chance you break the control spell on your bodies, you, at least, my lady, will still have to hang around. I suspect that this alone will keep our big friend put, but since iron is no problem for him, I'll cast one little insurance spell." Again he flicked his wrist, and Joe yelled.

"Hey! You're not going to leave us in the dark!"

"It is no matter," Boquillas responded. "You see, you are totally blind until I return. Do hang around and have fun. I have many questions to ask you under less pressing circumstances, and I know that Hiccarph, too, wants to question you on why you don't seem to exist for him. Until happier times, then—bye!"

With that, Esmilio Boquillas walked off, and they could hear him ascending the stone stairs to the cheerier part of the building.

When all sound of him had faded, Marge called, "Joe?"

"Yeah?"

"Is it true? Can't you see at all?"

"Not a thing. It's pitch dark to me." He turned his head toward her. "Can you see my eyes?"

She strained to see. There was only one torch, and no certainty of how long it would last. She gasped.

"Bad, huh?"

"Joe—all I see are whites. You don't seem to have any pupils at all."

He sighed. "Yeah. He sure wasn't taking any chances, was he?"

"There's still tonight, if he's gone long enough."

"Huh? What do you mean?"

"The last night of the full moon. Remember last night?"

"How could I forget it?" he responded grumpily.

"You'll change again. The spells will be off."

"What good's that gonna do? You're the closest living thing to me, so all I'll be is you again, right? Hanging here without any painkiller. Okay, maybe the iron wouldn't kill me, only silver, but what good does that do? Even if I slip out of these bindings by getting smaller, I still am no Macore."

"It's a chance, though. One we must take. This madman is going to destroy the whole world. Our only hope is to get Ruddygore in here before the Baron comes back. Otherwise Ruddygore will have nowhere to hole up, no safe seat of magic. The Baron and Kaladon will pick him off easily, even without their demon."

Joe sighed. "Yeah. Thanks a lot. It seems that an awful lot is hanging on very little here."

"That goes for both of us," she said glumly, looking at the manacles.

CHAPTER 14

OF MICE AND MEN

Castle dungeons must be dark, damp, and infested.
                                        —Rules, XVII, 114(d)

WITH NOTHING TO DO BUT HANG AROUND, THEY TALKED.

"Joe, do you think that even Ruddygore could take Boquillas on? With his demon, I mean?"

"I don't know. Ruddygore seemed to think so, so we have to go with that. I'm still trying to figure out how the Baron could move several large armies all the way up there without anybody noticing. At least that explains the squad we saw."

"And the missing and pirated boats. I wonder, though, if he really can pull it off."

"He probably can, at least the military part of it. They aren't ready for him with massed armies this time and a couple of weeks' notice on where he'll march. Oh, he'll do it, all right. What he probably can't do is win the peace the way he thinks. I wish that demon had brought him over some history books along with that Marx and Hitler stuff."

"That's true. Lenin in particular was a well-meaning visionary with real hopes for the future, but his system gave us Stalin instead. And there were a bunch of Hitler's friends and supporters who thought he was just a social reformer. By the time they found out, it was too late. Boquillas isn't Hitler or Stalin, but there's one around."

"Kaladon?" Joe mused. "I wonder if that's the plot."

"Maybe. Certainly he would be a better friend to demons than Boquillas in the long run. Do you think Ruddygore knows about Tiana's power?"

"I doubt it. If he did, he'd never have let her risk it all by coming with us. Damn! So much depends on your getting out of here! It's the Baron's only real mistake. That and bragging about where the transmitters were hidden. If he wasn't just putting us on. Anybody with his kind of mind can't be trusted to say his own name right."

"Oh, I think he was telling the truth. As he said, he needs to have them on and operating or it will tip everything off. Let's just be thankful he didn't return a few minutes sooner this morning, or we'd have no chance at all. He'd have discovered two of me in that room, and that would have been it."

Joe sighed. "Yeah. But I still wish I knew how to pick locks. How's that torch coming along?"

"Still going. I think it will last a while." Marge paused a minute. "Say, do you hear something?"

He cocked his head. "Water dripping."

"No, a little *scratch, scratch, scratch* type of sound."

They both kept silent for a long while, and finally he heard it, too. "What the hell *is* that?"

She thought a moment, then had it. "What else? Rats. Ugh!" Suddenly it struck her. "Joe! Rats! Around here!"

"Big deal. So we'll get nibbled to death."

"No, no! If we're very, very lucky, we might be able to attract them by biting off some of your cheese and letting it drop to the floor!"

"*My* cheese? Why not yours? At least you can see."

"No, I mean at the proper time."

He finally got the idea. "Fine—if we had a watch or a view of the sun. I don't know if we've been here for ten minutes or ten hours. The odds are just too slim. Besides, becoming a rat might get me out of here and even upstairs, but I couldn't activate the transmitters."

"You wouldn't have to. Just escape, find them, then wait until dawn. When you turn back again, you can use them."

"No good." He sighed. "When I turn back again, I'll be paralyzed and blind again, too, remember?"

She thought furiously. "Maybe not. At least, not paralyzed. I looked you over. The paralysis is a simple spell analogous to an injury. All your injuries faded, right? I think this will wear off, too."

"And my eyes?"

"That's fifty-fifty. It looks like a transmutation spell there, rather than an injury. If he'd just rendered your optic nerves inoperable, that would be one thing, but he took no chances. He changed the composition of your eyes. The curse isn't clear enough to allow me to guess on that one."

"Oh, great. So we have to hope that you're right and that I'll be able to move afterward. Uh-uh. Too risky. I'll try picking the cell door lock. Just as likely to fail, but more of a chance than the other way."

But as it turned out, he had little choice in the matter. After a while the skittish rats grew bolder, first showing themselves, then scampering about here and there, and finally checking out the leavings that had dropped on the cell floor from the prisoners' attempts to eat.

It seemed like an unpleasant eternity that they hung there, but finally, when both had more or less lapsed into sleep, sundown arrived.

The first Joe knew about it was when he was falling. Then he hit the floor with a force that hurt. Dizzily he got up, opened his eyes, and looked around. He was awfully low to the ground. He turned on four legs and saw behind him a long, bare tail; he knew for a fact that he had indeed changed into a rat.

He looked up at Marge, who seemed incredibly gigantic to him, and saw that she was still sleeping. He decided to leave her that way, since he'd be gone a very long time, anyway, and she would take a lot of comfort from his absense, far more so than from his presence.

In rat form, he found it absurdly simple to get between the bars and out into the corridor. His rat's eyes were quite good, he discovered, although that stairway was one hell of a gigantic obstacle.

It took him three hours, stretching and groaning and aching all the way, to manage the climb. He knew, somehow, that there was a far better and easier way, but he decided that the other rats might not take kindly to him, and probably couldn't tell him where it was, anyway.

Once on the main floor, which was mostly dark now, with only a few isolated torches left going, he made for the main hall and discovered that, while the previous evening he'd been short, now he was in the world where giants loomed.

Being four foot ten was a hell of a lot easier to live with than being six inches off the floor.

Disgusted, he relaxed and let the rat in him dominate. He began exploring, almost without thinking about it, and found a long, tasseled bell rope at one side of the bookcases. Using his handlike clawed feet, he tried several times and finally got a grip, wondering where and what he might be ringing, and started up.

It was a hairy task, and he fell several times, but eventually he got the hang of it and made it to the top row of shelves. Judging the distance as best he could, he made the leap, grabbed a volume of the Books of Rules, and almost pulled it off the shelf and himself with it. Fortunately, there were so many of the things that they were very tightly shelved, and he managed to pull himself up on top of the books and start to look behind them.

It didn't take him long to find the small jewelry box, hidden behind a row of the Rules; but after pushing several volumes out from the back and having them fall and crash to the floor, he waited nervously. He'd never really believed the place was deserted; but when a reasonable time had passed, he decided that it might be true.

He got behind the box now and started pushing it out with his head, using his neck muscles. It was tough going, but finally it reached the edge of the shelf, then dropped to the floor. It somehow managed to miss the pile of books down there and hit on a corner, coming open in the process. Among a lot of junk spilling out, he spotted both the earring and the necklace. *Halfway home*, he thought to himself.

It took him a lot longer to get up the guts to climb down, but he finally decided on the rope approach in reverse, and it worked, although he fell the last three feet to the floor. He was by this time one battered and bruised rat.

He scampered over to the two small pieces of jewelry and,

taking them in his teeth one at a time, he arranged them in a clear space, then settled down to wait until dawn. He was determined that, no matter what, he was going to wake up with those pieces near his head.

Marge heard sounds of somebody coming and moved her head to look. The torch was dying now, but it still gave off enough light for her to see by. She was apprehensive about those sounds, and she had no idea how long she had slept or whether it was night or day. The figure moved with agonizing slowness, closer and closer to the cell, and finally appeared.

"Joe!"

He grinned. "Yeah. You were right, kid. When I changed back, I moved perfectly. I sent the signals with no trouble at all. If there's anything out there, they're hearing it now. Just to make sure, I gave as much information as I could into both transmitters, along with the proper invitations."

"And your eyes?"

"I'm still blind," he told her. "That's what took me so long. I damned near broke my fool neck coming down those stairs."

"You shouldn't have tried. You should be up top in case Macore or somebody else comes. You can't get me out of here, anyway. Even if you had sight and a key, there's too much iron here for it to be safe, and besides, I'm still paralyzed."

"I had to," he told her. "I couldn't just leave you here not knowing. Don't worry, though. I can make it back up now. Even blind, I can do it a hell of a lot easier than as a rat."

She laughed, and he quickly filled her in on the night's work.

"Well, I'll go up now, for all the good it will do. Just stay here and pray the message gets through before our mad Baron returns."

"It will, Joe! It has to! After all this, we can't have failed in the end!"

"Well, we'll see."

"Be careful!"

"I will. Just stay here until I come back."

"Ha, ha," she responded sarcastically.

He stumbled a couple of times, but made it to the top without any real disasters. He felt lucky that the place was so small and therefore fairly easy to remember. That didn't keep him from stumbling and tripping over things he didn't quite remember, but it helped him get around.

Flags fluttered in the mild breeze, and the army, more than two thousand strong, now resplendent in full uniforms, waited in the fields outside the tiny town of Terdiera. The town itself seemed unnaturally quiet in the early morning sun, but it was often so just before a battle. All had gone well up to this point. The really dangerous part of sneaking in undetected and then assembling was over. Through the night, supply barges had shed their protective freighter's camouflage and offloaded all that was needed. Unit after unit had turned from ordinary civilians back into menacing military men.

The Dark Baron himself had arrived an hour before dawn. None had seen him arrive nor knew whence he'd come, but now he was here, resplendent in his shining black and gold armor atop his great black horse. With him, too, was his mysterious and equally armored adjutant, known by reputation only as the General. Few had ever seen his massive figure on its white horse before, but now they watched as both rode forward to inspect the field of battle.

The Baron looked out on the town. "I do not like this. It's far too quiet. Not even a rooster crowed, nor has a dog barked."

The General nodded. "We've sealed off the bridge on the Marquewood side, so they've no place to run to. The trolls have been raising Cain all night, but they'll quiet down. Send a patrol into the town and let's see what we're up against."

The Baron rode back and conferred with a leading officer. Six soldiers drew swords and proceeded slowly forward, followed by a dozen spread-out infantrymen armed with powerful crossbows. They met no resistance nor saw any sign of life, except an occasional bird and butterfly, as they advanced on the town. When they reached the first of the buildings, the cavalry stopped, and the infantry fanned out both to scout and to protect the mounted men. Only then did they proceed into the town.

It took them almost forty minutes to do a thorough search, but after the first quarter hour, they were pretty sure that no one remained behind. It was, in many ways, an eerie sight. Although a few things were missing in one place or another, there were still half-eaten meals on dinner tables and half-consumed tankards at the inn. All food and fires were cold, yet there was the distinct feeling among the men that the town's hasty abandonment could not have occurred earlier than the previous afternoon or early evening. In fact, dinner had clearly been at least in preparation when the alarm came. The captain ordered one of his men back to inform the Baron.

"I don't like this," the General noted. "It has a bad feel to it."

"It was your plan, remember," the Baron responded, knowing that the truth of the statement would make very little difference now.

The army marched into the town and quickly secured it, while the bulk of the infantry was told to establish safe perimeters to guard against an attack from the rear and to seal off any breakout.

Detaching a hundred and fifty battle-hardened cavalry from the main unit, the Baron and the General rode on down the road toward the dark towers of Terindell.

"Could they have all retreated inside the castle?" the Baron speculated.

"It's possible," the General responded, "even probable, if it were just the people who were missing. But they took their livestock and pets as well when they went, and that I don't like. The wind is right from the castle now. Such a crowd of people and animals should make an awful racket, yet I hear nothing save the birds."

They came around the bend to the castle gates and stopped. The gates were wide open. Inside, they could see no sign of a living thing.

Another patrol was dispatched, moving forward with agonizing slowness. Finally it reached the gates and halted for a moment. The officer in the front turned back to his leaders and gave a massive shrug.

"I'm going forward," the General told the Baron. "Stay here and wait for my signal." He rode confidently ahead, soon reaching the forward patrol. He stopped then, his huge, oddly cast helmet, which concealed every bit of his features, looking this way and that, as if giving some sort of impossible inspection of every stone. Finally he eased his horse across the bridge and entered the outer castle, the patrol nervously following. They passed through into the inner castle and then into the beautifully manicured inner courtyard and looked around. Nothing stirred.

"There is no life here except the usual parasitic animals," the General told the patrol. "No ambush. Nothing. Signal the Baron to come in and have guards posted on outer and inner gates."

The patrol quickly did as it was instructed, and the Baron moved forward and joined the General. They dismounted together and walked over to the simple, two-storey block building at the far end of the courtyard. On the door was a large scroll, held with two heavy nails. The Baron took it down, unrolled it, and read it with mounting anger and frustration.

"My dear Baron:

"Welcome to Castle Terindell. I hope that you and the boys won't make too much of a mess of it, since it's a very nice castle in a wonderful location. You can safely put up your troops here and be comfortable about it, as I will have no need for it in the immediate future. You should have no difficulty in defending it, as there is no enemy army anywhere nearby.

"I must thank you, though, for that brilliant infiltration plan. I admit that my military education is sadly lacking, and I would never have thought of it on my own. Of course, you must have realized that moving such large forces, even in small groups over a long period, would inevitably attract somebody's attention, and it did. When I saw just how ingenious the whole thing was, I embraced the plot wholeheartedly.

"It should be immediately obvious to one of your talents and intellect that it is far easier to move such forces downriver than up, and far faster. It therefore occurred to me that if you really wanted this place so much, it would be absurdly easy to swap. By the time you read this, Esmerada will be disposed of and Witchwood will be under my domain, but I suppose you expected that. However, at almost the same time, my forces will have seized control of the roads and river routes between Zhafqua and the Khafdis, giving us effective mastery of all Zhimbombe except for Morikay itself, which is totally besieged and cut off.

"In the meantime, my agents in and around your three armies have the ability and means to poison meats, fish, fowl, and water selectively, by nonmagical means. As long as your armies remain in and occupy the places they took today, all will be well; but should you take to the march, you will find the pickings slim. I'm afraid, too, that our effective blockade of the Dancing Gods at the River of Sighs has already captured more than a third of your fleet. The rest can not come up, while those that you have are trapped, as we sank a number of old ships in the main channel of the Rossignol after your supply boats passed and I'm afraid there isn't enough draft left to allow travel. Feel free to start removing my obstacles, but we sank a tasty cargo with them, so you'll find the river monsters rather dense, shall we say? And, naturally, I'm saving some other surprises so as not to spoil your fun.

"The civilian populations you now hold have all been given an effective poison antidote, but they remain your hostages, of course. I might remind you, though, that your attack on Sachalin has brought an additional and formidable sorcerer into the fight against you, so if *you* leave, you'll give our brother free rein to trample your army with all sorts of delightful scourges.

"I believe I have given you only one way out, and I shall be delighted to meet you in some neutral place to settle this. Bring your friend, too. Otherwise, have a nice day. Love and kisses, Throckmorton P. Ruddygore."

The Baron shivered in cold fury, then handed the scroll to the General, who read it without any visible reaction.

"Now what?" the Baron asked him.

"Well, I would say that we certainly underestimated the man," the General responded. "From a military standpoint, he's got us cold. He is quite right that it is far easier to enter a place than to leave it. We can't even depend on treaty to keep the waterways open, since nothing says he cannot blockade his own lands. We could certainly consolidate our forces into a formidable army, but we would then face a fighting retreat of over a thousand miles. There are harsh and difficult measures that could be taken, of course, including the wholesale elimination of the civilian population, one bit at a time, attempting to force terms, but we don't have enough force to hold this vast north country well enough to keep the majority from fleeing to the wilds and waging an endless guerilla action. In any such war of attrition, the carnage would be horrible, and we would lose."

"We could always retreat inland through Marquewood under a pledge of safe passage," the Baron suggested hopefully. "They would go for it, I think, just to eliminate the devastation we could cause."

"To what end, though? Ruddygore would be under no such constraints. It would be the Valley of Decision all over again, with all the elements in the enemy's favor."

"I suppose. Damn Ruddygore! He's thwarted us at every turn! Only my slow subversion by means of the books you imported from Earth through Hell has shown any measurable effect, and that will take decades, perhaps, to have any real impact!"

"He cannot take Kaladon now. Morikay may be besieged, but its seat of power is safe. The Council will be shocked enough by Ruddygore's audacity in eliminating Esmerada. They will not be kindly disposed to helping him topple yet another member. Even his friends will be feeling their own necks by now."

"True, but Kaladon is loyal to me only because he sees me as the way to expand his power. If he is in fact besieged, he knows that we have lost another round. I hardly think he will welcome me with open arms, or, if he does, with empty ones. No, if we are to recover from this, it must be as Ruddygore himself suggests. If I can eliminate the fat man, I can turn things around immediately. Then he has an unsupported army in the south, while we control a strong series of bases here. Eliminate Ruddygore and we win. Anything less and we lose. It's as simple as that."

"I concur. However, do you think he can be defeated? You faced him once in the Valley of Decision and fought to a draw. It was my analysis at that time that you would both have died, had the engagement not been broken off."

The Baron chuckled. "*You* are worried about *my* health? Kaladon would probably be more to your liking."

"Kaladon is as surely mine in the end as you are; but, unlike you, he wishes no meeting with Hell until forced to do so. He is a good schemer, but he is vain and egomaniacal in the extreme, without the intellect to control what he would have. Politically, the surviving Council members would move to fill the weakness. As I said, our fortunes are linked, and I believe that you are right. Where will you fight him?"

"No question there. I have the means to bring him to Wolf Island in a hurry, for I have two of his most favored agents there and a third certainly lurking nearby. I meet him there, on familiar ground to me, with hostages who just might distract him." He thought a moment. "Have the Bentar dispatch messages by their birds to the other units to secure and hold their positions but not advance until further orders come from you or me. Our unit here will make Ruddygore's suggestion and enjoy the comforts of this castle and the town. We will return to Wolf Island to prepare for the arrival of our fat friend. 'Love and kisses' indeed!"

The General laughed. "You must admit the man has real style and flair. Come! We will tend to the business that needs to be done, then fly to Wolf Island. With any luck, you can be home by midnight. *Then* we shall prepare to decide this thing."

CHAPTER 15

A FALLING-OUT BETWEEN OLD FRIENDS

Never give a sorcerer an even break.
—Rules, VI, 307(a)

IT WAS WELL PAST MIDNIGHT WHEN ESMILIO BOQUILLAS swooped down on the familiar shores of Wolf Island once more. He could see at once from the air that things had changed, and he didn't like it. In his flight back, he had diverted to check on the progress of Valisandra's southern expeditionary forces and he hadn't liked what he'd seen there at all. The border with Marquewood was now a very open one, with that nation's army pouring in behind the protection of the Valisandran advance parties, and the nearest really effective troops the Barony had were in Leander. The bulk of the regular and mercenary forces of Zhimbombe not involved in the north had apparently fought well, but had finally been forced to retreat to secure defensive positions within the city limits of Morikay. The majority of the forces south of the Khafdis could not be spared, or the region would rise in revolt behind them.

In other words, the Barony was in deep trouble.

And now, he saw, even Wolf Island was not secure. The castle he had left virtually shut down now blazed with light and warmth, with smoke coming from the two main chimneys. There was, in fact, a boat docked just down the island from the cliff side, a boat such as he'd never seen before, and decorated with strange writing and symbols. It looked large enough to have transported a small army, but the signs of such a force in and around the castle were absent. He was pretty sure whose boat it was and what was waiting for him. He was more or less ready, but he had wished for a night's sleep first. He was dead tired, and that was no way to go into a fight.

He landed just outside the castle as he always did and quickly transformed himself from great bird to his normal self. He was dressed now in his own formal clothes and he hoped for the courtesy of a switch of robes, at least. Hesitating only for a moment, he walked up and entered through the familiar gate and then the front door.

All the torches were fully refueled and lighted, but there was no sign of any large force. There was, however, the sound of habitation from the main hall area, and he headed for it.

A lone, huge man sat at the dining table, which was littered with the remains of a meal that might have fed four lesser men. The big man looked up, smiled through his white beard, and raised a wineglass to the haggard-looking newcomer. "Esmilio! Please, do come in and have a seat. You look dead on your feet!"

"Hello, Throckmorton. I see that you've made yourself at home here."

Ruddygore beamed and drained the wineglass. "I really must compliment you on your wine cellar. It is surely the finest I have ever seen, and certainly not what I expected in this remote locale."

"Glad you enjoyed it. Did you leave a bottle for me?"

Ruddygore chuckled. "But of course! I couldn't help noticing the Hobah '99. Really remarkable! I had thought I'd seen the last of that enchanting vintage. I took the liberty of bringing it up but wouldn't dream of touching it. Still, don't you agree that this is a fitting occasion for it?"

Boquillas was forced to smile. "Yes, I believe it is. However, I hope you will allow me the luxury of changing into something more appropriate and perhaps even a shower first?"

"But of course, my old friend! Of course!"

Boquillas looked the big man over critically. "You seem remarkably hale and hearty. I *had* thought that Esmerada would give a better account of herself than that."

Ruddygore shrugged. "It just must have been my day. Actually, I managed to get a little sleep through it all, so after that, plus a good meal and fine wine, I've never felt better in my life."

"I wish I could say the same. I assume your young friends are free?"

"Oh, yes. The blindness was a bitch to straighten out, though. Nice piece of work."

Boquillas sighed. "I should have put them both in suspended animation and have done with it. The result would have been the same, but at least I'd get a decent night's sleep."

"I am a bit surprised that you arrived this evening, despite seeing my boat. You could have waited until morning, after all. If it makes you feel any better, though, even the suspension wouldn't have helped in the long run. Not only are they smart and determined, the best I have, but one of them is a were."

Boquillas started to laugh at that, and then the laughter became louder and more prolonged. It was a minute or so before he got his self-control back. "A were! And last night was the last of the full moon! That's very good, Ruddygore! No, it is more than good. It is *genius!*"

"Yes, well, I wish I'd thought of it, but he managed to catch the curse all by himself. It did come in useful, though. Got him into the Dark Tower and out of your little jail. If you have to have a curse, I think that's the one to have." Ruddygore sighed. "I must say, however, Esmilio, that even with every signpost pointing to you, I continued to refuse to believe until the last moment that you, of all people, could be responsible for such carnage, cruelty, and destruction. It wasn't just an act. I'm sure of that. What changed you, Esmilio?"

"Frustration! Perhaps a little guilt, too, at having so much while the masses were in bondage!"

"But what do you know of the masses, Esmilio? You were born to wealth. Even had you not had the talent or the intelligence, you still wouldn't have had to work a day in your life. You're like every social revolutionary I've ever seen. You know no more of the masses, what they're like, how they think, act, and live, than a hereditary king."

"One does not have to be a woman to understand women's oppression. One does not have to be a soldier to know the horrors of war. Often I've gone out in full disguise, mingled with people from all walks of life all over Husaquahr, lived with the farmers and the merchants and the stevedores on the docks. I know more of them than you!"

"Indeed? So the rich boy went off in disguise and played at farming, or played at loading ships, all the time knowing that at any time he could materialize what he needed or, if need be, slink back to his family's banquet hall. You have never felt, nor can you ever feel, the hunger that comes from having no such fallbacks, no resources. You can never know the anguish of being a continual victim of society, pushed and shoved, without influential friends to bail you out or stay the whip's cruel hand. Even your emotions are intellectualized. The masses are a conceptual model, a mathematical construct like a good spell or an accountant's ledger. You can never know the human individual, for you can never experience what he or she experienced. As any actor, you can play the part, but you cannot be the man."

"And you can?"

"My mother was a prostitute. My father, I was told, was a common sailor, looking for a good time while in port in Todra. I grew up in the filth and squalor of the docks of long ago, which were worse then than now by quite a bit. I scrounged through the garbage for scraps to eat, but I was ambitious. Oh, yes. I could see the magic and I understood what that meant. Back in those days, Todra was a republic, and imported tutors taught the very rich and powerful in small groups on the tree-lined estates of the wealthy. One day, while still a mere lad, I was casing one of those places for a possible robbery when I happened on such a class. I was fascinated. I never did burgle the place, but I came back, day after day, for weeks and months, hiding in the trees and hearing the lessons. Basic mathematics. The classics, frustratingly discussed but which I could not read. Oh, yes, I can indeed, my friend, I can be such a man."

Boquillas was shocked. In all their conversations over the

years, he had never heard this before. "But—how did you rise?"

"Every society requires one thing to keep it from exploding. It requires a measure of social mobility. Surely you know that. In some countries it is the degree of literacy, or some sort of merit system within a political structure. For some, it is money. Here it is both money and magic, but you know that magic brings wealth. By my tutorial eavesdropping, I was able to manage and master some small spells. With that, I was able to demonstrate the art to certain magicians in the bazaar, who seemed impressed. They continued my education, as well as taught me to read, and from this I attained membership in the Society. From that point, I began truly to learn and rise. I really never regretted my origins, nor my price in my attainments. Perhaps my only regret is a lifetime of overcompensation for those early days of near starvation."

"I never knew."

"It was very long ago."

"But—you should have been my natural ally, not my enemy in this! Together we could have changed so much!"

Ruddygore sighed. "I see now my mistake, one that must be paid for. At some point I should have put aside my reservations about taking a fellow ranking sorcerer across and given you a tour of Earth."

"Is it so terrible?"

"Well, yes and no. But with all the modernities that technology brought them, there is more true happiness here than there, I would say. Many people yearn for our world and our life. Some of what we have here comes across to them as dreams, and they write glorious books with wizards and sorcerers, and all have their fairy legends. Most would be very disappointed with the reality here, I grant you, but as long as we remain fantasy, we remain an ideal they yearn for. It is ironic, I think, that they yearn for us, while just the opposite has happened to you. No, old friend, it's not worse than here over there, only very different. But, on balance, it is about even in its good and bad points. Those two you held here were from Earth, and from a particularly progressive part, and they both seem to be doing better here than there."

"So that explains . . . Never mind. You talk of Earth, but this is not Earth. Here we have magic! We need not fight,

Ruddygore! Together we can blend technology and magic to build a perfect world!"

Sadly, Ruddygore shook his head. "No, it cannot be. You would see it for yourself, were you not blinded by a beautiful but impossible vision. Technology and magic do not mix. The more of the former, the less powerful the latter becomes. There were as many fairies on Earth at the start as here, you know. They are mostly gone now—dead. They died from obsolescence. Their forests were cut down, their rivers dammed, their true work replaced by devices. You would kill them here as well, for they cannot change. They are not meant to change. And, with their going, our power, too, will vanish, for all new magic comes from faërie and its values and traditions and work. It happened on Earth, which once also frolicked with the djinn and had sorcerers and witches as great or greater than ours." He sighed. "I will make you an offer. I will send you to Earth, to a system run according to one of those books you got hold of. Live there as a commoner and see how far you get and whether you want it for Husaquahr."

It was Boquillas' turn to shake his head sadly. "It is much too late for that, even if I believed you, and you have been too full of tricks for me this day. I can neither give up my dream nor abandon my people who believe in it. Surely you must know that."

Ruddygore nodded. "Yes, I knew, but I had to try first. Why don't you go upstairs, shower, and change? Then we'll crack that fine old bottle and smoke a couple of good cigars. I do have your word that you'll be back shortly?"

Boquillas smiled and nodded. "Yes, of course. There is no purpose to prolonging this while good people are dying on both sides." With that he arose wearily from the table and made his way upstairs to his room. Ruddygore just stared after him, a sad look in his eyes and perhaps just a glint of a tear.

They stood facing each other on the wall, the tall, handsome Boquillas in brown velvet robes, trimmed in gold and silver, Ruddygore in his sparkling golden robes. Below them, waves lapped at the base of the cliffs several hundred feet down the sheer drop. The sky was clear and star-filled, the nearly full moon eerily illuminating the great lake.

Boquillas looked at the huge figure of Ruddygore and shook

his head. "This shouldn't have to be. If I win, I win it all. If I lose, you merely abandon this world to Kaladon, who will do it far worse than I."

"I think it does have to be," Ruddygore responded. "As for Kaladon, I will tend to him at the proper time. Come. It is time to put an end to this thing."

Boquillas bowed silently, his face grim, but he said nothing.

It began.

There was a seamless growth in the Count's figure, until it rose up and towered over Ruddygore, fluidly taking the form of a great and ferocious beast that stank and howled and gibbered and drooled. Ruddygore watched, but did not seem impressed. "Magic tricks," he muttered. "Ghoulies and beasties. No, Esmilio, we met this way on the fields of the Valley of Decision and settled nothing. Now face the curses you would bring to our land."

Massive explosions sounded all around the monstrous, gibbering shape, the concussion from their charges echoing menacingly against the castle walls and then out onto the lake like some eerie thunder. The creature became confused, disoriented, and began to swat at the explosions, then realized that it was on the wrong tack. It leaped upon the form of Ruddygore with a snarl, but he was not there. In his place was a massive, horrible machine, all gaseous fumes and grinding gears, sucking in the monster, sucking in and grinding it in sharp and nasty gear teeth.

The creature changed and became a terrible whirlwind, a tornadolike funnel cloud that sucked up and broke apart the machine with a thunderous roar. Overhead, immediately atop the whirling mass, appeared a great orange explosion that rapidly spread and grew until it covered the whole of the sky, setting, it seemed, the very air afire. As it descended, a blazing blanket, it drew up into the very oxygen below; with its force, it dissipated and swallowed the whirlwind. But it did not reach the castle proper, vanishing just above it and leaving the region oddly quiet.

From the sudden, deathly stillness came a huge shape, the great roc of ancient and terrible legend, its condorlike beak snapping furiously while from deep within its massive throat came horrible shrieks. It swooped and whirled around, searching for an adversary, and it found one, also coming out of the sky, a strange blackness that approached at impossible speeds and was gone again before even the tremendous explosive sounds of its passing struck the great and terrible bird of old.

But the newcomer had not passed in demonstration but rather had laid its eggs, dozens of them that now sped toward the roc from all directions, including from above and below. Frantically the bird tried to zoom up, then straight down, then from side to side, but those horrible eggs kept matching its movements and all the time coming closer, closer . . .

At least five struck the roc in its massive underbelly, exploding with incredible force, driving white-hot bits of metal into its flesh along with flaming jellied liquid that seemed only to eat into the creature while refusing all efforts to be extinguished. The roc reeled as seven more struck it, one in the head, and the force of the explosion there and the spread of the terrible burning jelly struck its eyes, rendering it blind. In panic, burning, it raced for the surface of the lake and dove beneath the placid waters, sending a plume of water thirty feet into the air as it did so.

Ruddygore, his face and eyes showing tremendous strain and concentration, stood on the castle wall and looked outward to where the roc had entered the water. Within a short time, the water was smooth once more, with no sign of the huge entry.

Now, though, great bubbles issued up along a wide area below the castle, as if some enormous creature was surfacing. When it did, it was more terrible than anything of the old legends, a monstrous mass of living green slime from which issued thousands of wriggling tentacles as needed. It continued to rise, its bulk so vast that it was soon almost the size of the entire castle. Ruddygore faced it impassively, not moving a muscle as stench-ridden, sucker-covered tentacles reached out for him.

From all around the beast, small white contrails broke the surface of the water, dozens of them coming in a semicircular pattern toward the beast's bulk. Just as the first tentacles of the kraken closed upon Ruddygore, the objects struck, all within a fraction of a second, sending up tremendous plumes of water as each exploded with a roar that made all previous detonations look like firecrackers. With the water, pieces of green slime went up as well, and the kraken roared its terrible agony and writhed in pain, its two giant eyes on great stalks glaring in hatred.

Ruddygore reached down, picked up a strange-looking object, and aimed it at the eyes. The thing shot more of the jellied flame, which this time burned on and into the water, and the creature groaned and thrashed in an unsuccessful attempt to quench the spreading fires that covered it.

Suddenly the kraken vanished. For a moment, all was silence again. Then there was a roar from the castle roof, and Ruddygore spun around to face an enormous dragon that reared back and shot hot, smoky flame at him. Boquillas was fighting fire with fire.

Ruddygore flung back his right arm as if about to throw something, but when he brought it forward, an enormous stream of water rose out of the lake and struck the dragon full force in the mouth. Suddenly the fat sorcerer was standing right on the castle wall, holding and guiding a gigantic pressurized hose that quenched the dragon's flame.

The dragon, its flame so easily extinguished while Ruddygore's fires had been unquenchable, roared defiance and leaped upon the man below, but suddenly the man wasn't there. The dragon missed and plunged over the edge of the castle wall, but there was no sound of an object striking the water.

Both men again stood facing each other on the outer wall, neither actually hurt, but Boquillas' fine robes looked slightly singed.

"It's called napalm," Ruddygore told him. "Just one of technology's little gifts to mankind."

But Boquillas was no longer there. Instead, the whole castle shimmered and seemed to change into a terrible, menacing jungle of carnivorous vines and animated plants. The transition was so swift that Ruddygore found himself suddenly held by strong tentaclelike vines that tightened and pulled in all directions toward gaping plant jaws. The abrupt change had obviously surprised him, and he showed real pain and discomfort, but only for a moment.

There was a sound like a thunderclap, and down from the sky rained a suffocating, yellowish cloud of gas. It quickly covered all the plants and the sorcerer himself; but at its first touch, the vines recoiled and the gaping mouths of the huge plants seemed to scream in dreadful agony. The jungle was suddenly in frantic, insane movement, screaming and tearing itself to bits as it died. The more it writhed, the more it opened its wounds to the yellowish powders.

Freed, Ruddygore, although slightly injured, did not pause. "Now smell the world of the perfect future! Breathe it and weep!" he cried. The air changed, and the stars and moon were blacked out. All around was a dense, wet fog that choked anything it touched, a fog filled with the metal particulates from a billion smokestacks and the noxious fumes of a hundred chemical and power plants. It was the condensation of all that had been pumped into the air by mankind's progress through the centuries, and it was more horrible than any monster of Husaquahr.

Again Boquillas was disoriented by the tactic, which was more terrible and incomprehensible to him than anything he had known. He tried to fight his way out of it, to rise above it, but it was so dense and so horrible that he could not seem to find a break in it.

Suddenly the way was clear, and he made for it, but it was not a pleasant clearing. Although the pretty farms and fields appeared lush and green and the little town looked both alien and very familiar with its small cottages and dirt main streets, it was a scene of total terror. Two armies, it seemed, were going at each other, but not in any formal way. The entire pastoral vista was one of pure carnage and disorganization, and men were falling from bullets so thick in the air that the entire countryside seemed infested with some sort of locust. When any man showed even a part of himself, though, those locusts struck and tore gaping wounds open, causing terrible pain and agony. Men fell by the hundreds, by the thousands, in an impersonal carnage that turned the little creek that ran through the fields and then through the town into a river of blood. Antietam Creek had become Bloody Lane.

Just as abruptly, the scene changed, yet somehow stayed the same. It was a horrible wasteland now, any trace of what it might have been before having been long obliterated. Shells burst in the air in an almost constant barrage of concussion and shrapnel, while men huddled in long trenches and died every time they tried to advance *en masse* just a few yards from those holes …

Then the sky was filled with a shattering roar as machines

of destruction flew over in so dense a formation that the city below seemed blocked from sunlight. Most of the people were below, in shelters against the rain of bombs, but nothing could protect them from this onslaught of explosions that created a firestorm above, rather than on the surface, sucking out the oxygen and killing them, men, women, children, old and young, dogs and cats, soldiers and bankers and janitors, as they huddled in their shelters . . .

Boquillas whirled, but the place now was a new place, without explosions or bombs. He saw rows upon rows of men so thin and emaciated they looked like what the line marching the road to Hell must look like, only these were human beings, some being forced to shovel out piles of human remains from enormous ovens, the remains of men, women, children, and none of them soldiers . . .

The sights sickened and appalled him at first; but after a while, their very sameness brought him a measure of respite, a crack in the chamber of horrors, allowing reason to resume command. Ruddygore was effectively showing him the evils of technology, but without any of the benefits, and he fought back in this Never-Never Land of the mind.

Gleaming cities of steel and stone . . . Highways that were ribbons of concrete stretching from coast to coast, spanning continents, filled with horseless vehicles in astounding numbers . . . Homes, powered and heated by oil, gas, even the sun itself, in tremendous profusion, and not a castle in sight . . . Huge symphonies in large, well-lighted halls of acoustical perfection, playing wondrously beautiful pieces . . .

Ruddygore, ready, counterattacked . . .

Family units all grouped around boxes from which issued moving pictures in full color, all hypnotically staring at the screen for hours on end, all watching incredible drivel . . .

A band on a huge stage entertaining tens of thousands of young people, but the band was dressed in weird, half-naked fashion, its lead singer's jewelry including razor blades for earrings; all their faces were terribly made up, while their hair was shaved in strange ways and dyed in greens and blues and reds. They were singing of death, destruction, and hopelessness to a crowd that was at one and the same time worshipping them, emulating them, and watching with that same hypnotic fascination as those in front of the little boxes . . .

Inventory, Boquillas commanded. And in his mind appeared fallout shelters, missile silos, satellite guidance systems ... Mutual Assured Destruction ... the hydrogen bomb ...

He located what he needed, targeted it, and aimed it properly. The great missile broke back through the atmosphere, targeted not on a city but on a single individual, its lenses and computers interacting to locate that one man, who, when spotted, turned to the onrushing death from the sky ...

Only it was not Ruddygore. It was a small, helpless beggar child with pitiful eyes, his hands still grubby and stained from rooting through dockside garbage. He looked up at the missile with sad, fatalistic eyes, then turned to Boquillas, who watched, horrified. The boy reached out, pleading with him, pleading ...

Count Esmilio Boquillas screamed and fell back against the battlements. Again back in his own world, under a starry, moonlighted night sky, he was not alone. The poor beggar child was still there, still approaching, those sad eyes boring down upon him. And now the child spoke, a halting, hurt sort of tone. "Please, my lord, why do you wish to kill me?"

Only a child, only a little child now. He could reach out, crush that child, beat in his brains, and toss him from the battlements to the cold waters below. He could, he could ...

"I cannot!" Boquillas sobbed. *"Hiccarph! Save me! Save me from the child!"*

Behind the child, abruptly, a ghastly shape formed, towering over both child and man, a rotting, stench-filled body filling out a grand costume of crimson and lavender, its eyes consumed with hatred and contempt. A gnarled, clawed hand reached out for the boy, then picked him up. The boy screamed as he was pulled into the air and mercilessly crushed in the foul hand of the demon, his body quickly limp and then reduced to a bloody mass of tissue which the demon contemptuously discarded. Then the demon stood there, looking down on Boquillas, and shook his head from side to side.

"Well," Hiccarph said casually, "he certainly had your number."

The Count, breathing heavily, pulled himself weakly to a sitting position and for a moment just buried his face in his hands. Finally he looked up at the demon and sighed. "It—it was horrible! Horrible! If he was that strong, why did he not take me in the Valley months ago?"

"Because he cheated," the demon told him. "First of all, he knew you very well indeed, while out there he was fighting an unknown enemy. But, most of all, he cheated. He brought in the weapons of Earth to face the magic of Husaquahr, and that was something he could never do in public, where all could see or feel or sense it. There would be those who would get ideas, and others who would like what they saw. Out here, it was a safer bet. Now, though, his soul is lost to the world. A pity, for I'd hoped to have him myself."

Boquillas looked up at his demon general. "He is dead, then?"

"I search high and low and cannot find him in the world. He is vanquished by his very trap that really won him the contest. He knew you well, knew that you were powerless to face down someone totally vulnerable, innocent, and defenseless. But when he chose that path for the *coup de grâce*, he also was most vulnerable to outside forces not so easily swayed."

Boquillas tried to get to his feet, failed, then tried again, clutching the battlement stones for support, and finally made it. He gasped and coughed as he did so. After a few seconds, he got some strength and took in several deep breaths. Finally he said, "Then we've won."

"Yes. We've won," the demon agreed.

"Well, not exactly," came a voice from the window nearest them. They both turned. Sitting in the window, looking fairly relaxed, was Joe de Oro, clean and rested, dressed in a breech-clout and sandals, and wearing his great sword.

CHAPTER 16

WHEN THE HURLY-BURLY'S DONE . . .

A woman has no fury like Hell scorned.
—Old Husaquahrian Saying

BOTH THE BARON AND THE GENERAL WERE STARTLED, BUT not particularly worried. Hiccarph reached out a long arm to

Joe and swiped at him as if swatting at a fly. Joe flinched, but the demonic hand passed right through him without effect, and he relaxed and smiled. "Having problems, fish-breath?"

"You're the one from the tent back in the Valley," the demon recalled. "I understand it all now. You're from Earth, aren't you?"

"Give that devil a cigar," Joe responded, gaining a little confidence.

"You are subject to the magic of Husaquahr, so I wouldn't feel so confident. You have no one left to protect either you or your female companion, who, I assume, is also from Earth."

"You're right on that," the swordsman conceded, "but not on the other. Ruddygore didn't think that a battle between two such illustrious sorcerers should go unappreciated by all except vagrant travelers from Earth and a notorious thief. He issued some invitations, and, what do you know, everybody accepted. You see, he sort of made a bet with each one, and even though you did him in, for which I will cheerfully see you in a worse hell than the one from which you came, he still won the bet. He was very busy at that convention making deals, you see."

Both the exhausted Boquillas and the demon were fascinated but hardly worried. "Indeed?" Hiccarph responded. "And what sort of petty magics can you find against *me*?"

"Just one," came a thin, nasal voice from behind the demon. The two on the battlement turned. While Boquillas simply frowned in puzzlement, the expression on the demon's face was terrible indeed to behold, and he uttered a groan that sounded like the death cries of a million damned souls.

The object of this was a small, pudgy little man in monk's robes, clean-shaven even to his very smooth scalp. He looked quite cherubic, but his expression was anything but amused.

"Mephistopheles," Hiccarph whimpered. "Wait! I can explain . . ."

"Explain what?" the little monk asked. "That you, a minor nothing over here in the backwaters, could unilaterally break the Compact and risk Armageddon without even his Majesty knowing of it? *Well, he knows now, Hiccarph!*"

"No!" the demon wailed. "How—how did you find out . . . ?"

"Ruddygore does a fair amount of business our way, usually with the minor elementals, of course, but enough to get messages where he needs to. He's been complaining about this for years, but we never believed him. We never believed that *any-one* in the demonic hierarchy could be both so clever and so utterly stupid at one and the same time. Finally, he offered a wager to us. Himself, his soul, all that he had, to the total and complete service of Hell, if he couldn't prove it to my satisfaction tonight. It had the approval of the Old Man himself, in fact. We usually get the average soul without bargains, as you know, but one of Ruddygore's caliber, right away and now, is very rare. The Old Man's going to be as pissed by missing that as he is with your rampant and reckless risk of the status quo."

"But I could have delivered this whole world to Hell!" Hiccarph whimpered.

"Bah! You idiot! We're winning *now*! We could lose the whole thing if we're forced into a premature Armageddon. Well, you'll spoil things no more, now or in the future, until Armageddon truly comes. An example will be made of you, Hiccarph, and a most terrible one indeed, I promise you, by the Old Man himself. Let's see how you like an eternity stoking fires in the dung pits we reserve for the religious zealots! And not as supervisor, either—as a common demon ninth class! And when Armageddon arrives, guess who's going to be right out front leading the first charge into Heaven!"

"No! Wait! I—" the demon screamed, but there was a sudden, near-blinding flash of light and both figures were gone, leaving only a very slight smell of sulfur behind that the wind quickly carried away. Again there was silence.

The silence, though, was broken by a low chuckling. Joe turned and saw Boquillas sitting on the battlement wall, looking highly amused. Finally the sorcerer said, "Well, that's that. Actually, I have to thank old Ruddygore, wherever he may be. Now the Dark Baron will put his plans into action without the meddlings of any Hellish princes—or ex-princes. Yes, indeed, it was quite a favor you just did me, and I appreciate it."

"Don't appreciate it too much," Joe cautioned him. "Old monkey wasn't the only onlooker, and I think it's time you met the rest."

Marge appeared now, looking every bit the Kauri once more, grand with her wings of power, flitting along the stones in true fairy fashion. Behind her came a rather large assemblage of people, all wearing varicolored robes that were made of fine materials and beautifully tailored.

Marge went over to Joe as Boquillas gaped. "You know the folks," she said lightly. "Fajera, Docondian, Sargash, Mathala, Brosnial, Careska, Jorgasnovara, Yiknudssun, O'Fleherity, Kaladon, and Esmerada?"

The Baron gasped. "*Esmerada*! But I thought Ruddygore had killed you!"

Joe looked at Marge quizzically. "O'Fleherity?"

"*Darling* Esmilio!" Esmerada oozed. "You know me better than that! I mean, given a choice between a fight to the death you might not win and a partnership, which would *you* choose?"

"So that's why he was so well rested," the Baron muttered. "You traitorous bitch!"

She laughed at him. "Oh, darling, you say the *sweetest* things!"

"To business! I have already delayed my departure from this rotten continent long enough," snarled a huge and powerful-looking black man in robes of red and yellow. "Although, I admit, the show was more than worth waiting for."

Boquillas was frankly too tired to care. "So what happens now, my fellow members of the Council?"

"You've been a *baad* boy, Essie," Esmerada scolded playfully. "Got to pay the piper. Playing with real demons in the real world is a no-no, and you know that."

"You and Kaladon in particular didn't seem so upset at the Barony when it was going your way," he noted sourly. "And you, Careska, surely didn't mind when we handed you Leander on a platter. Fajera, you weren't exactly turning the other cheek when you helped recruit the Bentar mercenaries. A fine lot you are! Most of you are blacker than I am!"

"Which is precisely the point," Fajera, the big black man, shot back. "You heard Mephistopheles. We've a long way yet to Armageddon, but you provoked it prematurely. At least half the Council is on the dark end of the art, and the other half doesn't know which way they'll finally go, but has some idea that you don't get this far and receive wings, a harp, and eternal thanks. Maybe Ruddygore got away with it because he was willing to give his life to stop you, but that's too high a price for me. You and your damned visionary dreaming almost got us screwed for eternity! Now you have to pay."

Boquillas sighed. "Yes, I bet Kaladon and the rest of you love that. Two vacancies to fill on the Council, and Husaquahr is yours with its armies in place. You like that idea, Sargash?"

"Enough. Temporal problems are for temporal resolution," a distinguished-looking woman in silver robes said. "The vote has been taken after evidence was presented on a proper complaint by a member of this Council, now deceased. Shall we agree on the sentence?"

"We are agreed," the rest chanted.

"Very well, then. Esmilio Boquillas, the problems of the world and how much or how little each of us gets involved in them are none of the affair of the Council as a whole. The Council is agreed that you have made a most grievous breach of the ethics of the art and hereby expels you from the Council, with loss of all rank and privileges, and from the Society, whose covenant you so violated. So say we all, and so do we all act in concert."

Boquillas just sighed and nodded.

The Council was quiet for a moment, each member's head bowed as if in prayer. Then they looked up again at the man who had been the Dark Baron.

"It is done," the woman in silver intoned. "Let us leave this place."

With that, they all turned and walked back along the wall, chatting pleasantly, and disappeared into the castle below.

Joe was disappointed. "That's *all*? They cashier him and that's that?"

"You don't understand, Joe," Marge told him. "They did the worst thing they could do to him."

Joe looked over at the man, who was still sitting on the stone wall. "He looks pretty good to me for a guy who just got scolded."

"Not just scolded, Joe. They took away his power. All of it! He has no more magical power than you do. Less, in fact. I doubt if he's even able to do a sleight-of-hand magic trick. They cut him off from the magic, you see. He's just an ordinary, totally human, totally nonmagical mortal now."

Joe brightened. "You mean I can bash him?"

"You could," Boquillas agreed, "but why bother? If you

wish to kill me, then do so now. Otherwise, I am going inside and going to bed." With that he got up, then walked away from them down the battlement walkway to the small door, through it, and back into the castle.

"Damn!" Joe swore. "He kills the best man in this crazy world and gets away with it! And I don't have the heart to take him on, not when he's *that* beat."

Marge grinned. "Well, we could always do likewise, you know."

"Huh?"

"There's still the bedroom in there, and we're still here. It will be a while before Macore gets back with a longboat to take you off, probably tomorrow sometime. In the meantime, Boquillas can't get off the island any more than you can, and all the others have already gone."

"But it's still the middle of the night!" he protested. "You're not sleepy and I'm not tired."

"And there's no full moon, either," she pointed out.

"Oh—I *see* . . ."

Together they went in by way of the window.

The weather turned bad the next day, delaying Macore's rescue boat. Ruddygore had sent the little thief back to the mainland before the battle between the two sorcerers because he feared too many people would be noticed and because Macore had no demonic immunities.

Boquillas slept solidly for more than fourteen hours, but Marge and Joe finally heard him moving about upstairs as he breakfasted on leftover pastries from Ruddygore's last meal. Both Joe and Marge felt pretty good, their only dark clouds the knowledge that Ruddygore was gone and that Tiana was still in the hands of Kaladon. That last seemed more unassailable an obstacle than ever; although Marge could ease some of the ache, she wasn't able to remove the problem from Joe's mind.

When Boquillas finally came down, he looked years older than he had looked the night before—just a tired old man. Joe reached for his sword, but Boquillas raised his hand wearily.

"Must we still continue to go through this?" he asked. "Please understand that now I am as much on your side as Ruddygore would have been, although, alas, without his power."

Joe frowned. "What do you mean?"

"I may have done all the dark things that you say, and I will surely roast in that pit for it, but what I did, I did for the most idealistic of reasons. With what happened last night, things have turned upside down. Is there still a pastry, by the way?"

Marge, who no longer felt human hunger, passed him a gooey one. "What do you suggest, then?" she asked.

"I know Kaladon and some of his plans. I know Morikay, too, and what's involved there. More than that, I still know more magic than practically anyone else alive."

"But what good does that do you now?" Marge asked him. "I mean, you can't use it, you can't practice it, and you can't even see it or protect against it."

"Quite true," he admitted, "but beside the point. Kaladon really isn't very good, either. Esmerada helped him rig his contest for the seat he holds because she wanted a share in the take, you might say. She's now been badly burned. Ruddygore had to get a sacred oath out of her to stop the fight, and that oath certainly removes her from any politics inside or outside Zhimbombe. We are, then, dealing just with Kaladon, whose power resides not in himself but in his ward."

"Tiana," Joe said softly.

Boquillas nodded. "Exactly. She has the power, but is totally under his control. She doesn't even have the knowledge to break the simple spell that binds her to him, although she has the power to break half of Husaquahr. So we are in a cul-de-sac, as it were. I can analyze the spell and show anyone just how to break it, but I can't see the spell. Break the spell, and any half-baked magician could tell her how to fry Kaladon to ashes. Ruddygore's fairy adept, for example."

"Poquah! Sure!" Marge responded, sounding enthusiastic.

"Kaladon's bound to make his move very quickly, before the armies start getting ideas of their own. That means both he and Tiana will have to come out of that castle, and I can guess by the way his mind works what he'll pull. It will take a pretty good adept to resist the spell, and even that will be chancy. However, that sort of thing won't work on a true fairy, so somebody of true fairy blood, preferably somebody who can also fly and defend herself quickly, would have to go there and examine that spell, sketch it *exactly*, and bring it back to me."

"I think I'm beginning to see where you're headed," Marge noted.

"Uh-huh. The trick then would be to get into Castle Morikay, if need be. Outside the castle, the defenses will be too much for any but the best sorcerers in the land. That means somebody has got to pull Ruddygore's trick—get into a castle you can't get into without an invitation if you harbor intentions against any of the occupants, invite in Poquah, say, and dissolve the binding spell on Tiana. Give me a couple of weeks with him, and I can teach him what he'll need to know. If my analysis of her latent powers is correct, and I'm sure this is what Ruddygore had in mind, the proper spells directed against an unsuspecting Kaladon could do to him what was done to me last night."

"You mean—take away his powers?" Joe said hopefully.

Boquillas nodded. "Not permanently, I think. That would take four or maybe five of the Council to do. But, Joe, if you had Kaladon unable to use any magic whatsoever for several hours, what would you do?"

Joe grinned.

"That's what I thought. Now this is going to be tricky, and I assure you that the odds are very much against it all going our way, but Ruddygore seems to have picked you two very well. Somehow, with a superhuman effort, he's matched you to various arcane bunches of Rules, so that, no matter how hopeless the situation is, you seem to come through. How anyone could do this, even in a thousand years, is beyond me, but he managed it, and I have to go with that."

Marge thought a moment. "You know—Ruddygore was always going off to Earth at odd times. I wonder if, somewhere over there, he hasn't got one hell of a computer working for him."

"Computer? You mean an abacus?" the Count asked, confused.

"One hell of an abacus, you might say," Marge told him. "Joe? What do you think?"

"I think this is crazy," the big man mumbled. "A couple of days ago this guy blinded me and chained us both up in a rat-infested dungeon; then last night he killed the only friend we had in this world; and now *we're* working for *him!*"

"Will you do it, though?" she pressed.

"Oh, *sure* I'll do it, but . . ."

CHAPTER 17

. . . WHEN THE BATTLE'S LOST AND WON

When cults convert more than ten percent of a population, they are to be considered a religion and are covered by Volume XXVI instead of Volume XCI.

—Rules, XCI, 494(b)

"IT'S LIKE NOTHING ANYBODY'S EVER SEEN," MARGE TOLD the small council of war two weeks later. "I've never been so alternately fascinated and repulsed by anything in my entire life."

They sat there, Poquah, Joe, Boquillas, listening intently.

"First of all, the siege is over. In fact, the war is over for all intents and purposes. The Barony has been replaced by the spreading new world of the Goddess."

They nodded, knowing some of this, but not firsthand.

"Morikay has been rechristened the Throne of Paradise and is the center of this expanding movement. It's an amazing thing to see it spread so quickly in so short a time. The official line is that the Dark Baron, who brought Hell to Husaquahr, was defeated by Ruddygore at the cost of Ruddygore's life. They made him a saint."

Boquillas chuckled. "It's a wonder he doesn't come back from the grave over that."

"Anyway, with Hell vanquished, so the line goes, the Creator sent the Goddess of Husaquahr, a true angel, to watch over us and see that it never happens again. Three guesses who the Goddess is."

Joe looked at her and nodded glumly.

"Anyway," she continued, "the Goddess came to banish all war from the world and to carry out the Creator's plan for us. She appointed the wise and benevolent Kaladon as High Priest of the new One True Church and established her seat on earth at Mori—sorry, the Throne of Paradise. She raised the siege by merely walking through the lines and letting all the soldiers see her. They fell down and worshipped her, even the mercenaries and half-breeds like the Bentar. She has since appeared in dozens of major towns and cities, including Sachalin, Halakahla, and other places, and every time it's been the same. Instant conversion, followed by the immediate establishment of a temple under a leader hand-picked by Kaladon. There are already huge statues of her all over the place, all of which attract crowds of worshippers. By the way, Joe, all the statues are full nudes."

"Naturally," Boquillas put in. "If she's a true angel, then she is without sin of any sort, and clothing would be inappropriate."

"If the statues are from life, that means she's changed a bit," Marge went on. "From what I understand, she's just about ten feet tall; and if you thought her proportions were large before—*wow*! Her hair also seems much thicker and about ankle-length, and she looks, well, smoother. Really angelic in the extreme. Of course, I never saw her personally."

"What of the fairy folk?" Poquah asked. "How are they taking all this?"

"The ones I talked to are mostly divided. Kaladon has sent emissaries to all the key tribes, offering peace and harmony and assuring them that the temples will preach a line that they're the children of God and are to be treated with honor and respect. Most of 'em seem willing to suspend disbelief and go along. A few are even debating whether or not the Goddess might be the real thing. The ones who have seen her haven't fallen down in worship, but they report an enormously powerful glow of pure white within her, more than has ever been seen."

"Pure white. Good touch. Perhaps I *did* underestimate Kaladon," Boquillas noted, mostly to himself. "And what of the distinguished members of the Council?"

"Esmerada has been given her own seat at Halakahla, taking over from Ruddygore. She seems delighted to go along with it all and is working to make Terindell a holy shrine, of all things! Sargash is still fuming over the siege of Sachalin, but she's decided that the handwriting is on the wall. She's not helping, but she's not obstructing, either. Word is that Kaladon and Esmerada have offered to back her candidate for one of the two vacancies on the Council, and that's bought her off.

Careska's head of the Church in Leander and she's been given a pretty free hand there, while Fajera is priming Todra for a visit by the Goddess real soon now. It's all happening so *fast*."

"But it's been planned for years, perhaps decades," Boquillas responded. "Kaladon is an incredible politician with an incredible mind set only on power. With the complicity of the rest, or at least noninterference, he'll soon have all of Husaquahr that's worth having under a single theocracy with himself at the helm. Oh, it will take quite some time to secure it all, but if the mere appearance of the Goddess can cause instant conversion and worship, then any time he gets a pocket of trouble, he just goes visiting. But tell me, what is this new doctrine like? Surely he has grandiose plans."

Marge nodded. "So far, the grand plan is limited to the Throne of Paradise, and that's just getting organized, but the pattern seems clear. Each cooperating sorcerer is more or less being encouraged to write his or her own holy book for the locals, tailored to their own aims and conditions, so that keeps the people happy. Kaladon himself seems to have his own vision. Whole parts of the city are being torn down by eager volunteer converts. Parks are being developed, and a style of building that reminded me of ancient Greece—sorry, I know most of you won't understand that—is going up. Big marble temple-style buildings. People work five days on their regular jobs, then two for the Church for nothing. They also are expected to go to services each night and get more holy instructions and they do. Half of what they earn goes to the Church and gets poured into the building and developmental programs, while Church leaders are organizing syndicates for all major industries, including shipping and farming."

"An integrated economy. Interesting. Continue."

"Well, what he's getting is a world of willing, worshipful slaves who won't even sneeze without permission, but who will do anything they are told to do. They also seem bent on a plan they call 'efficiency of form,' where people are being willingly turned into other creatures to do their work better. The centaur population alone is growing by leaps and bounds, since that's an efficient farm form, and the mermaid and suchlike population's going to grow under a harvest-the-sea program. There's a whole winged legion for transportation and communication, too. It's scary. And remember, I'm an empath—I can feel these people's insides. They're sickeningly joyful."

"That's to be expected," the former Dark Baron commented. "After so much war, suffering, and killing, they were ready for a savior, and he's given them one. Of course, Tiana's magic is reinforcing all this, but that just makes it easier. You were not, however, able to see her in person?"

Marge shook her head from side to side. "I tried to. Just missed her once. But she takes a leaf from your book and turns herself into a great white dove, or something similar, and gets places faster than I can."

"Hmmm . . . This complicates matters. Have you any idea how often she returns to the castle?"

The Kauri shrugged. "Hard to say. They're transforming the place into a really stunning supertemple, by the way, at least on the outside. All marble and spires."

Boquillas thought for a moment. "But you said Fajera was trying to arrange an appearance in Todra. Any idea when?"

"The Goddess is due to appear in the City-States—which are, by the way, mostly very cynical but very curious—next month. Does that help?"

"Yes and no. I hate giving him so much more time to establish and consolidate his program, but this has to go exactly right or it's no go. You'll be down there when she shows and give us a firsthand account, plus that all-important spell information. I've told you what to look for—the one string that ties her to Kaladon."

Marge nodded.

"I don't see why I have to wait," Joe put in. "I mean, in just a couple of weeks I'll be ready again to sneak in there. Should be particularly easy with all the workmen."

"Perhaps, but we can't take any chances we don't have to," Boquillas replied. "First of all, I don't want you meeting the Goddess. The spell would grab you, and that would be that. Secondly, we might catch Kaladon with the barriers down for a few days, even a week, but certainly not a month. He's bound to notice, busy as he is, that he has no protection. You're the key man, Joe, the only human we can afford to use in this operation. Marge and Poquah will handle the rest, but they can't get in without you."

"Okay, but I just get itchy sitting around here, that's all."

"Better itchy than lost forever," the Count warned.

Four weeks and three nightly transformations for Joe later, the conspirators held another meeting, this one far more pressing.

"I've seen her," Marge told them. "Man! Is she *something*! I tell you, I knew what was going on and I was immune from the spell she radiates and I still almost bought it. This empathic thing is a two-way sword. She radiated such, well, godliness that it almost overwhelmed me."

"It probably would have overwhelmed any other Kauri," Boquillas told her. "Your mind and your past are your strength."

She nodded. "Joe, she *is* ten feet tall and looks just like those statues all over the place. Also, every little blemish and imperfection is gone, and so is that great dark tan. She's almost blindingly smooth and white, and her hair's now silver—and I mean *silver*, not white or gray—and her eyes are a deep emerald green. She still has her slight German accent, but her voice is real soft and musical and super-sexy; yet it will carry in a square jammed with ten thousand people, somehow. You ought to see Kaladon, though. Wearing snow-white robes with silver trim, he looks like an angel from an old religious movie."

"You have the spell, I hope?" Boquillas prompted.

She sighed. "Damned hard to do, I'll tell you. That white inner glow is almost blinding, and I had to do it in daylight. Bless old Ruddygore's dark goggles! I doubt if anybody without 'em could see through the glare enough to figure out the pattern."

"A smart move on Kaladon's part," Boquillas noted. "Just in case some of the other councillors get ideas."

Marge passed him her sketch of the spell in colored pencils. "Took me five different appearances to get it all down," she told him, "and each time it was harder not to join the cult."

Boquillas studied the incredibly complex pattern for several minutes, then grabbed a pad and began sketching his own series of lines, shapes, forms, and relationships. It looked like kindergarten scribble to Joe, but Poquah in particular was gazing over the former sorcerer's shoulder and nodding.

"Can you do it?" Boquillas asked the Imir.

"Of course," the adept responded. "It is not difficult when

you diagram it that way, but I can think of no other mind save perhaps Ruddygore's that could have solved the pattern from so basic a sketch."

"I was a theoretician far longer than I was an activist," the Count told him. "In fact, Kaladon is cloddish enough or egomaniacal enough to have used a slight variation of one of my own designs. I suppose he no longer considers me a threat. Still, a wise teacher never tells his student *all* he knows." He looked up, smiled, and said to the Imir, "You have all the rest of the preparation. Joe, you have the latest reports from Poquah's and Marge's fairy friends about what's going on in Morikay. Let's see . . . Your next cycle is in eight more nights, right?"

Joe nodded. "Yeah, that's about it."

"And we have here from Marge evidence that our dear Goddess will formally and personally dedicate Fajera's temple a week from tomorrow." He sighed. "That's pretty dicey, and cutting things rather fine, but I think we might manage. No, I think we *have* to. If we let this go on another month, we won't be able to get near the place without being converted ourselves. Let's do it. Eight nights from tonight, Joe, you will be in Morikay, and so will Marge and Poquah. If your phenomenal luck holds, nine days from today we will free this world from Kaladon, not to mention Tiana."

"I can hardly wait," Joe said truthfully.

It was easier to get into Castle Morikay, or the Palace of the Angels, as it was referred to, than it was to stomach two days in the city itself. The building boom was amazing, with all sorts of bright-eyed men and women, aided by the Halflings of equal fervor, working like insects in a hive for the glory of the Goddess. How so many statues had been made in so short a time without a production line was beyond Joe and the others, and they were probably magical products, but it was both stunning and disturbing to see them, not only as decorations but actual objects of worship.

The people drove themselves with total fanatacism, calling one another Brother and Sister and praising the Goddess all the while they slaved. Even though he lay low and kept away from much contact, Joe got blessed more times than a Swiss guard at the Vatican. He had to admit, however, that, if it wasn't for the sheer fanaticism of the people and the fact that they looked malnourished and horribly overworked, he approved of the face lift in progress. It was still hard to tell just what the final thing would look like, though.

The great castle on the flat hilltop in the center of town was getting a new marble facade, its towers extended, and, in front, a tremendous statue of Tiana was being installed.

Still and all, Joe had the same distaste for this cult that he had for the cults back home on Earth. About the only nice thing he could say for this one was that at least they didn't ask for money all the time. In fact, he couldn't pay for anything at all.

Not that there was an awful lot to be had. Restaurants and cafes seemed a thing of the past, and inns were closed and deserted. He had to depend on the charity of some of the bright-eyed converts for what food he could get, and they were sharing obviously meager rations. The economic and trading system had been given a lower priority than the building of Kaladon's dream city.

As for the castle, or temple, or whatever it was now, passing through into the inner courtyard proved quite easy in the evening, since work never seemed to stop. As a mule, though, Joe put in one hell of a tough night's work and almost had it all go for nothing when they moved to take the animals out come daylight. Fortunately, animals worked better when fed, and there was an area inside the courtyard where the horses and mules could munch on hay. Near sunup, he positioned himself in the middle of a large group of animals and managed to change back unseen, although he was almost chomped and trampled getting out of the mob.

He wasted no time issuing his invitations with the earring he still had, and he prayed that the batteries hadn't run down. They had worked fine in a test the night before, but one never knew.

His problem now was that he was naked and unarmed in the midst of the enemy camp and he had no real way out. Boquillas' memories of the inner castle, though, proved right on the mark. After a few hairy near misses with some of the people inside, who did not look or act completely entranced, he found the right section and also found, to his relief, that it was still used as an inner storage area. In fact, it had been stuffed with lots of junk left over from the siege, causing him no end of trouble to locate a comfortable place. He only hoped that Marge would find him, preferably with a roast turkey or a thick steak.

Fortunately, the night's work as a mule, powering a complex pulley system for the main steeple, had tired him out so much that he just passed out for the day.

Marge got in, somehow, before nightfall, with a large cold cuts sandwich and a small gourd of water. It was better than nothing, and he ate the food quickly. As planned, they remained together until the full moon was again in the sky, making Joe once more a twin of Marge; but this time a different Marge was involved. The last time she'd been just a pixiewoman, but now she was a full Kauri again—and could fly.

That gave him the double immunity of the were's curse and a fairy form, as well as flying ability.

"Poquah?" he asked her.

"By midnight," she told him. "He's using some of his magical talents and coming in as a pilgrim worker."

"I just wish Tiana were back," he said. "I want to get this over and done with."

"She is back. Came here in midmorning, as a huge white bird with Kaladon perched on her back."

"Something symbolic in that."

Marge smiled and nodded. They settled down to wait in the dark storeroom for Poquah.

"You know," Joe remarked, "it's a wonder they don't do this sort of infiltrating each other all the time. Esmerada, for example, would love to replace the Goddess with herself."

"They would if they could," Marge pointed out. "Remember, it's only these neat little transmitters that make all this possible. Kaladon's people are watching for any strangers, and they'd prevent anybody new from talking to anybody outside. They check every working person coming up here thoroughly, too. No, Ruddygore's beaten the system with a were and some Japanese transistors. Nobody else has even one, let alone both."

"Maybe I should rent myself out to bite specific people, if being a were is so important."

They waited nervously for hours, but it was almost dawn

before the storeroom door creaked and a shadowy figure entered.

"I had real problems," the Imir told them as soon as they saw that it was indeed he. "The spells to detect other spells are very tight. This is a well-defended place, I'll have you know. I had to—radio, isn't that the term?—Boquillas for additional help."

"Boquillas! He's here?" Marge was both amazed and worried.

"He is. Hiding out in the cellar of a deserted inn just down the hill, and a good thing, too. He said either we do it or he might as well join the cult. There was no purpose in his staying away. I can communicate with him through Macore's little devices." He pointed to a small object, like a golden hearing aid, in his pointed left ear.

"Well, I just changed back, without even getting to fly once," Joe grumped. "Damn! What do we do now?"

Poquah paused, as if listening, then nodded. "The Count suggests that we either act straightaway or wait until dark once again. The rest of the time, the halls will be filled with functionaries."

"Take a chance and go now," Joe suggested. "I don't think I can stand another night in this place."

Poquah, nodding agreement, pulled up his hood and silently slipped away.

They almost went crazy waiting, but finally he returned after what not only seemed like but might have been hours. The impassive Imir was not in a better mood. "Problems," he told them.

"You couldn't get near her?"

"Oh, I located her, all right. The trouble is, Kaladon seems to be in the same room with her at all times. The moment I try to break the spell, he's going to be aware of it. Incidentally, you might be interested to know that, although the physical changes remain, inside here she reverts to her old height, which was still considerable."

Joe nodded. "That's a relief. But if Kaladon never leaves her side, we've got problems. How long will it take you to break the spell?"

"Only a minute or so. But that is a very long time if he knows immediately and can react. The lines of magic from me to her will be instantly recognizable to him and traceable back to me."

Joe thought a moment. "Well, we're in no position to have him called away. That means we have to distract or confuse him ... Hmmm ... Yeah. Why not? I've been Marge twice, so why not?"

"Why not what?" Marge asked him.

"Poquah, how hard is it going to be to sneak *me* into a place of concealment near where they're likely to be at sunset?"

"They handle business in a magnificently appointed throne room," the Imir replied. "Their bedchambers are right behind. A large study and apartment, actually. They take their meals there as well. Why?"

Joe told him his plan, and both Marge and Poquah were aghast at it.

"Still and all, it's an interesting try," the Imir said at last, "and our technical advisor recommends trying it if it is at all possible. I have a few spells of concealment and nonrecognition I've used before and just used now. I can get you in, and myself as well. But the Creator have mercy if you so much as sneeze."

"I'll take the chance," Joe replied. "Just be ready."

"Above all, do not look at her if you can avoid it," Poquah told him. "It is possible, even probable, that the conversation spell does not operate in here, when she is human and normal size, but we can't take any chances."

Poquah set up a watch and waited until the receiving room was clear of business and both Kaladon and Tiana had retired to the rear apartment for lunch. With the aid of Poquah's magic, Joe found himself able to reach the room with no trouble and he was impressed with the way it looked—like some reception area from the age of kings, with grand tapestries behind the velvet-lined throne of solid gold. He got behind the tapestries all right, then settled down as best he could for the long wait. Poquah would have to remain outside until after dark, lest Joe's curse go the wrong way. Even now there was a fifty-fifty chance of real problems.

Throughout the afternoon, it was maddening to hear the voices of both Kaladon and Tiana, the latter on the throne just in front of Joe, but he held onto what patience he could. As the afternoon wore on, though, he certainly wished he could go to the bathroom.

Tiana sounded wonderful but imperious. There was a lot of work to be done and lots of people to be seen. Joe was certain that the only reason he had escaped detection was because it would simply never occur to Kaladon that such a thing was even possible.

Several times, sometimes for long periods, Tiana would leave the throne, and many times both of them would leave the room and then return, causing Joe a great deal of worry. He had no clock, no window, no way at all to know what the situation was, and he could only wait and listen and hope.

Still and all, it worked. Tiana was, in fact, sitting on the throne at sunset, while Kaladon was tending to some paperwork across the room. Joe knew immediately that the change had occurred, smiled, leaned down, and picked up the small gold charm he'd taken in with him but not worn. "Go," he whispered into it, hoping that only the one on the other end would hear. He then got up, brushed back the impossibly long silver hair, and stuck the little gadget in his ear.

Outside, a door opened, and a man's voice said humbly, "Begging your worshipful Highness' pardon, but there is an Imir outside."

Kaladon was quick to get suspicious. "What? How did he get in?"

"I—I don't know, sir. I assumed—"

"You *assumed*! I should—no, wait. Send him in and leave us. I'm going to get to the bottom of this."

"As you wish, your Worship," the adept responded, then bowed to the woman on the throne and left.

Poquah entered without disguise, looking as impassive as ever. Nothing had ever seemed to disturb him, and he didn't appear to understand the meaning of fear. He bowed to the throne and to Kaladon. "I am Poquah, your Worships, formerly in the service of the late, sainted Ruddygore."

Here we go, Joe thought, knowing every possible meaning of fear.

"So you are Poquah," Kaladon responded. "I have heard a lot about you. How did you enter this castle without permission?"

"But, your Worship, I *had* permission," the Imir replied.

"Whose?"

The Imir pointed to the throne where Tiana sat, impassive as the fairy. "Hers," he said.

Kaladon turned to look, and as he did, Tiana rose and started toward him . . .

Then *two* Tianas were there, side by side, walking toward him.

"Wha—*what trick is this*?" Kaladon screamed, and Poquah watched the thin yellow band connecting him to the real Tiana. Watched as it wavered, moved, and seemed unable to choose between the two absolutely identical Goddesses.

The Imir struck. It was something that even Joe could see, because he had the same relative abilities as Tiana at this point; although, since his soul was different, he did not have her great magical powers.

Tiana herself seemed to frown and rock to and fro. Kaladon became suddenly concerned with reestablishing his umbilical link, completely forgetting Poquah, who was rapidly rewriting the magical script.

Once the link had been broken, even for a few seconds, Poquah's opening had begun changing the rest of the pattern that bound Tiana so tightly, so that Kaladon's link with the big woman would not rehook to her. Instead it wavered, then attached itself to the one pattern it could grab hold of—Joe.

Realizing his problem, Kaladon screamed and rushed headlong into the Imir, bowling him over onto the floor.

Tiana shook her head as if to clear it and blinked several times, as if awakening from a strange and terrible dream. She looked around in complete confusion, then saw the two fighting on the floor.

The yellow umbilical was attached to Joe, but it had no pattern with which to mate and so it only tickled a little. Tiana gazed very confusedly at him, gave a gasp at seeing herself, but did not know what to do, so she just stood there. Joe quickly moved around to the other side of her, in the process knocking the yellow magic band away as if it were a cobweb.

The protective spells taught him by Boquillas worked well, but the Imir was no match for Kaladon and was quickly brought to heel. He lay there unconscious on the floor, and Kaladon picked himself up, then looked with a snarl of satisfaction at the twin Goddesses before him. He stretched out his hand, and from it flowed a pattern of yellows, greens, and reds, completely covering one of them and freezing her into immobility, while the other stared wide-eyed, then seemed to realize exactly what was going on.

"First the imposter, then the Imir," Kaladon snarled. "Here is the pattern. Do it! I command you!"

"She would if she could, usurper, but she is only a double of me!" the unbound Tiana on the left said. "But thank you for the pattern!"

It shot out from her in blinding lights. Joe could only watch, unable to move from or do anything at all, but no help from him was needed. Kaladon was trapped in the complex mass of colors and textures. They held him, froze him, and bound him all at once, and then they started slowly to constrict, ever slowly but steadily, until the veins began to pop from his skin. Vessels burst under the pressure, bathing the frozen man in his own blood and continuing to contract until the pattern met, then dissolved, leaving a gruesome mess on the rug.

As Kaladon died, the spells binding Joe seemed to snap and then dissolve away. He could think and move once more and he let out a loud sigh.

Poquah groaned, rolled over, and made his way to his feet. Both Tianas just looked at him. Finally he got hold of himself, glanced over at the pulpy mass and, for one of the very few times in his life, he gave a slight grin. It quickly vanished when he realized it, and he turned to the two large women standing there.

"What is this all about?" Tiana wanted to know. "I do not remember anything since I was forced into Kaladon's presence . . ." She suddenly paused. "Oh, God! It was not a dream, was it? This strange religion, all those people . . ."

The Imir nodded. "Not a dream. In fact, a more humane version of the system might be just what Husaquahr needs. I'm not at all sure that it can be properly dismantled with so many on the Council in on it."

"Quite right, my friend," came a voice from the door, and in walked Esmilio Boquillas. "The spells hold, for they are Tiana's, not the late, unlamented Kaladon's, and she doesn't even know how to undo them."

Tiana was confused. "What? Who?"

The other Tiana grinned a very uncharacteristic Tiana grin. "I'm Joe, Tiana. This is a night with a full moon. Remember?"

She gasped. "Then that explains it! And you, sir?"

Boquillas smiled and bowed. "Esmilio Boquillas, Count of Marahbar, at your service."

"How'd you get here so quickly?" Joe asked him. "The whole outer castle is guarded."

Boquillas chuckled. "Poquah did it. You see, while I can no longer *cast* spells, I can be the easy recipient of them. It was a trifle. I had him cast several good spells on me for practice weeks ago."

Marge entered from the back of the room, looking confused, and stopped at the sights she saw.

Joe eased away from Tiana and over to a side where two rapiers were mounted decoratively on the wall. Boquillas glanced over at him and grinned. "Oh, you have guessed it. Yes, indeed, my friends, we shall yet build perfection in this world. One of those spells you used in freeing Tiana, my dear Imir, also subjected her to my direction. Come! Come! Do not feel dejected! The Dark Baron's plans come to fruition at last, that's all. There is nothing you can do about it."

Joe took both rapiers from the wall and checked out the heft and balance. "I think there is, Baron," he said in Tiana's sweetest voice. "I think you should have been in this room rather than assuming your scenario."

Boquillas' face clouded. "What do you mean?"

"I mean that you'd better take this rapier, you bastard! Poquah did no more than break the link before he was otherwise engaged. *He cast no spells on Tiana—she used Kaladon's own!*" He tossed the rapier to the man, who caught it deftly.

"Joe!" Tiana cried. "No! It is not necessary! With Poquah's aid, there is no problem!"

"I can handle him without you," the Imir responded, and Boquillas looked nervously at the two of them.

"No! This *is* necessary!" Joe told them. "Just get out of the way, all of you! It's time for this murdering bastard to meet his fate in the real world!"

Boquillas glanced over at the real Tiana. "If I order you to fling the same spell on her—er, him—that you used on Kaladon, I don't suppose you'd obey, would you?"

"Not a chance, old man," she responded.

He shrugged, raised the rapier in a salute, then leaped at Joe.

Joe was fortunate that Tiana was about the same height as he normally was and that her body was also trained as a swordswoman, with the proper muscles and reflexes. Although he had to remember to protect his chest a bit better, he had height and reach on the older man, as well as youth. He also, unfortunately, had six feet of flowing hair that threatened to trip him up.

Boquillas was no slouch as a swordsman, either. In fact, he was nearly brilliant, and they dueled back and forth across the chamber with little effect to either combatant.

Ultimately, though, the Dark Baron's strategy held true, as he forced Joe into a series of gymnastic moves that could not be done without tripping on that damned hair. Joe fell, cursing, and lost his rapier.

Boquillas made no allowance for honor. The rapier plunged deep into Joe's chest twice, spurting blood, and the stricken were cried out in pain.

"I think that is quite enough," another voice said, and Boquillas whirled, froze, and literally gaped at the heretofore vacant throne. The rapier dropped to the floor, and still he stood there, looking like a man facing his own death.

Tiana, Marge, Poquah, and Joe all stared as well, and only the Imir remained in the least bit unaffected by the sight.

Throckmorton P. Ruddygore, looking about forty pounds thinner and with a neatly trimmed beard, got up from the throne, an amused twinkle in his eyes. He was wearing his formal clothes, complete with opera cape, distinctive cane, and top hat.

"Joe, don't just lie there feeling killed. The rapiers weren't made of silver, and he had no power to make them so. Wipe that damned blood away and get up!"

CHAPTER 18

COMPLEX EVER-AFTERINGS

Never consider a sorcerer dead for good until you have seen him die a minimum of three times.

—Rules, VI, 303(b)

"DON'T LOOK SO STARTLED, ALL OF YOU," RUDDYGORE TOLD them. "Come back into the apartment with me and let's find something to eat in this mausoleum. Yes, you, too, Esmilio."

"But—I killed you! Or, rather, Hiccarph killed you! We all saw it!" the Count protested.

Ruddycore chuckled. "Oh, I admit I got a real mauling, but only on the psychic level, like our kraken and dragon and my replay of Earth warfare. I will also admit that, had I been that poor, starving boy, you would have had me; but he was just a construct, like the rest."

"He *couldn't* have been!" Boquillas protested. "It was *you* there! You as a starving scavenger! I know the Rules better than you! No construct may have a direct relationship to its creator."

"Could be you're right," Ruddygore admitted, "but, trouble is, Count, you're just too damned gullible. That life story of mine that I told you over good wine and better cigars was a total and complete lie. You're such a sucker for a bleeding heart I can't help but feel sorry for you, old boy. Come! Everyone! We must eat and relax and decide what to tell all those officials around here who are scared to death to enter the presence of the Goddess without permission, despite the commotion!"

"But where were you when you escaped the demon? Where have you *been* all this time?" Marge wanted to know.

"Where I could rest and bind my wounds and regain strength?" the fat sorcerer responded. "Where else?" And with that, he launched into a chorus of "I Left My Heart in San Francisco."

It was daybreak, but Joe and Marge had talked through the night, telling Tiana of their adventures and briefing Ruddygore on what he had missed. Meanwhile, Tiana gave orders forbidding interruptions in her best imperious manner, while fanatical followers still worked on rebuilding the castle and the city.

Boquillas remained the most silent of the batch, rarely offering a question or comment. He looked, and was, a totally defeated man and he knew it.

Finally it was dawn, and Joe changed back to his old self. He was delighted, as was Tiana, who hugged and kissed him. He finally broke away, laughing, and noted that three of them in the room were stark naked.

"That brings up an interesting series of questions," Ruddygore said at last. "We have to discuss all our futures here."

Everyone was suddenly very serious.

"Boquillas, I certainly owe you for helping dispose of Kaladon, although, as I promised, I was ready all in good time. I find, however, that I can not allow you freedom, considering your activities of this night. I think, perhaps, that you will come with me for a while, and we will take a little trip together."

The Count's eyebrows went up. "A trip? Where?"

"I'll give you back your health and your youth, so that you will have a chance to see how things really are. I'll prepare you with languages and I will even bankroll you. You are going to work for me, on Earth."

"Earth? Doing what?"

"Research and correlation. It would be a shame to let one of your intellect and experience go to waste. You like technology so much, I will introduce you to my computer section. Without them, all this could never have been possible."

"I *knew* it," Marge put in.

"Alas, you are also ready to experience a far different world from what you've ever known, as well as the Bangkok flu, stomach ulcers, and all the other pressures of day-to-day living. Still, it is better than you deserve." The sorcerer pointed at Boquillas, and he winked out and vanished. "Stuck him in storage until I have to go over again," Ruddygore told the others.

"And what of us?" Marge asked him. "What now?"

He sighed. "Boquillas was right, you know. Esmerada, Fajera, Sargash, and the rest will not be easily talked out of this cult thing. Nor, in fact, could you, Tiana, ever lead a normal life now. You have what you wished all along to have, much to my surprise. You are absolute ruler here. We can modify the harsh parts of this new religion,, but the others won't let us kill it, I'm afraid." He chuckled. "Besides, I *like* being a saint."

Tiana shook her head in wonder. "You know, all that time in exile, I dreamed of this sort of thing, although tens of thousands of statues of me fully nude are a bit more than I thought about." She laughed. "Well, then, so be it. The climate is tropical, and I certainly can no longer claim modesty after so many have seen not only statues but me in the altogether." She paused a moment. "But the responsibility it now gives me is staggering. I had not thought in those terms. My dreams were always of taking back what was stolen, not of what happened after."

"Of course, there will have to be *some* modifications," Ruddygore told her. "Let them continue to think you an angel, for they will, anyway, but we must restore their free will and sense of perspective. We must get the economy going again. Adjust the new status to the old so that it all works, but without war or mass slaughter, at least for a very long time."

She nodded. "Of course. You need only show me how to do it."

Ruddygore turned to Joe. "And what about you? What do you want now, Joe? I mean, really want. Long-term."

Joe thought a minute, then leaned over and hugged Tiana. "I want a goddess."

She seemed delighted and excited, and grabbed and hugged and kissed him all over again.

Ruddygore smiled. "A slight modification is in order, then. There will have to be one, anyway, to explain Kaladon's demise. You sent him to his Heavenly reward, that's all."

"She sure did," Joe noted.

"Goddesses do not have consorts, of course, and I think Joe ill fits the role of high priest. Therefore, we'll reaffirm some old-fashioned values and virtues. The Goddess shall have her God. You certainly look the part, Joe."

"Hey! Wait a minute! You mean there's gonna be a million marble statues of *me* in the nude?"

Ruddygore laughed. "And why not? When they see the attributes of both of you, you will be the sex idols of Husa-quahr."

"But I have no godlike power, and Tiana can't use hers," he pointed out. "And you're expecting us to rule a country directly and a church that goes out who knows how far?"

"There will be little trouble there. First of all, your new high priest will handle the mundane magical chores and advice, accompanied by his faithful band of adepts and hangers-on. And, because the potential for this is so fascinating, there will be a backup. A simple microcomputer, I think, with a number of hard disks, should hold the basics. With some nice color graphics, of course, so you can see the spells and how they're formed when you punch them up. I'll bring one back when I drop off Esmilio."

"But how will you plug it in?" Joe asked him. "And isn't that violating your own ideas on technology?"

Ruddygore winked. "The power source will be a new type of battery tapping a magical source. As you know, sometimes cheating on one's principles is necessary. Without doing so, we would now all be dead, at the mercy of the Baron's armies."

Ruddygore turned to Marge, whose expression was solemn. "Don't look so glum, my dear!"

"Nothing in that bag of yours for me, is there, Mr. Wizard?" she responded sadly.

"Soon the inns will open, the shows will restart, and all will begin anew," he told her. "You are Kauri, Marge, and that is a great responsibility, but also an important one. Fly, Marge, into the night skies! Play! Sing! Dance! The whole new world is at your feet, and you are truly free to enjoy it!"

She smiled and got up and walked over to them. "I'll miss you all terribly, though."

"But you can return any time, and there is always time for you," Joe told her. "Always."

They hugged and kissed, and then Marge left. Going down a hall and seeing an open door, she walked in and climbed up on the window. The sun was bright, and she lowered her goggles to keep the sleep away, then leaped out into the cool sky.

Back in the apartment, Joe sighed. "Will we ever see her again for real, I wonder?" He leaned over to Tiana and kissed her. "I know and I'm sorry, but we were pretty close."

She kissed him back. "I understand."

Ruddygore grinned broadly and got up. "Well, Poquah, it's about time we saw what they've done to our old home. But we'll be back, children, rather quickly. Until then, don't worry about any problems coming about. Everybody here will obey every order the Goddess gives." He sighed, yawned, stretched, and made for the door, then turned back to the couple.

"Don't worry about not seeing Marge again," he told them. "The Rules still hold."

Tiana looked puzzled, but Joe smiled softly, and that smile turned into a big grin.

"Yeah, that's right, isn't it? We've got at least one more great adventure left, haven't we?"

"Oh, yes, yes. At *least*," agreed Throckmorton P. Ruddygore.

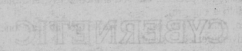

DEL REY ONLINE!

The Del Rey Internet Newsletter...

A monthly electronic publication, posted on the Internet, GEnie, CompuServe, BIX, various BBSs, and the Panix gopher (gopher.panix.com). It features hype-free descriptions of books that are new in the stores, a list of our upcoming books, special announcements, a signing/reading/convention-attendance schedule for Del Rey authors, "In Depth" essays in which professionals in the field (authors, artists, designers, sales people, etc.) talk about their jobs in science fiction, a question-and-answer section, behind-the-scenes looks at sf publishing, and more!

Online editorial presence: Many of the Del Rey editors are online, on the Internet, GEnie, CompuServe, America Online, and Delphi. There is a Del Rey topic on GEnie and a Del Rey folder on America Online.

Our official e-mail address for Del Rey Books is delrey@randomhouse.com

Internet information source!

A lot of Del Rey material is available to the Internet on a gopher server: all back issues and the current issue of the Del Rey Internet Newsletter, a description of the DRIN and summaries of all the issues' contents, sample chapters of upcoming or current books (readable or downloadable for free), submission requirements, mail-order information, and much more. We will be adding more items of all sorts (mostly new DRINs and sample chapters) regularly. The address of the gopher is gopher.panix.com

Why? We at Del Rey realize that the networks are the medium of the future. That's where you'll find us promoting our books, socializing with others in the sf field, and—most importantly—making contact and sharing information with sf readers.

For more information, e-mail delrey@randomhouse.com